I0632521

Bob Faulkner

The Buffalo Rock

Stand Up America, USA

ISBN # 978-0-6152-4176-0

Published by Stand Up America, USA

Bigfork, Montana

Printed in the United States of America

Acknowledgments

To Deb Legarra: Thank you for
diligently crossing
the t's and dotting the i's.

To Sarah Safford:
Thank you for making me look
literate.

To Tom Hays
and Rich Shedd:
Thanks for taking the time.

To Bill Brooks:
Thanks for the encouragement
and the K.I.T.A.

And
To my bride, Vicki, the love
of my life.
Thanks for being you.

1

Grant was lying, head down hill, arms and legs askew. With every breath, a bright red froth of blood coated his lips in a darkening patina.

"Don't move around too much, son," Tom said.

Fearing that Grant would drown in his own blood, Tom gently dragged his limp body into a depression formed when a giant ponderosa had toppled, ripping the soil from the steep hillside.

"This here is the only level spot on this whole mountain...and this big root snag will be a nice wind break till I get back."

Tom retrieved Grant's crushed Stetson and then scraped together a pile of soft dry earth and pine needles. Lifting the young man's upper body, he covered the mound with the hat and pushed it into place beneath Grant's head.

"I made you a nice pillow outta that new hat yer so proud of."

Tom glanced up at the clouds building over the mountains. He took off his coat and placed it over Grant's chest to cut the chilled wind.

"Looks like we're gonna get a little snow."

Grant smiled a silent thank you.

"Now I don't want you runnin' off this time. You stay right here while

I go get us some help. You hear?"

Grant smiled again, choking back a painful laugh at his friend's attempted humor.

"I broke the President's rifle!" Grant said.

"Hell, don't worry about that right now."

Tom placed the backs of his fingers against Grant's forehead. A worried look knitted his brow.

"You're gonna be fine. I'll be back just as soon as I can."

Grant listened to the cracking of brush and the crunching of pine needles as Tom disappeared down the steep slope.

Grant smiled through gritted teeth as a flood of pride sent a thrill of warmth through his body. He had faced danger and stood his ground. Even now, with the realization of the dire situation, he felt strangely unafraid. Tom had prevailed through worse situations than this.

With his good arm, Grant tucked Tom's jacket tightly around his shoulders. The frigid wind brought involuntary shudders sending pain searing down his arm. He grimaced, imagining the jagged ends of broken ribs gnashing together. A painful cough racked his body. His head throbbed. I must have hit my head when I fell, he thought.

He attempted to occupy his mind, studying the quickly rising billows of cumulus clouds refracting the late afternoon sunlight. The ever-changing tower seemed to infuse the pigment, in varied hue and accent, of the earth, rock and vegetation below. Roiling over the white crowned peaks, the clouds appeared to adopt the shape of a knight with a couched lance on a white charger.

His mind aswirl in memories, Grant could again smell the honeysuckle and lilacs, which graced the heavy hot afternoon breeze in the backyard of his childhood home in Baltimore. He could hear the shrill, siren like buzz of cicadas fulfilling their annual ritual. He could once more feel the cool grass beneath his back. In his reverie, he lay with his fingers laced behind his head watching the clouds with Cousin Bernice, each in turn giving interpretation to the ephemeral white formations suspended in crystal blue.

Tom had been right, Grant thought, as nickel-sized snowflakes touched lightly on his face, bringing him back to reality. The moisture provided some relief as he ran his tongue over the dried blood that coated his wind-chapped lips.

Watching the tops of the ancient pine trees bow to the power of the incessant mountain winds he wondered what his family and friends would think when they heard of his adventures. Would they apprehend the profound transformation he had undergone in these few short months?

The snowflakes stopped as the moisture-laden cloud passed beyond the ridge, pushed by the increasing wind. The sun shone momentarily through breaks in the filmy overcast. Perhaps the weather is changing, Grant thought as the shivering slowly ceased. Closing his eyes, a warm red glow engulfed him as the afternoon light filtered through flickering eyelids. Drifting in semi-consciousness, he could hear again the conductor's, "All aboard," which had begun his odyssey.

It had been a balmy morning in the spring of 1923, when Grant Sherman Collins boarded the train from Saint Louis to Fort Benton, Montana. He regretted now, lying here injured on the mountainside, that much of the aura of the journey had been lost in his focus on the asperities. He wished that he could relive the interminable layovers, dreadful food and inadequate accommodations of the train ride, which had been the first and only real adventure of his life.

There had been no moment of epiphany, he thought to himself. It had been, instead, a slow realization that his priggish insistence on propriety and creature comfort had left him isolated from things in life that really mattered. No wonder that other men considered him such a blue nose. Now, eye-to-eye with the specter of mortality, he wanted to taste, smell, and feel all that he could of this delicious world. Even the cold wind now seemed a delight.

He could clearly recall the first vestige of his transformation. The train had stopped at a small prairie town. Grant got off the train to see if his imagined Montana would fit the reality. In an instant, he recognized that the Big Sky glorified by Western aficionados was beyond the spare descriptive capacity of word or canvas.

With great excitement, he climbed to the top of one of the railroad cars so as to get a clearer view of the surrounding country. A breath caught in his throat as he scanned the horizons. The seemingly infinite plain melded into distant rolling hills, which diverged into purpling mountains rising to their snow mantled peaks. He realized that his unpracticed eye could not begin to calculate the distances.

The broken overcast allowed intermittent shafts of sunlight to bathe the faraway landscape in a prodigiously colorful cyclorama. The sky seemed so imposing; he could remember doubting that there were ever enough clouds to completely envelope the heavenly arch.

No wonder, he thought, so many aspiring artists chose Montana as the subject of their work. Even a rude rendition of nature's daily masterpiece was, in human terms, fine art.

Within the time consumed by a slow pirouette, his being was immersed in the panorama. Grant found himself uncharacteristically awash in a profusion of ambivalent emotions. Whatever might happen in the years to come, he knew that a part of him would always be in this moment.

A blast of steam and the simultaneous grinding of steel couplings jolted Grant from his preoccupation. The resulting lurch nearly toppled him from his vantage point as the train, after discharging the passengers, aligned the baggage and then the freight cars with the dock for unloading.

Clambering from his perch, he became aware of a chilled wind cutting through his light clothing. Re-boarding the train, he found a new admiration for a place he had only imagined a brief time before.

He could not clearly define for himself just why that moment had been pivotal. Prior to that stop, the trip had been a complete bore. Loading and unloading passengers and freight in nondescript small towns had held little interest for him. To relieve the boredom he entertained himself by making conversation with, and assessments of, his fellow passengers.

A few finely attired Easterners and Europeans provided momentary respite from his tedium. They were either looking over the country for potential opportunities or vacationing to experience firsthand the Western ambience. Like Grant, their experience was limited to what they had heard, read or seen in a Charles Russell painting.

There were also some not so finely attired Easterners and Europeans. They were traveling mostly in family groups coming west for promised opportunity, or the free land offered by the Homestead Act.

The drought years beginning in the spring of 1917 had bankrupted most of the early homesteaders, sending them packing. That land was again available and these newcomers hoped to beat the odds. These people were bringing with them everything they owned. Some even carried cages with poultry and small animals. Grant found this to be quite repugnant and had changed cars frequently to avoid the noise and odor.

The remaining passengers were people traveling to the small towns for business or to visit friends and family. Traveling salesmen with their sample cases occupied facing seats to play cards and pass the hours. There were also working men, miners and loggers, moving to new diggings or timber stands.

A laconic cowboy dressed in boots and a felt hat created a great a buzz of excitement when he boarded the train with a saddle slung over his shoulder. Grant changed his seat to get a better view of this living embodiment of the myth portrayed in a legion of motion pictures, books and paintings. As a child, Grant had read the works of Irwin and Erastus Beadle, Alfred Henry Lewis, Owen Wister and Ned Buntline. But this was a living breathing human being who, notwithstanding automobiles and electric lights, put a face of reality on those long ago read sagas.

It was early afternoon when the train arrived in Fort Benton. A chilly wind blowing from the northwest drove a sparse sleety rain through Grant's clothing. Snowflakes unexpectedly swirled in the driven rain, coming to rest on Grant's coat in momentary crystalline perfection. He wondered if there was a mercantile in the town where he might purchase some long woolen underwear.

Grant collected his luggage and looked around at the passengers who had detrained in Fort Benton. A well-dressed young couple, speaking what Grant believed to be German, ducked their heads into the wind and walked briskly toward a line of vehicles, both horse drawn and motorized, waiting nearby. He thought how odd it was that even with the rain, there was blowing dust stinging his eyes.

Two of the homesteader families had also alighted in Fort Benton and were huddled by the dock waiting for the freight car to unload their belongings. Grant carried his suitcase across the tracks toward the waiting vehicles. A tall middle-aged man wearing a long dustcoat was holding a sign, which read, "Grand Union Hotel."

The German-speaking couple was engaged in conversation with a man holding a sign advertising the "Choteau House." Their gesticulations gave

Grant to believe that they too were waiting for luggage to be unloaded.

Approaching the tall man from the Grand Union Hotel he asked, "Are you waiting for someone particular or may I have a ride to the hotel?"

"Mister, we seldom get anyone too particular around these parts," the jovial man replied in a drawling accent that was at once as agreeable as it was unfamiliar to Grant's ear.

As the big man picked up Grant's suitcase, carrying it toward the Chevrolet Touring Car, he spat brown fluid through his moustache and said, "Let's go. Reckon them honyockers won't be going to the Grand Union."

"Honyockers?" Grant asked as the big fellow put the suitcase into the car.

The big man seemed to ignore the question and Grant climbed into the back seat of the Chevrolet. The car had a leatherette top but no side windows. A sharp wind was blowing rain and dust through the Chevrolet as it coursed off the hill and down into the town of Fort Benton, making the ten minute ride to the hotel seem endless.

Grant's experiences during his week on the road had taught him to moderate his expectations. Although the sublime appellation, "Grand Union Hotel," had not raised his anticipation of the potential accommodations, he was pleasantly surprised when the car stopped in front of a three story brick and mortar building. The river front edifice was, Grant thought, more reminiscent of the structures one might see in the cities of the East than the wooden frame buildings more prevalent in the rural West.

"That must be the Missouri River?" Grant said.

"The mighty, muddy, Mo," the big man replied, pointing to the fire station a block away. "That ol' river is the only reason this town is here. Right along in front of the hotel is where the steamboats docked in the old days…had freight stacked from here to beyond the firehouse."

Grant entered the lobby with the big man in the duster carrying his bag. The interior of the hotel was, although aging, quite exquisite, with oak paneling and hand wrought railings on the carpeted staircase. The copper paneled ceiling reflected light from the recently installed electric chandeliers. The fine accommodations surrounded by Old West ambience brought renewed excitement for Grant's self-imposed task.

The broad shouldered man removed his duster as he walked behind the heavy oak reception desk. Turning the guest register so that Grant could sign and sticking out his hand he said, "Welcome to the Grand Union Hotel. Charlie Lowe is my name. You'll want a room I reckon…I got a nice corner with a river view."

"I must admit my surprise. This is such a beautiful hotel out here in the middle of nowhere."

"Yes sir. She was built in 1882 when Fort Benton was still a major port for the Missouri River trade. The folks that built 'er was tryin' to bring growth and civilization to the town. This ol' hotel was the center of social doin's for many a year. Still is for that matter. I reckon this is only 'the middle of nowhere' if you didn't know it was here."

Grant smiled at the polite rebuke.

"Do you have a restaurant?"

"You bet. Breakfast and supper. Darned good food too. We used to have a nice saloon till ol' Carrie Nation got her hooks into them Washington politicians. I was the bartender until Carrie's deeeevine ordination caused me to seek other duties or face dispossession."

"It is a pleasure to make your acquaintance, Charlie." Grant extended his hand. "Do you know Mr. Tom Thomas who owns a ranch near Fort Benton?"

"Tornado Tom? I surely do," Charlie said enthusiastically. "Saw ol'

Luke, that's his horse, over by the Masonic Lodge as we was comin' in. I bet you're that newspaper fella that sent the telegram to Tom a few weeks ago."

"Is that what you call him, Tornado Tom? I saw that name while reading a history of the Pony Express."

"People been callin' him that since I was a youngster." Charlie turned the registration book to look at the signature. "Don't know for sure why though...Grant is it?"

"I'm Grant Collins, Charlie. I'm a reporter with the Saint Louis Morning Star Newspaper. I am doing research for a story about the Pony Express and I saw Mr. Thomas' photograph in an old edition of the Muddy Water Press. The caption said he had been a Pony Express rider, the oldest still alive. I thought perhaps he might be able to help me."

Charlie's moustache turned up at the corners in a huge grin.

"Don't let Tom yarn ya now. That ol' boy's got more of it than the Abilene stockyards. When you get settled, I'll drive you over to the Lodge and introduce you."

"Which way to my room?"

Charlie pointed to the wide staircase ascending to the second floor.

"Right up those stairs and around to the left...and let me get that luggage for you."

Before Charlie could walk around the desk, Grant picked up his suitcase.

"That's fine...I can manage."

Freshening himself quickly, Grant returned to the lobby without unpacking.

Charlie wore a look of surprise as Grant came bounding down the stairs.

"You ready, already?"

Grant passed the desk walking toward the door.

"Let's go meet Tornado Tom."

"You must be in a real hurry to get buried in bullshit," Charlie said as he followed Grant out the door.

Half a dozen horses were tied to a rail and a like number of automobiles were parked outside the Masonic Lodge building as Charlie parked by the front door walkway.

"My grandfather was a Mason," Grant said, more to relieve his nervousness than to relay information. "So was George Washington I understand."

"Yep," Charlie said, "and so are most of the fellas in this county."

Entering the Masonic Lodge building Charlie escorted Grant to the dining room. There, about twenty men of varying ages sat around tables, playing cards and talking. The air was permeated by a combination of the smell of whiskey and tobacco smoke. The men were dressed in varying styles, from fine suits with spats, and skimmers, to dusty ranch wear with chaps and sweat soaked, sun bleached felt broad brim hats.

Grant immediately recognized Mr. Thomas seated at a table mid room playing cards. He was a more substantial man than Grant had expected. His face was like tanned leather from the years of living outdoors, reminding Grant of old sepia toned photos. He was attired in a quality dress suit of Western style and was wearing a huge broad brimmed beaver felt hat. Well-trimmed white hair contrasted the sunned brown of his face.

"This here is that newspaper fella from Saint Louie," Charlie announced in a loud voice. Everyone in the room stopped what they were doing to look in Grant's direction. "He's the one that sent that telegram to Tom some while back."

Tom Thomas arose from his chair and extended his hand. His tanned face was aglow with a broad and pleasant smile. As Grant took Tom's hand he was startled, not only by the strength but also by its tough leather like quality, so hard and calloused that Grant was sure one could strike a Diamond Match in his palm.

"Mr. Thomas, it is a pleasure to finally make your acquaintance," Grant said.

A wry smile lit the old man's face.

"Mr. Thomas? That was my father. You can just call me Tom like everybody else."

Grant was caught short by the exhortation.

"Why yes...uh, okay Tom."

"Good deal," Tom said, taking Charlie's arm. "Charlie, introduce this boy around and then get him something to drink, will you? On me!"

Turning his attention to Grant, Tom said, "Son, I'm catchin' some damned good cards here. Let me finish this game and we'll head over to the hotel for a palaver."

Charlie escorted Grant around the dining room, introducing him to each of the men in turn. Grant listened carefully as he attempted to make a mental note of the names.

When the introductions were complete Charlie asked, "What'll it be? You want some of the good imported Canadian or some of our hometown whiskey?"

"May I have a cup of coffee?" Grant asked.

Charlie filled a cup obligingly with coffee and then poured himself a brimming shot of the local rotgut whiskey from the makeshift bar set up on the counter of the kitchen's serving window. They sat at an empty table to chat, waiting for Tom to complete his game of five-card draw.

"Being close to the border like we are, we can get some real whiskey.

Hell, you can drive across near about anywhere you like and they ain't hardly got no border guards. Specially late at night. That imported is pretty pricey though. I just stick to the local stuff. It's cheap. I'll admit that it ain't none too tasty but it's whiskey just the same."

"Mr. Thomas...uh, Tom...said it was on him. May as well treat yourself."

"Naw, I'm used to this rotgut, and I wouldn't want to take advantage of Tom's charity. Besides, I might just get spoiled."

"Don't the police raid this place?" Grant asked.

Charlie took a sip from the shot glass and smiled knowingly.

"That tall thin fella next to Tom is the Sheriff. Ask him."

"I can see that prohibition is about as effective here in Montana as it is in Saint Louis, New York and Baltimore."

As Grant and Charlie chatted about incidentals, Grant learned a bit about the town and its people. Time passed quickly, and soon Tom rose from the table and walked to where Grant and Charlie were sitting.

"I skinned them boys like a mess a catfish." Tom said with a wink. "I need to take ol' Luke over to the livery. Poor ol' bastard's been standin' out there all day with no food or water. You got me a room for the night Charlie?"

"You bet," Charlie said.

"Well...would you follow me over to the livery in that fancy automobile and then you can take me and this young fella over to the hotel for supper?"

"You bet," Charlie repeated, walking toward the door.

Grant had anticipated meeting a seventy-seven year old man, doddering and enfeebled. When they walked outside, he was stunned to see Tom spryly mount his horse and gallop the three blocks to the livery stable. By the time Charlie and Grant arrived in the Chevrolet, Tom had liveried his horse and was waiting for them in the street.

Charlie drove to the hotel. As they walked into the lobby, Grant said, "Would six o'clock for dinner meet with your approval?"

"Six it'll be," Tom said as they walked up the two flights of stairs to their respective rooms. "Bring yer appetite...they've got some good vittles."

Grant put his suitcase on the bed and removed a clean shirt and silk necktie to wear at dinner. I should have unpacked and hung this clean suit earlier in the day so that it would have appeared less wrinkled, he thought.

He put his suitcase in the corner and then sat on the edge of the bed to scrawl some quick notes. He wanted to remember every moment of the day. He felt effervescent at his success and wished that he could share his excitement. He had just arrived in Fort Benton and had already achieved the cooperation of Tornado Tom. I will, he thought with delight, complete my work in a few weeks and be headed back to Saint Louis.

He put his notebook on the table beside the bed and flopped back onto the pillows, allowing himself to relax. His thoughts wandered as he lay entranced by the hypnotic rotation of the ceiling fan.

The time he had spent mining archives seeking a viable project for his writing seemed to be paying dividends. The grainy newspaper photo of Tom Thomas had sparked his imagination and had been a gem worth the search. His confidence was growing. Tornado Tom appeared to be the genuine article. The past two years of exasperation working as a newspaper reporter, he said to himself, were the dues one had to pay in learning the craft.

Closing his eyes he laughed at himself as he recalled his painful initiation, two years prior, when he first entered the offices of the Morning Star. He had arrived in Saint Louis by train on a sweltering afternoon in late July of 1921. Although rivulets of sweat were flowing down his torso, soaking the shirt beneath his suit jacket, he had been oblivious to the oppressive weather. He remembered feeling a chill of excited anticipation, as he stood on the swaying trolley en route to the offices of his new employer.

Notwithstanding the reputation of the Saint Louis Morning Star, Grant knew that many of his soon to be colleagues lacked his superior educational credentials. An elitist by upbringing, Grant considered the Star to be his 'second choice.' He had not received a response from the New York World, once owned by his idol, Joseph Pulitzer. Somehow, the acceptance letter from the Star had given him a false sense of superiority. He had illusions of fawning admirers welcoming him to their ranks.

Still carrying his suitcase, he entered the lobby of the Star offices with great excitement. He was anxious to meet Jonathon Kuntz, the owner and Editor-in-Chief. Reaching into his inside coat pocket, he removed his now soggy letter of acceptance, handing it across the counter to the attractive and fashionably dressed young receptionist. He knew that his voice had quavered when he said, "My name is Grant Collins. Is Mr. Kuntz available?"

The receptionist had reached across the counter and taken the letter from Grant's hand. "I'm Melinda Kuntz. Perhaps I can help you."

She read enough to satisfy her curiosity and then emerged from behind the reception desk saying, "Follow me."

Reflecting on the incident, he laughed at his naiveté. She had gotten the better of him in that first encounter; flirtatiously brushing against him as she unceremoniously escorted him to the newsroom.

"Mr. Kuntz, and yes he is my father, is unavailable. Hiram. He'll be your boss. He's in his office and he can take care of you."

Grant recalled that, as he was being escorted to Hiram's office, he had become aware of the stifling heat. Sweating profusely, his insides felt like gelatin as they crossed the open room. The buzz of conversation and clatter of typewriters filled the air.

"I always feel sorry for the new reporters," Melinda had said, as they approached a row of glass-enclosed offices adjacent to the newsroom. "The experienced men get all of the good stories, and you poor fellows end up being little more than glorified copy boys."

He knew that his face had blanched white, showing his discomfort, and he had not said another word for fear that a cracking voice would expose his anxiety. He also sensed that she was enjoying a perverse sort of coquettish bedevilment at his expense.

They entered one of the offices with gold leaf lettering inscribed on the glass, "Hiram Laidlaw Assistant Editor."

She handed Grant's letter to Hiram and walked toward the door.

"This is your new man. Columbia Journalism no less!"

Extending his hand and smiling nervously, Grant recalled how he was still expecting exuberant recognition of his academic achievement.

Hiram, obviously distracted, took a quick drag from his cigarette and peered at Grant over his metal framed glasses. Rising from his chair, he handed Grant the soggy acceptance letter without looking at it.

Grant's hand hung in mid-air as Hiram spoke.

"Let me give you a piece of advice Mr. Collins. God gave you two ears and two eyes...you'll notice, however, that you only have one mouth. Watch and listen a lot...and talk very little. If you learn just that today you may have a future with The Morning Star."

Recalling it now, it was almost humorous, but at the time, he had been mortified. He had remained silent, considering that Hiram seemed to have plenty to say.

Hiram walked from behind his desk, incredulously eyeing Grant's suitcase.

"Mr. Collins, you have more formal education than my five best reporters put together. Now I am willing to forget that, if you are. Don't let Columbia stand in the way of becoming a good reporter."

Grant laughed to himself. Whatever delusions of self-importance he had carried into Mr. Hiram Laidlaw's office were quickly laid bare to reality.

Hiram had taken him into the newsroom where they approached a disheveled character in a well-worn suit, a greasy fedora and a soup-stained tie. The man was pounding furiously on an old Remington typewriter. Hiram stood by respectfully waiting for the man to acknowledge his presence. When the man looked up from his work, Hiram said, "Shawn Newman, this is Grant Collins from Baltimore. He's the new man we talked about and you are going to help him hit the ground running."

Shawn Newman, a florid faced mid-forties fellow with an ear-to-ear smile arose from his chair and accepted Grant's handshake.

"Welcome to Saint Louis," Shawn said.

Grant remembered feeling a huge relief at the first friendly greeting he had received since his arrival at the offices of The Morning Star.

"Grant here just graduated from Columbia University," Hiram had persisted in a sardonic tone, "and I'm sure that he'll have a lot to teach us."

Shawn had offered some reassurance.

"Don't mind this grumpy old troll," he said, turning to Hiram. "You go back under your bridge Hiram and I'll show the kid around."

"Good," said Hiram, surprising Grant by extending his hand for a polite handshake.

Grant remembered walking away with Shawn when he heard Hiram say in a loud voice, "Welcome aboard Mr. Collins...and by the way, take the rest of the afternoon off and find a home for that suitcase. I appreciate your dedication, but you can't live here."

Shawn took him on a quick familiarization tour of The Morning Star building. After brief introductions to a few of Grant's new coworkers, Shawn said, "Look kid, I have a deadline. Go find a flop and I'll see you tomorrow."

Grant recalled the knot in his stomach and fighting back tears while walking the streets of Saint Louis. For the first time in his life, he had felt empty and completely alone in a new and uncertain world.

2

Awakening from his brief nap with a start, Grant dressed quickly. A feeling of excitement ran through him. It was nearing six and he looked forward to a productive evening, drawing out the golden nuggets of experience from the head of the remarkable gentleman who, he hoped, would be a new beginning for his mired writing career.

Grant approached the hotel desk.

"Have I any messages?"

A slight, pale man in an ill-fitting suit was seated on a stool behind the desk.

"You that fella from Saint Louie?"

Grant nodded.

"Ain't been no messages. Maybe you ain't near as important as you'd figured."

Grant smiled and turned to walk toward the dining room when he saw Tom coming down the stairs.

Tom again presented his hand, giving a solid greeting before they walked into the dining room to the accompaniment of Al Jolson singing "April Showers" on the hotel's Victrola.

Tom turned to Grant as they waited for a table and said, "Looky here ol' son...just what exactly is it that I can help you with?"

Before Grant could reply the maitre d' approached and said, "Good evening, Mr. Thomas. May I show you and your guest to a table?"

Tom looked at Grant, the corners of his mouth drooping in disapproval. Looking back at the frail young man in the black formal jacket, he said, "Leonard, how many times do I have to tell you, call me Tom, and yes, you can show me and the young gentleman here to a table...and thank you very much."

"Sorreeee Tommmm," the maitre d' said indignantly. "This way please."

Tom sat down and picked up his menu, watching Leonard's mincing steps as he walked back to his station.

"That swishy little shit," Tom said. "Always puttin' on airs...I've known that funny little bastard since he was knee high to a hop toad and he still tries to pass himself off as some fancy pants from New York City."

Grant ignored the invective.

"I saw your photograph and an article about you in the Muddy Water Press," he said. "The news piece reported that you had once been a rider for the Pony Express."

Tom smiled a broad grin.

"I most assuredly was...but that don't answer the question. What can I do for you?"

Grant returned Tom's infectious smile and continued.

"Well, you see Tom, I'm interested in a controversy regarding the first westbound ride of the Pony Express from Saint Joseph in 1860. The Daughters of the American Revolution honored a man named Richardson, but I found that the claim was in dispute. In my research, I've found the names of seven men, including yours, who were supposed to have made that ride. You are one of a few Pony Express riders extant. I'm hoping that you have some firsthand knowledge."

Tom studied the young man's face for a long moment.

"I am extant, thank God! And I do have firsthand knowledge...of a sort."

"What does that mean, 'of a sort'?"

"I wasn't in Saint Joe when that first rider started. I was out in Nevada. I carried that very first mochilla, sure enough, but other than that, I only know what I heard about who carried it on the first leg out of the stables in Saint Joe. Back then, it just didn't seem very important to anyone. No one figured we was making history."

"Perhaps you could tell me what you heard at the time...or more importantly, have you some other stories which might be of interest?"

"I got a passel of stories, if that's what you're lookin' to hear. I recall that I did get a letter from an old gal at the Daughters of the American Revolution about ten years back. They wanted me to come to some shindig at the old Pikes Peak Stables in Saint Joe. Letter said they was makin' a park out of it...but I was busy and never heard any more about it. So what kind'a stories are you interested in hearin', besides the Pony Express that is?"

"Your Pony Express adventures...frontier tales...like the stories which were told by Buntline about Buffalo Bill," Grant said.

Grant looked at Tom smiling in embarrassment.

"I thought perhaps you might enjoy being in print...and frankly, if the stories are verifiable and interesting it certainly won't hurt my career either."

Tom laughed aloud at the candor.

"That's puttin' 'er straight alright, and you know what boy...I'm really glad you showed up. I have about wore out every ear in this part of the country. No one wants to hear the bullshit stories of an old man any more. Even the kids don't want to listen. The kids these days have motion pictures with those dandy looking cowboys like Tom Mix and William S. Hart. Those fellas always shoot straight and ride fast and they always outsmart the Injuns and the bad guys...have you ever seen that William S. Hart in a motion picture?"

Grant nodded his head.

"You probably don't know this, but that fella had never been on a horse until about ten years ago when he came up here to my ranch to learn what a cowboy looked like. That sumbitch is from New York City. He didn't know which end of a horse the hay went in or the road apples come out of...then after I taught him how to pretend to be a cowboy, he never even let me be in one of them flickers. Now ain't that just the shit? I reckon I just lived way past my time."

Tom took a long drink from the water glass.

"To tell ya the truth, I used to be real jealous of the likes of Jim Hickock and Bill Cody. Now don't get me wrong, Cody was a good friend of mine, but he was sure enough in the right place at the right time...but maybe now it's my turn. Maybe you can be my Buntline. Hell, that story you read in the Muddy Water Press...that was one of the few times my name ever got into a newspaper."

Tom removed a small flask from his inside coat pocket and held it out to Grant. Grant waved his hand in polite refusal and Tom poured some whiskey into his half-empty water glass.

Tom held the glass aloft in the manner of a toast.

"Son...I'm gonna let you make me famous, but if'n you're wantin' all the details, this is gonna take some time. Tomorrow, why don't you and me ride out to my ranch. I have some things I got to get done before I go over to Shelby. You can stay out at my place and we will have plenty of time to palaver."

Delighted by the invitation, Grant lifted his glass of water.

"What takes you to Shelby?"

"Big fight! Hell's bells boy, where you been? I thought you was a newsman. It's been in all the papers. Dempsey is defendin' his title against that Gibbons kid on the Fourth of July. Every town around here has changed or cancelled their doin's on the Fourth so that all the men can go to Shelby."

"If I'm still in Montana, may I go to Shelby with you? My editor is quite interested in the controversy over the fight. I personally don't care much about the fight game. One man beating another senseless seems a bit primitive. I am, however, interested from the standpoint that my editor might look favorably on this trip if I produce something he considers newsworthy. I could kill two birds with one stone and have time to spare...if you wouldn't mind my company."

"You're welcome as the spring grass, and you might just enjoy it. It's gonna be the biggest entertainment to hit these parts since the whorehouse burned on a winter night back in the nineties."

Tom reached into his coat for the flask and poured the remainder of its amber contents into his water glass. He raised the glass again.

"I'll make another toast. Here's to new adventures and old metaphors."

Grant smiled and raised his glass. Tom had again surprised him. Concealed beneath the veneer of a hard-lived frontier life, the erstwhile frontiersman was more worldly and literate than Grant could have anticipated.

Tom took a drink and then nodded at a young man standing nearby.

"You ready to order, Tom?" the waiter asked.

"Yes sir, we are." Tom looked at Grant. "What you gonna have?"

The waiter wrote their orders on a small pad of paper, thanked them and turned on his heels toward the kitchen.

"So just exactly what is your 'career?' Before I go spending too much time telling you about me...you tell me about you. Are you an honest to God newspaper reporter? Pardon me bein' blunt, but...you ain't but hardly shavin'."

Grant looked stunned.

"Yes sir, I am a reporter. I am employed by the Saint Louis Morning Star."

"So what, in the name of Jesus, Joseph and Mary does a big city reporter like yourself find interesting about some old fart who once rode for the Pony Express? There must be a shit load of scandal and corruption to report in a city the likes of Saint Louis?"

Tom looked Grant in the eye.

"You're just too damned young and innocent lookin' to have been exposed to the harsh realities of man's inhumanity to man for very long."

"Not quite two years. I joined the Star not quite two years ago."

"Okay then, you must be pretty well connected, or something. How does a youngster like you get a reporter job with big time news rag like the Star?"

"Attending Journalism school. I graduated from Columbia in twenty-one...Columbia University...in New York City...then I was hired by the Star."

"I get the drift," Tom said.

"And you are correct, there is a great deal of corruption and there are endless stories of 'man's inhumanity to man' to be told in a city like Saint Louis, but I must be totally honest. I suppose my elbows are not sharp enough to compete in that arena...or maybe I don't really have the stomach for high binders in smoke filled rooms. At any rate, my true desire lies in the writing of fiction. As of now, I have no story to tell. When I was offered the job at the Star, I jumped at the chance. Most of the famous writers of the past half century have begun their careers as reporters. Even Samuel Clemens was a reporter before Tom Sawyer."

"So you really don't want to write a story about the Pony Express or someone like me then. You just want to make something up?"

"No sir, that is not my intention at all. You mentioned men like Hickock. Most of the accounts I've read are obvious embellishments of real events. I want to write the real events, however, one must learn of the real event before writing or embellishing upon it. My entire picture of Western life comes from the reading I did as a child. I must expose myself to the real people and places if I expect to write in a believable style."

The waiter set their dinner plates before them and said, "Can I get you anything else, Tom?"

Both men shook their heads and the waiter walked toward the kitchen.

"Then you plan to use my name and everything?"

"Oh yes. If we come to an understanding and I can make your story a salable work...and the facts are verifiable of course, your name will be on the story. I can promise you that. Just as Buntline did for Buffalo Bill."

Tom again lifted his glass.

"Then I'll say her again. Here's to you making me famous."

As they chatted Tom noticed that Grant had only picked over his food.

"You better stuff those groceries down your neck, boy. Tomorrow's gonna be a long day."

They finished dinner engrossed in conversation about President Harding's trip to the West.

"I don't want to hurt your feelings or nothin', but it's gonna take more than shakin' a few hands for a big city Eastern fella like Harding to understand how things are out here. I voted for him because he claimed he was gonna get the government outta my business. Now it looks like his pals are linin' their own pockets and the worst of it is that businesses like mine have got the cold nose of the government stuck up our asses."

"No offense taken, I assure you," Grant said. "I must admit that as an Easterner I am finding things to be quite different out here."

When they had finished dinner, Tom threw his napkin on the table.

"I'll see you at six for some breakfast and then we'll take a little ride on out to my place."

Shaking hands again, they retired to their rooms.

Grant undressed and collapsed onto the bed. He pulled the blankets up to his neck against the chilled evening breeze blowing through the open window. When he had finally allowed his body to unwind, he realized that he was nearly exhausted from his travels and the anticipation of his meeting with Tom. His only real worry at this point was the ride to the ranch. Grant had never been on a horse.

Tempus fugit, ergo carpe diem, he thought, reminded of a phrase from his first year Latin class. Men had, after all, been riding horses for thousands of years. It surely could not be that difficult.

"Time flees, therefore seize the moment," he said, translating the Latin phrase aloud in the darkness.

His anxiety subsided as his body relaxed, luxuriating in the sensuous touch and the smell of freshly washed bed linens. Smiling in the silence, he recalled Tom's question as to whether he was an "honest to God reporter." He was a reporter, but his career was less than he had dreamed of two years prior.

As Melinda had predicted, his first year at the Star was disappointing. His assignments were primarily human interest, the society page and obituaries. However, Melinda had shown an interest in him, and he began to receive invitations to dinners at the Kuntz home in addition to acting as Melinda's escort at many of the society functions attended by the elite of Saint Louis.

Socializing with the Kuntz family had brought about derision from his fellow reporters at The Morning Star. The inevitable teasing had, at first, made him angry. Insinuations of "kissing ass with the boss," and "keeping the boss's daughter happy," became a regular part of the daily patter of his working companions.

He had done no more than politely accept the invitations of Melinda and her family, as he saw it. He learned to cope by saying such things as, "Mr. Kuntz and I are on a first name basis you know. He calls me Grant and I call him boss."

He did feel badly that the men made unseemly comments regarding Melinda. Her chastity was beyond question, to the best of his knowledge. The relationship was purely Platonic and he had seen to it that proper decorum was maintained at all times...not that he hadn't allowed his imagination to cross the line on a few occasions. Then there was that scene at the train depot only days ago to think about. He had most assuredly bungled the good-bye and left some hurt feelings. However, Melinda must certainly understand that he had not acted with any malicious intent. Oh well, he thought, I will have to deal with her when I return to Saint Louis.

Remembering Tom's question regarding corruption and scandal in the big city caused him to wince involuntarily as he lay in the darkness. He had, in fact, been close to a story which may have been worthy of a Pulitzer Prize, had not fate, assisted by his own callow handling of the matter, allowed the opportunity to slip away. Why belabor the situation now? He was off to other endeavors. However, self-recrimination still seethed.

It had been so close, he thought. Remembering the incident, he could still smell the perfume and cigar smoke as he and Melinda entered the ballroom that night. It had been one of those endless charity affairs to which the wealthy elite seem to feel a moral obligation. Grant attended these functions because he enjoyed the opportunity to hear live music and dance. A part of him wished that he had possessed the guile to take full advantage of the contacts he had made through these social channels.

Melinda had quickly introduced Grant to Mr. Benjamin Tully, one of the city's Planning Commissioners as she was dashing off to powder her nose. Grant recalled feeling put upon as the rather large Mr. Tully, who had been drinking heavily, grabbed his arm and dragged him into an alcove.

"I'm told that Kuntz has great expectations for your career," Tully had said to Grant's surprise.

"I am pleased to hear that," Grant could hear himself saying. "But he hasn't shared that enthusiasm with me."

"And he hasn't shared it with me either," Tully went on. "I hear it through mutual friends...if you know what I mean." Tully had winked as he finished and Grant began to realize that this conversation had a hidden agenda. "And you could really make some friends around town if you could see your way clear to drop in a few stories about the great advantages to be had by this fair city if our urban renewal bond issue gets the nod from the good citizens in our upcoming election."

Tully's breath reeked of whiskey, and the cigar he insisted upon waving under Grant's nose, was nearly overwhelming. Grant had attempted to break away, but Tully's insinuation stopped him cold.

"A man with your education and connections could do quite well out of this. My associates in the banking and construction side of these projects will see some tidy returns on our investment in this campaign. And we believe in sharing the wealth, if you know what I mean!" Tully had winked again saying, "A well placed word here and there from a man in your position could garner a lot of appreciation when this comes to fruition."

Grant had found himself transfixed on Tulley's exposition. He cringed in the darkness beneath the crisp linens of his bed in the Grand Union Hotel when he recalled the embarrassment at his own gullibility and naiveté. Had he not learned anything in those years at Columbia? Guileless though he had been as a child, this education in which he took so much pride, was supposed to have made him a journalist. Live and learn he exhorted himself.

Although Tully had considered the conversation quite confidential, he was speaking in inebriated whispers heard across the room. Grant, at last getting his reporters feet beneath him, had stepped further into the alcove and whispered, "Ben...may I call you Ben...just exactly what is in this for me?"

As Tully began his reply, a rough looking man whom Grant recognized as an assistant to the Mayor appeared, cutting Tully's words in mid sentence. "The Mayor would like to have a word with you, Mr. Tully", he said in a stern voice.

Grant had not shared his feelings regarding the conversation with anyone. He had however, begun some discreet inquiries into the background of Benjamin Tully and his associates. He interviewed several former employees of Tully and his associated construction firms and banking interests. Although he had not found any reliable stand-alone source, Grant was soon convinced that this bond issue was a boondoggle designed to line the pockets of a few powerful people in the city, beginning with the Mayor.

He had been relieved when the Kuntz name did not emerge with any of the various threads of information he pursued. Deciding that the cumulative rumors, insinuations and the blatant offer of a bribe from Tully were sufficient to pursue an official probe by The Morning Star, he had gone directly to Jonathon Kuntz.

"These are some serious allegations," Jonathon Kuntz had said, his years of experience making him reluctant to leap into a political volcano without some compelling confirmation. "Have you discussed this with Hiram?"

"No sir," Grant had replied, knowing that his impromptu disclosures were outside of Kuntz's strict adherence to the established chain of responsibility.

Kuntz had then referred the matter to Hiram Laidlaw, who recommended that Grant work with Shawn Newman on the investigation. Hiram had insisted that Shawn was familiar with the intricacies of city politics and that he was, therefore, best suited to assist Grant in uncovering any impropriety.

Grant's muscles stiffened as he relived the discomfort there in the darkness of the hotel room. He recalled the exasperation and resentment he had felt while reading the edited reportage. His byline was attached to the published compositions, but the story bore little resemblance to notes he had submitted to Shawn. At that same time, the editorial page of The Morning Star was extolling the bond issue, the politicians and the proposed projects. He had found himself doubting his own senses.

Grant had long since accepted that he was not, by nature, a confrontational person. His staid upbringing had only served to augment this innate characteristic. So when Shawn invited him to dinner one evening after a long day of sorting obscure details into an intelligible draft, he accepted, deciding it was time to make a stand.

They ordered Coca-Cola as Shawn slumped into the corner of the booth, slipping a flask of whiskey from the inside pocket of his jacket. When the drinks were delivered, they ordered hamburgers as Shawn blatantly poured a strong shot into one of the empty glasses the waitress had set on the table without being asked.

Girding himself for Shawn's expected indignation, Grant said, "Shawn...I'm not accusing anyone of anything...and I'm reasonably sure that Mr. Kuntz is not involved in anything inappropriate. But these stories that are being printed with my byline are so bowdlerized that even I don't know who wrote them."

Pausing in expectation of a response, Grant noted that Shawn was staring directly into his eyes with an unchanging expression on his face.

"Am I expecting too much to seek an honest revelation of the collusion which seems to be a corrupting influence in our city's affairs?"

Shawn stared another long moment into Grant's eyes. Finally, he took a deep breath and lit a cigarette.

"Collins, my boy, surviving in an unjust world often requires compromises. Sometimes we get a little and sometimes we give a little. But we seldom get all we want, and truth and justice are most often in the eye of the beholder. Now I know you'd like to get yourself one of those Pulitzer Prizes...and you believe that corrupt politicians, especially those with a weakness in the grip of the grape should be easy pickin's. Ripe fruit on the low bows. Right?"

"I could scarcely have put it more eloquently. Yes. Once the cat is out of the bag I would think that a sense of civic responsibility would be the order of the day."

"Do you know where that expression about the 'cat out of the bag' originated?" Shawn asked.

Shawn had again looked Grant in the eye but did not wait for an answer.

"In the old days when food was scarce, the grifters would go through a small town offering to sell the hungry folks a pig. In other words, they had a sack or poke, which contained an animal. Now the grifters would claim that the animal was a small pig...that's where the term 'buying a pig in a poke' came from. They'd let the potential buyer feel the wriggling contents for a moment and then, of course, the negotiating would begin. After some hagglin', the con men would concede defeat to the superior negotiating skills of the rube, who would consider he had the better end of the bargain. Mr. Grifter would collect his money and fade away."

"So what has that to do with what is going on with Tully?" Grant asked.

"Well, sir, most often the animal in the sack was some hapless cat that the con men had caught on the way to town. Once 'the cat was out of the bag' the con was over. The swindlers would be forced into a hasty escape."

"I still fail to see what that has to do with my investigation?" Grant had said, recalling how angry he had felt at what he considered, at the time, to be Shawn's stalking horse designed to avoid answering his question.

"Well, my boy, unfortunately for you, this is politics, which means that nothing is what it seems. You see, you only got to cop a feel of that 'pig in the poke.' Trouble is that you jumped a step ahead to believing that the 'cat was out of the bag.'"

Shawn took a long sip of his whiskey and washed it down with Coca-Cola. Looking Grant squarely in the eye again, he smiled a knowing grin.

"Fact is that the pig, or the cat or the possum or whatever it was that you thought you got to feel...it's still in the poke, and very likely there it will remain."

Grant had stared blankly into Shawn's smiling face, not knowing what to say.

Remembering that revelation, he again felt the warmth of his cheeks in the darkness of his Grand Union Hotel room. He had been the rube and he had paid dearly for that 'pig in the poke.'

The hamburgers were delivered. As Shawn took a huge bite he chewed pensively. Swallowing, he said, "Grant...since we are on these pig analogies and since I am supposed to be showing you the ropes, let me explain my metaphor for politics."

Shawn washed down his food with whiskey and Coca-Cola. He then smiled again as he asked, "Have you ever seen a greased pig contest at a county fair?"

Grant nodded his head in the affirmative.

"Politics is that greasy pig. They grease that little oinker for the contest and then they turn him loose in an arena in front of a lot of otherwise sane and decent people. Then some of those folks jump right into the arena in their Sunday best and begin to chase his greasy ass while the others, the spectators...or voters, give encouragement and clap and laugh. Now everyone who actually participates in chasing that pig gets real dirty, but no matter who catches the slippery bastard, that porker ends up as the main course at the barbeque. I have heard it said that 'money is the mother's milk of politics', but I'll tell you lad...it is also the grease on the pig. Some chase the pig and some just sit on the sidelines and cheer. But in the end, everyone goes to the barbeque...be it by ignorance or design the barbeque goes on."

Shawn had then poured a shot of his whiskey into the empty glass the waitress had placed in front of Grant. Unaccustomed as he was to hard liquor, he recalled downing it in one swallow and nearly vomiting before he could dilute the acrid residue with a sip of Coca-Cola.

That conversation had made it clear to Grant that, in the bare-knuckle world of political expedience, his sheepskin from Columbia University was not worth the match it would take to light it afire.

Unfamiliar sounds of the night drifted through the open window of his hotel room as Grant recalled that moment in time. That was the tipping point at which he had made his decision to seek other outlets for his writing ambitions.

At last, exhaustion overtook his busy thoughts. As he drifted into sleep he congratulated himself for his good fortune so far in his meetings with Tom. The invitation to stay at Tom's ranch seemed a God send. Even his apprehension in anticipation of riding a horse soon dissolved into the blackness of his surroundings and he slept a dreamless rest.

3

Charlie Lowe was at the desk when Tom came down the main staircase and entered the lobby the next morning.

"Has that kid come down yet?" Tom asked.

"Ain't seen him," Charlie said, leaning across the desk to look up the stairs. "Tell me somethin'...you ain't really plannin' to take that tenderfoot to the ranch on J. D.'s knot-headed old roan are ya?"

"I reckon," Tom said with a wink. "Tell that boy I'll be in the dining room waitin' for him if he ever gets up. I got to have some coffee."

Tom disappeared into the dining room as Grant came down the stairs carrying his suitcase.

"Good morning Charlie! May I leave this here?" Grant said, holding his bag in the air.

"You bet...I'll keep an eye on it for you."

After breakfast, Tom and Grant went to the desk to settle their accounts.

"You gonna haul us over to the livery?" Tom asked, as he paid for his room.

"Yes sir," Charlie said. "It'll be my pleasure."

As Grant placed his suitcase into the car, the morning chill was again blowing through his light clothing.

"Charlie, would you mind stopping at the mercantile? I need to pick up a few things. The clothing I brought doesn't seem adequate to your Montana summer."

"You bet," Charlie said.

Looking through the selection at the mercantile, Grant purchased some red woolen long underwear, a warm sweater, a jacket and a pair of Levi Strauss blue jeans. He also bought a pair of high top work boots Tom recommended as more suitable for riding and wear around the ranch.

Charlie parked the Chevrolet beside the stable. Following Grant and Tom into the barn, he chuckled to himself when he saw a small roan horse standing saddled beside Luke.

They were met by a rail thin, weathered looking man whom Grant estimated to be at least as old as Tom.

"This here is J. D. He runs the livery, little as there is a need, these days," Tom said.

Grant was holding his new clothing under one arm and his suitcase in the other hand. He nodded acknowledgement.

"You can put on yer new duds in the empty stall there," J. D. said.

Grant went into the empty stall to put on his new clothing. He pulled on the stiff boots and came from the stall carrying his leather suitcase.

"Damned if you ain't lookin' real Western," Charlie said.

Grant recognized Luke, the horse Tom had ridden the day before. As he walked to the roan he asked, "Is this my mount?"

"That's the one," J. D. said.

Tom threw an old flour sack toward Grant.

"Put your possibles in there. You can leave that suitcase here with J.

D. It won't ride well on ol' Strawberry."

"I'll see to your belongings," J. D. said. "No one will bother your outfit here. I'll put your case in the tack room."

Tom mounted his horse while J. D. held the reins of the roan.

Grant quickly stuffed what he thought would be necessary from his suitcase into the cloth sack. J. D. helped him roll and tie the bag behind his saddle.

"Tom," Grant said, trepidation cracking his voice.

"What is it son?" Tom asked.

"I have never ridden a horse," Grant said.

"You know somethin' son, I ain't no psychic, but somehow I knew that."

Tom turned Luke so that he could watch Grant.

"Just put yer foot in the stirrup there and step right on up. J. D. will hold the reins till you get your seat."

Grant followed the instructions and when he was in the saddle J. D. put the reins around the horses neck and handed them to him.

"If you want him to go left, move the reins to the left and give him a nudge with your heel. If you wanna go right, do the opposite."

Luke began to walk toward the door of the livery barn.

"Giddy up," Grant said as he lurched forward in the saddle.

The roan laid his ears back, turning his head sufficiently to one side to see his rider.

"I don't like the look in this animal's eye," Grant said.

His knuckles turned white, holding the saddle horn as if it was deliverance itself. Strawberry began moving forward to follow Luke.

Tom turned his mount toward Front Street and Grant thought it odd that they were again passing the hotel. The roan followed about twenty feet behind with no urging from Grant. As they rounded the corner, Grant realized for the first time that there was a paved street in Fort Benton. Musing over this revelation he heard Luke's steel shoes begin to clatter as Tom's horse walked onto the paved roadway.

The roan walked to within a few feet of the pavement and stopped abruptly. Grant nudged the horse with his heel as Tom had instructed but the horse stood frozen. Its forelegs were stiff and its body quivered. Even in his inexperience, Grant could sense its fear.

"Tom," Grant shouted. "My animal has locked up and won't move."

"Give that hay bag a good kick in the ribs," Tom replied, without turning.

Grant was now aware that Front Street was lined with people on both sides.

"I did that and he's just standing here shaking."

Tom stopped Luke and turned to face in Grant's direction.

"Take the loose ends of those reins and whack him a good one," he said.

Tom turned his head so that Grant could not see his smile.

"Come on boy, we can't sit here all day."

"I'll give it a try," Grant said.

He took the dangling reins in hand and gave the quivering beast a resounding slap. The roan spun like a spooked dervish, rearing slightly as he reversed direction. When its front feet hit the dirt, he bucked, pitching Grant into the air. The horse crow hopped a few dozen yards, before stopping to look back. Strawberry then walked back to where Grant was lying on the dirt gasping for breath.

"Okay folks, we had our fun. Stand back and give the boy some air," Grant heard Tom say.

Grant looked around and realized from the looks on the bystander's faces that he had been the morning's entertainment. A young man of about fifteen was standing a short distance away holding the roan horse by its reins and smiling an empathetic smile.

"Sorry son, but every cheechako has his day. I reckon you are now an official cowboy," Tom said.

He held out a hand to pull Grant to his feet.

Feeling humiliated, Grant brushed the dust from his clothing as he looked at the faces in the crowd. Embarrassment mixed with fear, anger and physical pain left his head swimming in confusion.

"Ya see, they paved this street about two months ago and that horse you're ridin' has never got used to it. He is an otherwise trustworthy nag but there is somethin' about this pavin' that he just won't abide."

The young man who had been holding Grant's horse approached and handed him the reins. Grant's eyes were wide with unabashed fear.

"I'm not getting back on this animal," he said.

Tom put his arm around Grant's shoulders. He leaned close so that only Grant could hear. In a comforting and fatherly tone intended to instill confidence he said, "Grant, when ya get bucked off, you just gotta get right back on or you'll likely never ride again. I know you're embarrassed, but it'll be a whole lot worse if you don't get back on this glue pot. Besides which, you wanna go out to the ranch don't you?"

Tom forced the younger man to make eye contact. Grudgingly, Grant looked into Tom's eyes. He then turned and reached for the saddle horn.

"Here, let me hold them reins and you get back on just like ya did before. We'll take another street and get the hell on out of here."

Grant remounted and the two rode out of town, puffs of dust erupting from beneath the horse's hooves.

They rode in silence, Strawberry trudging slowly behind Luke. Although Tom's big gelding was capable of a ground-eating lope that could cover many miles in a day, Tom kept him at a walk allowing the younger man to overcome his fear and get accustomed to the feel of horse and saddle.

Pangs of guilt over getting this young dude bucked off on his first ride caused Tom to rein Luke to a stop. The roan closed the distance and stopped beside Luke without command.

Grant was staring straight ahead, still holding firmly to the saddle horn.

"Son...are you a believer in the baby Jesus?"

Grant, taken by surprise, responded without thinking. "Why...uh... yes. Certainly I am."

"Good! Then I can count on your forgiveness when I say that I am sorry about that joke back in town."

Tom watched Grant's face.

"Is there anything hurt besides your pride?"

Grant shook his head but said nothing.

Tom urged Luke gently with his spur and both horses began to walk.

"What is a cheechako?" Grant broke the silence.

"A newcomer, a greenhorn...a fella unfamiliar with the country."

"How far is it to your ranch?"

"About twenty miles, I reckon."

"Have you lived in Fort Benton all your life, Tom?"

"Not yet."

Grant laughed involuntarily at the quip.

"Let me rephrase that...how long have you lived in Fort Benton?"

"Me and my people came in fifty four. There was my ma and pa, my big sister Rachel, my big brother Derrick and my little sister Sarah. Benton was still a trading fort then. Belonged to the American Fur Company in those days."

Grant pictured the stereotypical paintings and motion pictures of the western migration.

"Did you come by Conestoga wagon?"

"Part way, but most of the trip from Saint Louis was up the Mississippi and the Missouri on a side-wheeler. Steamers only came up to Fort Union, which is over on the North Dakota border, back in those times. I was just a little younker then. 'Bout seven years old as I recall...and for a boy who had a heart for adventure I had sure picked the right ma and pa. Just gettin' on a steamboat was adventure enough for most folks."

Tom stopped Luke pointing to a cluster of white spots in the distance.

"Antelope!"

As Grant studied the foliage, animals began to materialize around the moving spots.

"I would never have seen those, had you not pointed them out."

"It takes practice; just like living in the city takes practice. You train your eyes to see little bits of movement. Back when I first came here, you learned to see or you starved. We had to depend on huntin' to live."

"I'll start practicing, just for the experience. So you came by steamboat to Fort Union?"

"To be honest, I was too young to remember the particulars. Things like the names of places and people, or the dates of incidents...that escapes me now. That was near seventy years ago. But I can sure as well remember some of the things that happened like they was yesterday."

"I believe that I can check libraries and steamboat company logs and other historical data for dates and places. What I would find helpful are your eye witness accounts of the events. I can do the necessary research."

"Well then, I'll just give 'er to you as best as I can recall. The first real excitement that I remember was on the steamboat headed up to Fort

Union from Saint Louie. We'd been on the river for maybe three or four days. It had been rainin' and I was makin' a pest of myself, as usual, going down into the engine room and talkin' to the fellas who was stokin' the fire. I was a curious boy and I was lookin' to see how everything on that riverboat worked. Mostly I was generally gettin' in the way...you know how young boys are when the rain keeps you from gettin' outside? It was close quarters on board and the only time we could get off that boat was when it stopped at the small towns for freight or passengers. There was also the wood stops. I damn nearly got marooned at a couple of the wood stops. I'd run off into the woods, get engrossed in some critter or whatever, and have to run like hell to make it when the whistle blew. Now it was just after we had put on a load of wood and as we got under way, the sun finally came out. We were havin' a beautiful day and I was up on the top deck with my folks when our steamboat rounded a bend in the river and came upon a mackinaw sittin' dead in the water, near about mid-river."

Tom, noting Grant's quizzical glance, did not wait for the question.

"A mackinaw was a flat bottomed freight boat, maybe forty to sixty feet long. They were mighty handy for floatin' the shallows and carried all manner of goods down the river from the trading forts. They were most generally built of the local lumber right on the riverbank site where the goods were to be hauled from. Now it was apparent when we came alongside this particular mackinaw that it was hung up on a bar. Our captain knew the channels and he stayed a couple hundred feet away from where the mack was hung...but even at a few hundred feet you could see the arrows stickin' out of that boat. Damned thing looked like Aunt Maudie's pin cushion...and there was blood from one end of that mackinaw to the other. From a distance it appeared that several of the men aboard were not movin', and a couple more were not doin' too well.

41

Our captain slowed the engine to hold the steamer in place and sent some of the crewmen in a row boat draggin' a tow line for the mack. I was intent on watchin' those fellas rowin' in the little boat when I heard a noise that sounded like a 'ping-ka-thunk' right next to my little punkin'. Bits of paint and metal stung the side of my face and I realized that somethin' had hit the cabin wall close to where I was standin'. About then I heard what sounded like a far off rifle shot."

Tom looked at Grant.

"I reckon you ain't never been shot at?"

"No...thank God! So the bullet hit before you heard the rifle?"

"You see, when a gun is fired at you from a distance the bullet actually gets to you before the sound of the gun. So the bullet hit that wall before I could hear the rifle that had fired it. Anyway...real quick there was a lot of yelling and men runnin' and my ma and pa was both hollerin'. I looked up the river and could make out a log raft with about five or six men aboard. In an instant I realized that they were Injuns on that raft and they was shootin' at us."

Tom rubbed his chin in thought.

"I put two and two together and figured that those Injuns had apparently been in a fight with the mackinaw men before our arrival on the scene. Looked like them redskins was floatin' right on down to finish the job too because right about then I heard someone shoutin' about Injuns and people were pointin' to the bank just a hundred yards the other side of the mackinaw. That was when I noticed another ten or twelve head of them Injuns on the bank of the river just down from where that boat was hung up. That bunch was horseback, and although we could see them pretty good I can't say for sure what kind of Injuns they were. If I had to guess I would say they were some breed of Sioux or maybe Rics. Fine lookin' bunch of men they were, too. Fancy feathered with war bonnets and all. They was quite impressin' to a kid from back in the settlements. I'd reckon that all them Injuns had been together when they attacked the mackinaw men. I kind'a figured that the men in the mack had been ashore tradin' when the Injuns decided to take the whole kit and caboodle. Somehow those boys had got clear of the fight and had started floatin' safely down the river. Considerin' the appearance of those men, all shot up as they was, and that boat all full of arrows, it was clear as to why they weren't payin' much attention to their navigatin'. I doubt anyone was steerin' when the boat hung up on the bar. I'd reckon those redskins had been followin' the mackinaw along the bank downstream on horseback. When they seen that the boat was hung up and there weren't enough healthy men to get 'er loose...they took advantage of the opportunity to finish off the white men and get that cargo. As I remember, there was a passel of trade goods in the mackinaw and I guess them Injuns was bound to have it. I reckon that they'd gone upstream and built 'em that makeshift raft to float down and get at those boys in the mack. I'd suppose that the Injuns had put their best warriors on the raft and then the rest of 'em rode back down stream to meet the rafters when they had finished their bloody work."

"What happened to the crewmen from the steamer...the men in the rowboat? What happened when they met the Indians on the raft?" Grant asked.

"Those steamboat crewmen who had gone over to the mackinaw must'a set big store by their hair. They wasted no time in throwin' the tow rope to the mackinaw men and churnin' some water with them oars gettin' back to the steamer."

Tom smiled to himself.

"Fortunately, there was only a couple of the Injuns who had old muskets. Even though they was loadin' and shootin' just as quick as they could, they was well outgunned. By that time most of the men on the steamboat who was armed began to take pot shots at them Injuns on the raft. I looked at my ma and she was white as fresh hung linens. My pa ran to get his rifle and by then all hell was a poppin'. Every now and then you would hear that 'ping-ka-thunk' of a lead ball hittin' the steamboat and a second later you would hear the report and see the smoke comin' from a rifle on that raft. My pa and all the men on the steamboat was firing as fast as they could load. It wasn't long, in that still mornin' air, that you couldn't see nothin' at all. Sulfur smoke so thick from all the shootin' that the men on the steamboat were forced to wait until a gust of wind would blow away the smoke before they could take aim for another shot. It was like a giant boiled egg fart at the Fourth of July fireworks. One of the men on the steamboat got shot in the hip and he was howlin' like a banshee. Worse yet, my little sister was bawlin' loud enough to raise critters from extinction. Betwixt her caterwaulin' and his howlin' the din was discombobulating."

Tom looked at Grant with a smile.

"I swear...the smell of smoke from that sulfurous gun powder and all the noise and wailing of the folks on the steamer was exactly what my young mind would have conjured up for a picture of Hades itself. I was expectin' any second to see ol' Beelzebub come dancing down that rail collectin' souls. It was, beyond doubt, the most excitin' thing my young eyes had ever beheld...and there I was, right in the middle of it. Can you even feature such a thing?"

"To be honest, I am not sure I would have been 'in the middle of it,'" Grant said.

"Well I nearly got run off. My ma hollered at me to take my little sister and go below...but there was no way I was gonna miss that show. Ma finally picked up little sister and ran below decks, but I stayed right there at the rail watchin' that fight."

Grant had removed a small notebook from his inside pocket and began furiously scribbling notes. His handwriting scrawled illegibly with each step of his hired horse.

"This here is interesting but it ain't the good stuff," Tom said.

Tom glanced sideways in an attempt to see what Grant was writing.

"It's a start." Grant replied. "I don't want to forget anything."

Grant looked up from his notebook.

"Were the men on your steamboat able to stave off the attack?" Grant asked.

Tom thought a moment, recalling his place in the story.

"Seems them Injuns weren't complete fools. At least not so stupid as to float that raft up to a steamer full of armed white men who figured on makin' them the guests of honor at the turkey shoot. Somehow those redskins got the raft out of the current and headed to the bank where their pals were waitin' with the horses. Pretty quick they got to the bank, jumped on their ponies and skeeedaddled. I watched 'em as they rode up to a rise some distance off and out of gun range. They proceeded to built 'em a fire and sat and watched what we was gonna do."

Tom watched Grant's furious scribbling.

"I told you this wasn't the good stuff. Hell...I was just a kid. I didn't even have a gun."

Grant finished his notes and then looked at Tom.

"Was the steamer able to tow the mackinaw from the sand bar?"

"It was...and when we'd towed the mack to the opposite shore it was a gruesome sight for my young eyes to behold. Two of the mackinaw men were dead and two were hurt awful bad. There was two more who were a bit the worse for wear but able to make do, and one fella had come through the fray completely unscathed. You know...that is somethin' that has amazed me since that very day and through the years...and all of the fightin' I was ever a part of. How is that you have a big fight with bullets or arrows flyin' everywhere, and some men seem to get hurt or killed and others seem to come through without a nick? I'll never understand...but anyway, the Captain put together a burial party to see to the dead. They didn't leave no valuables in the graves; not even clothes. I reckon they figured the Injuns, who was watchin' from the other side of the river, was just gonna dig them boys up anyway. Then the steamer re-supplied the men on the mack with powder and lead. Back in those times, no decent white man would leave another in the wilderness without weapons, at least powder and ball and the like. As I said before, that mackinaw was carrying furs and buffalo hides as I remember. I guess that's why them fine lookin' feathered devils was so anxious to have at it. It was first class trade goods for sure. It surely didn't take too much persuading to get three or four of the men on the side wheeler to accept an offer to help crew that mackinaw for a share of the profits in Saint Louis.

I remember that there was a doctor on the steamer who treated the wounded as best he could and then we set them boys adrift. I have no idea what ever became of them or their boat. I can tell you this...that was the first time I ever saw wild Injuns and it was also the first time I saw dead people who hadn't died in bed...and it was sure enough the first I ever watched men die in a violent way."

Grant was contemplative for a time.

"That must have been very disturbing for a seven year old child."

Thinking a moment Tom smiled, cocking his head to one side to look at Grant.

"I pissed my pants in all that excitement. Damnedest scare as ever a little shaver had."

Tom leaned back and dug into his saddlebag, removing a tarnished brass container. Grant could see that the oval box was about three inches by five and perhaps three quarters of an inch deep with a press fit lid. Tom reined Luke to a stop and Strawberry stopped without urging. Tom removed the lid and placed it in the hollow behind his saddle horn.

Tom offered the box, which contained cigarettes and matches, to Grant.

"Would ya care to put a nail in your coffin?"

"Oh, no thank you," Grant replied with a wave of his hand. "Tobacco makes my head spin."

"Good habit not to get into. I just smoke 'em now and then. Seems at my age, coughing is about all the exercise I get."

Taking a Diamond Match from the box and striking it with his thumbnail, Tom lit one of the Lucky Strike cigarettes.

"That is a very unusual cigarette box. It looks quite old. I have never seen anything like it," Grant said.

"It's an old timey fire starter box," Tom said.

Tom replaced the lid and handed the container to Grant.

Grant examined the box. Removing the lid to see its underside, he noticed that what had appeared to be a cap covering a piece of glass.

"Does this come off?" he asked.

"Yeah...just get your fingernail under the edge and lift up."

Grant removed the silver dollar sized brass dome to expose a magnifying glass.

"Mountain men used them boxes aplenty. Some called 'em Hudson Bay tobacco boxes. They were prized as trade goods in the old days. You'd see lots of them things around even thirty or forty years ago."

Tom pointed to the inset magnifying glass.

"See that glass? A fella could use it to start a fire or light his pipe on a sunny day, or maybe he could see to get a sliver out of his finger...or fix some small part in his rifle, if'n his eyes were getting' a might weak."

"I hadn't thought much about how the mountain men built a fire," Grant said. "I always heard the old saw about rubbing two sticks together or the bow and drill procedure."

"Mountain men carried flint and steel for starting their fires, mostly... but they'd use these boxes to carry their fire startin' tools and the kindlin'. If it was sunny they could use the glass to kindle a flame...if not he could use his flint even when it was cold. Fire could be life and death to a man out in the mountains."

Grant handed the brass box back to Tom.

"Yep, these here tinder boxes were common, but like a lot of things, you don't see much of them any more. I traded a little blood for this particular one, which is why I keep it as a sentimentality."

Tom calculated the pace they were traveling.

"I reckon we're about another hour to home. You wanna hear a bit more?"

"That is why I came to Montana," Grant replied.

"Let me see now...where was I? After we left the mackinaw adrift there wasn't much excitement, at least by comparison anyway. It took that steamer a couple three more days to get to Fort Union, where we joined up with a wagon train going on to Fort Benton."

"I saw the old docks outside the Grand Union Hotel in Fort Benton. Why didn't you just take the steam boat all the way to Fort Benton?"

"In those days, Fort Union was as far as they could take those steamers up the ol' Muddy Mo. They didn't begin to build boats with a shallow enough draft until later years. That was into the late fifties or early sixties I reckon."

"So you actually did come to Fort Benton by wagon train?"

"Couple hundred miles of it was by wagon train. Which reminds me...

I'm gonna let you in on a secret. I reckon you kind'a have a picture in your mind of wagon trains and all...which prompted your question?"

Grant nodded.

"In these new motion pictures they always show the wagon trains being pulled by horse teams running full tilt across the prairie...and then circling up to fight Injuns. The plain truth is that most wagon trains was actually drawn by oxen. Most of the work like loggin' and minin' and haulin' freight was done by oxen. Horses was damned expensive for white folk and they was treasure to the Injuns. Any horse left unattended for five minutes on the prairie would be run off by the Injuns or miscreant white men. Although oxen was cantankerous critters, they was strong and had stamina...but mostly they weren't likely to end up in the remuda of some redskin."

"A remuda? I don't think I am familiar with the term," Grant said.

"A remuda is a bunch of horses most generally belonging to one man. You might think of the term as bein' used to describe a man's personal bunch, pickin' one to ride each day. Like the drovers did on the big cattle drives. They didn't want to wear out one horse, so each man had a remuda. Injuns wealth was based on the size of his remuda, so there wasn't too many horses left standin' where the redskins could have at 'em."

"I get it. I see that the motion picture people are not doing us any favors as far as depicting history."

"Those motion picture folks are just entertaining and trying to make a buck. You can't believe much of what you see on the silver screen. But anyway...it was oxen that did most of the work on wagon trains and loggin' camps and farmin'. There was still plenty of buffalo back in those days, so the Injuns wasn't about to risk life and limb to steal a cow. On the other hand, a horse was a prized possession for any Injun...or white man for that matter."

"I must admit that had you asked me, I would have said that horses were the dray animals of the wagon trains. But you say the oxen were cantankerous?"

"I guess unwieldy would give a better picture. That was where the term bull whacker come from. Movin' oxen took a skilled hand. The bull whackers didn't actually whack the oxen though. A fella couldn't afford to injure his transportation. That would have been like whacking the brand new engine of your flivver with a sledge hammer. But the bull whackers got real good at crackin' a whip. They could sure enough get the attention of a bovine that was lollygaggin'. My ol' pappy could knock a fly off a beeve's ear and never draw a drop of blood. Fact is, that wagon trip from Fort Union was my first exposure to being a bull whacker...and I hadn't no more than just become a whippersnapper."

Tom chuckled at his own humor, drawing a smile from Grant.

"Did you have any Indian problems during the wagon train to Fort Benton?"

"We had a couple of brief meetin's with some Injuns on the way to Fort Benton but there was nothin' near as excitin' as that shootout over the mackinaw. The ones we met was mostly lookin' to do some tradin' for whiskey. That was the prime trade goods for Injuns."

"Why did your father choose Fort Benton? It must have been a very remote outpost in those days."

"My pappy had accepted employment with the American Fur Trading Company. He was a pretty fair hand at trappin' and huntin' and he could cipher well enough to be of value at keepin' their books."

Tom took off his hat to scratch the back of his neck.

"He was also a right smart carpenter and had a good head for all manner of buildin'. He would work on the maintenance of the fort when there was little else to turn his hand to. He even had me and my brother helpin' him in the makin' of mud brick with which to reinforce the walls of the fort. Adobe didn't burn like the wooden walls and it was much more resistant to arrows and bullets."

"So the family relocation was a matter of employment?" Grant said.

"Yes sir...and it wasn't long till pa had a reputation as being a good and fair trader. That gave him some advantage with the Injuns. And what with the other things he could do, such as the fact that he could handle a team of oxen or mules and he was a good shot with rifle and pistol made him worth what the American Fur Company was payin'."

"Sounds like one of those rare Jack of all trades sort of men."

"He was that indeed...and I never saw him show a sign of fear to the Injuns, or to any man for that matter. Of course, he was my hero, so I reckon I remember him well. Pa had got hired on by American Fur Company through some contacts of my mother's people. Fella by the name of Chouteau, after who this here county is named, got him the job. Now ol' Choteau was the American Fur Trading Company. He was the one who opened the fort to trade with the Injuns in eighteen and forty-six. I was given to understand that the Chouteau family was some sort of shirttail relatives on my ma's side, but I never verified it. According to my pa, prior to forty-six the fort had been called by various names and had even been moved up and down the river as they was seekin' the most secure place. There was a couple of other trading outfits that had tried to compete with Choteau but he had an ace up his sleeve in the form of a Missouri Senator by the name of Thomas Hart Benton. Seems ol' Benton greased the skids for American Fur to obtain the proper government licenses. There had been some dispute over the licensing of liquor...naturally. Chouteau and Benton were apparently pals and I would have to figure that some sort of shenanigan took place."

Tom took a last drag from the cigarette butt and pinched the lighted ember.

"Now ol' Benton himself is an interesting study. I guess you didn't hear much about him, but he left his mark on history and that's for sure. I mean besides having the little river town of Fort Benton named after him. You see, ol' Benton was the mentor and sponsor of Captain John C. Fremont who is famous for discovering and mappin' the Oregon Trail. Fremont also mapped the Great Basin and a whole bunch of California. Hell...they even named a city after Fremont in California, which is more than they even done for Benton. All Benton got was a little bitty ol' burg in Montana."

Grant looked up from his writing. Slowly, a realization was sinking in. The exploration and settlement of Western North America had occurred during the lifetime of his new acquaintance. Tom had, in some way, been involved in the American history that Grant had been taught in school; much of which had unfortunately gone in one ear and out the other.

"I remember Fremont from history class! Did you actually know Benton or Fremont?"

"No sir...I did not. But I did meet Kit Carson, and truth be known, it was really Carson who did the exploring and finding of the places Fremont got the credit for. At least as I was given to understand. I heard that Fremont couldn't have found his way out of a one hole shithouse, had it not been for Carson to guide him. The only time Fremont ever did lead a party in the mountains he got lost in a snowstorm and got half the men killed."

"So how did you come to know Carson?"

"Carson was an old man, by my standards, when I met him. He had some ranchin' interests in Colorado and I ran across him when I was scouting for the Army down around Denver. He'd come to buy some land and do some scouting for his own business. We had a chance to sit and trade yarns one rainy afternoon. He was a kind'a quiet, soft spoken fella and, to be honest, he really wasn't the one to say anything bad about anyone, especially Fremont. I heard the Fremont stories from other fellas who knew them both."

"Kit Carson!" Grant said in near reverence. "I did read all about him."

"Well I reckon this here ought to be the interesting part for you then. It seems ol' Fremont's wife also had a fondness for writing. Fremont would tell her the stories and she'd write it all down...then she began to publish the exploits of her gallant husband. Of course, her interest was in promoting her husband's potentialities. But in so doin' she also made ol' Carson famous because Fremont had spoken highly of Carson. And damned well he should have spoken highly of Carson, all things considered!"

Tom paused looking over at Grant, who was scribbling notes. He waited until it appeared that Grant's notes were complete.

"And where, you ask, did ol' Fremont's young bride come by the wherewithal to publish her writings about Carson and her heroic young husband?"

Grant looked at Tom waiting for the answer.

"Well sir...Fremont's wife was the daughter of, none other than, Thomas Hart Benton. The same Thomas Hart Benton who was the namesake of the old fur trade fort and the town of Fort Benton. Like I told ya last night, some of them boys just seemed to be in the right place at the right time or have the right writer. Ol' Carson, it seems, was one of 'em what with Fremont's wife and all."

Grant smiled at Tom's obvious envy. He realized that he was getting a different view of history than one was likely to receive in any classroom. He wondered just how much to take with a grain of salt but he was anxious for Tom to continue.

Tom squinted and looked around as if he was seeing the country as it had appeared seventy years earlier. He took a deep breath and looked at Grant. He swept his arm in an encompassing arc.

"This country around here wasn't called Montana in those days. We didn't get our statehood till eighty-nine. When my folks came here in fifty-four, all of this area east of the Divide was still known merely as the 'Injun Country.' It was a portion of what was then the Missouri Territory of that Louisiana Purchase."

Tom's eyes smiled for a moment as if some special place in his heart had warmed.

"It was fresh and new then. No fences, no roads, no people, 'ceptin' for the Injuns. Pappy used to say it was a thumb in the eye of royalty and a gift to free men from Tom Jefferson...it really seemed to tickle my ol' pappy that President Jefferson had bested that frog turd Napoleon in the world's biggest real estate deal.

I believe it was shortly after we got out here, within a couple of years, that the government changed the name of this part of the country and started calling this the Nebraska Territory."

Tom pointed to the west.

"Other side of the mountains, over around what is Kalispell today...or what we called the Flathead Country, that was still the Oregon Territory. Later on, in sixty-one I believe it was, they got another wild hare and started calling this here part of Montana the Dakota Territory."

Tom wrinkled his brow.

"If I recall correctly it was sixty-four when the government made up its mind to call the whole shebang the Montana Territory."

"Did your parents start the ranch when they got here?"

"No...that wasn't really possible then. You gotta remember that there was still a lot of Injun troubles in the fifties. We lived at the fort for several years while ma and pa saved up a stake. Then they decided to build the ranch. I say 'the ranch' but there wasn't any ranch then. There was just prairie. There was buffalo, antelope, deer, bear, the wolves, the wind...and of course the Injuns.

"So the hostiles were still present when your parents began to build the ranch?"

"Hell boy, them redskins was our only neighbors and of necessity we was tradin' with 'em all the time. Most of them people were just like you and me. Biggest difference I reckon is that they were folks who lived off the land. Most were just tryin' to make a livin' and feed their young'uns as any man would do. That's not to say that there weren't a bunch of 'em who were real assholes. I knew a few who just naturally needed killing. But then there was a lot of white men who were assholes who needed killin' too!"

Tom's eyes narrowed as his voice tailed off. A chill went down Grant's spine.

"The Injuns were a tough and proud bunch. They lived by the buffalo. They ate buffalo. They lived in buffalo hide lodges. They made clothes and weapons and tools of all manner from the buffalo. There wasn't no mercantile where those Injuns could go get a sack of flour and a pound of coffee. Everything depended on the buffalo. Even before the white man came, one bad winter could decimate the buffalos and the Injuns."

"I recall the stories of people shooting thousands of buffalo from train windows, leaving them to rot," Grant said.

"The buffalo was the life blood and the downfall of the Injuns. It was their dependence on the buffalo that made it so easy for the government to put an end to the Injun's freedom. The Great-White-Father in Washington just gave the order to kill off the buffalo in the name of Manifest Destiny...and that was pretty much the end of it. It only took a couple of years. Without the buffalo, the Injuns went from being the lords of the plains to being a bunch of drunken beggars living on worthless land that the white folks didn't want…and being fed scraps by crooked government agents."

"I really never had considered the lives of the Indian peoples. The history taught in school presents them as savages who required control. I just can't imagine that your family lived in close proximity to the Indians without great fear," Grant said.

"I never said that there wasn't fear. Pa kept a rifle loaded and a sidearm close at hand and he taught me and my brother and even ma and my sisters how to shoot center. But in those days the Injuns were a fact of life and we were on their land. By necessity we traded with 'em and except for my brother and sisters, those Injun kids were my only playmates. Some of them so called savages became real friends, but I'll tell you more about that later.

Hell, I near about grew up Blackfoot. I spoke Blackfoot as well as I could talk American…they taught me trackin' and stalkin' and makin' bows and arrows. I slept in their lodges and ate their food. It was a great life for an adventurous kid like I was. I spent about as much time with my pal Prairie Dog at that Blackfoot village as I did at my own home. His pa was the head man and he liked to summer the village close to our ranch. There was good huntin' and fishin' and foragin' for the women. Whenever my pa didn't need me to work, I was a wild Injun myself. I learned a lot of things that stood me in good stead in later years."

Tom lit another cigarette, exhaling the smoke slowly into the warm dusty wind.

"Believe you me, they didn't call them young bucks 'braves' for nothin'. With those young men, every day was a test of their manhood. Not like today where the government keeps 'em dependent on those reservations.

Those boys were tough and unforgivin' when it came to being a sissy...and what with my older brother, I reckon I grew up pretty tough. Bein' young, I learned real quick how to palaver with most of the Injuns we saw on a regular basis. You know how kids are? Race, religion and language ain't no barrier to a child. I picked up enough Blackfoot, Crow, Sioux and Shoshone to get by when I had to. This area we're in right now was inhabited mostly by the Blackfoot. They were a pretty ferocious bunch and even the Crows and the Sioux avoided tanglin' with 'em any more than was necessary to settle boundary differences.

All the various Injuns depended on huntin' and what vegetables they could acquire. The Injuns didn't really have settlements the way you might think of it. They were nomads in the true sense of the word. They made their homes where the larder was. Everything was seasonal for them. Hell, you could go to a village one day for a visit and if you came back a day or two later there wouldn't be anything there but cold fire rings. I mean to tell you that they could pick up and move in a matter of hours. It was stupefying to watch. Ask them fellas who were on the ridge overlookin' that village on the Little Big Horn. They told me that those ten thousand or so Sioux and Cheyennes vanished like morning mist."

"Coming from Baltimore and being raised in the twentieth century, it is difficult to imagine human beings living in buffalo hide lodges. It might not have been too bad in the summer, but the winter must have been hell, especially for the women with small children."

"I reckon you're right. The Injun women with little ones suffered the most, but on the other hand, they didn't know any different so they did the best they could. It was white women like my ma who really had to be tough in those days. They knew the difference."

"I just can't even imagine white people living in the middle of savagery and wilderness. Your mother must have been a remarkable woman."

"My ma, believe it or not, was a well brought up city lady, just like yours, I reckon. She was well educated and accustomed to civilized society. She did her damnedest to maintain civilization, even out here on the prairie. Taught all her children to read and write and cipher. She tried to give us all a bit of culture."

Tom smiled.

"I reckon that culture thing sort'a slid right on by me, except that she passed on her love of readin'. I would read everything I could get my hands on. Yes sir…I'll tell you that my ma was as genteel and courtly as ol' Queen Vic herself…and I know…I met Queen Victoria."

After his story about Carson, Tom was fearful that Grant would begin to consider his revelations no more than the exaggerations of an old man who was hungry for attention.

"You met the Queen?" Grant sounded incredulous.

"I'll get around to that, but yes sir. I did meet the old girl."

Tom thought for a long moment.

"And she could also be tougher than whang leather if the need arose."

Looking at Grant, Tom laughed.

"My ma, not the queen. Ma could birth a calf, cut firewood and shoot and skin a buffalo when left with no option. Her and pa figured they were gonna conquer the new land and build a dynasty of their own. They'd have likely done 'er too. Ma was close to havin' another child when she passed."

Grant was genuinely sympathetic to the tone of Tom's voice.

"What was the cause of your mother's passing, if you don't mind my asking?"

"I don't mind," Tom said.

Tom turned his horse from the main road onto a well-traveled trail leading to a gate in a barbed wire fence. Grant looked at the fence, which seemed to go for miles in each direction. On the surrounding hills of the rolling coulee country was a patchwork of pastures: corn, wheat, barely, oat and hay fields. Cattle and horses dotted the countryside. Interspersed among them, Grant could see the distinctive white rumps of distant antelope feeding in small herds. He felt a moment of pride that he was quickly training his eye.

"We'll take a shortcut," Tom said.

Tom dismounted to open the gate.

"Is this your ranch?"

"Part of it. This here is my bull pasture," Tom said.

Grant's eyes immediately widened and he looked around to see if any bulls were present. Seeing several large animals off in the direction they were riding, Grant grew uncomfortable. Except for the childhood stories, which told of bulls chasing picnickers from pastures, he knew nothing of livestock.

"Is it safe to cross here?"

Apprehending Grant's trepidation, Tom smiled.

"Just don't bend over, and don't wave no red flags neither."

Grant wrinkled his forehead and then broke out in a smile.

"I'd like to hear more about your family if you don't mind. You said your mother had passed away."

Tom was thoughtful for several long moments as he recalled the events of so many years before.

"I ain't spoke of any of this in years...but I reckon we need to start somewhere. Now you might want to put some of this in that notebook."

Tom took a deep breath, and sat silent for a long moment.

"I can't say for sure how long we'd been livin' out on the ranch...but it had been a couple of years. Pa had made a good start on a real house for ma, wood floor and all, and we'd built some pretty good outbuildings and corrals for the stock. My ma even had a garden. That garden and the wood floor house made her real happy. My pa and my brother and me would go up to the timber country and bring back lumber on a freight wagon, hew it and build what was necessary, or what ma figured was necessary anyway. My brother was six years older than me and he was a big, strappin' boy. Him and pa could do a lot of work in a day with a little help from me of course. I was strong and a good worker. I just didn't have no size and I was more of a Tom Sawyer kind of kid. Chasin' rabbits and fishin' was a lot more fun than workin', if you know what I mean.

I was about twelve comin' thirteen that summer of fifty-nine. My big sister Rachel had got married off to a fella who'd worked at the fort. By that summer she was livin' in Missouri with her new husband, Jacob MacGregor by name. Now ol' Jacob had saved all he'd earned workin' with the American Fur Company at Fort Benton. He'd come to call on Rachel and the next we knowed, him and Rachel was courtin'. Then right along he come to ask pa if he could have her hand in matrimony. Truth is that Rachel hated Fort Benton. She hated the West, the Injuns, the dirt and just about everything about the place. So pa gave them a wedding and Jacob took his savin's and my sister and opened a mercantile just outside of Saint Joseph. He did right well by Rachel and their children, but I'll tell you this...a more boring individual you would never hope to meet. All business...that was Mr. Jacob MacGregor. But then I wasn't married to the sumbitch, so what did I care?"

Tom looked at Grant who was furiously scribbling in the notebook.

"That ain't the stuff worth notin' neither," he cajoled. "But I am gettin' to it."

Tom stopped Luke again and removing the brass box from his saddlebag he lit another Lucky Strike.

"You came all the way from Saint Louis to talk to me about the Pony Express. The thing is that I would never have been a rider for the Pony Express except for what happened the spring of fifty-nine when I lost my mama.

It was a right pleasant spring afternoon, as I recall. My pa had put me to diggin' in the bottom a deep ol' hole. I was diggin' and puttin' the dirt into buckets to be hauled up. The hole was for a new privy he was buildin' for my ma. So it had to be deep but it wasn't none too big around...you know what I mean? Anyway, he was carpentering on the privy house; makin' a seat and buildin' the door and all while I was fillin' buckets with dirt in the bottom of that hole. I can remember lookin' up and just seeing a spot of daylight at the top and I figured I'd dug half the way to China. Now I wasn't ever too comfortable in confined places like caves and closets and the like...and this was really givin' me the dithers."

Tom's face was painted with an odd expression. He took a puff from his cigarette as he squinted, recalling the details.

"My older brother, Derrick, was off huntin'. Pa had a pack of some real nice Red Bone, Blood Hound mix that he'd had brought by steamer from Missouri as pups. They was not only good for huntin' but they was damned good watch dogs too. You could hear that throaty bayin' from a mile away. Pa kept them tied to little shelters around the house and they would raise a ruckus when anything, day or night, man or beast, come near. Anyways, Derrick took a couple of them hounds and was supposed to be bringing home some dinner...so it wasn't no pleasure type huntin' trip he was on, but I would still more rather to have been with him than down in the bottom of that hole. Let it suffice to say that I was lacking enthusiasm for the task.

I recall that I'd hollered up to pa that the buckets was filled and pretty quick he came and began haulin' the buckets full of dirt out of the hole and takin' it over to ma's garden. Ma was working in her vegetable garden with my little sister and as pa would pour the dirt, ma and little sister would spread it around, which likely helped to save my life."

Tom anticipated Grant's question.

"I'll get to that in a minute. You see, I was stuck down in that hole where I couldn't see nothin'. Well sir, it wasn't long until pa came back and started letting the buckets back down into the hole and I hollered up that I was gettin' parched, seein' as how I was sweatin' near to soakin' my shirt through. So pa let down a bucket of water with a tin cup and went back to building the shit house. While he was nailing the privy house together with some lumber we'd brought down from the hills, I started refillin' them buckets with dirt. Like I said, I didn't care much for bein' down in that hole. I felt like I couldn't breathe. Truth is I was scared of bein' in that hole. I got them buckets filled again and I hollered at pa and told him that I had to have some relief for a call of nature. I didn't want to break in that new shit hole whilst I was still diggin' in it. Pa never came and I hollered again that I needed some relief and that them buckets was all filled."

Tom took a deep breath and his brow furrowed.

"At about that time I heard a shot way off and figured it was my brother shootin' a rabbit or somethin'. Then I heard a couple more. I knew Derrick only had a single shot gun...and about that same time the hounds that were still tied up began to bawlin' like they did when somethin' or someone was comin'.

I was yellin' at pa tryin' to find out what was goin' on 'cause there was no way for me to get outta that hole, without him pullin' me up on a rope. All of a sudden I saw my pa peering down at me. He had an odd look on his face but he sounded real calm when he told me, 'There's Injuns after your brother and they're comin' this way.'

Then he told me in that same calm voice to be quiet and stay hid down in that hole till he came back for me. To my surprise, he proceeded to tip that shithouse right over onto my hole so as to cover it up. All of a sudden, it got real dark in that hole and my apprehension turned to cold fear. I knew there was no use to holler. Whatever was gonna happen, I was where I was for the duration."

Tom puffed his cigarette and was quiet for a long moment.

"I could hear pa runnin' and shoutin' at my ma and my sister. Then I could hear a lot of shootin', but that shithouse muffled the sound and I couldn't tell where it was comin' from. Then I could hear some Injuns hoopin' and hollerin'. I could hear horses runnin' and then there was some awful screamin' from ma and my sister. Them hounds began makin' that awful yelpin' sound. You know that sound a dog makes when it's bein' hurt real bad. I figured them Injuns was beatin' the poor bastards to death. I recognized the war hoopin' and I understood enough of the lingo they was shoutin' to know there was some Blackfoot heathens havin' some fun. Next thing, I heard the cows bellowin' and then more horses runnin' but I couldn't see nothin' and all I could do was sit there and pray. Pretty soon the shootin' and the hollerin' stopped."

Tom paused, his brow knitted in thought as he looked into the distance.

"Then the real screamin' began. I could hear my ma screamin' like nothin' I ever heard before. I could hear pa and my brother cussin' and callin' them red bastards all manner of names. I had never heard such language comin' from the God fearin' lips of either of them before. Then I heard each of them screamin' in misery in their own turn."

Tom's knuckles were white as he held his reins tightly and looked straight ahead.

"Then, all I could hear was the cracklin' of burnin' wood as the house and outbuildings got torched. I could hear them Injuns laughin' and havin' themselves a little celebration. They'd fixed some food...eatin' them dogs I reckon...they was really enjoyin' the party.

As for me...I can tell you that I was sure enough one scared turd down in that shitter hole. Time seemed to stop as I sat there shakin' like one of them little hairless dogs shittin' a peach pit on a cold mornin'. All I could do was hunker there lookin' up at the little streaks of light comin' around that half built shithouse my pappy had dropped over my hidin' place, just waitin' fer one of them villainous cutthroats to come and find me. I wanted to holler at 'em to come and get me so I could put up a fight. But I only had that shovel for a weapon and besides, much as I hate to say it, my throat was froze in fear."

Tom stopped Luke and dismounted.

"I have to get rid of some of that Grand Union coffee," he said.

He dropped his cigarette onto the dusty trail and extinguished the butt with the spent coffee. Grant stood shyly behind his horse to relieve himself.

They remounted and rode some distance in silence.

"It was early June, about this time of the year in fact. The days were long and I'll tell you that this one day in particular was real long. By late afternoon and into early evenin' there was still plenty of light. I could hear them bastards arguin' about whether they should make camp or get started toward home. I could tell by the palaver that they were Blackfoot, but I knew they weren't locals because the local Blackfoot was mostly friends and I didn't recognize the voices. I figured they were most probably Bloods from up north in Canada. I don't think I need explain to ya why everyone called that bunch Bloods.

Anyway, for some reason they finally decided to hightail it with their trophies and I could hear them gathering their booty to hit the trail. I was just about to breathe a sigh of relief when one of them wife beatin' mother defilin' bastards rode by and throwed a brand into that overturned shithouse.

That was the second time in my life I'd pissed my pants. Now this is also where the dirt in the garden comes in. Fortunately, pappy had hauled the dirt away so that the privy house lying there concealed the hole. That Injun didn't know the hole was there when he flung that brand. It was just an afterthought for him. He sure as hell didn't know I was there...but for me it was big trouble. But I reckon it would have been bigger trouble had they not all mounted up, gathered the stock and rode out. The last I heard of them boys was the rumble of the stolen horses and cows movin' fast as those sons-of-bitches drove 'em off."

"I thought the Indians didn't steal cattle," Grant said.

"I said they wouldn't risk life and limb to get 'em. This was an easy deal and those cows gave them groceries for the trip home."

Grant noted the differentiation.

"Anyway, when they rode off my fun really began. That brand laid there smolderin' fer a couple of hours and then slowly caught the half-green wood of that newly built shithouse afire. Smoke began to fill the hole and it wasn't long before embers were a rainin' down upon me. I dipped my hat and my shirt in the water bucket to help protect my hide and wrapped my kerchief around my face to help me breathe. I felt like I was gonna pass out but I was so scared I just kept fightin'. Real quick I took that shovel and began to waller out a cubby on one side of the shitter hole. I was hopin' all the while that the whole damned thing didn't come cavin' down upon my head. I was able to dig a shelf and get far enough under the ledge so as to avoid the fallin' chunks of burnin' wood...but I was nearly out of breathin' air.

All I could do was get my face as close to the bottom of the hole as

I could. I had my nose right in the dirt and I was able to take a little air from time to time. When I could get a breath, I'd take some handfuls of dirt and what little water I had and put out the burning embers in the bottom of my hole. It seemed like forever, but the fire finally died out and the smoke subsided.

That night, when the sun went down, I found out exactly what they mean when they say 'cold as a well digger's ass.' I was wearing nothin' but that cotton shirt, that I'd soaked in the water bucket to save my hide during the excitement of the fire. Now, with the sun quittin' on me I was sittin' there ten feet down in that would-be grave near about froze. The darker it got the worse it got...and the more my imagination ran wild...and when I say dark, I do mean dark. It was like bein' four feet down a cow's throat. When darkness came so did the night critters. I could hear animals growlin' and snappin' and draggin' things about and my imagination was runnin' wild trying to figure what was goin' on. I could tell that wolves and coyotes and coons was fighting over whatever there was to eat and I knew that the only thing to eat had to be my folks.

Most of my upbringin', what with a big brother and the Injun boys and all, had taught me that a man ain't supposed to show emotion or cry. That night, I couldn't have care less what I supposed to do. I cried...and I cried...until I finally shivered myself into exhaustion and dozed off to a fitful sleep. Unfortunately, things were about to get worse. When I woke up a few hours later, my mouth was so dry I could'a spit a cotton ball. On the good side, my pappy had dropped that bucket of water down the hole just before the Injuns had come, but I'd used a lot of it on my shirt and firebrands. I put my finger in the bucket and I reckoned there was about enough for a few swallows with a mite to spare, so I wet my mouth and saved a bit.

As it got light it also began to warm up. I was happy to have a little warmth until I began to figure out that the water I had wasn't gonna go too far in the heat of the day. I began to ponder the possibilities and it occurred to me to use that rope that pa had attached to the bucket as a means of escaping my entombment. I tied a chunk of that half burned wood on the end and tried to throw it out of the hole to see if it might catch on something solid so as to allow me to pull myself out."

Tom stopped the horses and smiled at Grant as if amused by the reminiscence.

"I must'a throwed that damned thing a hundred times, but it just never got any purchase and all I'd done was wear myself out. I finally gave up on the idea and sat as still as I could to conserve my energy. I'd wet my finger in the bucket from time to time and then wet my lips. I was trying to conserve the only resource I had available, but there I was in the bowels of hell, hopin' for a miracle.

The long day passed into night and that night was even worse. The darkness brought even more God-awful noises. I could hear the wolves, coyotes and coons and the skunks and the other critters growlin' and snappin' at one another and fightin' over things, things which my mind would not even allow me to imagine. I finally wet my lips with my last few drops of water, put my hands over my ears and slept an exhausted and fitful nightmarish half sleep."

Looking at Grant, Tom said, "I reckon you never really been hungry or thirsty?"

"No sir. I have lived a very fortunate existence."

"The next day when I woke up, the bottom of that bucket was drier than jerked buffalo hump. I knew I couldn't last too long and all I could do was look up at that sky above my grave and hope that someone would come by to find me. But in eighteen and fifty-nine, the likelihood of someone just comin' by was about as likely as me sproutin' wings and flyin' out of that hole."

Tom shook his head and chuckled to himself.

"I even got delirious enough to laugh at myself. I can remember sayin' that when they found me they could just say a few words and fill up the hole to cover me over. I'd dug my own grave and I'd dug 'er deep."

"Didn't you have any other neighbors, at all...besides the Indians?"

"Nary a one! And I was beginnin' to get mighty weak too. That third night, I was in more of a fitful unconsciousness than sleep. I was fadin' in and out and having dreams that were too crazy to remember. I'd wake up and forget where I was altogether...and then when I'd remember I'd cry myself back to sleep just wishin' I could die. I would have to say that the third night, I got a real clear idea as to the definition of misery. That was sure enough one long and awful night...maybe the worst of my life.

Three days and three nights...and that third night went on forever. Then, the beginnin' of the fourth morning I was fadin' in and out of reality when I suddenly realized that it was comin' daylight. By then I had just about given 'er up. I said one more prayer, not for me but for my folks and then I drifted off into total unconsciousness. I have no idea as to how long I was layin' there. When I came around again it was bright afternoon. I thought I caught some motion above me and when I squinted into the light at the top of the hole I could see that there was an Injun staring down at me but I couldn't make out his face against the bright light.

I got this sudden burst of energy as I recall, and I'll tell you this, if I'd had anything to eat in the previous few days I would have likely shit my britches."

"Was it the Blackfoot?"

"Sure as hell was Blackfoot...and thank God it was. It turned out to be one of the men from the village of ol' Limpin' Calf. Now Limpin' Calf and his people were Piegan Blackfoot and, like I said, they summered at a village about twenty miles from our ranch. Ol' Limpin' Calf himself was about my pa's age and he and my pappy got on real well. I guess you could say they was friends."

Tom thought a moment.

"You remember me sayin' that I had Injun playmates and all?"

Grant nodded an acknowledgment.

"Limpin' Calf was also the father of my best pal who was a boy by the name of Prairie Dog. Now me and Prairie Dog had been good pals for several years and we'd spend a lot of time together whenever Limpin' Calf moved his village close enough to our ranch for me and him to get together. The people in the village had started callin' him Rides With White Boy because me and him was always together. Limpin' Calf's bunch were the locals who claimed this area around here as huntin' grounds at that particular time."

"You say your friend was named Prairie Dog but they called him Rides With White Boy?" Grant asked.

"The Injuns had a different way of naming folks than you and I and the Christian world. A person could have a name given to them as a child and then do something...it could be something heroic, or something dumb or just something that stuck in the minds of their friends and family, and they would then have a new name. Like a man who wasn't too good at keeping an edge on his blade might get called Dull Knife. I even knew one fella they called Roots Make Him Fart. I reckon you can figure that one out...and you know'd he wasn't born with a name like that, but a fella would get named by his pals and the name would stick. Ol' Custer had a Crow scout they called White Man Runs Him. You don't reckon he was born with a moniker like that do you? So ol' Prairie Dog, as he'd been called as a child, became Rides With White Boy when we were about old enough to get into some real shenanigans together."

"So let me get this straight. These were Blackfoot, but different Blackfoot than those who had murdered your family. These Blackfeet were your friends and they came to rescue you?"

"You bet...this was my pal Prairie Dog and his pa and some men from their village. When I first saw it was an Injun I didn't know who it was so I was scared. But once I found out it was my friends, it was like the miracle I'd been prayin' for. These were my neighbors comin' by.

I was so weak with hunger and the lack of water and just pure exhaustion that I had one helluva time just tossing that piece of wood tied to the rope up to those fellas. I finally got it up high enough for them to grab on and got the rope tied under my armpits and they dragged me to salvation. There was about half a dozen young men from Limpin' Calf's village who had come to see what happened and I was damned glad to see 'em all. As they lifted me out of that grave, I was one happy boy. Leastwise till I got up to where I could see what had occurred."

Tom's face was sallow with the emotion of his recollections.

"The stench of death and the sights that I beheld upon comin' out of that hole is just beyond describing. What was left of my ma and pa and brother wasn't recognizable. Parts of 'em was still hangin' on the fence where they'd been skinned alive and left for the critters. The animals had dragged parts of 'em away and there was gore and dried blood all around. I wanted to throw up, but I hadn't eaten nor drank nothin' and that was probably a good thing. My Blackfoot friends was all sympathetic and they begun to help clean up and take care of my folks remains. Then it occurred to me that I didn't see nothin' at all of my little sister."

Tom's breath escaped in an audible sigh.

"I could barely walk and I was too weak to resist much when ol' Limpin' Calf told Prairie Dog to make a travois to take me to their village. You might say he was like a father to me. I had spent near about as much time in his lodge that past few years as I had in our house. My folks figured it was not only good fer my learnin' process but an insurance policy against hostile actions by the Piegans. It had worked for a long time, too. But unfortunately, them Bloods from up in Canada didn't recognize no immunity created by children. Them scalp liftin', woman killin' shitheads didn't have a qualm about cuttin' another Injun's throat as quick as a white man's. And they always sent their enemies to the afterlife in such condition as to ensure that they would never be able to fight again for eternity."

Tom stopped and it appeared to Grant that he was fighting back a tear.

"Bein' young, it only took a couple of days of good food and water at Limpin' Calf's lodge to get me on my feet. Then I set about to care for the remains of my folks and figure out what I was gonna do with myself. I loved Limpin' Calf and Prairie Dog and all them Injuns in the village, but I knew I couldn't stay with 'em. Limpin' Calf told me I was welcome to stay, but he gave me some fatherly advice when he told me that it would never work out for me...becomin' an Injun after being raised with white ways."

Tom's eyes narrowed as he thought back to his twelfth summer.

"As I regained my strength in Limpin' Calf's village, the old Chief explained that some of the men from his village had been huntin' and seen smoke the day that the Bloods had attacked the ranch. He was real careful to let me know that my pal, Rides With White Boy, was real upset and that he had wanted to come investigate right away. In fact, him and a couple of other of the boys who were my friends had started toward the ranch right off. But before they got too far they met up with that renegade band of Bloods.

Rides With White Boy recognized the horses and cows that the Bloods was drivin', but he could only listen to them brag on how they had took 'em away from 'many white men after a big fight.' The cutthroats was all bloody and a couple was wearing scalps on their belts according to Limpin' Calf. Prairie Dog knowed they was lyin', but what could him and a couple of kids do against that bunch? Them Bloods was men, seasoned warriors well known in their nation, and they had one helluva reputation.

Rides With White Boy told me that they was packin' my little sister along too. He was very ashamed that he had not killed them renegade bastards to get her back for me. But hell, like I said, he wasn't no more than just a kid...like I was. Even ol' Limpin' Calf apologized about my sister and all, but he had a small village and his people didn't want no trouble with that bad bunch. Especially considerin' that they was all of the same tribe...that bein' the Blackfoot nation.

So they pretended like they was real impressed with the big victory and all. By the tradition, they was more or less obligated to invite those no good sons-of-bitches to their village for a celebration. Of course, them Bloods had some whiskey that they'd got when they'd raided a small wagon party of traders before they hit the ranch. So that party lasted several days before them murderers finally wore out their welcome and headed back to Canada.

My friends, figurin' we was all dead anyway, didn't see no need in startin' a blood feud with their bad doin' relatives from up north over folks they couldn't bring back to life anyway. But when the Bloods finally headed north, Rides With White Boy asked his pa to ride with him and they came over to the ranch to say a ceremony over us, bein' as how we'd kind'a been considered family. Thank God they did. Otherwise, I would have been worm food for sure."

Tom took another long deep breath, the emotion showing on his wizened face.

"In a couple of days when I was feelin' spry, ol' Limpin' Calf made me the lend of a horse. He let my friends, Rides With White Boy and a couple other of the young bucks who were pals of mine come along to help clean up and see to proper services for my people.

We called 'em savages, but them folks took their religion seriously too. They faced death near about every day and they honored the folks they cared about and desecrated the ones they didn't. But it was a religious ceremony, none the less. The boys helped bury what was left of my folks and them Injun boys did their death dancin'. I greatly appreciated that ceremony, seein' as how that was all the funeral my family would likely ever get. Then they helped me salvage what we could of the tools and other family belongings. Not really knowing what to do with the stuff, we cached most of it down the crapper hole, then we put some boards over it and buried it so it couldn't be seen. I figured I would be able to find it if I ever got back that way. Then those boys rode into Fort Benton with me to let everyone know what had happened. I made it plain to all that it wasn't Limpin' Calf's bunch that done the dirty deed. I didn't want no trouble for Limpin' Calf's people. Hell...they was the only family I had left. I made sure certain that the whole town understood that Limpin' Calf and his Injuns had saved my life. You gotta remember that in those times, there were men who killed Injuns just for sport, and an excuse like the massacre of a white family would have been more than sufficient provocation for a bunch of yahoos to wipe out Limpin' Calf and his people. Even though they'd done nothin' wrong. I will tell you one thing for damned sure, when Rides With White Boy and those other kids waved good bye and headed back to their village, I was just about the loneliest, most miserable child as ever there was on God's green earth. I was real tempted to just go back to the village with 'em. But ol' Limpin' Calf had made it clear that I should go to Fort Benton and be with my own people."

Tom reined Luke to a stop at another gate. When he dismounted,

Grant sat for a long while in stunned silence. He had not taken any notes. His mouth was hanging agape. Even the dime novels had never portrayed the vivid emotion and the brutality of story he had just heard.

"We're almost home. You get that gate, would you son?""

Tom pointed to a cluster of buildings, predominated by a large Victorian style house, in the distance.

Grant was jarred from his bewilderment and quickly dismounted to help. He handed his reins to Tom. Releasing the lever he dragged the wire aside so that Tom could walk through with the horses. Tom mounted Luke and held the reins of Grant's horse while Grant closed the gate.

"Ol' Luke here has had a rough couple of days and I can bet that he is real anxious to get home. Now you hang onto those reins and get a good hold on that saddle horn."

Tom handed Grant his reins and waited patiently while the younger man prepared himself. Tom then pulled his broad-brimmed hat down tight on his head and asked, "You ready?"

"Ready for what?"

Tom turned Luke toward the cluster of buildings and gave the horse a prod with his spurs.

"Yeeaaa," he shouted.

The big gelding leapt forward into a dead run.

Grant's horse, not wanting to be left behind, lunged forward nearly unseating the unsuspecting neophyte. Holding the saddle horn with white knuckles, Grant could feel, for the first time, the power of the animal's undulating muscles as it broke into a full run. Putting his head down so as not to lose his hat Grant suddenly found himself in a state of near euphoria as the prairie sped beneath Strawberry's flying hooves.

4

Grant's horse came to a sliding stop beside Luke at a hitching rail near a stable. Grant was smiling with satisfaction as he dismounted.

"Tom, that was hugely exhilarating! It is a good thing that you warned me. I was nearly unhorsed when this animal burst into a run."

"Well sir, I'm happy with ya!" Tom replied.

Grant noticed a young dark complexioned boy of about fourteen years who had crawled through the corral fence and was leaning on the rail. The boy was accompanied by a black and white collie dog, which walked around Grant sniffing his new clothing and boots. Apparently overcome by some odor, which demanded his attention, the collie suddenly grasped Grant's leg between his front paws and began moving his pelvis in a simulated act of mating. Grant's cheeks turned crimson as Tom and the boy laughed.

"Well, it looks like ya meet with his approval," Tom said.

"Yer late, Grandpa," the boy said. "Everyone figured you'd met up with that newspaper fella and got drunk."

"This smarty aleck youngster here is my grandson. For want of anything better you can call him Little Tom," Tom said, putting his hand on the boy's shoulder. "And this here gentleman that your dog is so fond of is Grant Collins from the Saint Louis newspaper. He's come to interview yer grandpa about my days with the Pony Express."

Tom pushed the dog with sole of his boot, dislodging the animal from Grant's leg.

"That amorous critter there is ol' Dawg. He's Little Tom's pal."

Little Tom took the reins of both horses.

"Have they still got any warm groceries for a couple of half starved cowpokes over in the mess hall?" Tom asked.

"Yep," Little Tom replied. "Mom was savin' ya some food, just in case."

"Good deal. Come on Grant, we'll go over to the mess hall and get somethin' to eat. Then I'll settle you in."

Tom slung his saddle bags over his shoulder while Grant retrieved his flour sack.

"Mighty fancy luggage you got there," Little Tom said with a grin.

What had appeared at a distance to be no more than a cluster of ranch buildings had materialized into a small town. As they walked across a wide roadway Grant could not disguise his amazement. On the one side of the roadway where they had dismounted were various barns, outbuildings and stables overshadowed by several tall silos. Corrals and pens containing horses, cattle and sheep were spread over many acres.

Men on horseback were moving small herds of cattle or sheep from one enclosure to another. Vehicles were loading and unloading livestock while various pieces of farm machinery were coming from and going to work in distant fields. Grant's excitement grew as it became apparent that he would be observing, firsthand, a real working ranch.

The other side of the road could have been a residential neighborhood in any small town. Laid out in a four block grid and predominated by a

Victorian mansion, the well kept tree lined streets had been given names, "Nicolas," "Agatha," "Derrick" and "River" with signs so designating.

Tom pointed to the Victorian house three blocks away.

"That monstrosity down there is where I live. It is a monument to my ego and represents to them that sees it just what a pompous asshole I can be sometimes. I just had to keep up with the Conlon's ya know. Ol' Conrad Conlon helped settle this country and the sumbitch is richer than Job. Old bastard owns half of Flathead County, so I have to spend a lot of money on foofaraw so as not to be outdone. The smaller houses are for my family, the married hands who have families and our guests of course."

They crossed the road and walked toward a long wood frame building that reminded Grant of structures he had seen at military facilities.

"This big barracks affair here is the bunkhouse and mess hall. On down yonder is the boat docks and such along the river. The whole area with the barns and corrals and all is what we call 'The Compound.' Damned nearly a small city. Ain't it?"

"I thought it was a town when we rode in," Grant said.

They entered the mess hall door and Tom was greeted by a woman with long black hair and dark eyes whom Grant thought to be Indian. However, she bore a resemblance to Tom and greeted him with a hug.

"Daddy, I was worried about you."

Turning to Grant, she said, "You must be Mr. Newspaperman from Saint Louis."

Tom smiled as Grant was left standing speechless.

"This overly polite little lady is my youngest child, Susanna Cries Too Much. She'll answer to Sus," Tom said.

Tom put his hand on Grant's shoulder.

"This is Grant Collins. He's gonna make your old man as famous as

Bill Cody...so be nice to him."

Susanna put out her hand as a middle-aged man accompanied by a young woman entered the mess hall.

The younger woman approached Tom and also gave him an affectionate hug.

"Uncle Tom we were worried about you."

Tom smiled broadly, obviously deriving great pleasure from the attention.

"Grant Collins, this here pretty young darlin' is my grand niece Dixie Lee. She quit Vassar College just to come and learn about livin' on a ranch with her Uncle Tom. Now you be careful of her. She'll steal the heart right outta your rib cage, while it's still beatin'.'"

The warning was too late. Grant was dumbstruck. Even in a flannel shirt and blue jeans, Dixie's comely grace had overwhelmed him. Her skin radiated a tawny glow and flaxen curls framed a face that, for Grant, was a most beautiful portrait. When she offered her hand and said, "I'm pleased to meet you Mr. Collins," Grant's lips were moving in response but there was no sound. It was obvious to all that the young man was smitten.

Tom grabbed Grant's shoulder, forcibly turning him.

"And this strappin' lad, is my oldest boy, Nick. He kind'a keeps an eye on the place and makes sure that things get where they're supposed to be when they're supposed to be there."

As Grant put out his hand, it occurred to him that Nick's fair skin was in stark contrast to his younger sister.

"Good to meet you, Grant. How long you figure to be with us?" Nick said.

Grant was at last able to find his voice.

"I'm not sure. Your father is helping me understand what the frontier was like and I want to hear as much as possible. I could fill a tome with the stories I heard just riding out here to the ranch."

"Well sir," Nick replied, "make yourself at home and we'll do what we can to make you welcome."

As Grant turned, to his disappointment, the two women disappeared into the kitchen. Tom took Grant's arm and guided him toward a buffet table.

"Come on son, I'm starved. Let's get somethin' to eat."

They filled plates and then seated themselves on benches at a long table.

"Nicky is my business brain. He manages the whole shebang and keeps me from pissin' away the family fortune. He is a busy man trying to keep up with just that."

"Dad's just bullshittin', Grant," Nick said. "He's the one who made this prairie into an enterprise. I just happen to be lucky enough to have a job I enjoy. Being the ring master for this here circus is a full time profession."

"I can certainly see how that could be. This is such a vast country. The expanses nearly take my breath away. We rode for hours to get out here. How large is the ranch property?" Grant asked.

"Delaware," Tom said.

Grant looked across the table at Tom and then back at Nick who was seated beside him.

"He's not bullshittin' you now," Nick said. "It's about the size of Delaware."

Nick and Tom both laughed aloud at Grant's audible gulp and the stunned look on his face. Just then Susanna and Dixie came out of the kitchen and sat next to Tom at the table. As they approached, Grant's eyes were fixed upon Dixie. His mouth hung open.

"Catching flies, Mr. Collins?" Susanna asked.

Grant's mouth snapped shut as he looked at Susanna.

"Uh...no...I...I was just a bit amazed to hear about your father's vast land holdings."

"This land has been in the family for hundreds of years...actually," Susanna said. "My grandfathers on both sides died right here in this country."

Susanna's words hung in the air as she followed Grant's eyes. He was again staring at Dixie, who had diverted her gaze and was blushing.

Grant glanced around to realize that everyone but Dixie was staring at him.

Tom laughed as he and Nick stood to leave the table.

"Get your dishes," Susanna said.

Tom and Nick gathered their dishes and utensils obediently and headed for a window which opened into the kitchen. Small tubs had been placed on the window shelf for the dirty dishes. Grant gathered his own, following the other men to the window to deposit his plate and utensils.

"I'm gonna go get Grant settled in," Tom said, as he walked from the mess hall.

"We have dishes to finish," Dixie said, still blushing. "Hope to see you later, Mr. Collins."

Grant nearly tripped over his feet.

"Oh...ah, yes...later. I hope to see you later, also!"

"Give us a ride to the house, Nicky," Tom said, throwing his saddle bags into the bed of Nick's Ford truck. Tom and Grant sat on the tailgate for the three block ride.

Nick stopped the Ford in front of the large Victorian house. Tom and Grant waved and started walking toward the porch.

Nick's "See ya later," was barely audible over the noise of the Ford's engine.

Tom's home was, to Grant's surprise, the equal of any of the fine homes of New York or Baltimore. Paintings, primarily of western motif, decorated the plastered walls. The signatures of Charles Russell, Edwin Deming and Frank Tenney Johnson on original canvases were mute testimony to Tom's discernment, belying his course façade. An assortment of statuary, including a bronze statue of a cat from an Egyptian tomb and an original Remington, embellished elegant furnishings. The doors, entryways and handrails were hand carved, enhanced by Persian carpets protecting exquisitely inlaid hardwood flooring. Ornate electrical fixtures lit the rooms and illuminated tapestries hung in the hallways.

The enclosed double door entryway was designed to maintain heat on windy winter days. On each wall of the entry alcove were hat racks and coat hooks of various antlers and animal horn, mounted on carefully crafted oak backing. Benches beneath the coatracks provided seating while removing muddy boots. Boot pullers of oak and brass were positioned in front of the benches on either side. A heavy rough carpet in the center was intended for the cleaning footwear prior to entering the house.

When Tom closed the door behind them the inner door immediately opened and they were met by a dour woman in her mid-fifties who said, "Clean your boots or leave outside."

Tom attempted to kiss her cheek but the woman brushed him aside.

"You clean boots," she said again.

"This here smilin' beauty is Miss Koko," Tom said. "This is her house, and I'll warn ya right now, don't be messin' up nothin' or this here redskin is gonna get on the war path and lift yer hair. Huh Koko?"

The woman did not acknowledge and showed no emotion.

"She's been a cheerful darlin' like this since she was a baby," Tom said, carefully wiping his feet on the carpeted pad provided. "That's why her pappy called her Koko. It means 'night' in Blackfoot, and she was always about as cheerful as a dark night." Tom wrapped his arms around the woman to give her a hug, saying, "But I love her anyway."

Koko pushed him away and looked at Grant.

"You paper man?" she asked.

"Yes ma'am," Grant said taking off his hat.

"Hmmm!" was her only reply. She turned and walked through the door and down the hall.

"Show Grant here to the guest room, would ya hon?"

Tom then turned to Grant.

"You get settled in and I'll see ya out at that big barn later on."

Tom was pointing to a large building across the road. Grant looked through the window and acknowledged.

Tom disappeared down the hall while the unsmiling Koko showed Grant up the stairs to his room. She brought him towels and showed him the private bath. To his surprise it was complete with marble tile, toilet, shower, basin and tub. Grant was unexpectedly pleased.

Taking advantage of the time alone, Grant sat at a small desk in his room recording in his notebook everything that he could remember of the stories Tom had told. He wondered if he would be able to relate, in the written word, the color and emotion that Tom had painted so clearly in his telling. He attempted to imagine what he would have felt at age seven had he witnessed the violence that Tom had recounted during the fight over the mackinaw boat.

Lying on the bed and closing his eyes he found himself driven nearly to tears as he remembered the story of Tom's ordeal during the murder of his family. How would he ever capture, in writing, what this man had experienced? How would one paint a narrative picture of this young boy trapped in that pit and listening to the screams of his family as they died? How would he, with mere words, show the world the ambivalence of this young boy torn between his raging anger and his inability to even scream, his throat frozen in fear? What nightmares had accompanied this man to his bed for much of the past seventy years? Unable to rest he returned to the desk to finish his notes.

When he had completed the work of note making to his satisfaction, he went into the bathroom and luxuriated in a hot soapy shower intended to cleanse the road grime, trail dust and the smell of horse. He meticulously shaved and cleaned under his fingernails before taking advantage of a bottle of Bay Rum sitting on a small shelf above the toilet. Liberally bracing his freshly scraped face with the fiery fluid he slicked his hair and hoped that he would be seeing Tom's niece again that afternoon.

Grant looked at the new clothes of which he had been so proud only hours before. Now he found himself a bit embarrassed at the idea of seeing Dixie again wearing this worker's attire. But then what else could he do? These were the only clothes he had.

Sitting on the bed, he started to pull on his new boots, which had worn sore spots on his feet. Smiling to himself, he thought how odd it was that he would be wearing cowboy boots, an item he would not have considered as apparel just the day before. Forestalling the discomfort of pulling on the boots, he laid back on the pillows, mesmerized by the patterns of afternoon sun shimmering on the white ceiling; reflected by the marble top of the writing desk by the window.

Was it fortuitous providence that Tornado Tom Thomas had a niece? A beautiful young woman with whom, for the first time in his life, he had been instantly infatuated. Was he selling himself a 'pig in a poke?' He recalled the scene at the railroad depot with Melinda when he had departed Saint Louis. A confusion of emotions had been in his thoughts constantly for the past week. His impetuosity at embarking on his Montana adventure had surprised even him. He was sure that no one who knew him, even slightly, would understand.

He remembered his hours of research undertaken after the dinner discussion with Shawn. Perhaps he was not cut out for the blood sport of political reporting, but he was a damned fine writer after all. He had decided to find a vehicle for his skills that was more suited to his style.

Reflecting on the genesis of this undertaking, he recalled the article in a ten-year-old archived edition of the newspaper. The story had explained a controversy about the first westbound ride of the Pony Express. Having been an avid reader of Western fiction as a boy, the article had given him the idea that perhaps this might be an outlet for his talent and energy. Later he had come across an old picture of Tornado Tom in the Fort Benton newspaper. The accompanying story told how Tom Thomas had been a rider with the Pony Express. Grant had sent a telegram immediately to learn if the old man was still alive. Upon receiving Tom's reply he had spontaneously made the decision to travel to Montana to get a personal sense of the West and interview this legend.

He had met with his boss, Jonathon Kuntz, the next morning. Kuntz had asked if there was a problem. Grant had replied that he had a story he wished to pursue. The story, he explained would require that he travel to a small town called Fort Benton in Montana. Although Grant had hoped for a private meeting, Kuntz had walked him to the editorial office insisting that he had to "keep his finger on the pulse."

In his eagerness to pursue the interview with Tom, Grant had offered to make the trip at his own expense and without pay. He realized almost immediately that he had made a mistake when Kuntz walked him to a large map of the United States on the wall of the editorial office.

Mr. Kuntz had placed his finger on Shelby, Montana.

"Have you heard about the fight to be held in Shelby on the Fourth of July? Some kid named Gibbons from Minnesota is going to fight Jack Dempsey for his title."

Although Grant was vaguely aware of the event, he recalled his embarrassment when he was forced to dissemble. Seeing that Shelby was quite close to Fort Benton he told his boss that he had planned a visit to Shelby while in Montana to report on the fight.

It was a good thing, he laughed to himself, that he had no weakness for gambling. He would not be a very good poker player. Mr. Kuntz had certainly received the best cards in that deal.

With Hiram's approval, Mr. Kuntz had accepted Grant's request for the unpaid leave of absence. Grant made reservations and informed his landlady that he would be temporarily moving out. He told her that he would be back in about six weeks if the room was still available.

Early the next morning when Grant emerged from the rooming house, he saw Melinda Kuntz standing on the sidewalk beside a taxi at the curb.

"I'll drop you at the station," she said, a pained expression on her face. "Weren't you going to say good-bye?"

They got into the cab and Grant had stammered some incoherent nonsense about writing when he got to Montana.

"I really hate good-byes," he had told her. "I'm just not good at that sort of thing."

He could still feel the ponderous silence which had pervaded the ride to the station. When they arrived, Melinda had handed the driver a wad of bills she had been holding in her hand. To Grant's dismay she got out of the vehicle, telling the driver not to wait. She had then accompanied Grant to the platform.

Uneasy minutes passed as they waited for his train. Although he did not feel that he had ever mislead Melinda regarding their relationship, her distress at his failure to tell her he was leaving still left him with a sense of guilt.

"Did it occur to you Mr. Collins, that I might just miss you very much?" she had asked, facing him with a look that riveted him in place.

He had felt like a small boy fixed by the scrutiny of a disapproving school teacher. He had shuffled his feet, fidgeting with the coins in his pocket, trying to think of some clever repartee to break the onerous gaze, which held him like a fly on a web.

Without warning she had reached up and placed her hand behind his neck, pulling his face close to hers. Placing her other hand under his coat she held herself close to him in an intimacy he had never before experienced.

Startled, he was unyielding. However, her kiss had jolted him from head to toe. The warmth of her body against his torso began a melee of emotions and hormones leaving him light-headed.

Releasing her grasp, she had taken a step back and looked at him again, tears welling in her eyes.

"I'll be looking for that letter," she said, as she turned and ran toward the street.

He had nearly run after her, confused by a sensory tornado obliterating any attempt at rationality. Then the purpose of his mission had erased the brief flood of hormones. He focused on the more enduring need to fulfill his goals. But the sensations created by the smell and taste and feel of her still burned in his memory. He wished that she had been more forthright at some prior time when he was not about to board a train to Montana.

A soft knock at the door brought Grant from his daydream. Quickly putting on his shirt he padded to the door in his bare feet and opened a crack.

Koko was standing in the hall.

"Old man over in barn. You go now?" she said.

"Yes...I go...I didn't realize it was getting so late."

Time had passed quickly. It was late afternoon when he finally walked into the large barn Tom had pointed out earlier. Stopping in his tracks he saw Tom remove his head from the engine cowl of an airplane.

"I thought we'd lost ya. Did you find everything you needed?" Tom asked.

"Quite more than satisfactory, thank you."

Tom was wearing bib overalls, a denim shirt and a railroad engineer's cap. His hands were black with grease and there were stains on his face where he had wiped the sweat.

"Damned if you don't smell like a San Francisco whorehouse of a Saturday night," Tom said.

"I thought it was time to clean up a bit."

"Judging from the scent, I'd reckon that niece of mine made an impression. I told you to watch your heart, but don't worry, you'll be seein' her at supper. Now hand me that screw driver layin' on the floor over there."

Grant retrieved the screwdriver and placed it in Tom's greasy hand.

"Well you certainly don't look much like a cowboy or a mountain man right now. If a person didn't know better they might mistake you for a mechanic," Grant said.

"Reckon you're right...and a damned good one too."

Grant walked around the biplane, running his hand over the cloth fabric of the wing. Drawn tight by the dope and paint, the canvas had a surprisingly solid feel; a near drum like quality. Twanging the guy wires like harp strings, he looked at the narrow struts and wires holding the wings and landing wheels to the frame.

"May I look inside?" Grant asked.

He put his foot into the small step below the cockpit.

"Help yourself. Just be careful where you step on the wing. It's only cloth you know."

Grant recognized the compass and magneto switch, but he was unsure as to the function of the other gauges on the wooden dashboard. Looking at the unadorned interior of the old military training plane, he thought how fragile the entire machine appeared.

"Do you fly?" Grant asked.

He immediately felt foolish for the question.

"What I meant to say is…what kind of plane is this?"

Tom smiled his broad grin.

"Does a Blue Tick hound chase a coon? Damned right I fly, and this here is a Curtiss JN-4…commonly called the Jenny. I told you I had to get some things done before I went to Shelby. Well this is it. Needed to change the oil and make sure this thing is runnin' right. I got a lot to do the next few days so I wanted to get this finished. I don't let no one else work on ol' Jenny. That way, I got no one to blame if she don't do right. I just had her painted this red, white and blue last summer. Pretty as she can be. Don't you think?"

"Yes…quite beautiful, very patriotic. You mean you're flying to Shelby?"

"No, I mean we are flying to Shelby. Have you ever been in an airplane?"

Grant shook his head, taking a step back.

"This thing is little more than a canvas and wire version of the paper and string kites that I built as a boy."

"You'll love it. Hell boy…you ain't never had a ride like it. The only thing holding you back is fear and common sense."

Tom recognized the pallor of fear on the younger man's face. He decided to leave well enough alone and let him make up his mind.

"Where did you get it...how did you come by an airplane?" Grant asked.

"Won 'er in a poker game! About four years ago I was down in Great Falls when a fella came flying in to do a barnstorm show and give people rides. Later that night he showed up at the saloon and wanted to play some poker. Prohibition hadn't yet been ratified at the time. I was sittin' in the game and we was playin' five card stud. It was getting late and he was down to his last few dollars. I had three spades up and another in the hole and he was showing a ten, a king and the Ace. I figured to run him out of the game so I bet enough to take his whole wad. Damned if the boy didn't call me and push it all in for that last card. Well sir...he caught a queen of spades, which upped his odds and caused me a moment of discomfort, but damned if I hadn't caught my black seven, and everyone knows that a flush beats a straight. So I dropped two hundred dollars on the pot...just to shut him up. He sat there lookin' at me for a while and then he smiled and said, 'I'll put up my airplane against your four flushin' two hundred, Grandpa.'

You could'a heard a pin drop. Everyone knew that there had been a time when callin' this old boy a four flusher could have painful consequences...and so it did. I flipped my fifth spade onto the pot and said 'Show me where my new airplane is.' That kid looked like he'd been hit up the side of his head with a dirty sock full of dog shit."

"How did you learn to fly?"

"Next morning, when we was both a little more sober, I bought him some breakfast and told him I'd pay a fair wage if'n he'd teach me to fly. He agreed, so we flew up here to the ranch and he stayed for about six weeks until I could handle it on my own. I really got to likin' the kid, and I damn near gave him the plane back...except for two things."

"What were the two things?"

"First thing is that anyone who calls me Grandpa better be a member of this family. The other thing is that he should never have called me a four flusher. Was a time I might'a killed a man for that. Besides, I was gettin' so I liked the ol' Jenny. Most fun I ever had with my britches on. Now let's go get ready for some supper and give you a chance to drool and look silly in front of that niece of mine."

Walking toward Tom's house, Grant felt weak in the knees at the thought of flying in an airplane with this old man who seemed to have no fear. Riding a horse was one thing, but going into the air with nothing but wood and canvas to keep one there was another matter. Attempting to hide his trepidation Grant, repeated to himself the motto of his Latin professor, *Tempus fugit, ergo carpe diem.*

"What's that?" Tom asked.

"Nothing! Just talking to myself."

5

The dining room, with its elegant furnishings, fine china and crystal was grandiose. Tom, seated at the head of the table, had placed Grant at the end opposite in the position of honor. Grant took his seat and surveyed with surprise the diverse group around the table. All were dressed in work clothes similar to his own attire, although Dixie had put on a summer dress. How incongruous this party looked, he thought, dressed in rough work clothing in these splendid surroundings.

When everyone was seated, Tom stood, raising a glass of wine.

"I hope that you all will join me in a toast to welcome our guest, Grant Collins from Saint Louis. Grant is a newspaper fella and he is trying to write about life on the plains in the frontier days."

Everyone at the table raised a glass and acknowledged Grant.

"Now you all know that modesty prevents me from talkin' too much about myself," Tom said, rolling his eyes.

He waited for the laughter to subside.

"While Grant is with us you can feel free to share with him anything that you think might be worth recording in that notebook he carries around with him."

Grant accepted the toast with trained propriety and studied the faces around the table with a near clinical criticality. He had always imagined himself a liberally educated and open minded man, accepting all races, creeds, colors and religions without prejudice. Now he found himself perplexed to realize that he had not, in his entire life, shared a meal with anyone but upper middle class white society.

As he looked at each of the faces in turn, one white another brown, he was sure that his thoughts were perceptible. He felt the need to say something that would convince this disparate family of his genuine egalitarianism.

Grant raised his glass.

"This is certainly an eclectic group. I hope that I have the opportunity to get to know each of you and hear your views about…uh…Tom and…the West…and the ranch…"

His voiced tailed off in a nervous quiver. He took a sip of wine, thinking to himself that this toast was the most incredibly asinine and pompous thing he had ever done. He felt as though he was shriveling in the harsh light of each enigmatic stare as he glanced at the faces around the table.

Grant set his wine glass on the table as he surveyed the eyes, which were fixed upon him. The foot of the goblet balanced momentarily on the tines of a fork and then toppled, sending a purple wave across the starched white linen table cloth. The sound of shattering crystal brought Koko hurrying from the kitchen. Grant, Dixie and Susanna leapt to their feet to dam the spreading tide with their napkins.

Koko toweled the liquid and swept the shards of broken glass into an empty plate.

"No harm done. You ain't the first to ever break a glass at this table," Tom said.

Dixie could see the anxiety imprinting Grant's face.

"Why don't we go around the table and each of us will introduce ourselves to Grant and tell him about our family?" she said.

Tom raised his glass.

"As Mr. Roosevelt would'a put it, 'that is a capital idea my dear.' And bein' as how it was your idea, why don't you just start 'er off."

Grant was not only thankful for the respite from his discomfort but again found himself unable to take his eyes off of Dixie, who was seated immediately to his right.

Dixie was now nearly tongue tied with the giddy exchanges of eye contact and stage fright. Everyone at the table was now focused on her, having followed Grant's unswerving stare.

"That's not fair Uncle Tom," she protested. "You should go first. You're at the head of the table."

"All right then, you're off the hook, but there ain't no use for me puttin' my two cents in the pot. Grant is gonna get to hear plenty from me in the next few days. We'll go clockwise. Rom can start 'er off."

All eyes turned to a man in his mid-fifties who was seated to Tom's left. His copper face, with the distinctively chiseled features of his Indian ancestors, was deeply etched from years of working outdoors. His dark hair was showing streaks of grey.

"I'm Rom, Romulus...Romulus Horsens. Tom here is my uncle. I run the livestock end of our ranchin' business."

Romulus looked at Dixie.

"Dixie's grandma kind'a helped to raise me and my brother for a while when we was little boys back in Saint Joseph...after our father died. Later on, we moved here to the ranch and then Uncle Tom looked after us when we lost our mother and step pa. My brother Remus and me live in the red brick and white place on the next street over. He's off workin' tonight.

He's in charge of the farmin' side of things here on the ranch. He does the raisin' of feed for the stock and some grain and hay to sell at market."

"It's a pleasure to make your acquaintance, Rom," Grant said.

Rom looked into Grant's eyes.

"And you can sleep sound tonight, I'm only half eclectic...I think. Hell I ain't took a scalp in near thirty years. It's against the law ya know," he said with a wry smile.

Everyone laughed as Grant's cheeks again showed crimson.

As Rom finished his introduction, Koko entered the room carrying a huge platter bearing a prime rib roast. She set it on the table in front of Tom and returned to the kitchen. She emerged almost immediately with another tray containing potatoes, gravy and vegetables. She set it on the table and again walked toward the kitchen door. As she passed Tom he reached out and gently took her by the arm.

"You go sit down and eat some dinner with us," he said, pointing to an empty chair at table. "You've done your maidly chorin' for now."

Koko pulled her arm free and returned to the kitchen.

"Lots of work to do," Koko muttered.

"Damned woman! You'd think she liked nothin' better than bein' a servant," Tom said.

Tom rose from his chair to carve the roast.

"Go ahead Nicky. Your turn!"

"Grant and me already met this afternoon," Nick said. "You already know Tom is my dad. Rom's mother, who was my Aunt Sarah...Dad's sister...she sort'a helped with raising me when my mother died. I reckon it sounds complicated, but you'll figure it out."

Nick looked at the pale, middle-aged woman seated to his left.

"This pretty young thing next to me is my childhood sweetheart and wife of twenty seven years, Phoebe. We have two girls who have both married and gone off to the big cities with our grandchildren. That didn't make us none too happy, but that's life in the modern world."

Grant nodded a greeting to Phoebe, who shyly returned the nod and immediately looked down at the table.

Dixie again interceded, knowing that Phoebe would not say a word.

"Grant and I met this afternoon also," she said.

Tom was passing plates with thick slices of roast beef around the table.

Dixie handed Grant a plate and set another for herself.

"Tom is my uncle and that's about all Mr. Collins needs to know for now," Dixie said.

"Okay then, have all the women in this family turned into shrinking violets? How about you Sus? Have you got anything to tell our guest about this 'eclectic' family?" Tom said.

"You're in no danger from me either. My Blackfoot mother absolutely forbade the scalping of white boys. However, if my brother was around it might be a different story. He's still pretty much of a wild Indian. Dad told you this afternoon that my name is Susanna Cries Too Much. When I was born, the song "Oh Susanna" was my mother's favorite, and according to Dad I cried a lot when I was an infant. So she gave me what she thought would be a good American name."

Susanna looked at the stocky, balding man to her left.

"This is my husband, Caleb Johannsen. I take no credit for any hair he may have lost in the last sixteen years, other than that which wifely nagging just naturally brings to a man...and I hear that you also met my son Tommy this afternoon."

Caleb Johannsen nodded at Grant but said nothing.

Grant returned Caleb's nod, then looked at Little Tom who was smiling.

"Dawg likes him," the boy said.

Susanna laughed, obviously having heard the story.

"I'm not shy," Susanna said, "but I live with two men who can go a month without exchanging two sentences, so don't expect a lot of conversation from either of them.

Caleb and me take care of the dude ranch and outfitting business. I don't know if Dad told you but we have people come from all over the world to ride horses, play cowboy and have a real Wild West experience. We try to make them feel as much like a cowboy as they can stand for as long as they're here. We also have people who come to shoot their guns on the range and some who hunt and fish.

Lately, we've been getting a lot of science people who come to look for the fossils. Ever since they started finding dinosaurs and such around here, we have been really busy; and then there are some who just come to see the country."

"That sounds to be quite a handful," Grant said.

"It is a full-time job. Dixie has been helping me with some of the chores since she got here. But me and Caleb handle that part of the ranch business with some hands we hire as guides and labor on a seasonal basis. The rest of the year we take care of the maintenance around The Compound and the guest quarters."

Susanna looked at Grant.

"So now you tell us about yourself and why you're here and what you want...and just how old are you anyway?"

Grant was caught off guard. His face blanched. He stammered for a moment and then gathered his best voice to respond.

"Well, I work for the Saint Louis Morning Star Newspaper and I came to Montana to interview your father for a..."

Grant was interrupted in mid sentence by Koko who had entered the room carrying a tray of desert.

"We already know all that," Koko said. "Answer what she asked you."

Grant looked toward Tom, who was thoroughly amused by the young man's discomfort.

"It's your problem, son," he said.

"Oh yes...by the way," Susanna said, as she put her arm around Koko's waist, "she won't introduce herself, but this is my Aunt Koko, and I guess you also met her earlier today."

Koko stood, her eyes fixed on Grant. "You answer now?" she asked.

"I'm twenty three," he blurted. "I'm from Baltimore, in Maryland. My father is a doctor. I attended Columbia, where I received my degree. I have been in Saint Louis for two years working for the newspaper."

Grant looked around the table. All eyes were now upon him.

"Are you married or engaged?" Susanna asked.

Koko stopped at the end of the table with an armload of dishes to await his answer.

"No! I'm single and I live alone in a rented room in Saint Louis. That is if it's still available when I return."

"Don't let these women buffalo ya Grant," Tom said. "You let this bunch back you into a corner and they're just like a pack of wolves. They'll tear a fella to pieces."

For the first time in his life Grant laughed at himself.

"Yes, I believe you're right. Give them the upper hand and they get brutal, don't they?"

Grant glanced at Dixie.

"Okay then, I'll tell you my purpose in being here...that is if you're still interested."

"Let's hear it," Rom said.

"Does everyone know who Joseph Pulitzer was?" Grant asked.

Dixie, who was well aware of Pulitzer, again came to Grant's aid.

"Why don't you just explain," Dixie said.

"Since I was a small child I've wanted to be a writer, but my parents were hopeful that I would become a doctor like my father and grandfather. When I attended Columbia I studied journalism, and I'm sure that they believed it to be just a lark. But I decided, against their wishes of course, that I would become a journalist and hopefully an author. If I fail to become an author...and famous, then I suppose I will have let them down."

His voice tailed off as he realized how egotistical the statement sounded.

"So how is Grandpa gonna make you famous?" Little Tom asked.

"To be a really famous author these days, it helps if a person wins the Pulitzer Prize."

"So what's this Pulitzer Prize," Susanna asked.

"It is a special award given each year for writing. It is named for Joseph Pulitzer who was a Hungarian who came to America during the Civil War to be a soldier."

"Why did he care about the Civil War if he was a foreigner?" Little Tom asked.

"He didn't really care about our Civil War. He just wanted to be a soldier. He was seeking adventure. Mr. Pulitzer was seventeen at the time. He had tried to join the French Foreign Legion. He'd also tried the Army of Austria but had been refused because of bad eyes and poor health. When he heard that the United States was looking for soldiers he found a recruiter in Hamburg, Germany and signed on as a substitute for an American who had been drafted. President Lincoln had implemented a draft when the army was short handed, but the wealthy and influential people didn't want their sons to go to war, so they passed a law permitting drafted men to hire a substitute."

"You mean this Pulitzer fella was hired by some rich coward to fight in his place," Rom said.

"It was something like that. This law spawned a whole industry. There were men who traveled all around the cities of America and Europe recruiting substitutes for wealthy draftees. The standard bounty was three hundred dollars, which in those times was a great deal of money. The recruiters would promise the potential substitute whatever it took to get a signature on the enlistment, perhaps fifty or a hundred, then the recruiter would keep the rest of the three hundred dollars for themselves. Some men signed up for no pay whatsoever. Joseph Pulitzer was one of those."

"White men never made much sense with things like that," Rom said.

"And why would anyone be that dumb?" Little Tom asked.

"He didn't know about the money at that time," Grant replied.

"You mean he got took?" Little Tom said.

"I guess you could say that...but anyway, he boarded the ship to America and during the voyage he learned about the money. Of course, when he realized that he had been cheated he decided that he would get the money himself, so he jumped overboard in Boston harbor and swam to shore. The story goes that he met some German speaking men who were joining the Lincoln Cavalry Regiment, which was being formed in New York. They assured him that many of the men in that regiment spoke German and that he could do well with them. Not speaking any English he decided to join with them and to keep his own three hundred dollars."

"So he got his three hundred dollars and got his adventure too?" Rom said.

"That's correct. And when he had served honorably and was discharged after the war he decided to stay in the United States. He learned to speak English and became a newspaper man and eventually bought the Saint Louis Post-Dispatch newspaper."

"Is that why you went to work in Saint Louis?" Susanna asked.

"In part, yes. When Mr. Pulitzer died in 1911 he was very rich. He left a lot of money to pay for the Columbia Journalism School. He also set aside some money for a prize for the people who do the best writing each year. They started awarding those prizes in 1917 and now, if you want to be somebody in the writing business, you have to win a Pulitzer Prize."

"I still don't see what that's got to do with Gramps?" Little Tom asked.

"Well, Little Tom, I think that your grandfather may know things that are noteworthy enough to write about. And those things may warrant my winning such a prize."

"Mercy sakes alive, Dad!" Phoebe said. "I always thought you were just telling tales."

"Yeah Grandpa, who would have thought anyone would have cared what happened in the olden days?" Little Tom added.

"Ya see how it is Grant? 'The olden days,'" Tom repeated. "A man can't win...not even with his own flesh and blood. Well I got news for all of you...this here Grant is gonna make me famous and then you'll all be sorry about makin' light."

"Com'on Dad," Susanna said. "Don't get your long johns in a knot. Those were the olden days and most of the people you have talked about are dead. How were we supposed to know you really did anything anyone would care about nowadays?"

"There are those who will always be interested in history," Grant said.

Dixie rose from the table.

"The wind has finally died down. I think I'll get the evening air."

With that she disappeared through the kitchen door.

"Would anyone care to join me in the den for a glass of brandy and a fine Cuban ceeeegar?" Tom asked.

Romulus walked toward Tom's den, but with the exception of Little Tom, whose acceptance of the offer was nullified by his mother, Tom's invitation seemed to fall on deaf ears. Each of the families left for their respective homes.

Grant excused himself. "I need to use the powder room," he said.

Grant walked to the top of the stairs where he waited until things were quiet. He then slipped out through the kitchen.

Although the hour was late, Grant was surprised to see that in this northern latitude there was still daylight as he walked around the house in hopes of finding Dixie. She had crossed the wide roadway and was headed to the stable where Tom and Grant had left their horses earlier in the day.

Before Grant was able to catch her, two young cowboys came out of the stable where they stopped to talk. Grant watched for a moment, thinking that perhaps he should just wait until in the morning when he would have another chance to spend some time with her.

Carpe diem, he reminded himself as he walked to where the three of them were engaged in animated conversation.

"Well, good evening again, Mr. Collins," Dixie said with some delight.

"Boys, this is Grant Collins from Saint Louis...he's here to write a story about my Uncle Tom."

"Howdy," the taller of the two said as he put out his hand in greeting.

"Howdy," Grant replied.

"No," the young cowboy said. "That's what they call me, Howdy. Howdy Dunbar. What's yer handle again?"

"Grant...Grant Collins...from Saint Louis."

The other man glowered at Grant through narrowed eyes.

"This here is Buck Horton," Howdy said.

"Nice to meet you Buck," Grant said.

"Yeah!" Buck said, squeezing Grant's hand tightly enough to cause pain.

"Would you care to take a walk with us, Grant?" Dixie asked.

"I'd love to," Grant replied.

Grant immediately found himself strolling on the far side of Buck who had moved quickly to walk on Dixie's right side. Howdy was on her left leaving Grant to trail along.

They came to a corral where Dixie took carrots from a sack she was carrying. Feeding the carrots to a small brown and white horse, she said, "Uncle Tom gave me this Pinto. She is just so sweet, isn't she, Buck?"

Buck shuffled his boots in the dust. "Yeah, I guess," he muttered.

Little Tom's black and white dog approached the group and eagerly accepted the scratching of his ears from each of the people in turn. Dixie bent over and put her arms around the dog's neck. The animal pressed his head hard against her shoulder soaking in the affection. When she rose, the dog walked slowly around Grant who stood stiffly refusing to acknowledge the animal's presence. The dog then proceeded to grasp Grant's leg as he had earlier in the day, moving his hips while a look of euphoria glazed his eyes.

Dixie giggled and the two cowboys burst into laughter when Grant's attempts at dislodging the amorous canine were met with warning growls. Grant froze in place, his face a mask of bewildered humiliation.

Dixie began walking away, Buck and Howdy juxtaposed at her sides.

Grant remained, feeling it prudent to stand in place until the dog had concluded whatever gratification he was deriving.

"Coming, Grant?" Dixie shouted over her shoulder.

"I'll be along shortly," Grant replied.

Dixie and the two cowboys disappeared among the buildings.

Grant heard Howdy saying, "Ol' Dawg seems to have a genuine affection fer that boy, don't he Buck?" Laughter echoed through the outbuildings.

"See you at breakfast then," he heard Dixie shout.

"Breakfast then," he replied.

6

The distant sounds of shouts and whistles, mingled with the bellowing of cows, awakened Grant before daylight. He arose quickly, hoping to see a real cattle drive in progress. Barely able to make out the shapes and forms in the pre-dawn dust, he realized that the legends of the life of a cowboy continued into the twentieth century. Hard work and long days seemed to be their lot.

Before the glow in the eastern sky could reveal the details of men and cattle, the herd had moved away from The Compound, disappearing onto the prairie. Grant dressed in the slowly increasing illumination of the rising sun coming through the window.

He left his room in excited anticipation of meeting Dixie before she started her day. As he descended the stairs he chided himself at the thought. He had known the young woman less than a day. Why could he not get her off his mind?

"You drink coffee?" Koko said from the kitchen as he came down the stairs.

"Yes ma'am," Grant replied as he entered the dining room.

"Good morning," Tom said, pushing aside a copy of the Wall Street

Journal.

"It appears that the stories of ranch life are true. I tried to see the cattle drive but they were gone before daylight," Grant said.

"Can to can't...that's a day for a workin' cowhand, and it hasn't changed in my years," Tom said.

Dixie entered the room and sat opposite Grant at the table.

Glancing at the newspaper on the table, she said, "The President is going to Alaska?"

"They say he's going to try out that new Alaska railroad the government put all that money into," Tom said. "Guess he'd best be careful. About the only thing a fella might get in Alaska is a case of pneumonia."

Koko poured coffee for all and then silently left the room.

"So how was your evening with your new friend?" Dixie asked, sipping her coffee.

"The bee's knees," Grant said.

"It looked like the cat's pajamas," she smiled in reply.

"What?" Tom looked at each of them.

"Never mind, Uncle Tom," Dixie said. "It's new slang. Grant said he and Dawg had a good time last night and I told him that is nice."

"Was that dog of Tommy's bein' affectionate again?" Tom asked.

Dixie stood and walked toward the door.

"Something like that," Dixie said. "Well gentleman, I hate to leave such stellar company, but I have to go help Susanna. Twenty-three skidoo."

"See you later?" Grant said, rising as she walked from the room.

Before Grant could sit down, Tom stood and walked to the door.

"How would you like to go for a little walk? I have something you may be interested to see."

Grant followed Tom out of the back door and toward a grove of trees by the river. As they approached the trees and topped a small rise, Grant could see an ornamental iron fence surrounding a small cemetery. An outhouse, built of rough lumber and complete with a half-moon carved in the door, stood in the middle of the burial area. The rows of graves had fresh flowers and were well maintained. Tom opened the gate and held it so that Grant could enter.

A shiver ran down Grant's spine. "This is where it happened?"

"Yep, this is where it happened. And right there, under that shithouse is where they're gonna bury me when my time comes. Near sixty-five years ago I got a reprieve from that grave. I figure when my time does come it is only fittin' that I pay back the reaper by goin' to a spot where I'll be easy to find. I built that shithouse with my own hands about fifteen years ago, and it looks just like the one that pa was puttin' together that day years back."

Grant was momentarily shocked at Tom's matter of fact attitude. Then he smiled, beginning to appreciate the ever present sense of gallows humor.

"Are these the graves of your family?" Grant asked.

Tom smiled.

"Yes sir...my whole family is here. The ones that's dead, that is. That's my pa and ma, my brother, two wives and a child. Reckon it won't be too long till I join 'em," Tom said.

Knitting his brow, Tom looked around.

"This here is the spot where I was diggin' those many years ago. This was where me and the Injun boys buried my folks, so I decided to just leave it like it was and make our family cemetery right here."

Tom opened the door of the privy house.

"Of course, I'm gonna have the most prominent headstone. Don't you reckon?"

Grant looked into the small building. He was surprised to see that the privy was fully outfitted, complete with a new roll of toilet paper. He looked into the hole beneath the seat.

"A very nice facility. I assume that is 'the' hole." Grant said.

A wry smile lit Tom's face.

"That's her, but I'd appreciate it if'n you didn't use it though. I guess you can understand why," Tom said.

"You told me about going into Fort Benton with your Indian friends, but you didn't tell me how you got to Saint Joseph to join the Pony Express. For a twelve year old boy to travel and face the world alone must have been frightening."

Tom thought a long moment as if recalling where he had discontinued the story.

"I got to admit that I was a might bit upset and more than a little scared when my folks was killed. I just didn't want to stay in Benton. The folks there was good to me. They fed me and gave me a place to sleep and all, but I figured I would go down river and see if'n I could find my big sister, Rachel. She was the only kin I had left.

You recall me explaining to you about them mackinaw boats? One of my pa's old friends told me that there was a group of hide hunters who was in the process of buildin' a mackinaw. He said that they was fixin' to start a float to Saint Louis in about two weeks hence."

Tom walked out through the gate and over to a couple of large cottonwood stumps. Indicating that Grant should have a seat, Tom sat on one of the stumps.

"Well sir, I went and found those men and they were a rough lookin' bunch. Buffalo hunters...and you could smell them and their outfit for a Montana mile. One real big fella seemed the boss and he reckoned they'd take me along outta the goodness of their hearts, what with me bein' a poor orphan and all."

Tom lit a cigarette and thought a few moments.

"So I threw in with 'em...turnin' my hand to whatever work needed doin'. It took about three weeks to finish the buildin' of the mackinaw as I recall. It was getting into July and the river was droppin'. So we had to make haste to get to floatin' before it was too late. When we headed down the muddy Mo, it took us several days of floatin' before we got to Fort Union. Them hiders did some tradin' and got themselves some whiskey and a little bacon for our beans. A lot of the people at Fort Union had known my folks and they was real sympathetic and offered to help in any way that they could. One man especially, warned me to watch out for this bunch I was floatin' with. He never said just why but he didn't like the look of 'em, and maybe I should have took heed."

"Did you have valuables which would have interested them?" Grant asked.

"You might say that...but it weren't no pocket full of money. We set out from Fort Union figurin' it would take somewhere between four to six weeks to get to Saint Louis."

"The first couple days there wasn't much happened. The river was flowin' big and the boat was movin' right along. We had a tail wind, which was keepin' the skeeters off us, and we was makin' good time. That seemed to keep everyone in good humor. I was just tryin' to earn my keep helpin' with whatever needed doin'. I'd sit on the bow and watch for snags and such. When I'd see anything I'd holler to the oarsmen and the big fella who had proclaimed himself the helmsman. I could see after a few days that the others gave the big man, whose name was Burl, a wide berth. I reckon I was too young and too dumb to be scared. At night it was dangerous to try to float so we'd pull her in and tie her up. No one wanted to be floatin' at night 'cause of the snags and bars. But then of course, when you was in close enough to shore, the skeeters would eat on you and you were takin' the chance that the Injuns was gonna put the sneak on you. So you was damned if you did and damned if you didn't. Either way you went you was bound to be wrong."

Tom snuffed out his cigarette and looked at Grant, a strange stare in his eyes.

"As I remember now it was about the third night out from Fort Union. We'd found us an island late in the afternoon and decided to tie up. There was a lot of driftwood on that island and a little breeze was keepin' the skeeters at bay. I started a fire and we was planning a good meal.

Best part of that island was that the water was deep enough to keep the Injuns from gettin' at us. I went and gathered enough wood to keep the fire all night and one of the oarsmen started fixin' some bannock bread with the beans and bacon. It was a right cozy camp. After we ate a good meal the men was smokin' their pipes and drinkin' some whiskey and tellin' tales the way men will do around a fire.

Long about dark everyone began to get his blanket and find a place to ease up for the night. I made myself a spot by a big cottonwood blow down and it wasn't long before I was dozin' off. I was half asleep when I heard some rustlin' around and then I heard one of the fellas say, 'Let the boy be Burl, he's just a kid.' Next thing I know that big bastard has got me by the arm and is draggin' me over that log. Like I told ya before, I was only twelve and just a little slip. I felt like I'd been grabbed by a griz. At that point I wasn't sure just what his intentions were, but about that time one of the oarsman by the name of Benji jumped up from his bed and came to help me, shoutin' at big ol' Burl, to leave me alone. Burl let go of me sure enough and then hit that Benji so hard his teeth flew out of his mouth. Blood splattered all over everything. Poor ol' Benji just crumpled into a heap and all Burl had to say was that he hoped the sumbitch would be able to row the next day. I figured that poor bastard was goin' under from the look of him. And the worst part was that he was the only one of 'em who had stood up for me.

Well sir...I begun to run from Burl, and bein' as how I was fast, he was havin' problems catchin' me, but my problem was that we was on a little ol' bitty island. Why...you couldn't have hid a pregnant piss ant on that little sand spit. I looked around to consider my options and they wasn't none too good. I could swim for it and either drown or get left in the wilderness, or I could cozy up with Burl for the evening, which really wasn't very appealing! I picked up a dead limb from the firewood pile and was preparin' to whop ol' Burl alongside the head if he came at me again...and he sure enough did come at me again.

Now he was not only big but he was quick as a game cock. He jumped up and kicked me so hard my ears was ringin' like a hot shoe hit with a cold hammer. Then he picked me up and headed to the boat where he was beddin' for the night on some hides. I was really gettin' scared. He throwed me over the gunwale and jumped in that boat right behind me. When he pulled off my suspenders and started skinnin' me out of my britches I lost all doubt as to what he had in mind to do."

Grant was taking notes and Tom waited until he looked up from his work.

"Now I had seen the bulls breed the cows. I even knew how the chickens made eggs and the dogs got puppies, but when it occurred to me that I was about to be Burl's brood sow my mind began a full throttle preparation for the worst while at the same time tryin' to figure a way out of this mess. After seein' poor Benji get mashed like a roach on a stove hood, it was obvious that there wasn't no talkin' my way out and he had sure enough already skinned off my britches. He had my shirt bunched up behind my neck so as to prevent me from escapin' or even turnin' around. Then he commenced to un-pants his own self.

However, to get his own britches off he had to drop his suspenders, which meant that he had to change hands to keep a hold on me. When he changed hands he throwed a little slack in my shirt and as he dropped his drawers I could feel somethin' hard bumpin' against my bare bottom."

Grant's was staring at Tom, his eyebrows raised.

"No I ain't talking about what you're thinkin'. It was the elk horn handle of his skinnin' knife. He'd loosed his grip just enough to give me some room to move and right quick, I reached back and grabbed that knife and came out of the scabbard with it before he even knowed I had it. I didn't waste no time neither. Without lookin' I just started stabbin'. I stuck that knife right where he was preparin' his weapon to stick me. Now it's up to you. You can decide whether you want to put some this in your book."

Grant, who was sitting in stunned silence, returned to the notebook and pencil.

"I could feel that knife blade hittin' bone and instantly I could feel the blood runnin' down the back of my bare legs. That big ugly boy rapin' bag of shit let out a shriek like a dog treed mountain lion. He loosed his grip on my shirt and I jumped out of that boat with my bare ass shinin' in the firelight. Then and there I decided he was gonna have to kill me if he intended on satisfyin' his desires. Like I said, for a big fella he was quick and it wasn't long till he'd got his britches up from around his ankles and he was out of the boat and after my skinny little ass like a honyocker's wife in the chicken yard catchin' Sunday dinner.

Scared as I was I could see that he was bleedin' like a throat cut hog and I figured that in addition to stickin' him in the gut, I'd likely cut that big artery next to his balls."

"The femoral artery," Grant mused.

"Now it occurred to me that if I could hold him off long enough, at

111

the rate he was bleedin' he'd start to get feeble before too long. Thank God none of the others were in it with him. That gave me the chance to run him all over that island, and at the rate he was bleedin' I figured I could hold out the pursuit longer than him.

Sure enough, it wasn't but a little while and he began to get puny. I could see that there was blood everywhere you looked. Pretty quick I started taunting him and doing all I could to get him to chase after me some more. Then, he tipped right over like a heart shot buffalo. He was layin' there floppin' around and whinin' like a little girl. I had no sympathy for his plight to be real honest."

"I feel no sympathy now," Grant said, a look of shock still glazing his eyes.

"I just sat there on a log, starin' at that overgrowed boy lovin' sumbitch. I looked him right in the eyes smilin' like a peccary eatin' a prickly pear. There was blood like jelly pilin' up between his legs and I figured he was fixin' to meet his judgment. Then it occurred to me that his friends might not take kindly to me killin' their friend. They hadn't helped him catch me, but that didn't mean they was gonna approve me killin' his miserable ass. He was, after all, kind'a their boss. Now all them fellas, except for Benji who was still out cold, were standin' there lookin' down at ol' Burl with a kind of sympathetic look. I jumped in the boat and got my britches and my boots on and prepared for the worst. I still had Burl's big ol' skinnin' knife...just in case."

"Did this Burl fellow die?" Grant asked.

"You bet! Oh, he hung on for a bit but it wasn't long till he quit movin'. Then I heard one of the others say he figured Burl for dead. There was a long silence as the three of them sat around the fire lookin' at one another not knowin' what to do. I went and got a rag, which I wet in the river, and went to help Benji. That poor bastard was hurt damned near about as bad as ol' Burl. But I guarantee you that ol' Burl wouldn't have been near as sympathetic for Benji, or the least bit worried about his condition. He was just one mean son-of-a-bitch.

So I was washing Benji's face and seein' to him when he finally came around, chokin' and spittin' out teeth. As bad hurt as he was he actually started cheerin' through his busted teeth when he learned ol' Burl had gone under. So those men talked it over and Benji was on my side. To my surprise they all figured that I'd had the right to do what I'd done. Even more surprising, they figured I'd done them a big favor. They took a vote and decided that if I would take some of Benji's chores and help with the rowin' and the helm the rest of the way to Saint Louis they'd split Burl's share with me. Now figuring that I'd started out with nothin', a piece of Burl's share was better than what I'd had goin' in. I was happy as a hound lickin' the bean pot."

Tom stopped and sat looking at Grant waiting for a comment.

"Would you really want this story to appear in print?" Grant asked. "I have been sitting here trying to remember my twelfth year and what I did and what I was like. I was just a child...a little boy. I can't imagine myself in that situation having that presence of mind and the emotional wherewithal to carry on under so much duress and to actually kill a man."

"It ain't as if I had a choice, Son. I was just a little boy too, but that's the hand I was dealt, and them was the cards I had to play. You might just be surprised at yourself if'n you was to be put in a situation where you was out of options."

"I just don't know," Grant replied. "I just don't know."

"Well, anyway, you got the story. If you write it fine, if you don't want to that'll be fine too. The good side of the story is that at least when I arrived in Saint Louis I wasn't destitute. Those men kept their word and cut me in for a share. We ain't talkin' no paltry sum neither. Burl also had a .31 Colt's pocket revolver with a short barrel and of course that skinnin' knife I'd killed him with. I reckon those boys figured them weapons were my entitlement, because they gave me that knife and pistol in addition to the money. When they'd sold the hides and we took that boat apart to sell the lumber I came out with a pretty good stake fer a younker. I reckon I walked away with near the equivalent of two or three year's wages for a workin' man of the day.

Benji and the other fellas turned out to be square shooters and when we'd settled accounts and went our separate ways I was sorta sorry to lose their company. By then it was nearin' the end of July or getting into early August I reckon. I decided to head up to Saint Joseph to see if I could find my big sister, bein's she was the only family I had left. Now if you remember right, Rachel is Dixie's grandma."

"It must have been heartbreaking for her when you told her about the family," Grant said.

"She grieved the longest time, but life goes on. Her husband, the borin' feller I told you about, he let me turn my hand to workin' around the store and such. He even had me goin' to school for a bit."

"I suppose it was well that you had the guidance of a grown man. Education is important," Grant said.

"I reckon it was, but I could read and cipher about as well as any at the school, because of the tutorings of my ma and pa...and I got real antsy just sittin' and listenin' to the same ol' three R's from the school marm every day. Of the few months I was supposed to be attendin' that school, I reckon I was unattendin' as much as I was attendin'.

Ol' Jacob, Dixie's grandpa, would get onto me about going to school and workin' and such, but even with our differences about my education and so forth, I finally decided that Jacob, other than being a borin' fella, was a pretty good kind'a man as far as honesty and havin' my best interest at heart."

"I would think you were lucky to have a businessman to mentor you," Grant said.

"In many ways that was surely true. And, I was surely not wantin' to carry my money around with me. I wouldn't have trusted a bank in those days and what with the ruffians and road agents I decided to invest it with Jacob. You should'a seen his face when I showed him that money. You would'a thought that money was postcards from Paris from the look on his mug. After some explainin', not about how I'd kilt ol' Burl to earn the share mind you, but about the fact that them fellas had cut me in for my work, ol' Jacob saw me in a new light. He invested that money for me and saw to my savin's for some years thereafter. Did well by me too!"

Grant put away his notebook and pencil and sat pensively for some moments.

Tom stood and stretched his arms above his head.

"Let's stroll over to the mess hall and see if'n they got any handouts."

They returned to the house later that afternoon.

"Grant, you'll have to excuse me a while," Tom said. "I have some business which needs my attention. I'll see you at dinner, if that's okay with you?"

Grant went to his room to work on his notes. Writing while the emotion is still burning, he thought, is the best way to capture all that this story has to tell. The time passed quickly as he wrote. As the light in his room dimmed he noticed that the afternoon sun had passed his window and was moving to the western horizon. Putting away his notebook, he indulged himself, soaking in a nearly scalding bath until the still warm water began to feel chilled. Meticulously groomed for dinner, he hoped that his preparation would not go unnoticed.

"Did you garner any award winning gems today?" Dixie asked as Grant entered the dining room.

"I'm not sure as to award winning, but I have discovered gems," Grant smiled.

Grant was surprised when Koko, who had served dinner, joined them at the table.

"Young man smell nice," she said, causing Grant to squirm uncomfortably.

"He'd best be careful," Tom added. "I may have to come down there and kiss him my own self."

Nick and Phoebe had joined them for dinner. As they finished desert, Nick asked, "Dad, are you going into town Saturday night for the dance?"

"Ya know son, the widow Barnaby has gone to Boston to visit with her daughter and I don't reckon any other of them old hens is worth the strut of a fine rooster like myself. I think I'll just take a pass on that."

Tom then turned to Grant.

"Grant you need to get that horse back to J. D. at the stables. Right?" Tom asked.

When Grant nodded his reply, Tom looked at Dixie.

"This young filly here would probably enjoy a turn around the dancin' floor, don't you reckon? And as a matter of fact, I got another horse that needs to go to J. D. at the livery anyway."

Looking at Nick, Tom inquired, "You gonna drive in Saturday?"

"Me and Phoebe are going in the afternoon so she can do some shoppin'."

Tom looked at Grant, then at Dixie.

"Why don't you two ride them horses into town for me? Then Grant can get the rest of his possibles from J. D. at the stable. Then on Sunday Dixie can ride back out here with Nick and bring Grant's luggage."

"And where will I be on Sunday when they bring my luggage out here?" Grant asked.

"Well...you're gonna be goin' with me to Great Falls in the airplane."

Tom looked at Nick.

"Bring Grant out to that big flat on top of the mesa by the railroad station about ten o'clock Sunday. I can pick him up there."

"Okey-dokey! I'll have him there at ten on Sunday," Nick said.

Grant had hoped to spend some time that evening with Dixie. However, the hour was late and the party retired for the evening.

7

Saturday morning was cool and clear. Grant arose early to shower and dress. Dixie was already seated having breakfast with Tom when Grant entered the room.

"Better sit down and grab some vittles," Tom said. "This is gonna be a big day for you two. Ride clear into town and then dancin' and all."

"Yes, Uncle Match-Maker, we have the picture," Dixie said. "May I ask why you are taking Grant to Great Falls?"

"Wanna watch Dempsey do a little trainin'. He's got his trainin' camp in Great Falls and there just might be some kind'a story in it for Grant. Besides I got a vested interest in this here contest."

"Vested interest?" Grant asked,

"You see, last fall I flew down to Helena to have a chat with some of the boys in the legislature. There were a bunch of us havin' a toddy one evenin' when I ran into a loud mouthed Irishman by the name of Mike O'Halloran who claimed to be a fight promoter. He seemed like a decent enough sort although he was full'a bullshit to his eyebrows. Just the sort of feller I can abide."

Tom winked at the two.

"Now this O'Halloran was sort'a insinuating that he was gonna promote some fights around Montana, which sounded to me like a pretty good idea, from a business point of view. We was chattin' and I told him that I had flown down to Helena in the Jenny. He was just beside himself. Said he'd never been in an airplane and could I give him a ride. Next thing ya know we are headed up to Shelby where I have a few friends who I figured might just be interested. When we got into Shelby I called an old friend of mine by the name of Mulroney who just also happens to be the Mayor and a part owner of the bank. I also own a piece of that same bank myself."

"So you also have banking interests?" Grant asked.

"That's a story for another time…Well I got these two Irishmen together and the bullshit was flyin' fast and furious. One thing led to another and delusions of grandeur accelerated by the whiskey took over the conversation. They got to talkin' about land booms and how they could make Shelby a big city overnight and God knows what all. The next thing ya know O'Halloran makes a telephone call to Tommy Gibbons' manager and asked would he like to fight Dempsey in Shelby, Montana. The kid's manager didn't hesitate. He tells O'Halloran that if we can get Dempsey to Shelby for the fight, Gibbons will fight him for nothin'. Now I'll be damned if that didn't start the cow pie rollin' down the mountainside."

Tom took a sip of coffee.

"You mean that Gibbons is fighting for nothing?" Dixie asked.

"You bet he is," Tom replied. "Kid's past his prime and figures it's do or die for his boxing career. Didn't make no nevermind to Dempsey. He's sure enough gettin' his share. Next thing I know, that damned fool Mulroney has let O'Halloran talk him into sendin' Dempsey a telegram offering three hundred grand to come to Shelby for the fight, which of course, Dempsey found hard to resist I'm sure. Anyway, Dempsey's manager, a fella by the name of Doc Kearns, wanted a third up front. So we had to send him a hundred grand right away. Then he wanted another third a month before the fight...and the last hundred big ones before the champ ties on the gloves on the Fourth."

Tom took another sip of coffee.

"Speakin' of damned fools, I let Mulroney talk me into dippin' into the bank funds to send Dempsey the first hundred grand. Worse yet we dipped again for the second go. Now we gotta hope that O'Halloran's promotin' is as good as his bullshittin'."

"Do you have a lot of your own money in the venture?" Grant asked.

"Way more than I like havin', not to mention the bank's money. I hope you liked that beefsteak the other night. We may be eatin' beans around here from now on," Tom concluded.

Dixie's face was painted with concern. "You won't get in any trouble, will you Uncle Tom?" she asked.

Tom rose from the table.

"I'll be fine darlin'. You kids have nice day ridin' to town and enjoy the dance."

Looking at Grant he said, "I'll pick you up at ten Sunday mornin'."

Grant and Dixie walked to the corral where Little Tom was waiting with the horses.

"Dad told me to saddle these two and have 'em ready for ya," he said.

As they mounted the horses, Buck came out of the stable and walked toward them.

Dixie smiled when she saw him.

"Good morning, Buck. I haven't seen you for several days."

"Me and Howdy been gettin' the camps ready fer the dudes. I rode all night to get back here for the dance. I was hopin you was gonna be there."

"I'll be there," she replied. "Grant and I are returning these horses and then we'll be going to the dance. I guess we'll see you there."

"Sure enough," Buck said through clenched teeth. "I'm gonna catch a ride with Nick this afternoon."

Buck stood in front of Strawberry, staring directly into Grants eyes.

"You be real careful Dude, a fella can get hurt ridin' on these wild horses. Even just ridin' into to town."

"Thank you for the advice," Grant said.

Buck stepped out of the way.

Grant's gelding followed the lead of Dixie's mare as the horses plodded along the road that divided The Compound. They rode several miles in silence.

"Is this the way to town?" he asked.

"That's the main road just beyond the gate," Dixie replied.

Grant saw a large gate where the ranch road intersected the main road. The gate was framed by primeval pine logs, a Western rendition of entrance gates seen at Southern plantations. The log which formed the top of the arch was hewn across the front and deeply inscribed with the words, "The Buffalo Rock Ranch."

"I hadn't seen this gate when your uncle brought me out to the ranch. We came in by another way...I guess we took a shortcut. Is there some rock formation called Buffalo Rock nearby which gave the ranch its name?"

"No," Dixie replied. "A Buffalo Rock is a type of fossil which was sacred to the Indians. Remember when Susanna told you about the fossil hunters at dinner the other night?"

Grant nodded.

"One of the types of fossils they have found are ancient sea shells which the Blackfoot Indians considered to be magic. They believed that finding those shells could give them power over the buffalo. Hence, they called them Buffalo Rocks. Uncle Tom called this place by a few other names in the early years I'm told, but his second wife, Susanna's mother, who was Blackfoot, talked him into calling it 'The Buffalo Rock,' and that's what he's called it ever since."

They rode some distance when Dixie again broke the silence.

"You didn't really tell us much about yourself at dinner the other evening. You told us about Mr. Pulitzer and about your aspirations, but you never really told us about Grant Collins."

He smiled to himself, hiding his joy at the thought that she might just be showing an interest in him.

"I'll strike a bargain with you," he said. "You tell me about Dixie and I'll tell you about Grant."

She reached out her hand in an offer to shake on the agreement.

"You have a deal, but you go first."

"Uh huh," Grant protested. "You said less than I did. I don't even know your last name."

"Anderson...Dixie Lee Anderson."

"Good start, but not good enough, Miss Anderson. You can surely think of more than that. For example, how old are you?"

"I'll be twenty in the fall," she replied. "Nearly an old maid."

"And, born, raised, school, family; why are you here in the middle of Montana?"

"Well, I was born in Missouri, in Saint Louis as a matter of fact. My father is an attorney."

Grant interrupted.

"Anderson. Are his offices in downtown, close to the newspaper office? First name William? Does he know Jonathan Kuntz?

She nodded her head with no hint of surprise.

"I met your parents at a charity event some months ago. Very distinguished looking gentleman, quite a handsome couple. They are well thought of in the city I am told. Small world, isn't it?"

Dixie smiled a knowing smile.

"How is the Kuntz family? Melinda must be quite the socialite these days. I hope she's learned to dance."

"Yes, she dances quite well," he said, taken by surprise.

Grant thought quickly, perplexed at the way women could leave him feeling guilty when he had nothing to hide.

"And did the two of you dance often?" she pursued.

"No, not often. I did escort her occasionally and we are friends," he stammered.

"She is quite a beautiful girl," Dixie said.

"Yes...yes she is quite attractive."

"We grew up together you know. Our families were close. She is a couple of years older than I, which gave her the advantage with the really handsome boys."

Dixie looked directly at Grant to study the impact of her words. Seeing that her wiles were having an effect she put the back of her hand against her forehead.

"And now, she's seen you first, and again she has me at the disadvantage," she said in dramatized melancholy.

"No...uh no. She has no advantage, we are only friends."

Embarrassed at his own blithering, his mind raced to the scene at the station just a week prior. Dixie couldn't possibly know about that.

"So, I may have a chance after all?"

"Yes...uh...yes you do. I mean..."

"My my, aren't we the conceited one," she said with an affected pout.

"I didn't exactly mean that you..." his words tailed off and she could see that it was time to offer some relief.

"I know what you mean, Mr. Collins."

"You're having me on. Right? You must have inherited that sense of humor from your Uncle Tom."

"Speaking of Uncle Tom," she said, "wasn't that just a charming piece of match-making he orchestrated at dinner?"

"Speaking for myself, I was grateful. I hope you're not too put off by the arrangement?"

"Well...this little ride to town will certainly give us a chance to know one another. So where was I? Oh yes, I was telling you the story of my life. My father is the great nephew of Bill Anderson. That is the Bloody Bill Anderson...of the border conflicts during the 'unpleasantries of the sixties,' as my father calls the Civil War. My father has never surrendered. He is still fighting the War of the Rebellion. He even belongs to some silly secret group who call themselves a clan. They wear robes and hoods and act like fools when the moon is full. Have you heard of the K. K. K.?"

"You mean the Klu Klux Klan?"

"That's his group," she said, her embarrassment now apparent.

"It just hit me," he said tossing back his head in laughter. "Dixie Lee, of course. General Lee fighting for Dixie. That is nearly as outrageous as my grandfather insisting that I be named after Grant and Sherman."

Grant guided his horse close and put out his hand for another handshake.

"Shall we call an Appomattox?"

"So that is how you came to be Grant?"

"My grandfather was a surgeon in the camps of both Generals Grant and Sherman during those 'unpleasantries'. My father is also a doctor, as I said at dinner. The entire family is very disappointed that I decided to pursue a career in journalism. The consensus seemed to be that it is quite an inelegant life. My father asked, 'Why would a well turned out young man concern himself with the goings on of the great unwashed masses?' My mother actually fainted and injured herself when I announced my intention to go to St. Louis."

"Is she alright? Was it a serious injury?"

"It was a serious injury, but she is fine now. She and my cousin were seated at the piano when I told her and she fell from the bench and sustained a concussion. It was quite serious at the time. I delayed my trip to Saint Louis a few weeks until she recovered."

"And why did you choose a career so repugnant to your family?"

"I love to write...and I wanted to be my own man."

"Are you?" she asked.

"What?"

"Are you your own man?"

"Not yet, but I am going to be. I believe that as long as one is living on family money or employed by another, it is impossible to be your own man. I am pursuing a path that I hope will take me to an independent life. All of the greats, from Shakespeare to Samuel Clemens to the present day popular writers such as Fitzgerald, had difficulty becoming independent."

"That certainly is a lofty ambition," she said, looking into his face. "I do believe that you will stick it out, but I suppose it is nice to have family money to fall back on."

"In all honesty, I have not forsaken the family fortune, just in case."

They laughed together in mutual understanding.

"Your Uncle Tom told me that you attended Vassar. The Buffalo Rock Ranch seems a long way from Poughkeepsie. Why did you come west?"

"Coincidentally sir, you are not the only one with ambition. I would also like to be a writer...poet actually. But I became bored and overwhelmed at school and wanted to have some real life experience outside of the artificial Victorian cocoon that a young middle class woman must endure. I actually wanted to go to Europe, but my father was hearing none of that."

"I wouldn't say as how I could blame him."

"Your Victorianism is showing, Mr. Collins."

"One does hear some rather disturbing things about Europe, especially France."

"Ahhhh...Paris, The City of Light. I shall visit there someday. But for the present, I had heard stories about the family ranch for years and decided that it might give me a chance to at least meet some real people. My father was agreeable to that. He thinks that Uncle Tom will take good care of his little angel."

"I would say that your father made a wise choice. Of course, I must admit to some bias in the matter."

He shifted in the saddle so as to look her in the eye.

"Frankly, I am quite pleased that you are here."

"The feeling is mutual," she said, looking at him with a bashful smile.

They rode a while in self-conscious silence.

"I had planned to go back to school this fall, but I have been working on some poems and short stories and I have decided to wait until next year. Uncle Tom said that I can stay as long as I like. I try to make myself useful."

"You'll have to show me some of your work," he said.

"I haven't actually finished anything worth sharing," she said. "You are lucky to be a man, working at a newspaper...and it was a stroke that you sought out Uncle Tom. I hadn't even thought of his story, or the history of the ranch as something worth writing. I am jealous, but then I think I prefer poetry to anything historical. I'll wager a lot of what he has told you is very violent. Isn't it?"

Grant thought a long moment and then, without answering the question, began to recite a poem.

"And so you see, to old V.C., Our love shall never fail. Full well we know that all we owe, To Mathew Vassar's ale."

"You know the Vassar theme song," she said in surprise.

"I knew several fellows who were seeing Vassar women and it's hard to forget the rhyme. Besides, there is certainly no shame in building a college with brewery money. Besides, I rather enjoy drinking songs for that matter. You may not know, but Pulitzer funded Columbia with a publishing business built on the Yellow Kid, which was some scurrilous journalism in its day and Vassar made his fortune in brewing. They each turned what some may call 'ill gotten wealth' to a good purpose. I think Vassar's drinking song should be held in reverence."

"I've always thought it quite funny that the favored institution of higher learning for well bred young ladies was built with booze and was known for a drinking song. I was just surprised that you knew it," she said.

"Speaking of drinking songs, just before I left Saint Louis I read an article from our Washington correspondent that Congress is considering a bill to declare Scott Key's poem, 'The Star-Spangled Banner' the official anthem of the United States. The tune they've chosen is an old English tavern song. The Vassar women shall never again have to hang their heads."

They both laughed again.

"When I return to Vassar I hope to have a different perspective about life. I don't think college professors are any better off than the young women they supposedly teach. They live in a cocoon of their own. But I am hopeful that a couple of years out in the Land of the Shining Mountains will give color to my writing. Something it's lacked until now. Perhaps then, Vassar can polish my style."

"Well, you are certainly in some good company," Grant said. "Edna St. Vincent Millay won the Pulitzer this year for her poetry, and she'd just finished at Vassar six years ago."

"She's my inspiration. Have you read her work?" she asked.

"Only excerpts. I am planning to read her writings when I return to Saint Louis. I am trying to read all of the Pulitzer Prize winners."

"You'll love her poems," she said.

Dixie cocked her head to one side.

"Do you hear a motor car coming?"

"I believe I do," Grant replied.

He stopped his horse to look behind them and listen.

"It might be Nick."

They could see the cloud of dust behind them and soon a new Packard convertible was closing the distance. When Nick honked the horn both of the horses began to prance and turn in nervous circles.

Grant's knuckles were white from holding the reins so tightly.

"I hope this animal doesn't go insane again," he said.

"Turn him to face the car," Dixie said. "He'll be less likely to spook if he can see the car coming. He's seen cars before. It is just the pavement he doesn't like."

"You know about that...the incident in town?" he asked.

"You're doing fine. Don't worry about it," she reassured with a smile.

Nick stopped the Packard beside them.

"Where have you been? We thought you were lost," Dixie said.

"Had a few chores to finish this morning," Nick replied.

Buck was sitting in the back seat with a scowl on his face. Grant's horse was turning in circles prompted by the tight rein he was holding.

Buck stepped from the car and took Grant's reins.

"Let him have some slack. You're givin' the poor nag a crick in his neck," Buck said.

Buck pulled the reins from Grant's grip.

"There ya go. Just hold him easy. He'll settle down," Nick shouted above the noise of the engine.

"Thank you," Grant said, as Buck got back into the car.

Grant moved his horse next to Nick's window.

"Would you reserve a room at the hotel for me when you get to town?" he asked.

"Sure thing," Nick replied.

"Save me a dance tonight Buck," Dixie shouted.

The blue convertible disappeared into a cloud of dust.

"Are you seeing Buck?" Grant asked.

"No more than you're seeing Melinda," she replied. "We've gone to a movie and danced a few times. You know how that is...don't you...just friends?"

"Was it a good movie?"

"Quite good...recommended by Little Tom. Douglas Fairbanks in Robin Hood."

"I haven't seen that flicker. Maybe I'll catch it when I get back to Saint Louis."

They rode in silence for another mile.

"I remember these trees," Grant said, referring to a small stand of cottonwoods beside the road. "I don't think it's too far to town now."

"It's not. Wanna race?" Dixie said with delight, "On the count of three. One, two, three...go."

She slapped her horse with the reins and the mare sprang into a run. Grant again found himself hanging on to the saddle horn as the gelding began his pursuit.

The horse had no trouble finding his way to the stable. When Grant rode into the barn Dixie was ready to dismount. J. D. took Grant's reins and looked up with a smile.

"Glad ta see ya made it. Nice horse huh?" the liveryman said.

"Yes, quite a nice a nice horse. How much do I owe you for his rental?"

"Don't owe me nothin', Son," J. D. replied. "I made eight dollars off'n the bettin' so I figure I'd owe you if anything."

"Betting?" Grant asked.

"As to whether this lazy little roan could buck you off. Most didn't think so...but I'd rode him enough to know that he's pretty quick. He done 'er just the way I figured," J. D. replied.

Dixie looked at Grant and smiled.

"Western humor takes a bit of getting used to," she said.

J. D. walked into the tack room and came back carrying Grant's leather suitcase.

"Reckon you'll be needin' this to get purdied up fer the dance. In fact, I think I hear Nick comin' to get ya."

Just then Nick's Packard was framing itself in the open stable door.

Grant noticed that neither Buck nor Phoebe was in the vehicle.

"I managed to get a couple of rooms but they was fillin' up pretty fast. Would ya mind bunkin' in with me and we'll let the girls have the other room?" Nick said.

"That will do nicely," Grant agreed.

"I'll drop you two off at the hotel and go get Phoebe. She went to do some shoppin'," Nick said.

"It's still early," Dixie said, "could you drop me at the mercantile and then take Grant to the hotel. I'll go shopping with Phoebe."

"Sure thing," Nick said. "I'll be back to pick you girls up in about an hour."

Nick drove to the Grand Union Hotel and he and Grant went to their room. After changing into a suit more appropriate to the occasion, Grant went to the desk to send a telegram to Jonathan Kuntz.

"DEMPSEY TRAINING IN GREAT FALLS-STOP-TRAVEL THERE TOMORROW-STOP-HOPE TO GET INTERVIEW-STOP-ANY INSTRUCTIONS-STOP- COLLINS"

That evening, before the dance, the four dined at the Grand Union. Nick then drove them to the Grange Hall. It appeared to Grant that the entire county must be in attendance.

As they walked onto the grounds Grant could see that a wooden bandstand and dance floor complete with lanterns to provide ambience for the dancers had been constructed. The Fort Benton orchestra was playing a variety of timely and old favorite music. Folding wooden chairs surrounded the dance floor to accommodate those who wished to sit out a dance.

Inside the hall, refreshments in the form of punch and ice cream were being served by the ladies of the Grange. As they entered the Grange Hall they met Buck who was holding a cup of punch. He was wearing a new, albeit ill fitting, suit and a fresh bowler hat.

"My, aren't we dapper tonight," Dixie said.

Buck's face reddened.

"Damned if you ain't the cock on the walk. Get yourself a new suit, did ya Buck?" Nick added.

"I got it today over to the Mercantile," Buck said proudly. "Milt had it ordered out for me...said it was the latest style."

"By golly," Nick continued, "you're the spitting image of your hero. You look just like that old picture of Butch Cassidy that was in that magazine a couple months back. You and Howdy ain't fixin' to rob no trains now are you?"

Buck's knuckles whitened around his punch cup. Sweat became visible on his already flushed face and he began to mumble inaudibly as he shuffled toward the door.

"I don't reckon I ever saw that picture," he said, his voice breaking.

Grant did not want any unpleasantness and he could see that Nick, much like his father, was not willing to quit his pursuit of a laugh at Buck's expense. Grant had also detected the odor of whiskey on Buck's breath.

"Would you care to join us for refreshments," Grant said politely.

Before Buck could answer Dixie said, "Yes, do join us. We're going to have a wonderful evening."

Taking Buck's arm Dixie walked him toward the refreshment table.

After refreshments, they walked to the folding tables and chairs surrounding the dance floor.

"The band is surprisingly accomplished," Grant said. "Quite professional, in fact."

When he heard the first bars of his favorite song, Grant took Dixie's hand.

"You do Charleston?" he asked, as she followed him to the floor.

They danced the Charleston, the Fox Trot and several more of the popular dances. Nick and Phoebe joined them on the floor, leaving Buck sitting with an angry scowl. When at last a slower song was played Grant felt a tap on his shoulder.

"I'm cuttin' in," Buck said.

He elbowed Grant to one side.

Grant looked at Dixie and shrugged.

"Why yes, of course," Grant said.

"You sure are lookin' beautiful tonight," Buck said, the whiskey slurring the compliment. "I'd dance with ya more but I can't do all them fancy steps like that sissy city boy does. 'Bout the best I can do is a cowboy shuffle."

She glanced at Grant who sat watching them wrestle their way around the floor.

"You're doing fine," she reassured, propping him up. "I can teach you all the steps some night after work, if you'd like."

"I'd like that a lot," he replied.

Another Foxtrot tune began to play.

Grant was on his feet as Buck walked toward the chairs. As they passed, Buck turned and embraced Grant so as to whisper in his ear.

"You know I'm gonna kick yer sissy civilized ass all the way back to New York City...or wherever it is ya came from. Don't you know that?"

Releasing his grip Buck staggered from the floor and disappeared into the darkness.

"What did he say?" Dixie asked.

"Just boy talk! Judging from that barley corn waltz and the smell, I would say that Mr. Horton is quite intoxicated."

"I wouldn't antagonize him. I have heard some stories. He has a rather unpleasant reputation for losing his temper," Dixie said.

Grant and Dixie danced to most of the songs. When the band struck up the strains of "Good Night Ladies," Grant again felt a tap on his shoulder.

Buck, bleary eyed and unsteady, leaned close to Grant.

"I'm cuttin' in again, city boy."

When Grant turned he saw Nick, who was standing behind Buck, nod his reassurance. Buck again attempted to elbow Grant out of his way but lost his balance and stumbled.

"Don't push me you sumbith," Buck slurred.

He cocked his fist to swing at Grant but before he could throw the punch, Grant moved in close and grabbed him around the upper torso. Buck's intended blow veered impotently skyward as he lost his footing. Grant sat him on the dance floor.

Nick immediately grabbed Buck's jacket from behind.

"Okay pardner, you've had enough fun for the night," Nick said.

Nick turned to Grant.

"I'll take him over to the livery and let him sleep it off. I'll be back to get the three of you in little while."

"Do you need any help?" Grant asked.

"No, Nick don't need no help, but you're God damned well gonna need help," Buck slurred.

Nick half carried Buck toward the Packard.

8

After breakfast at the Grand Union, Nick drove Grant to the top of a long smooth mesa adjacent to the train depot.

"Ol' Buck was pretty drunk last night. He even slept in his new Butch Cassidy suit." Nick said. "He's full of himself and he thinks he's in love with Dixie...moons around worse than a day-old dogie."

"And a 'dogie' is?" Grant inquired.

"That's a calf or a young horse that's lost its mama," Nick said.

He then looked at Grant's face and smiled. "If I was to come to Baltimore, I reckon there would be a lot for me to get my mind around. Don't you?"

Grant nodded in thought.

"I would give ol' Buck a lot of walkin' room though...he can be a mean bastard...and I wouldn't take him lightly," Nick said, his tone serious.

"I certainly don't want any trouble, and I haven't done anything to provoke him...not that I know of."

"Well watch your step anyway. Ol' Buck don't take a lot of provokin' sometimes."

Grant cocked his head to one side.

"That sounds like your dad coming in the airplane."

Squinting into the morning sun, they saw the reflection on the airplane's white wings as Tom banked sharply to align for a landing on top of the mesa. The Jenny seemed to hang in the still morning air as it glided, feather-like, toward the road which crossed the top of the mesa. As it touched down the plane bounced once, then settled on the two main wheels. Slowing quickly, the tail wheel touched the earth and Tom turned sharply, stopping the plane about forty feet from Nick's Packard. Motioning to Grant, Tom did not shut off the engine.

"You'll take my suitcase to the ranch?" Grant shouted over his shoulder as he ran to the plane.

Grant climbed onto the wing where Tom handed him a leather helmet and goggles. As he pulled on the helmet, he could feel the fear in the pit of his stomach as the cloth wing beneath his feet vibrated in rhythm with the engine. Grant stowed his flour sack luggage and climbed in. He fastened the buckles of the safety belt and glanced around the small cockpit.

"Are you ready?" Tom shouted from the rear seat.

Grant waved his hand and then grasped the wooden frame tightly, bracing his feet against the floor.

Something moved against his shoes.

"Get your feet off the rudders," Tom yelled above the noise of the engine.

Fearing to touch any of the controls, Grant pulled himself into a ball as the Jenny began to roll slowly forward, turning into the fresh tracks on the dirt road surface that the plane had left on landing.

Grant watched as a red handled lever on his left side began to move forward in concert with the engine turning faster and faster. The engine grew louder as the plane increased speed. Grant glanced around at bushes and rocks moving ever more rapidly in his periphery. He hoped that none were tall enough to hit the wings. He felt himself lurch involuntarily and realized that the tail of the Jenny had lifted. Suddenly the rumbling of the rubber tires on the dirt surface ceased and the sagebrush, rocks and grass began to fall away beneath the wings.

Nick waved as they circled above. Tom then turned to fly over the town, dipping a wing as the Jenny passed over Fort Benton. Grant could see the Grand Union Hotel and the three blocks of macadam paving on Front Street, which had been the source of such humiliation just a few days prior. He laughed at himself. At least he would be remembered for having provided the town with some real entertainment.

Nick's Packard now looked like a small toy as he drove off the hill toward town.

Following the Missouri River, Tom did not climb beyond a thousand feet so that Grant could see the wildlife and farms along the way. He dropped low and circled the hulk of an ancient steamer which had attempted, without success, to navigate the ever changing course of the river beyond the docks at Fort Benton in some prior time.

Grant marveled at the scenery below, viewed as he had never imagined it would appear. From the air, the town and road and river appeared to be a miniaturized exhibit one might see at the fair. He began to calm down and enjoy this new world. When Tom made a tight circle around a roaring giant waterfall, Grant could clearly understand how the Corps of Discovery had been left awestruck at the sight of the millions of gallons of cascading white water more than a century before. These Great Falls had found no better name than the description given to the tumbling torrent by Lewis and Clark.

As they flew a figure eight over the city of Great Falls, Grant was surprised that it was much larger than he had expected. After the aerial tour, Tom flew low over a ranch house a few miles from town. Waggling his wings, several people could be seen waving from the ground. Tom circled and landed the Jenny on a road some distance from the house.

Grant stood in his cockpit and could see a yellow Stutz Bearcat careening toward them, dust roiling from beneath the wheels. He and Tom stepped down from the plane as the Stutz slid to a stop a few feet from the plane. A large man of about sixty, dressed in work clothes, tipped his hat.

"I told Gert that was probably you when I heard a plane...and it's hard to miss that red, white and blue Jenny," he said.

Tom put his foot on the running board and shook hands with the man seated in the car.

"How the hell you been, you old horse thief?" the man said.

"Better'n you and that's fer damned sure," Tom replied.

Tom put his hand on Grant's shoulder.

"I want ya to meet Grant Collins from Saint Louis...and this here is Bernie Gregory. Richest bastard in three counties and he still don't quit."

Grant shook hands with Bernie who was still seated in the Stutz.

"What brings ya to Great Falls?" Bernie asked, looking at Grant.

"Grant here's a newspaper fella," Tom replied before Grant could answer. "I hope he can help promote this damned fight."

"We need all the help we can get, and that's for certain," Bernie said. "Get in, let's go have a drink and say hello to Gert."

Tom sat next to Bernie while Grant stuffed himself into the 'mother-in-law' seat in the rear.

When they arrived at the house a heavy women with a huge smile came to the driveway.

"Mr. Thomas, you better get over here and give us a hug," she shouted.

"Gert," Tom said, prying himself from her bear hug, "want ya to meet

Grant Collins."

Gertrude Gregory shouted hello to Grant as he extricated himself from the folding seat.

"You boys gonna stay with us ain't ya? You ain't gonna find a place in town. All the reporters have taken every room that was available."

"How the hell could we refuse an invite like that," Tom said. "Give me the chance to drink Bernie's whiskey. I say hell yes and what's for dinner?"

Bernie put his hand on Tom's shoulder as they walked toward the house.

"What did you think of that bottle of whiskey I sent over for Christmas?" Bernie asked.

"It was just right, Bernie...just right," Tom replied, a twinkle in his eye.

"That was some damned fine Scotch whiskey," Bernie ranted. "What do ya mean, 'it was just right?'"

"Well, sir," Tom grinned, "had it been any better, you wouldn't have sent it to me, and had it been any worse, I couldn't have drunk it. It was just right."

Everyone laughed as Gert showed them into the house. The three men entered a room with a large stone fireplace, over which hung a portrait of Bernie and Gert. The likeness had been painted over an enlarged photograph of the two, taken in their younger years.

The room was furnished with fine heavy leather furniture. Persian rugs protected the polished hardwood floors, which showed evidence of marring by high heeled boots. The heads and hides of animals unfamiliar to Grant adorned the walls.

"Aren't those African animals?" Grant asked.

"Yep," Bernie replied. "Gert and me took us a safari about six years ago. Damnedest time as I ever had. It was like the old days around here before the buffalo was gone. There was critters everywhere. Everything from elephants to little antelope no bigger'n a jack rabbit."

"This is a huge lion's head," Grant commented, closely examining the mount.

"That thing scared the shit out of me, but ol' Gert shot the son-of-a-bitch and it dropped dead right at her feet. Had she not been there I would'a run like hell," Bernie laughed.

Bernie poured tumblers of Canadian whiskey and when they had toasted and discussed the upcoming fight, Bernie said, "You can use the Stutz, Tom. I ain't goin' to town fer nothin'. You might as well enjoy something nice for a change."

Bernie winked at Grant. "That Stutz is like the best horse you ever rode...or the best filly, if you get my drift."

"Well, by God, I'll just take you up on that too,' Tom said, draining his glass. "How do I get to Dempsey's training camp?"

"Stop at the Moose Lodge. Our honorable Mayor and Doc Kearns are hangin' around over there to hide out. They won't let the news boys in there so they got a little privacy.

Tom started the Stutz and Grant climbed in beside him.

"What is the largest newspaper in this area of Montana?" Grant asked.

"Great Falls Gazzette is about as big as I can think of," Tom replied.

"Do you suppose there is any chance of an outsider getting work as a reporter?"

"You lookin' fer work, are ya, son? I thought you had a job in Saint Louis."

"I am just looking at possibilities."

"This couldn't have nothin' to do with my niece...could it?"

"I suppose I did have some thoughts about your niece when I asked the question. Perhaps it is time for me to view the future with a more multi-dimensional perspective. I have only thought of myself to this point in my life. One has to consider that there may be room for another in one's plans for the future."

"Ohhhh, sweet Jesus, the boy has fallen in love. Son, that's a disease that will either cure ya or kill ya. I reckon right now you ain't sure just which."

"I must admit that I have some very unusual feelings."

Grant could feel the Stutz make a faltering shutter as the engine backfired.

"That damned Bernie and his 'best horse I ever rid' bullshit. It'll run good if ya feed it. This damned fancy son-of-a-bitch is outta gas."

"Worse yet, she's about to throw a shoe," Grant said, pointing to the right front tire.

Tom stopped the Stutz and jumped out to look at the tire.

"Fanciest automobile in the Western United States and a man can't get to town in the damned thing. Look in that rumble seat compartment and see if'n there ain't some tools back there. You've got a good young back and some knees that don't creak. How's about jackin' up this thoroughbred pile of nuts and bolts and removin' that tire before it gets any flatter?"

Grant placed the jack under the axle and was raising the front of the Stutz when they heard the rumble of an approaching vehicle. Grant stood and saw an army surplus Ford transport truck.

The truck stopped and a tall young man opened the passenger door and got down. "Howdy, Tom," he said. "You likely don't remember me. I ain't seen ya since I was just a kid. I'm Coyle...Bernie's nephew."

"Yeah, sure I remember ya now," Tom said, shaking the young man's hand. "Damned if you didn't get to be a big'un."

The other man had alighted from the truck and approached.

"This here is Jesus. He works for Bernie too. Good hand with the horses but he don't habla English too good."

"Nice to meet you, Jesus," Tom said nodding. "You wouldn't happen to have a can of gas in that truck would ya? Or a siphon hose?"

The tall young man shook his head and pursed his lips.

"I didn't reckon we was gonna be that lucky," Tom said.

Jesus had walked to the Stutz and gently nudged Grant to one side.

"I change tire reeeel queek. You not need for get dirty, Señor."

Tom nodded and Grant moved out of the way. A few minutes later the young man had the spare on the Stutz and the tools put away.

"When we get to town I'll send Harvey out with some gas for ya, if'n that's okay. Or you can ride in with us and send someone out for Uncle Bernie's Stutz."

"Just send us a can of gas," Tom said. "I'd hate to leave your Uncle Bernie's prize possession unattended out here in the wilderness. You know what I mean? Might be some miscreants lurkin' about who'd up and steal it."

As the two young men drove away Tom climbed into the Stutz.

"Well at least the sumbitch ran out of gas under a shade tree. Might just as well take our comfort on these leather seats while we await our rescue," Tom said.

"How long do you suppose it'll be?"

"It'll be a while, that is if it's Harvey they're sendin'."

"Do you suppose you have time to tell me about how you became a rider for the Pony Express?"

"Not only yes, but hell yes to that. Let me think a minute. I told ya about the mackinaw ride with Burl and the boys. And I think I told you about Rachel and Jacob and going to school and so forth."

Grant nodded and Tom's eyes squinted in thought.

"Well, it was like I told ya. I was workin' for Jacob around his mercantile, kinda makin' myself useful. And of course, I was doin' the things boys do, huntin' and fishin' and gettin' into mischief. And so I passed the winter of fifty nine and sixty in Saint Joe."

Tom leaned back and lit a cigarette. He blew a ring of smoke and watched as it disappeared in the breeze.

"One morning, it was late in the winter as I recall...this was maybe February of sixty, I was sweepin' out the store and shootin' the breeze with one of the local youngsters when a man came in and asked could he post a notice. He said that he was lookin' for men to do a job of work. Now you got to remember that work was hard to come by in those days...so I asked him what kind of work it was he was offering. He told me they was gonna be startin' an overland mail route in a couple of months and that they'd be needin' riders and wranglers and hands for various positions. The fella then looked at me and asked could I ride a horse. I told him that I'd growed up on a ranch in the territories and that I'd rode since I was a weanling. Then I told him that my folks was killed and I came to Saint Joseph to stay with my older sister. His eyes lit up and he handed me a copy of that flyer. It had the location of where to report and he told me they were gonna be givin' special dispensation to orphans; bein' as how it would likely be dangerous work and all.

I read that thing and told Cooter, that was the kid who was hangin' out in the store, Cooter LaRue...that we'd ought to go down to the stables and talk to 'em about them jobs. I was about tuckered out with store work and I figured that bein' an ophan, I'd get that 'dispensation,' even though I had no idea as to what that meant."

"That advertisement must be in an archive somewhere," Grant conjectured.

"I reckon it would be. That notice was posted all over Saint Joe...all over the country for that matter. Now ol' Cooter had a mule, or rather his pappy had a mule, which he could borrow, and Cooter fancied himself a horseman. I didn't even have a horse, so him and me rode down to the stables bareback and double on that mule. We got to the place at the appointed time to see if'n we could get us a job. I don't know how many men there was but I never saw so many fellers all wantin' to do the same thing at the same time. Must'a been a couple hundred of 'em all lined up and quiet as if they was in church, not wantin' to miss anything that was said by the men who was doing the hirin'.'"

Grant began writing in his notebook.

"Now we're gettin' to the good stuff, best you write this down. They had about fifty or sixty head of what appeared to be some pretty good horses in a corral and the rumor was goin' around that they was gonna give each of us a test. They was wantin' to see, could you really ride or were ya just bullshittin'. This was supposed to pay good wages and there were those who would lie, and then there were those, like Cooter, who was just delusional.

They was promisin' to pay fifty dollars or even more, dependin' on the post ya got assigned to. Fifty dollars a month was a lot of money, believe you me. There was many a hard workin' family man in those times would have kissed yer ass with a howdee do every morning for fifty dollars a year. Christ all mighty, you can believe it when I say that there was some serious competition for them jobs. There was men of all ages and descriptions and even a few women showed up, but they weren't likely to get a fair shake. No one figured women was tough enough for a job like that, so no one took 'em too serious...besides, having females around some remote outpost would'a been nothing but trouble the way most had it figured."

Tom sat a long moment and then looked at Grant with a smile.

"And now they're gonna let 'em vote. Can you imagine? Things sure have changed.

Anyways, first thing they done was weed out everyone that was too big. Some of them fellas was hired as wranglers and such but they was to heavy in the saddle to be riders.

Next thing they done was put everyone in small groups to sort'a make a competition outta this test. Then they made us jump onto one'a them horses bareback and ride around in a little arena. That was the end of most of the bullshitters right there. I'd say we lost about a third of that bunch 'cause they couldn't stay astride an unsaddled horse makin' quick turns. Bareback ridin' is harder than it looks, but I'd been ridin' with Injuns for a couple of years, so it didn't seem like nothin' for me.

Then each of us had to saddle and bridle as quick as we could and then mount and ride around that little corral. The company had a saddle maker build 'em a bunch of special saddles. These saddles was similar to a regular stock saddle only a whole lot lighter. Near as light as a jockey saddle but more the cowboy style with a horn and all. Had the skirts cut to a minimum and a special tree that didn't weigh hardly nothin'. During that saddlin' test they weeded out another big bunch of them fellas. Some of those men had little experience on a horse, bareback or saddled and their fumblin' was obvious enough. Pretty quick that bunch was gone too. No one laughed though because this was all being done very serious. It was real serious because of the money and all."

Tom paused to take a puff on the Lucky Strike and allow Grant to finish his notes.

"However, I got to admit that I didn't really consider it all too serious...

as to the money that is. It was an adventure for me. Hell, anything was better'n workin' in a store. Money didn't mean nothin' to me when I was a kid. It was the adventure that I was lookin' for. Then you've also got to remember that I was still a kid and I had just lost my folks. Sweepin' out a store gave a young fella too much time for thinkin'. I reckon that adventure was my way of dealin' with the grief. I was still feelin' pretty miserable at having lost my folks."

Tom looked at Grant as if he was embarrassed at the having admitted a weakness.

"I was always pretty competitive. So I done my best but I never figured I'd get picked, just bein' a kid and all."

Tom stepped out of the Stutz to stretch his legs.

"They sent ol' Cooter packin' right off. He didn't make it through the saddlin' part cause he had only ridden that mule while his pappy was plowin' mostly. He found out soon enough that ridin' a quick horse was a bit different. I could tack up in a hurry and get mounted without difficulty. I was just a little bitty slip of lad, but agile as a monkey in those days."

"That was too bad about your friend, Cooter?" Grant said, looking up from his notebook.

"Yeah...it was too bad but he wasn't the only one. There was men there with families and responsibilities and you could see in their eyes that gettin' asked to leave was just breakin' their hearts. Some had tears in their eyes.

It's hard for us, sitting here in this Stutz Bearcat wearing fancy clothes and eatin' good food everyday, to picture what it was like back in sixty. That Pony Express job was offering remuneration sufficient to set a man up for his life if he stuck at it for one year and minded his pennies. It was a God's plenty for any workin' man and that's the truth of it. When they'd weeded that bunch down to about fifty, they told us straight up that there would only be about ten of us who would get picked in the end. That's when I figured I was done for. I reckon that's why I remember it so well.

They set up a race where each man was given four horses. Then they took us in groups of five and we had to race each other head to head. We all had to start with our saddles and tack layin' on the ground. You had to saddle up that first horse as quick as you could, ride about a quarter of mile to another horse, which one of the other men was holdin' for you, take the saddle off and put it on the second horse and then ride back to the other end to third horse and do the same thing. When we got to that fourth horse, it was pretty obvious that some of those boys was way behind. I thought it was kind'a fun but I didn't figure I had a chance until we was on that third leg and I was a half a length in front of my bunch. When all was said and done I was one of the twenty or so who was left for the finals.

Gettin' that far commenced to get my competitive spirit aroused and I figured, what the hell, I can do this as good as any of these fellas. Then I really let 'er rip. I was not only one of the ten who got picked, but I'd finished first in that bunch. Wasn't long before all those other fellas started callin' me 'The Little Tornado.'

Time went along and that name stuck with me. Wherever I went they started callin' me Tornado Tom. To be honest, I took a shine to the handle and never discouraged folks from usin' it. Kind'a set me apart and made me feel good, if ya know what I mean?"

"You are recorded in the archives of the Pony Express as Tornado Tom Thomas," Grant said.

Tom scratched his chin and smiled.

"I didn't know that. At least I got some remembrance. Anyway, I got the job and you should'a seen ol' Jacob's eyes when I told him I was an oath swearin' member of the Pony Express. Word had got around by then what the Pony Express was all about. At first he attempted to dissuade me, mostly because of my sister I reckon, but I was bound by then and he was truly impressed when I told him I would be gettin' one hundred and twenty five dollars each month. I didn't tell Jacob or Rachel but it seems that the company was sending me to one of the most dangerous parts of the route, so I was getting a bit extra. It was the Paiutes, but I'll tell you more about them a little later."

"You mentioned swearing an oath," Grant asked.

"Yes sir...seein' as how we was contractin' to carry the United States mail the Company of Russell, Majors and Waddell swore us to an oath. Carrying that mail was serious business.

After they swore us in they gave us all a Bible, a Sharps carbine rifle and a pair of Navy .36 caliber Colt's revolvers. We was obliged to pay for the guns out of future earnin's. However they gave us that Bible. They also gave us a bugle with which we was supposed to announce our arrival at each remount station. We didn't have to pay for that neither."

Tom resumed his seat in the Stutz.

"Now I'll tell ya Grant, most of them fellers were rough and the spirit of the Lord did not reside in too many of 'em. But I reckon before the brief days of the Pony Express was over, there was more than one of those Bibles that got put to use. I'd reckon them Bibles got more use than those guns or bugles."

"Well, Tornado Tom," Grant said, "I have a question, which originally prompted my investigation into the Pony Express. Do you have any guess, 'of a sort,' as to who made the first ride westbound from Saint Joseph?"

"Can't help ya with that son. I wasn't there and to tell ya the truth I don't know who was. Like I told you at dinner, I got a letter about ten years back from the Daughters of the Revolution wantin' to know if'n I was still alive and would I accept their invite to attend some doin's about it at the old stables. I was busy at the time and couldn't go. I wouldn't have been no help with their problem anyway. Best I can say is that it was a man by the name of Fry. Johnny Fry. I didn't know the fella. But that's what I was told at the time...if I recall correctly. I do remember on that first run across country someone mentioned his name. Any more than that I just can't say."

"It really doesn't matter, I suppose. I could have impressed my boss but I think that he's going to be happy with my product, whether or not I answer that question."

"Well, you see, the way it worked was that they had to have men all along the line when that first ride started or there wasn't no one to take the mochila on for the next leg of the route. That's why there wasn't too many riders around the headquarters in Saint Joe for that historic occasion. They was sittin' in shanties all the way across the prairie clear to California just waitin' for their turn."

"Mochila?" Grant said. "You have spoken of a mochila several times. What was it?"

"Mochila, it's a Mexican word I reckon, meaning the pouch or some such thing. It was a special built leather covering that went over the saddle, like a leather saddle blanket that went on top of the saddle. It had holes cut out so that the saddle horn and cantle stuck out but the leather covering was the actual saddle seat. There was four special made cantinas or pockets or boxes, whatever you want to call 'em...two on each side...one in front of your leg and one in the back...and ya put yer legs down between them boxes in the stirrups and sat on that mochila to hold the thing in place while you was ridin'. The mail was put in those pockets, which had little locks and only certain station keepers had the keys for those. It was bad trouble for the rider who tried to get into the mochila. Bad trouble!

The mochila was designed so that a horse could be saddled, ready and standin' when a rider got to the remount station. That was why they had those special saddles made the same size. It was also why they only hired little fellas.

Each rider was only allowed two minutes at a stop. He'd pull off the mochila, put it on the saddled mount, take a sip of water and a quick piss and he was flyin' again. All the saddles was built the same so it wasn't like each man needed his own or nothin'. I often wonder what happened to all them saddles. One'a them saddles would'a made a fine keepsake if a fella had thought to get one when the organization went toenails to the sky. But, as I have said, I wasn't no more than a kid and that sort'a thing... things like souvenirs never even occurred to me. I don't suppose there is any of them saddles left around today. You might check that museum in Saint Joe.

Another thing about that mochila was that if your horse got hurt or kilt, a man could carry that mochila to the next station, bein' as how it was real light and all. It was the responsibility of the station keeper and helpers to go out and get the saddle off the dead horse. Speed was all that mattered to the men who ran the Pony Express. Life, limb and horseflesh were secondary considerations."

"You were making one of the higher wages. if I understand correctly, and you mentioned earlier that it was because of the Paiutes?" Grant said.

"You bet. I wasn't aware when they told me I would be workin' in Nevada that there was big Injun trouble brewin' and that the Paiutes was ready to take to the war path. Seems that those Injuns was a might bit disenchanted with the way the white folk was treatin' their land. Killin' buffalo fer the hides and leavin' the meat to rot and choppin' down the nut trees that the Paiutes relied on for winter fare. A whole bunch of 'em had starved that winter of fifty-nine and sixty. So we had no sooner got the Pony Express started than them Paiutes decided to make life uncomfortable for us. We'd started out with a real bang according to the station keepers. We was makin' some good times cross country and the newspapers was braggin' on us real big.

We'd been at it about a month, I reckon, when I had my first taste of a Paiute's sense of humor. I'd been told that if they caught you, they'd skin you alive and feed your ass to the ants. The Paiutes was primarily in the Nevada and California border territory, and like I said, they was in an ugly mood by the time we got to carrying the mail. The folks runnin' the Pony Express knew damned well that there was an Injun war brewin', so we got some extra pay for the privilege of dyin' on that part of the route.

Now I was assigned to a place called Friday's Station when this particular incident occurred. I had picked up the mochila and headed east. As a rule, each man would ride about seventy-five to a hundred miles, dependin' on the country. The remount stations were spaced out in ten to fifteen mile legs so we would ride an hour or so and then change horses and ride some more. I reckon that sounds like kind'a harsh workin' conditions by the standards of today, what with all our modern conveniences, but for us it was actually looked upon with great enthusiasm and pride. Truth is that each rider only rode once or twice a week so there was long periods of boredom. I did a lot of readin', some liked playin' cards and then there was always shovelin' the old horseshit out of the corral. We'd do a little huntin' and gatherin' wood, that kind'a thing. I liked to keep myself busy so the station keepers liked havin' me around. I would always be doin' something helpful, just to keep busy."

Tom paused a moment.

"Sorry...I lost my train of thought there for a minute. So I'd started an eastbound ride and I'm out about two and half hours from Friday's

Station and comin' up on Buckland's Station when I get this eerie feeling runnin' up and down my spine like spirit fingers was playing the piano on my backbone. Wasn't long before I could see smoke rising on the desert where the station was supposed to be, and I don't mean from the woodstove neither. Schedule or no schedule, Buckland's sure didn't look like a good place to head for. I deviated from the trail and headed for some high ground where I could have a look see before I went bustin' in on something that there might not be no bustin' out of. I can't say I was scared right then, but I was damned cautious.

Well sir...I come up the backside of the ridge and sat a few minutes. I could see the station was burned down and I didn't see no one movin' around. I figured to ride in from around the hill and at least have a quick look. When I got close enough to where I could see the station, it was plain that there hadn't been much of a fight. Them Paiutes must'a took those fellas by surprise. There was nothin' left except ashes and mutilated bodies. I knowed most of those men so it was hard to see."

A pained expression crossed Tom's face.

"My little ol' head was swimmin' with the remembrances of the year before when I saw my own kin hangin' from fences, gutted and skinned like so many slaughtered sheep. I took one quick look around and decided to high tail it for the next station. Knowin' Injuns like I did, I knew damned well that they had some lookouts on a ridge somewhere just waitin'. I don't mind tellin' you that by then I was one scared child."

"Had the Paiutes taken all of the horses?" Grant asked.

"Good question, the fact is that they'd not taken all the horses. They had left one. Nice lookin' long legged roany gelding. All saddled and ready too. Just like it had been left by the station folks before they was killed.

Had I been one of those boys from the East, like ol' Cooter, who didn't know much about Injuns, I reckon I would have got suckered. But

I knowed damned well that there weren't no Injuns leavin' no horses standin' around unless that horse be just on the short side of lame. You can bet that pony would have been easy catchin' fer them Paiutes had I been dumb enough to throw the mochila on him. But I'd spent enough time with the Blackfoot to know Injun ways. I thought about that fresh horse, that's for sure...but the trail had been pretty flat and my pony wasn't near played out so I decided to dance with the one who brung me.

I duly considered the circumstance and figured it was best to leave that big roan tar baby right where he was and high tail for the next station and hope for the best. I can still remember that pinto I was ridin'. Looked a little like that one Dixie calls Cupcake. He was a tough little mustang with a big heart and I was thankin' God for every step he made past Buckland's Station. I put him into a lope and figured I'd ease him along to see what was gonna happen. Sure enough about three miles out I see dust comin' off the sidehill just below the ridgeline up ahead and off to my left. I knew right then and there that I was in for a race. I kicked that little mustang up a gear and he was movin' along right smartly. Then I could see that them Paiutes was comin' in at an angle to cut me off.

There was a low piece of ground betwixt me and the Paiutes who comin' down off the ridge. Kind of an arroyo or wash or big gully place if ya know what I mean. I turned that pinto to the left and rode toward the hills them Injuns had just rode out of...like I was gonna make a run for those hills. As soon as I turned off the trail, I could see that they was turnin' to their right to cut me off. They was hopin' to get me in the narrows at the head of that arroyo. Figuring I'd snookered 'em temporarily, I rode like hell until we lost sight of one another. When I hit that low ground and they couldn't see me, I cut back hard to my right and headed down that arroyo to the main trail. I was usin' all that poor little pony had to offer. Struck me that maybe them Paiutes weren't near as smart as the

Blackfoot or the Sioux to fall for an old trick like that. Maybe that's why you never heard quite so much about 'em."

"That was a very clever concept for a thirteen-year-old boy," Grant said.

"Clever...but unfortunately, not perfect. I did manage to get the jump on 'em but it wasn't long before they'd seen the error of their ways and got back into hot pursuit. Now I knew that it was a matter of keeping that pinto on his feet for another six or seven miles and hopin' that none of them Injuns had foreseen my plan. I kept wondering if there was any of them Paiutes that had got ahead of me. I knowed for certain that was any of them layin' in wait along the trail; I would surely be decoratin' an anthill before sundown.

I reckon I was pretty lucky as none of them Injuns were in my front, but my little cayuse was gettin' about as low on gas as this here Stutz. Mile by mile those Paiutes was gainin' ground on me...about a quarter for every mile I'd ride. It wasn't long before I could actually hear their pony's hooves pounding along behind me."

"I'll bet you were happy to have those weapons you'd been issued?" Grant said.

"I didn't have any weapons. I had quit carryin' the damned things 'cause they was too heavy. Besides, the company policy was to run for it if you could, so the weapons was just one more thing to slow you down. Most of the boys didn't carry weapons, except for a knife and maybe a pistol. That rifle they gave us was just about useless. It was single shot and shootin' from horseback was a waste of time. Besides which, it weighed way too much if a fella wanted to make speed. Had I been carryin' that rifle, them redskins would have had me sure. Even the pistols were way too bulky for my skinny little ass and way too heavy unless carried in a saddle holster. However, I got to admit that right about the time I heard those Injun pony's hooves, I was wishin' that I had me one of them six shootin' Navy Colts. I knew that little mustang didn't have much left and just about the time I figured I was done for, damned if I don't see the smoke comin' from the next station."

Tom read the look on Grant's face.

"Not the burnin' down smoke but cookin' smoke. I knew then that if I could keep my little cayuse on his feet I had a pretty good chance. I was hopin' that them Injun ponies was gettin' as played out as my pinto. I knew that the fellas at the station would have guns and I was hopin' that they'd be lookin' out for my arrival. Now you remember that bugle I told ya about that the Pony Express gave us to signal our arrival?"

Grant nodded.

"Well I didn't have that sumbitch either. All that folderol was too heavy and bulky to pack along. Like I told you, the company policy was to use speed to avoid trouble and to avoid a fight at all costs. Travel light and travel fast was our way of lookin' at it. But anyway, my only hope was that the fellas at the station would see the dust and know that I was coming with an escort…and I was really hopin' that they was gonna deter my riding companions with some hot lead.

I was maybe a mile and a half from the station corral when I heard the swish of an arrow past my ear. I knew that sound real well. One of them redskins had got close enough to get off a shot with his bow and it looked like he was pretty damned good with the thing too. I would likely have put some gravy stains in my buckskin britches had I not been so preoccupied with spurring that little mustang; just hopin' that he had one more mile left in him.

Then I heard another swish, and somethin' hit me in the right side. I could feel the cold shaft of an arrow against my skin and the warm blood runnin' down my rib cage. I looked down to see the arrow head stickin' out of the front of my shirt and I figured I had taken it right through the lung. But then I took a deep breath and what do ya know, I could breathe. My elation was short lived, however. About then another arrow hissed past my ear I could hear two of them Injun ponies, one on either side about to overtake me.

I glanced back over my shoulder at the one on my left...he was the one with the bow. The one on the right was closer and I could see that he was wielding a war club ready to bash my brains out. I caught the motion out of the corner of my eye as he was preparin' to give me a good wallop. I glanced back at him again and I was just about to duck to avoid the blow when that little mustang lost his legs and piled up like a cowboy's britches on the whorehouse floor. I went sprawlin' hat over boot heel. Lucky for me that cayuse didn't land on top of me. Luckier still was that the redskin missed with the war club and all them Injuns went thunderin' on by where I was tumblin' through the sage brush.

I'd had the wind pretty well knocked out of me and I was figuring as how I was a goner when I heard a gunshot from off a ways. I'll tell you son, those bangs and whizzin' bullets could have been angels singin' as far as I was concerned. I had made it into rifle range of the station. Them boys at the station weren't the best shots in the world but they was comin' close enough to make it real uncomfortable for them Paiutes. At first them Injuns thought they was outta range and they was gonna be real brave and began to parade around like shootin' gallery ducks. Finally, one of the men at the station got the range and I saw one of the Paiutes fall off his horse.

That was enough for most of those redskins...most of them others decided that prudence dictated a hasty departure. All except for that one with the club. He must have been especially brave or really pissed off because he headed straight back at me, raising that weapon with businesslike intent. We was close enough to look into one another's eyes and I figured he had me sure. He was just about to bash me when I heard a thud like someone hittin' a ripe watermelon with the blunt end of a splittin' maul. His head just near about exploded.

When the rest of them Injuns saw their buddy's head evaportin' they decided I wasn't near as worth killin' as they'd previously thought. At least they all got the hell out of there in a hurry and headed back the direction they'd come. I was just standin' there all alone."

"Had your horse stumbled from exhaustion?"

"No sir. One of them redskins had put an arrow right behind his ribs. It must'a just missed my leg. I don't know when he'd been shot but he had sure enough made one valiant attempt to get me home before he died on his feet. I looked at the poor critter and saw there wasn't anything to be done for him. I sat there for a minute and thanked God and that pinto pony for my life. I was a damned lucky kid. I think about that tough little critter from time to time. If there's a horse heaven, then I reckon he's there."

Tom paused a moment and then turned to look at Grant.

"I took my first scalp that day. I don't even know why I did it. It just seemed like a natural thing to do. I went over to that Paiute...the one with the club, and lifted his hair. It wasn't none to hard 'cause half his head had been blown off. I just grabbed a hank and skinned his head like a possum. Then I pulled that mochila off of the Pinto and ran like a turpentined tom cat for the shelter of that station."

Grant sat in stunned silence just staring at the man in seat next to him.

"I reckon it sounds a little brutal when you talk about it in terms of the way things are today...with the Injuns and all. But things like that were just a part of livin' in those days. Dyin' being a part of livin' and brutality bein' a part of the dyin'."

"Were you injured? You said an arrow had hit your side and you were bleeding."

"That arrow had gone through my shirt and cut the skin. I was bleedin' all to beat hell but I wasn't really hurt none. Gettin' the wind knocked out of me when that pony went down hurt worse than anything else. Them fellas at the station were talkin' about what a hero I'd been and makin' a big doin's over my wound and that scalp and all. They was really bumfuzzled that I had took that scalp, bein' as how I was just a kid.

I was a little embarrassed by all the hoo-hah to tell ya the truth. But I was thinking about gettin' back to Montana and showin' off that scalp to Prairie Dog, if you want to know the truth. I figured he'd took a few by then. Been a year since I'd seen him and I knew he'd gone through his comin' of age ceremony. That was a big doin's for Injuns."

"What did they do about delivering the mail?"

"Well sir, I told 'em about the massacre at the last station and explained that the Injuns were blood in the eye, genuine on the war path. The station keeper reckoned that it would be best if I stayed the night and then they'd have a couple of the men reconnoiter the next mornin'. I wasn't ever much for sittin' around so I rested up a bit and asked one of the fellas to saddle me a pony. They tried to talk me out of it but I was headed for the next station down the line."

"That was pretty brave, under the circumstances."

"Pretty damned stupid was what it was. Had I been thinkin', it would have occurred to me that them Injuns know'd the schedule. They'd been watchin' those stations for weeks before they began the attacks.

The station wrangler had saddled me a big ol' long legged, well muscled thoroughbredy lookin' gelding with a deep chest. That fella, he swore that this was the fastest mount in his corral.

I put on the mochila and jumped in the saddle to see what he could do. Now I hadn't no sooner gathered that horse up under me in a good rhythm when here came them Paiutes off the hills and right after my dumb ass. I didn't see 'em at first. They kept quiet and stayed in the low ground till they had rode up close behind me and then they started that war hoopin' that you city folks think of when you think of Injuns in the movies...and they figured they had me caught for sure.

When I finally heard 'em right behind me, they was whoopin' that victory sort of holler. I right away figured that if it was the same bunch that had chased me earlier, they had to be ridin' horses, which was about done in. I put the spurs to this big ol' thoroughbred and sure enough he ran like Omar Khayham winnin' the Derby in seventeen. Wasn't long before them Injun ponies was plum tuckered. I just loped right on into Sand Springs to bring the mail and warnin'. It occurred to me later that I sure as hell had not wanted to get caught with that bloody scalp lock hangin' on my belt. Them Paiutes would have taken exception to that for sure."

Grant found himself sweating from the excitement of the story and the warm afternoon. Tom looked at the sweat showing on his face.

"Sure is gettin' mighty thirsty out here. Ain't it? I hope that damned Harvey didn't forget us."

"I have read that Wild Bill Hickock and Buffalo Bill were riders with the Pony Express. I know there were many men distributed over a large territory but did you ever meet either one of them?" Grant inquired, wiping his face with a handkerchief.

"Yeah, I knew 'em both. Cody was about as nice a fella as a man could hope to meet and about as big a bullshitter as ever lived. He was one self-promotin' son-of-a-bitch...and that's for certain. He wasn't but a year or two older than me and when we were at the same station, we was kind'a pals. Did you know he made one of the longest rides of any of us Pony Express riders, according to what was said back then? Near about three hundred miles as I understood."

"Did the two of you remain friends?"

"We did. In fact, I got a letter tellin' me that ol' Bill just died here a couple years back. They even have a museum with the history of his exploits down in Wyoming. And far be it from me to denigrate the intrepidity of my old friend, but the fact is, he only rode for a couple of months for the Pony Express and then he had to go home to take care of his ailin' mama.

But he was sure enough an army scout during the war and a damned good one at that...and he killed a heap of buffalos. But there was some of them stories that even he had to laugh about, and he wrote 'em. I worked in his Wild West show for a while back in the eighties."

"How about Hickock? He rode with the Pony Express also as I understood it. What was your opinion of him?"

"Big Jim Hickock surely worked for the Pony Express, of that there is no doubt. But he was way too big to run the mail. He must'a been near two hundred pounds when I met him. He was a stock wrangler and station agent but he was never a rider."

"So the fact that he was with the Pony Express was exaggerated in the dime novels?" Grant asked.

"No...just the part about him bein' a rider was exaggerated. I liked ol' Jim but he was a scary fella. He was about ten years older than me and when I met him he already had a reputation as a gamblin' man, a drinker and a gun fighter. I run across his path in the spring sixty-one, just before the war started. He was tendin' the stock at Rock Creek in the Nebraska Territory."

"I noticed that you call him Jim. Why was he known as Wild Bill?"

Grant asked.

"I don't have no idea. It was a handle someone stuck on him and that was the name which became famous, but I don't know where or when. His name was James Butler Hickock. I can tell you that with certainty.

Let me explain how I met Hickock and some background so you can understand what was doin'. The Pony Express was owned by an outfit by the name of Russell, Majors and Waddell. Those men had spent fortunes gettin' the Pony Express up and runnin' and they was bound to make 'er a success. Now Mr. Honest Abe Lincoln had been elected President and he was about to be inaugurated. Russell, Majors and Waddell, who was his supporters, intended to see to it that his inaugural address got to California as quick as possible. There were a couple of reasons they wanted this particular message to get to California in record time. First of all, it was good advertisin'. But more important was the fact that some of the Southern states were beginning to secede from the Union. California gold could have made the Confederacy pretty viable if California had decided to secede. No one knew for sure what California was gonna do. I reckon the owners of the Pony Express supported the Union because they made mighty preparations to see to it that ol' Abe's speech got to California before that decision got made. Those fellas spared no expense, I'll tell you that. They hired a whole bunch of extra men and had a saddled horse standin' every ten miles along the entire Pony Express trail."

"I have never heard this," Grant said. "This wasn't taught in school."

"Son, I reckon there's a whole lot they ain't teachin' in school."

"I suppose you're right," Grant replied. "The war seems so long ago and far away that no one seems to care much what happened in those days. But you were saying about Hickock?"

"Wild Bill was only Big Jim the wrangler when I met him, leastwise that's what I called him. Like I said, he already had a reputation and people were a little leery of him. But at that time he was just a fella lookin' for work like a lot of other men. He sure wasn't nothin' special to the folks who ran Rock Creek Station...just another hand wrangling horses, as far as I could tell. But he did have a reputation and I guess because of that, he didn't like to go about unarmed. If ya saw Jim, ya saw that big ol' Whitneyville Dragoon pistol he wore in a wide belt for all the world to feel. Big Jim was another of those self promotin' sorts."

"So you never called him Wild Bill?"

"Nope...never did. Not even after he got to be known as Wild Bill, I just called him Jim. He was a fine lookin' specimen of a man, I got to admit that. Tall, six foot three or more I reckon, broad of shoulder and he walked with a confident gait. Always looked a man right square in the face with them blue eyes that seemed to look right through you. Preened that long silky hair he cultivated like some kind'a exotic bird. Ya knew when you met Jim that he was different. As I said, he was already a man and I was still a slip of a younker when I met him. He took a likin' to me and seemed to look after me, so I wasn't scared of him...but most men gave Big Jim a wide path and talked real polite when in his presence, even though he wasn't no more than a wrangler."

"So the two of you were assigned to Rock Creek for this special run of President Lincoln's inaugural address?" Grant asked, writing furiously in his notebook.

"That was the way she happened. Now I'd just been at Rock Creek a day or so when 'Wild Bill' come into the bunk house and noticed my Navy Colts layin' on my bunk. I'd been packin' them damned things around for over a year."

"Did you carry them after the Indian attack?"

"Nope, I did not. I did however take to carryin' ol' Burl's thirty-one caliber pocket pistol that the boys gave me. That little revolver brought comfort more than once during long lonely stretches on the prairie, especially at dusk and during the night where every bush seemed to come alive.

But because of my size, them damned Navy Colts was just too heavy to tote along, no matter what the danger. However, Mr. Hickock, who was a big man, took a shine to them things and began to badger me to sell him them guns. He took notice that I didn't carry them Colts, and he got a hankerin' to have 'em. That Dragoon was impressive to carry but he reckoned that two new Colt's Navy thirty-six calibers would be even more intimidatin' and the two of them weighed less than that horse pistol he'd been packin' around. Did ya ever see any photos of Hickock?"

"Yes, I've seen several. I do remember the long hair and pistols in his belt."

"Well, them was my pistols. Yes sir, ol' Hickock, in addition to tendin' the Pony Express stock, had come to the job with a small string of his own horses too. He'd won that remuda in a poker game is what I'd figured. I didn't own a horse of my own. Had they fired me from the Pony Express for any reason, I reckon I would have had to walk home or buy a horse. So after some persuadin', he traded me one of his ponies and twenty dollars gold for them Colts. I figured I'd made a good deal. They wasn't nothin' but a nuisance for a man of mobility like myself. In addition to the damned things bein' too big for me to carry. I had never liked the look of them anyways. Just a personal preference thing, I reckon.

Now those ivory grips that you see in the photographs didn't come till later on. He had 'em made special for them guns. And if you saw the picture you know that he displayed them guns to the world in such a way as to let anyone who was in doubt know for sure that he would use 'em, which brings us to the killin's at Rock Creek."

"I do remember reading about Wild Bill Hickock's Rock Creek

shootout," Grant said.

"Well sir, them guns were no sooner in the possession of Mr. Wild Bill Hickock, as you like to call him, than he'd shed that big ol' Dragoon's pistol and took to sportin' them more wieldy Navy's in a cross draw arrangement in his belt...just like in the picture."

"I do recall from the photo that he wore those guns with the handles reversed," Grant said.

"That was the way he wore 'em. Now near about anyone with a brain bigger than a thirty six caliber pistol ball could have predicted that Big Jim Hickock wasn't gonna wait long before showin' off those shiny new extensions of his personality. He was struttin' around like a turkey gobbler makin' the world aware of his lethal beauties, when sure enough, here comes a fool lookin' to tempt fate."

"Wasn't that the McCanles gang?" Grant asked.

"I reckon that depends on your definition of a gang. What I saw was a fella by the name of Dave McCaulas, too drunk to hit the floor with his hat, come walkin' up to Rock Creek Station carrying a big ol' sign that said, 'Try them guns on me Mr. Hickock.'

Now I didn't know McCaulas, nor anything about the dispute he was havin' with the Pony Express company, but I can tell you that comin' to the station armed and drunk was about the dumbest thing he ever done.

As I understood the story, McCaulas had owned the place and started the stage coach station a few years before. He even built himself a toll bridge to get a few extra dollars out of the enterprise.

Anyway, ol' McCaulus had been contracted by folks from Russell, Majors and Waddell to use the stage coach facility as a Pony Express Station. It was a good deal to start because McCaulas already had the stage coach station. The company, it was said, had agreed to let him run the place. I don't know what transpired between the parties but somehow ol' McCaulas got aced out and they brought in another man by the name of Wellman to run the Rock Creek operation."

"So where did this McCanles gang story get started if the man's name was McCaulas and it was a business dispute?" Grant asked.

"Dime novel bullshit artists and the lawyers for Russell, Majors and Waddell is all I can tell ya. And I ain't even sure that the shootin' was about the business dispute. There was also a rumor that Big Jim had been playin' some horizontal hokey-pokey with Mrs. McCaulas. That was also a part of Wild Bill's reputation. So your guess is as good as mine...and I was there. The one thing for sure is that Russell, Majors and Waddell didn't want no blight on their company and after seeing to it that Big Jim got off in court, the dime novelists made a legend outta the story that just grew almost by itself.

I can still remember that morning as if it was yesterday. As I said, it was early spring and there was still a pretty good chill in the air. A couple of us had finished chores and was sittin' in the office by the wood stove when I heard angry voices outside. I looked out the window and McCaulas was out in front with his boy. McCaulas had a kid who was about my age at the time.

There were a couple of other fellas with McCaulas too. Friends of his I was told. I reckon that was his gang. They was talkin' real loud to Wellman and pretty quick there was a shoutin' match goin' on. McCaulas and the men with him was all carryin' rifles and McCaulas had his coat throwed back to expose a pistol in his belt. The whole caboodle of 'em had been drinkin', except for his kid. McCaulas was obviously drunk and in a bad mood. He was ravin' about bein' cheated and that he wasn't plannin' to take it sittin' down. He was sure enough spoutin' that 'Try them guns on me Wild Bill' kind'a talk that can get a fella killed, if'n ya know what I mean."

Tom lit a cigarette and let the smoke drift into the warming air.

"Now ol' Big Jim was a cool customer. He wasn't given to shoutin' or even arguin' as I recall. He went over, opened the door and stood right there lettin' them guns in his belt do all of his talkin'. The warnin' was sure enough clear if there had been anyone willin' to listen.

A fella didn't have to be none too smart to know that things was about to get ugly. Watchin' Jim stand there with his elbows bent and his hands restin' lightly on them revolvers, I was struck by his lack of emotion. I could plainly see his hands weren't shakin' and his eyes were fixed on them men like a rattle snake fixes a gopher.

McCaulas was nearly screamin' by then and I heard him ask Wellman if'n he'd hired himself an assassin. Then the dumb bastard really waved that red flag at the bull."

Tom turned to look at Grant.

"I don't suppose you have ever been at a real donnybrook. The kind of confrontation where two men are really gonna try to kill one another?"

"No...I guess I never have."

"When things like this happen there is more of a feeling in the air than a tangible happenin' that can be written down and described. It is just this feeling that things are goin' south. And this was one of those times. I moved over to look out the window as McCaulas yelled at Wellman, 'You tell that beady-eyed pig fucker to stay out of this.' Now when he said that, he kind'a pointed the rifle at your Wild Bill."

"You mean he aimed the rifle at Hickock?"

"No sir...there was no aimin'. He was just gesturin' with the rifle like a fella would do with his finger or a stick. I don't think he had any intention of shootin' or anything. The rifle wasn't cocked and he was just holding it loose at the balance. His finger wasn't even near the trigger. However, for Mr. Hickcock that was about all the incitement necessary to try out them new Colts of his. I heard a shot and ol' McCaulas crumpled up and fell in a heap at Wellman's feet. I looked over and Big Jim, movin' like a cat. He was on the porch with a revolver in each hand and the lead was flyin'. Before them fellas got their rifles up to their shoulders they was all dead, all but the McCaulas' kid...and I reckon that Mr. Hickock didn't want that on his conscience.

I looked around and everyone just stood there for a long, long time. Then Wild Bill walked out to where the three of 'em was layin' in the mud. He looked 'em over like they was dead buffalos and then he walked toward the bunkhouse sayin' that he had to go clean and reload his new Colts. McCaulas' kid was bawlin' and I plumb felt sorry for the boy. I can assure you of one thing. I never after wanted to get crossways of Mr. Big Jim 'Wild Bill' Hickock after seein' what happened to them fellas at Rock Creek that day."

Grant's mind raced. Could this larger than life Western hero have been this flawed? Was this a true account of this historical event? Tom could see the questions playing on Grant's face and he sought to assure.

"That's the way she happened boy. Swear it on my Pony Express Bible."

Just then the dust of an approaching vehicle could be seen. The truck passed and then turned around, stopping behind the Stutz. A pallid thin man in greasy coveralls stepped out of the vehicle without turning off the engine.

"What'd you do, Harvey, stop for a couple a beers?" Tom said.

"Naw, Tom," Harvey replied, ignoring the good natured chide. "I was puttin' some tires on for one of them Eastern fellers who drove all the way to Montana from Illinois to see Dempsey in this fight. He wore out two sets of tires on the way."

Harvey retrieved a gas can from the flat bed of his Ford truck and poured the contents into the Stutz.

"Harvey, they tell me that you're the best damned mechanic in Montana. Is there any truth to that rumor?" Tom asked.

"Well, I can fix a broke motor if'n that's what you mean Tom," Harvey replied.

"Why is it then that your machines always appear to be on their last gasp? Look at that Ford you're driving. I've seen better automobiles sitting on crates in some honyocker's barnyard. Sort'a like the story about shoemaker's kids, I reckon. Huh?"

Harvey smiled and shook his head. He got back into his vehicle.

"Let me get ahead of you Harvey," Tom shouted. "I don't want to eat dust all the way to town!"

Tom started the Stutz and pulled into the road. Harvey's vehicle was soon enveloped in dust.

9

The Moose Lodge dining room was crowded. Grant could hear the men, who stood in small groups drinking and discussing the upcoming fight.

Tom approached a well-groomed and distinguished looking gentleman who was smoking a cigar and holding a glass of beer.

"Rodge, I want you to meet Grant Collins," Tom said, pulling Grant forward. "This is Rodgers Wesley. This gentleman is the Mayor of the fine metropolis of Great Falls."

Grant proffered his hand as Tom said, "And this is Grant Collins from the Saint Louis Morning Star. He's here to interview Dempsey for his paper and maybe get us a little advertisin'...and to make me famous, of course."

The Mayor laughed, then turned and tugged at the sleeve of a pug faced man in a bowler hat.

"Doc," he said in a loud voice, "this young man is a reporter from the Saint Louis Morning Star. What's the chance of getting him an interview with the champ?"

Turning to Grant, Mayor Wesley completed the introduction.

"This is Doc Kearns. He is Mr. Dempsey's manager and if you want an interview with Dempsey, you will have to talk to him."

Grant shook Doc Kearns' hand and said, "I understand that Mr. Dempsey is a busy man, getting ready to fight...but do you think it might be possible to speak with him?"

The expression on Doc Kearns face never changed as he looked Grant in the eye.

"These guys are payin' the tariff so if they want you to interview the Champ, I'll set it up, but I'll tell everybody one thing right now..."

Kearns looked around until the room had fallen silent.

"If we ain't got that last one hundred G's in hand by day after tomorrow, the Champ is gettin' on a train to somewhere besides this Shelbyburg."

Grant felt his stomach tighten in excitement. This may be a scoop after all, he thought.

"You mean you may cancel the fight?" Grant asked.

"You're damned right we may cancel the fight. I don't want to do it, but a deal's a deal and I have to look out for the Champ," Kearns said.

Tom put his hand on Kearns' shoulder and said, "O'Halloran's in Shelby with Mulroney right now makin' the final arrangements, Doc. Don't go gettin' yer knickers in a knot. Hell, you gotta lot of good faith money already, don't ya. And truth is that the money ain't due till fight day anyway."

Tom's pleasant way seemed to placate Kearns for the moment.

"Okay, Tom," Doc said, "bring the kid over to the training camp in about an hour and I'll set it up with the Champ."

Tom took Grant's arm and started walking to the door. As they crossed the room a young man grabbed Grant's sleeve.

"You the fella that jerked the slack outta Buck's rope at the dance last night in Benton?" he asked with a grin.

Grant looked puzzled and shook his head.

"No, I ahhhh, I didn't do anything to Buck."

The young man persisted.

"That ain't the way I heard it. Word is ya kicked the shit out of him. Knocked that no-good son-of-a-bitch right on his ass."

Before Grant could make another protest, Tom pulled him toward the door.

When they were outside, Tom asked, "Did you have some trouble with Buck last night that I ought to be knowin' about?"

Grant shook his head.

"Buck got drunk and fell down. There wasn't much more to it than that. Then Nick took him to the livery to sleep it off...and what's that all about with Doc Kearns...and canceling?"

They climbed into the Stutz.

"Remember me tellin' you about them lame brained bastards promising Dempsey the three payments of a hundred thousand each before the fight? Well, the last payment is due the morning of the fight. Of course ol' Kearns is trying to scare shit out of everyone so we'll come up with the cash early. He's afraid he's gonna get stiffed...and it could be he's right."

They drove to Harvey's gas station.

"Harvey, would you fill this filly up with gas and fix that spare tire for me, and I'd appreciate it if you could fix me up with a can of gas and a piece of hose. I have to take some gas with me for the Jenny."

"I'll get 'er ready for you, Tom," Harvey said.

Tom and Grant crossed the street to the hotel.

"We'll have a cup and by the time Harvey is done we can go over to Dempsey's trainin' camp. I reckon you'll wanna be usin' a phone or at least sendin' a telegram?"

Grant telephoned Hiram from the hotel, reporting his scoop regarding the possibility that the fight might be cancelled. Hiram thanked him and assured him he would get a byline in the evening edition. He and Tom killed an hour having coffee before driving to Dempsey's training camp.

Doc Kearns had rented a house on the edge of Great Falls with several acres of land and a stable. Dempsey performed his public training regimen twice each day, in the morning and afternoon, with the press invited to observe. The remainder of the day was reserved for Dempsey's peace and quiet.

Grant quickly realized that because of Tom's influence he had received a special courtesy for this private interview with the Champ.

Tom stopped the Stutz in front of the house and Doc Kearns came out to greet them.

"The Champ is doin' his little rituals," Kearns said, walking toward the car. Kearns then looked Grant in the eye. "Before you go out to meet him, you gotta swear secrecy, you know...off the record, about certain things anyway."

Doc winked at Grant.

"Anything that Mr. Dempsey wants to be kept secret will be confidential with me."

"You understand, the Champ is a little superstitious? He thinks some of his rituals could help him win the fight. Okay?" Kearns said.

"I will certainly be discreet and respect Mr. Dempsey's privacy," Grant said.

"Good! If the Champ tells you somethin' is off the record, it's off the record." Kearns pointed to the barn and said, "Go on out there. He's waitin' for you...and what you see here stays here."

Doc and Tom walked toward the house as Grant went to the barn.

Grant apprehensively entered the stable where he found the heavyweight boxing champion of the world sitting on a wooden crate staring at four large horses tied in stalls along one wall. He was wearing a warm flannel shirt and wool trousers with a Turkish towel draped over his head and tucked into the shirt collar.

When Demsey looked at him, Grant was taken aback. Dempsey's face was covered with a foul smelling greasy substance that was noticeably unpleasant from several feet away.

"Doc says you get a special interview," Dempsey said. "I don't give special interviews...but Doc says you're with one of the money guys so I'll talk to you until I finish what I'm doin'."

Dempsey looked at Grant for a moment.

"Doc told you the rules about what you see here stays here...right?"

The Champ was sitting with several buckets placed strategically around the crate he was using as a seat. He was slowly petting a puppy he was holding on his lap while never diverting his gaze from the horses. To Grant's relief, he made no attempt to shake hands.

"I really appreciate your time, Mr. Dempsey," Grant said, embarrassed that his voice sounded obsequious. "That's a cute puppy. Did you bring him with you?"

"Naw, some trapper fella brought him by the other day as a good luck charm. He's a wolf. Fella killed the momma and took the little cubs out of a hole. I hope to hell the little bastard is a good luck charm."

Dempsey looked up at Grant. A wisp of smile played on his face.

"It would be downright humiliating to get my ass whipped by some nobody farmer of a has-been who never was. Especially in a place where no one with a fifty dollar bill for a ticket ever heard of."

Suddenly Dempsey bent forward and placed the puppy on the floor, staring intently at one of the horses.

"Hand me one of those buckets, would ya?"

Grant picked up a bucket and pushed it into Dempsey's outstretched hand.

His eyes riveted on the horse, Dempsey moved forward talking to the animal in an odd high-pitched voice.

"Easy boy...easy. I ain't gonna hurt ya."

Moving slowly to the animal's side he moved the bucket beneath the horse's distending penis. Grant noticed that the horse was stretching and arching his back and it occurred to him that the animal was about to urinate. He stood amazed at what he was seeing. As the gelding unsheathed and began to discharge a stream of urine, the world champion of boxing was holding a bucket carefully catching the animal's foamy yellow excretions.

When the horse had completed nature's call, the five gallon pail was about two thirds full. Dempsey quickly returned to the crate where he had been previously seated. Placing the bucket on the corner of the crate, he straddled the wooden box so that he faced the bucket. He then pulled up his shirt sleeves and to Grant's bewilderment, plunged his hands into the still steaming translucent yellow fluid.

Dempsey smiled for the first time.

"Hot horse piss. Makes your hands tough. I ain't sure what's in it but I hear that you'll never hurt your hands when they've soaked in it. I do it every day before a fight. I rented these big horses special."

Grant could not suppress a chuckle at the spectacle. He was thinking that he had a great human interest piece.

"I know what you're thinkin' but you can't print it. This is my secret formula and I don't want the word gettin' out to every pug in the world who wants my title."

Grant's excitement dwindled to disappointment.

"Your secret is safe with me, Mr. Dempsey."

"Of course, I ain't too sure that anyone else would have the patience I do. I sit here for hours waitin' for one of these boys to piss. Ya have to know what to look for. I only use these geldings 'cause they're gentle and I have learned just when to get the bucket ready. First, he'll start to stretch a little and then he begins to hang his pecker out. The timing has to be just right. The stuff has to be fresh and warm or it loses its potency."

Grant stifled and chuckle.

"I won't print a word if you have an objection. Would you mind if I write about the wolf?"

"Naw, this wolf is just for luck and I don't care who knows about my luck. It's only my trade secrets that I'm tryin' to protect. Like this grease on my face. I suppose you're wonderin' about that too?"

Grant smiled and nodded his head. "I assume that's the strong odor I smell?"

"Yep. It's some kind'a bear grease that the fella who brought me the wolf cooked up. He claims to be married to an Indian woman. Says this is an old secret recipe the Indians used to make their skin tough back in the old days. I've got to admit that even if it didn't make your skin tough it would sure make people avoid hittin' you. I can hardly stand bein' around myself with this stink."

Grant laughed as the humor relieved the tension of the interview. He began to see the human side of the man they called the Manassa Mauler.

"I don't care what they tell you, anyone in the fight game is a superstitious bastard," Dempsey went on. "Back in my bare knuckle bar room days, before all these fancy gloves and rules and ropes; I saw a lot of really odd things. I fought a great big Negra one time and he was a tough son-of-a-bitch. He'd whipped all comers, and I was pretty sure that he was gonna give me a match. At the time I had a man who was sort'a settin' up my fights and managin' things that way. He'd done a little checkin' and found out that this colored boy had been struck with seizures a couple of times as a youngster. You know what I mean, eyes rollin' and floppin' around on the floor."

Dempsey looked up at Grant.

"My manager fella found out that he'd apparently went to some voodoo lady who fixed him up with a dried frog in a leather pouch. He always wore that thing around his neck and he believed that frog was gonna keep him from havin' those seizures, at least according to what this fella had learned. The day of the fight came and that bar room was packed. There was a lot of shoutin' and yellin' and bettin' of course. We squared off in the middle of the floor, looking each other in the eye and damned if that nigger didn't hit me four times before I'd got in a lick. It was like bein' kicked by a Percheron mule. I sure as hell wasn't lookin' forward to twenty-five rounds of them punches."

The wolf pup curled up against Dempsey's ankle.

"Poor little fella. I reckon he's lonesome for his mama."

Dempsey looked up at Grant.

"I got to thinkin' about that frog pouch bouncin' around his neck and wondering if it really did him any good. As he ducked and stepped close to swing at me, I saw an opportunity. I jumped at him and grabbed him in a clinch. Before the referee could get us separated I got a hold on his bag with the frog and held tight. He had it tied on his neck with a leather thong and it took a couple of jerks to break it off. It cut his neck when I jerked it loose and sent blood streamin' over his shoulders.

I held that pouch right in front of his face so he'd know that I had it. His eyes got real big and I knew I was gettin' to him. I knew I had the advantage. I stuffed that pouch down the front of my pants and he looked at me like I was pissin' on his mother's grave. While he was lookin' at the front of my pants I proceeded to lay on a couple of right hands that had to have hurt him because they sure as hell hurt me. I reckon losin' that dried frog took all the fight right outta that boy. I hit him one more good one and he had a seizure right there and fell to the floor unable to continue. Now I never forgot about that and that's why I don't go around tellin' you news fellas my secrets to success."

"Don't worry, Champ," Grant assured, "Your secrets will be safe with me. But you have to give me something that I can print. I would really like to use the bare knuckle story...the superstition angle."

"Hell yes, that was a long time ago. And write up the wolf pup story. People will like that. Good public relations and it will be good for my image. Animal lover and all that little old lady stuff. And you can tell the world that I just had my twenty-eighth birthday and that if I fight Tommy Gibbons, I am gonna give myself a birthday present and knock that son-of-a bitch right out of the ring."

"If you fight?"

"That's Doc's end of the business, but he contracted for three hundred grand. We got two of it, and he's not making any commitment until he gets that last one hundred thousand from the yokels who set this thing up. Just between you and me though, I'm just about pissed off enough at Gibbons and his big mouth to fight the bastard whether I get that money or not...but I leave all of the business to Doc. We'll see."

"It would certainly be a shame to disappoint all of your fans at so late a date," Grant cajoled. "What has Gibbons done that has made you angry?"

"I read in the papers that he's braggin' that he's gonna knock me out. Now I don't know if it's braggin', but he also said that he thinks I am afraid of him. I think he's just tryin' to get his own courage up by twisting my tail. He's sure pissin' me off. I can guaran-damn-tee you on that. If there's much more of that shit comin' from that punchy old bastard, I'll go over to that little Shelby place and beat the shit out of him for nothin'."

"When do you plan on making the announcement?"

"That's Doc's job," Dempsey said, removing his hands from the bucket. "Piss is gettin' cold. Besides, it's time to get something to eat."

The Champ removed the towel from his head and dried his hands. He picked up the wolf pup and began walking toward the house with Grant. Doc and Tom were standing by the Stutz. As they approached, Doc said, "Tom Thomas, this is the Champ, Jack Dempsey."

Tom stuck out his hand to shake but Grant stepped between them.

"Mr. Dempsey is protecting his hands from injury prior to the fight. He isn't shaking hands until after the bout."

Tom nodded and Jack Dempsey smiled at Grant's diplomacy.

"Nice talking' to you kid. Hope you got enough for a story. Remember, no secrets!"

Tom started the Stutz and as they drove into town, Grant said, "Could you take me by the hotel? I would like to call the paper again with some updates."

"You bet," Tom said. "Then we'll head out to Bernie's."

It was after working hours in Saint Louis. Grant expected that the call, for which he told the operator to reverse the charges, would go directly to the editorial offices. When he heard Melinda's voice say "Good evening, Morning Star, how may I help you?" he felt an instant queasy knot in his stomach.

"I have a call from a Mr. Collins in Great Falls, Montana," the operator said. "Will you accept charges?"

Grant's mind raced as he heard Melinda accept the call. What was he going to say? He considered hanging up and pretending to have been accidentally disconnected. He was reaching for the cradle when he heard clicking in the receiver as the operator disconnected from the line. Grant could hear the tears in Melinda's voice.

"I was here late tonight...checking the mail. I just knew that letter you promised would be here today."

"Melinda!" he said in as cheerful a voice as he could muster. "What a pleasant surprise. It's good to hear your voice. How are things in Saint Louis?"

"Hot! Everyone is getting ready for the Fourth."

She said no more, creating an intentionally uncomfortable silence.

"Well...you know Melinda, these small towns out here in the West...it is so difficult to get to postal service. I was going to mail a letter from Great Falls. It is a fairly large village and they have a post office and everything."

"Oh...I understand perfectly," she said. "Would you like to speak to Hiram?"

"Yes. I have some news about the Dempsey fight, which he may want for the morning edition."

"I'll ring his office...and give my best to Dixie Anderson when you see her. She's an old friend you know. By the way, does she dance any better than she used to?"

The click of the telephone sounded like a cannon shot. It took Grant a moment to realize that Dixie had obviously spoken to someone in Saint Louis. The world is becoming a small place indeed, he thought. The days of hiding in the Old West are certainly over.

When Hiram answered the phone, Grant gave him the details on the wolf pup and the story of the dried frog.

When Hiram had completed his notes, Grant said, "By the way, Dempsey is really angry at Gibbons. He said that Gibbons is 'a has-been who never was.'"

"Is the fight on or off?" Hiram asked.

"It is still uncertain," Grant said. "I am going to Shelby tomorrow. I should have something for the late edition."

Grant decided to hold any more of the story until he had an opportunity to speak to Tommy Gibbons.

1 0

After dinner, Bernie and Tom sipped Canadian whiskey and told tales of their experiences on the frontier. Grant was sure that the stories had grown more outrageous with time, each trying to outdo the other.

Tom handed Bernie his glass for a refill. "Bernie, I could tell you about somethin' that even you never had the chance to see."

Bernie's eyes rolled as he poured the tumblers full.

"Give it your best shot, ya old fart...and this better be good."

"Pigeon hunting!" Tom said.

"You think I never shot a damned pigeon. I been clean to Africa, for cryin' out loud. You better have a couple more shots of this whiskey."

"Earlier today, I was just tellin' Grant here about the Pony Express days."

"You senile old bastard, everyone knows you was with the Pony Express. I heard that one a thousand times. What about the pigeons?" Bernie pursued.

"This is somethin' that I got into right after the Pony Express ended. Now I know you never heard this before and I'll guarantee you never had a chance to do any of it."

Tom turned to Grant.

"I gotta fill Grant in on how this came to be. Bernie has heard most of this...but you remember what I was tellin' you about carryin' Lincoln's inaugural speech? Well it wasn't long after that the War of the Rebellion was gettin' started in earnest. That last few months with the Pony Express was filled with some real unpleasant situations. Some of the Southern states had already seceded from the Union and it was hard for the men with the Pony Express not to take sides. Shortly after that hoo-hah with your Wild Bill Hickock at Rock Creek, Lincoln was inaugurated as president and everyone with half a brain know'd there was gonna be some trouble. Lookin' back, it was quite a historical event transportin' that speech across the country, I reckon."

"What hoo-hah with Hickock?" Bernie asked.

"I told you about how Hickock shot the shit out of them boys at the Rock Creek Station," Tom said.

"Oh...that!" Bernie replied.

"Well sir, shortly after Lincoln got into office, some of them hotheaded Southern boys fired on Fort Sumter down in South Carolina and the fuse was lit. All across the Pony Express line the talk was about the Union raisin' an army to prevent the secession. Ol' Abe Lincoln started an all out recruiting campaign. Of course that pissed off the Southerners and several more states seceded. Now personally, I had no real political beliefs at the time. I called myself a Southerner but that was just out of respect for my folks who was Southerners.

But the feelin's was runnin' high amongst the Pony Express men. Some was Yankees and some, like me, considered themselves Confederates. Truth be known, there was several...what you might call petite rebellions... right within the Pony Express. There was quite a few men hurt and a couple even killed arguin' over the right or wrong of secession."

"Hell, I didn't know that," Bernie interrupted.

"Bernie, I could fill an entire library full of the shit you don't know anything about. Just shut up and learn somethin'...now where was I. Oh yeah, I had the misfortune of bein' at the Marysville station that summer of sixty-one when the westbound mail came in and the rider, who was due for relief, started braggin' on how the Rebels had whipped the Yankees at a place called Manassas Junction. It was later called the battle of Bull Run by the Yankees. You probably heard about it in school."

Grant nodded and Tom continued.

"A couple of Union fellas took exception to his braggin' and pretty quick there was some angry shoutin' amongst the men...then a fist fight broke out between a stock tender and one of the other riders who was layin' over at Marysville like I was. Those boys was havin' 'em a real good shin kickin' contest, rollin' around in the horseshit and gougin' each others eyes enough to make mine want to water.

We was all watchin' and hootin' and hollerin' when some dumb bastard yelled 'Whip that Yankee's ass like we done 'em at Manassas,' and that was all she wrote. Another one of the Yankee fellas hit the Reb who'd hollered and then someone else hit someone else and you can only imagine."

"I suppose you was right in the middle of it?" Bernie said.

"No, sir...now you got to remember that I was just a little bit of a turd in those days. I was lookin' around for someone to hit but all them Yankees was one helluva lot bigger than I was. Next thing I knowed they was all fightin' and then sure enough...someone pulled out a gun."

"Had this sort of rancor occurred prior to the Fort Sumter incident?" Grant asked.

"Never did...we'd all been pretty much friends up until then."

"You mean to tell me that there was a fight and you weren't in it?"

Bernie said.

"I didn't say I didn't get in it...but you got to remember that I was just about big enough to be a nuisance in a fist fight amongst grown men...so I ran over to my pack and got that pocket pistol that I'd received upon the demise of my unrequited despoiler."

"Your 'unrequited' what?" Bernie interrupted again.

Grant looked at Bernie and recognized that he had not heard of Burl.

"That's another story completely. He can tell you that some other time. Finish the story of the gunfight, Tom," Grant said.

Tom gave Grant a grateful nod.

"I'd no sooner obtained that weapon than sure enough the shootin' started so I hurried back to the corral and hunkered by a rain barrel at the corner of the buildin'. I could hear the crack as bullets whizzed past my ear every little once in a while...so I was hidin' as best I could. Then I heard another one of the stock tenders let out a scream that scared shit out of me. He was hollerin' that he'd been gut shot. That sort'a put a damper on the fun."

Grant looked at Tom, incredulity obvious on his face. "Fun?" he asked.

"I kept lookin' for where the bullets was comin' from, with every intention to shoot me one of them Yankees, but, ya know, I just really didn't want to kill any of those men. I knew 'em all and I didn't see no reason for killin' any of 'em. Yankee or not. As I sat there aimin' that pistol at this fella I'd known for near a year, I commenced feelin' like a fool. Thank the Lord it was over as quick as it begun. That poor stock tender was gut shot and everyone knew he wasn't gonna be leaving Marysville alive. No one ever owned up to shootin' that poor bastard either. I ain't really sure if anyone would'a known had they done it. Being as how there was so much confusion. That unfortunate tender never got any medals or credit…but he was sure enough killed at the Battle of Marysville and there's no doubt in my mind that it was the same kind'a fightin' that happened all around in the great Civil War."

"My grandfather was a doctor in the Army of the Potomac," Grant said. "He still has nightmares about the bloodshed."

"Any man who's been witness to wholesale death and don't have his sleepin' habits altered by the visions, is a man whose company I would not want to keep.

I reckon we should all be glad that war the turned out the way it did, though. Had the Confederacy succeeded it wouldn't have been long before some European king would have got his boot on the necks of them high toned Southern aristocrats and created himself a monarchy right here on the soil of the good ol' U.S. of A. Then there would have been another fight and who knows what would'a happened then, but that's another story.

As far as the Pony Express was concerned, the end came when they strung the last of the wire for the Transcontinental Telegraph. Everyone that worked for the Pony Express knew it was comin'. We knew they were stringing wire as fast as they could. So it didn't come as no surprise in November of sixty-one when they told us we was drawin' our last pay."

"Just like that?" Bernie asked.

"Just like that! As for me, havin' nowhere else to go, I headed back to Saint Joe and figured to ease up with my sister and ol' Jacob. So I again found myself keepin' store and behavin' about half-civilized. Jacob said he reckoned to tame me down after all. But my boots was still full of ants and I had a hard time standin' still behind that counter.

Now Missouri was a border state and it was a mess. Most of the folks who lived around Saint Joe was sympathetic to the South but the area was under the control of the Yankees. Bein' young and stupid and filled with patriotic fervor for my Confederate roots, one day I get a wild hare up my ass and run off to join the army of the rebellion.

I jumped on that pony I'd got in trade from Hickcock and headed south. I was real lucky too. I found me a Confederate Cavalry unit. I was proud as a peacock when I told the Captain that I wanted to join up and fight for their freedom to own slaves. Now the stupidity of that idea was too difficult for a prairie boy to wrap his mind around at the time. It's still a mind twister if'n ya think about it a little.

That grey coat Captain looked at me and just laughed. Told me right out that as bad as the Confederacy needed men they wasn't yet in the business of robbin' some mama's cradle. He did, however, relieve me of my mount, saddle and all, which he claimed as the eminent domain of Jefferson Davis's noble purpose. He then thanked me for my contribution to the Confederate cause and sent me hoofin' it back to Jacob's store."

"You still ain't said dog squat about no pigeons," Bernie interrupted again.

"Hold your water, I'm gettin' to it. Now I had just about resigned myself to clerkin' duties in that store when one day some fellas came into Jacob's store who claimed they was outfittin' themselves for a pigeon hunt."

Grant and Bernie looked at each other and then at Tom.

"Yeah, I know! The only pigeons you two ever saw was the filthy critters that inhabit farmer's barns and the tall buildings in the big cities. Hell, those things ain't even American pigeons. They was brought here from Europe like them English Sparrows and the Starlings. I'd reckon that bringing those critters made them European folks feel more at home; havin' some familiar critter they could look at out their windows and all. The pigeons I'm talkin' about were the Passenger Pigeons."

"Passenger Pigeons. I read about those in school. The last one died in a zoo. In fact it may have been in Saint Louis," Grant said.

"Yes sir, you're right. Last one died in seventeen in the zoo in Saint Louie. I read about it in the paper. They're all gone now, and that's for sure...and I reckon I had a hand in it. Seems near impossible lookin' back on it now. They flew in their millions and no one ever figured that there was any way to kill 'em all, like the buffalos. Who would have thought just sixty years ago that you could bring that host to near annihilation in just a few years? Still don't seem possible. That's why I keep those few head of buffalo on the ranch. To remind me of how tenuous existence really is."

"For Christ sake, Tom! Don't be so damned morbid. Get on with the yarn about the pigeons," Bernie said.

"Them pigeons was bigger than barn pigeons by near about half with beautiful colors," Tom said.

"We learned a bit about them in biology class. Even the professor had never seen a live one. Just paintings," Grant said.

"Well if I seen one, I saw ten million of 'em or more. That's no exaggeration...maybe twenty million. They were mostly east of the Mississippi in those hardwood forests. But as many as they were, they had a couple of real bad flaws in their strategy...the way I seen it.

First, they was a real pretty bird and the ladies liked to put those feathers on their fancy Sunday-go-to meetin' hats. Then you add to that the fact that they were a right tasty meal for every predator in the countryside, includin' people and the biggest problem of all was that they just needed way too much room and food, just like them buffalo.

The farmers up around Illinois and Indiana and Michigan would pay men to go kill as many as they could. In addition, the farmers was cuttin' the trees for plowing where the pigeons roosted and nested to raise their young. Good God almighty...there was thousands of acres of trees bein' cut every month. You could go to a forest in the spring and walk for miles in virgin timber. When you went back in the fall the place would be bare fields ready for the plowin' in spring. It broke my heart, to be honest. But progress is progress and people seem to place the big premium on it. But the final clangs of the death nell for them pigeons came when the fancy folks of New York City decided that those birds were a real delicacy for eatin'.

At about that same time they was buildin' miles of railroads across that territory. The Union needed the railroads for movin' troops and supplies. What with easy access and easy transport, them birds was done for. Any time you get a market, there is some man with a hankerin' to fill that need for a profit. And that was exactly what this bunch of Confederate hooligans that came into Jacob's store had in mind to do. They was headin' north to catch that flying delicacy, which the big city folks would pay good Yankee gold for them squabs to put on their dinner tables, not to mention those feathers for their ladies' hats.

I gotta say this right up front. A more disreputable and unlikely looking bunch of entrepreneurs you have never laid an eye upon. About half of them were draft dodgers. They didn't want to fight in anybody's army and they didn't want to march to nobody's tune...whether that be Dixie or the Battle Hymn of the Republic. They was just lookin' out for themselves. Most of 'em was refugees from a circus that had winter quartered down around Milledgeville in Georgia. When the war came, some partisan volunteers had appropriated all of their horses in the name of the Confederacy, which I had a real sympathy for, considering my similar experience. And the railroads in the south had been taken over for military use. The owner of the circus and his family had stayed on to take care of the other animals, but he couldn't pay the rest of the hands, so he let 'em go. We even had a midget. Tough little bastard. He could bust your knee and leave you a cripple if you crossed him. They were clowns and magicians and trick shooters and roustabouts. You wanted to be real careful playin' cards with that bunch."

"Magic tricks," said Bernie. "That where you learned those magic tricks?"

Bernie winked at Grant and put his hand to his mouth in mock confidentiality.

"Don't ever play poker with this old bastard either. He can not only pull a silver dollar outta your ear, he can pull a third ace out of his ass, while you're watchin'.'"

"I learned magic tricks and a whole lot more," Tom said.

He looked at Grant and then at Bernie.

"Ya know boys, as I said before, money wasn't any too important to me in those days. But an adventure was worth everything. And these fellas was promisin' somethin' new, which sounded to me like an adventure. Of course, my sister and ol' Jacob considered the idea to be about the dumbest thing they'd ever heard of. Hell, they figured I had a good job with Jacob. My prospects at the store was lookin' mighty good. I had a sizeable bank account to see to my future, what with Burl's share of the mackinaw profit and my savings from the Pony Express money and all. Jacob and Rachel was just bumfuzzeled by the idea of going off to hunt pigeons. But go off to hunt pigeons was exactly what I planned to do.

Now this band of pigeon hunters was led by a one eyed fella who had been runnin' the sideshow when the circus broke up. He was also the sideshow strong man and you could tell right off that the others respected him. I'll tell you that he was strong. He had a horse that he'd trained for his sideshow act. They told me that the horse would sort'a lay on his shoulders and let him lift it off the ground. I never saw it but the others said it was quite impressive. I don't reckon that the Georgia

Cavalry ever appreciated the true talents of that animal but then they probably didn't have anyone who could'a picked it up anyway."

Tom smiled and took a sip of his drink.

"Two of the draft dodgers had hunted pigeons before...as hired hands with another outfit. They knew what we needed in the way of equipment, and they was using the money they'd earned as hired men to buy a share of this operation. They was also supposed to act as guides.

I took some of my stake money, which Jacob was holdin', and me and those boys put ourselves together an outfit. Nets and guns and gunpowder and wagons and all sorts of paraphernalia those boys said would be necessary to the success of our venture. With me joinin' up there was a baker's dozen of us. We figured if we got too busy we could hire extra men as day workers when needed. I let 'em all know right up front that I wouldn't be taken lightly. I told them that I had been doin' man's work with the Pony Express and I showed 'em that scalp I took in Nevada. I let 'em know that my money was every bit equal to their own and that I'd expect a full share. Jacob confirmed what I said to 'em and you could see they was rightly impressed when Jacob drew us up a legal paper to ensure my position with the enterprise. I also took to carrying that thirty-one caliber Colt in my belt, just in case any of those bigger fellas had funny ideas."

Tom winked at Grant.

"I reckon you know what I mean?"

Grant smiled and returned to his notes.

"So we was off to the pigeon hunt and it was nothin' like anything I had done before or have done since. It took us the better part of three weeks to get into the really good huntin' grounds. First we had to find the birds. Then we had to figure out a way to get the meat and feathers transported to the cities. About six weeks into our venture we come upon a stretch of forest, which was close to Lake Michigan. It was a right good setup because we could send some of the meat on barges through the Great Lakes to the cities and when we was too far from the lake we could ship by rail.

Set up as we were we went to huntin' pigeons. Truth is that those birds had some habits which made huntin' 'em a pretty easy endeavor. They roosted all in one place it seemed like...and they made so damned much noise on the roost that a blind man could'a found where they was. They even built their nests all in one area so we didn't have a whole lot'a travelin' once we'd encountered our quarry."

"The biology books were sorely lacking in the details of those birds. What are the things you remember most about them," Grant asked.

"They were a beautiful bird. Unlike barn pigeons, they were noisy as hell. Like I said, you could hear 'em for miles. A pair of them would build a nest and it appeared to me that both the cocks and the hens would set them eggs after the hen laid 'em. The eggs hatched in two or three weeks. I don't know as how anyone ever checked on how long it took...but I do know that when the babies hatched both the ma and the pa would feed the young for about two more weeks. Then they'd up and leave the little bastards to fend for themselves. Those youngsters would get hungry and come floppin' out of the nest and hit the ground unable to yet fly. They was earth bound for a few days while they was getting their wings and Holy Jesus, it were a picnic for the predators.

Bears and coons and foxes and skunks and bobcats and badgers and who knows what all would just wait under those trees for them young pigeons to fall right into their mouths. Shit, oh dear, more than once I wondered how there was so many of 'em with the numbers that was taken by the critters.

That's what I mean when I say that we didn't see no way a few men huntin' could kill 'em off. There was just so many of the damned things. The squabs, as the New Yorkers called them little ones, was easy enough to hunt. When they was fallin' from the trees a man could walk around pickin' them up and filling sacks faster than the boys at the wagons could draw and feather the damned things. The birds that could fly took a little more huntin'. First we had to locate where a bunch would be roostin'. Then when they'd leave the roost in the mornin' to go feed, we'd set our nets, which would string for a mile by their roostin' trees. When they'd fly to those trees late in the evening to go to roost, they'd hit those nets and get tangled and either be stuck or fall to the ground. Then when it was too dark for the ones that had made it into the roost trees to fly away, we'd set off the punt guns."

"I haven't heard that term. What on earth was a punt gun?" Grant asked.

"That's a big shotgun...and I mean big. It was more like a small cannon. We had a slew of 'em, each of which held near a pound of shot. Took all day, sometimes a couple days, to hang the nets and load them guns. When the birds finally roosted, we'd shoot all them guns at one time. When we'd let 'er rip at them birds up into the roosts the damned things would come down like rain. I even heard of some fellas who invented some kind'a machine gun to kill those pigeons. That was way before they had any such weapons for the battle field."

"You must have been out there all night pickin' up those critters," Bernie said.

"I just figured that staying up all night pickin' up those birds was a dam site easier than diggin' for gold. How many men did you ever know, Bernie, who really made any money diggin' for gold?"

"None...as I reckon," Bernie replied.

"Well, I'll tell you this, we made a petite fortune killin' those birds.

But even as easy as it was, after a while a man just gets tired of the smell and the feathers and the killin' day after day. At least I did. After about a year I had a real fat poke and belly full of killin' those pigeons. I settled up accounts with my companions, interesting companions though they were, bought myself a good horse and made my way back to Missouri."

"Well, I guess ya got me," Bernie admitted. "I never saw anything like what you're talkin' about. All I ever saw was those damned pigeons around the barn."

Tom finished his glass of whiskey.

"Show this boy to his room, Bernie. We gotta get up early and take off before it gets too hot or the wind gets too big."

11

Tom studied the sky in every direction as Bernie drove them to the Jenny.

"Looks like we might get some weather," Tom said.

Grant wriggled his way out of the rumble seat and closed the cover. "Is it going to be a problem? Perhaps we should wait a while."

"Yeah, Tom," Bernie said. "Maybe you should wait it out. It feels like a little wind is coming up already. You could get blowed around and find one of them clouds is full of rocks. It's spitting rain already."

"I gotta get up to Shelby and straighten out this money deal before O'Halloran puts us all in on the poor farm. Doc Kearns is talkin' about pullin' out on the deal and he already has two hundred thousand of our money. I think payin' up the other hundred to save the two we're out would be good business at this point!"

"I agree. If you don't get it fixed, this could get expensive. But it ain't worth gettin' killed over neither. Let's have some breakfast and see if it blows over," Bernie said, looking at Grant.

"We'll be alright," Tom said, pulling on his helmet. "She looks pretty good up to the north."

Bernie noticed the pallor of Grant's face.

"This boy looks a little peaked," Bernie said.

"He'll be okay once we get in the air. He's just new at this."

"Okay, you stubborn old coot. Give 'em hell and good luck," Bernie said.

He swung the propeller and ran out of the path of the airplane.

Gusts of wind swirled clouds of dust into the air as Tom turned the Jenny into the wind.

Grant could feel the blood pulsing behind his eyes as he gripped the wooden frame on each side of his seat. The rumbling beneath the wheels sounded deafening as the Jenny picked up speed, bouncing on the dirt road. His body involuntarily jerked with every quick movement of the airplane.Sitting rigidly still, Grant realized that the rumbling had ceased and that there was only the sound of the engine and the wind. He breathed a sigh of relief as Bernie's Stutz on the road below got smaller and smaller.

Tom circled to ensure that everything was running properly and then turned the Jenny north. Grant looked at the fabric on the wings and realized that it was flexing, buffeted by gusts of wind which cause the plane to lurch in unexpected and frightening jolts. He renewed his grip on the wooden frame.

The coulee country north of the Missouri River breaks was an expanse of sculpted prairie. Grant was soon engrossed in the scenic beauty, noting the difference in topography from the flight along the river into Great Falls. He felt a queasy nausea as the light plane careened in a pitching waltz with the errant winds.

As if they had flown through an invisible barrier, the Jenny began to glide smoothly on the morning air. Grant's excitement returned when he saw what he thought was a small town in the distance.

"That little burg up ahead is Shelby," Tom shouted.

The plane circled low over Shelby, and Grant could sense the tremendous energy being expended by the small town in behalf of the hoped for fight enterprise. He could see a huge wooden stadium under construction. Trucks and wagons unloaded lumber from flatbed freight cars parked on an adjacent railway siding. Men appeared like ants, pursuing the single minded purpose of assembling the bleachers and a platform for the fight arena. The entire scene was, to Grant, inconsonant with this tiny village in the middle of the prairie.

Tom flew a crisscross pattern over the activity pointing to various things that he thought might be of interest. After noting the wind direction from the movement of the American Flag in front of City Hall, he made one more pass over the bustling activity to be sure that he had been seen by people on the ground, and then flew to a pasture on the edge of town. Turning the plane into the wind, he pulled back on the throttle, gliding toward a ranch road which crossed an open field.

Grant again found himself holding his breath, every muscle taut, until the tires touched the dirt and the tail skid aligned the plane with the roadway. Rolling to a stop in a cleared area, Tom and Grant got out of the cockpits and stood in the shade of the Jenny's wing.

"What a difference in the weather in just a few miles," Grant said.

"Little summer storms. They're usually just local, like that little blow down by Bernie's. I figured we'd be okay if we could get ahead of it. If a man is traveling on the ground, he is at the mercy of the weather and terrain. Of all I have done in my life, there is nothing quite like flying to give a fella a feeling of freedom and discovery. Even in the days of the open prairies before the fences, when you'd ride over a hill and not know what you was gonna see. It didn't equal that feeling of release a man gets when he swoops over a hill and sees the world in a way he never saw it before. Kind'a that eagle's eye view and a fella in the air can actually outrun the weather. Nothin' to equal it!"

"I suppose that the initial fear is the worst part. Once one is acclimated, it is quite exhilarating."

"Better'n that sprint on horseback?"

"Just different...perhaps not better!"

Tom put his hand to his ear.

"There'll be someone along shortly...I hope...to take us into town."

"Quite a spectacle! Is all that construction just for this fight?"

"Yeah, and that ain't the half of it! In addition to the two hundred thousand we gave Doc Kearns already, we've spent at least that much more on the lumber and the labor and the promotion of this thing.

From what I gathered talkin' to Kearns, it looks like Mulroney and O'Halloran are tryin' to bluff him out of his last hundred till after the fight, when we have the gate money just for a little insurance. Either that or they've pissed away more than we'd planned and they don't have the cash, in which case I have really got to get everyone headed down the same trail or we're gonna have a financial train wreck."

Grant cocked his head to listen.

"I hear a car coming."

"Good. At least we don't have to stand out here in the heat all day."

A Ford touring car came into sight and stopped close to the Jenny. A large man in an expensive suit and wearing a carnation boutonniere in his lapel stepped out of the car.

"Thomas, me boy! It's glad I am you're here. Flyin' in like ya did, you're the closest thing to an angel that my eyes are likely to behold."

Tom shook the man's hand.

"Grant Collins, this purveyor of the blarney is Roy Mulroney. His honor is the Mayor of Shelby, Montana. And Mr. Mulroney, this fine young gentleman who accompanies me is Grant Collins from the Saint Louis Morning Star newspaper. He's come all the way to Montana to tell the story of my very interesting life. While he's here I'll expect that you'll be setting up an interview with Gibbons. Grant also has to justify this Montana adventure with his editor."

"Sure and begorra, consider it done. And it's a pleasure to make your acquaintance, Mr. Collins," Mulroney said, pumping Grant's hand.

They climbed into the car.

"What in the name of Saint Patrick's serpents is O'Halloran tryin to pull?" Tom asked.

"I think our friend O'Halloran has become drunk with his power. Seein' as how he hasn't any of his own money in this show, I'm not just sure why he's nettling Kearns the way he's doin'. It appears that he's attemptin' to bullshit the bullshitter, if you get me drift. Doc Kearns doesn't seem the type to be trifled with, but O'Halloran thought we could stall him until after the fight and use the money for promotion. Had he kept his fly trap shut we'd have been the better for it. Kearns has near killed the ticket sales and many of the trains have already cancelled. Perhaps, with your charmin' persuasion, you can put a plug in O'Halloran's blow hole and if Kearns says it's on within the next twenty-four hours we still have a chance to recoup our losses. As far as a profit is concerned, well..."

"We went to Dempsey's trainin' camp yesterday and Kearns is sure enough smokin' hot under his grease-stained collar. Dempsey apparently leaves the business to Doc, so he is gonna go along with whatever Doc says, as best I can gather," Tom said.

"Dempsey told me he is angry at Gibbons about things Gibbons said in press interviews. He said he was mad enough to fight Gibbons without the extra money up front...but then as you said, he is leaving it to Doc Kearns," Grant said.

"Why didn't ya tell me that before, boy," Tom said. "Hell that might just change the complexion of this here predicament."

"You had spoken with Mr. Kearns so I assumed that you knew about it," Grant replied. "How could this change the situation?"

Roy Mulroney looked at Grant in the back seat and then at Tom.

"Like the lad says, if Dempsey is lettin' Kearns hold the reins on the business end, what difference does it make?"

"Well, let me explain this in dog shit simple terms to you boys. Dempsey is a man of great pride. It appears he's already sore about Gibbons defamin' him in the newpapers...and it shouldn't take too much to push him over the edge. You set up that interview with Gibbons and let's us find out just what Gibbons has got to say."

Tom turned to Grant.

"I am assumin' that you're gonna make sure that Dempsey gets an ear full, or an eye full, before Doc's final decision gets made?"

"Dempsey doesn't consider Gibbons a worthy opponent. He is really upset with things Gibbons has said. As a news reporter, I can't take sides, but I will certainly report whatever Gibbons says to me," Grant said.

Tom looked over at Mulroney and winked.

"There you go, looks like this might work itself out," Tom said.

Mulroney parked the car in front of the Elks Lodge and the men entered the crowded bar. Tom approached a round faced man of squat stature wearing a disheveled suit and crushed felt hat.

"Tommy me boy," the man said proffering his hand. "And it's glad I am to see ya. We've a wee bit o'difficulty...or have ya heard?"

Tom looked at Grant.

"This is the famous Mr. O'Halloran."

As Grant put out his hand, Tom said, "Mike, meet Mr. Grant Collins of the Morning Star Newpaper in Saint Louis. Watch what ya say to him.

He's one of the few honest men left on earth...I think."

Tom then took O'Halloran's arm.

"Excuse us Grant but we need to talk some business."

Pushing O'Halloran by the elbow Tom disappeared into an anteroom.

Grant approached the bar to order a cup of coffee. A young man of about Grant's age touched his arm, causing a start.

"Aren't you the fella that came up from Saint Louis to interview Tornado Tom about the Pony Express?"

"Why yes, that seems to be the worst kept secret of the entire countryside."

The young man smiled and slapped Grant's shoulder.

"Can I buy ya a drink?"

"Just coffee if they have any."

"Coffee it is. Any fella kick the shit outta ol' Buck Horton has got a free drink comin' on me."

"Wait a minute," Grant said.

Grant turned and held the young man's arm.

"Who told you that? Buck is fine. He just got a little drunk the other evening."

The young man looked at Grant with a grin.

"Don't be so modest. What the hell, it don't make no difference, the story got around now and I'll buy ya a drink anyway. If it ain't so...it outta be."

Just then a tall thin man with a moustache wearing a badge approached Grant.

"Are you Grant Collins?" he said in a gruff voice.

Grant turned quickly to face the man.

"You're under arrest for frequentin' an establishment where liquor is bein' served."

The muscles in Grant's stomach tightened and his face blanched as the officer's face turned to a smile. He stuck out his hand.

"Just funnin' with ya, kid. Don't tip over on me now. I'm Delmer Driscoll, Chief of Police of this here city. The Mayor asked me to take ya over to see Gibbons."

Grant swallowed hard and tried to laugh.

"Oh! That was very kind of the Mayor," Grant said as he followed the Chief to the car.

"You must be some kind'a special reporter to get your own private interview?" Delmer said. "Most of the press boys are stuck over in them train cars waitin' for the regular press conference every day."

Delmer pointed to the line of railroad Pullman cars being used as press offices and living quarters for the journalists.

"Those press fellas are about to go nuts tryin' to find out if this thing is on or off. I guess that Doc Kearns figures he's got Shelby by the balls and he ain't lettin' go till he gets a squeal."

Driving to Gibbon's camp, they passed the flurry of building activity Grant had seen from the air. He recalled how the view of the arena from Tom's airplane had conferred upon the scene a surprising miniaturization of people and objects.

When viewed at ground level, in concert with the din created by the hundreds of men busying themselves in the construction, this fifty thousand seat stadium at a prairie crossroads might have been a fantasy penned by Lewis Carrol.

Delmer stopped the car at a ramshackle house on a hill overlooking the town.

"Reckon this was the best the kid could do," Delmer conjectured. "I'll be back to pick you up in about an hour."

Grant got out of the car and walked around the house where he was met by a massively built man in his thirties. Shirtless, he was working on a punching bag that had been hung from a tripod on a level spot behind the house.

"Are you Collins?" Tommy Gibbons asked.

"Yes sir. I'm from the Saint Louis Morning Star."

Two children were playing in the yard. A woman came out of the house and asked, "Could I bring you some refreshments?"

"This is my wife," Gibbons said. "Would you like some coffee or tea or lemonade or somethin?"

"Lemonade would be just wonderful, Mrs. Gibbons," Grant said.

Tommy Gibbons removed his gloves and walked to a cluster of chairs.

"This is where I do my daily news conferences. These reporters are about to drive us crazy. I brought the wife and kids so they could see me take the championship."

"So you are confident that you will beat Dempsey?"

"Sure as the Fourth of July."

Gibbons picked up two chairs and set them by a small table.

"Have a seat...we'll talk."

A young boy of about six climbed into Gibbon's lap.

"Damned right I'm confident," Gibbons repeated. "Mister, I been fightin' all my life and I never got a break. This is my break and I intend to take advantage of it."

"I suppose that a man in your business has to have confidence. Do you suppose you may be overconfident?"

Tommy Gibbons ignored Grant's question.

"I hear ol' Dempsey's got a wolf pup in his trainin' camp for luck?"

"Yes, he does. I saw it."

"Well you can tell the world that I brought my tiger pup for luck too. Huh, Tiger," Gibbons said, hugging the giggling boy on his lap.

"Have you heard that Dempsey may call off the fight?" Grant asked.

"I think they're scared. I've seen Dempsey fight but he's never seen me. He only knows what he's heard. Now he's stuck. The only way he can stay Champ is to back out of this fight. What the hell, he's got these cowboys for a couple a hundred G's. He's got everything to lose and nothin' to gain by fighting me. I wouldn't blame him if he just turned yellow and left for New York on the midnight flyer."

"Do you really believe that he fears you?"

"God damned well better believe I think he's scared...and you can tell him I said so."

Gibbons looked at Grant and asked, "Are you a regular boxing reporter?

"No sir," Grant answered. "This is the first fight I've covered."

"So you've already talked to Dempsey?"

"I spoke to the Champ yesterday."

"I'll bet he looked scared!" Gibbons said.

Gibbons hugged the child again and then set him on his feet. He then rose from his chair and motioned Grant to follow.

"Since you ain't a regular boxing reporter, I'll give you some things to look for when you're reportin' on the fight. Come on over here a minute."

Gibbons posed Grant in a boxing stance.

Grant smiled nervously at the huge muscular man.

"You're not going to hit me are you? I know you boxing fellows don't like journalists but there are limits."

"Naw...I ain't gonna hurt you none."

Standing opposite Grant he raised his hands, fists clenched loosely.

"See how I have my left hand up and out? Well that's the way Dempsey gets his jab in your face. It comes at you quick and his glove is twisting so he cuts you up with those little jabs that look like they don't hurt."

Gibbons faked several jabs and then threw a right, which stopped half an inch from Grant's nose, causing him to flinch involuntarily.

"Easy there, Collins! I said I ain't gonna hurt you."

Putting his hands up again, Gibbons faked another left.

"Then ol' Dempsey comes at you with his power like this..."

Gibbons then faked several more punches with his right hand.

"Now those rights not only look like they hurt...they do. But I got some moves of my own."

Tommy Gibbons once more posed Grant, who had dropped his hands.

"Now you try what I just done."

Grant tried to put the pattern of jabs and punches together in his mind. He then began to spar with the aging prize fighter.

"Good! You learn quick. Now try that right hand."

Grant swung his right hand as Gibbons had done, but found it countered by a left as the fighter's right hand again stopped a hair's thickness from his jaw.

"If a fella swings at you like that," Gibbon's said, dropping his hands, "put up your left and throw your right to catch him off guard. I watched Dempsey do that and he's not gonna be ready for my moves."

Grant then sparred a slow motion mock round as Tommy Gibbons demonstrated his skills.

Grant heard the sceen door slam.

"Don't you hurt Mr. Collins now, Tom," Mrs. Gibbons said as she carried a tray out of the back door.

Sweating in the late morning heat they sat to drink the lemonade she had placed on the small table in the yard.

"Like I told you, Collins, Dempsey never seen me in a fight. He only has two options. Fight me and become the former champion or get on the train and haul his ass back to New York City with his tail between his legs."

As Grant walked to Delmer's car, he found himself secretly hoping that the likable young family man would prevail in the fight. Gibbons had invested his entire future on this one day. As big and strong as he was however, Grant gave him little hope for a win against the proven talents of the Manassa Mauler.

Delmer drove Grant to the Elks Lodge where Tom was at the bar with O'Halloran and Mulroney.

"I hear you're becomin' a local celebrity," Tom said.

Grant looked puzzled.

"Not that I am aware of."

"Seems that misunderstandin' you had with Buck, has got everyone in three counties talkin'," Tom said.

"But nothing happened," Grant said. "Buck was drunk and he tried to throw a punch...but he fell and Nick and I helped him off the dance floor."

"Humility is very becoming in a young man these days," Mulroney said. "And I'll tell ya laddie, no one in this county would mind seein' Mr. Buck Horton get his comeuppance for the change."

"Come on Mr. Mayor," Tom said, "let's go shove some grub down our necks."

Tom picked up his glass and took a swallow of beer. He then turned to Grant.

"We're gonna be the guests of the Mayor tonight. He has thoughtfully invited us to stay at his home. Otherwise, we'd be sleepin' under those railroad cars where your fellow reporters are stayin'. There ain't a camp cot nor a floorboard that ain't got someone sleepin' on it tonight."

"Mr. Mulroney, have you a phone I could use? I have to update my editor on the story. I'll make it a collect call," Grant said.

"Sure, and you're welcome to use it. And what did Mr. Gibbons have to say that might be of interest to the public?" Mulroney asked.

"He thinks he'll win if the fight goes and he says that he believes Dempsey is afraid of him. He thinks that is why Doc Kearns is trying to call off the fight. He thinks that Dempsey will get on the train a go back to New York rather than lose his title," Grant said.

Tom's face lit in a smile.

"You are gonna to put that in your newspaper...I hope."

"That's the story. So that is what I am calling in," Grant said.

Tom turned to Mulroney and O'Halloran and raised his glass.

"Gentleman, the fight will go on, money or no money. I guarantee it."

Mulroney wrinkled his brow.

"Trouble is, about half those trains that were scheduled to come are cancelled and most of those fifty dollar duckets are unsold. Doc Kearns still hasn't given the go ahead and at best we can hope to get a little of the gate."

"So cross your fingers and let's go get somethin' to eat," Tom said.

Tom drained his glass and walked toward the door.

1 2

It was late in the afternoon of the next day when O'Halloran rushed into the Elk's Lodge to announce that Doc Kearns had called to inform him that Dempsey was boarding the train to Shelby in the morning.

The town exploded with the news. Bands appeared from nowhere and began to play while hundreds of men began a snake dance several blocks in length through the streets of the small town. As the evening progressed, the fireworks display intended for the Fourth of July was set off a day early. A party, the likes of which Grant had never witnessed, besieged the normally quiet village in a continuous uproar through the night.

"I told you Dempsey was gonna fight," Tom said, raising his glass in a toast. "There was no way he'd let this Gibbons kid call him a coward and then not fight. It would'a ruined him. Man's gotta save his pride, even if it costs money. That's just the way it is. Trouble is now, it's gonna cost us money too. But maybe we can at least cut our losses tomorrow at the gate."

The others raised their glasses and toasts went all around.

"May I use your telephone, Mr. Mulroney?" Grant asked.

After the toasts, Grant and Tom walked to Mulroney's home where Grant telephoned Hiram for the final edition. Breathing more easily with the uncertainty at an end, Mrs. Mulroney fixed dinner and everyone was able to relax.

After dinner Tom and Grant sat on the front porch listening to the cacophony of celebrations.

"Son, there's somthing that I been meanin' to tell ya and I don't know exactly how to put it." Tom said. "I want ya to be careful around Buck. He can be a dangerous man."

"I gather that he has some reputation."

"Well sir, the way I see it, there's more to it than that. Truth is, even if Buck was an otherwise affable gentleman, which he ain't, you just can't have two roosters in the same hen house.

I reckon ya know that he's moonin' over my niece with about the same degree of fervor that you yourself are demonstratin'. Now that tends to make a man's thoughts go awry even if he's normally an even tempered fella and I can guarantee you that Buck ain't normally even tempered. I don't know what happened the other night at that dance, but it has got blowed all outta proportion in the rumor mill. Lotta folks don't like Buck. He's kicked the shit outta 'bout half the young men in this part of the country at one time or another. That don't make him none too popular for starters and I'll tell you that he's one mean son-of-a-bitch when it comes to a fight.

He near killed a kid right here in Shelby about three years ago. Got the boy down and stomped his face till he didn't have a nose left and most his teeth was gone. Took a couple other good men to pull ol' Buck off the kid. There seems to be sumthin' lackin' in Buck. He seems to enjoy hurtin' people way beyond what's needed to win a fight. So what I'm tryin' to explain to you is, don't give him no opportunity to bait you into a fight.

He'll hurt ya...maybe kill ya."

Tom's face lit up with a smile to break the somberness of the warning.

"And then you wouldn't be able to write my story. I gotta look after you."

Grant looked dismayed. "I haven't found physical confrontation a necessity since I was seven years old. What makes you think I would pick a fight with Buck?"

"I don't think you would pick a fight with Buck but that don't mean that he ain't gonna pick one with you. Fact is that he already has...and young men being young men, you're gonna have to fight him if ya get painted into a corner. Just don't let him paint you into that corner is all I'm tryin' to tell you."

Grant sat silently, understanding the words without fully comprehending the serious nature of Tom's admonition.

Just then they heard the creak of the screen door.

"Could ya go for a nightcap," Mulroney said, as he walked onto the porch with a bottle and glasses. "Thought I'd come out and catch the evening air and hold Communion with a prayer that those trains are filled with money tomorrow."

Mulroney set the glasses and bottle on the table.

"What da ya think, Mr. Thomas? Are we all gonna be headed to the poor house this time tomorrow night?" Mulroney said.

"Damned well could be. We really dodged the musket ball with ol' Doc Kearns. I still believe it was Dempsey who made the decision to fight. Now Kearns has gotta bet on the gate just like we do. Course, that dumb bastard is the cause of the cancellations with that on again off again waltz he was dancin' with the press boys. Serve him right if his cut is as skinny as our own."

"Did you have a word with young Grant here about Buck?" Mulroney asked.

Tom nodded.

Mulroney looked at Grant.

"He's mean as a badger, that one. Since the word's got round 'bout your differences I'd be awful careful. Ol' Tom here dealt with plenty like him in the old days I'd imagine. Huh Tom?"

"That was a mighty long time ago Roy. Now I'm just an old fart tellin' stories to newsmen and hopin' to see my name get famous before I die. But I did run across a few like him in my day. Funny thing is that Buck is always real respectful around me...and he is one helluva good hand."

"Did you know that Tom had hunted Passenger Pigeons?" Grant said, looking at Roy.

"That's one I hadn't heard or I must'a been too drunk to remember when he told that one. But then he is a bit of a bullshitter you know."

"When I was huntin' them pigeons, the best part of Mulroney was soakin' into a flea bitten straw mattress in the County Cork."

Tom handed his glass to Mulroney.

"Pour me another, Mr. Mayor, and I'll tell ya how I got myself into the great Civil War."

Mulroney laughed a huge belly laugh and poured Tom's glass full of whiskey.

"And ya know why the North won that war, don't ya lad?" Mulroney said to Grant.

"I think it was because the Southern states had insufficient resources to continue the conflict," Grant said.

"No, me boy, it was because the Union had all the Irishmen from New York City. They was accustomed to fightin' every day since they were children. The Irish lads actually enjoyed dressin' up in them fancy suits for the fightin'. Not like at home in New York where they killed one another in their plain old raggedy assed street clothes every day just for the entertainment."

Tom laughed with Mulroney.

"Much as I hate to admit it, I reckon that he ain't so far from right on that one," Tom said.

"So you did serve as a soldier in the Civil War?" Grant asked. "I thought they took your horse and sent you home."

"Leave it to me to overcome rejection," Tom said with a wry grin. "Yes sir, I was a soldier in the great War of the Rebellion...on both sides. Like I was tellin' ya the other night, I'd had a belly full of killin' them Passenger Pigeons, so I went back to Missouri and headed to Saint Joseph to see my sister and Jacob. I reckon you remember me tellin' you about the kid who rode the mule with me down to the Pony Express on hiring day?"

"You mean Cooter LaRue?"

"Yep! That was him. Well, he was still hangin' around Jacob's store and I had no sooner got home and hung my clean shirt on the nail when he comes to me real secret like and tells me that he's gonna join up with the Confederate Army. They wasn't doin' too well and he reckoned to turn the tide.

As I said before, most of the folks in that neck of the woods was sympathetic to the Confederacy, but the area was completely controlled by Yankee troops. Now ol' Jacob, my brother-in-law, was enough of a politician to keep the Yankees happy and still remain friendly with his neighbors. To tell you the truth, I don't know for sure just what his politics were. But I did know that if I was to be found out as a Confederate, it wouldn't have gone easy on Jacob or my sister."

"You mean the Union Army would have punished your sister if you were a soldier in the Confederate Army? How could they punish the families?" Grant asked.

"Shit oh dear, my boy! I guess you only heard the Yankee side of that story. Hell, the Union was shootin' men and boys who was just suspected of sympathizin'. And they was puttin' women in prison if they had kin folk fightin' for the rebels. In fact, that was how the Yankees created one of their own worst nightmares. Didn't you ever hear of Bloody Bill Anderson?"

"Dixie told me that he was her father's great uncle, but I don't really know much about that portion of Civil War history," Grant replied.

"The story goes that the Yankees had imprisoned a bunch of Confederate sympathizin' women in an old dilapidated buildin' somewhere south of Saint Joe. This old buildin' they was usin' as a jail supposedly collapsed. It killed and maimed a bunch of them women and girls. As I hear it, some of Anderson's women folk was in that collapsed buildin' and ol' Bill went out of his mind. I don't know if them Yankees killed the girls on purpose or not...I doubt it. But they sure lit the fuse on the powder keg of hades when they done it. Bloody Bill, who was workin' with Quantrell's Raiders, took his bunch and went to murderin' and rapin' and pillagin' all along the border. He was the scourge of Kansas. And the more he done the meaner them Yankees got and it was just one big terrible circle drawn in fire and blood.

Now to say the least I didn't want any of my kin gettin' hurt because of anything I was doin'. So when I joined the Confederate Cavalry, I just used a pseudonym, kind'a like you writer fellas do. Bein' a kid it was just another adventure to my way of thinkin'. Anyway, me and that Cooter kid slipped away and headed up to Fort Smith in Arkansas to join the men in grey in their glorious quest.

We both lied about who we was when we joined up. I told Jacob and Rachel I was going off pigeon huntin' again so that they wouldn't have to lie or have nothin' to confess, even if they was asked. I told Cooter to tell his folks he was goin' with me on the pigeon hunt. Everyone knew that I'd been off huntin' pigeons for near a year and that I had made a lot of money. So I figured there'd be no suspicion on Rachel and Jacob or on Cooter's folks for that matter.

You remember me telling you about how I'd tried to join the Confederate Cavalry earlier on in the war and how they took my horse and all?"

Grant shook his head in acknowledgement.

"They had not been interested in me then because I was too scrawny and they had plenty of men. Things was different by sixty three. I had growed a lot in that time and the Confederacy had lost a lot of men. They wasn't near as picky and they must have really been in a pretty bad way in the cavalry. They took ol' Cooter and it didn't appear to me like he could ride any better than when we went to join Pony Express. I reckon that the Confederate Army fellas needed riders a whole lot worse than Russell, Majors and Waddell had back in sixty. I can tell you one thing for sure…they sure as hell wasn't payin' near as good…and the pay was in Confederate dollars besides. I reckon you know that Confederate currency wasn't worth wipin' paper in a shithouse."

"It was early spring when we joined and those first few months we didn't do nothin' but drill…drill…care for your horse, clean your rifle and drill some more. We played some baseball and I did what readin' as I could find things to read but it was just awful. I can't say that I was well suited to army life. First of all, I didn't like bein' told what to do every minute of the day and night. I was accustomed to goin' and comin' as I pleased and doin' things the way I wanted to do 'em.

Even though I'd had bosses with the Pony Express, they mostly left you alone and respected what you was doin'. And once you was in the saddle there wasn't no one tellin' ya how to do your job. But, be that as it may, I was in the army and they told you everything to do and when to do it, from cleaning your gun to usin' the latrine."

"So what's this big story about your great adventures in the Civil War?" Mulroney asked. "Sounds like all you did was go camping and play with your gun. Didn't you do any fightin' at all?"

"Yes, sir, and I'm comin' to that. One day about the end of June we was on a patrol out of Fort Smith lookin' to see what we might see. That was the job of the cavalry, providin' reconnaissance information. They called it 'intelligence.' I always thought that to be a bit odd, seein' as how none of it seemed too intelligent when you were there. Anyway, we was out on patrol providing intelligence to the high muckety-mucks at headquarters.

Well, sir, we come upon a Union supply train headed south from Fort Scott up in Kansas to resupply Fort Gibson down in the Injun Territories... in what is now Oklahoma. That particular supply train was bein' guarded by the First Kansas Colored Infantry. That was the first Negra soldiers I'd ever seen. Most of my Rebel comrades could barely contain themselves. They was all braggin' about bein' real anxious to get in there and kill them some niggers. As it turned out, that Yankee supply train was bein' held up at a place called Cabin Creek. The creek was runnin' high because of recent rain and therefore it was impedin' their progress.

Our Captain sent some riders to report back to our main column and request that they send some reinforcements so we'd have enough men to attack the Yankees. That was war as I saw it. The Yankees was stuck waitin' for the high water to recede and we was stuck waitin' for reinforcements... so we was all just waitin'. That's mostly what war is about for the soldiers. Waitin'! Unfortunately for us, it happened that the Grand River, which our reinforcements had to cross, was also runnin' high. That detained the reinforcement column leavin' us in a pickle.

Next thing we know those black Yankees, the ones my fellow Confederates had been so anxious to exchange lead with, was attackin' us. They cut loose with their artillery and followed with a couple of cavalry charges and then come those colored infantry troops. My Confederate brethren learned 'em a real lesson that mornin'. Them 'niggers' that my fella gray coats was so anxious to set upon came chargin' in behind that artillery barrage and turned our ranks to chaos.

We had already got scattered a bit with the cavalry charge but we was proceedin' to regroup when the Lieutenant leadin' my outfit saw what he figured was a weakness in the Yankee line. He took it upon himself to mount a counter attack and we was proceedin' to form up for a charge when one of them explodin' cannon shells landed right in the middle of our bunch.

I was knocked right unconscious and my horse was killed under me. I don't know how long I lay there but when I came around there was screamin' and shoutin' and moanin' and the clashin' of metal. I knew that men was fighting it out, bayonet to bayonet."

"Was ya badly injured your own self?" Mulroney asked.

"Just the general hurtin' of the fall and gettin' the wind knocked out of me and I'd busted my head when my horse came rolling over with me. Other than that I could still move. But I was hurtin' bad enough to take most of the fight out of me. The worst part was the explosions. The Yankee infantry hadn't yet got to where we was and the artillery shells was still landing everywhere around us and those things shook the ground enough to set your teeth on edge. I don't give a damn what anyone says, for the soldier who does the fightin', the artillery is the worst of it. You don't know when it's comin' or where it's comin' from.

When I got my wits about me, I looked around for Cooter. I could see his horse floppin' around there lookin' like a busted water melon. I crawled over to see how he was and he was layin' face down about half way under his animal. I grabbed Cooter's arm and the back of his coat to pull him from under his horse and..."

Tom stopped, took a deep breath and choked back a tear.

"When I pulled, his arm come off in my hands and as he rolled over I threw up all over him and what was left of that floppin' animal he'd been ridin'. His face was completely gone. Just gone! Just bloody red meat with white sinew and bone showin' through. I wretched all I had, then I wretched some more.

Since there was no helpin' Cooter, I reckoned I'd get myself out of there before one of them Yankees come by to stick me with his bayonet. I started to crawl, just hopin' no more of them shells landed where I was. I crawled a couple of yards keepin' my head down with my nose in the dirt and as I rounded a dead horse, I come upon my Lieutenant. He'd had a leg blowed near about off and was sitting there, just very business like, with his pocket knife, amputatin' the remaining chunks of his leg...which was hangin' from a stump just above the knee.

I couldn't believe my eyes. You could see that the ligaments and tendons was tough to cut. It had to hurt like all holy hell, but he just kept cuttin' till the whole thing fell away. Then he looked over at me and said something that I'll never forget. In a voice, which had a real gentlemanly quality to it, he asked, 'Would you twist this belt very tightly around my leg trooper? Otherwise, I think I'll bleed to death.'

All of a sudden I was oblivious to what was goin' on around us. I found a bayonet and took that officer's belt and twisted it tight around that stump that had been his leg. Then I just sat there with him until one of them darky soldiers come upon us. That colored soldier was lookin' for survivors and he had his bayonet ready for business. I figured sure he'd skewer me and be done with it but he looked me in the eye and then he looked at that Lieutenant with the stump of a leg and he just couldn't do it. In fact, I learned a real lesson from that. A lesson about how willin', or unwillin', a man is to kill another man, even if the other seems to have it comin'. I guess he saw I was just a kid and near about scared as he was...and that Lieutenant sure as hell wasn't no threat to no one. So he took us prisoner. He even let me get my canteen off'n my dead horse, as it was terrible hot in that June sun."

"So it was your opinion that the black soldiers had acquitted themselves well enough in the battle?" Grant asked.

"Acquitted my ass! They flat put it on us. Whupped our Rebel asses to a fare-thee-well."

"And what did that Negro gentleman do with a child soldier like yourself and a one legged officer?" Mulroney asked.

"They gathered up the ones of us who could walk and marched us to Fort Gibson where they put us in a stockade. I never saw that Lieutenant again. I don't know if he lived or died.

There was only seven of us that they took prisoner at the battle of Cabin Creek according to some history books. But there was more than that at Fort Gibson. I'm sure of that. However, there was more guards than there was prisoners. It was obvious to me that them blue bellies, even them black ones, weren't no better off in the boredom department than we was."

"Were you treated well in the detention camp?" Grant asked.

"I sure as hell learned somethin' about man's inhumanity to man. Some of them Confederates was bein' real assholes with them darky soldiers. Some of 'em seemed to forget that we was the prisoners. In return they was gettin' treated to some of their own. Some of them colored boys was just fresh off plantations. There wasn't no doubt in my country mind that they knew a thing or two about whuppin' ass. It occurred to me that a little New Testament wisdom was in order, so I treated them Negro soldiers just like I wanted to be treated. All in all I come out pretty good.

Some of them Rebel boys, especially the ones that was getting' them ass whuppin's, was a might annoyed with me, but I decided I better look out for my own hide. The news and rumors about the progress of the war circulating around the prison camp, was makin' it sound real bad for ol' Jeff Davis and the Confederacy. The Yankees had taken Fort Smith in my absence, and we were hearing about places like Gettysburg and Vicksburg and the like.

At that point I really didn't give a good chili bean fart about who won. I never owned a slave. Never even wanted to own a slave and all I could think about was Cooter's face, or his lack of a face, and I just wanted to be left alone. I wanted to get on a horse and just ride across that prairie and not hear anything. No cannons, no orders, no nothin'. Maybe just go listen to the sound of God, that's what was on my mind. Now I never been real religious, but that was one period in my life when I did a whole lot of prayin', what with there bein' a real lack of anything better to do. And I suppose that my attitude was rewarded since my time as a prisoner of war didn't really last none too long."

"Did they parole you?" Grant asked.

"Not exactly. But I did have a stroke of luck. It wasn't but a month or so and the Yankees shipped us from Fort Gibson over to Fort Smith where it was rumored that they was fixin' to send us to a place called Camp Douglas up in Chicago. That Douglas was a regular prison and the things I heard about it didn't make it sound none too appealing."

"And what was it that you'd heard?" Roy asked.

"I was hearing terrible stories about men dyin' of starvation and disease and the filth and the stink. It was near as bad as Andersonville the way I heard tell. Maybe worse, 'cause the Yankees could afford to at least feed those poor bastards. Being in a prison camp in the North or the South wasn't no picnic and that's the truth of it.

But, like I said, I had a stroke of luck and my prayin' got answered. When we got to Fort Smith I saw a fella who had been a pretty good friend. We had rode together on the Pony Express line. Well sir, he saw me in the monkey cage and imposed on the Captain to let him talk to me. I reckon you heard about the 'dead lines' and all, so he was bein' a might cautious. Well, they let me out to talk with this fella and me and him got to jawin' about the Pony Express days and then he told me that the Union Army was real short on Injun scouts out in the West. He told me that if'n I was to swear an oath of allegiance and promise to become a good Yankee he could get me outta that train ride up to Camp Douglas."

Tom looked at Mulroney and Grant with a grin from ear to ear.

"What would you have done? My pal apparently told that Captain about me growin' up out on the prairie with the Injuns and that I was able to palaver with the redskins and that I was a good rider and a fair shot.

Damned if the next day they didn't come and get me outta that stockade and took me to the see a Colonel. He was a decent feller, explaining that I would be sent west to act as a scout. He told me they didn't really want Confederate converts in the regular war...didn't trust 'em. But he said I would be assigned with some outfit or another out on the frontier and that I would have to sign up for two years in exchange for a full pardon and citizenship. That sure as hell sounded one helluva lot better than layin' around in a Yankee prison camp with the grim reaper sittin' on the foot of your bunk for God knew how long. That ol' Colonel made me swear an oath and the next thing ya know I was a 'galvanized Yankee' on my way to fight the Injuns."

Looking at the faces of the two men, Tom considered how the story of switching sides might sound less than patriotic to Mulroney and this young reporter. It had not occurred to him until he told the story aloud just how unprincipled and disloyal it might sound to a loyalist listener of either persuasion.

"Like I said boys, I never owned a slave and had no intention to do so. I was a Southerner by birth but not necessarily philosophy. Hell, I was from Montana when all was said and done. And my sister Sarah and ol' Jacob would'a been put to some pretty harsh treatment had the Yankees found out who I was, what with me wearin' that gray jacket. Switchin' the way I done gave my family some small amount of protection, seein' as how the Yankees had pretty much took control of the border states at that point in the war."

Tom thought a moment before a smile lit his face.

"Besides, I come from a long line of deserters and side switchin' sons-a-bitches. As I understand it, my mama's great grand pappy fought in the Revolutionary War with the Hessians. He was in New Jersey when ol' George Washington and his boys took that famous boat ride. According to the family legend, him and his whole outfit was drunk as New York Irishmen on that particular Christmas night."

Tom held out his glass for a refill as Grant and Mulroney both laughed.

"I reckon them Hessians figured that the Continental Army was about done in, so getting drunk seemed the thing to do. Next thing my grand pappy knew there was Yankee Doodles holdin' him and his bunch at bayonet point and hardly a shot had been fired. I was given to understand that most'a them Continental soldiers hadn't loaded their muskets 'cause the weather was too wet and they didn't figure the damned things would shoot anyhow. Well sir, my great grand sire was taken prisoner in his under drawers and sent back across the Potomac in one of Washington's boats. Story goes that he was pretty damned well impressed by the pluck of them Continentals and figured he was bein' treated better by the Americans in the prison camp than he was by his own folks anyway. Not only that, the Yankees promised him a piece of land, which he could never have hoped to get back in Germany, so he became our first 'galvanized Yankee'."

"You mean there were more?" Mulroney asked.

"Well, there was the matter of my pappy's grandsire. That would'a been my great grand pappy Thomas. He was an unwillin' conscript with the British forces when they sailed off to New Orleans with the intention of whippin' Andy Jackson's rag tag rabble. He was jerked from the streets of Liverpool with not too much in the way of a future and not a whole lot of a past neither. Did ya ever hear about that battle at New Orleans?"

Grant and Mulroney both acknowledged that they had.

"Well, my grand pappy was one of them lucky young fellas who got to occupy the center of that British line, which famously charged into the wrath of hell and Andy Jackson.

You might say that the British had some pretty bad generalship. Ol' Andy had set his boys in near impregnable fortifications and those Red Coats was no better off marchin' across that low ground than those roosted Passenger Pigeons I was tellin' ya about. Jackson's boys shot them Englishmen to pieces. After the Red Coats abandoned the field and skedaddled, the Americans walked through the killin' field pickin' up whatever the Brits had left behind. It was said that the bodies was stacked as high as a man's head. Turned out that my ol' grand pappy had been hit in the leg and was buried under a bunch of dead soldiers. He was just damned lucky that someone heard him yellin' and pulled him from that carnage. I was told that he'd nearly drowned in the blood and all but suffocated. Jackson's men took him prisoner, patched his leg and sent him off to a prisoner camp to recuperate.

Now as it turned out, the whole battle was a waste of time. Wasn't long before they got the word that the British had signed a treaty ending the war before that battle even got fought. So ol' grandpappy walked with a limp the rest of his life for nothin'. But to make the long story short he got to figurin' that goin' back to Liverpool with a bad leg and no skills to sell wasn't gonna serve him none too well...so he decided to become a Yankee himself. Like I said, I come from a long line of 'galvanized Yankees' and I reckon I should be proud of it. We always came out on the right side, at least so far anyways."

After a good laugh, Mulroney raised his glass.

"Gentlemen, with that I'll call it a night. It's gonna be a long day and we're only gonna get a couple of winks before the headaches begin."

13

The Fourth of July sun scorched the dusty streets of Shelby. The population of the small town had grown overnight. Its usual one thousand residents was nearly ten thousand with a steady stream of vehicles leaving a fog of dust hanging in the still dry air.

Delmer had hired extra men who walked the streets futilely attempting to control the traffic. Spontaneous fist fights among young men, still inebriated from the all night party, took these surrogate deputies from their duties of directing the massive flood of carriages and automobiles. Insufficient jail space gave them little choice but to reprimand and release the drunken participants. Those who chose to be belligerent with these substitute enforcers were handcuffed to lampposts. Some, if combative, found themselves unconscious in an alley, out of the public view.

Notwithstanding the throng at hand, by early afternoon it was obvious that the on again, off again nature of the news of previous days had dissuaded many a would-be spectator.

Tom and Grant walked to the fifty-thousand seat arena with Roy Mulroney, where O'Halloran was closely monitoring the proceeds at the gate.

"Looks like Doc Kearns announcin' his intention to go home without fightin' has really cut our throat on the gate," Tom said. "Those trains should have been loaded with money this morning but there just ain't no trains."

The massive assemblage of residents from the surrounding towns was milling about the entrance to the freshly assembled wooden arena. The tickets being sold were for the inexpensive seats high on the stadium benches. Those without the price of admission begged for a few cents here and there. Soon, a melee erupted as tensions rose with the temperature.

Mayor Mulroney, took note that most of the fifty dollar seats remained empty only minutes before the scheduled fight time.

"Might as well let our good neighbors see Dempsey fight. It's fifteen minutes till show time and I've about got a riot on my hands. Let 'em in," Mulroney said.

With that the deputies removed the barriers and announced open seating to all.

Tom and Grant, forewarned of the announcement, had entered the arena and sat at ringside.

O'Halloran entered the ring with a megaphone to announce the first of five preliminary bouts.

Tom stood to look around at the crowd.

"A fifty thousand seat arena and it's one third full. And seventy percent of these sons'a bitches didn't pay. Hang on to your hemorrhoids. This ain't gonna be pretty when the bookkeepin's all done."

"Are you in serious financial trouble?" Grant inquired with genuine concern.

"Hell, yes. I ain't gonna lose the ranch or nothing but I own enough of the bank to make it hurt. Mulroney buried us in this deal and the bank may just go belly to the sun. Then I'll have to make that up to our neighbors who have their money in the bank. That worthless bastard Mulroney may just have to get a real job if he ain't careful. Bein' Mayor don't pay nothin' you know. He makes his livin' off the bank."

The preliminary bouts had attracted unknown fighters from across the country to get their names before the public at what had been anticipated to be a world class event.

Grant recorded the names of each fighter in his notebook and a brief description of the blow by blow encounters. This, he thought, would give Mr. Kuntz a potential reason for reimbursement of his expenses at the very least.

Just then Grant could smell the strong odor of whiskey and he could feel a hand on his shoulder.

"Afternoon, boss," Buck said from behind them, a hand on each of their shoulders.

"How ya doin' Mr. Buck?" Tom asked, glancing over his shoulder. "Where's your partner in crime?"

"Howdy went to find us some good whiskey. We've been drinkin' that home made shit all night and it's about to make him sick."

"Well, you boys take 'er a little easy. We still got work to do tomorrow. Leave a little of that whiskey for the next time," Tom said.

Leaning close to Grant's ear Buck said, "I hear tell ya kicked my ass at that dance the other night. I ain't takin' too kindly to hearin' stories like that."

"Well...uh, no, that isn't true," Grant said, his voice cracking.

Tom stood and turned to face the young cowboy. "Let 'er be, Buck. I'm here to enjoy this fight and I'll just have to catch one of yours some other day. Now go find your buddy and stay outta trouble."

Buck's eyes narrowed with Tom's admonishment. "Sure enough boss,"

Buck said through clenched teeth.

He then glowered at Grant. "We'll see you later, Cheechako!"

Buck disappeared into the crowd.

"You remember them dime novel stories about gun fights and grudges and shootouts in the streets?" Tom asked.

Grant nodded his reply.

"This is just the way these things always get blowed outta any proportion. I have seen many a man killed for less than we're talkin' here. Hell's bells son, I may have to put you on a train for Saint Louis before this is done. Ol' Buck ain't intending to let it lay, and that's a fact."

"But I didn't do anything and I didn't say anything," Grant protested.

"That's right...but right don't always keep a man alive. There ain't no William S. Hart gonna bring justice to the likes of Buck. Just stay outta his way and I'll have a talk with him when we get back to the ranch."

O'Halloran's megaphone gave a hollow sound to his voice as it reverberated through the wooden stadium. His tone was authoritative as he announced the main event, giving the vital statistics for first the challenger and then the champion.

Grant saw Mrs. Gibbons and the two children being escorted to their front row seats. He quickly walked over to pay his respects.

"I wish your husband all the best today. Tell him I sent my regards," he said.

He returned to his seat thinking how drawn and pale the poor woman looked.

"She is a very nice lady. This must be most unpleasant with all the press and name calling and the brutality," Grant said.

"Guess she knew what she signed on for," Tom conjectured. "Had it been me, I would have left my wife and children at home."

Grant's sympathy for Mrs. Gibbons was well founded. Even to his inexperienced eye, the bout was a terrible mismatch.

Dempsey did not overwork himself, but with each round Tommy Gibbon's face became less recognizable. Any chance that the challenger would knock out the Champ diminished with every hammer like blow from Dempsey's meticulous and incessant attack. By the tenth round people were leaving the arena. The final bell was heard by just a few die-hard fans.

Grant and Tom tipped their hats to Mrs. Gibbons as they left their ringside seats. Walking by, Grant noticed that the tears, which ran down the face of Tommy Gibbon's son, were etched red as they streamed through the spatters of his father's blood.

"This is a terrible business," Grant said.

"Terrible but profitable, except for this particular fiasco of course! Fightin's been a profitable business since way before the Romans and I can assure you that as long as there is money to be made, it will never end. Jack Dempsey would have been a hero in the Coliseums of Rome and a hundred years from now there will be a man just like him who will be a public hero.

What with the do-gooders and all, I'd reckon someday that they'll outlaw things such as chicken fightin' and dog fightin' and even bull fightin', but as long as two men want to beat each other senseless for money, there will always be a Dempsey and a Gibbons; and guys like me and O'Halloran to put up the money."

As Tom and Grant made their way out of the arena they were met by Nick who was accompanied by several of the ranch hands.

"We got here too late for those fifty dollar seats," Nick said.

"Too bad! But then the fight wasn't worth two hoots in Hades anyway. That Gibbons kid was way out of his league with Dempsey," Tom said.

Tom looked around and then took Nick's arm.

"Can you give me and Grant a ride out to the Jenny? I'm so pissed off, I don't even want to talk to Mulroney or O'Halloran until I get a rein on my thoughts."

As they walked to Nick's Ford, Buck sidled up to Grant. "See Gibbon's face after that fight? You're gonna be seein' one just like it in the mirror one of these first mornings."

Ignoring Buck's words Grant climbed into the back of the Ford truck with the ranch hands. Buck sat across from Grant glaring purposefully through squinted eyes. Grant diverted his gaze but he could feel the hate in Buck's stare burning a hole through him.

As Grant climbed out of the truck, Buck said in a low voice, "Be seeing you soon, flatlander."

Although he did not hear what Buck had said, Tom could see anger in Grant's eyes. Deciding to ignore the situation until he could speak to Buck alone, he walked toward the Jenny.

"Me and Grant here is gonna be home before dark. We'll see you fellas tomorrow."

A young cowboy called Elmer had jumped from the truck and stood ready to swing the Jenny's propeller as Tom walked around the plane, checking each cable and every inch of canvas.

Tom then picked up a handful of dust and let it fall slowly through his fingers.

"We'll head that way...into the wind," he said.

He and Grant put on their helmets and goggles and climbed onto the wing.

When they were strapped into the cockpits, Tom gave Elmer the thumbs up sign and the engine coughed and then convulsed, belching smoke before commencing a rhythmic roar. Allowing the engine to warm up, Tom went through his checklist.

He pushed the throttle forward and the Jenny began to taxi into the light wind. They waved at the men in the truck and the Jenny began to pick up speed.

The now familiar sound and feel of the airplane becoming light on her wheels gave Grant a thrill. He allowed himself to relax as he recognized the sensation of the tail lifting off the ground.

Speeding along the dirt road, the plane was about to become airborne when, to Grant's horror, he saw part of a wooden post lying in the roadway ahead. As the Jenny passed over the large piece of wood he heard a loud cracking thump and realized that, although they had hit the post, it had been simultaneous to the airplane lifting off of the ground.

The plane seemed to be flying normally and Grant was unperturbed.

"I think we busted the landin' gear. Can you see that wheel?" Tom shouted.

Grant unfastened his seat belt and raised himself, hanging on tightly, to look over the side. To his dismay he could see a part of the left wheel turned sideways and hanging by the retaining wire.

"It's broken," he said.

"How bad does it look?" Tom said.

Grant turned his hand to describe for Tom the condition of the wheel.

"It's turned like this and broken clear off the undercarriage."

Tom nodded his head and motioned Grant to sit down and put his on his safety belt. He did not seem to be concerned, giving Grant cause to relax. Surely, he thought, Tom knew exactly what to do.

"I'll worry about it when we get home," he heard Tom shout from the rear seat.

The late afternoon air was clear with bumpy convection currents causing Grant to grasp the wooden cockpit frame with every jolt. He could hear the dangling wheel bumping against broken wood with each bounce.

Grant would have thoroughly enjoyed the flight as the coulees slid smoothly beneath the JN-4, except that the thought of having to land with no left wheel was building into dread. Realizing he was holding a death grip on the wooden frame, he consciously forced himself to relax.

When they had been in the air about forty minutes, Grant noticed that Tom was making a slow sweeping turn.

"Everything you can see down there is The Buffalo Rock Ranch," he heard Tom say. "I'm gonna fly around a little while and burn off some of this gasoline...we sure as hell don't need it on this landing."

Cattle dotted the landscape, assembling in the coulees where they watered in small creeks. Elk, antelope and deer scurried at the sight and sound of the approaching plane.

Tom turned to fly along a row of bluffs broken by pastures where men waved at the plane from small covered wagons, which were their homes, as they tended herds of sheep.

Grant could hear the broken wheel make another cracking sound as Tom banked the plane steeply to fly low over a large brown bear running from a bloody black and white carcass.

"Calf killin' son-of-a-bitch! I reckon that'll ruin his dinner," Tom shouted.

The huge bear ran into the cover of a grove of trees.

Just beyond the grove, Grant could see an Indian tipi beside a small lake. Buffalo were feeding and rolling in the dust on the hills around the lake.

"Are Indians living there?" he shouted over his shoulder.

"No, that's my hideout," Tom shouted back. "When I get sick of people, I come out here and do a little fishin' and look at my buffalo and pretend that things never changed."

Tom's cavalier tone in the exchange gave Grant a sense of confidence. How serious could this be? Tom did not seem the least upset.

They passed over the tipi and lake and soon Grant could see the Missouri River ahead. When he saw the buildings of a small town in the distance, he realized that it was The Compound.

His stomach again tightened and he could feel the trepidation rising. He knew that the moment of truth was drawing near. Unconsciously he grasped the wooden frame on the inside of the cockpit. He realized that his entire body was shaking with anticipation of the unavoidable meeting of machine and earth.

Tom made several very low passes over The Compound to get the attention of anyone who might be available.

Grant could see people emerging from the houses and mess hall pointing at the airplane. Holding their hands cupped around their mouths, Grant knew they were making warning shouts, but they could not be heard.

"I think they are telling us that the plane is falling apart," Grant shouted.

Tom made a wide turn and then aligned the nose of the Jenny with the dirt road, which ran through The Compound. An American flag flying on the mess hall indicated that he was headed into the wind.

"Thank God the wind is right," Tom shouted. "At least I got the sun at my back. I'll need to see everything I can for this here landin'. Hang on tight and cross your fingers."

Grant's apprehension rose in direct proportion to the Jenny's altitude. His knuckles were blanched white, holding to the frame. He watched the details of the gravel road grow ever larger as he peered over the nose of the crippled aircraft. Having no control he could only watch as the red handle of the throttle moved toward him and the engine slowed to an idle.

When the Jenny's right wheel touched down, Grant could feel the rumble of gravel against the rubber surface of the tire. He could also hear the intermittent scraping of the broken landing gear bouncing on the gravel surface and hitting the bottom of the plane. The Jenny flew along the dirt road for some distance in an upright attitude, tail high as Tom used the throttle to add intermittent spurts of power.

Grant was just beginning to feel a sense of relief when the left wing dipped toward the ground as the broken landing gear bit into the dirt. Catching the brush beside the road, the wing crumpled, spinning the plane into a ground looping halt. The Jenny came to rest, nearly inverted, with the tail in the air and the propeller plowing dirt as it brought the engine to an abrupt stop.

Momentarily stunned and disoriented, Grant found himself hanging head down, held by the seat belt. Surprised that he felt no pain, he was having difficulty seeing. Blinded, he wiped at his goggles and then ran his hands quickly over his head in an attempt to discover the source of the wet sticky warmth.

Grant ripped the goggles from his face and looked quickly around. Covered in blood, he could smell the strong odor of gasoline and see the liquid fuel pooling on the ground beneath the hot engine. Panic gripped him. He tore at the seat belt wildly attempting to free himself from the imminent inferno. When the seat belt at last released he tumbled headlong to the ground scrambling like a wild thing escaping the jaws of a predator.

Stopping some yards from the plane, he looked back to assess the damage. He could see that Tom was hanging motionless from his seatbelt in the rear cockpit. Feeling thoughtless and cowardly, he ran back to the Jenny and climbed onto the wreckage. Reaching into Tom's cockpit, Grant hastily unfastened the seat belt, all the while praying that the airplane did not burst into flames. As the belt loosed its hold, Tom began to fall and Grant became aware of another person helping to catch the old pilot's limp body as he slid from the Jenny's cockpit.

Grant lifted Tom's legs as the other man grasped him under the armpits. The two carried him a safe distance before laying him gently on the ground. Tom's face was covered with blood from a gash on the forehead sustained when the Jenny came to its violent rest.

Grant took an inventory and realized that he was uninjured. The blood on his face had come from the wound on Tom's head, dripping on him as they hung in their seat belts.

Tom's eyes slowly opened. Still dazed, he looked around at the crowd that was quickly gathering.

Grant felt himself pushed aside as Susanna, who had run from her house, knelt by her father's side.

Dixie, out of breath from her sprint, fell to her knees beside her uncle.

"Give me something to put under his head," Dixie said.

"Can you hear me dad?" Susanna asked.

"I can hear you. I reckon I must not be dead."

Susanna put her head on Tom's chest and gave him a hug.

"Please don't fly that thing any more. You're going to get yourself killed in that contraption."

Susanna had barely finished her sentence when the Jenny erupted in flame, wood and fabric fueling a withering inferno, accelerated by the gasoline.

Tom raised himself onto one elbow to watch his treasured Jenny disintegrate into a pile of ashes.

"Well, I won't be flyin' her for a while, I reckon that's for sure," Tom said.

A Ford pickup truck stopped close to where Tom was lying and several men walked toward him.

"You alive, boss?" one of the men inquired of his blood covered employer.

"I'll live," Tom replied as the men lifted him to his feet.

Tom shook his head and pursed his lips. He took one last look at the crumbling remains of his airplane, then turned from the searing heat as Susanna and one of the ranch hands assisted him to the back of the truck.

Others in the crowd were also moving away from the scorching heat as Dixie walked to Grant and put her hand to his head searching for the source of the blood.

"Now let me see what's wrong with you," she said.

"I didn't get a scratch. All of this blood came from your uncle's head."

"Well, that's a fine how do you do," she fumed. "I don't know why I'm concerned anyway. You're old enough to know better than to fly around the countryside on a dilapidated assortment of wood, wires and canvas."

Grant was stammering in an attempt to answer Dixie's tirade when the man who had helped him remove Tom from the Jenny stuck out his hand.

"I'm Remus Horsens. You must be that newspaper fella they've all been talkin' about."

Grant shook Remus' hand.

"Yes, sir. My name is Grant Collins. Pleased to make your acquaintance."

Grant looked at the man with a quizzical stare.

"You met Rom. He's my twin brother. That's why you think you've met me before."

"That's right, Rom told me he had a brother," Grant said.

Remus then turned to Dixie.

"This boy still looks a little wobbly legged to me. He did save Uncle Tom's life you know. I reckon you could throw a little slack in that rope."

"I'm sorry," she said, taking Grant's arm. "I was just worried about you and I let my emotions get the better of me. Can you walk?"

"I'll be fine," Grant said, thankful that Remus had interceded.

Remus and Dixie escorted Grant to the truck. A young cowboy drove them all to Tom's house where several of the ranch hands helped Tom into the house. As they came into the entryway, Koko, who had obviously been crying, put her arms around Tom's neck and gave him a long embrace.

"Old fool," she said as she released her hug and walked away.

"I still love you too darlin'," Tom said as she disappeared down the hall.

The men helped Tom to his room as Susanna called Doctor Philburn in Fort Benton for advice on the care of her father's injuries.

"Damned if you must'a drove a hundred miles an hour," Tom said as the the doctor entered his room.

"You're one of the few in the country who can afford to pay my bill," Dr. Philburn said, looking at the laceration on Tom's forehead. "I can't pass an opportunity like that. Besides, you got me for thirty-three dollars at that poker game."

Dr. Philburn stitched Tom's head and gave him an envelope of pain pills.

"Tom," Dr. Philburn said in a serious tone. "You have a pretty bad concussion. I'd advise taking it easy for a few weeks. I know you hate to hear it but you aren't getting any younger."

Tom smiled at his old friend as he looked up with a smile.

"I reckon to throw the first handful of dirt on your coffin and maybe outlive another sawbones in this town before I'm done," he said.

Dr. Philburn returned the smile with a twinkle in his eye.

"You may do it at that, but for the next few weeks, take it easy," the doctor said.

Susanna knew that her father was injured more seriously than he would admit by the mere fact that he was willing to stay in bed.

14

Other than brief visits to offer his best wishes and concern, Grant left Tom to rest and recover. He spent much of his time during the next week transcribing notes, attempting to record each detail of Tom's stories while they were still fresh in his mind.

He did feel some sense of guilt at using the opportunity of Tom's disability to spend time with Dixie. Her obvious display of concern at the plane crash had encouraged him. The two spent many hours together discussing their families, commonalties and differences, acquaintances and friends, likes and dislikes, their ambitions and hopes for the future.

Time passed all too quickly as Grant found himself surrendering to an unreasoned giddy euphoria he felt each time he thought of this intelligent, self assured and elegantly beautiful young woman. Every waking moment seemed to be spent in arranging the occasion of his next opportunity to be alone with Dixie. He had never before enjoyed the company of another person in the way he felt this need to be in her presence.

Early one morning Grant sat at the small desk in his room. He was enjoying the cool morning breeze coming through the window and filling pages with notes. The morning sun provided perfect illumination for his transcription. His heart raced at the sound of the knock at his door. Dixie had suggested the previous evening that they might take a ride around the ranch one day. He nearly ran to the door in his borrowed slippers.

"Are ya up and about, boy?" Tom said as Grant opened the door.

"Yes, sir," he answered, hoping that the disappointment in his voice was not apparent.

"When you're ready, come on down to my den. I'm feelin' a world better today. Maybe we can get ya caught up before you forget all of what I told ya before. I know you're anxious to get this writin' done and head on back to civilization."

"I'll be right down," Grant replied.

He dressed quickly and retrieved his notebook.

Walking down the stairs he was thinking how wrong Tom was. He suddenly had no desire to go back to Saint Louis, or anywhere else in 'civilization' for that matter. Staying at The Buffalo Rock Ranch suited him just fine.

Grant had not previously gone into Tom's office. The room was, to his amazement, a fascinating dichotomy of modern business paraphernalia and museum quality antiquities. An Edison dictation machine next to the Underwood typewriter on a portable table in one corner with the telephone and a neatly kept set of books on Tom's desk, seemed in stark contrast to the exhibits of Aboriginal artifacts adorning the walls and hung from the ceiling.

Koko entered with sweet rolls and coffee, which she placed on a small table in front of a leather sofa. Ignoring the two men she entered and left the room like a soundless apparition.

Grant prowled the room, absorbing the unusual displays which represented the history of the life of his new friend. A gamut of weapons, from stone headed spears and antler adorned war clubs, to beautifully engraved modern firearms, were displayed so that Tom could see them when seated at his desk. Grant hoped that Tom would give him a complete explanation of the ceremonies and stories surrounding the feathers, bones, wood and stones which comprised the primitive creations.

Even more intriguing were the photographs, many with signed inscriptions. Buffalo Bill Cody, Annie Oakley, Chief Sitting Bull and President Theodore Roosevelt were prominently pictured in Tom's company at various places and stages of his life. Any lingering doubt of the old man's veracity was completely annulled as Grant slowly scoured every inch of each display with a critical eye. The very room was bona fides, in and of itself.

Tom seated himself in a large leather arm chair and gestured for Grant to have a seat.

"Sorry I ain't been of much count as a host the last little bit," Tom said, pouring coffee and offering Grant a sweet roll. "Maybe Sus is right, maybe I am gettin' too old for my flyin' machine. But then I reckon that's a moot discussion since there ain't nothin' left but a few wires and a scalded engine. I'll miss her though. I may have to get me a new one."

"I'm just thankful that you're alright," Grant said. "I have to admit that I acted in a very cowardly way after the plane crashed. When we were ready to land, I was very frightened. When I smelled the gasoline after the crash, I ran away like a rabbit and left you there in the plane. It took every ounce of effort I could muster to go back onto the wreck."

"Well, son, you didn't have no corner on bein' scared. I reckon my stomach had a few knots in it when we was glidin' onto that road. But I was worried most about hurtin' you. I'm glad you was alright...and as to bein' cowardly, let me tell you somethin'. Every man is afraid when his life is in danger. It ain't bein' afraid that makes a man a coward, it's what he does when he's afraid that makes a man what he is. Now the way I hear tell, you done a mighty brave thing out there. Which I reckon makes you a hero. So don't go sellin' yourself short."

Tom stared for a moment, lost in thought.

"I was tryin' to remember last night where I'd come to in the story of the Pony Express. That rap on the noggin seems to have befuddled my thoughts. I've been tryin' to tell the story in the order in which things occurred so as to not get too confused. I think I told ya about the pigeons. Right?"

"As a matter of fact I was just transcribing my notes and you were telling Mr. Mulroney and me about your conversion to full fledged American citizenship after your incarceration following the battle at Cabin Creek."

"I'm with ya now. I've had some really odd dreams the last few days. Yes, sir...let's see now. After I was swore in, they gave me some Yankee money as the regular enlistment bonus and a brand new blue uniform. They told me to get shed of that gray coat. They also gave me a brand new Colt's forty-four Army revolver, which they said I was supposed to return to 'em when my two years as a scout was over. In fact that's the one right there."

Tom pointed to a pistol on the wall. Without pausing to elaborate he continued.

"One of the first things I did when they let me outta that stockade and off that post was to go to Fort Smith and find myself some regular civilian clothes. Scouts wasn't required to wear the uniform and I'd about had all of the standin' tall in a uniform as I could endure. I really preferred buckskins, when they could be found, and of course the buckskins sort'a made the image of the scout. A fella had to look the part you know. Unfortunately, during the war years in the East, it was downright difficult to come by even so much as a hide shirt. I was forced to settle for a wool jacket, some wool britches and a cotton shirt.

While I was in town in Fort Smith buyin' duds I run across a Yankee veteran who was beggin' in the store. Poor fella was missin' his right arm. Said his whole outfit got caught nappin' by Stonewall Jackson's boys at a place called Front Royal. He reckoned as how he'd run about six miles with his arm blowed off. The arm was gone just above the elbow. He surely didn't want to end up in one of those Confederate prisoner camps.

When he got back to the Union lines the doctors cut off what was left of his arm and then the army cut him loose. They'd told the poor bastard he was of no more use to 'em. He was feelin' pretty sorry for himself and I couldn't say as how I blamed him none...lookin' back on it now. Seems he'd been a farmer before the war but he didn't want to go home and be a burden to his folks. So he'd headed west to see if he couldn't seek his fortune in the territories. But it looked to me like all he'd found so far was the bottom of a bottle. I felt sorry for him, sure enough, but I was a callow and self centered newly minted scout who was all full of himself and that one armed fella was carryin' a nearly new Henry repeatin' rifle. Did you ever hear about those?"

Grant shook his head.

Tom pointed to a brass framed lever action rifle hanging above the pistol.

"The Confederate troops really hated that rifle, except when they could liberate one from a dead Yankee of course. They called it 'That damned Yankee rifle they load on Sunday and shoot all week.' You've got to remember that most of the shootin' irons of the day was muzzle stuffers. The regular issue for both sides was a fifty-eight caliber rifled musket. A really good soldier could load and shoot about three times a minute...maybe four, so a repeatin' breech loader was really prized. I surely took a shine to that gun, figuring there was goin' to be some Injun fightin' in my future. I had that enlistment money they'd gave me when I converted, so I thought maybe I could buy that rifle. Now I had no intention of takin' advantage of a cripple, but I noticed right off that he had a problem handlin' that rifle, bein' as how he only had one arm and all. So I reckoned in a way I might be doin' the man a favor takin' it off his hand."

"How positively Christian of you," Grant said with a smile.

"Like I said, he was beggin' for drinkin' money. So I told him I wouldn't give him charity just for drinkin', but that I was willin' to bargain on that rifle. I explained my situation and told him I was headin' out west to be a scout and that I'd likely be fightin' Injuns. I reckon, after all, he needed that whiskey more than he needed that rifle, because he didn't negotiate too long before strikin' a bargain and headin' for the nearest saloon.

As I recall it now, I wasn't there at Fort Smith but a few more weeks when several companies of Ohio cavalrymen intended as replacements for a Colorado Cavalry outfit, rode into the fort on their way west. They was there a day or so when the Colonel who had proselytized me for the Union sent for me and said that I would be assigned to the Ohio boys to act as their guide and scout. He introduced me to that Ohio Colonel who showed me a big Army map. He pointed to where he was supposed to be takin' his troopers. I knew pretty well where it was as I had ridden close to the place when I with the Pony Express. I figured it couldn't be too far south and west of where the old Julesberg Express Station had been."

"Where was the Julesberg Station, today that is? What state?" Grant asked.

"It's in northern Colorado. I had talked to a couple of scouts about that country and in lookin' at that map, I decided to take those boys right up the Platte River country. The terrain out across Nebraska and eastern Colorado is just a big ol' flat prairie. Flatter than a stomped fritter with occasional bluffs on the sides of the old river channel. I figured it would be the easiest country to cross with the supply wagons and it was the best ridin' and the best grazin', plus we would have water for the stock on the trip west, which I figured was gonna be about eight weeks with this column of cheechakos strung out half way to Arkansas.

Now the South Platte really ain't much of a river...as rivers go. It's shallow and muddy, dependin' on the time of the year. One of the honyockers who'd come up the Platte with a wagon train said of that river, 'It was too thick to drink and too thin to plow.' The main thing that I didn't like about the look of the country was that the hostiles could get on a piece of high ground, such as there was, and see you comin' for twenty miles, especially with the dust that column of farmers was raisin'.

There were two things that changed a lot during my time with them Ohio soldier boys. First of all, when the word got around that I was freshly converted to salutin' the Stars and Stripes, them blue bellies was a might bit suspicious as to my loyalties. I'll be gettin' around to how that come to change in a minute.

The other change that occurred amongst them boys was their attitude about service on the Western frontier. You see, those plow boys and their commander didn't know war paint from wheel grease about Injuns. They only knew what they'd read in the newspaper and what the Army had told 'em. At first they was happy about goin' west, havin' heard the casualty numbers from places like Antietam Creek and Gettysburg, they figured they was gettin' outta the real fightin'. Once we got to Injun country, those boys learned quick that those 'savages' wasn't no pushovers neither. They also found out that them Injuns didn't line up in nice straight ranks and come marchin' in to be mowed down like wheat. Not like those poor bastards in Pickett's outfit at Gettysburg. That movie hoo-hah about those Injuns riding around like gallery ducks while the cowboys shoot 'em off their horses is plain ridiculous. The Injuns was brave, sure enough, but they wasn't stupid.

Because of my concerns about our visibility and gettin' my outfit ambushed, I always kept a sharp eye out for movement on the ridges and smoke and such. As we began to get into Cheyenne country, I'd ride on out ahead of the column, sometimes I'd get two or three days out, just to see what might be brewin'. On those scoutin' trips I would usually take three or four of the soldier suits with me to use as messengers just in case I had to get word back to the Colonel in a hurry.

Now, remember that I was only nearin' sixteen by then and these soldiers were usually a couple of years older than me, so even though they was kids themselves it would really rankle them that I was telling 'em what to do, me not bein' an officer or nothin', especially with me bein' a Reb convert and a kid myself…and besides which, they just plain didn't trust me.

For some reason, the hair was standin' up on the back of my neck one morning and I told the Colonel that I was goin' out to do some lookin'. I got me five soldier suit volunteers and headed up river to have a look see. We'd rode all day without seein' nothin' and it was gettin' late in the afternoon. I had those cheechakos ridin' single file and real slow just below a ridge on some wooded high ground. That hair on my neck was still up and I was lookin' for sign and a secure place to hole up for the night. Off yonder, down by the river, I seen some smoke and when I put my glasses on it I could see what appeared to be a pretty busy lookin' Injun camp with a good sized remuda feedin' near by.

I took my boys and I dropped off into the low ground and put the sneak on that camp just to see if'n I could get a closer look. I bellied down on the backside of a hill about a half a mile away and looked 'em over real good with my binoculars. I didn't see no women and no kids. Just men, and they was loungin' around by the fires and cookin' their own food and such. They'd built some wickiups and they had some deer carcasses hangin', but I could tell it wasn't no village. I'd seen enough of Injuns to figure this was likely as not a war party which had seen my column and was just layin' in wait for us to ride into their ambush. I picked one of the soldier boys, who was ridin' a big ol' long legged bay horse that appeared capable of runnin'. I told that boy to ride back to the column quick as he could and tell the Colonel that we was about to encounter our first hostile action. Then I took the other four and found a creek comin' down from the trees. There was a little canyon near the top, which I figured would hide us till the Colonel got close with the column.

Then I told them soldier boys to ease up and get some rest and we ate hard tack and watered the animals and then I had the boys let our critters graze just keep 'em quiet. We took turns gettin' some shut eye and then a while after mid-night I slipped down to have another look.

I was expectin' to see a sleepin' camp, but when I looked over that hill, the fires was burnin' bright and in my glasses I could see that they was gettin' ready for somethin'. They was cookin' and eatin' and readyin' themselves to leave that place. I hurried back up the canyon and told the boys to saddle up. I told 'em we was gonna charge them redskins."

Tom smiled when Grant looked up from his notes.

"I could see the ghostly white of fear on their sunburned young faces glowin' in the dark. They was one scared bunch...but then so was I.

Fortunately, there was a slight breeze blowin' in our direction. I didn't want them Injun ponies catchin' wind of us and raisin' a ruckus before I could get my plan into operation. We walked our critters down behind that hill and I went to have another look and sure enough those Injuns was finishin' eatin' and packin' up. It was clear that they was fixin' to ride and I didn't want them boys on horse back without me knowin' exactly where they was. I figured they'd have a few of the hard to catch horses and a dominant mare hobbled or tied, but the rest was just loose in a grassy meadow near the river.

Now it was about half a mile to that camp so I set them four soldier boys, two on each side so that we was five abreast and about fifty yards apart. I told them to ride real easy until they heard me shoot. That was to be the signal to charge. When we was about two hundred yards from that meadow, I let out a holler like a Blackfoot and fired a shot while I was putting the spurs to my horse. I know them others was scared, but bless their hearts they stayed right with me, shootin' and hootin'.

Them Injuns didn't know whether to wipe asses or skeedadle. With the exception of about eight or ten head, which was hobbled or tied, we ran off their whole remuda...fifty or so head I'd reckon. That, of course, put most of them Injuns afoot. We proceeded to run them animals clean out of the area before any of the Injuns could get mounted and make a pursuit."

Tom smiled at his at the recollection.

"Besides, I think they was plum bumfuzzled and didn't want to go chasin' into the darkness not knowin' what they was chasin' after."

"Were these Cheyennes that had planned the ambush?" Grant asked.

"Turned out that they wasn't plannin' no ambush at all...at least no ambush of my column. We rounded up the herd and drove them ponies around the back side of a low mesa, so as to head back toward the column. About five miles from the Injun camp it started to get light and we come across a herd of buffalo feeding toward the river. When I finally got to lookin' at the horses I realized that they wasn't Cheyenne. They was Ute ponies. Then I put two and two together.

The Utes lived way south of where we were and they wasn't too welcome by the Cheyennes, but it was comin' on fall and they was on a buffalo hunt to get winter meat to see 'em through. It occurred to me that they hadn't pursued because they figured it was Cheyennes that had run off their horses and they didn't want a war. I'll bet they was pissed off at daylight when they saw shod ponies had run off the stock and knew it was whites what had done it."

"So they were only waiting to ambush the buffalo when they came close to the river and they were completely unaware of your army column?" Grant said. "Were your comrades disappointed to learn that there had been no danger?"

"Hell's fire, I never told 'em."

Tom chuckled when Grant looked up.

"Them plow pushers didn't know a Ute from a Fugawi anyways. I just kept my mouth shut and let them tell the story when we got back to the main column. We had; after all, acquired near fifty head of horses for use by the United States Cavalry and diverted an imminent attack. At least that's what my citation said when they gave me and my soldier suits a medal. Them soldier boys began to show me a whole new respect.

Wasn't no way I was gonna spill that stew pot. Fact is, I was always sort'a proud, not of that medal but of my comrades and of their deed. Hell's fire, how many men do you know that would have ridden into a camp full of hostiles to run off their stock without regard to life or limb? And the thing I was really proud of was that somehow I managed to get that circus of an army column all the way to Colorado without losing a single one of my soldiers."

The door to Tom's den opened.

"How's your head doing Dad. Still got bees a buzzin'?" Nick asked.

"No, son, I think I'm gonna live. Come on in."

Nick entered and took a seat at the coffee table.

"Coffee's all gone I reckon," Tom said.

"Don't matter," Nick said. "Koko's cookin' some steaks and taters for lunch and I just stopped by to see if we needed to make funeral arrangements."

"No, sir, I think the hole under my shithouse will remain empty for a bit longer. Anyways, I was just tellin' Grant about my days with the Army as scout down in Colorado. How long we got till lunch?"

"It'll be a few minutes," Nick said. "Go on with the story. I don't think I have heard much of this myself."

"Well you see, I'd taken a bunch of Ohio Cavalry up the Platte into Colorado country and we'd had it pretty soft as far as the Injuns was concerned on the ride west. However, when we did get to Camp Collins, as it was known at the time, the troubles was intensifyin'. Over the next couple of years I lost a bunch of those young troopers. We were at it with the Cheyennes and the Arapahos almost constantly.

Now them southern Injuns weren't a whole lot different than the Blackfoot. They had some different ceremonies and the language wasn't exactly the same but all in all they had come from the same ancestry and it wasn't hard for me to figure 'em out, havin' been around the Blackfoot as much as I had. One thing was sure, they'd steal anything that wasn't growin' a ten foot tap root and they took big delight in hangin' around just out of gunshot range and givin' them Easterners a bad case of the vapors.

I'd reckon I must'a been in a hundred skirmishes during those next couple'a years. I wouldn't even try to remember 'em all. One I can recall because it was the clincher for me as far as gettin' the respect of the soldier suits and it also involved that Henry rifle."

Grant walked to where the rifle hung on the wall for a closer look.

"If the Civil War was still in progress, why were they sending all of these soldiers to Colorado?" he asked.

"Settlers and gold. The settlers and miners was movin' to the country and they was complaining to the government about the Injuns. Of course, it wasn't helpin' none that some of the assholes who was complainin' was shootin' Injuns just for sport. Any Injun showin' up around what those white folks considered to be their private property would get their hides ventilated. Those Southern Cheyennes took real exception to being shot on sight and they was causin' a lot of problems all around that part of the country. There was one chief by the name of Roman Nose who had a big followin' of tough dog soldiers. Seemed as though they loved nothin' better than a good fight and what with the settler's avarice and stupidity, Roman Nose wasn't plannin' on makin' peace with nobody. That country suited them Cheyennes and Arapahos just like it was and they was willing to fight to keep it that way. Then there was the huntin'. Buffalo was at the root of it. The hunting rights and who owned the land. Those were the things that the fightin' was mostly about in the West.

But there were two old chiefs who were trying to make peace. Ol' Lean Bear and Black Kettle could see that they was losin' the war of attrition. But they was havin' trouble keeping a tight rein on their own young dog soldiers."

"So there was no consensus among the Indians in dealing with the white migration?" Grant asked.

"Politics is politics. Whether it's taking place in a buffalo hide tipi or a big dome in Washington City. Have you ever seen any group of human bein's who could come to a consensus? It's damned hard to get two men to agree as to where to go get a drink, if they're given a choice."

"If I may interrupt," Grant said, looking Tom, "what is a dog soldier?"

"These men were the toughest of the tough, the bravest of the brave.

They were members of a warrior society like King Arthur's Knights of the Round Table. They were assigned the dubious distinction of being the last line of defense for the villages. Like the knights with their chivalry, these men had a code of their own. They wore a sash around their waist to identify to all that they were among the honored few, and each man carried a sacred arrow in his quiver. When one of these men walked through a village, the children were in awe of him like the kids of today might be in awe of Dempsey.

Now that sash they wore, it drug on the ground, and it was like that for a purpose. When they were called to duty to defend the village, they would take that sacred arrow out of their quiver and nail that sash to the ground. Talk about your last stand...that was it. Once he'd nailed that sash to ground, he could either win the day or die right there fightin'. Tough bastards!"

Grant was writing as fast as he could when Koko opened the door. The men all rose and followed her to the dining room.

"I'll tell you more about Black Kettle in a bit...but I have another story to tell you first. Now this requires me givin' you a little background information, so you can understand why this here incident happened.

You see, when the army built a fort, the first few months was generally easy pickins as far as huntin' meat for the men, fodder for the livestock and firewood, the resources necessary to the maintenance of a large number of men and animals. With each day that passed them resources got a little farther away. Once that fort was established it wouldn't be long till they would have to send men for miles to obtain those resources. Once the game like deer and elk and buffalo was shot out and the grass all grazed and the wood was burned, it required a trek to get those things. Contrary to what you might have seen in the motion pictures, them Injuns wasn't complete fools. They knew that all they had to do was wait and pretty soon a bunch of greenhorns from Ohio would be straggling away from the revetments in search of hay or firewood without so much as a thought the presence of them hostiles."

Tom looked at Grant with a huge smile.

"No, sir...those Injuns did not know that these soldiers was from Ohio."

"I got it," Grant said, as they all laughed.

"One mornin' the Captain told me to go with a detachment of troops, which was to be led by a young lieutenant by the name Braithwaite. Now Braithwaite was older'n me but he was still no more than a kid officer. I was a kid but I'd lived a lot in my sixteen or so years. He was a kid who had been to school and that's all.

I don't think we had any West Point officers on that post, least as I recall. The army had all the best of their officers fightin' the War of the Rebellion and the Injun's wasn't any too much the concern of ol' Honest Abe in sixty-three and sixty-four. So we got boys like Braithwaite, who was supposed to lead soldiers. Bein' sworn to my duty, I done what the Captain said and went to saddle my cayuse. It was another one of them mornings when the hair began to stand up on the back of my neck. I ain't never been real superstitious, but somethin' told me to take along some extra ammunition.

I'd made it a habit that whenever I could get 'em I would stock up on the cartridges for that Henry rifle. Some of the men would kind'a joke with me about bein' the regimental armorer, or bein' a packrat, but I figured I'd keep a store none the less. I grabbed a couple of leather pouches full of them cartridges and put one in each saddle bag before we left on our wood gatherin' chore. There was a small stand of mixed timber some miles from the fort and I led that lieutenant and the boys over there where they commenced to choppin' and loadin' pack mules and wagons.

Braithwaite was standin' around there real official like and I was kind'a helpin' the boys tie the packs on the mules when I saw some Injuns out about four or five hundred yards.

Braithwaite hollers 'Mr. Thomas, do you see the hostiles?' I could tell by the tone in his voice that he was lookin' to win himself a medal. 'Yes, sir, lieutenant. I see 'em just fine. And if'n ya want my advice you'll leave 'em be.' Course, he wasn't havin' none of my advice. He starts to shout orders, tellin' the bugler to sound assembly, and gettin' the men mounted. I could see that he was intent on pursuit. He was near frothin' at the mouth when I rode up beside him and tried to calm the boy down. I tried to explain that those Injuns was just decoys and that somewhere in those surrounding arroyos there was gonna be a whole bunch who wouldn't look quite so defenseless up close.

'If you are afraid to fight Indians Mr. Thomas,' he says in his best patronizin' tone, 'then why don't you ride back to the fort and let these brave men do their duty without your interference.'

Now had I been about half smart I would'a done just exactly that. In fact, knowin' that none of them boys was gonna tell this story anyway, I could'a just rode on outta there and gone to California and the army brass would'a figured I'd been taken by the hostiles. They would'a gave me one of them posthumous medals that a fella gets when he's dead and I could'a been a free man. I'll never understand what it is inside a man that makes him do really stupid things in the name of God and country and his fellow human beings. Knowin' full well that I was gonna be dead by afternoon I pulled in beside that arrogant prick, said a prayer and was preparin' to ride 'Half a league, half a league, Into the Valley of Death, Not to make reply, Just to do and die.'"

Grant again found himself surprised at the erudition of his ill spoken friend.

"Did you enjoy Tennyson?" Grant asked in surprise.

"Some," Tom answered. "But real men don't die in glory. Those poems by Kipling and Tennyson? By God, you'd think that the rattle of the battle was a wonderful thing. Well, I hope to shout that it ain't. It's a terrible thing and I'm happy that Nicky and the other boys didn't have to experience that particular thrill. Of course, my youngest son would love to go to war...but..."

Tom stopped, allowing the thought to fade into silence.

"Maybe I'll read that Tennyson fella," Nick said. "I might'a missed somethin'."

"You ought'a read Tennyson. He's worth the time. But take my word for it son, you didn't miss nothin'when it comes to war.

Anyway, sure enough them Injuns went exactly where I'd figured they was goin', right up the mouth of a big curvin' coulee with steep sides that was perfect for an ambush. Before we got too far into that mess, I signaled a halt and bein' the scout all the men stopped. Ol' Braithwaite come ridin' back to me just madder'n hell.

'Mr. Thomas, we have them cornered now. Why are you stopping,' he says loud enough for the whole Cheyenne Nation to hear. So I try to explain to the dumb bastard just what this here coulee, which I had previously scouted, looked like and why it might be a good idea to put some troopers along the ridge on each side, just in case. He starts spoutin' a bunch of falderal about splittin' his force and military tactics when the old Sergeant decided as how maybe he wasn't lookin' to get kilt that day neither. He tells Braithwaite, in a real respectful tone, that he was in agreement with the scout and that it might be a good idea to get some troopers on the high ground so as to prevent the escape of them savages from the coulee.

I suppose my diplomacy wasn't near as good as that ol' Sergeant's, but then he'd been kissin' them brass asses a whole lot longer'n I had. I took a couple'a men with me, and that Sergeant took a couple with him up the other side and it was agreed that Braithwaite would keep the troopers quiet and in place until we'd got into position on the reverse slope on the tops of the ridges on either side. We synchronized our watches and decided that about forty minutes would give us time.

Now ol' Braithwaite was sure enough bound and determined to have his scalp adornin' the lodge pole of one of them Cheyenne warriors. Twenty minutes hadn't passed...hell, we hadn't got half way around the ridge when I can hear the shootin' start. I told the boys with me to hurry along and we finally got to the top of the ridge. But by then that coulee was so full of smoke from all the shootin' that ya could hardly see who was doin' what.

I looked across the coulee and I could see the Sergeant, and he and his boys commenced to cut down on them Cheyenne from his upwind vantage point. About then I heard one of the fellas that had come up with me sayin' 'Oh shit,' and a couple of them Cheyennes had come out of the brush and was draggin' him off his horse. I pulled out that Colt forty-four and proceeded to discourage their attack, although not before the trooper had sustained a pretty good head wound from one of them Injun war clubs. He was still conscious so I set him to watchin' our backs, while I put the other two on firing points off a promontory of rock that had a commandin' view of the coulee below.

I remember kind'a laughin' to myself and when one of them troopers asked me what was so funny I told him that there sure wasn't no danger of them Injuns escapin', what with the way we had 'em surrounded and all. I guess it was what they call gallows humor but them boys laughed with me as we rained hell's fire on the 'red heathens.'

The fight had gone on for a few minutes when a good gust blew the smoke clear from the bottom of the coulee and I could see that the Lieutenant and his men were pinned in a brushy wash right in the bottom. They had a little cover but not much, and every time one of the troopers moved he would draw some attention from them Injuns by way of a bullet or an arrow. Within a short time I knew all them troopers was gettin' low on powder and ball because the boys with me sure didn't have much left neither. Thank God the Injuns had mostly bows and arrows and the few firearms they had was old trade rifles.

That was when I was real glad I had decided to bring those extra cartridges. I had what amounted to an artillery position on that promontory with that Henry Rifle, and once the smoke cleared I was able to pour death and destruction on them Cheyennes long after everyone else was seriously short on shootin' materials.

Those Injuns wasn't just sure how many troopers we had up there what with the amount of fire comin' at 'em and I kept movin' around just to keep 'em guessin. That ol' Sergeant had conserved his ammunition too, smart ol' soldier that he was, so between us we was able to convince them Cheyennes to seek refuge away from that coulee bottom. It was a good thing that little breeze kept the air clear or those Cheyennes would have overrun Braithwaite and the boys in short order.

There was three of them poor boys killed and we had five more with wounds that required the attention of the doctor at the fort. Braithwaite got an arrow through his right lung, which earned him a hero badge and trip back to Ohio. There wasn't any of them troopers who was sorry to see his backside. But one thing was for sure. After engangin' in Lieutenant Braithwaite's version of the Charge of the Light Brigade, them troopers looked at me in a whole new way. I never heard another word regardin' bein' a pack rat with them cartridges neither.

I sometimes think of that poor fella with one arm. I wonder whatever become of him? I had never even found out his name or what he was doin' in Fort Smith. But I am glad he was there 'cause otherwise I would never have had that Henry and it sure enough saved a lotta lives during its career with the cavalry."

"When I was a child I would read the dime novels. I often had bad dreams after reading the stories of children dragged from the corn crib and tomahawked by bloodthirsty savages, but then I suppose that there were terrible stories on both sides," Grant said.

"Yep, it was on both sides. We civilized white fellas did our share of givin' little Injun children nightmares as well, and that's the truth. The worst I personally witnessed was in the fall of sixty-four. I'd been a scout a little over a year by then and to tell ya the truth, I'd go to the villages with the officers for one thing or another and it would make this old boy homesick. The look and smell made me want to head for Limpin Calf's village and just be free and wild."

Tom thought a long moment.

"Did you ever notice how smells can bring up memories of things that you'd never have thought of otherwise? Nearly like it runs a motion picture in your head. Well, sir, we'd be in some village and I'd watch the young boys wrestlin' and playin' war and I wished I could see Prairie Dog and eat some of his mama's food and hunt some buffalo that was gonna get used for more than hump'n hide."

"Hump and hide?" Grant asked.

"Back then the white folks had took a hankerin' for buffalo hump stew. They even had it in restaurants and it was quite the thing. Men would kill the buffalos by the hundreds for no more than their hump and the hide. Sometimes they'd take the tongue. Leave the rest to rot on the prairie. Made for lots of feed for the buzzards, jaybirds and magpies, but left the Injuns with empty bellies and tears in their eyes. Like I said before, that's what most of the Injun fightin' was all about. They had the huntin' grounds. We wanted the huntin' grounds. We had more people and more guns than they had and there was no where else for the Injuns to go. We won!"

Tom looked at his plate and sat silently. He then looked at Grant.

"You're talkin' about havin' nightmares as a child, I'll bet there's a little piece of Injun war history which gives those little red skin children a nightmare or two even today. This was that story I was gonna tell you about Black Kettle. It was late fall of sixty-four and we got called up to support a bunch of Colorado volunteers who was supposedly goin' to rout a band of Cheyennes down at a place called Sand Creek.

Now them Cheyennes was lead by a Chief by the name of Black Kettle. I'd met him a couple'a times while I'd been with the Army. Black Kettle knew he couldn't win a war and he just wanted to be left alone. He preached it to his people and he did all he could to live in peace. He even had an American flag flyin' on his lodge. These Colorado Volunteers was commanded by an ambitious religious fruitcake by the name of Chivington. How that crazy bastard ever got into a position of commandin' army troops is just beyond me. I went with my Captain, fella by the name of Soule, to the briefin' and Chivington's intention was clear. Get rid of the Injuns. Captain Soule wrestled with the problem all night and when we got to the Sand Creek camp at dawn, he told all of the regular army troopers to stay out of the fightin' and to shoot only if they was shot at. But they wasn't shot at. The camp was asleep and outside one tipi I could see a great big American flag.

My gut was wrenchin'. Chivington's volunteers was all drunked up and they rode into that village and just started slaughterin' those folks. I thought real serious about shootin' some of Chivington's men, but the army would have had me shot for sure had I done so. I got off my horse and sat there watchin' with tears in my eyes. Little children was beggin' for mercy and them bastards just stove in their heads, laughin' all the while. I could see ol' Black Kettle runnin' around wavin' that big ol' American flag of his. How he kept from bein' kilt was a mystery to me.

I finally just turned away. When the shootin' died down Captain Soule ordered his troopers to head back to the fort. A couple weeks later ol' Chivington is writin' letters to Washington and makin' speeches sayin' as how Captain Soule and his soldiers is a bunch of cowards who had run away from that glorious battle at Sand Creek without takin' a scalp. The city of Denver put on a parade for Chivington and his volunteers and those murderin' poltroons displayed their hard won scalps for all the good citizens to see. Made them cheechako sodbusters real happy but they had no idea what had really happened.

Now to really pull the cork outta the jug, ol' Chivington finagled a deal to have that Captain Soule come into Denver. Conveniently for Chivington, Captain Soule got himself murdered while he was in that fair city. Rumor had it that it was one of Chivington's pals who done the dirty deed.

I heard that the murderer was passin' through on his way to California and Chivington covered his tracks. Captain Soule got branded a coward and the whole incident got reported to Washington as a victory for the Colorado Volunteers.

It was a damned good thing justice had her blindfold on tight that day. Of course, that stirred up the Cheyenne dog soldiers and we had a whole new Injun war to fight. I did what I could to keep my boys alive over the next year and I kilt me a bunch of Injuns, but I had lost any illusion that killin' Injuns was a glorious enterprise...as you have probably noticed by this 'eclectic' family."

Tom sat sat silently for a long moment looking into space.

"I was comin' up on my eighteenth birthday and I'd already had three relatively successful careers. I was about to end the obligation to the United States government, which I had signed back in Fort Smith, and I had no idea as to what I was gonna do next. It was lookin' as if I was about to become an eighteen year old has been. One thing, however, had been eatin' at me for the past six years and that was the whereabouts of my little sister. I'd put on some size and I considered myself a man by that time. I thought maybe I'd go have a look see as to where she was and what had happened to her. Besides, like I said, I was also kind'a homesick for to see ol' Limpin Calf's village and my friends, especially Rides With White Boy who I called Prairie Dog. I wanted to see how he'd growed up and if'n he'd even remember me at all.

Just by coincidence, that spring the Army sent me with a detachment of troops to the Dakota Territory where Ol' Red Cloud's Sioux was raisin' hell over the buildin' of forts on the Bozeman Trail. The gold fever was spreadin' to Montana and Ol' Bozeman had staked a trail that was openin' the new gold fields around what is now Helena.

The trouble was that the Bozeman Trail ran right through the Powder River huntin' grounds and the Lakota, and ol' Red Cloud was none too happy with that idea. Not only that, but the Sand Creek massacre was still stirrin' up the warriors of the whole Sioux Nation. Ol' Chivington had sure enough given them redskins all the excuse they needed to kill white folks. So here I was headed back to Montana, but I wasn't plannin' on bein' with the army for long. I now had me a clear mission. I was gonna find my little sister."

"Did you desert again?" Grant asked with a smile.

"Hell, no! My time was near up and I had told 'em when we left Colorado headin' to the Bozeman Trail that we was gonna part company at the end of July. So the Colonel had brought along another scout to replace me. He wasn't no where near as good as me, but he was a scout."

Tom smiled at Grant and Nick with a twinkle in his eye.

"I got me a sure enough letter from the Commandin' Officer statin' my honorably discharged status as a citizen of these United States."

Nick stood and picked up his plate.

"You story writers and story tellers are gonna have to excuse me," he said. "You fellas have got the day to dawdle. I got me a passel of work."

Tom and Grant picked up their dishes and followed Nick to the kitchen.

"I'll see you at dinner then, and don't work too hard," Tom said.

1 5

Tom walked into the den and poured himself a tumbler of Scotch whiskey.

"I'm gettin' a little headache. Maybe a sip or two of The Glenlevit will belay the pain. Would you care for a snort?"

"No, thank you. I surely won't get any work done then," Grant said.

"Suit yourself but this here is the finest Scotch Whiskey a man can illegally import."

Tom picked up his glass and walked to the door.

"Let's go sit on the porch. There's a breeze in the shade and I haven't been out in a week."

Tom sat in a wicker swing while Grant sat in a chair with his notebook.

"Let me see now...where was we?"

"You had been detached to the Bozeman Trail and taken your discharge I believe."

"Oh, yeah, my discharge. Well sir, I kissed my soldier suits good-bye and I was gonna be a free man again. I had fulfilled all of my obligations to God and country and I was headin' off to find little sister. We was somewhere down around what is now the town of Sheridan, in Wyoming, on the Bozeman Trail when my hitch with the army was up. I decided to head north. I had heard that they was buildin' a town called Bozeman just a couple hundred miles north from where we were.

Now you might just find this interesting. The army unit I was with had stopped for a few days to camp close and give comfort to a wagon train that was in the process of turnin' back because of the Injun troubles.

I figured to spend a day or two socializin' with the settlers and maybe do a little tradin'. I got to talkin' to the wagon train scout who introduced himself as Gabe. He'd decided he'd seen enough of that country behind him and he was gonna ride on ahead in the hopes of seein' somethin' new. Seems as some big money men with an interest in mining was gonna pay him top dollar for findin' gold diggin' grounds and he'd only taken the wagon train job because it was headed the way he travelin'. Told me he was fixin' to head up through a range of mountains to the north to see could he find any likely lookin' spots for the findin' of that yellow metal that is the root of so much insanity.

Even though he was an older fella, we kind'a hit it off, bein' of the same profession and all. He was real impressed with me speakin' Injun, specially Blackfoot. In fact he had a few stories about his own encounters with the Blackfoot. Claimed he got on well with them though. So we decided to ride together a spell. I guess each of us was figurin' it would be nice to have someone who could shoot the middle in case we crossed paths with some hostiles.

That train he'd been guidin' had a back trail you could'a followed in the dark and my soldier suits had 'em a new nanny so me and this fella named Bridger took off to see what we could see."

"Was that theeee Bridger?" Grant asked, furrowing his brow.

"The one and only Bridger. In fact, that range of mountains he was headed for is now called the Bridger Range on the maps, if you look. But you've got to remember that back then his name wasn't no where near as well known as now. He was just a scout and hunter like a hundred others at the time, although a damned successful one at that. He was one helluva business man and he'd made a good livin' at his fort sellin' necessities to the pilgrims on the Oregon Trail. But he liked the free life of scoutin' and huntin' and I guess if that's in a fella, there just ain't no gettin' it out.

Well, sir, Bridger and me took off north and the second day we saw some Injun sign that had us sittin' tall in the saddle and keepin' our eyes peeled. I had, of course, heard of Bridger, but as I said, he liked to be called Gabe, and it was a comfort to me to have a man like him to watch my back. He was damned good at his business and he could read sign like you'd read words in a newspaper. He did have one problem though, his eyes was goin' dim and he couldn't see nothin' too far off. Said that was a bother to him and he was glad I was along as well to see the distant ridges. I heard later on that it was just a few years after we met that he got so blind that he had to quit the mountains and let relatives care for him. Damned if that didn't break my heart. Reckon that'd kilt me if'n I was at the mercy of relatives.

So anyway, me'n Bridger is ridin' along and about the third day we come upon a camp with a couple of covered wagons. As if that white canvas on them wagons wasn't advertisement enough, they had smoke billowin' to be seen for miles.

Bridger figured it'd be best if'n we was to take a wide detour around those folks and avoid whatever trouble they was lookin' to bring upon themselves. However, bein' young and foolish, I said to him that it was only Christian to warn whoever it was. After all, they was sendin' smoke signals to the Crow and the Sioux which, if they was to be read, would be a quick ticket to the tomahawk barber shop.

Not only that, but it was late in the day and gettin' on to time for us to make a camp. I was kind'a hopin' they might have someone cookin', who was better at it than me or Gabe.

We skirted around the camp and hid our horses. I finally walked close on foot and sure enough it was just a bunch of cheechakos, women and all, with wagons and several head of oxen. Without announcin' my presence, I went back to the horses and got Bridger. We rode on in big as you please figurin' to do those greenhorns a favor.

When we was still a ways out I hollered 'hello in the camp' and at about that same time a musket ball cut a gouge outta my left side right through my belt and shirt. Damned nearly took my knife right off'n my belt. It took out a chunk right here where the fat is."

Tom grasped the fatty flesh above his waist.

"Of course, in them days I didn't have a lot of fat, and I can still feel the burnin' of it to this day. Hurt like fifteen kinds of hell, and that's for sure. Bridger had spun his horse and was makin' tracks and my cayuse, not wantin' to be left behind, had near about put me afoot tryin' to follow. I reckon you know what that feels like?"

Tom laughed as Grant looked up from his notebook.

"Yes...I remember it well," Grant smiled.

"When we was outta range ol' Bridger pulled his pony to a halt and said, 'Now that was one helluva scoutin' job you done back there. Lucky you ain't got us kilt.' I was too embarrassed to even try to justify my lack'a discernment to Bridger, but I was shore as well mad enough to hanker a bit of get-even on the sumbitch what had shot me. Ol' Bridger gets the idea that he'll take the horses and ride a wide circle around that camp out in the open. Figures that will draw their attention and they'll have to reckon they'd kilt one of us. While he was ridin', I spent the rest of the daylight puttin' the sneak on that camp.

I could smell the cookin' and my stomach was grumblin' loud enough that I figured they could have heard it in that camp. Come dark, they settled in, leavin' one to stand guard while the others laid down for some sleep. The one guardin' was sittin' there silhouetted in the campfire like a fool and I was gonna get close and put a pistol ball in son of a bitch but I just had that feelin' creepin' up my back that it wouldn't be a right thing to do. Least wise not till I figured out why they'd shot me. So I watched a bit and pretty quick the guard, who was wrapped in a blanket against the night chill, walked over to where they'd made their latrine and squatted.

I couldn't have asked for nothin' better. I had a leather thong in my possibles bag and I got me an idea. I pulled out that leather strip, which was about two feet long. I figured if I could get up on that guard while he was preoccupied I could choke him unconscious without makin' a sound and without doin' the poor bastard too much permanent damage neither. I was always a soft hearted humanitarian like that you know."

Tom flashed a big smile.

"Well, sir, I put the sneak on that guard and my plan went perfect. I applied my garrote with the deftness of a conquistador. Now I was expectin' the possibility that the guard was gonna shit all over everything, considerin' the circumstance, but what happened next nearly scared the shit outta me.

When I dropped the loop and jerked the ends of that garrote, the guard let out a shriek that went down my spine like shatterin' glass. Now I had figured this was some fella fixin' to empty his bowels and that is what I was prepared to deal with. But it wasn't no fella at all. It was a female takin' a piss...and she'd put her elbows on her knees and was holdin' her fists up to her chin when she squatted down with that blanket wrapped around her. When my loop tightened, it wasn't no where near her neck. It was around the backs of her hands and she was able to get plenty of air. She was screamin' and hollerin' and writhin' around. Then I heard other women's voices and more screamin' and hollerin' and it wasn't but a minute and I'm lookin' down the barrel of a musket for the second time that day.

I wasn't about to let go of the only thing between me'n tarnation so I grabbed both ends of that strap in one hand to hold her in place in front of me and drew that forty-four, which I'd plum forgot to give back to the Army when I'd departed. Damned if me and musket man didn't have us a Mexican standoff.

I was pointin' my Colt over that woman's shoulder and peekin' around her head just enough to see that the bead of that fifty eight was right in the middle of my forehead. For a long moment it was so quiet you could'a heard a hummin' bird fart. I was wonderin' what to do next when that silence was broken by a thunderous click as someone cocked a pistol behind me and off to my left. I was just about to make amends with my maker for all my misdeeds, when I heard Bridger's voice sayin', 'Either let that gun roar or you'll die with her loaded.'

I reckon that fella cherished every breath he was takin' 'cause he dropped that musket like it was a rattler he'd picked up by mistake. Trouble was he left 'er cocked and the damned thing went off. The next thing we hear is another woman...and she's squealin' like a pig in a pitfall. I loosed my grip on the garrote and when the blanket fell away that girl was standin' there with her bloomers down around her ankles and right funny look on her face. She grabbed her drawers and pulled 'em up and Bridger walked close enough to be seen in the fire light.

We was both tryin' to calm them folks and make heads or tails of what was happening, but the other woman was screamin' bloody murder so as to be heard for ten miles and she wouldn't shut up.

Finally, ol' Gabe told them all to be quiet and sit down. Sittin' them folks down seemed to calm things a bit. Even the one who'd been shot cut it to a whimper. When we got 'em all quieted down we learned that there was five of 'em, women that is, and two men. When the girl who was shot had finally stopped the bellowin', I went over to take a look at the wound. Turns out it weren't a whole lot worse than mine, only on the other side. The bullet had grazed her right tit, taking off a chunk of meat and bent a couple of ribs. It had also scorched the inside of her right arm but it wasn't no where nearly fatal. Bein's she was a whore, I reckon she had some interestin' stories for her clientele in the years to follow.

Once everyone had calmed down I suggested that they maybe put on a pot of coffee and warm up some of what they'd had for supper. My stomach was still growlin'. One'a them girls dished up some buffalo hump and beans and after me'n Bridger filled our gullets we began to learn just what it was that them folks were doin' out here in the middle of Red Cloud's huntin' preserve.

The fella in charge, Kennedy was his name if I recall correctly, he was a saloon keeper and whorehouse tender. Well, you gotta know that where there's gold there is bound to be folks who wanna get some of it without standin' knee deep in a cold creek all day. Whores and whiskey are things that can bring forth them nuggets quicker than a dredge in El Dorado.

I guess I don't have to explain why the ladies were there, but ol' Kennedy also had that wagon full'a whiskey and various gamblin' paraphernalia. The other fella with them was all beat to pieces and it was obvious that someone had really worked him over. He claimed to be a photographer by trade, who had come to take pictures of the minin' and loggin' and ranchin' and Western life in general. He said he had a special interest in gettin' photographs of Injuns.

I told him and the rest too, that if'n they hung around out there in the open for another day or two, they'd get all the Injuns they wanted to photograph. But then he tells me that he can't take any photographs because some miscreants had made off with his camera and beat the hell out of him besides.

After some prodding ol' Kennedy proceeded to tell us that until recently, he and his flock of fallen angels had been holdin' forth down around Denver relieving the Cherry Creek strikers of all that extra weight they was packing. He said that it appeared those Cherry Creek pickin's was getting slim so he'd hired a guide and was hopin' he could get his whores and whiskey to a place called Bear Gulch, while the iron was still hot. He figured to have first refusal on all that hard dug yellow treasure rumored to be coming out of Montana."

"Bear Gulch?" Grant asked.

"It's just a ways from Helena, where the Capital is today. That gold was what put Helena, and I reckon like a lotta other places, on the map so to speak. Now, ol' Kennedy tells us that his guide had seemed to know his business and they'd been makin' good time when they met up with some scalawags who was operatin' under the guise of buffalo huntin'. Them hunters had eased up a night camped close to Kennedy's party and during the night they all wanted to consort in Kennedy's coop of soiled doves.

Now it should come as no surprise that in the midst of the revelry, a deck of cards miraculously appeared and pretty quick Kennedy and this photographer fella was pickin' the feathers from the cock robins who had come consortin'.

Turns out that this photographer fella could not only develop photographs like magic on a plain blank paper, he was apparently comin' up with some card hands that seemed to appear like magic...if'n you get the drift. I have no idea as the original intention of those buffalo hunters, but at some point in the festivities one of those fellas took exception to the extraordinary adroitness of that photographer.

Betwixt the girl's favors and Kennedy's whiskey, most of the money that those fellas brought with 'em had already changed hands. When that photographer got too lucky to suit one of them hunters, it got real mean. They beat the holy living hell outta that card sharp photographer and then they whipped on ol' Kennedy a bit for good measure.

The guide had attempted to intercede and one of them hunters had put a shot in that poor bastard's liver for his trouble and then they'd beat him right to death. When the smoke cleared those skinners proceeded to relieve Kennedy's party of everything that could be carried. Took their mules and horses and left 'em with a dead guide and that photographer fella near about dead."

Tom's eyes twinkled as he smiled at Grant.

"Don't worry much about not understanding females at your age. I ain't never claimed to know nothin' about women. A woman's mind is as mysterious to me as the origins of the universe. But one of them girls actually told me that to her way of thinking those fellas just weren't all that bad. When I asked her the reasonin' for such an opinion, she reckoned that seein' as how they'd left 'em a rifle, with which to defend themselves against the savages, and the oxen to get them to their destination, she figured they was real kindhearted souls.

Even in my youth it occurred to me that for some women, a fella didn't need shining armor to exceed their expectations. I'd have to reckon that her forgiven attitude enabled her to make a livin' as a whore. The way I had it figured them boys leavin' that rifle was an oversight and them hide hunters had no use for a bunch of yoke broke cattle anyway.

Now ol' Kennedy goes on to explain that they had spent that day buryin' the scout and tendin' to the photographer and not much concerned about the Injuns. When me'n Bridger come ridin' in, ol' Kennedy figured them hunters was comin' back to finish them off to cover the crime, so he took that shot at us without even seein' as to who it was. Considerin' his circumstance I was forced to forgive and forget and then me'n Bridger found ourselves impaled on the horns of another dilemma. Although this bunch of greenhorns wasn't our responsibility, I reckon me and Gabe both felt some moral obligation to see that they got to someplace safer than where they was.

I also got to admit that there was the small incentive provided by one of those dancehall divas in distress. When she found out that I was shot, she'd offered to doctor me some and I was surely not opposed to havin' her do so. She washed my wound and put a patch on it made from some of her own cotton underwear. Now, I was unaccustomed to the wiles of women in those days, and I had yet to acquire a weakness for barleycorn... or the temptations of the flesh.

Before the night was out, however, that blue eyed angel of mercy had definitely shown me the ways of those temptations, and I have been hop scotchin' across the pavin' stones of hell as often as possible ever since. I won't go into the details but needless to say I felt a certain obligation to see to the welfare of that fair maiden and her wayfaring companions, so me'n Bridger rode along with 'em for a few days.

You don't need to write about it, seein' as how he can't speak for himself, but I reckon ol' Gabe was also recompensed for his trouble over them next few nights.

Now the photographer fella got to feelin' a mite better and we was movin' along making some miles when we come upon a United States Army outfit, which was headed to Bear Gulch. Seems some miners had made a request to Washington for some protection from the hostiles. The officer in charge knew Bridger and I'll be damned if that slick talking ol' rascal didn't shuck them cheechakos off to that soldier suit, which relieved us of any further moral responsibility.

I am forced to admit, however, that ridin' away from the warm comfort provided by that comely young maiden, shopworn though she was, took about as much backbone as I ever had to muster. That was near sixty years ago and I still think about that darlin' from time to time."

"Did you ever see her, or any of the others again?"

"Nary hide nor hair. However, that brings me to the brass box with the magnifier in the lid that I showed you the day we rode out to the ranch."

"I remember. The one you carry your Lucky Strike cigarettes and matches in."

"That's the one. Although I never again laid eyes on that darlin' denizen of the dens of inequity, she was the one who gave me that box for a remembrance. I reckon she'd likely pilfered it from one of her payin' paramours, but I kept it just the same. It always reminds me of those shinin' times of my youth."

Another broad smile lit Tom's face.

"Anyway, we headed north and I have not an idea as to whatever became of them folks. Me'n Bridger only rode together a few more days. He told me that he knew of a pass through those mountains...the ones which now carry his name...and he reckoned that would be a shortcut to Fort Benton. He headed me in the right direction and then went off to seek those gold diggin's for them moneyed clients of his."

Grant heard footsteps and looked up to see Dixie walking toward them.

"And how's my darlin' neice this fine afternoon?" Tom said.

"I'm doing quite well, thank you," she said. "What have you gentlemen of leisure done to entertain yourselves?"

Dixie kissed her uncle on the forehead.

"We been story tellin'...but I was just gettin' ready to go lay down and take a nap. Maybe you can entertain this young buckaroo while I get some rest. In fact, when you have some time, why don't you take him for a ride and show him around the ranch?"

"I'd love to. We had discussed it last evening. Cupcake needs some exercise and so do I...but it is up to Mr. Collins. Would you like to take a ride in the morning?"

"I would be delighted. I would like to go see your buffalo up close," Grant said.

"You'll enjoy it. It's just like ridin' back a hundred years," Tom said. "I'll see the two of you at dinner."

16

Grant felt a strange elation as he walked toward the mess hall. I have never been in love, he thought, but this must be the feeling. I can't seem to stop thinking about her.

His thoughts were interrupted by the horn of Nick's Ford.

"Would you like a ride?"

"Thank you, I would...and good morning," Grant said, as he climbed into the truck.

"Good mornin' your own self," Nick said. "What's on your schedule for the day?"

"Dixie and I are going for a ride around the ranch. I haven't really seen much of it yet, except from the airplane."

Nick stopped the Ford and turned to face the young reporter.

"I want to thank you for pulling Dad out of the plane. That was a very brave thing to do."

"It was instinct...an automatic reaction. I assure you that bravery had little to do with it, but I appreciate the thought."

"Well, I thank you none the less. To hear Remus tell it, Dad wouldn't have made it without you."

Grant followed Nick into the mess hall. To his dismay, he saw Dixie seated at one of the long tables with Buck and Howdy. Tom had instructed Grant to stay away from Buck, so he walked to the buffet table as Nick approached the three.

"You boys takin' the day off are ya?" Nick said.

Howdy jumped to his feet and walked toward the door.

"No, sir," Howdy said. "We'll see ya'll later."

Buck also stood, but did not move toward the door.

"You need a special invite, Buck?" Nick asked.

"No, sir," Buck said in a low tone of resignation.

He followed Howdy to the door.

"And since you boys are dawdlin' anyhow," Nick shouted after them, "saddle Dixie's horse and my sorrel mare for Grant."

"Will do, boss," Howdy said.

Nick and Grant filled plates and sat at the table with Dixie.

"And just what kind'a adventure have ya planned for our new range rider?" Nick asked.

"I thought we would ride out to the lake. Maybe see the buffalo…and maybe Grant would enjoy looking for fossils?"

"That would be splendid," Grant said, "Dixie told me about the Buffalo Rocks. She says there are many fossils to be found on the ranch."

"Sure enough are," Nick replied. "We get professors and museum folks from the East come out here to look for them dinosaurs and whatever. Caleb and Sus have got their hands full with a bunch comin' this next week. Damnedest thing I ever saw. These fellas get themselves college educated and then come to Montana and work like railroad coolies."

"I believe they would call that science," Grant said. "They think that their coolie work is furthering man's knowledge."

"Might could be," Nick replied, picking up his plate and silverware, "but it's still the damnedest thing as I ever saw. You kids have fun. I'll see ya later."

The morning was cool with a breeze pushing the chilled air through light clothing. Grant was glad that he had put on his long underwear.

When he and Dixie walked to the corral, Nick's mare was saddled and tied next to the little pinto gelding that Dixie called Cupcake.

"What a beautiful morning for a ride," she said.

As they approached the horses, the black and white dog came out of the stable and ran to meet them. Dixie bent down and cupped her hands around the dog's ears scratching vigorously and speaking in a high-pitched voice. The dog seemed to melt.

When she had finished and stood erect, the dog headed for Grant, who stepped up onto the first rail of the corral. Holding some bacon and a biscuit for the dog's approval, Grant stepped to the ground, keeping the bribe just out of reach. He then broke the offering into small pieces to keep the animal busy as he attempted to mount his horse.

Grant untied the lead rope and placed his left foot in the stirrup. He stood to swing his leg over the horse's back. As he did so the saddle slipped, dropping Grant on his back in a fresh pile of manure. Dixie could not conceal her laughter as Dawg ran to lick Grant's reddened face.

"Buck," Dixie said, laughing. "Buck left your cincha loose."

Dixie walked to the horse and pushed the saddle back into position.

"Let me show you."

Hooking the stirrup on the saddle horn she demonstrated how to check and tighten the girth cinch.

"I would suggest that you always tighten it yourself before you get onto any horse," she said.

"I really have a lot to learn, don't I?"

Grant could feel the cool moisture left by the wet dung on his back and was embarrassed by the odor, which accompanied the stain.

Dixie turned him around to see his back.

"It'll dry. Don't let it bother you too much, everyone has to learn. You haven't been around animals. Even more importantly you haven't been around people like these. Cowboys have a different sense of humor than you are accustomed to. Just relax and take it as it comes. You may even get to enjoy it. Now get on that horse before Dawg gets romantic again."

They mounted the horses and Dixie lead the way as they rode out onto the open prairie.

As the horses plodded along, Grant said, "I'm already enjoying it."

"Enjoying what?" Dixie asked.

"You just told me to relax and enjoy it, take it as is comes. Well I'm already enjoying it."

"As am I," she said, turning her face away from him.

"I'd like to know something," he said.

"You ask and I'll try to answer."

"Why were you so mad at me after the plane crash? It wasn't really my fault you know?"

"You looked an absolute fright. Your face and clothes were covered with blood and I thought you were terribly hurt."

"Do you always become angry with people who are seriously injured?"

"Well, maybe I was worried about you. Maybe I wouldn't want to see you hurt. It may even be that I like you, at least enough so that I wouldn't want you injured."

"Well, maybe I like you too, but I wouldn't be mad at you if you were hurt."

"But you weren't hurt. You were doing a dumb thing flying around the country with Uncle Tom and I didn't sleep for a week while you were gone."

"Next time, you might just tell me you're worried without being so harsh."

"Next time, Mr. Collins, don't do dumb things."

She laughed as she urged her horse into a trot.

Grant's horse followed and he saw the white canvas of the tipi in a grove of trees beside the large pond. The day had warmed. A small herd of buffalo gathered to cool in the glade began to run at their approach.

"Look! Buffalo! There are the buffalo," Grant shouted.

"I told you we might see them. These are Uncle Tom's pets. He keeps them to remind him of the old days. He doesn't let anyone hurt his buffalo."

"I saw all of this from the airplane, but I never dreamed how beautiful it would be. You do know that there is a large bear that lives in those woods?"

"Uncle Tom told me to keep an eye out."

Riding to the edge of the pond, they let the horses quench their thirst. They then tied the horses in the shade and loosened the cinch straps so that the animals could rest. Dixie removed her saddle bags and spread a blanket in front of the tipi.

"Koko fixed a picnic. Roast beef sandwiches and eggs. There's tea in that canteen if you'd care for some."

Grant stopped in his tracks when she removed a Colt revolver from the lunch sack and placed it on the blanket.

"Where on earth did you get a gun?"

"I told you, Uncle Tom told me to keep an eye out for that bear."

"He is a man who gives warnings seriously,' Grant said, laughing nervously.

"He said it was 'just in case.' He showed me how to shoot it last summer. 'In case' I wanted to go riding alone."

Grant walked to the shore of the ancient pond. The water had been impounded by beavers. For many generations, the animals had dammed a rivulet, which originated at a spring about a half mile upstream. Although copper toned from the annual leaf litter, the small lake was crystal clear. He could see many fish darting about and he wondered how many men and animals had fed on this bounty of trout and slaked a thirst in these bronze hued depths.

"It really warmed up since this morning," he said as he walked toward the blanket.

Grant prepared to sit down for their picnic. Dixie held her hand palm out.

"Hold it there, stinky boy. You're not eating lunch on my blanket smelling like that. Didn't your mother teach you anything?"

Grant's face was a blank stare. His cheeks reddened.

Dixie suppressed a laugh. His look was that of a small boy caught with dirty hands at the dinner table. His obvious discomfort was quite endearing.

"Go wash the shirt and it wouldn't hurt to wash the red woolies too… maybe?"

"But I would have to…" he gasped.

"Mr. Collins," she said in feigned exasperation, "I have three brothers… one older and two younger. I seriously doubt that the sight of your manly torso is likely to wither me. Queen Victoria passed along about twenty years ago you know. I, too, have gone to college and I am a big girl. Now, go take a bath!"

Grant unfastened the ties on the tipi door and entered to undress.

He emerged with his shirt modestly wrapped around his waist, carrying his red union suit. The light breeze on his bare skin felt sensuous. He ran to the pond making "Oh-oh" sounds, his soft bare feet unaccustomed to the rocks and rough plants. He dropped his clothing on the shore and plunged into the cool depths.

Enveloped in the luxurious, near decadent, feeling of freedom, he floated in mid-pond, at once wishing that she would join him while shamed of his thoughts.

His modesty had prevented him from looking at Dixie after coming out of the tipi. When a movement caught his peripheral vision he looked over to see her standing at the waters edge, ready to dive into the lake. She was wearing only her ankle length cotton under drawers and a mercerized lace sleeveless vest.

"You're not the only one who gets a swim."

He heard her laugh before she disappeared beneath the water.

Grant was frozen in stunned disbelief. Except for the renderings in the Sears catalog he had not seen a woman in undergarments since he was a child. Treading water, he watched for her to reappear.

Something touched his leg and he pulled away reflexively. He could see the bright copper outline of her white cotton clothing beneath the surface as she pursued him into shallower water. When he stood chest deep, she emerged in front of him laughing.

"Did you think a creature had you?"

He was speechless; his eyes were riveted on the contour of her breasts. The semi-transparent garment outlined the pigmentation of her erect nipples, causing the breath to catch in his throat. When she moved close, putting her arms around his neck, a thrill shook his body and he could not fill his lungs with air.

"You smell much better," she purred into his ear.

She held herself tightly against his naked skin. The touch of her body beneath the gossamer undergarments sent a pulse of jolting hormones surging through him. Electric waves began in his scalp and continued down his spine culminating in uncontrolled erotic excitement.

He held her close, kissing her face and neck. His hands moved over the warmth of her skin, which was protected by flimsy cotton garments as unrelenting as chain mail armor.

She returned his kisses, pressing her thinly shielded and eager flesh tightly against his naked arousal.

She squeezed him in a tight embrace and then pushed him to arm's length.

"I'm convinced," she said.

He stood, looking at her face, mystified by the comment.

She wrapped her legs around his thighs, floating with one arm around his neck. Slowly she moved her hand down his body, softly touching his erect organ.

"You like me more than you're admitting."

"I love you," he coughed.

He pulled her tightly to him, still fearful to return her bold touch.

"Do you," she teased, securing a clumsy grasp on his erection.

"I do...yes I do," he said in a raspy whisper.

Holding him in the embrace of her legs, she slowly moved her hips in rhythm with his undulating body, her hand now squeezing his member as they moved in unison.

Locked in this embrace, their hips moved in an untried and ungainly primal urgency. Her grip became tighter, her hand moving with the rhythm of their bodies.

He was now unaware of anything around him, consumed by the desire to consummate this primordial rite. He could feel her breath become rapid and shallow, her heart beating tumultuously as her hand moved with the motion of his body.

His passion was now urgent and he was about to tear away the filmy cloth separating him from his instinctual goal. Her hips moved in rhythm with his insistent drive as he held her so tightly that she could barely breathe.

To her dismay his entire body was suddenly rigid. He remained motionless for a long moment, his face an agonized mask. His orgasm left him convulsing intensely. Weak legged and shaking he slowly released his suffocating grip. A pained expression still distorted his face. His eyes glazed and his breath came in deepening gasps. She pushed away in alarm.

"Are you alright?" she asked.

The fear was obvious in her voice. She slowly put her arms around his neck and, again held him close.

The strength began returning to his legs as he stared blankly into her face for a long moment. A smile crossed his lips and she could feel his convulsing body begin to relax.

"Are you sure you're okay?" she asked again.

"I don't believe I have ever been better."

He pulled her to him, holding her with all the strength he could muster.

"May I ask you something?" he said.

"What?" she asked, "And don't squish me to death."

"Would you marry me?"

She giggled and pulled away, swimming toward the shore.

"Don't you think it might be a good idea to know one another for at least a few weeks before making such a monumental decision? Besides, I'm not sure I love you yet."

She walked onto the bank and picked up Grant's clothing and began washing the stained shirt and underwear.

"But I will perform this wifely duty of doing your laundry just this once...just to see how it would feel."

Grant went into the tipi and put on his pants and boots, then joined Dixie on the blanket for lunch.

As they ate, Dixie's curiosity over came her.

"What happened to you...out there in the water? I was really frightened. You looked like you were in such pain."

"Are you a...well uh...a virgin?" Grant asked.

"Of all the impertinent personal questions!"

She looked Grant in the eye, a storm of emotion running through her mind.

"But then, I suppose, given the circumstances I do owe you an answer...and the answer is, yes."

He said nothing as she continued to look into his eyes.

"I must admit, however, that a few minutes ago, had you not been taken with that seizure, I may have been talked out of that...being a virgin that is! Except for my brothers I had never touched a naked man before. It was not what I expected. Thank God for cotton undies or seizures."

"It wasn't a seizure," Grant said.

"Well, you most assuredly appeared catatonic. You couldn't even speak. I was fearful that you would drown. If it wasn't a seizure...then...?" her voice tailed off.

A glimmer of recognition lit her eyes as she looked at him with an unabashed boldness.

"I guess you're not then."

"Not what?" he asked.

"A virgin?" she replied. "So tell me, were you a virgin before our incident in the water?"

"I suppose men aren't supposed to admit their inexperience, but yes I am. Or I suppose I was, depending on your interpretation of the event."

"Was it really painful?" she asked.

"It was grand! I would highly recommend it," he said.

"They have secret birth control classes for the girls at Vassar you know. Parents never hear about them. I guess I thought I knew more than I did. Even in those classes they don't just banter about terms like 'orgasm' and such. Even though we learned a bit, there is still a lot to know...it would appear. I didn't know that a man behaved that way when he...well, you know what I mean. I'm sure that Margaret Sanger would have given me exemption for our minor indiscretion. That could certainly be considered birth control...I think!"

Grant watched her face closely as she spoke, causing her to again divert her eyes.

"Did you have any similar occasions with...or rather; did you ask Melinda to marry you?"

"I assure you that Melinda and I were only dance partners, although I suspect that she may have had other ideas. But the answer to your question is, no. So will you think about marrying me? I didn't ask only in that moment of passion. I really have fallen in love with you."

An awkward silence followed.

"Do men always react so...I'm not sure of the proper word here... intensely...when they make love?"

"Counting today," he said, "that made once for me, but I'll keep you informed if I acquire any further information."

They both broke into laughter as he took her arm and pushed her onto the blanket. They kissed a long kiss. She pushed him away and looked into his face.

"I don't think you need any further information on the topic today, however. We had better be heading home...and, yes, I will think about it...your proposal that is."

Their clothing had dried in the afternoon sun. They dressed and readied the horses while Dixie packed her saddle bags. When she had mounted her horse she noticed that the tipi door was open.

"Tie the tipi door shut. The buffalo will get in there and make a mess and then Uncle Tom will skin us both alive."

17

Grant and Dixie walked to Tom's Dodge Touring Car, which was parked in front of the house. Tom started the car and drove toward the mess hall.

"How was the ride yesterday," Tom asked.

"We saw your buffalo. I had seen one in a zoo, but I had no idea that wild ones still existed. One is really huge."

"I reckon they ain't really wild. They can't leave the ranch because of the fences, but they're as wild as they can be under the circumstances. Did ya close up my tipi?"

Dixie winked at Grant and laughed.

"Yes, we closed up your tipi. But I think that cow buffalo with the funny horn knows how to untie knots."

"I'll tie a knot in you, young woman, if them buffalo crap in my tipi... and I'm feelin' spry again so don't try me on."

"We know, you're a very mean old man," Dixie said.

"Would ya care to take a ride with us over to the diggin's?" Tom asked.

"I have to go earn my keep," Dixie said. "Susanna and the girls need some help. I'm going to be the poor working girl today."

"What are 'the diggings'?" Grant asked.

"Caleb has a group of scientists from Chicago out at The Bone Yard," Dixie said. "They're looking for dinosaurs."

They dropped Dixie at the mess hall.

"Well, gentlemen, I'll see you both later," she said as she walked away.

Tom turned the car toward what appeared to be trackless prairie. Soon they were meandering through the sage brush and cactus in wheel ruts worn, first by wagon, and now by the tires of automobiles.

"I'd told you before that we had these scientist fellas come to dig for bones. So we started callin' it 'The Bone Yard.' It's a place where the earth turned itself upside down and sideways. There are fossil bones to be dug right near the surface. Them scientists say that some of those things have been in the ground there for near a hundred million years. Hell, that's longer than I been around here."

"I'm anxious to see this place," Grant said.

"Speakin' of my buffalos, I seen in the paper that President Harding finally got to Alaska and drove the last spike in that railroad, which crosses the wilderness. Sort'a sad! They make these parks like Yellowstone and that new Glacier, but it just ain't the same as when the country was wild and free. Once they put in railroads and the roads are open and the people come...makin' a park is about the same as buildin' a great big museum. Nothin' there is really free. The critters is dependent on us to take care of 'em. All these do gooders can talk about keepin' it natural, but it ain't natural. I seen it when it was natural...and there ain't no park ever gonna be natural after white men set foot in it."

"I was raised in the city with paved streets. I can't remember when there was no electricity or telephones. For me those things seem normal.

But I can certainly see how you might sometimes find modernization more a bane than a boon. For me, it was a thrill to see fenced buffalo. I can't imagine what this must have looked like when you first saw it. You are right. Nothing is really free in a park. It is just a museum with live exhibits."

"That's for absolute sure. You've read some history I reckon?"

Grant nodded.

"The early days of these United States, in my opinion, was the freest time for men in the recorded history of the human race. Think about it. From the times of the earliest Bible stories and on to the Egyptians and the Babylonians and then the Greeks and Romans and on to the history of Europe and Asia, there was always some kind'a king who owned the ground and governed with an army. The royals and the land owners would kill a man for attemptin' to hunt somethin' for his family to eat...hell, they'd kill a fella for a trespass. But the early days of the United States, especially after we sent ol' King George packin'; them was shinin' times."

"Even after the Revolution, we had an army and a government, didn't we?" Grant said.

"Oh, we sure enough had us a government and an army. But if ya take a good look at the history of that hundred years...say between 1790 and 1890, just think about what that government and army was'a doin'. They was openin' the land and helpin' folks get all the land they wanted for free. The army was defendin' settlers, even squatters, not runnin' 'em off the land...all except for the poor raggedy assed Injuns of course. Son, I can still mind the time when I could get on a horse right here where we are and ride for a month without seein' a fence."

"As I recall the Indians did receive special note in the Constitution regarding taxation," Grant said with a smile.

"I reckon the poor bastards never got taxed, but that was damned poor compensation for the price they paid. When you consider that they was stone age people when ol' Columbus supposedly discovered 'em... and when you consider that the white men brought guns and swords to fight stone tipped arrows and spears, you got to give 'em credit. They held their own for near four hundred years. In fact, when they got the horses from the Spaniards and started tradin' for modern weapons of steel, they actually advanced themselves considerable. But they, just like them Passenger Pigeons, had a big flaw in their strategy. They always seemed to be livin' where the war was."

"Don't people at war always live where the war is?" Grant asked.

"Nope! At least not us Americans...with the exception of the Confederates, that is. In any war, the folks who lived where the war was just about always lost. Let's just consider a white man's war that you've some familiarity with. In the great Civil War, what was the main objective for just about all the major battles that stick in our minds? Most of them battles was named after towns. Right?

Did you ever hear people make the comparison of takin' something from someone else by saying 'Like Grant took Richmond?' Well ol' Grant went after Richmond because that's where the families of the big chiefs were. You get at the women and kids and there won't be much fight left in the men.

That's been the strategy of the every conqueror from the Romans to the Spanish. Take the war to where the other fella lives. They can't fight when they're busy protectin' the women and kids. Well, the Injuns lived on the prairie. That's where their food and homes and their families were. They fought a good fight for near four hundred years but, as Sand Creek and Wounded Knee showed, they lived where the war was.

The soldiers in the blue coats had a home to go to after the battle. But the Injuns was fightin' in their own livin' rooms and kitchens. It's real hard to be a good warrior when your watchin' your kids and your women get their noggins bashed in. Sort'a takes the fight out of a fella. Think about this...what do they usually call folks who are livin' where a war is, even today?"

Grant thought a moment and then shrugged.

"Refugees!"

The Dodge topped a rise and Grant could see a group of people working with pick and shovel near several trucks and cars.

"That'll be The Bone Yard," Tom said.

The group was oddly dressed in an assortment of work clothing and jungle garb. Observing the straw hats and pith helmets, Grant laughed to himself thinking that these people looked like the treasure hunters in a Tarzan movie he had recently seen.

As Tom and Grant emerged from the car, Caleb approached.

"Howdy Grant. How's the writin' coming?"

"Just fine! Not nearly as labor intensive as your work I can see," Grant answered.

"What brings you out, Dad?" Caleb asked.

"Just wanted to show Grant some of the things we do when we ain't chasin' cows on The Buffalo Rock," Tom answered.

One of the men wearing a pith helmet quit digging and walked toward them.

"We've had a splendid morning, Tom. How are you feeling? We were told that you'd had a mishap and were under the weather."

"Spry as a yearlin', Doc," Tom answered as he stuck out his hand to greet the man. "Grant, this is Doctor Dedman Mossback from Chicago."

When they had been introduced, Professor Mossback said to Grant, "I hear you're a newspaper reporter?"

"Yes, sir. I'm getting some background for a story on Tornado Tom."

"We may just have the scientific scoop of a lifetime. I am just beside myself with excitement," Mossback said.

Professor Mossback walked toward the spot he had been excavating.

"I believe we have unearthed an ancient creature, which would have been about the size of a railway engine."

The outline of a huge rib cage was beginning to appear where the Professor and his colleagues were working the earth.

"I am assuming those are its ribs, in which case it would certainly have been a monstrous creature," Grant said. "Have you identified the animal yet?"

"No, that's what is so exciting. It may be some species about which the world is completely unaware," Professor Mossback said.

Tom walked around the giant ribs, arms across his chest, scratching his chin.

"Did you know that critters like this gettin' unearthed by the wind was some big medicine for the Injuns back in the old days?" Tom said.

"You mean you've seen things like this before?" Mossback said.

"Seen a plenty! I been tellin' Grant here about the Injun wars and how the West was won and all that hoo-hah. In fact, I was tellin' him that most of the fightin' was about the hunting rights...and so it was. But there was another element to the Injuns bein' so protective of the ground, especially from here to the Black Hills. Each year these prairie winds blow away a lotta dirt. Over a period of time, if a fella is around the same place for a while he begins to notice things. Well, them Injuns noticed that these critters was slowly comin' outta the ground and it spooked 'em some.

They lived by hunting so they knew what an animal looked like, inside and out. They had skinned many a deer and elk and bear and buffalo and they knew that there was no critter around these parts that would'a fit them bones so they could only imagine, just like you and me, what the damned things looked like. They reckoned that these was critters from the spirit world and they had devised themselves some ceremonies to deal with 'em. But as much as they was afraid of them monsters, they was also just as protective and that was what began a lot of the conflict when the white men began diggin' for gold.

The Injuns figured that the miners was diggin' up the spirit world and that they just might release some of them critters before their time. Not wantin' something that size running through the village, they would take to the war path to run the miners off...and those reasons somehow never got through the heads of the white men."

"Could you show us others you've seen?" Mossback asked Tom.

"You're lookin' at your best deal right here Doc," Tom answered. "Hell, some of them I saw was years gone by and the wind and rain has long since released them from their restin' places."

"Did you happen to see the news from Egypt?" Grant asked.

"An undisturbed tomb of a Pharaoh. Complete in every detail. Carnarvan must be jumping with joy. He's invested a fortune in that dig," Mossback replied.

"I would hope that with all of the interest in King Tut, my editor will be quite pleased with your dinosaur story. Can you supply me with photographs?" Grant asked.

"I should say we can. Perhaps we can get together for dinner tonight. I can fill you in on all of the details then. Are you dining in the mess hall?" Mossback asked.

"Yes...the mess hall it is," Grant said.

"You'll join us...won't you Tom?" Mossback asked.

Tom nodded, still looking at the huge outline of bone.

"Good oh, then," Mossback replied, patting Grant on the shoulder.

"See you tonight and I'll even stand you a toddy."

"Not him Doc," Tom chuckled.

Cupping his mouth with one hand as if to conceal what he was saying, Tom pointed a thumb at Grant.

"Tea totaler, you know," Tom said.

Tom started the Dodge, driving in the wagon ruts toward The Compound.

"I had no idea that the Indians had known of the dinosaurs."

"Now, I didn't say that they knew about dinosaurs. What they knew about was skeletons. After all, they skinned and boned all kind'a critters in their day-to-day life. So they was pretty well familiar with anatomy. It didn't take much of a stretch of the imagination for them to figure that a skull that was three feet long had to belong to a big son-of-a-bitch."

"Didn't it occur to them that they had never seen any animal that large?" Grant asked.

"Sure it occurred to 'em. But then, like I explained before, there's a lot of folks who've never seen God, but they believe. Right? Just like you and me...and we never even seen a skeleton of God. Well sir, they wasn't takin' no chances neither."

The early afternoon sun was heating the prairie and Tom stopped beside a small creek. He handed Grant a canteen.

"Son, your knees is much better'n mine. Scrape the scum off that crick and fill this thing up. I'm about parched."

Grant knelt beside the stream, laying the canteen gently on its side. Slowly he submerged the canteen as the clean clear water flowed into the container.

"So you actually did spend time with the immortal, Jim Bridger?" Grant asked.

"Sure as chili beans will make you fart. But like I said, it was only a few days. I probably wouldn't have even knowed his name except that the soldier suits told me who he was. He wasn't a man to brag. While we was together I just called him Gabe. Like I said, that was what he went by. But he sure enough saved my life 'cause I'd bet a dollar against that chili bean that ol' Kennedy would'a blowed my head to kingdom come had it not been for Bridger. That pimp was scared and that makes a man dangerous."

"But you never saw any of those people again? Not even Bridger?"

"Would have liked seein' Bridger again but I never did. Now me'n that lady visited quite a few times in my young dreams, but I never had occasion to go to Bear Gulch, and I have no idea as to what happened to any of them others. Remember, I was on a mission and Bridger was on a job of work, and Kennedy and his girls were going to find gold...in the miner's pockets, of course. Bridger was a good man and good company but he was headed his way lookin' for diggings and I was headed to Fort Benton to start a search for little sister."

They drank from the canteen and then got back into the car. The Dodge lurched down the dusty two lane track.

"After Bridger'n me split up, I headed toward where he'd told me there was a pass through the mountains. I rode slow, usin' all the cover of the terrain that I'd learned from the Injuns and from bein' a scout. A man alone wouldn't be no match for any kind of Injun that may have inhabited that country and there was all kinds of Injuns in those particular hills. There was Rics and Gros-Ventre and Crows and Sioux and Nez Perces and Flatheads, not to mention the Blackfoot who scared the shit out of all them others. I was lucky that the weather was bein' real nice and by the third day alone, I was pretty well along my way to that pass ol' Bridger had pointed out to me.

I was pokin' along keepin' a sharp eye when those hairs started standin' up on the back'a my neck. I'd learned by then not to ignore that warnin' and I could see there was about a half dozen buzzards circlin' the trail that headed into the pass. All of my senses was on full alert and it wasn't long till I could smell death floatin' on the breeze comin' down the canyon. I figured that whatever it was, it was not too far ahead and it was pretty near to the trail I was usin'.

I sat there real still for quite some time just smellin' and listenin' and then I heard some magpies squabblin'. I figured there couldn't be any livin' people any too close to whatever it was, or them magpies wouldn't have been hangin' around. I slipped off my pony and walked real slow and quiet, hopin' I could see the thing that was dead before somethin' saw me.

I come round a big rock, where the trail turned, and I could make out a dead mule and a couple of human bodies on a flat spot ahead. After takin' a careful survey of the scene, I didn't see no movement except the magpies. Real slow I went in to have a look. The sight I beheld wasn't any too purty. By their clothes, which the Injuns had throwed all around, I knew they was all four white men and they had paid dear for trespassin' in Injun country. From the look of the arrows in that mule I figured it was Crows. They'd had themselves a real party too.

It appeared to me that it took those four men a couple days to go to mercy from what I could tell. You could near about hear 'em screamin' still...if'n you knew the signs to look for. Them Crows had took near about everything of use that those men had been carryin'. However, they had left some stuff which they'd seen no use for...and guess what I found?"

Grant put his hands palm up and shrugged.

"There was a camera and the possibles that you needed to make photographs. I reckon them redskins couldn't make out a use for it so they just left it where it was. They hadn't even busted it up. Maybe they figured it for magic. I reckon they'd seen cameras before but they was still superstitious about 'em.

Did you know that ol' Crazy horse never allowed a photo to be taken of himself. Thought it would steal his spirit.

As I pondered that scene of blood and gore, it occurred to me that maybe a court of poetic justice had convened for Kennedy's guide and that photographer...and them Crows had been judge, jury and executioner.

The Injuns had kilt a mule and fed on it for several days whilst they was enjoyin' the company of those buffalo hunters. Had I not known that bunch for the no good murderin' scum that they was, I would have likely felt sorry for those men and seen to their burial and all, but I reckoned as how justice had been served, what with the way they'd done Kennedy's guide and all.

I got to studyin' that camera, the likes of which I'd not seen. It was brand new, a big ol' box affair with a bellows on the front and a fine lens. There was a tripod and some boxes and bags of paraphernalia. I was tryin' to figure out how I could take it along with me...thinking maybe it might come in useful in doin' what I had to do. But there wasn't no way I was gonna load that junk on my horse and walk. Just as I was ponderin' the problem, my cayuse let out a whinny that made me figure he'd winded another horse.

It went through my mind that them Crows had backtracked or seen me or somethin'. I knew I was in a real bad spot. If I was to make a run for it I would have to guess as to the best direction and bein' as how I was unfamiliar with my surroundings, I would'a just been runnin' blind. I weighed the possibilities real quick and decided that I'd let them Crows come to me and fight it out right on the spot...takin' comfort in that Henry Rifle as I did.

I tied my animal so that the Injuns couldn't run him off and then I hunkered behind an old deadfall log with a big rock to my back. I sat there hardly breathin' for a couple of minutes and then I could hear the clatter of rocks and I knowed there was a critter on the hill to my right and I figured they was makin' their move. I got a glimpse of an animal through the brush but I couldn't make out a rider. Then my horse whinnied again.

I was barely breathin' as I got that Henry cocked and pointed and started countin' my last minutes on God's green earth. Time went creeping along. After a time, the weight of that rifle had my arms quivering from the strain. Beads of sweat was flowing, and big drops of the salty liquid was drippin' off the end of my nose and onto that gun."

Tom smiled and looked at Grant.

"You know, it's really odd what comes to a man's mind at a time like that. Just try to guess what I was thinkin'?"

Grant shook his head, his heart racing at hearing the story.

"I was thinking about how that sweat was gonna rust my rifle and maybe make it inoperable. Damndest thing to think of at a time like that. But I recall it like yesterday. Anyway, I pointed that rifle in the direction of that movement and waited for my doom."

"So what did the Indians do?" Grant asked, unable to contain himself.

"There wasn't no Injuns. It was a damned ol' mule come bustin' out of the brush to seek the company of my horse. When I'd quit shakin', I kind'a put together what had happened. The Injuns had apparently run that mule off when they'd kilt the other one for eatin' purposes. Poor critter was still wearin' her pack saddle."

"If horses were of such value, why did the Indians chase the mule away?" Grant asked.

"Now the Southern Injuns, Commanches and Apaches and even the

Kiowas and the Utes seemed to favor mules. In that desert country a tough ol' mule was an asset. They even bred mules to use and traded 'em to the settlers. But the Crows and most of the others of the northern tribes didn't care much for mules. Thought of them mules in the same way one of you college boys might think of a homely girl."

Grant looked at Tom and smiled.

"And just how might that be?"

"They'd make use of a mule in a pinch, but they wouldn't want to be seen ridin' one."

Grant laughed in spite of himself.

"Well, sir, I caught that mule and she was damned glad to be caught. She was wantin' company and she wasn't goin' too far from my horse. When I'd gathered myself and quit shakin', I cleaned and oiled my rifle first thing. Then I looked around and decided that since I had me that mule, I might just as well pack along the camera and whatever else there was worth packin' on that old molly.

I got to lookin' at the remains of them mean bastards and thinkin' about what they'd done to Kennedy's party and especially the guide and I decided to leave them to the scavengers. The murderin' bastards wasn't worth a buryin' as far as I could tell. Not a Christian attitude, I'll admit, but them miscreants needed killin' anyway. And them magpies and buzzards needed a feed too. So I packed up that mule and got back on the trail through Bridger's pass. I continued movin' real slow so as I was to avoid trouble with the hostiles, so it took me the better part of ten days to get all the way to Fort Benton country."

18

The car lurched violently and then came to an abrupt halt, pitching Grant against the glass windshield.

"God damned badgers! Why can't they dig them holes somewheres besides in my road? I bet I've kilt a half dozen horses over the years because of them things diggin' holes where they oughtn't."

Tom took a shovel from the luggage compartment and looked at the left front wheel sitting axel deep in the collapsed earth.

"Looks like backin' out will be the easiest."

Tom began to dig a ramp beneath the running board of the Dodge. Grant took the handle of the shovel.

"You don't appear to me to be well suited to workin' with a shovel, boy," Tom said.

"I'll have a go at it," Grant said.

When Grant had freed the tire, Tom started the Dodge and began to back out of the badger hole.

"Get on that front bumper, son. Lift and push at the same time...I think she'll go," Tom said.

Tom spun the tires as he backed out of the hole, throwing dust, which covered Grant and his clothing. Grant returned the shovel to the trunk and got into the car.

"Damned if you ain't a sight," Tom laughed. "You look like you just rode in from west Texas after a long cattle drive."

Grant stepped out of the car to brush the dust from his clothing and wipe his face. He then sat down and took out his notebook.

"You told me that your ride to Fort Benton was relatively uneventful. When you got to Fort Benton, after you found the mule, were any of the people whom you had known still around? It had been nearly six years if my calculations are correct."

"By the time I'd got back up to this country, I had pretty well growed up and haired over. I'd growed a foot and I had a beard and I'd filled out my frame some. There wasn't no one around who even recognized me. I saw a few folks whose faces I recognized, but I decided that for my mission it was maybe the best thing just to keep my identity a secret.

You would have been amazed at how quick news could spread across this prairie. Seemed faster then than now...and today we got telephones and all. I sure as hell didn't want word gettin' about that I was gonna look for my sister. Dependin' on her circumstance I wanted my comin' to be a surprise to them Bloods who had took her.

Now over the years I've seen plenty of folk who was lookin' for relatives taken by Injuns. Most of them folks had a pretty unrealistic expectation of what they was gonna find...and most was sore disappointed in the end. You got to remember that I knew them Injuns pretty well, so I wasn't harborin' no illusion that little sister was gonna be ready for a cotillion, if'n I could find her, and if'n I could get her back at all.

She'd been about eleven when they took her so I figured she was nearin' seventeen. A squaw at seventeen was a woman...likely as not married and doin' woman's work. What with haulin' wood and cookin', skinnin' buffalo and tannin' hides to make her man's moccasins, not to mention havin' babies. Remember, these women had their babies where there wasn't no doctors or clean sheets or anything that you might think of today about a woman givin' birth."

Grant had not even considered the intervening years and the fate of Tom's sister. Tom could clearly read the look of disdain Grant wore on his face.

"Yes, sir, I reckoned I knew that if'n she was still alive, she was gonna be real eclectic," Tom said.

The revulsion on Grant's face changed instantly to embarrassment. He returned to his pad and pencil.

"I'd rode on into Fort Benton needin' supplies and I figured I could get the local folks to give me a readin' on what the Injuns was up to. That town had really seen some changes. In those intervening years they'd built shallow draft steamers that was able to get clear up to Fort Benton. That town had become a buzzin' beehive of activity. I couldn't believe my eyes. There was folks of every shape, size and description.

Now there still wasn't no fancy hotel like the Grand Union back in those times. In fact, I'll bet you figure that Benton was pretty much the cow town you read about in them dime novels. Right?"

"I, uh, yes. It was a Western town, and I picture the cow town of Wister's description."

"Well sir, for your information, Fort Benton was a sea port city."

"A seaport?" I hadn't thought of that."

"It was a sure enough cow town, but it was a sea port city too. Furthest inland seaport in the history of the world. Like any seaport in those days, or even today for that matter, it was rough.

That stretch of Front Street along the river...across from where the Grand Union and the Fire House stands now...that was called the

'Bloodiest block in America.' A man could get himself into bad trouble with very little effort and many did just that.

There was the usual assortment of hide hunters, mule skinners and fresh faced cowboys lookin' for a little fun, but there was also seamen and stevedores and cutthroats who had done their killin' in ports around the world. Shootin's and cuttin's on Front Street was as reliable and about as frequent as the horse turds. You recall that nice park-like area in front of the Grand Union Hotel? Well, all up and down that stretch of river bank was where the boats were loaded and unloaded. Stacks of cargo filled that area for half a mile. And across Front Street from the river was a string of saloons and gamblin' dens that would'a put fear into the Prince of Darkness himself.

If a fella needed some dental work, all he had to do was stroll into one of them dens of iniquity with a crossways look on his face, and he could about count on gettin' a couple of extractions...free of charge. Yes sir, ol' Fort Benton had changed considerable from the time I'd left in fifty-nine."

"Bloodiest block in America!" Grant said to himself as he scribbled.

"Now as I was ridin' into town, coincidentally, I passed a photographer's shop. Fella had just set up in town and was doin' a thrivin' business. He saw me ridin' by with that camera and all...and stopped me to make some conversation. Now at first I was tryin' to get away from him 'cause I didn't want any attention drawn to myself. However, he was a hard one to get shed of and he invited me into his shop to show off some of his special techniques. It turned out to be a blessin' as I'll tell you later...but he inadvertently showed me quite a bit about that photography business, while he thought he was showin' off to a fellow professional. He taught me about usin' the camera and even sold me some supplies for my outfit. I told him I was goin' out to find some Injuns to photograph and he told me that there was Blackfoot about and that I had better hang on to my hair with both hands if'n I was goin' to get pictures of 'em. He told me that a young chief by the name of Bloody Spear was the big cheese in those parts and that although this Bloody Spear would trade with the whites, he was one ferocious Blackfoot.

I asked about Limpin' Calf but the photographer said he'd only been in town a short time and that he hadn't ever heard of such an Injun. Now I was glad to hear about the Blackfoot being in the area 'cause I hoped it was my pal Prairie Dog and his pappy's people. It did worry me some about this new chief Bloody Spear, 'cause I'd never heard of him, and it was also worrisome that this fella hadn't heard of Limpin' Calf. I was sort'a worryin' that maybe a young Blood warrior had come down from Canada and took over the area.

Well, sir, I got myself supplied with some grub and a few necessities and headed out here to the ranch where I figured to camp a few days. Things hadn't changed at all. It looked just the same except that the graves was growed over with weeds. I retrieved the things we'd cached down that crapper hole those years before and started ponderin' how I was gonna meet up with ol' Prairie Dog, if'n he was still alive, without gettin' separated from my hair."

Tom squinted a moment in thought and waited for Grant to look up.

"When you was a kid, did you and your pals ever have secret codes and places to hide and so forth?"

"We certainly did. I suppose all young boys do those things."

"Well, we did too. I reckon it's hard for a city boy to picture what it was like, but me and those Injun kids did the same thing. Only difference I reckon is that we had miles of prairie, fast horses and smoke signals... and hidin' places that no one but an Injun could ever have found. The

Injun people pretty much gave their children a free rein on life until they was old enough to be wives or warriors, so me and them kids just had us a good old time."

"I envy that," Grant said, more to himself than to Tom.

"I cold camped a couple nights here at the ranch...sort'a visiting with my folks and doing for their graves and all. I'd even bought some flower seeds in Fort Benton to brighten up their restin' places, not sure if I'd ever be back to this place. Now, while I was seein' to my ma's grave, I unearthed a real unusual stone. It looked like a sea critter, only bleached white with time and it had a hole right in it. I remembered having seen one years before at Limpin' Calf's village. I was told that it had big medicine and I'd heard it called a Buffalo Rock. I remembered that the Injuns put big store by 'em. Since I'd found it on my ma's grave, I tied it on a thong and decided to wear it around my neck for a token of remembrance.

At the time I had no earthly idea how that fossil stone would change the outcome of my immediate mission and my whole life for that matter. After payin' my respects and seein' to the graves, I decided to ride out to one of them secret places that me and those Injun boys had played in when we was kids. It was an outcrop of rock that made a natural fortress. I'm sure you and your pals made forts too. Now this here was a real big ol' fort. In fact, it was big enough to be the real thing...sheer walls that dropped off on three sides with natural revetments and just a small entry through a bulwark of upturned granite to defend. A young warrior's dream come true, be he redskin or white...or man or boy. And we was the only ones that knew the ways over and through those rocks to get into our secret hideout."

"Our forts were mostly apple crates or furniture covered with old bed clothing," Grant said.

"It was a different world, I reckon. Since that fort had been our secret meetin' place and we'd spent a lot of time there, I figured to send our secret signal and then hole up in the fort hopin' that, if my pal was anywhere close enough to see the secret smoke, he would know it was me and not go pokin' my hide full of holes before I got a chance to explain myself.

After first lookin' about to see was there any sign of hostiles other than Blackfoot, and findin' no evidence of recent activity in the area, I eased into our fort and tied my critters.

I prepared some defenses, just in case, and fixed a cold meal to see me over...not knowin' how long I might have to wait. When I was set up, I struck a match, said a couple of amens and sent that secret smoke signal. Now I had no idea at all what would happen, but youthful folly won the day, and there I was just waiting for God knows what.

It was early afternoon when I signaled. I, real quick, put the fire out... just in case the wrong folks came lookin' to find me. I didn't want to make it too easy to get into the fort in case it was Crows or some others I wasn't none to anxious to make the acquaintance of. I kept a sharp lookout all around until it started comin' dark. I hadn't seen any movement on the prairie except for some antelope and few stray buffalos and some elk.

When the sun sank below the hills it started to get a mite chilly. I couldn't build a fire and I didn't want to encumber myself with a blanket, so I gritted my teeth and leaned back against a rock, puttin' my forty-four in my lap and my Henry Rifle across knees, which brought some comfort.

It was a moonless night as I recall, with a skiff of overcast clouds just sufficient to block out what starlight as might have been of value. The darkness of the night magnifies every sound, and this darkness was suffocating as it spread itself over my being like blackstrap molasses. Once it was plumb dark, I had no idea as to the time."

Tom pointed to Grant's wristwatch.

"We didn't have no fancy doodads like that in those days. If a man had a big ol' pocket watch he was likely a rich fella. Train robbers loved 'em. Only time I used a watch was when we had some need in the army, like those binoculars, then the officers always made sure to get 'em back."

"This watch was a gift when I graduated from Columbia," Grant said proudly.

"Most folks got those today. Hell, I even got a couple of them things myself, but we didn't have wristwatches then. In fact, I didn't have no watch at all...and the night wore on like a Sunday service with a wind bag preacher. What with the cloudy sky, there was no way of measurin' time.

I know that I dozed off a couple of times during those long hours, and I can remember waking from one particularly disturbin' dream. That dream is as vivid in my mind today as it was that night near sixty years ago. In my dream Ol' Limpin' Calf, in a fine bonnet of eagle feathers and adorned with white weasel skins, comes riding out of an eerie fog, well mounted on a huge prancin' ghostly white buffalo. Behind him was my folks in a sort of a parade...and they was astride silver white horses and wearin' white furs and finery befittin' the crowned heads. They was all smilin' and noddin' and wavin' like they was the grand marshals, and their animals glided silently by me on a carpet of camas flowers so thick that the animals seemed suspended and movin' as if being drawn along by the turnin' of the earth itself.

I ran and I hollered as loud as I could, but they took no notice of me. The faster and harder I ran, the more I seemed to be falling behind...as if the part of the earth where I was runnin' wasn't a part of that ground over yonder where their mounts were glidin'.

I felt small and weak, like I was a child, but I didn't want to look like a sissy in front of Limpin' Calf and my pa and brother. But I wanted my ma to cradle me and give me comfort. I ran faster and faster and they just kept gettin' further away until they was all swallowed up in a misty fog which seemed to be colored a pale purple by a brilliant and unearthly glow from that carpet of camas flowers.

When I woke up I sat bolt straight. I was actually breathin' hard like I'd been runnin'...my buckskin shirt was wet clean through with sweat, and I looked around in the dark, not knowin' where I was or what I was doin' there. It surely took a couple of minutes for me to get my mind workin'and realize where I was."

Tom looked over at Grant.

"Did you ever have that happen to you where you had a dream so real it took a while to figure out that you had woke up from it and it was only a dream?"

"Yes. I've had the feeling. It breaks the tie of reality. It can be frightening."

Tom pursed his lips as he shook his head.

"I wasn't sure how long I'd been sleepin', and when I got my senses back in my head I was hoping I hadn't missed anything that was gonna be my end. Then I thought I heard somethin', that is to say that I sort'a felt somethin' more than hearin' it. It felt like there were hoofed animals, big ones, movin' close to where I was. My senses were so keen now that I could feel the vibration of the ground through the cheeks of my ass. The vibratin' quit near as quick as it started and I commenced to figure that I was lettin' my imagination run away with me...what with that strange dream and all. Then I heard my horse snort and him and that mule began to paw around like they was gettin' spooky.

Back in the 'olden days,' as my grandson would say, horses was always a problem. Unlike automobiles, which you can turn off and walk away from, horses have to be tended. My dilemma in goin' to our hideout was what to do with the critters? That mule had bonded to my horse, so if'n I left her tied somewhere, she would have raised hell to be heard in half the territory. If I left both the horse and the mule and walked in to our fort, there was the danger that some predator might get 'em or some passin' Injuns would find 'em and take 'em for their own. And then there was the problem that if'n I needed to make an escape in the event that it turned out not to be my friends who came to the smoke, I would be afoot and helpless. Damned if I did and damned if I didn't!

So there I sat, quiet as I could, just prayin' that neither of those two jug headed broomtails would let out a warning for any possible belligerents that might be puttin' the sneak on me.

Now about that same time the hair on the back of my neck was puttin' through a person to person call to my better judgment. I was sittin' stark still and was barely takin' a breath. It was as dark as four feet down a cow's throat, and since I couldn't see nothin' anyways, I real quiet laid that Henry down beside me. I picked up the Colt, bein' careful to muffle the click as I brought 'er to full cock...then I got ready, settin' that forty-four on my knee to relieve the shakin' of my hand.

Time dragged as I peered into the dark, attemptin' to make out a shape...any shape...and I all of a sudden realized that I was holdin' my breath. When I let that breath out, it sounded like thunder in my ears. I was bone sure that the presence I was feelin' there in the darkness knowed I was there too. Then I heard a sound that near about made my heart leap."

Tom placed the back of his hand against his lips. In the manner of an exaggerated kiss he made a sharp sucking sound.

"That's sort'a what a prairie dog sounds like when he barks...and that was Prairie Dog's side of our signal. He'd make his prairie dog sound and my answer was to try to sound like a prairie chicken rooster on the strut."

Tom cupped his hands around his mouth and made a raspy sound in his throat by rapidly sucking air over his vocal cords.

"Now, I'll tell you that I was only too happy to signal back, when I heard that prairie dog sound. Trouble was that my voice had changed and my prairie chicken sounded more like a stomped toady frog"

Tom laughed at the memory and Grant looked up to laugh with him.

"Lucky for me my toad frog sage hen got the job done. Turned out that it was my friends. Next thing I knowed there was Injuns all over me, whoopin' and hollerin' and havin' a good laugh at how they'd counted coup on my snorin' young ass. I was sure enough happy that they was my friends 'cause had they been hostiles, my animals and my possibles, includin' my scalp would have surely been under new ownership.

We had all changed a heap over those years, and I had no idea, there in the dark, which of them redskins was which. I couldn't tell my best pal from any of them other boys who was chantin' and dancin' as they built a fire.

They had a little fun with me for a few minutes until we had fire light to see and although he had changed considerable, I finally recognized Prairie Dog by his crooked nose and the scar on his lip when he smiled.

He'd broke his nose and split his lip as a younker. We was out huntin' and he was holdin' the horses while a couple of us had gone to chase a deer. He was standin' in front of a horse that had his head down feedin' when we come sneakin' back to scare him. Trouble was that we scared that horse too and he jerked his head up and hit Prairie Dog right in the face. Broke his nose and cut his lip and he was bleedin' like a rain barrel with a bullet hole in it. After he got done bein' sore about the joke, he was right proud. Those was his first scars. Injun without no scars wasn't much of a man to their way of thinking. Anyway, we finally got the fire goin' so that we could see one another and he had to admit that had he seen me under a different circumstance, and had I been in the company of other white men, he wouldn't have knowed me either.

We exchanged the usual 'How you been doing' and all and then he said that the village was at a new summer place closer to the river and that we ought'a go on over there. After we palavered a while, he signaled and pretty quick a couple of youngsters brought the horses. When we rode into the village it was just comin' first light. The mornin' fires was bein' built for cookin' and it was just like comin' home. It smelt good and felt good and we sat around the fire and talked well into the day. No man ever had a better homecomin'."

The Dodge topped a small rise where Grant could see the ranch road leading to the main gate. As the Dodge bounced down the gentle slope toward the road, Grant saw a large cloud of dust billowing on the road in the direction of The Compound.

Tom stopped a few yards from the road. He and Grant got out of the Dodge and Grant could now make out a horse drawn wagon traveling at high speed.

"Is that a wagon from your ranch?"

"It's Buck or Howdy workin' one of the teams. I got me a couple of racing wagons, which we'll be takin' up to Canada here in the next few weeks for the Calgary Stampede. You ever been to a rodeo show?"

Before Grant could reply, the wagon passed, pulled by four horses running at full speed. The discordant clatter of the steel rimmed wagon wheels and thundering hooves sent a thrill down Grant's spine, causing him to involuntarily shudder. The din subsided as the wagon disappeared into a wake of dust.

"No. I haven't seen a rodeo. We didn't have many cowboys in Baltimore when I was a child."

Grant waved his hand in front of his face, attempting to get a breath in the choking dust.

"I would think that running those poor animals at breakneck speeds while pulling a vehicle would be extremely dangerous."

"You got that right. Wheel comes off and a man could get himself kilt. Worse yet you might hurt your horses."

Tom leaned against the Dodge and lit a cigarette as they watched the cloud of dust grow smaller in the distance. The rumbling of the wooden wheels on the gravel road began to fade as the wagon disappeared.

"That was Buck driving the wagon," Grant said.

"Looked to be him! For a young feller, Buck's one helluva teamster. Just seems to have took to it natural. He may not be worth tits on a bull frog when it comes to dealin' with people, but he's about as good a hand with critters as ever I've seen. What with the plane wreck and all, I never did get a chance to talk to him. Have you had any more problems?"

Grant shook his head, deciding that the incident with the saddle was not worth the mention.

"I've not heard of the Calgary Stampede. Is it an annual event?" Grant asked.

"Not only that, but it appears that they're gonna be doing it every year."

Tom looked obliquely at Grant and raised his eyebrows.

Grant paused for a long moment and then smiled.

"Only kidding. Right?" Grant said.

"Yep...only kiddin'! They've been doin this rodeo, which they call the Calgary Stampede, for about ten years now. It started out as a kind'a fair and agricultural exhibition. Then someone decided to have a few rodeo events. Next thing you know, all the cowboys in the United States and

Canada want to go to Calgary to show off.

You know son, cowboys are a real strange breed, even today. You take a young hand who does real hard work from can till can't, in all sorts of weather for very little pay and give him a day off...and what does he do? He goes to the rodeo. Of course, I reckon men do that with just about any endeavor. Lumberjacks do the same damned thing as far as showin' who can chop wood the fastest. These days it's automobiles. One fella drives his car real fast and another fella bets that he can drive faster. Next thing you know, someone builds a racetrack in Indianapolis and you got yourself a five hundred mile race. Boys will be boys."

Grant could hear the rumble of the wagon wheels and feel the slight vibration of the ground as a cloud of dust reappeared.

"It sounds like the wagon is coming back this way," Grant said.

"From the look of the dust he's got 'em smokin'. This is the first year that they've done a chuck wagon race for the Calgary rodeo. I got a call last fall from the promoter askin' if I'd bring a chuck wagon along to ensure they had a few participants. I provide some of the steers and rough stock for the rodeo. The fellas who promote the thing know that I can't say no to a bet, so I set Buck and Howdy to puttin' together a couple of chuck wagons. We had a bunch of parts and pieces of some old army supply wagons, which was layin' around. Now they're workin' with the teams."

Tom's voice was slowly rising so as to be heard above the clatter of the wagon's noisy approach. The din of steel rimmed wheels and iron clad horse's hooves drowned out the conversation. Grant again shuddered involuntarily at the noise. The wagon disappeared in a dust cloud headed toward The Compound.

Grant and Tom got back into the car. Tom waited until the dust dissipated before turning into the road.

"Buck and Howdy both like to rodeo, so basically I been payin' them boys to do what they'd normally be doing for nothin'. I got about two dozen cowboys I'll be takin' to Calgary. I like to hear it when they announce my boys and tell the crowd that they're from The Buffalo Rock."

"I can understand the cowboys showing their skills at roping and riding and so forth, but who in the world dreamed up a chuck wagon race?" Grant asked.

"Back in the days of the open range days we had a roundup Spring and Fall. All the outfits would meet in a central location where everyone would make camp. That was where they'd sort the stock, do the brandin' and in the evenin' they'd have 'em a little sociability.

Well, naturally the chuck wagon drivers had some preferred spots. Most liked to get close to the water and as near as possible to where the action was to set up their outfits. After a couple'a years they was racin' to see who'd get them choicest spots. But the big race came when the roundup was over. It became tradition that when all the stock was branded and the work was done, the chuck wagon teamsters would race to town for a drink. Last outfit to the saloon had to buy for the house.

Lloyd Clarkson, who sort'a manages the rodeo up in Calgary, told me that some of those old chuck wagon drivers got together and decided that they wanted a piece of the rodeo action...so there you are. Like I said, boys will be boys."

"You say you've built two wagons. Are both going to race?" Grant asked.

"Maybe so. Howdy is gettin' the hang of the drivin', but mostly I'm takin' two outfits so as to adhere to the Thomas rule of eventualities."

Tom was smiling as he watched the road and waited for Grant's question.

"And 'the rule of eventualities' is?"

"The way I got it figured is this, anything I've got a spare part for will never break. That second outfit is primarily for spare parts, which means that the other'n most likely won't break."

As Tom stopped the Dodge beside a large corral, Dixie was climbing onto the wagon seat. Buck started the horses forward and circled the corral to the gate.

Passing the Dodge, Dixie shouted, "We're going to cool out the team."

The wagon rumbled toward the pasture gate becoming smaller and smaller as it slowly moved toward the horizon.

Grant could feel the blood rushing to his face and he could hear his voice crack when he said, "Those are fine looking horses in your team."

"Yes sir, some'a the best around."

Tom looked at Grant, worry wrinkling his brow.

"Are you okay boy? You appear a bit peaked."

"No...no...I'm fine. Just a little dry I think," Grant lied, disguising the gut wrenching nausea. "I think I'll go have a bath before dinner."

"Good idea," Tom said. "Get in on the hot water before the women get to it. Besides, that dust bath I gave you could use some scrubbin'."

Grant stepped out of the Dodge and began to walk toward the house.

"By the way," Tom said. "Sunday we're gonna have a little rodeo here so as to give the boys some practice before we head up to Calgary. We always have a fun day and you can even try some cowboyin'...if'n you're a mind."

"Yes, I would enjoy that. I've not seen what happens at a rodeo so I would like to come. I don't know about cowboying, but I'll see if there is anything that I might like to give a go. I'll see you at dinner then?"

"Don't forget, we'll be havin' dinner with them bone diggers at the mess hall. You can join us there or else you can have Koko rustle you some grub if'n you're feelin' poorly. Whatever suits? You surely don't look none too good."

"I'll see you at the mess hall," Grant said.

Grant hurried to his room, his hands shaking and a sickening knot below his heart making it difficult to breathe.

He took off the dusty clothing and stood under the hot shower. His body was trembling and a strange feeling of nausea swept over him as he remembered Dixie passing in the wagon with Buck.

I do believe I have succumbed to the green-eyed monster, he thought. He soaped his hair and watched the brown dusty residue turn to mud and run down his legs.

"If this is love, then I don't want it," he said aloud to himself. "Just let things be as they were before I ever met this Dixie girl."

That evening when Grant met Professor Mossback's party in the mess hall, Tom, Caleb and Susanna were already seated, making light conversation. Grant's insides shook and the knot in his stomach grew tighter when Dixie did not join the group. He forced himself to engage in the conversation, attempting to ignore the nausea, which killed his appetite.

He scolded himself silently. After all, he had no claim on this young woman. One somewhat intimate encounter did not give him any right to expect her undying loyalty. She had said that she wasn't sure she loved him. She could go riding with anyone she pleased. Eat your dinner and enjoy the company, he told himself again and again.

He took notes of Professor Mossback's discovery and verified that he had the names of the Professor and the assistants spelled correctly in his notebook. He then gave Mossback the address where photos could be sent for publication.

Susanna noticed that Grant was only picking at his dinner.

"Grant, you don't look well. Is there anything I can get you?" she asked.

"No, I think maybe it was too much sun today. Would everyone excuse me...I'll be fine."

Leaving the mess hall he walked toward the river, completely consumed in an inferno of confusion. He walked down the wooden steps cut into the steep bank, which formed a stairway leading onto the dock where several boats were tied.

"What a pitiable dolt you are, sir," he said aloud. "She's made you no promises and you've made none to her. You're here to record the story of a lifetime, not to romance the locals...but then...I think I just might have fallen in love with this girl."

Staring at the muddy water for a long moment he attempted to get a deep breath.

"If this is what love is all about, why would anyone want any part of it? I certainly do not. I have never felt so absolutely wretched in my entire life. I hope that she and this Buck fellow have gone off in that wagon and eloped," he said aloud.

The words, spoken aloud, turned distress to antagonism. A mosquito buzzed around his ear. In his anger, he swatted at the insect with a vengeance intended to smite his frustration. The momentum of the ill planned blow landed a resounding slap to the side of his own head causing his ear to ring.

"Damn her, anyway," he said, hearing the words echo across the river on the still evening air.

As the harshness of his words sank into the swirling water, he heard footsteps behind him on the wooden planks of the dock.

"Why Mr. Collins, I trust that I am not the 'her' to whom you refer. If so, I'll be happy to slap the other side of that flesh covered bone you call your head."

"Dixie," he nearly shouted in joyous surprise. "I've been looking for you."

"I'd gathered as much from that conversation you were having with yourself. So what seems to be your quandary?"

Her fragrance enveloped his senses in the still evening air. Tawny hair framed her tanned face and a light colored print summer dress lent a glow to her features in the golden wane of the summer sunlight.

"You are an absolute fantasy in this light," he said.

His voice sounded weak in his own ears.

"Well, I'm glad you at least like the way I look. Isn't there anything else you could find to like about me?"

Without waiting for him to reply she walked to where he stood and put her arms around his waist.

"Hold me. It's getting cool."

He wrapped his arms around her, feeling a protective urgency. Holding each other tightly they stood, silent in the gathering dusk, oblivious even to the ubiquitous mosquitoes.

"So is it true?" she whispered.

"Is what true?"

"Do you really think that you love me?"

Grant held her for a long moment, but made no reply.

"I just rode along with Buck to cool the team and see what the wagon was like...and to tell him that we could remain friends but that I wouldn't be seeing him anymore.

He became quite angry...belligerent actually. As you said during your conversation with yourself, 'I made no promises.' Not to Buck...not to anyone. I never led him to believe that we were any more than friends."

She hugged him tightly.

"When we got back from cooling the team, I took a long hot bath to think about you and me...and that is why I was not at dinner."

"And what did you decide...about 'you and me'?"

"I am very worried about you. Buck is very upset and you know already about his reputation. I don't trust him. I want you to promise that you won't do anything to provoke him."

"Why is everyone so concerned that I will provoke Buck? I have no reason to do that."

"You already have," she said, looking into his eyes and then kissing him.

"And how did I do that?"

"By making me fall in love with you."

She put her arms around his neck as they shared a kiss, holding each other in a silent acknowledgment that a mutual threshold in their young lives had been crossed.

19

The summer days were passing quickly. Although Grant was working on Tom's story, he had fallen into the routine of ranch life and was enjoying the surroundings and the company. His immediate return to Saint Louis no longer seemed a priority.

Dixie, he thought to himself, had made a tremendous difference in his view of the world. He lay awake each night listening to the cacophonous ticking of the Baby Big Ben alarm clock on the table beside his bed. Conscious efforts to focus his thoughts on the original intention of his business trip were frustrated by unavoidable imaginings. His primary consideration, despite his best attempts to complete the work, seemed to be in finding ways to spend time with Dixie, while avoiding a potential confrontation with Buck.

He had become a part of Dixie's evening ritual, taking treats to her horse after dinner. It presented the opportunity of sharing time together and talking of the many things that might be. Grant had even become friends with Little Tom's dog.

Although Buck no longer spoke to Dixie or sought her out for these evening excursions, Grant could often feel unseen eyes burning holes in them from a distance.

One evening after their walk, when Grant and Dixie entered the house, Tom came from the den and said, "And what have you two been up to?"

"We went for a walk. It's a beautiful evening...except for the mosquitoes," Dixie replied.

"Come on in the den a minute. I was gonna show Grant somethin' the other day and plumb forgot."

As they entered the den Tom walked to the wall behind his desk and took down a small frame containing a fossilized sea shell with a deteriorating leather thong strung through a hole. Grant took the frame and held it in the light of the lamp to get a close look at the details.

"This is the Buffalo Rock fossil you found at your mother's grave," Grant said.

Grant handed the frame to Dixie.

"Yes, sir, like I told you, I found that rock the day before I went to meet up with my old friend Prairie Dog."

"This is what the ranch is named for?" Dixie asked.

"Well, darlin', the Blackfoot put big store by a stone like that. They believed it had magical power over the buffalo."

"So what power did they attribute to the stone?" Dixie asked.

"It is a complicated story, but I was tellin' Grant about how I found it on my mother's grave and that right after that I went to meet Koko's daddy who was known as Prairie Dog. I didn't know he was Koko's daddy when I went lookin' to find him. But anyway, I'll tell you about the rock.

When I met up with Prairie Dog and the other Injun boys who'd been my companions as a child, we went to their village and we had one rip roarin' reunion. We had us a bull session that lasted near a week. Now

I ain't rightly sure just when it happened but at some point during that gabfest, my life and status with them Blackfoot took a big turn. One of them boys noticed that fossil tied around my neck and you would have thought I had just been elected president of the Blackfoot Nation.

I didn't understand it at first. The men were all whisperin' around the fire and sort'a pointin' in as discreet a way as they was capable. Then my friend, Prairie Dog, asked me how I had come by the stone around my neck. He told me it was a Buffalo Rock and that it held big medicine and that bringin' it to the village was cause for celebratin'.

That night there was a big doin's and ceremony. All the youngsters was called to the fire to sit and listen. The Injuns didn't have writin', so all of the history was told in stories from one generation to the next. One of the old men of the village, who was a kind'a designated historian, told the story of the Buffalo Rock...not just for me but for all them kids...and all the folks for that matter. He asked if he could borrow it from me so as to pass it around so that the youngsters could see what it was and feel its magic as he told the story. I reckon that's the story that interests you, huh?"

Dixie nodded her head in anticipation.

"Seems that before the Blackfoot got their horses...in the olden days... huntin' the buffalos was a downright difficult proposition. Bein' afoot, they couldn't catch the buffalo and when the buffalo took to moving fast during the migrations, they was left hungry much of the time. Other than man power, or woman power as it was, they couldn't carry much in the way of extra meat and supplies and shelter. The only dray animals they had was dogs, which they used to pull a small travois. Back in them misty times, or so the story goes, there was one old woman who was very poor. Her robes was full of holes and her moccasins were near about to fall off her feet. In fact, the whole village was in dire straits, accordin' to the legend told that night.

The buffalo had gone away and the hunters had to walk farther and farther from camp, but even then, they couldn't find nary a one. This poor old woman went out one day to gather buffalo chips for her fire and as she walked along she heard singin'. It was a beautiful song and pretty quick she figures out that the singin' is comin' from a strange rock...and that rock, well it was singin' right to her. 'Take me,' the rock sang to the woman. 'Take me for I have great power.'

So the old woman takes the rock back to her lodge and tells her husband of the song. She shows him the rock and she tells her husband to gather all the men together as the rock had instructed her to do. She then tells him that the men are supposed to sing a special song which she would teach them...and if they was to sing the song...well it would bring the buffalo back.

You might know that her husband figures the old squaw has had a couple of the candles on her chandelier blowed out, and at first he just ignores the old gal. However, he's about hungry enough to try anything himself, so he gets all the men together with their rattles and amulets and bones and drums and such...and they all sat around a fire and began to sing the song which the old woman taught to 'em.

Then the old woman told the young men to go gather buffalo chips and put them in a line and sing a special song to them. Now the whole village really begins to figure the old woman for a loony...but bein' hungry as they was they went along anyway.

Then she began to wave a buffalo robe over the chips as the young men sang. As with any good legend, on the fourth wave of that robe, them chips all turned to buffalo. As it happened, they was camped by a big ol' cliff, which the Injuns call a buffalo jump, and the young men drove the herd, which was bein' led by an old cow...and the whole damned herd jumped off the cliff and the people was never hungry again."

Tom paused while Grant scribbled notes.

"It was, to those Injuns, a real religious story. I would reckon that it was about the equivalent of Moses and the burnin' bush and I was a happy boy to have found such a treasured article. I told them how I'd found it at my mama's grave and that it was a real meaningful keepsake to me. They was all real sympathetic, but I could tell that each and every one of them was sure enough hankerin' for that stone which hung around my neck...even though they wouldn't say nothin'.

I would'a probably given it to my pal, Prairie Dog, but he never asked and I wasn't gonna offer, bein' as how it was a keepsake of my ma and all. During the days that followed we talked about the old times and I learned what Prairie Dog been up to...and I told him about all of my adventures. He was especially interested in 'the white man's big war,' which is what the Injuns called the Civil War. They'd heard a lot about it while tradin' at the forts.

When I explained some of those battles like Gettysburg and Antietam, they couldn't believe that the white men had killed off more of each other than there was Injuns on the entire prairie. I can bet that it set ol' Prairie Dog to wonderin' how long they could last with that many white folks yet to come.

He was also real taken with my story about those pigeons. There weren't any of them pigeons on the western prairies and he'd not seen those and never hunted them. They'd all heard about the pigeons but not one of them could even imagine critters that numerous...exceptin' for the buffalo before the whites came of course.

I was about to ask Prairie Dog about the new chief that I'd heard about in town when he told me that they didn't call him Prairie Dog or Rides With White Boy no more. He'd earned a new handle and that was

Bloody Spear 'cause of the many fights he'd won. Like I told you, being a warrior was the most important thing to the Blackfoot. They actually went out lookin' for war and it seemed they had a special dislike for the Crows...and Crows hated the Blackfoot. So there was a war goin' on just about all of the time.

He told me that he had killed some white men too, mostly those hump and hiders, and that he didn't feel none too bad about doin' that. I didn't say nothin' because I'd killed or helped in killin' a passel of Injuns and I'd killed them Injuns for a whole lot less than takin' my food, I reckon. He seemed real proud of the name Bloody Spear. I could tell he was dyin' to tell me his war stories but he was tryin' to be polite not brag...but I wanted to hear it all.

I nearly choked up when he told me that ol' Limpin' Calf had been took by the pox about two years after I'd gone south. He said that half the tribe had come down with it over those next few winters. A whole bunch of new white men had brought no end of trouble for his people...not the least of which was the pox...and of course the whites wanted the army to come in to protect 'em from the hostile Injuns."

"So your friend Prairie Dog was now Bloody Spear and he was the chief that the people in Fort Benton were fearful of?" Grant said.

"It sounds like this story is about to get ugly," Dixie said.

She kissed her uncle on the forehead as she walked to the door.

"I'll see you gentlemen in the morning," she said.

She closed the door behind her.

Tom waited until his niece had left the room.

"That was him, but he wasn't a chief like you might think of it in white folk's terms...more of a holy man...like his pappy before him. That was why I'd been honored for the Buffalo Rock. The people of the village gave credit to Bloody Spear for bringing the luck of that fossil to the village, because he'd been friends with me. I know it sounds strange but those folks had their beliefs just like we do.

Now I never, for a minute, figured it was gonna cause a stir...telling Bloody Spear about my dream...but we was laughin' about how they'd put the sneak on me when I was waitin' at the old rock hideout. They claimed they could hear me snore a hundred yards. Some had even commenced to calling me Winter Bear. So, by way of conversation, I told them about the dream I'd had about Limpin' Calf and my family. When I'd finished, you could have heard a feather hit the floor of that tipi. I could tell by the looks on the faces of the men around the fire that they was seein' some real significance in such a dream.

Top that off with bein' blessed by findin' that Buffalo Rock...and the fact that I had the dream when they was puttin' the sneak on me...and this was turnin' into some really big medicine for Bloody Spear and his folks. Different ones of 'em was interpreting the dream in different ways. I figured it was mostly their wishes that they was hopin' would be fulfilled. Kind'a like sayin' a prayer. That night they chanted and danced and sang the holy songs, and we went to the sweat lodge so that they could think on it and maybe see the vision."

Grant looked up from his notes.

"Now I can see by the look on your face what you're thinkin'. Just a bunch of superstitious savages. Right?"

Grant felt as if Tom had read his thoughts. His brow wrinkled.

"Well, let me put this into a point of view that you might just understand. Every human bein' has some sort of belief system. There's folks that'll walk a mile out of their way if they see a black cat cross their path. I've seen intelligent people who was beside themselves after they broke a mirror. And there's a heap of civilized and educated folks who bow down to little plaster statues of the baby Jesus and his mama, and their ain't a livin' soul who knows what either of them looked like.

I saw some Rabbi fellas once in the big city who dressed in black and carried a rolled up parchment in a velvet pouch. Reckon they considered that parchment to be sacred. But truth be known, their reverence for that holy scroll didn't appear to me to be a lot different than a Blackfoot's reverence for his medicine bundle.

There's even some folks, I'm told, who think that cows are sacred...and they don't even eat the damned things. Blackfoot thought the buffalo was sacred. Only difference is that the buffalo actually meant life and death for them which would give that reverence a little more significance in my book.

Now, I personally believe in Jesus because that's what my ma and pa taught me. But that don't mean that I got no regard for the beliefs of other folk. And them Blackfoot rituals was a pretty potent kind of medicine for them that took it serious. So before you get too high and mighty in lookin' down your nose at them redskin rituals, you'd best take a look at what you believe and the rituals you practice."

Grant sat momentarily stunned as if he had been slapped.

"I suppose that I was raised with an attitude of superiority in such matters. I can't begin to tell you how fortunate I feel to have been allowed into your world, to see things from your perspective and to attempt to understand things that were only words in books. I have learned so much these past weeks. I do look at things in a whole new light."

Tom smiled.

"You're young. Don't be too harsh with yourself. You have a lot to learn and those are the things they couldn't teach you at that Columbia University."

"You mentioned a medicine bundle. They didn't teach that at Columbia. Could you enlighten me?" Grant said.

"Within the warrior society of the Blackfoot, just like in ours, men could move up and down the ranks by deeds and in some cases by politics. Then there was the instances of just plain old buying your way up the ladder. The Injuns didn't have money in our way of thinkin', but they had things valuable to trade, like a good bow or a horse or even a woman.

A medicine bundle was generally a collection of sacred and magical items, like amulets and maybe an eagle bone whistle that had been used to warn at a battle or a pouch of tobacco and a pipe for making peace. Wasn't no prescription for what was in it. That was more dictated by who owned it. The bundle was generally wrapped in a beaver hide and was opened on special occasions. On the occasions when the bundle was opened, the story of each item would be told by one of the old men. It was every bit as sacred to the Blackfoot as the Holy relics in Rome...near about the significance of a communion service or high mass.

The next few weeks was some shinin' days in my life. First thing we did was go on a buffalo hunt. I suspect that there was some doubtin' Thomas types among the young men who wanted to test out my Buffalo Rock. I reckon I got lucky. We'd no sooner left the village and we come upon a bunch of buffalo that was movin' through the area.

I got credit for killin' twenty seven, although the credit should have gone to that Henry rifle. I was really an honored member of the village then and some women built me a right nice tipi lodge of my own...what with all them extra hides they had. I was even offered a wife, which made for a right sticky situation. I didn't wanna hurt no one's feelin's or have anyone believin' that they was being rejected or nothin'. I managed to talk my way outta that one by sayin' that I couldn't be takin' a wife until the mission I had set for myself was complete.

Then, one night to my surprise they held a big feast. Damned if I wasn't the guest of honor. They took me to Bloody Spear's lodge and that ceremony went on for who knows how long. Couple 'a three days maybe. Seems that the dream I'd had and findin' that Buffalo Rock which had proved so successful on the hunt had also made big medicine for me in the status of the village. I was presented a new name and a medicine bundle of my own...an honor which I can't even begin to describe."

Tom sat mute for a long moment.

"I near about cried when I come to find out about that medicine bundle. When an old man told the story about each item, it turned out that this particular bundle had belonged to Limpin' Calf. You see, Limpin' Calf had not only been a great warrior but he was medicine man and a kind'a shaman. Limpin Calf's medicine bundle, with a sacred pipe and amulets and such, was the equivalent of the Arc of the Covenant for those folks, if'n you get the drift.

My new name was One Who Dreams. In Blackfoot the translation for dreamin' and havin' a vision was pretty much the same. When the story of my name and each item in the bundle was told by the old man, the pipe was smoked and the items in that bundle was then blessed with the smoke. Sweetgrass was burned and there was much ritualizin' and singin' and dancin'. I don't reckon that a priest or holy man from any religion ever had a ceremony more solemn and significant. Folks danced for days, goin' without food or water. They was hopin' to have a vision 'cause they figured that with me bein' around, the visions might come to someone else."

"That was very generous of your friend to give you his father's medicine bundle," Grant said.

"Now that medicine bundle was sure enough the rightful property of Bloody Spear, but since he'd failed in havin' a vision he had an ulterior motive in givin' it to me. He hoped that my vision and that Buffalo Rock would rub off on his village. That was kind'a his duty, what with him bein' a recognized leader. The people came first.

It was, however, about the biggest honor I ever had…and that's for sure. I ain't sayin' that everything was sunshine and flowers mind you. There was some in the village who was resentful of my presence and some who hadn't liked me even when I was a kid. I'm sure there were a couple of them boys who would'a lifted my hair and claimed that Buffalo Rock and that Medicine Bundle as his own had it not been for Bloody Spear. But then, I got on well with most of the folks and for a brief period in my life I was treated with the greatest of respect. I renewed old acquaintances and made some new friends of folks who had joined Bloody Spears bunch since last I'd seen them…and I met Bloody Spear's new wife and his new baby, little Koko…sourpuss that she was even then.

Well sir, I was in that village a while and I finally got 'round to tellin' Bloody Spear what my intention was as regarded my little sister. It turned out that he'd been harborin' some bad feelings about his Blood cousins from the north himself. Not only that, but he'd had a couple of minor disputes with the bunch that took my little sis, but he didn't seem none to anxious to piss 'em off neither. When he explained it, I understood his thinkin'.

First of all, he'd lost a few men in the recent fightin' with the Crows and he didn't have the warrior strength to make all-out war with the Bloods. In addition to that, the Bloods was, after all, of the same tribe, and besides, he had his hands full with the Crows and the buffalo hunters, not to mention the United States Army. He didn't come right out and refuse to help but he reckoned he was gonna have to think on it a bit. I didn't push none 'cause I couldn't blame him. He had to look to his own village first, after all, and we didn't even know if Sarah was still with that bunch up north, or if she'd been sold or killed or what. So don't get thinkin' he was fearful. However, he did tell me one thing that gave me hope. He said he reckoned that Sarah must still be livin'. I had to puzzle on that a bit and then he said that, had she gone under, she would have been with Limpin' Calf and my ma and pa and brother in the vision. I reckon that sounds like foolishness to you...but it was plumb serious to Bloody Spear."

"I wouldn't disparage the beliefs of the Blackfoot in any way," Grant said.

"I also reckon you just see these Injun villages like you'd figure a small town would be set up. You got your Mayor and the Councilmen and so forth. But it wasn't really like that. There was politics sure enough, but a person could achieve status in a couple'a ways in the Blackfoot Nation. Bein' a great warrior and accumulatin' wealth in that way was, of course, big medicine. Or a person could get status by bein' spiritual and havin' the vision or maybe by some good works in helpin' others in the group. In that way, men and women could get status and respect. Women not as much as men though 'cause they wasn't warriors. But they could achieve status none the less.

Another thing to remember is that any particular piece of real estate, even on these vast prairies, could only support a small number of folks. Edible plants and huntable game had to be conserved. So the Injuns spread themselves thin over the ground that was available...and even at that there really wasn't ever very many of 'em. So a particular tribe might be broken into eight or ten villages spread over hundreds of miles so as not to excessively burden nature's stores from year to year.

The head man, or 'the chief' as we like to call 'em, was almost more like a feudal lord than a governor. He mediated disputes and held council when there was a big war'a brewin' or trouble that would be a detriment to all of the villages. He sort'a oversaw the doin's of the tribe. Then in each village there was a chief...like Bloody Spear. That chief was responsible for leadin' the people to where there was food and water and buffalo robes and safety and such.

Now, whereas Bloody Spear and Limpin' Calf before him, was local village leaders, they weren't neither one of them a big chief...and unlike the feudal system, any individual or family in the village could just up and go somewhere else if'n the chief wasn't doing his job. So you might have a family in one village one year and another village the next.

Now, as to the politics, it worked like this. Before any big decision, like startin' an inter-tribal war could be undertaken, Bloody Spear would have been obliged to go for a sit-down consult with his big chief. At that time the big chief was a great warrior by the name of Spotted Horse. Another thing that would have made it tough on Bloody Spear, politically speakin', was that the fella who had led the raid on my folk's ranch was a big chief his own self. He was the equivalent of Spotted Horse, who was a Piegan, only he was the leader of those Bloods up in Canada. He went by the name of Puma, which roughly translated to Ghost of the Mountain as the Injuns called the Mountain Lions and his village was up in the area north of what is now that new Glacier Park."

"So Bloody Spear had to play politics," Grant said.

"You bet! Just like any group of folks today. And to keep his position a fella had to play his politics right or he ended up an outcast or worse yet...dead.

So I was bidin' my time as far as Sister Sarah was concerned. I was goin' huntin' with Bloody Spear and the boys. I even went raidin' on the Crows and took a couple of scalps.

I was doin' magic tricks for the kids. You know, makin' stuff disappear and pullin' feathers out of their ears and all...and getting' some good photographs of the people in the village. Gettin' some practice with that camera I'd acquired.

It was late in the season by then and the geese were already bunchin' up for the trip to the south. By then, I'm kind'a figurin' that maybe I'd be waitin' for spring to get headed up to Canada, not knowin' when my friend was gonna talk to Spotted Horse and all.

Then one afternoon, fate throws me a trump card. Who comes ridin' into the village but that very same big chief, ol' Puma, from up north and a party of about twenty of his young warriors. When I figured out who they was, I real quick told Bloody Spear and all the people in the village to play it quiet as to who I was.

I didn't want them knowin' quite yet that I was looking into the whereabouts of my sister. We pretended like I was just learnin' the language so that I could play dumb if'n it suited. Bloody Spear told ol' Puma that they was helpin' me get some photos and that I was bein' honored because I had shown some big medicine, which was namely some magic tricks and that Buffalo Rock of course.

Just for bona fides, I performed some prestidigitation, and I wore that Buffalo Rock outside my shirt on a thong where it could be seen and admired while them cutthroat bastards was in the village drinkin' themselves to oblivion. Seems they'd wiped out a party of hide hunters and got themselves some whiskey. I could see in their eyes that near about any one of them murderin' slime would'a cut my heart out to have that Buffalo Rock.

Then a plan commenced formin' in my head. I decided to spread some sweet frostin' on the bait provided by the Buffalo Rock...and attempt to get myself an invite to Canada. I started to flaunt my medicine bundle and I really put on some magic for them blackguards. I got one of the youngsters in the village and swore him to secrecy...then I performed my famous levitation trick. I had that child floatin' on thin air the likes of which would have made Houdini himself proud.

Then ol' Bloody Spear surprised me by spreadin' it on real thick about what a sacred individual I had become to his people. I could feel the jealousy just boilin' around that camp. Those Bloods had them a passel of buffalo robes they was packin' on a bunch of horses, which they'd stole from the hiders...and they had stringers of bloody scalps. They was sure enough in a braggin' mood. In addition, to the hide hunters, they'd raided a village of Crows and killed all but some women and kids, which they'd brung along to raise or trade or use for slaves."

"This may sound naïve," Grant said, "but I hadn't associated the Native Americans of the plains with slavery."

"It wasn't only the plains Injuns that had slaves. Hell, boy, there was a bunch of Injuns who fought for the Confederacy, so as not to lose their black slaves. I never gave it much thought but I reckon them redskinned Simon Legrees just never got the recognition they deserved."

Grant's face lit up in a smile.

"Perhaps Mrs. Beecher Stowe made those stories up and was therefore unaware that Indians had participated. She should have done her research," Grant said.

"I reckon you could be right," Tom said. "That's why I didn't want you just makin' up no stories about my life. You might leave out somethin' important...but anyways, the only thing that had me worried at that point was that one of them young Bloods would get liquored up and cut my throat to acquire my magic."

"Weren't you under the protection of Bloody Spear and his people?" Grant asked.

"That offered some protection but once them redskins got into their liquor there wasn't no tellin' which way they was likely to blow. Hell, when those Injuns got drunked up they was just as likely as not to kill their own brother. As soon as the drinkin' started in earnest, I took to my lodge to sit out the party. But every few minutes, one of them boys from the Blood village was comin' to me offerin' to trade everything but their grandpappy's soul in exchange for that Buffalo Rock. I had a couple of my old pals from our childhood days sleep in my lodge and sit with me to smoke...and thus I kept a low profile...and when confronted with a trade by some drunken Blood, I just claimed 'I no speakin' Blackfoot.'"

"I guess I don't understand how these people coming to the camp of Bloody Spear worked to the benefit of your plan to rescue your sister," Grant said.

"Well, sir, like I said, them Bloods had raided a Crow village in addition to killin' some white men...and then they'd rode right into Bloody Spears village leavin' a trail that could have been followed by those Ohio plow pushers I'd scouted for.

It didn't take too much calculatin' to figure that before too long there was gonna be more folks ridin' into that camp and they wouldn't be comin' to party. There was bound to be some pissed off Crows lookin' for their children and revenge and then there might damned well be the United States Cavalry comin' to find out who was killin' white folks in their area of responsibility. Let's just say that Bloody Spear's requirement for diplomacy wasn't near as urgent as it had been before ol' Puma brought the threat of annihilation to the doorstep of his village.

Fact is that Bloody Spear was madder than a wolverine with his tail in a snare. First thing he had to do when them outlaws moved on was to move the whole village to a safer place...which wasn't no easy doin's what with the winter comin' on fast. And he still had to get in one more buffalo hunt to feed his folks through the cold times ahead."

"Those people must have been really tough. The tribulations you describe, when one thinks of the women and children and the old people involved...it is just heartrending," Grant said.

"And heartrendin' it surely was. But cryin' after the spilt bourbon wasn't gonna see to the needs of the folks who was needin' took care of. So we moved the village clear up into the south fork of the Flathead Valley where there was some winter huntin' and sheltered sites for the village.

The Flathead Injuns who lived there were a mean enough bunch, but Bloody Spear reckoned they wasn't the measure of the Crows when it come to war, and they seemed a bit more willin' to trade and get along than the Crows would have been, under the circumstances. So it was really the only choice ol' Bloody Spear had.

Now all this movin' gave me a chance to start formulatin' a plan to go north and get my sister and sure enough when I put my mind to it, a plan came to me. Bein' a white man, of course, I had some needs for things that a fella just couldn't find out in the wilderness. As the village was bein' moved, I rode into Fort Benton with my pack mule and got some supplies for my own comfort...such as tobacco, some long johns, a new pair of suspenders and some extra cartridges in addition to a few other things I thought might come in handy if'n I ever got to Puma's village. Then I rode with Bloody Spear to see Spotted Horse and have a confab with the old chief about the situation with Puma's bunch.

Spotted Horse didn't figure that all of his Piegans together would have been the match of Puma's Bloods and he really didn't want no war. However, he did take to account that them Bloods had put Bloody Spear's Piegans into much danger with their reckless behavior and poachin' on Bloody Spear's ground.

Ol' Puma was such an arrogant bastard that he'd done all them things without seekin' the permission of Spotted Horse. The old chief reckoned that maybe Bloody Spear had a right to get some back, if'n he could do it without creatin' all-out hostilities. So, as your ol' school teacher used to say, we put on our thinkin' caps and come up with a plan.

First thing we done was to get the people moved. Then we hunted our Fall hunt, and damned if that Buffalo Rock wasn't with me again. We got enough meat to see everyone in the village through the longest winter. After the buffalo meat got jerked and hung to dry, the women commenced makin' the pemmican and other stores to get the people through the cold times.

Then me and Bloody Spear began to plannin' in earnest. We decided on some appropriate trade goods and gifts and began our preparations. I told Bloody Spear about a few tricks I was keepin' up my sleeve. For example, I'd found myself a copy of the Old Farmer's Almanac while I was in Fort Benton and I'd got me a real good idea from that book. Plus, I'd bought some other things which I explained to my friend might just come to some value.

We had to plan careful so that he wouldn't be faced with nothin' unexpected when we got to our business. Now to my surprise, Bloody Spear come up with an idea or two of his own, which was really outta character for a man as devout as I knew him to be. Anyway, we figured we was armed with as good a plan as we could conjure and as it was now gettin' late into the fall, Bloody Spear and me decided to ride north and take our chances with the snow.

Now I was a pretty fair hand at findin' my way around the country, but them Injuns always amazed me. Ol' Bloody Spear rode straight to that Blood village like he'd had a map drawn in his head. Turned out that Puma's village was about twenty miles from that Fort Macleod up in Canada.

It took me and Bloody Spear several days to get up to the village and as we traveled we was polishin' our strategy. For my part of the deal, I wanted to get back my little sister and for Bloody Spear's part he wanted to get even and give ol' Puma a little what for.

I would reckon that you're probably wondering why it was just the two of us goin', considerin' the gravity of our mission.

Well, sir, we wanted to show some good faith. To make them Bloods think we was just comin' for a social call and had no hostile intentions. We didn't want to ride in with a gaggle of warriors and arouse suspicion... and besides, our plan only required that we sell Puma a pig in a poke. Are you familiar with that sayin'?"

"As a matter of fact, I am," Grant said. "One might even say that I have a PhD in that concept."

Tom looked at Grant with a quizzical smile.

"Hmmmm!" Tom said. "Well, as it went, the last night we camped, we went over all the details to make sure as to what our signals was gonna be...kind'a like when we was kids. We was both feelin' good when the next day we rode right into that village like we owned the place. There was some real excitement when we come riding in. Lots'a shoutin' and kids chasin' our horses. There was also some not so happy faces in the crowd and them hairs on the back'a my neck was a constant reminder that this could be some serious business. But we ride right up to the lodge of ol' Puma and announce ourselves like we was family. He had, after all, extended the invite. But even at that, he had a look on his face like he'd stepped barefoot on a dog turd. Blood may be thicker'n water but it can still be spilled if'n you get on the wrong side of some mean bastards like these.

Now, I ain't gonna try to explain the whole inner workin's of a warrior society, but when we arrived, all of the senior men got an invite to come and sit around Puma's fire and smoke with me and Bloody Spear. One'a the warriors that was present was a fella by the name of Angry Bear, who Bloody Spear recognized as Puma's son. He was a couple'a years older than me and Bloody Spear, and Bloody Spear told me that he'd been one of the young men along on the raid when my folks was killed.

I didn't know him and he hadn't been with Puma's bunch when they came to Bloody Spear's village some weeks before, but there was a few others that I did recognize and they was givin' me some dirty looks. The jealousy was pretty clear.

But the welcomin' went on for a day or so and then I unpacked my camera and started to get with the business at hand. I was doin' my magic for the folks, like pulling a tomahawk outta the ear of their best warrior and such, and takin' pictures of various ones, while Bloody Spear was learnin' what he could.

While I was takin' pictures, I saw a squaw who I knew right off was a white girl. When she looked at me I could see my ma written all over her face. I could also see that she'd got beat some...bruises and such. I knew sure certain it was Sarah. Soon as she saw me she went right into her lodge. I figured that she'd been told to keep clear of me, but I was sure that she didn't recognize me, which was a good thing.

I told Bloody Spear that I'd seen her and then he gave me the bad news. He said that Sarah was Angry Bear's woman...Angry Bear bein' Puma's son, and they had twin baby boys. I knew right then that this was gonna be a whole lot tougher than it had seemed when I was plannin' this adventure."

Grant looked up from his writing pad.

"Romulus and Remus?"

"By God, we may make an investigatin' journalist out of you yet son. So, let's see, then I talked it over with Bloody Spear and told him that maybe it was best that he just ride on out and let me have a go at getting Sarah by myself. Just leaving that camp in one piece with our hair was gonna be tough, but packin' along the wife of Puma's son was beginnin' to appear near about impossible...and gettin' two babies out besides...well I reckon you can see the difficulty.

Discouraged as I was, my good pal Bloody Spear bucked me up. He reckoned as how he had confidence in our plan. He figured that if my medicine held out we'd make 'er just fine. I wasn't quite so confident in that medicine but we set about to work our scheme.

Now as it turned out, although ol' Puma was surprised that we'd paid him a visit so soon, he was right happy about it. He had a hankerin' for my magic and he was wantin' to know more. That was good because at least we had his interest. But I needed to get the ol' boy alone. Remember me telling you about that almanac I'd got in Fort Benton? Well, I was workin' on a timetable that was gonna have to be kept close or the whole plan was gonna come apart like a wet loaf of bread. You see, I'd read in that Old Farmer's Almanac that there was gonna be an eclipse of the sun and it was gonna occur just four days hence of the day we'd arrived. So we was down to about two days of settin' the stage for the big event.

That next mornin' I go to Puma and tell him I'd like to get a picture of him and me and his lodge. I'd showed Bloody Spear how to take a picture with that camera and he got a good one of me and ol' Puma together. I reckon Puma at least trusted me that far 'cause I got them photographs and developed them to a print right there. Then I told Puma that we should sit and smoke together as I was hankerin' to learn the secrets of his leadership success and longevity. Tried to pump the old fart up a little and play on his vanity.

I convinced the old boy that we had to be alone so as not to share the magic with all the men who might be after his position. Now, I'll tell you one thing for certain, if you're gonna try to trade somethin' away from a man and he values that thing and he's expectin' somethin' of value in return…it's a damned good idea to give more than he thinks he deserves. I don't think Puma would'a give a roasted rats ass about me takin' Sarah, even her bein' his daughter-in-law and all, but to give up his two grandsons, that was gonna take some doin'. I was pretty damned sure that Sarah wouldn't go nowhere without those children, so me and Bloody Spear decided that we had to convince Puma to take his reward in the next world or the happy hunting grounds as they say in them dime novels...and you know how folks are about their hope of heaven?

If we could make Puma believe that his reward would be in the next life, just maybe we could get outta that place alive and avoid the war. After all, he wouldn't know that he'd been bent over the stump until after he was dead. Sounded fool proof!

I finally got the invite to come to Puma's lodge and smoke. That was just what I'd hoped for and the timin' couldn't have been no better. This was the day of that eclipse. Even though I had no watch I knew from the book that it was gonna get real dark that afternoon and seein' as how it was a bright sunny day, it was perfect.

I stalled ol' Puma until about noon by the sun. Then I told Bloody Spear to come along and we went to see Puma carryin' with us my prized medicine bundle and that camera. I set that camera up outside Puma's lodge and we went in to set our plan in motion.

When I laid that bundle wrapped in beaver hide on the robe between us, ol' Puma's eyes lit up like the Aurora Borealis. He knew then that he was gonna be privy to some really big medicine and he run all the women and everyone else outta that lodge.

I started real slow to unroll that bundle and bein' as nonchalant as you please I put them items of interest there between us for the power to be felt. Real slow I got that tobacco pouch and started in to pack that pipe for the smokin' and you could see in his face that this was just like Christmas. I handed that pipe over to Puma and give him the honor of the first smoke. He takes a brand from the fire and lights 'er up...gets a good snort...and don't appear none too anxious to hand it on. When he finally did hand that pipe to Bloody Spear his eyes was rollin' and he was soarin' with the eagles."

"What was it about the pipe that put him into such an extraordinary reverie?" Grant asked.

"Well, you see, one of them items I'd acquired whilst I was in Fort Benton was a quantity of opium. Now you've likely heard the reputation that the Injuns have for bein' real susceptible to the effects of whiskey. Based on what I knew of what opium did to white men, I kind'a figured that maybe it would discombobulate ol' Puma's brains for certain. I was only hopin'...but I was sure as hell right. I'd been real careful to tell Bloody Spear that whatever he did he was not to take that smoke into his lungs. I explained that it was magic beyond any he'd ever seen and beyond my control. When he saw the effects on ol' Puma he knew I was sure enough right about that. You see, I'd packed the bottom of that pipe bowl with the opium before we got to Puma's lodge. I just put the tobacco on top so that when she was lit up, the fumes would go right to his head."

"So you drugged the old chief?"

"All's fair in love and war, my boy," Tom laughed. "And that ain't the half of it. When his eyes got to rollin' and he looked like he wanted to tip over and slip into dream land, me and my pal start tellin' the ol' boy about the great mystery of my camera and how I could steal a man's spirit if'n I was a mind. Then I proceeded to get out that picture me and him together and showed him.

Of course, what I'd done was make two copies. In the one he was clear as day. In the other I'd blurred him some while I was doin' the developin'. He was just barely visible in the photo and I told him that I could take away or replace his spirit any time I was a mind to do so. With a little sleight of hand I exchanged them photos just to show him the jeopardy that could come upon him without warning. Of course, him bein' drugged to a stupor didn't hurt my presentation any.

Then I reckoned it was gettin' on to the time to really put it on him. I let the ol' bastard get a few more puffs on that pipe and then we took him out to where I had that camera set. Only this time I didn't get no pictures of people. I pointed that camera at the sky and me and Bloody Spear told him to get all his men to start a dance."

A huge grin covered Tom's face.

"Now did you ever see a drunk who didn't want to have party?"

"No, I don't suppose I have," Grant affirmed.

"Well that ol' Injun wasn't no different. He started dancin' and all his people begun to dance, even though they had no idea as to why. I kept tendin' that camera and sayin' a little prayer of my own that this was the right day and time...and sure enough it begun to get dim. I told the ol' fool to keep that dance goin' and before too long it was downright dark.

I told 'em to build a big fire and that if they kept that dance'a goin' I'd bring back the sun...and damned if I didn't. Even my pal, Bloody Spear had to marvel at that magic and I'd told him it was comin'. I also told Bloody Spear not to be lookin' at the sun. I'd read in that book that if'n you looked when the sun was dim you could go blind. Damned if a bunch of them Blood bastards didn't do just that. Too bad! But I reckon they was outta the murderin' business after that. It really gave the aura of magic and that's for certain.

While it was dark I snuck back into Puma's lodge and put some more of that opium in the pipe and then went back to my post by the camera. When it come back to light I told Puma to keep them folks dancin' lest the sun leave again for good.

I kept that bunch dancin' all afternoon and the whole night until they was about wore to a frazzle. Now I'd tried that opium myself at a Chinaman's place when I was with the Army down in Colorado. I was sure that ol' Puma was gonna have some sort'a vision when he finally got some rest...and sure enough he did.

Next day as the effects was wearin' away, he sent to have me come and smoke some more. He'd sure enough had a vision and he was wantin' to trade no matter what the cost. By now he'd plumb forgot about that Buffalo Rock, and he was bound on havin' my medicine bundle and the magic within. So I tucked that bundle under my arm and went to see what he had to offer. In my best broken Blackfoot I told the ol' fart that I couldn't palaver well enough to bargain and I sent for Bloody Spear to act as my intermediary.

Now Puma was an overconfident ol' pirate but he wasn't dull. He knew that if harm was to come to me or Bloody Spear he'd have himself a war on his hands. And even though he had the strongest bunch for the fightin', it would still be costly in lives. So the negotiatin' was begun... along with the smokin' of course. I was actin' like I hadn't an idea as to what was goin' on while Puma was makin' his offers. First he offered some horses and Bloody Spear just laughed and told the ol' thief that the white magician had more horses than any man could ever ride.

Then it was furs, and then weapons and finally women. Bloody Spear kind'a took the bull by the horns when the women got mentioned. 'Which ones of the women would be in the tradin', he asked. Puma was beside himself by now, and not thinkin' real clear what with the opium and all. He said he'd give any squaw in the village.

Bloody Spear got uppity and acted real offended. He told Puma that most of the women in his village lacked beauty and grace. He told the old boy that the white man didn't favor his dark skinned girls. Bloody Spear told him that the white man favored light eyed women who were young and strong.

The old fart looked for a minute as if someone had kicked him in the balls. He explained in his most offended manner that the only woman like that in the village was married to his boy Angry Bear and that she had given him two grandsons. At that point ol' Bloody Spear showed his real talent as a diplomat. He comes right back at Puma and tells the old bastard that since this white woman and her children were of such value to him, nothin' less would be a fair enough trade. After all, he tells the old chief, this white man has a Medicine Bundle guaranteed to pass on magic to take him to the next world as the greatest of all warriors. Of course, he was so pie-eyed from that opium that he figured he was already half way there.

Puttin' on the best hurt look he could muster, Puma told Bloody Spear that the deal was done. Now just to show you what a disreputable sumbitch the ol' boy was, he tells Bloody Spear that his boy ain't gonna be none too charmed with the idea of losin' his family, so we're gonna have to trick him. Like I said before, blood is thicker'n water...but..."

"You mean that the old chief was willing to cheat his own son out of his family for a mere thing?"

"Now you're beginnin' to get the picture. Yes sir, treachery ain't the exclusive purview of white folks you know. The desire for power is a siren song that has brought many a man to disrepute. He sure enough sent that kid of his with a huntin' party on a real wild goose chase. He'd conjured up some bullshit story for Angry Bear that he needed some eagle feathers and a Big Horn ram for the dark sun magic. He sent them boys off in search of two of the most difficult critters on earth there is to catch. He figured that whilst Angry Bear and the young warriors was gone, he'd make the exchange and send me and Bloody Spear down the trail with little sister and those babies."

"My hat is off to you, even though it was a deceitful thing to do. You managed to rescue your sister and avoid bloodshed. That was a masterful stroke," Grant said.

"The deceit was even worse than you're imaginin', on both sides. Like I told you, we'd convinced ol' Puma that he'd get his reward in the afterlife, what with that Medicine Bundle and the magic and all, and that was exactly what he was gonna have to do...wait for the afterlife. The reason he was gonna have to wait is because that bundle I gave the ol' renegade was just a bundle of junk. Other than that opium, there wasn't no more magic or significance to that package than the value of the beaver hide at any tradin' post.

However, it turned out that sword was cuttin' two ways on the deal, and I was about to learn a great lesson in horse tradin' my own self. You see, gettin' little sister outta that Blackfoot camp was still gonna prove an ugly chore.

As it turned out, my little sister Sarah was as happy there with them Injuns as a grizzly on gut pile...and damned near as mean. She had no intention of leavin' that place. Puma's word or no Puma's word...she dug in her heels and wasn't goin'. It was good that I could palaver in Blackfoot 'cause she'd lost a lot of her English.

She made it downright clear that although she remembered and missed her ma and pa and she still remembered me as a child...and although she would always love those memories, she was stayin' with Angry Bear. Wife beatin' sumbitch or not, she let it be known that she harbored no desire to go anywhere except with him. So even though we didn't have to fight our way outta that village, we was fightin' with little sister every step of the way to get her and them two babies onto the horses and outta there."

"Did it surprise you that she wouldn't want to go with her own family? Grant asked. Before Tom could answer he said, "If she wanted to stay, why didn't you let her alone?"

"Now those are good questions. First of all, there was a mind-set in those times about white women and Injuns. There was no Christian man who would leave his sister to the mercy of savages. Much as I loved my Injun friends and the Injun ways, I had been raised as white Christian man with mores that left me committed to an irreversible course of action. Lookin' back, I should have left well enough alone. I was ambivalent even then, and that's for certain. But I'd gone so far as to cause my friend Bloody Spear to commit religious violations of his beliefs to get this woman back to white civilization...and gettin' her to civilization I was bound to do. The worst part for me was the hate in that girl's eyes whenever she looked at me. Like I said before, we're all the subjects of our beliefs, and hate or no hate, little sister was goin' home. I didn't see that I had no choice."

"I have read enough to understand the ethos of the times and I suppose you are correct that we are acquiescent to our beliefs," Grant said.

"Yes, sir, unfortunately that is what's so. But anyway, me'n Bloody Spear get headed down the dusty trail just as fat, dumb and happy as we could be. We got little sis between us so that she can't run off and we're just takin' it slow and easy because of the babies. Second day out we start to see pony tracks. Bloody Spear and me get to lookin' at the tracks and become aware that we've got ourselves some company there in those mountains...and our company is a Blackfoot huntin' party.

This was what I meant when I said that the treachery sword was double edged. Seems when ol' Puma sent Angry Bear and his bunch on the huntin' party, he didn't tell us where he'd sent 'em, and we was so happy to have won the tradin' that it never occurred to us to figure he might be puttin' one over on us.

Me and Bloody Spear got hit with the reality of the situation at about the same time. Ol' Puma had sent the huntin' party to be right in the middle of our escape route. That disgraceful ol' horse thief had it figured that if'n Angry Bear and that huntin' party killed us for stealin' his woman and children, he could talk his way around a war with ol' Spotted Horse and have his medicine bundle and our scalps too.

Now them old hairs on the back of my neck begun to tingle.Sure enough, I come around a bend and right there in the trail ahead was Angry Bear and about five of them fellas he'd rode outta camp with. I was leadin' the way and pullin' the pack mule. Little sister was behind me pullin' a pack horse with the children and their possibles and Bloody Spear was bringin' up the rear to make sure she didn't just vamoose back to where we'd come from.

When Angry Bear saw it was me, him and his boys all got big smiles. They was just as happy not to have encountered hostiles in their path as I would'a been. Then little sister comes around the bend and the entire mood of the situation took a turn. Havin' seen those tracks earlier, I had my Henry restin' on the saddle horn in front'a me and just by instinct I raised her up and snapped off a shot.

Ol' Angry Bear must'a been packin' some medicine of his own 'cause I just plain missed the sumbitch...but I managed to kill the fella that was behind him. Now I knew that Bloody Spear hadn't yet rounded the bend in the trail, and I was hoping that the shot was gonna warn him that the fight was on and to get ready for it.

At about this time I got an inklin' of why they called that boy Angry Bear. That man got a look on his face like I don't think I'd ever seen before. I swear that his cayuse must'a been blind 'cause he took that pony from a dead stop to a full run in the forty yards that separated us and ran that poor dumb animal right into my horse. We both just went sprawlin' through the saplings and when we hit the ground he was all over me like a bad odor. I guess I was lucky that I'd landed on my back 'cause I could at least see him. But he was astraddle of my chest with his knees pinnin' my arms to the ground and he had me by the throat.

Now seein' as how I'd got the wind knocked outta me from that collision, he wasn't havin' much trouble chokin' the breath right outta me. I heard a shot and I figured that Bloody Spear was probably a little busy, so I wasn't expectin' no help. I could hear little sister hollerin', but I sure as hell wasn't countin' on no assistance from her.

Me'n Angry Bear was nose to nose, and I could smell his breath as he was screamin' at me in Blackfoot, 'You will die white man and I will have your magic. You will not take my woman,' and such like that. By that time the chokin' was havin' an effect and things was getting' fuzzy. My head was swimmin' and this was turnin' into a real serious situation.

Now ol' Angry Bear was wearin' a quiver'of arrows, which had got all catawampus when we'd tumbled from our mounts. I was just takin' my last gasp when my hand fell upon feathers. I realized that I had one'a Angry Bear's arrows in my hand. I scooched my hand down the shaft enough so as to get a bit of leverage and then turned it just that little bit so it was pointed at his behind. I shoved that arrow point about three inches into his hip bone. He let out a holler that could'a been heard in Texas. He let go his grip on my throat and commenced tryin' to wrestle that arrow free from my hand, which he had pinned to the ground with his knee.

A couple'a breaths and I was able to renew my strength and while he was turned and distracted with tryin' to pull that arrow out of his ass, I got my right arm loose and was able to get him by the throat. Now I knew that it was gonna be way too long for him to feel the effects of me chokin' on him and he was a pretty strong ol' boy. When he turned his head to look at that arrow, I let go of his neck and grabbed hold of his hair. I jerked him sideways hard enough that it should have broke his neck...but like I said, he was tough. However, the pulling of his hair had enough momentum to put him on his back with me on top. Trouble was that he had pulled that arrow out of his butt and was holdin' the business end so as to preoccupy my time with pinnin' his arm to keep from gettin' stuck by the arrow myself.

Little sister was caterwaulin' like she'd done on that river boat. The babies was squalling from all that excitement and the shootin'...and now I could hear Bloody Spear doin' a chant that I took for his victory whoopin'.

Just when I thought I was gettin' the upper hand, I felt somethin' rip my back and felt a pain like a hot poker had been jammed against me. I was keepin' my eye on ol' Angry Bear's face and when I felt that pain I saw him kind'a smile. He seemed to relax just a little, which loosened his grip on the arrow we was playin' tug'a war with.

I could feel someone jerkin' on my collar tryin' to pull me loose from Angry Bear, but when he relaxed just that bit, I took the advantage and wrenched that broken piece of arrow away from him and in one motion I stuck it into his eye. Must'a went right into his brain 'cause he jerked a little but the fight was gone...and the truth is that fight was gone outta me too. I just keeled over and fell beside him.

When I looked up, Bloody Spear was holding Sister Sarah's arm. She had a bloody scalpin' knife clutched in her fist. Damned if that woman hadn't tried to kill me. She'd laid me to the bone along my shoulder blade and had come real near my spine."

"What were the other Indians doing?" Grant asked.

"Now ol' Bloody Spear had took care of his own end of this deal. He'd shot one'a the Bloods with his single shot rifle and had plumb ruined the day of another with his famous bloody spear. The other three had apparently decided that it really wasn't none of their business, I reckon.

They decided to just watch. After all, by the rules I was considered a Blackfoot and Bloody Spear had been knowin' a couple of those men since they was children. I reckon those other Injuns figured that there was nothin' to be gained by gettin' themselves hurt or killed over a family feud."

"So no one stopped you after Angry Bear was killed?"

"Nope! We was free as geese. Unfortunately, I was pretty well stove up and it took Bloody Spear a day or two to get me to where I could even ride. Angry Bear's friends hauled his carcass off and little sister was actin' as bitter as a pie cherry. She did her whole howlin' ritual...the ceremony that wives of Blackfoot braves do when their old man is killed. You'd have to see it to understand what I'm talkin' about. Caterwaulin' and throwing dirt about. Near about as raucous as an Arkansas holy roller.

At that point, I was beginnin' to feel real bad about havin' kilt ol' Angry Bear the way I'd done, but at least I'd fulfilled my manly obligation, as I'd seen it at the time. I got my sister outta the Blood village and we'd avoided a war. So you might say that the mission was accomplished, even though it was, in some ways, a real disaster all around.

Puma got stuck with a Medicine Bundle that had all the powers of gopher fart. Allowin' as how he wasn't supposed to get he reward until the next world, I reckon he was real disappointed when he died. Worse yet, he'd lost his son and both his grandsons and there wasn't a shittin' thing he could do about any of it in the way of revenge. So I felt like I'd squared the deal just a little bit for my folks. But little sister was one unhappy squaw. She hated my guts and she wasn't fit company for a rattle snake for the longest time...and of course, Rom and Remus lost their natural pappy. I reckon I felt as bad about that as anything.

Bloody Spear ended up with the best of the bargain. He got himself some give back to those Bloods for endangerin' his people and he didn't end up havin' a war."

Grant was writing furiously and Tom sat silently until he looked up from his notes.

"What did you do with your sister and the children then?" Grant asked.

"It's late boy. I'm about wore out. Been a long day! Remind me where we was next time we talk. It's easier for me to take it a step at a time. I'm tryin' to get everything down in order. Makes it easier for me to remember and for you to record."

"That's well. I was about to get writer's cramp anyway. I walked down to your docks the other evening. I didn't know you had boats. That is a very nice facility."

"Some of our dudes like to fish and I kind'a enjoy it myself now and then. Good way to relax and get your mind off the world. Have you ever caught a Paddle Fish?"

"I've never caught a fish of any kind. I have never even been fishing. It's always seemed a rather strange form of entertainment to me. I have always wondered at the excitement people experience from such a sport. I even read Walton but it didn't inspire me."

"Well then, by God we'll see to it that you get to catch a fish before you leave the Buffalo Rock."

Grant raised his eyebrows in a look of dismay.

"That sounds delightful," he said, with a note of sarcasm.

"Well, I'll see you in the mornin' then. I think Koko is fixin' some breakfast if'n you're up. Turn out the lights when you go to bed."

Grant sat alone, allowing the events of the last few days to assimilate in his mind. Hearing the creak of the wooden floor boards under Tom's feet in the silent house he smiled to himself. He could sneak into Dixie's room but the entire household would hear.

His face reddened involuntarily as his Victorian mores quickly overwhelmed the carnal conspiracy he was conjuring. He silently uttered a prayer, hoping for redemption, but the thought of her yielding to his lust could not be obliterated. He crept to his room, certain that all in the house were feeling his urgency.

2 0

Tom was on the dock stringing braided line through the guides of a heavy split bamboo fishing rod when Grant came down the steps. Little Tom was seated in one of the boats tying heavily weighted treble hooks onto other rods, which were carefully laid across the boat seats.

"Ready to catch yourself a spoony?" the boy asked.

"I'm ready to catch whatever there is in this river," Grant replied. "I wouldn't know a spoony from Moby Dick."

"A spoony is a Paddle Fish by rights. Some call them spoonbills but I just call them spoonys," the boy answered.

"Well, let's go catch us one'a them spoon billed paddle whackers," Tom said.

Tom put his hand on the boy's shoulder for balance as he stepped into the boat.

"I brought this strong backed younker along to use as a motor. I figure I'm old enough to earn a free ride now and then. Huh, boy?" Tom said.

Little Tom shrugged as he rowed the boat into the slow moving current.

"Just got these new fishin' outfits by mail order," Tom said.

He handed Grant one of the split bamboo rods with a new reel attached above the cork handle.

"Fella named Benson builds these in Kokomo, Indiana. Supposed to be the best a man can buy. I guess we'll find out today."

Tom cast the weighted hook into the greenish brown waters of the Missouri River. Waiting until his line went slack indicating that the weight was on the bottom, he made a protracted sweep with the heavy rod. He then reeled the slack line and repeated the process.

Little Tom let the oars float freely as he stood and emulated his grandfather.

"That's the way she's done," Little Tom said.

"But what are we using for bait?" Grant asked.

"Ain't no bait. These big bastards just cruise along on the bottom. You're just tryin' to get the hook and a fish in the same place at the same time."

Tom had no sooner finished his sentence when his rod bent and the handles of the reel began to spin as he put his thumb on the rapidly rotating spool of line to slow the momentum and prevent the line from becoming an unmanageable tangle.

"Just like that," Tom said.

Tom grinned broadly, as he raised the severely strained and pulsating rod and slowly turned the handles of the reel in an attempt to bring the unseen quarry to the boat.

Tom looked at Grant who was still seated in the front of the wooden boat.

"Come here and take this rod," Tom said.

Grant did not move but looked at Tom.

"Stand up and get this rod," the older man said.

Grant rose and reached for the rod.

"Put your thumb on the spool like I got mine," Tom said.

Grant nearly toppled out of the boat as the fish swam rapidly upstream in a powerful run.

"Now keep your thumb on the spool or you'll get one helluva bird's nest if that fish runs like that again and causes a backlash."

Grant could feel the burning heat of friction as the spool of line spun beneath the pad of his soft thumb. He glanced at Tom and the boy, certain that his thumb was blistering. Not wishing to appear a sissy in the presence of his companions he continued to hold the pressure.

Concentrating on the task he became aware of a thumping sensation being transmitted through the line and into the rod produced by pulsations as the large fish propelled itself forward with its muscular tail.

The fish exhausted its run and Grant could feel it beginning to yield to the insistent pressure of the bending rod. He quickly turned the handle of the reel and began to retrieve the line lost when the fish had surged away from the boat. As he recovered the line he could feel that his adrenaline was flowing and his heart was beating rapidly in the excitement.

The rod and reel seemed unwieldy in his hands, and he thought that he must appear quite clumsy in his efforts to bring this unseen creature from the depths. Suddenly the fish, which appeared to be about three and a half feet in length, breeched the surface and sent water flying with a powerful splash of its broad tail as it dived again to the bottom of the river.

Only moments before he had been completely unaware that such a creature existed on the face of the earth. Now his entire existence was invested in winning this primordial battle. He kept pressure with the bent rod as Tom had instructed, reeling in the line when the pulsating thumps diminished. With each surge the animal's strength ebbed. Grant watched in amazement as the oar-shaped snout and head of this prehistoric creature wallowed at the surface, its energy spent.

"You done good for your first one," Little Tom exclaimed.

Little Tom dipped the fish from the river's surface with a long handled net.

"He's a big one, sure enough," Tom said.

As the fish beat an intermittent tattoo with his powerful tail on the wooden floor of the boat, Grant sank to his seat in triumphant fatigue.

"Perhaps I'll reread Walton," he said.

Grant was pleased with himself when he looked at the smiles on the face of his companions.

Little Tom lifted the heavy fish as high as he could.

"Take a look at that. He's a dandy...you gonna try for another?"

Tom was already busy heaving the leaded hooks.

"I'm not exactly sure just what it was about the battle, but it seems to take one's breath and get the juices flowing," Grant said.

"Good," Tom answered. "Get off your ass and start chunkin' hardware. You can't catch nothin' sittin' there thinkin' about it."

Grant took one of the rods and made some tentative casts in an attempt to coordinate the release of the hook with the use of his thumb as a brake to avoid tangling of the line. Within a short period he began throwing the heavy leaded hooks with some proficiency as the three fishermen pursued their prey in quiet confidence.

Little Tom broke the silence.

"So you gettin' some good stories outta grandpa?"

"Very good! I can barely keep up the notes. I wish I could write more quickly. Maybe some day they will invent a recording device for reporters which can be carried along on interviews. Wouldn't that be a marvel?"

"You ought'a be inventin' a thing like that," Tom opined. "That'd make you a fortune and you wouldn't have to even do the writin'."

"Did he tell you about bein' in the war and about Buffalo Bill?" Little

Tom asked.

"Yes, he did, and he told me about being a scout with army," Grant said.

"Did he tell you how he took my Aunt Sarah and my cousins to Saint Joe on a river boat and got into a big fight?"

"No, but he told me how your Aunt Sarah nearly killed him," Grant replied.

"You mean Aunt Sarah tried to kill you grandpa?" Little Tom asked.

"Oh, yeah. She sure enough did that. Cut me right to the bone. Damn nearly kilt me for sure. Hadn't been for Aunt Koko's pappy I would'a likely gone under. But it was out of grief and misunderstandin' more than meanness. I never was mad at her over it."

"How did Aunt Koko's dad save you?" Little Tom asked.

"That would'a been your great, great Uncle Bloody Spear by name. He was there when it happened and pulled her off me. Then he doctored me some. But the truth is that after a bit even Aunt Sarah, who was my little sister, finally come off her high horse and commenced to feelin' sorry for me. She even helped Bloody Spear patch me up with poultices and the like. I was laid up for several days. Things was real different back in those 'olden times.' You likely didn't know that Aunt Sarah had been kidnapped by the Bloods, who was a mean bunch of Blackfoot up in Canada. Same bunch that kilt your great grandpa and grandma. I was trying to save Sarah. Trouble was that she didn't want savin' at the time. That was why she'd cut me like she done."

"So your sister had a change of heart and helped to doctor your wounds?" Grant said.

"Yes, sir, she did. Then me and Bloody Spear took her and the kids to his village. It was big excitement when we rode in. All of Bloody Spear's village knew about my folks havin' been kilt all those years before and how the Bloods had taken my sister so I guess none of them was any too surprised.

The women was all real sympathetic to my sister and of course when they saw that horse with a papoose hangin' on each side, why I thought they'd rip the poor animal in two gettin' at them babies. Those women was arguin' to see who'd get to hold 'em next. Them little fellers was sure some cute little turds. And when I thought about, it I was real sorry about killin' their pappy the way I'd done...but it had just seemed like a real white thing to do at the time. Remember, I was lookin' for some revenge when I'd started out to get my sister."

"Are you talkin' about Rom and Remus?" Little Tom asked.

"Yep, they was just babies when I took them from that Blood village to Saint Joe."

"So the people in Bloody Spear's village accepted your sister and her children?" Grant asked.

"Yes, sir, they took 'em in like they was their own. Which they was...in a way. Hell, almost everyone in the village knew the children's daddy and my sister could speak Blackfoot better'n I could. Anyway, it was comin' on winter by then, and I was still hurtin' so we eased up in the village until breakup.

I was still an honored guest in the village and my sister was treated right fine. She lived in my lodge and had herself plenty'a babysitters. Those little boys got more attention than twin lambs born at the county fair. People was pickin' 'em up and pettin' them little boys constantly. Why you'da thought they was the only children them women had ever seen. Even the men was fond of them babies."

"Didn't that make taking them away a bit difficult? Why couldn't they have stayed with Bloody Spear's people?" Grant asked.

"My intention was to return my sister to her rightful place in white civilization, such as it was, and I'd come too far to be dissuaded from the purpose at that point. Like I told you, you have to look at what I done through the prism of the times. Those was the days of Manifest Destiny and a Christian point of view that just wouldn't allow me another choice. Come spring I was healed pretty well, so I packed her up with Romulus and Remus, as I'd took to callin' them babies...considering that their mama was mean as a she-wolf...and headed for Fort Benton to get a boat for Saint Joe.

Sister Sarah come along pretty peaceable like by then. I think she still had a spark of curiosity about the civilized world, and her family, although she'd not seen them since she was a little bit. I told her that we was gonna go stay with our big sister Rachel.

We got one of the first boats downriver that spring. Of course our fella passengers was the usual assortment of miners, gamblers, adventurers, hide hunters and trouble makers that you was likely to find in this part of the country in them days. My biggest concern when I booked the cabin on the boat was for the health of those babies. Disease kilt many a child and I was feelin' pretty much protective of them boys by then. A couple of days downriver and I realized that I was gonna have another problem. There was some miners who'd come up from Bear Gulch to get the steamboat back to the settlements. They had apparently lost some of their party in an Injun skirmish and as it turned out they wasn't none too fond of Injuns, which they was more than willin' to explain to anyone who'd listen.

Sarah was still pretty much dressed in Injun clothes with her hair fixed Injun style. And there wasn't no foolin' anyone about what breed them two little tykes was, with their black hair and dark eyes. I was tryin' to ignore the miners, figurein' that sticks and stones can break your bones and all that. So I told sis to stay in the cabin as much as possible to avoid difficulty.

One mornin' it was real warm and, unbeknownst to me, she'd decided to get a little air on deck. She'd strapped Romulus on her back and was carryin' little Remus in her arms and just strollin' along lookin' at the river, mindin' her own business all in all.

I was sittin' up front on the upper deck havin' a chat with a young man who claimed to have been haulin' freight on the Mullan Road. Said he'd made a pretty good poke and was headed back to Kentucky to visit family and enjoy some of that money. I was interested in his stories of freighting as a possible business venture once I got sister and the boys to Saint Joe.

A ruckus interrupted that conversation and I reckon I would'a paid no mind but I heard my sister's voice and jumped up to go see what was happenin'. Now them miners had either got up early or stayed up late but they was already drunk, and it was only mid mornin'. As I got to the back rail of the upper deck, one of them miners had hold of Remus and was yellin' 'Let go'a that little heathen. I'm gonna teach him to swim.'

Now for the benefit'a clarity, I need to remind you that in those times it wasn't no crime to kill an Injun...even a little bitty one. Well, I took them stairs in one slidin' jump and when I was close I shouted at the feller to 'unhand that baby.' Of course, there was a dozen other folks shoutin' at the big sumbitch, too, and he was ignorin' everyone. So I hauled back and landed a good punch right in the back of his neck. I figured I'd likely break his neck and kill him. To my surprise he turned around to face me like he was completely unaffected. Needless to say, that turn of events required a new plan so I real quick planted a kick right to the place where I figured it'd do the most good. Sure enough, he grabbed his friends and dropped to his knees like it was mornin' mass."

"Was Remus injured?" Grant asked.

"No, but he was surely pissed off. Screamin' like a little Injun."

Tom laughed at his own humor.

"Now I figure that I'm dealin' with a drunk and that this miner fella is likely gonna go sleep it off and that's the end of the situation. Just about the time I'm congratulatin' myself I hear Sarah hollerin' in Blackfoot to look out behind me. About then, I find myself countin' the celestial wonders of the Milky Way. Someone had pole axed me from tall and although I was on my feet I couldn't see a thing. All I could do was put my arms up to protect my head and hope for the best.

I could feel the pushin' and shovin' around me and I could hear voices…and every now and then someone would land a blow on me. Fortunately, none of those punches was too serious. Somehow I managed to keep my feet and I was just swingin' like a windmill to fend off whoever was poundin' on me. When the red fog behind my eyes started to clear I realized that the young fella with whom I had been conversin' had come to my rescue and was at least holdin' them miners at bay, although he'd took some good licks himself.

When my senses come to me, I realized that I'd probably hit him at least a couple'a times myself. So now me and him was facin' three of them big bastards while, luckily, the fella I'd emasculated was still conductin' his Sunday services on his knees.

When I'd gone up on deck that morning, I had left my forty-four and that Henry rifle in the cabin, not anticipatin' that I'd be fighting for my life before noon. I didn't even have my knife with me and neither did that freighter, who was dressed in new city clothes."

Tom looked at his grandson and winked.

"That was the last time I ever got caught naked anywhere, anytime…if you know what I mean. So these here fellas have now got us outnumbered three to two and we're backed up against the back rail of that steamer.

I kind'a take a quick look around for friendly faces in the crowd, or any implement which might be useful as a weapon when I notice that one of them big fellas has now drawed out Bowie knife and I figure we're about to get quartered for camp meat.

I told you them Blackfoot was some fierce fighters. Well I reckon they pass it on even to their women. The next thing I see is little sister, still carryin' them babies, walk up behind the biggest of them miners. He all of a sudden hollers and starts doin' what appears to be a war dance in a pool of blood right there on the deck.

When he let out the holler, that other miner who had the knife took a run at us, tryin' to push us over the side. By fortuitous circumstance we just sort'a teamed up and took his own momentum and heaved him right over the stern and into that churnin' paddle wheel. Never seen him again! So now the other fella took a look around and decided that, what with the change in odds and all, he'd just see to his friend and leave us alone."

"What had happened to the large guy with the knife? The one doin' the war dance?" Little Tom asked.

"Seems Aunt Sarah had relieved one of the bystanders of his skinnin' knife and, babies notwithstandin', she'd proceeded to stick that big sumbitch right in the kidney. He lasted about a half hour before he bled to death and then joined his friend who'd gone into the river through the paddle wheel."

Tom looked at Little Tom and grinned.

"You just don't wanna get crossways of a Blackfoot woman, even if she's white...huh."

"You can say that again. I sure try not to get my mom too mad."

Tom and Grant both laughed.

"That's probably a damned good policy to stick with, boy. Anyways, it was a real ticklish situation for the boat Captain after that incident.

Again, I got to remind you that Injuns just wasn't real popular with most folks in those days. Not that they're much better off today. But at least it's against the law to kill 'em. In those days, killin' an Injun wasn't near as serious a matter as it would be to poach a deer today. No jury would ever convict a white man of killin' an Injun, but on the other hand they'd hang Injuns wholesale for stealin' a few head of cows. So little sister, lookin' like a squaw and packin' two black eyed babies, became the object of some talk of lynchin'.

I went immediately and armed myself for the inevitable and locked her and them kids up in the cabin. Sure enough the bitchin' started. The other passengers wanted us to be put off the boat and they didn't give a good God damn where. The Captain was a decent fella though. He knew there was a small settlement a few miles down river. Although he didn't normally stop there, he decided that he'd maroon us where we at least had a chance of lookin' out for them baby boys."

Little Tom hooked a fish, which was not quite as large as the one Grant had landed. When the fish was at the boat, Tom netted it for the boy and then picked up his rod.

Grant watched, thinking of Tom's story about the fight.

"Considering that those miners had started the fight, it seems a bit unjust that they would have put you off the boat. Why didn't the Captain put those men ashore?" Grant asked.

"Unjust! I just told you boy, there wasn't no justice where Injuns was concerned. And most'a the good folks on that boat figured little sister was an Injun. And she had kilt a white man. And I was damned lucky that they didn't just lynch her. Anyway, the Captain put us ashore at a little settlement that was just below where the Platte River comes into the Missouri. Wasn't much of a place...couple'a soddy buildin's and some tents mostly.

When I'd booked passage on that steamer I was figurin' we'd have accommodations and food so I was a might ill prepared when they put us ashore. Nary a hank of canvas to keep off the rain, nor a bean for our dinner."

"What did they do with the young man who'd come to your aid," Grant asked.

"Oh yeah...I near forgot. They'd told him he could stay on the boat but he decided that he'd be best off not havin' to face those miners who was still healthy so he got off with us. Said his name was Herman Houston Horsens. Seems his pappy had fought in the Texican war and had a spot in his heart for ol' Sam Houston. But that's a story for another time. He told me that they called him Sam. I just took to callin' him Horse Sense.

He'd kind'a took a shine to Sarah, so I ain't real sure that the fear of them miners was his total reason for comin' along, but whatever his motivation, there we was without transport, shelter or the prospects of a meal...but guess who saved us?"

"How would we know, Grandpa?" Little Tom said.

"Those babies...Romulus and Remus. Now I ain't sayin' that the folks in that settlement was any more or less sympathetic to Injuns than was most folks, but women have just got a natural weakness when it comes to children. And them good Christian ladies was not about to leave those baby boys to the vagaries of the wilderness. When I told 'em how I'd rescued Sarah from bein' kidnapped by savages, a couple of them ladies took her under their wing and saw to it that we all got fed and had a place to sleep. We was at least outta the weather.

I'd learned enough about life by then to know that charity has got its limits. I had about decided we was gonna have to start hoofin' it to Saint Joe when a mackinaw pulled into that settlement to ease up for the night. A more disreputable lookin' crew of reprobated itinerants you have never beheld. Several was miners from the Cherry Creek diggin's in Colorado, which was petering out by then...and there was a young fella who'd been huntin' meat for the minin' camps and restaurants in Denver. There was also a couple of trappers who'd been huntin' the head waters of the Platte and they was goin' to the big town to sell what plews as they had caught. They was one rough lookin' bunch and I was sure as hell not of a mind to be lookin' for trouble after the rhubarb on the steamboat. But me'n ol' Horse Sense decided to wander down and assess the possibilities anyway.

They had them some whiskey, naturally, and they invited us for sit and swig. When everyone was feelin' the glow in their bellies from ol' John Barleycorn, I decided to lay my hand on the table face up and see if anyone was gonna call. I put it on the line...told them all about my sister Sarah and the two baby boys and the steamboat fight and figured the chips was gonna fall where they was gonna fall. Turned out that three of them fellas was family men themselves and one of the trappers was married to a Ute squaw. He had a couple of half-breed children of his own. Damned if they didn't take us right to their hearts and right on into Saint Joe. They was not only helpful but mighty protective too. Just goes to show that you can't judge the book by the cover."

"I'll wager that your older sister was really glad to see you," Grant said.

"She was glad to see me...that's sure enough...but..."

"But?" Grant asked, taking note of Tom's comment.

"But...as to sister Sarah...well, that was a different matter. I had written a couple of times while I was out in the Colorado Territory to tell them where I was and that I was scoutin' for the army. I had never said nothin' about my service to the Confederacy. I figured it could have done them no good to know and would have caused them to lie if it had been questioned. That could have done some real harm, as I told you before.

As it turned out, in my absence, ol' Jacob and Rachel had achieved some real status in their church and the community, mostly due to Jacob's handlin' of business matters and in part due to the fact that I was with the Union Army and a real hero and all...at least as big sister had told the story. Now what with her lofty station among her grandiose friends, ol' Rachel wasn't none too anxious to be introducin' a sister who'd been befouled by savages and she sure as hell didn't want to have no half-breed bastards hangin' around her doorstep."

Grant's face blanched in embarrassment. He gave Tom a pained look as he nodded toward Little Tom who continued casting from the middle of the boat.

"He's heard this story," Tom said. "If he ain't heard it, he needs to. Besides, he ain't no half-breed, are you Tommy?"

"I'm' a quarter Blackfoot," Little Tom grinned. "And I reckon I ain't no bastard so you don't have to get yourself all embarrassed over me."

Grant smiled in relief.

"So your older sister was cruel to Sarah?" Grant continued.

"She come right out and told poor Sarah that she should have stayed where she was or kilt herself. She let it be known that she didn't appreciate this woman who had been soiled by Injuns comin' to muck up things for her social circle. I don't think I ever got so mad in my entire life. I was so far beside myself that I could'a been twins.

When I'd finally scraped myself off'n the ceiling, I gathered together my most profound diplomatic voice and I asked to speak to Rachel and Jacob alone. When I got them two outta earshot, ol' Rachel begun to lay into me for bringing 'that woman' into her home. Jacob stood there lookin' like a turkey on Thanksgivin' morning, 'cause he knew by lookin' at my face that I was about to drop a turd in his bride's punch bowl.

Damned if I didn't cut loose with both barrels. First I let 'em know that sis didn't have no choice in the matter. First of all, she'd been kidnapped and raped, and second I'd drug her kickin' and screamin' back to arms of her lovin' family. I also told them, in no uncertain terms, that I had never seen such an offendin' lack of Christian charity in my entire days...and that included my time amongst them savages that Rachel kept referrin' to. I told them in detail about how I served with the Confederate Army and that I wasn't no more than a galvanized Yankee who'd been pressed to service for the Union. That was one barrel. Then I give them the other.

I told ol' Rachel that if'n she continued in her attitude of malignant insensitivity to the needs of our little sister, come Sunday mornin' I was gonna march myself into that church she was so proud of and tell that highfalutin' congregation the entire story. I asked ol' Rachel what she figured them fine Christian folk was gonna think after hearin' that not only was little sister a Blackfoot concubine but little brother was a Confederate turncoat.

Ol' Rachel turned whiter than the Tetons. That woman was mean spirited but she sure as hell wasn't stupid. She could see right off that bein' a good sister was likely a better course of action if'n she wanted to continue relations with those haughty ladies of the faith. It wasn't no time at all before she was tellin' her fancy friends how she'd beseeched her war hero brother to go save little sister from the humiliatin' degradation of life among the primitives and return that beloved young woman to the breast of a Christian family who could love and care for her and her children. Much as it made me wanna throw up, I figured it was still better for Sarah and the boys, even if it was a pretense."

"In the meantime, what was your new friend, I think you called him Horse Sense...what was he doing?" Grant asked.

"Well, he was sure enough took with little sister and he was kind'a moonin' around like a young fella I seen doin' around here lately."

Little Tom chuckled.

Grant's cheeks reddened and he attempted to ignore Tom's humor.

"Did he stay in Saint Joseph with your family?"

"Not right then. Like I said, he had been headed to Kentucky to see his folks and let them know he was well and such. So once we got Sarah and the boys settled in at Rachel's place, he lit out. I told him that I was cookin' up some business in which he might wish to be a part so when he headed to Kentucky, he promised he'd be back before low water.

I'd judged his eyes when he was sayin' his 'so longs' to Sarah. I figured rightly that I'd be seein' him again sooner than later. Now I wasn't back in Saint Joe a day when ol' Jacob started in on me again about workin' with him in the business. With the railroad through and the blessin' of the Army, he'd been expandin' things and he was into lumber and cattle and all manner'a mercantile. He took me to his office and showed me the books and damned if he hadn't been takin' right good care of my money as well. He'd invested it like he said he would, and I found myself with a right fine bankroll for a young man who'd not yet voted.

I thanked him for the offer of partnerin' up, but I had to tell him that I just couldn't abide that flat country and all those fences. I wanted to see them hills and ride open country where you could go a week without seein' another soul. He told me that progress was comin' and that it'd all be fences and towns everywhere before too long. Of course, I knew he was right, but I was bound to hang onto some wild as long as I could. Besides, I had a plan for startin' my own freightin' outfit up in the territories and I still had dreams of a ranch.

I gotta say this, what ol' Jacob lacked in personality, he made up for in plain ol' discernment and intuition when it come to business. I explained what was goin' on with the mines and the settlers and the need for freightin' and all, and he could see the possibilities. Turns out that he threw in with me and wanted a piece'a that action. You see, up in Fort Benton...in fact all along the Mullan Road, a good freight wagon would fetch near eight hundred dollars and a well broke jerk line six-up of fine Missouri mules was worth near fifteen hundred dollars."

Grant wrinkled his forehead.

"Jerk line...six-up?"

"That was six mules that was broke as a team and they would be driven by a man ridin' one of the wheel mules. Wheel mules was the ones nearest the wagon. The rider would control the whole shebang with a single line and a whole lot'a hollerin'. A jerk line team could be any number of animals but a good team was usually a six-up for the average freighter. I just used a six-up as a measure because it was kind of a standard rig.

Now my plan was to build wagons in Saint Joe and buy the mules there in Missouri and then ship the outfits up to Montana on the steamboats. Even with the freight charges for the steamboat it was still cheap by territory calculations and those Missouri mules was highly prized. I had it figured that even if the freightin' business wasn't all I hoped it'd be, I could always sell the outfits to some other aspirin' entrepreneur for a good rip. So me'n Jacob employed a wagon builder and started assemblin' freighters to be shipped the followin' spring.

I went and rented me a little house which was close to Jacob and Rachel's place but far enough so as to afford me a bit'a privacy and time by myself. What with Sarah and the boys and Rachel's children gettin' bigger, it was a might cramped for my taste around her place."

Grant had put his rod down and was writing furiously.

"There's the boys with the truck," Little Tom said.

Grant looked to see one of the trucks from Tom's ranch parked beside the river. Little Tom rowed the boat to the shore, and Buck backed the truck close to the water as Howdy waved directions.

Each of the men helped in lifting the boat into the back of the truck.

"She's an easy float down but that rowing home is a hairy bear. Lot easier to just ride home in the truck," Tom said.

The rods were carefully wrapped in canvas and the fish were covered with wet burlap.

Howdy and Little Tom climbed onto the back of the flatbed while Tom and Grant got into the cab.

Buck put the truck into gear and turned onto the road.

"Didn't git too sceered by them sea monsters did you?" he asked.

"He caught that big one," Tom interupted, before Grant could respond. "How'd it go with the teams? They beginnin' to work?"

"Yes, sir, I figure to win that practice race tomorrow," Buck replied.

They drove to the ranch in silence.

Buck backed the truck toward the river, close to the docks to unload the boat.

A wiry man with long dark hair, wearing a felt hat, moccasins and a print shirt approached. A wide belt with a large knife in a leather sheath held the shirt around his waist. The young man looked like an Indian character from a Russell painting. Watching his loose-gaited stride as he walked toward them Grant imagined that this was much the way the Indians would have looked when they roamed freely on this prairie.

"You buckin' tomorrow?" Howdy shouted.

"Yeah! I thought I might teach you cowboys a thing or two," the man said.

"Howdy, son," Tom said. "So you're gonna go rodeoin' with us, huh? I'm glad you came. Come over here and meet Grant Collins from Saint Louis."

Tom turned to Grant with a smile.

"This here is my youngest boy Derrick. He stays over at Browning."

"I heard about him. He's a reporter," Derrick said.

He looked at Grant without offering a handshake.

"I hear you're writin' the story of the famous Indian fighter."

Tom ignored his son's obvious provocation.

"It's good to see you, son. Looks like you wintered well. How's your uncle and his family?"

"He'll see the elk hunt," Derrick replied.

"Good to hear. Tell him I sent my best. You goin' to Calgary with us or did you just come to teach these boys somethin' tomorrow?"

"Thought I'd go to Calgary," Derrick answered. "I need the money."

"I always like to see a man with confidence," Tom said.

They walked to the rear of the mess hall to clean the fish.

It was nearing dusk when Grant heard a car stop in front of the house. He and Tom were in Tom's office and Grant jumped to his feet and started to the door.

"Relax, boy," Tom said. "She'll be in quick enough. Don't want to let her think you're too anxious. Gotta kind'a keep them women guessin', you know. If they been shoppin' in town, she ain't give much thought to you anyway."

When Grant heard the front door open and close, he could no longer contain himself. He jumped to his feet and walked quickly to the entryway.

"Did you ladies have a nice day in town shopping?" he asked.

"Hi! How was the fishing?" Dixie said.

"Very exciting," Grant said. "Did you find anything of interest?"

"As a matter of fact, I did," Dixie said.

"Hi, Uncle Tom," she shouted as he walked quickly up the stairs. "Let me freshen up and we'll talk at dinner."

Tom, Grant and Dixie sat at one end of the long table.

Koko began serving dinner. She stopped to look at Grant.

"You catch this fish?" Koko asked.

"Yes, ma'am," he answered politely.

"I eat some. Maybe good," she said, uncharacteristically setting herself a plate at the table.

Tom's eyes twinkled.

"You mean you're gonna eat dinner with me?" he asked.

"No," she answered with the hint of a smile. "He catch fish. I eat with him."

"Damned obstinate squaw," Tom muttered under his breath.

"Susanna said that Derrick is here?" Dixie said. "Why didn't he have dinner with us?"

"He wanted to sleep in the bunkhouse and talk to the men, I reckon," Tom said.

The disappointment in Tom's voice was obvious. Grant could see the distress in his eyes.

"He seemed angry. I hope I didn't do anything to offend," Grant said.

"He wants to be Indian...like in old days," Koko said. "He not happy man."

"That's why he lives at Browning," Tom said. "That's the Blackfoot reservation over there. He lives with his mama's people. Tries to live like the free days but all he accomplishes is findin' disappointment for himself. Then he gets drunk and fights and raises hell and gets throwed in jail. I don't know what to do about him. He's a damned good cowboy when he wants to be. He can ride damned near anything with four legs... when he's sober...which, unfortunately, ain't too damned often. I reckon it's somethin' that he's just got to work out for himself."

"He mentioned an elk hunt. Does he enjoy hunting with his family?" Grant asked.

"He does work for Caleb now and again," Tom replied. "When we get dudes who want to hunt, Caleb hires him and his uncle to do the guidin'. He's a sure enough Injun when it comes to readin' sign. He's a real good hand when the evil spirits ain't got him."

"This fish is wonderful," Grant said. "Thank you for a glorious dinner Koko."

"You catch 'em, I just cook 'em," she said, her eyes aglow with the compliment. "You get surprise, too. I go get it."

Koko left the room and returned with a large round box and set it on the table in front of Grant.

"This from Dixie," she said.

"I swear to the Lord," Tom said, "Koko must be sweet on you. That's the most I've heard her talk in ten years."

Grant sat staring at the box, a look of consternation clouding his face.

"Is this a special occasion, my birthday perhaps?"

"Just open it ya ninny," Tom said. "Never look a gift horse in the mouth."

Grant lifted the lid from the box to reveal a large beaver felt Stetson hat with a snakeskin band.

"Well, now, that is just beautiful!"

"I heard you were going to the rodeo," Dixie said. "You can't go to the rodeo in a city hat."

"Well, thank you very much. I am truly honored."

"Did you know that I bought one of the first Stetsons ever sold? Back in the sixties," Tom asked.

"I wasn't aware that the brand had been around that long," Dixie said.

"Yes sir. Ol' John Stetson had himself a shop in Saint Joe and I just happened onto the place when we was gettin' wagons built to ship to Montana. I went in there and got myself one'a them big brimmed 'Boss of the Plains' fur felts he was makin'. You've probably seen pictures of 'em. Buffalo Bill had his picture made while he was wearin' one."

"I didn't know you had shipped wagons up here from Saint Joseph," Dixie said.

"Sure enough did," Tom replied. "Me'n your grandpa and Uncle Horse Sense shipped mules and wagons and built us a freightin' company. We was runnin' jerk line outfits supplyin' the miners, the small settlements and even the honyockers who was brave enough to build them a place out in Injun country."

"And what, pray tell, is a honyocker," Dixie asked.

Grant was relieved that she had asked the question because it seemed that he was usually the one who was showing his ignorance.

"Honyocker, as I know it, was a bastardization of some German word for 'chicken chaser,'" Tom replied. "There were a lot of Squareheads and Norwegians comin' to this country for the homesteads and somehow the cowboys started callin' 'em honyockers and the name stuck."

"I had heard that Uncle Horse Sense died while driving a freight wagon," Dixie asked.

"Yeah, but that wasn't till years later. In fact, we shipped the first of them outfits up here in sixty-five, as I recall, right after the war. In those days, ol' Fort Benton was a wild and wooly place. I've heard tell that it was worse than Wichita, Dodge City or Tombstone. Hell, the Barbary Coast in San Francisco was civilized compared to Fort Benton in the sixties. But me'n Horse Sense got five full outfits, an outfit bein' a wagon and a six mule team, to Fort Benton that first year and started haulin' freight. Hired us some experienced teamsters and we was doin' well on the financial end.

After the first year ol' Horse Sense got lonesome and asked could he go back to Saint Joe and court my sister Sarah. I figured that if he put no more value on his scalp than to try and tame that white Blackfoot, I'd give my blessin'. Off he went on the last boat of the summer and damned if he wasn't back the next spring with a couple more wagons and teams and a wife and two children too."

"You mean Rom and Remus?" Dixie asked.

"Yep. He was a good daddy to them boys. I think he loved them like they was his own. He did his best for them and taught them all he could. And he was damned good at that freightin' business. Wasn't long before I got bored and started lookin' to find somethin' more excitin' to take my interest...but ol' Horse Sense stuck to 'er and made us a pile of money. While he was doin' that, I got asked to kind'a be the town sheriff in Fort Benton. There was a lot of Injuns still comin' to town to trade, and the white men around that town were rougher'n a dry cob on a sore behind... if you'll pardon the expression."

"I do the dishes now. Too much talking," Koko said.

"I'll help you," Dixie said.

The two gathered the dishes and disappeared into the kitchen.

"I'll see you all in the mornin' then," Tom said, stretching his arms over his head. "I'm goin' to bed."

Grant sat at the table listening to the women talking in the kitchen as they washed the dishes. When they had finished Dixie and Koko walked through the dining room toward the stairs.

"Young man waiting for you," Koko said with a smile. "I go to bed now."

"My...my...my," Dixie replied. "I do believe you're right."

Koko disappeared into the hallway headed to her room and Dixie sat at the table with Grant.

"I want to thank you for the hat," he said. "That is the best gift I have ever received. I was surprised."

The look on Dixie's face became very serious.

"You be careful tomorrow," she said. "Don't get talked into playing cowboy. It is very dangerous business, you know. After all, I wouldn't want anything to happen to that new hat."

She stood and turned to walk toward the stairs.

"It will be an early day. Get to bed," she said.

Grant turned her around and kissed her.

"No, sir," she said in a playful tone. "I know what you're thinking. I'll see you in the morning."

She gave him a hug and a quick kiss and went quickly up the stairs.

2 1

The new Stetson was stiff. The threads of the new leather sweat band imprinted Grant's forehead. He removed the hat and massaged his brow.

A young cowhand who was passing watched with a grin.

"That's a right fine piece of headgear ya got yerself there, cowboy," he said.

"That is a fine looking hat. I'm glad I got it for you," Dixie said.

"Yes, sir, she's a dandy," Tom agreed. "Have you decided whether to give 'er a try in the rodeo today? Only things holding you back is fear and common sense."

"I haven't yet decided," he said, looking at Dixie. "I've ridden horses quite a bit now. I think I have a good handle on the situation. I may give it a go."

Dust hung in the still air of the hot morning. A steady parade of automobiles, horse drawn wagons and trucks of various sizes churned the powdery dirt road, which led into the rodeo corral.

Grant walked toward the arena with Tom and Dixie to observe the preparations. He reminded himself of the dangers of allowing pride to outweigh good judgment. His mind raced. He hoped that he would not show fear, if the reality of that moment arrived. He reminded himself of his recently adopted motto. "*Tempus fugit, ergo carpe diem*," he muttered to himself.

"What was that?" Tom asked.

"Just thinking out loud," Grant said.

They walked toward the chuck wagons where several men were helping Buck and Howdy in preparing the teams and checking to ensure that all of the equipment was in working order.

Dixie took Grant's arm and stopped, pulling him around to face her.

"You don't have to participate in this. These men have been doing this all their lives and they understand the risks and, even worse, they actually enjoy it."

"I really am looking forward to giving it a try. I am pretty tough you know."

"Okay, Mr. Tough Guy," she said. "But please...don't do this if it is on my account. You don't have to impress me...and please don't let these cowboys talk you into anything."

As they walked past the men who were working on the wagons Grant could hear derisive comments from the group.

"All hat and nary a cow," a voice said.

The men laughed and Grant heard another say, "Boss's city cowboy, ya know."

"Big hat full of chicken shit is what I'd reckon," said the voice of a third.

"I'd like to see that New York cowboy on ol' Rambunctious," Grant could hear Buck say.

"Who is old Rambunctious?" Grant asked.

"Rambunctious is one of Uncle Tom's herd bulls. Supposedly one of the best. He also uses him in the rodeo. He even takes him to Calgary. I don't think he has been ridden more than a handful of times...and some real experts have tried. He has crippled several cowboys. Everyone says it is only a matter of time until he kills someone."

"Do those men all ride the bulls?" Grant asked.

"Just ignore them. They'll get you into something you don't want to do," Dixie said.

They walked toward a row of narrow holding pens along one side of the large rodeo arena. The pens were separated by drop down gates. A hinged release gate spanned the length of each enclosure which opened into the arena.

"These are the bucking chutes," Dixie said. "The rough stock animals are driven single file into the chutes. Then the small gates are closed behind each to separate them and hold them in place. Then when the rider is mounted the animals can be released one at a time through that wide gate on the front.

"Rough stock?" Grant asked.

"Bucking horses, steers and bulls. You've never even seen a rodeo, have you?" she asked.

"No, I told your uncle that."

As they approached Grant watched horses being driven into the chutes.

"They're ready to start. Let's get a good spot on the fence," Dixie said.

She took his hand and led him toward the tall arena fence.

Grant watched as the cowboys climbed onto the chutes, assisting one another in saddling the horses. He watched as the men who were to ride stepped down into the chutes, slowly lowering themselves onto the saddles. Grant could see that each man was grasping a rope secured to the halter of his mount.

"Derrick drew first ride," Tom said as he stepped up onto the fence.

Grant looked at the chute in time to see Derrick nod his head. In a blur of action the wide gate swung open and the horse emerged in a frenzied leaping kick. The animal spun, coiling every muscle and then exploding with undulating fury in an attempt to unseat his rider who was holding tightly to the rope.

A whistle blew and Grant asked, "Is that the signal to dismount?"

Dixie pointed to a cowboy who had been sitting on his horse at the far end of the arena. At the sound of the whistle he spurred his horse into immediate pursuit.

"Not exactly. That's the eight second whistle. It means that the ride is complete. Then the judges decide what sort of score the rider is to get. If he doesn't stay on for the eight seconds...no score...the ride was all for naught. If he does ride the eight seconds, he still has the problem of dismounting. That is why they use a pick-up man."

As she spoke the pick-up man paced the wildly bucking bronco and urged his horse to run close alongside. Grant could see that Derrick had released his hold and leaned toward rescue. Grasping the cantle of the pick-up rider's saddle, he flung himself sideways onto the rump of the running horse as the pick-up man reined to slow his mount and turn from the flying hooves. When the bucking horse had moved a safe distance away, the Derrick dropped to the ground to the applause of the crowd.

"I told you that boy was a pretty good kind of cowboy," Tom said proudly.

A second pick-up rider then caught up to the still bucking horse and released a sheepskin covered strap from the horse's flank. He then drove the horse from the arena.

"That didn't appear too difficult," Grant said.

"It ain't, if you know what you're doin'," Tom said.

Dixie was about to speak when a second rider nodded and again the arena was filled with the shrill whinnies and discordant unfamiliar sounds of a horse attempting to relieve itself of an unwanted passenger. Grant counted. One, two, three when the cowboy was vaulted into the air, landing on the ground in flurry of scrambling arms and legs. In an instant the young man was on his feet and running to the safety of the fence.

"That didn't appear too pleasant," Dixie said.

Just then Grant felt a tug at his pant leg.

"Come on," Little Tom said. "You got a little practice on J. D.'s roan. You should do pretty good at this by now."

Grant looked at Dixie. Disapproval was burning in her eyes.

"You're going to regret this," she said.

He shrugged and stepped down from the fence.

Little Tom led him to the chutes where he climbed the rails to observe the procedure. He could not ignore the thrill of excitement as one by one the young men would nod and a chute would open in an explosion of dissonant sound and dust. He watched in fascination as each man, no matter how hard the fall, would jump to his feet. Some would run to avoid the crushing hooves. Some seemed nonchalant, standing as if ignoring the danger. Some would retrieve a lost hat, brush themselves off and walk stoically from the arena.

"It's yer turn, Dude...chute three," Little Tom said.

Grant climbed the fence behind the third chute. He looked down on the saddle cinched into place. He could smell the strange odor of the horse as it peered up at him from its confinement with a wrathful eye. It had to be, he thought, the smell of fight or flight emanating from animal. He wondered if this horse could smell the element of fear coming from his own body.

Little Tom handed Grant a glove as he climbed the fence.

"I reckon you'll be needin' this," the boy said.

Grant put on the glove and looked at the strap around the horse's flanks.

"What is that strap for," he asked.

Elmer and Howdy were standing on the chute as Grant, stepping one rail at a time, eased himself down onto the waiting saddle.

"It's a flank strap...or what we call a buckin' strap," Howdy said. "Sort'a pisses him off and makes him buck harder."

Grant sat on the saddle and kicked his feet from side to side until he finally found the stirrup openings and tested his weight in the foothold.

"This is your first time, huh dude?" Elmer said.

"Not exactly, but this is my first official try."

Grant looked up to see Tom's face.

"Grant," Tom said in a stern voice. "Take some advice. Hold the rope with your right hand and the saddle swell with the other. Everyone knows this is your first try and this ain't gonna be a rockin' horse ride like that ol' knot-headed roan. Just try to stay aboard and get the feel of what it's like while the animal is buckin'. You can develop your professional form after you've rode two or three. When you hear that whistle, start lookin' for the pick-up rider. When he comes beside, just try to jump over onto the back of his horse. Good luck and hang on tight."

Elmer placed Grant's hand into position on the halter rope while Howdy stretched the rope taut to provide leverage.

"Do like the boss told ya now. Get a good hold on that swell. If you just stay on this hay bag for eight seconds, you'll be doin' better'n I done my first two dozen tries," Elmer said.

"Two dozen tries?" Grant said, looking at the horse's angry eye. A sudden panic removed all confidence. Grant took a deep breath. He forced the muscles in his shoulders relax. Concentrating on the instructions, the confusion of fear dissipated. He held the rope tightly with his gloved hand.

"Go on," Grant heard Howdy's voice. "Get a grip on that saddle. I'm just like Elmer, I hit the dirt a bunch before I ever made eight seconds on a bronc. Don't try nothin' fancy. I'll pull the flank strap when you say when...now hold tight!"

Grant put his hand on the saddle, feeling for a firm hold.

"Okay," Grant said, dipping his head.

The sound of squeaking gate hinges grew into thunderous confusion as the horse erupted from the enclosure. Grant lost all awareness of time and space as he held with all his strength to the rope and saddle. The fences and faces were a hazy blur. He gripped with his legs as his arm, which held the saddle, felt as if it was becoming disjointed. The horse made high-pitched squealing sounds interspersed with rhythmic deep breaths as it kicked, leaping and bucking.

The shrill of the seemingly distant whistle was lost in the disorder. His surroundings seemed momentarily obscured. Then he realized that he was on the ground in middle of the arena. Instinct impelled him to stand. As he rose to his knees he could see the horse moving toward him. The animal was still bucking wildly. The pick-up man, who was attempting to loose the flank strap, veered his horse to avoid Grant but the bucking animal continued course. Grant was sent sprawling. He felt a burning pain as an errant hoof came down on his leg as the animal passed over him.

Driven by adrenaline, he jumped to his feet but found himself unable to run. His head was spinning, his vision an orange haze. After a moment, his head cleared and he could hear the applause of the crowd. He bent down to pick up his hat. He waved as he limped toward the gate.

Howdy, Elmer and a dozen other cowboys were waiting, pumping his hand and offering congratulations.

"Damned if'n you didn't cost me a dollar," Howdy said.

"Me too," Elmer said. "The boss had confidence in ya, I reckon."

As the cowboys returned to the chutes, Tom approached Grant with an outstretched hand. Seeing that Grant was favoring his right leg Tom frowned.

"Nothin' broke, I reckon?"

"As you might say, my leg is a bit bent but not broken."

"That's a long ways from the heart...ain't likely to be fatal. You didn't hurt that writin' arm now did you?"

"No. I think I'll be fine. I didn't know it had lasted eight seconds...and I never saw a pick-up man. I was too busy trying to fly. I guess it doesn't count since I cheated but those other men seem impressed."

"Hell son...I'm impressed, but then I knowed you had it in you."

"So you bet on me this time?"

"You was lookin' pretty determined. I always take the odds. Come on, we'll go get ready to watch the wagon race."

Grant followed Tom toward his car. Dixie was waiting for them. She stood in front of Grant, concern etched on her face.

"Was it as easy as it looked?" she asked.

"No. I was knocked cuckoo...and I'll have a charley horse, but at least I can say I did it."

"Good. I'll say you did it too and now we have nothing left to prove. Right?"

Tom was sitting behind the wheel of the car.

"Get in you two. You can discuss Grant's rodeo career some other time. Let's go over and make sure everything is ready for the wagon race."

Four of Tom's neighbors had brought chuck wagons and teams to participate in the practice race. Excitement filled the dusty air as horses pranced nervously. Several men worked on each of the teams checking the harness and hitch. Tom motioned to Buck and Howdy.

"Now listen careful, this here is just a rehearsal. I know both of you wanna win, bein' as how you're racin' against your buddies and all, but this one don't count. Don't go bustin' up the equipment or killin' the stock for this practice deal. We wanna win up in Calgary. So don't break nothin'."

When the two men had walked back to the wagons Tom turned to Grant.

"In Calgary they will be racin' right in the rodeo grounds. It'll be a damned dangerous situation. I got this practice set up out here in the open where everyone has got someplace to go, just in case. I just want to see how ol' Howdy is gettin' the hang of the team and the wagon. Buck's doin' pretty good if he don't get over enthusiastic."

Nick, who had been designated starter and judge, arranged the six wagons in a row behind a line he had created using a roll of toilet paper. The wagons accompanied by outriders on horseback were to remain behind the line until Nick's starting signal. The race course was a designated prairie track Nick had marked using old tires painted white.

"They're gonna run four laps around them tires," Tom said.

The drivers strained, planting their feet against the wagon boards to hold their teams. The outriders signaled their readiness as some of the horses turned in tight circles.

"How will they know…," Grant's question was cut short.

He was startled when Nick fired his revolver and the wagons rumbled into competition. As the wagons neared the halfway post of the first lap a team from one of the neighboring ranches was well into the lead with another running second. Grant looked at Tom who was shaking his head.

"I shoulda drove one of the damned things myself," he said.

As the wagons with their outriders neared the end of the first lap, Howdy's team had advanced into second place and was moving swiftly to overtake the leader. Buck was struggling to maintain fourth position.

At the midway post of the second lap, Howdy held second place while Buck was moving slowly to overhaul the fourth place wagon. Using his whip with ferocity he came alongside the fourth place team. When the horses were neck and neck it appeared to Grant that Buck intentionally swerved his team toward the opponent. The driver wore a startled look as he turned from the race course into a rocky patch of prairie. The right front wheel of his wagon struck a large rock, splintering the wooden spokes and dropping the axle into the dirt. The wagon pitched over and flipped end over end sending the driver headlong into the brush.

Tom started his car and drove to where the young man lay, bleeding from the head. As Grant, Tom and Dixie got out of the car the young driver sat up and said, "Lucky it was my head. I could'a broke somethin' real serious."

The three laughed as several people ran to assist the young man. Tom looked at his neighbor.

"I am sure as hell sorry about that Mathew. I'll send Buck and Howdy over to help ya get 'er ready for the rodeo."

The man looked at Tom shaking his head.

"Don't send Buck. I don't think we'll race with Buck no more, Tom. He done that on purpose and I don't want that mean son-of-a-bitch on my place."

"I'll say it again, I'm sorry Mathew. I don't know what else to say. I'm glad your boy ain't hurt."

Tom, Grant and Dixie watched as Howdy and his outriders crossed the finish line in first place. They got into Tom's car and drove directly to the corrals to congratulate Howdy on his win.

"And now we have the real show," Tom said.

"What do you mean, the real show?" Grant asked.

"We always save the bull ridin' to the end. If someone gets busted up ridin' a bull he's generally done for the day," Tom said.

When they reached the wagons Grant could hear Howdy shouting at Buck.

"Did you run that fella off the track like they said?"

"Naw pardner...it were an accident. My team just got away from me for a minute," Buck said.

"Well, that would'a been a damned mean thing to do Buck. You could kill a fella like that," Howdy said.

Tom and Dixie walked toward Buck's wagon. Grant walked up to Howdy, who was unhitching his team.

"Howdy, that was a magnificent job. You were certainly the champion today."

"Thank you, Grant," Howdy replied. "You done a good job your own self on the buckin' horse. He was a mean one."

Howdy stopped what he was doing to look at Grant.

"And I'll tell you somethin' else...don't go gettin' crossways of Buck. You know he's just jealous 'cause Dixie likes you better'n him. He's my pal and we get on okay, but he can be a mean sumbitch. I ain't just sure if he didn't run that driver into them rocks a'purpose."

"I appreciate your telling me that Howdy. I keep getting warnings about him."

As Howdy continued to unhitch his team and tend the horses Grant seized the opportunity. He grabbed the heavy harness and helped Howdy put it in the wagon.

"Are you going to ride the bulls?" Grant asked.

"Yes, sir. I am. I do a little doggin' and rough stock ridin'. I'm hopin' to make some money up in Canada...and those bulls are where the big money gets made."

"Dogging?" Grant asked.

"Bull doggin'. Wrestlin' a steer to the ground in as short a time as possible."

"I haven't seen that," Grant said.

Tom and Dixie returned to where Grant was helping Howdy with the harness.

"You done good today, son. I'm right proud of you. I think we'll just give you a run up there in Calgary," Tom said.

"Well, thanks boss. I sure would like to have a chance at it."

"You got 'er...now let's go see the rest of the show," Tom said.

Grant stood on the fence with Dixie to watch the calf roping and then the bulldogging competition.

"Howdy told me he will be in this bulldogging contest," Grant said.

"There he is. He'll be one of the first," Dixie said.

Grant looked to see Howdy, who was on horseback, ride into the arena. He maneuvered his horse beside a narrow chute. Grant could see that Howdy's horse was quivering in concentrated anticipation as the chute door was pulled open and a large steer burst forth into a dead run. The steer had gone no more than a few yards when Howdy dropped from his horse onto the back of the steer and placed the crook of his right arm around its horn. Twisting the animal's head and digging his heels into the dirt, Howdy pulled the large animal off balance and rolled it onto its back.

"What a super human undertaking," Grant said.

"I told you these were some tough fellows," Dixie said.

"And when it comes to doggin', Howdy's one of the best," Tom added.

Grant stepped down from the fence to see Little Tom running toward him. He felt a knot form in his stomach as the boy approached.

"You gonna draw fer a bull?" he panted.

"No...uh, I don't think so," Grant stammered.

"Well ya done good on that bronc and he was a real tough one. Onlyest difference is that these critters got horns."

Elmer was standing close by.

"I never seen but a damned few who ever lasted eight seconds on their first bronc ride," he said.

Grant realized that bravado was overruling his better judgment. Words sprung from his mouth involuntarily.

"Okay! Sign me up," he said.

Tom caught Grant's arm.

"Son, you'd best think this over. Don't get hoorahed into somethin' you might regret. These are a tough bunch of men and they're around these animals all the time. They know what they're gettin' themselves in for...and believe me, they get hurt a plenty. I ain't tryin' to scare ya, but this is gonna be the longest eight seconds you could'a ever imagined. I'd much prefer ridin' a cayuse to cow any old time...and these damned bulls will try to kill you."

Dixie then grabbed Grant's other arm. As he turned he could see the tears in her eyes.

"Please don't. I thought we'd agreed that you don't have to prove anything."

Grant thought a moment, his common sense gaining the upper hand.

"Oh...alright, I'll go tell Little Tom to take me off the list."

Grant walked toward the group of men who were preparing to draw names from an inverted hat Nick was holding in the air. As he approached,

Buck stepped in front of him.

"I guess you ain't near about as chicken shit as I had ya figured for."

Buck then turned to the crowd of cowboys.

"Hey everyone, look'a here. Ol' Dude is gonna show us how to ride a bull."

Grabbing Grant's arm Buck pushed him through the crowd toward Nick.

"Let the cheechako get the first pull," Buck shouted. "We want him to get a real fair shake don't we fellas?"

The assembled cowboys were cheering and shouting. Grant knew he could not refuse. To do so would be a complete humiliation. He reached into the hat as if it contained a nest of scorpions and gingerly removed a folded square of paper, handing it to Little Tom who was assisting Nick with the drawing

"Rambunctious," Little Tom announced to the throng.

The cheer from the assembly was as much in thanks as in excitement. To a man, each was happy that he had not drawn that scrap of paper. Grant stood staring into space as the remaining contestants moved to pick a name from the hat which no longer contained the scorpion. Little Tom read the names, one after another, and all of the men moved off to gather gear and load the chutes.

Grant felt light-headed as he walked toward the pens, which resounded with the bellowing of angry animals. As each was moved into its respective chute, holding gates clanged into position behind them.

"You're going to do it?" Grant heard Dixie's voice behind him.

"I didn't have any choice," he said, looking stunned.

"Well you'll excuse me if I don't watch," she said.

Tears streamed down her cheeks as she ran toward the house.

He took a few steps after her when he heard Nick shout, "Hey, Grant, could you give Howdy a hand on chute two?"

As he headed back to the pens the adrenaline began to flow. He felt nauseated but he had made the decision and this was something he must do. He climbed the fence to stand beside Howdy on the top rails.

"What do you want me to do?"

"You see that strap?" Howdy said.

Howdy was pointing to a length of flat woven rope lying on the ground beside the chute.

"Help Elmer tie it around his flanks. It's a buckin' strap, like on the broncs. Critters are real sensitive around the flanks, kind'a like you and me. Anyway, it sure as hell makes 'em buck better. Take that stick and push it through the chute over to Elmer. He'll fasten it on top."

Grant looked through the chute at Elmer. He fastened the rope to a stick, then pushed it under the bull. Elmer grasped the end and then climbed to the top of the chute where he secured the strap loosely around the bull's flanks.

Elmer waited until Grant had climbed to the top of the chute, then handed him the end of the bucking strap.

"Now you hang on tight to that end," Howdy instructed. "When the gate opens you pull it as hard as you can."

The bull was throwing himself wildly against the sides of the chute. A cowboy whom Grant did not know slowly lowered himself to the back of the unpredictable beast. Howdy helped the man fasten the flat rope securely around his right hand and when the man nodded, the gate was thrown open. Grant jerked with all his might on the end of the flank strap, until it flew from his grasp by the weight of the bull. The animal jumped into the arena. Grant began to count to himself as he watched the bull heave and twist, throwing its head with every leap. Several men, who had opened the gate, were now acting to haze the animal, diverting it from the fence. The hapless cowboy became airborne on the count of two and hit the ground face down beneath the raging animal.

Grant was horrified as the cowboy attempted to crawl away beneath flying hooves only to have both of the bull's hind feet come down, one on each side of the man's buttocks splitting the crotch of his pants from beltline to beltline. Just as Grant was sure that the man had been seriously injured the bull bucked away, chasing one of its tormentors.

The downed rider scrambled for all he was worth and rolled under the bottom rail of the fence. He jumped to his feet, climbed the fence and waved to the crowd. In his excitement he was blissfully unaware of the brown stain on his cotton underwear, showing through the rip in his pants, contradicting his ebullient smile.

Grant assisted several more of the participants, and was enjoying the excitement of the work.

"It's your turn Grant. Chute number one," Nick said. "And good luck and hang on tight!"

Grant felt instant nausea overwhelm him. In the excitement of helping the other riders Grant was not aware that his bull had entered the chutes. When he climbed to the top rail and looked at the animal below, his breath seemed to stop. His ears buzzed and his vision momentarily blurred. The animal's massive bulk left little room on either side of the chute for a man to place his legs. Rambunctious had huge horns as wide as the chute. A heavy board had been placed through the rails and across the back of the bull's neck.

"That board is so he can't throw his head up and get you before the gate opens," he heard Buck say.

Grant looked around and Buck was standing on the top rail holding the end of the flat rope.

"Come on, cowboy," Buck said with a smile. "This here bull ain't gettin' no younger." Buck then turned and shouted, "Howdy, get the flank, would ya."

There was no way to put this off now, Grant thought, as the sights and sounds around him faded into a jumble. The time had come. Grant eased himself onto the rails of the chute, just above the back of the huge bull. His senses began to clear. He could feel control returning to his muscles.

"*Carpe Diem*," he said aloud.

"What's that?" Buck asked.

"Just a good luck saying."

Grant looked into Buck's eyes. He could feel the disdain.

As his senses began to return, he noticed a marked difference between this animal and the horse he had ridden earlier in the day. When he had mounted the bronc he had been able to sense the fear of the animal and although he had also been afraid, his fear had been mitigated by the sense that the unhappy animal only wanted to flee.

Rambunctious was different. He smelled...that was sure. In fact, he smelled atrocious, Grant thought. But there was no sense of fear. No sense of flight. As the animal peered obliquely up at his potential adversary, the only thing Grant could sense from the beast was animus. Grant smiled inwardly, thinking he had never before been caught between two such malevolent sets of eyes. Buck and Rambunctious.

As Grant balanced on the rails above the animal, Rambunctious bellowed and flung himself wildly within the confines chute. He threw his head, breaking the board intended to restrain him.

"Bring me a goddamned board with some size," Buck shouted. "This big sumbitch is gonna kill someone before we even get the gate opened."

Elmer appeared with a heavy lodge pole. He placed it through the rails behind the bull's head. As Grant again balanced on the chute he experienced for himself the gallows humor so often displayed by Tom.

He looked into the red-rimmed eye of the confined brute. The animal was slathering slimy secretions from his nose as he emitted low snorting sounds. Grant smiled. Looks like the boiler gauge showing this locomotive about to blow, he thought. As his buttocks touched the animal's back he could feel the moist heat of quivering muscles awaiting emancipation.

Grant felt a hand on his shoulder. When he turned, Howdy was smiling in genuine encouragement.

"This is gonna be different than that horse this morning. You ain't got no saddle for one thing and when you get off this bastard your troubles have just begun. You got to concentrate like you done earlier. It's all in your head. Now, if ya can get off and get to your feet, run like hell. This mean bastard will freight train your ass right through the fence, if'n he gets the chance. So don't give him the chance."

"Get that flank, Howdy," Buck shouted again. "I'll get him tied on."

Grant laid his hand, palm up on the rope, as he had seen the others do.

"I rosined her up real good for ya, Dude," Buck said. "You ain't got no saddle, like Howdy said. This rope is all you got!"

"Thanks," Grant replied.

Grant noticed that Buck wrapped the rope just as the others had done, completing the wrap with the tag end between the ring and little fingers. Then Buck took another turn of the rope and put the tag end under the back of Grant's hand.

"There...that'll hold ya," Buck said.

Buck pushed Grant's head forward in a nod and shouted, "Unbox this ox!"

Grant's feet were still on the rails as the gate opened and instantly his world was spinning confusion. He was instantly unaware of anything that was happening around him. He pulled himself tightly to his right hand and gripped the furious mass of muscle called Rambunctious with all the strength his legs could muster. Without knowing why, he grabbed his hat and waved it above his head.

Rambunctious had come out of the chute spinning to the right and kicking his hind legs high in the air. In mid-flight he changed direction, flipping his head to the left. A fist sized glob of mucous hit Grant's face intensifying his disorientation.

Reversing direction, the bull swung his head up and back striking Grant a glancing blow on the forehead with end of his horn. Stunned and knocked from his seat, Grant's right hand remained tied securely to the violently undulating mountain of an animal. He was now being whipped around like a flag in a high wind as Rambunctious continued his furious gyrations. Cowboys jumped into the arena in an attempt to free the rope. Efforts to slow the violent gyration of the infuriated Rambunctious were futile. Derrick and Howdy, at much risk to their own safety, pulled the tag end of the flat rope, freeing the now near unconscious Grant from the wrath of the unforgiving beast. As Grant fell prostrate to the ground, Elmer and Howdy grabbed his arms and dragged him into the chute, closing the gate.

After a few perfunctory attempts to run down and gore some of the men who had jumped into the arena, Rambunctious trotted, pride intact, to the exit chute and his manger of hay.

As clarity returned to Grant's eyes, he saw Derrick standing over him holding his new Stetson. It was the first time Grant had seen the man smile.

"I had to save this for ya. All in all, them was two pretty good rides for a cheechako."

Derrick extended his hand and pulled Grant to his feet. He handed Grant his hat and walked away without another word.

Hearing loud voices, Grant looked toward the chutes where Howdy, standing on the ground, was shouting angrily at Buck.

"You tried to kill that fella, too," he said. "What the hell were you thinkin' about?"

"Naw, Howdy. He's just a dude and he don't know what he's doin'. I was just tryin' to help him," Buck said.

"Maybe so, Buck, but that was a real bad wreck...and your brand is all over it," Howdy said.

Howdy turned to walk toward the corrals. Grant waited until he approached.

"Thanks, Howdy. I think you saved my life. If there's ever anything I can help you with, you let me know."

Howdy stopped, took off his hat and scratched his head. He thought a long moment and then looked Grant in the eye.

"Ya know, Dude, I'm almost beginnin' to like you...and no offense, but you sure as hell have pissed on a hornet's nest."

Howdy looked at his hat and then back at Grant, his brow furrowed.

"I think it's best if'n you just let us take care of the cowboyin', and we'll let you take care of the boss's story writin'. I think we'll all be better off."

"Perhaps you're right," Grant said.

Howdy then put on his hat and tipped it back on his head.

"I'll see ya later, Dude. You take care of yourself."

Grant walked toward the house. As he passed the barn, Dixie bolted from behind the building. She ran to Grant and threw her arms around his neck holding him tightly. They stood for a long moment. Grant took her arms and held her away so as to see her face. Her eyes were red and her cheeks swollen.

"What is that awful slime on your face?" she asked.

"I think Rambunctious used my face for handkerchief."

"I couldn't help myself. I had to watch. It was horrible. I thought you were hurt...or worse. Are you alright?"

"A bit battered, but yes, I'm fine. What's the matter? You appear to have been crying."

The look of distress, which had clouded her face, was instantly replaced by hurt and anger.

"Grant Collins, I am never going to speak to you again as long as I live."

She turned and ran toward the house.

Grant stood for a long moment in bewilderment, watching as she ran toward the house.

"Now I have no idea as to what I've done wrong," he said aloud.

He turned to walk back to the rodeo arena and he found Tom standing behind him with a look of concern.

"You okay boy?" he asked.

"A little sore and bruised but I think I'll live."

"Good," Tom said. "That was a pretty good whippin' ya took out there. And I do mean whippin'. You looked like the business end of a mule skinner's black snake there for a few seconds. You sure you didn't hurt your writin' arm now did'ja?"

Tom smiled.

"No, I think I will be able to continue with our story."

"Women," Tom said, looking at Grant in unusual seriousness. "You'll never understand 'em."

"You heard Dixie?"

"No need bein' embarrassed about not figurin' out a woman. They just don't think like you and me. Best to let her be until she cools down a bit. Then with a little appropriate bowin' and scrapin' a fella just might get back into her good graces."

Tom lit a Lucky Strike.

"You know boy, a woman is kind'a like a good horse. About the time you get to dependin' on some cayuse, the sumbitch will run off and leave you afoot in the middle of God's country. If you go chasin' after the bastard, he'll head for the hills and you'll never see him again. But generally, if he likes you, and you let him be, he'll find his way back to camp and come to get his ears scratched...needin' the company as much as you do."

Grant could not help but laugh at the analogy.

"I'll take your advice," Grant said, laughing. "When she deigns to speak to me again I will appropriately bow and scrape and perhaps I may again find favor."

"Posies can't hurt nothin' neither," Tom said. "Let's go over to the mess hall. I can smell the barbeque from here."

The bull riding had concluded and the crowd at the arena had thinned. Most were going to the mess hall where Caleb and Susanna had prepared a steer on the barbeque. Kegs of beer were packed in ice from the newly installed refrigerated lockers and the crowd ate and drank until late into the night. Grant remained at the party, mingling with Tom's guests, listening to the tales of cowboys, young and old.

The house was dark and quiet as Grant softly closed the front door. Removing his boots, he crept up the stairs. The barely audible creak of the wood beneath his feet resounded in his ears like the screech of an ungreased wagon wheel. Silently closing his bedroom door behind him, he turned on the lamp at the small writing table where he sat and began to scribble notes. He wanted to record the day's activities, and the stories he had heard at the evening festivities, while still fresh in his mind. No one in Baltimore would believe the story of his adventure as a cowboy.

Sore and exhausted he undressed for bed. Looking at his clothing he smiled. He could not recall having been so thoroughly dirty in his life. Rodeo arena dirt, mixed with sweat had soaked to the skin. Too late for a shower, he thought, and modesty be damned. He stripped to his bare skin and climbed between the crisp sheets, allowing his body to melt into the sensuous smell and feel of the cool clean linen. Pulling the blankets tightly to his neck he quickly drifted into deep slumber.

He awoke with the strange feeling that someone was in the room. Holding his breath in the inky darkness he listened for any sound. Deciding that it was his imagination, he rolled onto his back. Something touched his face. He sat straight up, grabbing at the unseen intruder.

A slight fragrance in the air told him that it was Dixie.

"What are you doing?" he asked.

"Shhhhhhhh...you'll wake the whole house," he heard her whisper.

As he released the grip on her arm he was aware of the pain and soreness from the battering his body had endured during his encounter with Rambunctious.

"Ohhhhhh...that hurts," he said.

"I'm sorry, about being mad and shouting at you," she said.

She pulled back the blankets and slipped into the bed next to him.

"Does it hurt a lot?"

"Well, it feels better now," he said.

His heart was beating rapidly from the startled awakening. Now the adrenaline and testosterone were pumping through his trembling body as she leaned on one elbow and gave him a lingering kiss. He lay unmoving, not wanting to break the spell as the tip of her tongue searched his parted lips for a response. Inexperienced as a lover, he held his breath until he was nearly faint. Moving his head slightly he broke off the kiss.

"You don't know how happy I am that you're sorry."

She snuggled close to him and put her head on his right shoulder.

"Does that hurt when I lay here?"

"No," he lied. "It's just fine."

They lay quietly in the darkness. Long moments passed. Neither was quite sure of what they should do next. Dixie slowly ran her hands over Grant's chest and stomach. She was wearing a full length cotton nightgown so that his nakedness had not been obvious. When her hand touched his naked flesh she sat upright and giggled.

"You're naked...do you always sleep naked?"

"Well...uh...it was late and I didn't have a chance to take a bath and my clothes were dusty and my underwear was filthy and I hadn't really expected to have company, if you must know."

She threw back the blanket and arose from the bed.

Grant, thinking that she was leaving said, "I'm glad you didn't go to bed mad. Will we have breakfast in the morning?"

"I wasn't really mad," she whispered. "I was just worried about you."

Grant waited to hear the door as she was leaving. In the darkness he could hear her moving back toward the bed and when she pulled the sheet over them he realized that she had removed her nightgown.

"Now we're both naked," she giggled.

"Not so loud," he cautioned. "What if your uncle hears us?"

"He'd probably shoot you. He's very protective, you know."

"Well, that would certainly put an end to what appears to be a budding romance," he whispered, choking back a laugh. "You know that your Uncle Tom is one of the wisest men I have ever known."

"And what makes you think that,"

Raising up on one elbow and placing a hand on each side of her face, he kissed her softly. Then scratching her gently behind the ears he asked,

"Does that feel good?"

"It feels just wonderful."

She closed her eyes and purred.

"Yes ma'am...your Uncle Tom is real philosopher."

"How so?"

"Just take my word for it."

Tentatively, he moved his fingers along the inside of her arm, then down her waist to her hip.

"And I have to tell you something else," he said.

"And what do you have to tell me? Maybe I don't want to know."

"I told you at the lake, I have never made love to a woman...and I am frightened to death...and I don't know what to do next...and..."

The volume of his voice was rising with each admission.

"And what if you got in the family way and were humiliated and what if I'm no good as a lover...and..."

Dixie put her fingers over Grant's mouth.

"Shhhhhhh. Not so loud...and now I have two things to tell you," she whispered. "First, I have never made love to a man, either. That was the truth! I guess that was pretty close at the lake the other day. But I wouldn't say it really counted. Would you?"

Grant shook his head. His body was shaking with nervous energy.

"The most important thing that I have to tell you is that I have decided that I really do love you," she said in a near shrieking whisper.

She pushed him back onto the pillow.

"Breathe," she said.

She kissed him. He could feel her body warming as a flush of perspiration caused skin to cling, one to the other. She pressed her breasts against his heaving chest as he kissed her. He kissed her ear, then her neck, then her throat. His untrained hands made clumsy explorations, massaging gently as per instructions in a book once read in secret shame.

He lifted himself onto one elbow and pressed her onto the pillow. Each of them trembled in quivering spasms as his lips caressed her breasts in fulfillment of a mutual fantasy. With each kiss and every touch, shared temptations grew in urgency. Electricity shot through him as he allowed his fingers to explore imagined places, knowing for the first time the silky wet warmth of womanhood. An intoxicating sweet musk filled the space around them with an overpowering force that could no longer deny the joining of their bodies.

Ungainly collisions of conflicting limbs seeking purchase and position were ignored as each sought relief for innate demands of the flesh, which could no longer be denied.

Shuddering, as if in the grip of seizure, each fought the impulse to loudly proclaim their mutual delight as a never before known ecstasy completed the coupling. They held tightly to one another until collapsing in indulgent exhaustion.

Neither of them was aware of time passing as they lay in the dark listening to the other breathing in rhythm. Finally, the crowing of the rooster told Grant that Tom would soon be up and about.

"I do love you, Mr. Collins," she whispered.

"And I love you back, Miss Anderson," he said, holding her tightly and kissing her. "But before we both lose someone you love...namely me...you had better get back to your room. I know Koko will be up any minute now."

Dixie slipped into her nightgown and gave Grant another quick kiss. Opening the door wide enough to peek through the crack, she dashed to her room down the hall as Grant breathed a sigh of relief.

22

"Okay, everyone, get a shoulder under this thing and growl," Buck said.

Grant found an unoccupied spot on a wheel of the chuck wagon and began to push. Slowly, the wagon inched up the ramp toward the flat bed of the trailer. When the wagon neared the top of the ramp, the strength of the straining men began to ebb. The wagon rolled ever more quickly down the ramp coming to rest in its original position.

"Suppose we turn the wagon around and get a couple of the horses hitched to ropes. Wouldn't that facilitate pulling the wagon onto the trailer without getting anyone hurt?" Grant said.

There was a long silence as all of the men looked at Grant.

"I was jest gettin' ready to do that," Buck said. "Ain't no use all of us breakin' our backs like this. I'm glad ya explained it so well to these others, Dude."

Buck and several of the men walked toward the corral, while Howdy went with two other men to get the harness.

Grant looked at Tom with a shrug.

"I didn't mean to annoy Buck any more than was necessary but it seemed so obvious."

"Don't worry about it, son. I hadn't even thought of it myself to tell ya the truth. It'll stick in his craw for a bit but then most things do with Buck. I just don't know what I'm gonna do about him. Forty years ago a fella like Buck could'a done okay. There was plenty of places a fella like him could go in those days. Places where no one would have cared who he was. He would have likely joined up with someone like his hero, ol' Butch Cassidy or the Dalton boys or some such riffraff and ended up stretchin' a rope or takin' his scenery in some institution of confinement filled with suitable company for his likes. But these days things have changed. They say John Wesley Hardin shot a man for snorin' too loud. And I'd reckon Buck has pretty much that same disposition if given a free hand. I reckon that men like Buck have been around since the beginnin'. Bible says there was Cain, you know. If Buck weren't such a damned good hand I'd fire him right now."

Grant looked around at the array of large trucks and trailers assembled for the trip to Calgary.

"This is some fine equipment for ranching purposes. I noticed Bernie had some of these trucks also," Grant said.

"We got all these trucks and trailers and the like after the war. The government, bein', real watchful of our tax dollars, was given this stuff away for pennies on the dollar. These Ford trucks have got a lotta miles left in 'em. We haul all manner of critters and cargo on these things. They was built extra heavy for the military and they are damned fine for ranch vehicles."

"It's late in the day, are you loading the animals also?" Grant asked.

"We won't load the critters until the last thing before we leave tomorrow. Don't want 'em on the trucks any longer than they've got to be."

The men returned with horses and harness. Ropes were attached to the wagon tongues and soon the two chuck wagons were tied securely on their trailers.

"You boys have put in a good day," Tom said. "Come on over to the mess hall and I'll buy you all a beer."

"Thanks, boss," Buck said. "And thanks, college boy. I don't know what we'd have done without ya."

Grant and Tom walked toward the mess hall as the men put away animals and equipment.

"You mentioned the other evening that you were becoming bored with the freighting business even though you and Horse Sense were making a lot of money. The last we spoke you said that you were pretty much leaving the business up to him. What were you doing while he was freighting?" Grant asked.

"Oh, yeah! Like I told you, ol' Horse Sense was a damned sight better at the business end of freightin' than I was, so I let him kind'a take it over. That was in about the mid-sixties and I had just begun gettin' together a herd to start an open range ranch operation here abouts. Me'n Horse Sense started buildin' a ranch house, mostly for his family. In fact, that place there at the end of Agatha Street where Rom lives was the first one we started. Him and Remus lived there ever since."

"I was wondering how you came to name the streets until we went to the cemetery. I assume that the streets were named for your mother, father and brother?"

"Yes, sir. Nicholas was my pa and I named Nick after him too. Agatha was my ma and the third street was named for my brother Derrick. I also named my youngest boy after him. It took us a bit to get that house built, but my little sister had lived in a whole lot worse places than a tent. She never complained a bit. In fact, she seemed right happy. Ol' Horse Sense didn't believe in beatin' women, and she had sure enough had her share'a beatin's when she was with Angry Bear."

"Is there a reason you didn't name your daughter Agatha."

"When Susanna was born there was a song that was real popular about 'Oh Susanna, Don't You Cry For Me.' Susanna's mama really liked that song and Susanna cried a lot when she was tiny. Danny started callin' her Susanna Cries A Lot, in the fashion of an Injun name. I figured it was fittin' so we put it in the family Bible.

"When you speak of an 'open range ranch,' I assume that there were no fences. How did one know whose cows belonged to whom?"

"Nope. No fences. A fella would brand his stock and turn 'em out and then all of the open range ranchers would get together when the calves were born and round 'em up and brand 'em so we'd know whose was whose. The calves would be with their mothers so a fella could be pretty sure it was his, if'n the mamma had his brand. We'd generally emasculate the little bulls and turn out the best bulls we could find to take care of the cows. Then we'd sell off the steers when they was growed enough to load out for beef in Chicago. That was what I was tellin' ya about with the chuck wagon races. That was pretty much where the races started, during the roundup and brandin' time. Like I said, those boys would be boys."

"When did you have time to be the Marshall in Fort Benton?" Grant asked.

"Let's go have a beer and I'll tell these youngsters about that. Most of them is too young to remember anything about cowboys except what they seen in a Tom Mix movie."

Several men had tapped a keg of beer and set it on a picnic table close to the mess hall. Tom and Grant each poured a glass of beer and sat at one of the tables. The other men had soon joined the group. To Grant's surprise, Tom knew about each man. He knew their families, or where they were from and what they had done before coming to The Buffalo Rock. There was an obvious mutual respect.

"Grant here was asking me about the old days of open range ranchin' and my days of marshallin' in Fort Benton. Any of you fellas interested in hearin' that?" Tom said.

The group fell silent and each man pulled his seat close.

"Since we didn't have no fences to mend and my brother-in-law, who we called Horse Sense, was seein' to our freightin' business, I had a little time on my hands to spend in Fort Benton. By that time I'd developed a fondness for poker. I'd learned some card tricks while I'd been pigeon huntin' in the early sixties and it didn't hurt my luck at the game, if'n you know what I mean."

The men laughed as Tom winked.

"I was also becomin' friends with the town fathers, that is to say that if a bastard of a town like Fort Benton could'a been said to have a father. I was bankin' some real money. I even helped to start the Cattlemen's Association.

One day, some of them city fathers come to me and asked would I take on the job of town Marshal, mainly because the rest of the bunch was scared shitless to get anywhere near that job. The previous two Marshals had got themselves kilt and there just weren't no takers for the position. Not only that, it didn't pay enough to buy a good bottle of whiskey a month.

Now I'd made the acquaintance of a young buffalo hunter by the name of Caldwell Hart. He was tough and seemed a fearless young fella. I told the Mayor that I'd take the job if'n they would allow me to hire young Caldwell as my deputy and pay him a sum worth his while. Well, sir, I offered eighty a month and found. Ol' Caldwell could hardly refuse, even though Benton was a tough ol' place. But winter was comin' and

Caldwell figured it was sure better'n freezin' your ass skinnin' them stinkin' buffalos.

We didn't rightly have us a jail or even an office. We had a shack across from where the Grand Union now stands. We had a little windowless room where we could lock up the miscreants if we had to. But I tried not to do that any more than was necessary. Me'n Caldwell took turns at walkin' the streets and tryin' to keep things under control. Of course, I liked playin' a little poker my own self, so I was generally available when things went awry."

A huge grin lit Tom's face.

"Bein' a Marshal and all, led to me meetin' the first woman I ever fell madly and passionately in love with."

Grant's scribbled furiously without looking as the others laughed. All the while he could feel eyes burning holes in him. He looked up to see Buck glaring.

"Her name was Dumont. Eleanor Dumont. Now for them that don't know, she was also known as Madam Moustache. There's a picture I cut from an old magazine in my office in case you'd like to see what she was like. Of course, that picture wasn't taken till later in San Francisco. She was a darlin' young thing when I encountered her in Fort Benton. Truth is that she was a fine lookin' filly in 'er day. She had real fine black hair all over her body and it was the oddest sensation when ya'd rub your fingertips real lightly all over her...and she had that little moustache which was kind'a different for a fancy lady. And that woman had a pair'a balls bigger'n that ol' Rambunctious, figuratively speakin' of course."

The men laughed loudly.

"She could drink, cuss, play cards and shoot better'n most of the men I ever knew. And when it come to lovin', well she could present a cornucopia that would leave a fella in a state the likes of which he'd hope to not recover. Me'n that woman would play cards all night till she'd drink me under the table and then she'd make love to me till time for her to go back to work."

"What sort of work did she do?" a young cowboy asked.

"She ran the best whorehouse in Fort Benton. I do believe that your education in history has been sorely neglected, son. Madam Moustache ran whorehouses in every boom town and mining strike during the middle of the last century. But I got to tell ya one real interestin' thing she done, which made her a legend in Fort Benton.

Now you boys got to remember that Fort Benton was as much a seaport town as a cow town. A whole lot of the town's wealth came up the ol' Muddy Mo on steamboats. There was also a whole lot of bad things that came up the river on those boats...things that Fort Benton could stand to live without. Well, one day a rumor hit town that there was a boat steamin' into Fort Benton with the pox."

"You mean Smallpox?" Grant asked.

"Smallpox. Sure enough. Now that boat was loaded with all manner of goods which was sorely needed and there was sure as hell a load of people on board who wanted to disembark for the minin' grounds. But the pox is somethin' that'll put a scare into the bravest of souls. And frankly, no one knew just exactly what to do about the situation.

I do recall that we was all in the saloon swillin' rotgut and discussin' the legalities of the situation when sure as hell we hear the whistle blow. Here comes that infected steamer. I reckon that the captain would have been mighty happy to be seein' the ass ends of anyone suspected of having the pox. Of course, he also had cargo he was responsible to unload and money was most likely his big motivator...pox or no pox.

Now I got to tell ya that this was one of the damndest things I ever saw. Ol' Elly, which was what I called her, went stompin' outta that saloon as soon as she heard that whistle. As she walked by two fellas who had revolvers stuck in their belts she reached out and grabbed them guns. One'a them guns was a regular Colt forty-four and the other was one'a them LaMatt nine shot forty-two caliber pistols that had a sixteen gauge shotgun barrel in the middle of the cylinder. Damned sure if a person couldn't have started a war all by their lonesome with one'a them things. She marched her pretty little self right over to that dock with a pistol in each hand and when they started to put the gangway down she let go a shot from that Colt forty-four at the steamer bell. Well, of course that got everyone's attention and then she hollered up to the captain, 'Haul up the plank and get your disease carryin' asses outta Benton, right now.'

Of course, the captain took exception to this little bit of a woman givin' orders the way she was doin' and he told his boys to lower away. Now the second shot came outta that LaMatt. It was just a lucky thing for that Captain that the gun was set to fire the shotgun blast and that he was far enough away that the pellets from that short barreled LaMatt just sort'a stuck in the skin of the Captain's face without doin' a whole lotta damage. Lucky he didn't lose an eye or nothin'. Ol' Elly hollered up at him, 'Now ya know what ya'd look like with the pox. And if ya don't get this barge movin' real quick, yer gonna find out what you'll look like with some port holes in your hide. Now get the hell on outta here.' Well, sir, the Captain decided that this woman wasn't makin' no idle threats. He put that steamer around and headed back the way he'd come."

The men were regaled with Tom's tale, laughing uproariously. Tom looked around with a smile, enjoying the attention.

"Let me ask you...would you have stayed with a crazy lady puttin' holes in yer hide?"

"You're right, Boss, that woman had her some balls," Howdy said.

"So anyway, I always figured they should'a put a monument to her memory bein' as how she saved the town and all. But then she wasn't nothin' but a whore and people just don't seem inclined to wanna pay homage to a whore."

"Were there gunfights in the streets the way they tell 'em in the books and show 'em in the flicks?" Buck asked.

"There was sure enough gunfights in the streets but they wasn't nothin' like ya see in the motion pictures. The times I'm talkin' about was still in the sixties and most fellas didn't even carry a gun in a holster like the fancy lookin' rigs you see in the flickers. Men wore their britches held up by suspenders then. Most didn't wear a belt to hold up their pants. If'n they wore a belt it was to hold their shirt so the cold didn't blow in and then they'd carry a knife on that belt. Guns was usually just stuck in their belts and the only ones with holsters was fellas who'd got one from the army, like I did. And those hats ya see in the movies, I never saw one like that in those days. Those cowboy hats in the motion pictures are designed to show off the faces of them movie actors. They ain't much count for workin' hats. You boys know that. Fellers wore hats to keep off the sun and rain. Those hats we wore had a utility, and still do here in Montana. Not like movie cowboys with their brims turned up to show their mugs. Now the gunfights was generally at real close range. Hell, most of the gunfights I was witness to weren't no further than across the poker table. It was just lucky that most of them fellas was too drunk to hit a piss pot in pecker range...so there wasn't near as many kilt as there could'a been."

"Did you arrest a lot of the men who were in gunfights, Boss, or did you just ventilate their hides?" Elmer asked.

"I personally never had much desire to kill anyone...not to say that I hadn't had my sure enough fair share of doin' so, what with the great War of the Rebellion and the Injuns and marshalin' and all. I sure as hell wasn't willin' to get my head blowed off in the name of altruism and you can take that to the bank. I can't really say as how I enjoyed killin' a man, but I did so when it was him or me.

I found that I could deal with most of the problems I encountered as a marshal with an implement I called Armageddon. Now what I done was get me an old pick axe handle that some fella had broke and discarded. I cut that thing off to about a foot and half and had the smith drill a hole in it for a leather lanyard. I even carved a fancy handle, kinda like those billy sticks ya see the city police carryin' around these days. Whenever one'a them boys started gettin' froggy with me, I didn't give him no chance to jump. I'd real quick lay ol' Armageddon right alongside the man's head. If'n it didn't knock him down it would sure as hell take most of the fight out of him."

"Why didn't you just use your gun to pistol whip 'em like the marshals in the dime novels do?" a young cowboy asked.

"I done that once. Cost me a new gun barrel and near about cost my life. That was what prompted me to make ol' Armageddon in the first place. One day I was sittin' in the shack with Caldwell and we hear some shoutin' and a disturbance. Bein' peace officers, me'n Caldwell run down about a block and there was a couple'a fellas in the street, whippin' on one another over who knows what. One of 'em seemed to be gettin' the best of it, bloody as he was, so I told Caldwell just to hold back and watch. Figured I'd let 'em wear themselves out. First thing ya know the fella who was spittin' teeth reaches under his coat in the back and pulls a hog leg. He didn't even hesitate. I guess he didn't want to lose any more of them teeth 'cause he let 'er smoke right in the other fella's face. Well, I wasn't about to tolerate a cold blooded killin' so I real quick run up and pole-axed that sumbitch from behind with the barrel of my Colt.

He hit the dirt and started writhin' around and grabbin' his head, which was squirtin' blood like a leaky fire hose. So I kicked his pistol outta reach and me'n Caldwell took him down to the marshal's shack to cool off a little. Normally, we would only hold a man until they could have a fair trial and hang him, but it turned out that the other boy was might lucky. That bullet had took a chunk outta his left ear about the size of your little fingernail...and he had some powder burns which had give him a tattoo. I reckon he lived with that for the rest of his natural life, but other than that he was fit.

Now the moral of this here tale has nothin' to do with that fella's tattoo. The disaster came when I next had to use my Colt, which as it turned out was the very next day. About a week earlier there was a real wild eyed fella come to town to whore and lose his money at the poker tables. I reckon that was his intention 'cause he had surely enough succeeded to do both in a damned quick hurry. Then he commenced to claimin' that the games was rigged and the whores, one of whom was my very own sweetie pie, Elly, had robbed him of his bankroll. One thing lead to another and it wasn't long before some fella runs into my office, if ya could call it that, to tell me that the crazy bastard had just kilt the bartender and was threatenin' to slit Elly's throat, if he could he find her."

Tom took a long drink from his beer as the men sat silently intent.

"I never considered myself to be cowardly but there are times when a fella would just rather go somewheres other than where he has to go. After hearin' the circumstances, which I was facin', that was one'a them times. I figured this boy was gonna do it the hard way no matter what I said, so I checked the percussion caps on my Colt and started down the street to do my duty.

Now I hadn't walked but about ten steps when, kawhango...a bullet goes whizzin' past my ear. I looked down the street that there was that crazy miner with gun in hand trying to assassinate yours truly. When a second shot threw dirt in my face, I just knew that this was about to get real shitty.

There was a substantial post holdin' up the roof over the boardwalk at the next buildin' so I right quick run over there and got behind it. I was real careful to brace my arm against that post and rest that Colt so as to take a steady aim. Now I'd used that gun a lot and knew just how and where she shot, so when I squeezed that trigger and that fella was still pointin' his gun my way, to say the least I was bumfuzzled. I thought that maybe he was just too drunk to know he was dead...so I took another careful aim and let fly again. Damned if he didn't crank another shot my way, which took a chunk outta my right calf just above the boot. It was a long ways from my vital organs, but it hurt like the dickens.

I started gettin' real worried 'cause he was steady walkin' toward me. I knew it wasn't gonna be long before any advantage I'd held in distance and accuracy would be out the window. So I lined the bastard up one more time real careful like and dropped the hammer. Just lucky for me he was just passin' a store front window and I saw that bullet break that glass about a foot to the left of the sumbitch. Now this was not a situation where a man could contemplate the possibilities for too damned long. I just took it on instinct that a real quick adjustment was in order. I cocked that hog's leg, aimed about a foot to the right of his brisket and let 'er rip. The details ain't real important but we'll let it suffice to say that he didn't come no closer and he didn't shoot again."

"What was the cause of your bad shootin', Boss," Howdy asked.

"Seems I'd bent the barrel of that Colt over the hard head of that damned cowboy the day before, and it near about got me kilt. So I got myself a new barrel for that gun and afterwards I built Ol' Armageddon, which I always carried just for good measure. So when ya see them cowboys whackin' each other in them movies...or read them stories about the old marshals whackin' some miscreant on the head with his revolver, you can take all that bullshit with a pinch of salt. Heads are cheap and guns are expensive. Ol' Armageddon served me well."

Tom smiled and looked at the faces of the men.

"In fact, ol' Armageddon saved me one time in a kind'a odd sort'a way. I'd only been Marshaling about a year and I'd just got the new barrel on my Colt. I'd done some practicin' with that new gun barrel and I had 'er lined out so I knew where she was shooting, just in case.

One day a fella got off the steamer from Saint Louis and I do believe he was about the biggest man I've ever seen. He was lookin' fer work as a stevedore and he claimed to have been a longshoreman from Shanghai to San Francisco and all points east.

I was sittin' in the office one evenin' when Caldwell staggers into the shack with his nose situated over close to his right ear and his eyes was closin' fast. I got him over to the docs office and the best I could get of the story was that the big fella who'd just hit town hated the law and that's why he'd come to Fort Benton. He'd been told that there wasn't no law and he could do what he liked.

Apparently poor ol' Caldwell had tried to explain that the rumor wasn't true. It seemed that the big sumbitch took offense to Caldwell's explanation. The worst part, accordin' to Caldwell, was that the fella went about unarmed. He didn't carry no weapons, not even a knife...which he let everyone know. He also let it be known that his favorite sport was 'makin' invalids of law dogs.'

Now the way I saw it, cripplin' my deputy was sufficient offense to go to jail, but the problem was that with no deputy to assist, I was gonna have to bring this giant troublemaker to justice all by my lonesome. You see boys, committin' an offense and bein' held to account was two different matters back in old Fort Benton...and the prevailin' belief back in those days was that if a man didn't have a weapon, then no weapon should be used against him. So this big bastard was just havin' himself some fun usin' about three hundred and twenty-five pounds of solid muscle for a weapon...a weapon that couldn't be countered with the use of no gun.

I was, to say the least, in a quandary about what to do. I had me a sleepless night and I'll admit that I avoided Front Street when I figured the brute would be about. Him workin' as a stevedor during the day gave me a chance to keep account of his comin's and goin's, but I was not lookin' forward to a one-on-one encounter...I must admit.

Then one night the inevitable occurred. A lady poked her head into the shack to report a disturbance. Without thinkin' I jumped up and headed in the direction she was pointin'. Just as I was gettin' to the saloons, an enormous shadow stepped into my path and I knew I was about to take a float down shit river with no oars. As he stepped into the light I was surprised to see just what an angelic face the fella had. He looked like he ought'a been in a choir robe. However, he had a voice that sounded like thunder over the mountains when he smiled and said, 'I been waitin' to meet you, law dog.'

My stomach felt like it was makin' buttermilk. He's lookin' me square in the eye, only he's lookin' downward. 'Your deputy was gonna put me in jail the other day, but he never got around to it. I reckon you're lookin' to get a chance, huh?' he asks me with a great big innocent grin.

Now I kept Ol' Armageddon hangin' by the thong on my gun holster. When I dropped my hand, the big bastard threw up his hands and shouted, 'I ain't armed, law man. I don't carry no weapon and them folks over there watchin' will have to say that I never threatened you with no weapons.'

Of course, I realized that he was right and that shootin' the sumbitch might just get me hung...them was a part of benefits of bein' a law man in those times. Then an idea occurred to me. I eased ol' Armageddon off my gun butt and put it in my left hand behind my back...leaving my gun hand free just in case.

We stood lookin' at one another for a bit and then I stuck that hunk of hickory wood out in front of me and took a step back. 'Now you ain't plannin' to beat on old Archie with that stick, are ya Marshall?' he says as he put up his hands. I reckon he'd probably been lumped with a club more than once.

'Maybe I will,' I tell him. 'Kind'a evens the odds a bit,' I says. Then I took that stick and sort'a waved it in front of his face. Dumb bastard grabbed Armageddon quicker than an organ grinder's monkey can take your penny. Holding that club up for all to see, he smiled real big in surprise. It didn't occur to the dumb bastard that he had just unknowingly armed himself with that deadly weapon. He then proceeded to raise it above his head with the apparent intention of knockin' my brains into next Wednesday.

I don't think I ever drew faster. I put a bullet right through the middle'a his guts. The crowd that had been watching actually applauded...and that big sumbitch stood there for a good minute, still holding Armageddon in one hand and his guts in the other. When he finally toppled over, he laid there lookin' up at me like he couldn't believe what had happened. I don't think there was much grievin' for his miserable ass. It took six men to tote his bulk over to the doc's office."

"Did he die?" asked a chorus of voices.

"Nope! He recuperated and was never a problem for me after that. He did, however, give up the eatin' of spicy foods, I heard."

Everyone laughed.

"It was actually kind'a funny. He always hung around wantin' to be my friend after that, and I did use him a couple of times when the goin' was tough and I needed some muscle. But there was no doubt, somethin' about the fact that a half ounce bullet could lay this three hundred pound giant low had changed his outlook on the way he entertained himself."

Grant looked around at the smiling faces and again caught Buck's cold stare. He looked back at his notebook, completing what he was writing.

"What time is it getting' to be? Maybe we'd best get some supper and get in the hay stack. Gonna be a long week ahead," Tom said.

The men followed Tom into the mess hall door.

2 3

Grant stood in the gray light of pre-dawn watching as people bustled around him, loading equipment and animals, checking vehicles and packing necessities for the long drive to Calgary.

He was relieved when Susanna shouted, "Grant, could you give us a hand?"

Dixie and Susanna were carrying suitcases and canvas bags of rodeo equipment. Grant took all that he could carry and followed them to a truck where a man was loading luggage.

"Aren't Caleb and Little Tom coming to Calgary?" he asked.

"Tommy's coming, but Caleb's staying here to mind the guests. We hired extra people for the week."

"Do you do something in the rodeo or is Tommy riding?" Grant asked.

"I barrel race," Susanna said. "I don't think you have seen that yet."

"I am going to help her with her costume and tack," Dixie said.

Dixie placed her suitcase on the truck, and then turned to squeeze Grant's hand as she walked back toward the house.

"I feel utterly useless. Everyone is busy with something and all I can do is watch," he said.

"Are you packed?" Susanna asked.

"I packed last night. I didn't want to hold things up."

"Then put your things in the truck and go over to the mess hall. We'll meet you there in about fifteen minutes," Susanna said.

Grant walked toward the house and retrieved his suitcase from the porch. He handed it up to the man loading luggage on the truck, then walked toward the mess hall.

"How's Grant doin' this fine morning?" he heard Tom say.

"Just fine. Are you driving one of the trucks to Calgary?" Grant said.

"Hell, no," Tom chuckled. "You and me are gonna be comfortable. We're takin' my car. I pay these boys to be uncomfortable and seein' as how you ain't gettin' paid at all, we might just as well take our comfort."

Tom looked around at the busy people. Elmer was passing by carrying a saddle and a canvas bag.

"Tell everyone to be sure to eat a good breakfast," Tom said. "It's a long drive to Calgary and dinin' facilities along the way ain't none too good."

"Will do, boss," Elmer said.

"I'm supposed to meet Dixie and Susanna at the mess hall in a couple of minutes. Would you care to join us?" Grant asked.

"You bet," Tom said.

The mess hall was crowded. Tom and Grant were soon joined by Dixie and Susanna. When they had finished breakfast, they walked toward the convoy of vehicles where final preparations were being completed. Engines roared to life, and the horses and cattle voiced displeasure at their traveling accommodations.

"You want to drive, Missy?" Tom said. He put his arm around Susanna. "You're always wantin' to run the show anyway."

"Heck, yes, I'll drive," Susanna replied.

Tom and Grant got into the back seat of the car.

"Just make sure you stay out in front. I don't want to eat dirt," Tom said.

Dixie was seated in the front with Susanna. Grant reached his hand forward to give her an affectionate pat her shoulder.

"Ya know, son, she ain't near as pretty as my ol' Elly, but then it's damned hard to find a woman with a good moustache."

Grant and Tom both laughed aloud.

"And just what is that supposed to mean?" Dixie asked.

"Ain't nothin' that would concern you. You'll have to read it when this young fella writes my book," Tom said.

The car bounced slowly along the dirt road leading the convoy.

"You haven't told me how you came to meet Nick's mother. Was she a local girl in Fort Benton?" Grant said. "I hope you don't mind my speaking of her, Susanna."

"This family doesn't have any secrets...at least nothing worth hearing. You should know dad that well by now," Susanna said. "In fact Dad, I don't think I ever heard the story myself. How did you meet Angelica?"

"Backin in the olden days, when I was gettin' our open range herd built up, and helpin' Horse Sense with the freightin' now and then, I was also enforcing the laws of Fort Benton, just for some excitement. Bein' marshal also helped to pay for my poker playin' and such. Now we'd brung quite a few wagons and mules up the Big Muddy by that time and the freightin' business was doin good. Dixie's grandpa was still shippin' outfits with some regularity. In fact, we had so many that we had wagons that was just sittin' around with nothin' to do. They was easy enough to sell, but if we'd sell 'em, then we'd run short if'n we had large amounts of cargo for the Mullan Road. This was also about the same time as the big railroad boom. Hell, them gandy dancers was layin' ties and steel rails faster'n they was layin' the dancehall divas on payday night. Ooops! Sorry ladies."

Susanna looked at Dixie.

"I don't know why he apologizes. He is completely incorrigible and no one takes offense anyway," she said.

Dixie smiled and then looked fondly at her Uncle.

"I find it rather endearing. Don't you?"

"Well, sir, I saw me an opportunity to have a little fun and make a few dollars at the same time," Tom said. "So I told the Mayor that he'd have to get another marshal, who turned out to be Caldwell...and off I went to huntin' buffalo for the railroad gangs. The rail gangs needed a lot of meat, and an outfit to go huntin' was expensive.

I already had everything I needed...wagons and mules, a good grub stake and so forth. So off I went. Now and again I'd get a message from Horse Sense that he needed some of the wagons for something or another and we'd have to swap around some wagons and stock a bit...but we was doin' pretty well, all in all.

I went around to the railroad crews and if they didn't have a meat supply, I'd sign 'em up and hire me some hunters and skinners. In fact, I had three boys who come to work for me, one you might just have heard of. His name was Barclay Masterson. He became a newspaper fella himself. I read some of his articles. He died just a couple of years back. He went by the name of Bat...Bat Masterson?"

"I have heard that name. I think he worked for The Telegraph," Grant said.

"That's him. He had an older brother named Ed and a buddy by the name of Wyatt Earp. I thought that was about the funniest name I'd heard. Sounded a little like someone throwin' up after you drunk too much whiskey. But I didn't say nothin' to him. Never found it to be to anyone's advantage to make light of another man's name.

Anyways, a little side story to that was Earp gettin' himself into a big shootout down in Arizona. I believe it was Tombstone back in the eighties. Him and his brothers shot up a gang of miscreant rustlers and horse thieves. That story was in all the newspapers. I reckon you wouldn't remember that, being as how it was thirty years before you was born. I suppose one of these movie makin' people will do a whole motion picture about that big shootout some day. I was just never in the right place at the right time for gettin' in the papers.

Well, anyway, I set those fellas, Earp and the Masterson boys, up with a rig and put them on a fair split of the profits. Young Bat was the best shot of the three, and I loaned him a Sharps fifty and gave them boys a wagon and team to haul their meat and hides. They done good by me and I thought I was fair enough with them. I heard later that they'd all got into the lawman business in Kansas and other places...as well as gamblin' and managin' whores and what not. Ed Masterson got himself kilt down in Dodge City while marshalin'. I don't know what's become of Wyatt Earp. Last I knew he had gone to Alaska and cashed in big on the gold strikes in the nineties. I still got that ol' Sharps fifty I loaned to Bat. Remind me to show it to you next time we're in my office."

"Dad, he was asking how you met Nick's mother," Susanna said.

"Hold your water. I'm gettin' to it. Ya see I'd been at the buffalo huntin' for a couple of years and just like them passenger pigeons, the buffalos was startin' to get a little scarce by then. It occurred to me that if'n we kept up the killin' at the rate we was goin', them things was just gonna disappear too. Not only that, but the Injuns was gettin' mighty disconcerted by the fact that we was decimatin' their movin' mercantile... that, bein' the buffalo herds for you college educated children.

I'd decided I was gonna start shuttin' down the huntin' business, and

I just happened to be down in Wyomin' puttin' an end to some contracts with the railroads. This was the mid seventies and the Sioux was gettin' mighty feisty about bein' told that they had to go down to the Oklahoma strip and live on a reservation. Ol' Sittin' Bull's bunch along with Crazy Horse and a bunch of Cheyennes from down south had all got together for a powwow. They just didn't seem to understand what it was that Uncle Sam was wantin' them to do.

Them Injuns, bein' riled up as they was, had already burned one of my rigs and killed two fellas who were workin' for me. So I sent word to Horse Sense to come to Wyoming territory and bring some drivers, and we'd just take all our equipment back up to Fort Benton. By comparison, the outlaws and Injuns along the Mullan Road and in the local areas was tame compared to those Sioux. Besides, we was startin' to get a pretty good herd of cows goin' on the ranch by then and the railroads was beginnin' to stifle the wagon freight business.

Well, sir, ol' Horse Sense shows up with my sister Sarah and some drivers. We begin to gatherin' our equipment and settlin' our affairs and gettin' things in order so that we can head north for home. We had twelve men, countin' me, and Sarah of course. We had eight wagons and about seventy head of stock to drive. On the way north we had to pass about fifteen miles from the old Fort Fetterman. I knew some of the men stationed there. I had soldiered with 'em, so I figured to ride on over and learn what I could about what the Injuns was up to. I wanted to know what we might run into goin' north. I told Horse Sense to go on ahead and that I'd catch up to him the next day.

When I got to Fetterman, all hell was shakin'. General Crook had brought in near about a thousand men to enforce the government order that Crazy Horse and Gall and Sittin' Bull move their folks onto the reservation. The boys I'd soldiered with said that there was maybe several thousand Sioux and Cheyenne gettin' ready for a big Sun Dance and that there was gonna be big trouble. The boys introduced me to Crook and told him who I was and that I'd done some scoutin' in days past. Crook reckoned as how he'd heard of me, and he told me that there was a couple of other army columns comin' in from Fort Lincoln and Fort Ellis to catch the Sioux and Cheyennes in a pincer movement somewhere in either the Tongue River country or on the Rosebud."

"Weren't you worried about Uncle Horse Sense?" Dixie asked.

"I surely was, he was headin' right up into the Tongue River country... so I didn't even spend the night. I headed out across the prairie figuring it wouldn't take long till I'd cut their trail and catch up to 'em, just in case they might need some help. It was mid-afternoon by then and I was movin' along briskly when I see dust ahead. Well right off it occurs to me that if'n I can see dust, whoever it is that's comin' toward me can see mine. So I stopped. I got off my pony and walked along just below the crest of a high edge on a coolie and just watched the dust cloud get closer. I walked far enough that I figured if'n they was after me, I'd have a bit of advantage in the terrain.

Like I said, this was the mid-seventies. By this time I'd got me one'a them Schofield break open forty-five caliber pistols that was a whole lot faster for loadin'...especially on horseback. I also had me one'a them new Model 1873 Winchesters in the .44-40 caliber. So I was feelin' comfortable in my fire power."

Tom winked at Grant.

"Of course, I had me two saddle bags full of ammo for them guns... just in case. I got my cayuse down in the wash and just watched. It was pretty obvious that the rider was headed to Fort Fetterman. When he got close enough that I could make out horse and rider, I got my spy glass and took a careful look. My stomach made a real turn. It was one of the fellas that had been with Horse Sense and I knowed that this was not a good thing."

"Had he abandoned them?" Dixie asked.

Grant smiled, thinking that it was pleasant to have someone to ask the questions that were on his mind.

"He'd abandoned 'em alright. But I couldn't say as how I'd blamed him none. I rode outta that coolie and caught up to him to see what was what. He said that he had barely escaped with his hair. Seems ol' Horse Sense had sent him for help. They'd been accosted by about seventy-five head of drunken Rics and ended up in a fight."

There was a silence as Grant and Dixie looked at one another.

"And what is a Ric?" they asked in unison.

"Aricara," Tom said, in a matter of fact tone. "The Aricara hated the Blackfoot. Blackfoot had run 'em off their huntin' grounds some years before and the feud had never ended. The Rics got on well enough with the Crows and even with the Sioux...but they all hated the Blackfoot. So anyway, this fella tells me that they'd happened upon a Ric huntin' party.

Horse Sense had apparently told everyone to just to keep their guns ready and keep an eye on the Injuns while he went to palaver. One of the drivers was a know-it-all bastard who'd scouted for the army. He figured he knowed Injuns. So he tells everyone to relax 'cause they was just Aricaras...and nobody ever had no trouble with the Rics. So I reckon Horse Sense let down his guard.

Now Horse Sense should'a knowed better because him and little sister both knew that the Aricaras hated the Blackfoot. Sarah still pretty much dressed like a squaw even then, bless her little heart.

Turned out that all them Rics wanted was whiskey. They wasn't really lookin' for a fight. But when one of them warriors heard little sister talking Blackfoot, the hammer dropped and the bullshit stopped.

This fella that I had stopped on the trail said that he had kept his saddle horse tied on the freight wagon he was drivin'. When them Injuns got hostile, Horse Sense told him to get the hell outta there and go for help. That fella had done about the most sensible thing he could. He got the hell outta there amidst the bullets and arrows and headed to Fort Fetterman."

"Did you go back to the Fort for help?" Susanna asked.

"Nope! I got me another idea. I figured them Injuns was aware that one'a the men had escaped and that the fort wasn't too far off and I was hopin' that Horse Sense and the others had been able to keep the Injuns at bay.

I'd noticed that this fella had a couple of big hanks of picket line rope tied on behind his saddle. He'd tied it on his critter that mornin' when they broke camp. So I tell this driver to go get himself a great big pile of sage brush and bushes and tumbleweed and whatever, and I done the same. Then we tied them brush piles in bundles and dallied to our saddle horns with the picket rope.

I told that fella to stay off about fifty to a hundred yards from me and we'd go ridin' right into the fight like we was a whole regiment. I knew that pullin' them brush piles would keep our cayuses runnin' with no problem and it would sure as hell raise some dust.

Off we went, leavin' a trail' that looked like the Seventh Cavalry was comin'. I was just hopin' that those Injuns didn't notice that there was no bugle call as we come ridin' in. Now those Rics was some good fighters when they had to be, but that bunch was mostly drunk and they was lookin' to hunt, not fight. When they saw that cloud of dust'a comin' from the direction of the fort, they figured it was the whole United States Cavalry ridin' down upon 'em. Better part of valor and all. They skedaddled, and thank God they headed south."

"Were Uncle Horse Sense and his men alright?" Dixie inquired.

"There was two fellas who had been hit...one with a bullet and one with an arrow. Both the wounds looked less than life threatenin'...and I didn't reckon either man would be dyin' from what I saw. So Horse Sense got everyone hooked, hitched and started dustin' a trail north. I'd learned there was an army column marchin' south and I hoped to link up with them for protection.

That took care of Aunt Sarah and Horse Sense, but now I had another dilemma to deal with. While I was at Fort Fetterman, Crook had asked would I take charge of his Crow scouts and go along on the campaign to get Sittin' Bull's bunch and the Cheyennes back to the reservation. Seems them soldier boys had them a battle plan which they was calling a hammer and anvil. They didn't want the Injuns escaping up to Canada. So they had it figured that Crook and Gibbon were gonna be the anvil on the west and south and then Terry with Custer's Seventh Cavalry was gonna be the hammer to crush those rebellin' redskins by comin' in from the east.

I told Crook that I wasn't signin' on for no more long term enlistments but that if'n he'd take my word that I'd stick with him till the job was done, I'd have a go at the scoutin' job after I'd seen to my folks gettin' up north safely.

Now this was early in June and it was startin' to warm up real good. I figured that Sioux camp was gonna be somewhere up in the cooler river bottoms, either in the Rosebud or the Bighorn country."

"Are you talking about Custer's Last Stand?" Grant asked.

"That's what they called it, sure enough. But the glorious Mister Custer was only one part of that whole operation. Ya see, Gibbon was comin' down from the north and west with his infantry, which was why I wasn't none to worried about Sarah and Horse Sense. Crook was supposed to come from the south...that hammer and anvil thing I was talkin' about.

So anyway, I ride up to the Yellowstone with the wagons and then I told Horse Sense to go on ahead and I rode back to Fort Fetterman in time to join up with Crook on his foray to the north, actin' as a temporary scout.

On the second day, just before we got into the Rosebud River, ol' Crazy Horse and a couple'a hunderd of his men caught us with our britches down right at breakfast. Now whereas the soldier suits was carrying single shot Springfields and a Colt sidearm, those Sioux warriors was packin' repeaters of all descriptions. We had 'em outnumbered, but they had us outgunned and they took us by surprise.

That was another of them times that I was glad I had a saddle bag full'a ammo. Those poor soldiers with them single shot rifles was gettin' off about one shot to ten for the Injuns. Even worse was the fact that the army ammunition wasn't worth the weight of the lead. The cases were copper and the empty shell casings would stick in the rifle chamber about every other shot, leavin' those poor soldier suits to pry out the empty with a knife...if he had one. It was brutal. I don't know how many of them soldiers was killed but we took a beatin'.

I found myself a defensive position with about twenty soldiers in some deadfall timber and since I had that Winchester and a saddle bag of ammunition, we only lost one man. That fight went on for near about six hours. To make a long story short, the anvil got a might bit bent and we had to go back to Fetterman to get straightened out and resupplied. Of course, we didn't have no way of knowin' what was goin' on with the other parts of the operation, namely the hammer. There wasn't no telephones nor nothin' in the olden days."

Susanna looked at her father in the rear view mirror and smiled.

"As it turned out, Gibbons' men were still headin' east to play anvil and I guess you know that Custer fulfilled his destiny as that hammer...

and he was a sure enough hammer if you ever talked to anyone who served under the sumbitch. He was a glory hound and I'll tell you that he got about all the glory any man could ask for on that June afternoon in seventy-six. Of course, he took a lot of fine young fellas with him while he was establishin' his place in history."

"In your opinion, would Crook have been able to save Custer had he been at the Little Big Horn?" Grant asked.

"Maybe...maybe not. First off, Custer had got out ahead of Terry's column and was all by his lonesome with the Seventh. Appeared to me that he was gonna grab the glory all for himself before anyone could catch up to share it with him. But then there was no way of communicatin', so there was just no way to meet up with any precision over the distances that we had to travel.

It is my opinion, however, Custer would have likely taken on the battle whether anyone was comin' to his aid or not. Killin' all them Injuns was gonna be Custer's ticket out of the shit house. If you recall your history, he'd got crossways of ol' Ulysses Grant and I think he was plannin' to run for president his own self. But the coulda, shoulda, woulda's don't make a dime's worth of difference now. Crook's boys had not only got whipped pretty good themselves, but his soldiers had shot up most of the ammunition which they'd brung along. We had so many dead and wounded by then that goin' on to the Rosebud would have been a fool's errand. It took us two days to just limp back to the fort. Like I told ya, information was scarce and communication was poor. Crook asked if I'd take a couple of scouts and go make an assessment of the situation. I did it...but I should have just said no. Those were some real bad days.

I took three Crows with me and we headed toward the Rosebud movin' through the country real quiet like. When we was just south of the Little Big Horn River we come across somethin' that none of us had ever seen before. Me'n them Crow warriors was kind'a befuddled by the sign. There was a trail, which had been left by a group of rapidly movin' people. Crows reckoned it was Sioux. You could see the tracks of the travois and horses and the dogs, which in and of itself wasn't none to unusual. What was unusual was the number. There must have been somewheres between five or maybe ten thousand of 'em. Injuns seldom got together in huge numbers like that. Just feedin' the horses would have been a burden on a camp that big, leave alone trying to feed that many people. So I figured it had to be the bunch that I'd heard the rumors about at the fort. The bunch that was having the Sundance.

We followed for a while and then the trail showed that they had begun to break into smaller and smaller groups. Some went east, some went south and some others had headed back to the north. They'd just scattered to the winds. One of the Crows suggested that we just leave well enough alone as far as followin' them Sioux and go on back to see where they'd come from...and I had to agree. Catchin' up with 'em wouldn't really have been in our best interest, after all. So we commenced to backtrailin' to see where they'd been and what they'd been doin'.

The back trail led right into the valley of the Little Big Horn. When we topped a rise, which was about three miles from the Little Big Horn River, there wasn't no doubt in my mind that what we was about to find was gonna be right unpleasant. The smell of death was about enough to make ya wanna puke. Even from a couple of miles away you could see the buzzards and the crows circlin' in clouds above a ridge.

They call that place 'Last Stand Ridge' nowadays...but it was just a smell-bad ridge the day we found it...and it was sure enough a horror. We could see men movin', so rode on in under a white flag. I found Major Reno, who was in command. He looked like hell. He walking around like he was feebleminded. They was tryin' as best they could to do for the dead, who had been mutilated in a fashion not fit to describe. I told Grant before, that the Injuns left their dead enemies in a condition so as to make it impossible to come back and fight in the next life. None of them fellas came back, I'd reckon.

I sent one of my Crows back to Crook, and another to find Terry and then made myself useful in settin' a defense in case the Sioux should return. Benteen's boys was just comin' off their piece of high ground about three miles away. They was pullin' the packs with the Gatlin' Guns... the ones Custer should have had with him. Reno's boys was just beat to pieces. I walked along the ridge and it was plain to see how Custer had left men in small defensive positions, which is just where every one of 'em had died. Like I said, they was pretty well mutilated except for ol' Custer himself. The Injuns had took his clothes but they hadn't really butchered him. Squaws had stuck sewing awls in his ears. The Crows said that was so he'd be able to hear better in the next world. I reckon so he'd be able to heed a warnin'. It was pretty gruesome.

One thing I can tell you for sure about 'Custer's Last Stand.' Had the hammer and anvil scheme worked out, Colonel George Armstrong Custer would'a rode through that Injun village like hog fat through a goose gullet and killed every man, woman, child and dog and then gone back to Washington and bragged about the deed. And I don't reckon they would'a called that Sittin' Bull's Last Stand."

"How could you look at such a thing Uncle Tom?" Dixie asked, tears in her eyes.

"Well, ya see darlin', that was my business in those times. I didn't really have no choice. It was the soldier boys that I felt sorry for. I still think to this day that if'n those boys had been given decent repeatin' rifles, that the whole outcome could'a been different...but what the hell do I know? I was just a scout. Not a general. I heard later that the some army supply big-wig was afraid those soldiers would waste too much ammunition if they was to be given repeaters. Ain't that just the way some government fool would have it figured? They'll piss away a million on somethin' that ain't worth dog squat and then worry about some soldier who is fightin' for his life usin' too many bullets."

"I don't want to hear any more about this stinking hill," Dixie said. She squinched her face in disgust. "I thought you were going to tell us about Nick's mother."

"Oh, yeah, I'm gettin' to that. Like I told ya earlier, I hadn't made no commitment to the General Crook or the army beyond the Rosebud campaign. The Injuns had scattered all over creation...and seein' as how that anvil and hammer deal hadn't worked out anyway, I decided to take my leave of military service and ride over to the Deadwood gold strike in the Black Hills.

I'd heard a rumor from some of the soldiers at Fetterman that Big Jim Hickock, better known to you folks as Wild Bill, was holdin' forth in that camp. So ride to Deadwood I did. Sure enough, Big Jim was there... playin' poker and scarin' the bejesus outta the local gunslingers and ne'er-do-wells who was hangin' about. Those minin' camps and boom towns always had their share of scum like that.

There was so many mischief makers hangin' around that they'd even asked Hickock to be marshal of the town. I got to admit that I was glad to see the old boy. Hell, it had been fifteen years or more and we had a lotta catchin' up to do. I said to him 'I see you're still wearin' them Navy Colts,' to which he replied that they had served him well and saved his life on more than one occasion and that he wouldn't trade 'em for nothin'. He had carried 'em through the Great War and he was accustomed to their company.

We played some cards and drank some whiskey and I was even thinkin' about stakin' a claim on the gold strike hill, seein' as how it looked to be some rich diggin's.

Big Jim, however, reminded me about just how much hard work there was to pickin' and shovelin' and how much easier it was to just get the gold from the miner's pokes in a card game.

So we had another drink and fleeced some of those hard workin' miner fellas outta their hard-earned nuggets with a few hands of five card draw. Now I was only plannin' on stayin' in Deadwood long enough to say hello and exchange a few lies with Jim about how good we once was, when I got struck by lightning right in the lobby of the best of the flea infested hotels in Deadwood.

I was whiling away some time, waiting for Jim as I recall, when a fella carries in some luggage from the afternoon stage coach. An older gentleman, very distinguished lookin' sort, comes to the desk requestin' a suite. The clerk was bein' about as polite as he could be...considerin' his laughin' and all...trying to explain that they didn't even have a room, let alone no suite. I was sort'a chucklin' with the rest, when in walks this portrait of feminine pulchritude. Now she goes to stand beside this old man. I was sort'a standin' there with my big mouth hangin' open thinkin' that this has got to be some sort'a really rich old bastard to have a wife like that, when he tells the clerk that he needs the suite for him and his daughter.

Now I was never real suave with the ladies but I figured I'd best move real fast because there was about twenty-five hundred men in the town of Deadwood and about fifty women, most'a whom was whores, saloon girls or washer women. So I walk right up and introduce myself to the gentleman and offer my services for whatever endeavor he might be considerin' in such an outta the way place.

Of course, I was dressed like a damned ruffian in buckskins and mocassins and, to say the least, my presentation lacked polish. But as luck would have it, ol' Hickock come walkin' down the stairs lookin' like he was ready to do a show in New York City.

Well, sir, I grabbed Jim's arm and real quick introduced him and of course everyone in the country had heard of Wild Bill Hickock. So Mr. Herschell Devine introduced himself and his daughter Angelica. I informed them that me'n my friend Wild Bill Hickock was at their disposal should they come to need for anything while visitin' Deadwood.

It turned out that the old man was kind'a on his last legs and that he had come to Deadwood to make some money so as not to leave his family destitute. He'd apparently been a rich New York investment type and had got fleeced by some of his more astute associates."

"You never told us that Angelica was rich," Susanna said.

"Well, she sure as hell wasn't rich when I met her. Her pappy had lost his fortune and he somehow thought that he could get rich again in Deadwood. I reckon he'd been readin' too many advertisin' posters and dime novels. Anyway, me'n Jim imposed upon that hotel keeper to make a decent accommodation for the Devines and then we set out to explain to ol' Herschell the realities a diggin' for gold. As it turned out, the old boy was in such bad condition that Angelica, who was his youngest of five daughters, had come along to take care of his medical needs. Angelica's mother was doing poorly in New York and Herschell himself had the consumption somethin' awful. Seemed like the losin' of his fortune, bad health and plain old age was takin' its toll.

Of course, bein' a 'know-it-all' rich sumbitch from New York City, he didn't put much stock in the advice that me'n Hickock was tryin' to give him. So it wasn't long before what little money he had left had been transferred to the grifters who were sellin' promises and salted claims.

In the meanwhile, however, I had took to squiring Miss Devine around the town, such as it was. Before too long we had took a shine to one another. I was near about thirty years old by then and I decided that I needed a wife to help me with the ranch and to settle my wild ways; and so without no further ado, I up and asked for her hand in matrimony.

Now her pappy was near apoplectic when I put that to him. He commenced to tell me that he was lookin' for a proper Jewish gentleman for his baby daughter and that I, ruffian and plainsman that I was, just wasn't a suitable prospect as a husband."

"Angelica was Jewish?" Grant asked.

Tom looked at Grant, detecting a tone of condescension in the question.

"Son, your egalitarianism is showin' again," Tom said. "Yes, sir, young man, you find yourself amongst one of the most 'eclectic' collections of genuine characters that you could have ever imagined. In addition to Injuns, I don't reckon your family has consorted with too many Jews neither. Huh?"

Susanna was watching Grant in the rear view mirror.

"Don't worry Grant; I don't think Jew rubs off any more than Blackfoot."

Dixie's mind raced as she sat in silence. What a difference this last year with Uncle Tom and her cousins had made in her life. She had, after all, grown up inculcated with the teachings of the Klu Klux Klan; and Vassar was no bastion of social equality.

"I think his...our...education is getting broader by the day," Dixie said.

"We'll see when he writes his stuff," Susanna said.

Grant looked at each in turn, not sure how to respond.

"Well, he can write this," Tom said. "The only thing I knew about Jews at the time was what I'd read in the Bible. Abraham, Moses and Jesus and all them stories. The only thing I cared about was that she was a right pretty thing and that I was in love."

"So how did you convince her father to let you marry her?" Grant asked.

"I didn't. The old bastard died. When he found out he'd been took by the grifters I guess his heart just gave out. Tipped over on a faro table at the Number Ten. That was the same saloon where ol' Hickock got his brains blowed out about a month later. When her pappy died, I guess she figured I was the next best bet to look after her...and she had grown fond of me...so she agreed to marry me. She wanted to have a Jewish ceremony but it seemed that Deadwood was real short on Synagogues and Rabbis and such. We got the Mayor to say the 'Do you take this and do you take that' and all that legal hoo-hah. Then I bought about as nice a carriage as could be found in those parts and drove my new bride back to Fort Benton. Considerin' the hardships of that trip and the condition of the ranch at the time, she turned out to be a tough and patient bride."

"You say Hickock was killed a month later?" Grant said.

"About a week after we pulled out, the way I heard it."

Tom thought a moment.

"I remember some sneaky little rat faced bastard annoyin' Hickock while I was there. I didn't really put much store by any danger for Big Jim. Hickock's eyes was goin' bad from a social disease he'd acquired in his younger days, but I figured he could have took that dog turd with both eyes shut. So I was real surprised when I heard the little rodent had shot ol' Hickock in the back of the head."

The caravan had been moving for several hours when Tom saw a bridge crossing a stream ahead.

"Sus, pull over and let's let everyone get a stretch. We need to water the critters and I could use a little break behind a bush my own self," Tom said.

Buckets of water were carried from a nearby stream for the animals in the trucks and everyone stretched their legs and saw to personal needs.

Tom looked up and down the line of vehicles.

"Is everyone watered up and ready?" he shouted.

The engines starting soon turned to a roar as Susanna put the car in gear and moved slowly forward, waiting for the caravan to fall into line.

As the vehicles found a rhythm, Dixie asked, "Where did you live when you brought Angelica to Fort Benton?"

"We lived in town for a while. Then I got some hands to work out on the ranch and we built that little house which is next to Remus' and Rom's place. By the time we got it built, Angelica was pregnant and little Nick was born that next spring. Horse Sense was still doin' well with haulin' freight to the places where the railroads hadn't yet reached, and the cows was doin' their job buildin' up a herd. Those was some shinin' times for us white folks, but things was changin' for the Injuns.

Bloody Spear's people was really beginnin' to suffer from the lack of buffalo and everything bad that happened to any honyocker's chickens got blamed on the Blackfoot. If a drunk fell off his horse and broke his damned neck, you could bet that some Injun was likely to get hung."

"The last Blackfoot village was on our ranch, right?" Susanna asked.

"Yep. I'd told Bloody Spear to cut himself out a steer when he needed to feed his folks and it went okay for a while. But after the Little Big Horn, the army started gettin' down real hard on the free roamin' Injuns. Moved 'em all to reservations, even Bloody Spear and his folks had to move to Browning. Of course those crooked Injun agents was stealin' their food and damned near starved the whole bunch to death."

Tom furrowed his brow.

"But there wasn't much I could do. You know what they say about 'you can't fight City Hall.' I took food to 'em as much as I could but it wasn't near enough.

However, the open range ranch was doin' well. In fact it went real well for about the next five years and then things started to fall apart. We had a couple of real bad winters and lost a lot of the cattle. There wasn't but a few buffalo left around the ranch by then and a few of the Injuns who hadn't been corralled commenced to killin' what cattle I had left to feed their families. That's the way it is with farmin' and ranchin'. Feast or famine.

And then the worst of all things happened. Nick's mama got real sick. She took the cholera. Don't know if she got it in Fort Benton while she was gettin' in groceries or if she got it from the water, but whatever did it...she got it. Little Nick was four or maybe comin' five and all of a sudden me and him were all alone. I just kind'a went crazy. I commenced drinkin' too much and really bein' a fool."

"How could you take care of little Nick if you were drunk?" Dixie asked.

"I didn't! Thank the Lord for Sarah and Horse Sense. They took the poor little fella and cared for him while I was off trying to get myself kilt. I went on a runnin' drunk that lasted a couple of years, and I did some real bad things during those days. I never robbed or nothin' like that, but I stayed real drunk about half the time...and I stayed about half drunk all the time. Played poker and I lost a lotta money and got into too many fights to even want to remember. I reckon I might even have kilt a few men."

"Uncle Tom, that just sounds so absolutely out of character for you. You mean you killed innocent men for no reason?" Dixie asked.

Grant glanced up from his notes to see the look on Tom's face while

Susanna studied her father's face in the rear view mirror.

"Now I ain't sayin' it was for no reason, and I'm none too proud of it neither. It was the way it was and that's what Grant wants to know. But I was a real miserable bastard and that's for sure. I even went back to buffalo huntin'. Not so much to make money but I just felt comfortable in the companionship of the few ruffians and hooligans who were still in the business of killin' buffalos. The misery and the stink of death in buffalo camp was a perfect sanctuary for a lost soul.

I reckon the real irony of the whole thing is that Nicky stuck with me through it all and Derrick went his own way. That kid had all there was to have from me when he was a child, even though him and Susanna lost their mama too. I think I done fair by Derrick. Didn't I Sus?"

"Derrick's just trying to be what you were then, even though he doesn't know what that was...or why," Susanna replied.

"There was one good thing that come outta all that misery," Tom said.

Tom stared out the window for a long moment.

"Are you going to share the one good thing?" Dixie asked.

"I made me a good friend. Funny how things like that happen. It was over in the Dakotas in the early eighties. I'd partnered up with a couple of wild assed hide hunters who liked their whiskey about as much as I did and we'd took to runnin' together. There was still a few buffalo left over in that Dakota country then. I took a couple'a wagons and teams and we were just wanderin' the prairie shootin' whatever buffalo as we could find and hittin' every little town that had a saloon and a poker table. We'd been out on the prairie a month or so and we had us a pretty good load of hides to peddle. In addition, we was smellin' so bad we couldn't stand each other any more.

There was a railroad spur through a town they called Little Missouri.

We figured they'd have some whiskey and a bath, and we could unload our hides for shipment on the railroad and sell what fresh meat as we had. Now this Little Missouri wasn't really much of a town. It was no more than a collection of shacks. But they sure enough had a hotel and a saloon. We sold our hides at the mercantile, resupplied with necessities and got rooms. Then I spent a couple of hours soakin' off the stink of buffalo in some hot soapy water and soakin' in some of the local rotgut.

After a couple hours of sleepin' in a real bed I was ready to have a go at the poker table, which was a twenty-four hour a day operation. I went to the bar and got myself a drink and it was just my luck that the first fella to pass out drunk at the poker table was the one sitting with his back to the wall.

Now owing to the fact that I'd been livin' a dissolute life for those past couple'a years, and the fact that my friend Hickock had got himself shot in the back of the head; I always preferred to have my back to the wall. I got in the game and I'd been playin' poker for a couple'a hours. Just about long enough to get a little bored. Next thing you know, in walks this cocky little dude wearin' eye glasses and some fancy lookin' tailor made dude clothes that cost more than that saloon."

Tom turned to look at Grant smiling broadly.

"It was sort'a like the first day you got off the train in Fort Benton. You know what I mean?"

They all laughed.

"It didn't take anyone too long to figure that this fella wasn't from around Little Missouri. I had seen him earlier in the day over at the hotel. He'd just got off the train and was checkin' in at the hotel desk at the same time we was. I didn't really pay him much mind. I just figured him for some Eastern swell and he held no interest for me.

So anyway, this little fella with the cocky strut goes up to the bar and orders himself a cup'a coffee. Man, you could'a heard a pin drop. Now there was somethin' in his attitude that told you that he was accustomed to havin' his way, so the bartender was damned near apologetic about the fact that he didn't have no coffee. So the little fella asked, real polite mind you, could the bartender make some...and the bartender said that he would."

"That sounds civilized," Dixie said.

"Well, let me tell you somethin'. I don't care what saloon you're in, even today, there is always some fella who is lookin' to see if he can start a problem. Little Missouri wasn't no exception to that rule. Pretty quick a big ol' cowboy, who was just drunk enough to be tough, walks up to the little dude and says 'Only a side saddle sissy of a son-of-a-bitch from New York City would drink coffee in the saloon in Little Missouri. I think you ought to buy the whole house a drink.'

That little fella didn't even pay him no heed. He just stood there waitin' for his coffee. So the big man walks over and grabs the little fella's shoulder and sort'a spins him around."

"Weren't you going to help the little man, Uncle Tom?" Dixie asked.

"Let me tell you somethin' darlin', in those days, and I guess even today, the secret to longevity was mindin' your own damned business. Now if'n the big fella had threatened the little guy with a knife or a gun, I might'a took some interest. But a man gettin' the shit kicked out of him in a saloon was pretty much as regular as sunrise in a town like Little Missouri. Stickin' your nose into the affair could even get you kilt. I reckon I just wasn't that anxious to die...at least not that day. Maybe I was too sober, but I especially wasn't willin' to get kilt for some Eastern dandy with an arrogant attitude. You have to consider the times. A dude gettin' hoorahed in a saloon was't gonna make the evening edition of the newspaper, so I went back to my cards. Well, sir, the little man had turned back to the bar and was just ignorin' the big drunk. Then I heard that cowboy say, 'Best you buy the house a drink or I'm gonna take them glasses off'n your face and stomp your ass through the floor.'

Now that kind'a got my attention, so I started to watch to see what was gonna happen next. There was a real long silence and then the little fella took off his glasses real slow and careful, folded 'em up and handed 'em to the bartender. Then he says to the bartender in a real refined accent 'Would you hold these for a moment while I address this issue with our inebriated friend?'

That bartender didn't know what to say but before he could even put the glasses in his shirt pocket, the little fella turned to face the cowboy and put up his dukes just like ol' Jack Dempsey. That cowboy got a great big ol' smile on his face and says 'So you got a little fight in you, huh?'... but before he finished what he was gonna say, that little man had hit him about four or five times about the head and shoulders. The bigger man was wobblin' around and his eyes was rollin' in his head. Then, to my surprise, that little man took the big cowboy over and sat him down in a chair and said, 'I hope I haven't hurt you.' It was about the funniest damned thing I think I'd ever seen."

"You thought that was funny?" Dixie asked in disgust.

"Now, you gotta keep in mind that there wasn't a whole lotta entertainment back in those times and anything that broke up the monotony was worth watchin.' But I was really curious after the little fella put the lickin' on the cowboy so I cashed my hand and went over and offered to buy him a cup. I commenced to asking where he was from and such. Well you ain't gonna believe this, but he said his name was Theodore Roosevelt and that he was, in fact, from New York City. Said he'd learned his boxin' skills on the team at Harvard University, don't you know. He was a cocky little bastard but we had an instant affinity and as we talked, I learned that he was lookin' to shoot himself a buffalo and whatever else he might encounter. I told him that it was tough livin' on a hunt and asked was he sure he wanted to live like a red savage for a few weeks. He said he did and so I invited him along with my party. He turned out to be a real good shot, even though his eyes wasn't none too good, and he was an affable companion.

He sure enough kilt a couple of buffalos and an elk and bear. That man seemed to have more fun than a week old colt frolicking in the spring grass. Never have I seen a greenhorn take to primitive livin' like ol' Teedie."

"Teedie?" Grant asked.

"Yeah, I know, everyone called him Teddy. They even named a stuffed bear after him by that moniker. But he hated that. His family and close friends called him Teedie and if'n you know'd him well enough to be a friend you called him Teedie. Well, I can tell you with a great deal of pride that I was one of the folks in this world who called him Teedie.

So that was the good thing that came out of all that misery, darlin'. I made me a friend and I value my time with that man to this very day."

24

Tom strained his eyes, attempting to see a familiar landmark in the headlights.

"Where do I turn to the rodeo grounds, Dad?" Susanna asked.

"There should be a sign right up here pretty quick," Tom said.

"I see it," Dixie said, as the headlights illuminated a large board with a hand painted arrow and the word 'STAMPEDE.'

The caravan of vehicles from The Buffalo Rock parked beside the arena. Vehicles of other participants and competitors were already unloading wagons and animals. Tom found the night watchman and was given a list of corral spaces and assigned parking for his group. Nick, carrying a clipboard, conducted his usually efficient attention to the details and necessities. Lanterns were lit and the trucks were backed into position to unload the horses and cattle.

"Okay folks, we got an hour or so till daylight. Do the best you can at gettin' unloaded until the sun comes up and we get some light," Nick shouted, as he walked among the vehicles.

It had been a day and a night on the road. The morning sun revealed a small city of tents and trucks, which would be their sleeping quarters and dressing rooms. Tarpaulins were hung to provide shade for people and the animals. By afternoon, the group was ready for the show.

Tom walked through the camp ensuring that all was in place. Many of the cowboys had put on clean shirts and new hats in preparation for a visit to the city.

"If you fellas are goin' to town, I don't want no fightin' and if'n you get yourself throwed in jail, just remember that this is a foreign country. You ain't got no rights here. And I ain't goin' no bail for stupidity. So have fun but behave yourselves. I'm sure you can get plenty to drink and find a cat house or two without gettin' locked up. And don't forget we got stock to tend and equipment to get ready before each show. Other than that, go have a good time and God save Calgary."

The men began to disperse, headed for the biggest city that some had ever seen. Tom walked to where the chuck wagons were parked.

"Could you men come over here a minute," Tom said.

Both walked toward the boss and Howdy asked, "Yes, sir, is there a problem?"

"Nope! No problem. But I want you fellas to look out for one another and make sure that your outrider crews keep themselves in line. They're gonna give us some practice time tomorrow and we don't need anyone too hung over to ride."

"Gotcha boss," Howdy said. "We'll be ready."

Tom grabbed Buck's arm.

"I don't want no trouble, Buck." Tom said in a low voice.

He turned the young man so as to look him in the eyes.

"You gettin' my drift?"

"Yes, sir," Buck said.

Tom walked to the shade of the tarpaulin where Susanna and Dixie were sitting with Grant sipping iced tea.

"You don't need to give us a warning Dad," Susanna said with a laugh.

"Dixie and I are going shopping."

"Shopping...shopping? Is that all you women folk ever think about? Well, go on ahead, 'cause tomorrow it's gonna get real busy around this place. So get all the foofaraw you need because there ain't gonna be much time for the next couple'a days."

Susanna and Dixie walked to the car and drove out of the parking lot in a cloud of dust.

"They sure as hell ain't wastin' no time gettin' to them stores are they?"

"I am beginning to think that shopping is the distaff equivalent of a sport. Like rodeo or baseball," Grant said.

Tom looked up and waved. The promoter of the Calgary Stampede was walking toward them.

"Hey, Lloyd, I want you to meet my friend Grant Collins from Saint Louis down in the state of Missouri," Tom said without rising. Grant shook the man's hand and then sat down.

"Have everyone ready to go by about eleven tomorrow for the practice race," Lloyd Clarkson said. "Then, day after tomorrow I want to make sure we get all the events completed early enough so that we can run the wagons the last thing. That'll keep the crowd hangin' around till the very end."

"Well, I reckon you gotta sell them peanuts and soda water and beer," Tom said.

"I want to thank you for bringing your crew, Tom," Lloyd said. "I don't know how this chuck wagon race deal is gonna work out, but if it goes good this year we'll try it again next year."

"I brought a couple'a dandies. Good teams and good men. I got several boys who are goin' to compete...and Susanna's gonna ride the barrels and Derrick is ridin' the rough stock. He wants to win so's he don't have to get no money from me. You know how that goes?"

Tom's faced changed from a smile to a mask of concern.

"Well, Tom, I got a couple of children of my own and they all have their own way of making us miserable. Derrick might find his way some day. He's just going to have to decide whether he's going to be a cowboy or an Indian. By the way, I hear you've got a couple of real cracker jack rough stock riders you've been keeping secret."

"You just get out your cashbox 'cause I think I've brought some pretty good hands this year."

Tom laughed as Lloyd walked away.

Grant took a sip from his tea.

"If you don't mind my bringing it up again, it sounded in the car as though the death of your first wife changed your attitudes about living. I know you were probably not wanting to tell me the whole story with Susanna and Dixie along. Was there anything that you left out?"

"Son, there was a whole lot of that story I left out. Fact is that there's a whole mess of them days that I don't even remember. Like I said, I was drunk. If there was ever a part'a my life that I regret, that was it. I was a rounder and bounder and a whore house hounder. I know that I goaded more than a couple of men into fights. I don't know how I lived through it. I was as bad as ol' Buck in some ways, maybe worse. I gambled thousands of dollars playing cards. I'd get caught cheatin' and either the men at the table knew me and said nothin', 'cause they were in fear, or some dumb bastard would call me on it and I'd pull on him.

I didn't say this in front of Susanna, but when Angelica died, a bit of me died too. During them years my soul was dead. I just didn't care about nothin'. Truth is that I was hopin' that one of them fellas would pull faster'n me and there would be an end to it. Now, don't get me wrong. I didn't become a criminal or a nuisance to the towns I visited. At least not like the dime novels portray, but I was sure as hell one mean fella. I reckon I was just wantin' to commit suicide and I didn't have the gumption."

"I noticed that when you spoke of Mr. Roosevelt, you sounded very respectful. He must have been quite a presence in your life."

"Yes, sir, he was a little giant of a man. And I reckon that in a way he saved my life. He sure as hell turned it around at least. You see, when I met him in Little Missouri and he put a whippin' on that cowboy; truth is that I wouldn't have cared had that big bastard beat him to death right there on the barroom floor.

Had he got into the poker game. I might have just kilt him myself... what with his highfalutin' attitude and all. But when we'd had some time to spend together, he gave me a whole new way of lookin' at life. I never was much one for talkin' about my problems, or the things that were eatin' at me. I'd lived pretty much inside my own head since my folks had been kilt when I was a kid. I always liked people, but I'd seen so many die that I just couldn't allow myself to get too close to anyone. I wouldn't let myself care too much about anyone 'cause I figured that they'd probably not be around long enough to make caring worth the while.

Do you have any idea as to what I'm tryin' to explain to you? I was by nature an affable sort, but I just never let myself care about anyone too much; especially after Angelica died."

Grant sat for a long moment in silence.

"I think I do understand much more than you know. To be honest, I was a very lonely child. My parents, although they weren't killed, were quite distant. I too, have lived inside of my own head, until recently. Yes, I think I do understand."

"By God, I believe you just might. I guess we do have somethin' in common after all."

"To be honest Tom, being a part of your family for these weeks and hearing your stories has been a catharsis for me. It has changed my life forever."

"That's near about the most humblin' thing another man ever said to me."

Tom lit a Lucky Strike and took a sip of his tea. They sat a long while in silence.

"So you're askin' yourself, how did the future President of the United States save the life of some shiftless drunken buffalo hunter in the Dakota Territory. Right?"

Grant nodded as he took his notebook from his pocket.

"Like I told you, we took ol' Teedie on a hunt. One night we was havin' some hump stew for dinner, which was what we had about every night, and ol' Teedie asked could he cook up a special dish. He fried up a concoction of taters and onions and some other things that was about the best tastin' thing I ever ate.

So we're sittin' around the fire and jawin' and he tells me that his wife had taught him how to cook those spuds and such. So I ask about his wife and damned if he don't tell me that his wife had died. Then he tells me that he had a child who was bein' cared for by relatives. I got to feelin' a kind of kinship with the little fella then and I told him of my situation. He went on to say that he'd really loved that woman a lot and that he'd taken this adventure trying to get away from the pain in his mind. Now I ain't sure just why, but somethin' in my head clicked. I looked at this hopeful and cheerful little fella who had been some big wig politician in New York City. I knew he had more money than he could spend, and yet, it occurred to me that he was in the same old leaky boat that I was ridin' in. Only difference was that he wasn't lettin' it turn him into a whiskey soaked dung heap without a genuine human feelin' left. He was standin' tall, which was hard for Teedie. He was gettin' on with livin' and not makin' no excuses. I even found out that he'd been pretty sick as a kid and that he'd had to build himself from the ground up. I gotta tell you that I was inspired. I begun to look at him like he was ten feet tall."

"I guess that presidents are always inspiring," Grant added.

"Hell, he wasn't no president then. He wasn't no more than a kid like you. But I'll tell you this...you could see that he was one smart sumbitch and that he was gonna go places. In fact, while he was there in Dakota he got involved with some locals and started his own open range ranchin' association. That gave me the idea and that's how I come to start the association around Fort Benton.

The truth is that I kind'a liked the man and he thought that my Pony Express stories and all the Injun fightin' hurly-burly was 'just marvelous' as he would say. I don't know how it come to happen, but somehow me'n ol' Teedie become good pals. Why I even had dinner at the White House. Now there ain't many an uncurried, uncouth, scrufty ol' fart like me that can say that...and prove it. In fact, President Theodore Roosevelt slept in that very room your usin' and wrote at the same desk. Now what do you think about that?"

Grant smiled, looking up at Tom. He thought to himself that he had never met a person who could so honestly relate personal feelings and bare his soul so completely.

"I take it then that you returned to your ranch and began to rebuild your life after your meeting with the young Mr. Roosevelt?" Grant asked.

"That I did. Now understand that this didn't happen overnight. I got together with the bankers and the other ranchers and we started us a cattleman's association. That was when we started the roundups in an organized sort'a way. I came back to the ranch and was seein' to the care of little Nick, under the supervision of his Aunt Sarah, who was like an ol' mama bear where that boy was concerned.

The ranch was growin' again by then, and the freight business was in good hands with Horse Sense. Then one day I get a telegram from an old partner from the Pony Express days. Like I told you, I had made the acquaintance of Buffalo Bill. Bill Cody had started a Wild West show and he was lookin' for some of the old timers to kick the thing off and get it started right. He called it his 'Congress of Rough Riders.' Claimed he was gonna take the whole show to the crowned heads of Europe. Now I'd settled down some but that was more than I could resist. So I asked Sarah would she take care of Nick for another while and she reckoned that since I was gonna get to go to Europe, well she'd have to be understandin' even if'n she was jealous."

"So you actually traveled abroad with the Buffalo Bill show?"

"Yes, sir! That was when I bowed and made the acquaintance of ol' Queen Vic her own self, like I told you that first day. I'll tell you, them was some shinin' times. Most'a the folks in the show you'd never have heard of, but there was some really interestin' people who traveled with us. None the least of these was ol' Sittin' Bull himself. Killin' Custer wasn't no disgrace in my book. I liked that old Injun."

"You mean the Sitting Bull from the Custer massacre? I thought he had been killed by his own people."

"He was...killed by the reservation police. Of course the Injun agents had put 'em up to it. But that wasn't till a few years later. What an ironical turn that was. Back in seventy-six I'd followed his tracks out of the Little Big Horn. I would likely have helped put him on that reservation on the Oklahoma strip, or kilt him, had Crazy horse not put Crook's outfit in a sling.

Now here we was as travelin' companions and better company you'll never know. He was a grand ol' man. I enjoyed our time together and seein's how I was one of the few who could palaver in Sioux, he enjoyed talkin' to me. It was the oddest thing to go out into the cities of Europe and the big cities in the East with him. He was just so amazed at how the white folks built houses, one on top of another. And money didn't mean a damned thing to him. We'd walk the streets of a city like New York or London and he'd go get all of the money Cody paid him, and have it changed to coins. He'd give them coins to the children that would come to look at his fancy outfit and beg for money. Cody always asked that we dress up in our Wild West outfits. Of course, they weren't real frontier outfits. They was just costumes that ol' Cody had cooked up to sell the show. But it was sure enough an adventure that I was glad I got to take.

Had some other interestin' folks too. There was Annie Oakley, who I'm sure you must'a heard of, and there was other Injuns and we even hauled along some buffalo. Why ol' Bill had even hired a bunch of Cossack Russians just for the color. Yes, sir, it was quite a spectacle."

"I suppose we must all live in our own times, but I do wish I could have seen Buffalo Bill's Wild West Show...or even better, to have seen the Wild West."

"Best you can do now is write about it so that folks don't forget. Let's go walk around the exposition grounds and see if'n we can't find us somethin' worth eatin'."

Tom stood and dropped his cigarette butt, grinding it into the dirt with his boot. Grant rose to follow and realized that his stomach was growling. His mouth was watering from the smells drifting from the many concession booths.

2 5

A gray horse sprang from the chute, leaping high into the air. Grant recognized Derrick's long dark hair when his hat flew off. Tom climbed the fence to stand beside Grant.

"Watch this kid of mine. He's sober and he might just by-God win this," Tom said.

Derrick leaned back on the horse and raised his feet high so that his spurs were touching the horse's neck. When the horse kicked his hind feet into the air, Derrick's long hair swept the animal's rump as his head bent back in the effort to raise his spurs.

"The judges will like that...gettin' them spurs up high like that," Tom said.

The eight second whistle sounded and Grant knew by the approving roar of the crowd that the ride had been exemplary. The pick-up man spurred his horse alongside and Derrick leaned to grab the cantle of the his saddle. He rolled onto the rump of the pick-up horse, and then slid to the ground to loud applause.

Tom cocked his head, listening as the announcer with the megaphone gave Derrick's score.

"I told you he could do 'er. Got a little bit of the old man in him. Those other boys will have to go some to beat that. Now if he can make some money on the bulls, he'll be able to do a little braggin' around the ranch."

"Howdy also did well on the saddle broncs and Elmer won the calf roping. I would say that The Buffalo Rock has acquitted itself well, so far," Grant said.

"Don't forget Susanna. She won the barrel racin' like a real champ. She's got some of the old man in her too. Now ol' Buck ain't doin' too good at nothin'. I don't know what's the matter with him, but he's sure enough in a sour mood."

"Really, I hadn't noticed," Grant said with a wry smile.

Tom looked at Grant, then returned the smile.

"I took note of the fact that you have been avoidin' my mild mannered wagon driver."

"I am just following instructions and being prudent."

"Good idea. So what do you think of the rodeo show. Hell of a deal, ain't it!"

"I was thinking, as I have watched, that this will help to color my writing. One of the things I have found quite amazing is the toughness of these men. Some, I am told, make their living doing this. I would never have imagined such a thing. They perform strenuous and dangerous acts for the pleasure of the crowd, with no guarantee of any pay whatsoever.

One of the men got bucked off a horse and I know he was injured, but he walked from the arena waving. When the announcer told the crowd, 'Give that boy a hand, folks, that's the only pay he'll get today,' it hit me like a ton of bricks. He's going home injured, with no money for his effort and he's still willing to do it again. Amazing!"

"Some is cut out to the life of a cowboy and some ain't. It sure ain't an easy way to make a dollar. Let's wander over and watch 'em draw for the bulls. I'm kind'a hopin' that none of our boys draw Rambunctious.

I've decided I ain't gonna use that bull in the rodeos no more. He's gonna hurt someone just sure as hell. He near about put you under, but then I'd reckon Buck gave him a hand on that deal. That bull just seems to have an agility that I never saw in an animal like that before. He ain't necessarily mean when he bucks a man off, he don't usually go try to freight train him or nothin'...but when a fella is ridin' on his back, it is almost like he can read a man's mind. He surely does have the will to win. I reckon I ain't even gonna say nothin' to no one about it. I'm just gonna put the old boy out to pasture and let him make baby bulls."

They approached a group of men gathered around Lloyd Clarkson. Each in turn would reach into Lloyd's hat to draw the name of the bull he was to ride.

A small wiry man with his hat cocked onto the back of his head reached into the hat, looked at the scrap of paper and said with a grin, "I got him!"

A cheer arose from the group as the man strutted toward the chutes.

"I reckon he got Rambunctious," Tom said.

"Why is he so happy?" Grant asked.

"The better the bull, the better your chances of getting a good score, that is if'n you can ride him for eight seconds. That skinny kid is a Texican by name of Edge. Razor Edge they call him. He's one of those you was talkin' about. He travels the country makin' his livelihood riding rough stock, so he's got it figured that if he can ride Rambunctious, he's got this thing won...not to mention the braggin' rights. There's a sayin' you hear at the rodeos. 'Never was a bull that couldn't be rode and there never was a cowboy who couldn't be throwed.' I reckon that Razor kid is figurin' to be one of the few to put Rambunctious in his place. Only been eight."

Susanna and Dixie joined Tom and Grant, climbing the fence for a better view.

Dixie squeezed Grant's arm affectionately.

"I am certainly glad that you've proven your manhood and you don't have to reprise your last performance as a cowboy," Dixie said.

"I am only riding the fence this time," Grant said.

Grant watched the bulls enter the chutes and smiled inwardly, thinking that his pride and ego had nearly killed him at the ranch.

"Here comes your favorite bull now," Susanna said.

The chute gate burst open with Razor Edge sitting erect, concentration fixed on his face. He was holding one arm aloft and matching the nimble moves of the giant beast with equally agile counter moves.

Rambunctious came out of the chute and made a quick turn to the right and then an equally quick turn to the left, completely spinning in each direction. The young cowboy appeared to be enjoying the control he was displaying, well centered and matching the animal's violent contortions with subtle shifts of weight and balance.

The massive bull then made a high kick in the air with his hind feet throwing his head rapidly back and up as Razor leaned into the extended motion.

The poll of the bull's head made contact with the face of his young rider, blood spraying from his nose and mouth. Razor Edge tumbled to his right with his hand momentarily held fast in the flat rope hand hold. His body swung in an arc and when the rope released its grip he was sent flying across the arena.

Grant looked at Tom who was ashen faced.

"I knew that was gonna happen. I shouldn't have brought him along."

"You can't blame yourself, Dad," Susanna said. "Everyone knows what they are getting into. If Razor had made the ride, he would have been a hero."

"I know you're right darlin', but it just don't make me feel no better."

When the last of the riders from The Buffalo Rock Ranch had completed his ride, Tom said, "Come on kids. Let's go help get the wagons ready. This is gonna be a show."

A few of the men were limping and some were favoring obviously injured arms, but to Grant's surprise, everyone was working without complaint. Buck and Howdy, who had each ridden a bull, were readying their teams. Each shouted orders to his six outriders as final preparations were completed.

The announcer could be heard shouting into his megaphone.

"Gentlemen, get your wagons to the starting line and let us parade for our audience."

The seven wagons began to move into the arena, accompanied by the outriders. The cheering of the crowd became a deafening roar. The competitors paraded around the arena several times, allowing the audience to view the entries.

Spectators picked their favorites and wagers were exchanged. Soon the official starter began to form the wagons on a line side by side in preparation for the start.

The announcer again shouted through his megaphone.

"Could we have complete silence? Please folks, we need complete silence so as to give all of our drivers a fair chance at a good start. Now this is going to be a five-lap race around the arena track, and all six of the outriders have got to come to the finish line with the wagon. That's the rules. Now let's have some quiet and we'll get 'er under way."

The crowd obediently quieted. The arena went silent, except for the noise of the horses fidgeting nervously in their harnesses. The starter raised his flag and held it for an interminable moment. When the starting shot was fired, a roar went up from the crowd and the clattering rumble of hooves and steel rimmed wheels became a discordant din.

Buck had anticipated the starter's shot and when the wagons entered the first turn he was leading by a neck. However, when they rounded the turn into the back stretch another team pulled alongside and took a small lead.

Howdy had slowed to avoid colliding with another wagon and was coming into the main straightaway in fifth place.

Grant put his hand on Dixie's arm and said, "It looks like Buck has decided to win this."

Tom overheard Grant's comment.

"I told you that boy has got what it takes. He's one helluva teamster."

The wagon, which had been in front of Howdy, made a sharp jog to the right while in the straightaway, and Howdy was able to move to the inside and pass into forth place as the wagons came out of the turn.

Buck whipped his team into the back straightaway, now holding second place. Pulling alongside the first place team on the outside, Buck made a move to the inside. He urged his team into a tight turn forcing the inside wagon into the infield, running the team over a barrel, which had been placed as a marker.

The crowd booed its disapproval.

"Damned that guy," Tom said. "He can't never do anything on the square."

Howdy had passed the third place wagon on the straightaway and was now able to pass the second team as its driver fought to regain control after the animals had collided with the barrel.

Tom was screaming, unheard, at both Buck and Howdy as they entered the third lap running first and second. The driver who had hit the barrels was regaining control and he was challenging Howdy for second place. Howdy steered his team to the inside when Buck went wide on the second turn of the third lap. Urging his team with whip and shouts, Howdy pulled alongside Buck's team which was now running all out.

"Go, Howdy. You have it now!" Grant shouted.

In his excitement, Tom was beating Grant and Dixie on the back.

The third place team, which Buck had forced to run over the barrels, was again overtaking Buck and Howdy who were running side by side. All were running headlong down the straightaway.

When they approached the turn, Buck reined his team so as to press Howdy's wagon into the marker barrels. Howdy held a tight rein and refused to give way in his position on the track. Buck continued to maneuver his team closer to Howdy's wildly running animals. The left front wheel of Buck's wagon moved into the path of the right rear wheel of Howdy's.

Howdy, using his whip, picked up the pace. The rapidly spinning wheels of the two wagons touched. The momentum of Howdy's rear wheel caused it to climb the front wheel of Buck's wagon sending the back of Howdy's wagon erupting into the air.

Howdy catapulted from the driver's seat, arms and legs flailing the air. His body caromed across the backs of the two teams, dropping to the ground beneath the wheels of Buck's wagon.

Dixie and Susanna shrieked in horror.

"Oh, sweet Jesus...he's kilt for sure," Tom said, as the four began climbing the fence into the arena.

The official with the flag attempted to slow the wildly running teams. Grant felt a sickening knot in his stomach as two more of the wagons ran over Howdy's lifeless form before the race could be halted.

Howdy's body lay twisted into a grotesque caricature of human form. His battered face was unrecognizable. Dixie cradled his head in her lap.

Buck, who had reined to a halt, ran to kneel beside Howdy. He picked up the young man's hand.

"I'm sorry ol' partner," Buck said. "It was an accident. I didn't mean nothin' by it. You know that don't ya, Howdy?"

Tom stared into Howdy's face, knowing that his worst fears were realized.

"Take 'er easy boy," Tom said. "We got a car comin' to get you to the hospital. You're gonna be okay."

Howdy looked up at Buck and then at Grant, who was also kneeling next to him. Grant did not know what to say. He had never seen a person so severely injured.

"You know somethin', Dude?" Howdy rasped.

Grant started to say something, but before he could speak, Tom reached down and closed Howdy's eyes.

Grant felt a bitter sorrow and anger as he looked up at Buck. Before he could say anything, Buck stood and turned to Tom.

"You know it was an accident boss. We was just all too crowded on them turns."

Tom looked at Buck. A lump in his throat kept him from responding.

Buck looked at Dixie who continued to cradle Howdy's bloodied head. She stared back without expression.

"You know Howdy was my pal, don't you?" he asked.

"Yes. I know he was your friend. I can't talk about it right now," Dixie said.

Tears streamed down her face as Buck shuffled uncomfortably in her gaze. He then walked toward the race officials. Lloyd handed Buck the winner's trophy, while several other cowboys stood around him shaking his hand and congratulating him.

"That's a bit nonchalant, considering that he just killed his best friend...wouldn't you think?" Grant said.

Tom put his hand on Grant's shoulder.

"Let it be, son. Ain't nothin' to be gained by stirrin' that pot right now. We all knowed it was a dangerous amusement."

Howdy's body was loaded into the back of a truck. Lloyd Clarkson accompanied Tom to the hospital where he received permission from the Canadian officials to remove Howdy's remains to the United States. When the paperwork was complete, Tom sank into the seat of Lloyd's car with an exhausted sigh.

"I never heard Howdy talk much about kinfolk. I did hear that he had an uncle down by Great Falls. I sent Bernie Gregory a telegram. Maybe he can locate whatever family as there might be," Tom said.

"What do you reckon to do with that Buck fella, Tom?" Lloyd asked.

"I don't know, Lloyd. I always liked Buck even though he had a bad reputation and he is as mean as a weasel. I give him every chance to get over whatever it is that's eatin' at him but I think that chance just cost a fine young man his life. So I just don't know. I'll have to think on it a bit I reckon."

When Lloyd drove into the rodeo grounds it was nearly deserted. The bustling activity of previous days was gone. The competitors and stockmen had loaded their livestock and equipment and departed for the trip home or the next rodeo. Only The Buffalo Rock crew waited somberly for word to start the long drive to Montana.

Dixie ran to Lloyd's car and embraced Grant. They stood for a long moment holding each other. Tom passed the word to prepare the already packed vehicles for the trip home.

Buck walked to where Tom was talking to Lloyd. He stood quietly until Tom and Lloyd had finished their last minute farewells. When Lloyd walked away Tom turned to look Buck in the eyes, attempting to read his feelings.

"What's gonna happen now, Boss?" Buck asked.

"What do you mean, 'What's gonna happen now?' Nothin' as I know of," Tom said. "What's done is done."

"So they ain't gonna arrest me or nothin'? I mean, it was an accident and all, but I thought maybe them Mounties might want to talk to me," Buck said.

"No, sir, it's all done and settled. They wrote it down as an accident. I reckon you don't have to worry none. Go get your truck ready to roll."

Tom walked up and down the line of vehicles telling each driver to ready themselves for the trip.

"Do you feel like drivin', Sus?" Tom asked.

The engines of the trucks began to come to life.

"I'll be alright, Dad," she said, looking at her father through swollen eyes.

Susanna started the car. Grant and Dixie climbed into the back seat while Tom sat in the front. The fatigue and anguish was obvious on his face. The caravan of vehicles moved slowly out of the rodeo grounds and onto the road south toward the United States.

Tom could hear Dixie crying in the back seat. He turned to look at her.

"Darlin', rodeo is a tough business. Hell, ranchin' and raisin' livestock is a rough business. People are killed every day. I really liked that Howdy boy and I hope the good Lord has a special place for him in the beyond. I know you ain't accustomed to this sort'a thing...but dyin' is as much a part'a livin' as bein' born. Just honor his memory and let him go, or else your mind will take you to places that you can't afford to be."

Dixie sat looking at Tom through red and swollen eyes.

"Buck killed him to win the race," she said.

Her words filled the car like thunder.

"Yes, he did," Grant said. "I'm not certain that it was his intention to kill Howdy, but he surely killed him; and he seems to have no remorse. I have never felt such anger at anyone in my life."

"Well, I'll tell you all somethin' right now. I got to agree that he don't seem none too upset considerin' that Howdy was the only pal he had in this world, but let it go. That sort'a pent up discontent will only poison your own soul. This is gonna have to be dealt with and I'm the one who has to do it. So let's get off the subject for now 'cause this is gonna be one long ride home. Find somethin' else to occupy your mind."

26

The sound of honking horns caused Susanna to stop and look back at the slowing caravan. They had ridden in silence for hours. It was nearing late afternoon.

Susanna backed the car to meet Elmer who was running toward them.

"Boss, looks like three of the rigs is havin' some tire problems. We're gonna have to stop awhile."

"I knew it was too good to last," Tom said. "Not a problem comin' and three at once goin' home. Them split rims ain't gonna be done in a hurry. Have the boys see to the stock and tell everyone to break out the groceries."

Elmer started to walk toward the trucks.

"Oh, Elmer," Tom shouted. "Have someone bring up a table and some chairs. We'll have us a picnic. I might just as well set a nice table like them noble European folks who come huntin' with me years back. I hope you fellas been workin' on your tire pump muscles."

"Will do 'er, Boss and I reckon as how we'll see about them muscles."

"Did you know that your Uncle Tom had been to Europe?" Grant said.

Grant hoped the question would take Dixie's mind off of the pall which pervaded the aggregation.

They walked into the shade of a large roadside tree for relief from the afternoon sun. Tom looked at his daughter and his niece. He lit a cigarette and then leaned against the trunk of the giant cottonwood.

"You never told me you had gone to Europe. What were you doing there?" Dixie asked.

"I was a member of Buffalo Bill's Congress of Rough Riders and a part of the big show Bill put on before the crowned heads. That was before Susanna and Derrick come along," Tom said, also hoping to lighten the atmosphere. "I was one of the sharpshooters with Annie Oakley and the rest. We'd also shoot the buffalo...with blanks of course; and chase the Injuns down and run 'em outta the arena."

"So how did you come to take European royals on a hunting trip?" Grant asked.

"Well, like I was tellin' you, Bill Cody invited me and some others to join him on a tour of Europe. Now that was a hard offer to turn down and I'll tell you this, I sure did have me a good time. I won't go into the details of the various forms of entertainment that they got available over there in Europe, especially in France, but let it suffice to say that we had us a real good time."

"Just leave it to our imaginations," Dixie said.

"So as to the fellas I took huntin'. It happened like this...we was comin' close to endin' up the tour and we was travelin' through Germany and Austria when Cody comes over to me one day to say that he'd recommended me for a job of work. He asked if I would talk to one of these rich European fellas about comin' to America for a little huntin' expedition. It turned out that this fella was the boot lickin' lacky of the Grand Duke Ferdinand of Austria. This fella says that the Grand Duke had a hankerin' to go kill himself a buffalo and a grizzly bear. The Duke had heard all about the Montana Territory, and Cody told him I was the number one man in that country to use as a guide. Cody must'a spun him a yarn 'cause he thought I was the next thing to Kit Carson himself.

Now to be real honest the thought of playin' wet nurse to a bunch of lace wearin' dandies was about as appealin' as passin' a kidney stone, but I'd been drinkin' a bit and I figured I'd just send this jaybird packin' by sayin' somethin' really outrageous. I looked this fancy boy right in his monocled eyeball and told him that I couldn't even consider the offer for less than one hundred thousand dollars."

Tom looked at the three in turn.

"Do you kids have any idea what a hundred thousand dollars would buy back in the eighties? That would have been the equivalent of nearly half a million dollars in today's money. I figured he'd disappear like a cinnamon bun in a room full'a fat ladies. I'll be damned if'n ol' Cody hadn't convinced him that I was the only man for the job. He grabbed my hand and said in a thick accent, 'We will contact you for all the arrangements.'

I was left sittin' there with my mouth hangin' open and lookin' like a fool when Cody come by and asked how the deal went with the Grant Duke. I said 'Bill, I don't think it could'a gone no better and I don't want to bore you with the details.'

I didn't want to tell Cody that I'd just made a contract for more money than he was personally gonna make on his whole tour. As it turned out, Cody was happy, 'cause he'd made the Duke happy and I was findin' myself real happy to know that I'm about to be the best paid guide in the entire history of buffalo huntin', as far as I could tell."

"You charged those people one hundred thousand dollars for a buffalo hunt?" Susanna said.

Tom's eyes twinkled as he looked at his daughter.

"Yes ma'am. You didn't know that your old man was the premier buffalo hunter of these here prairies, I reckon. But the truth is that I did charge that dude one hundred thousand dollars and that was just for a six-week hunt. I told the Grand Duke's dandy that I was a busy man and I couldn't spend my whole career showin' the likes of him around the countryside. I'll tell you this much, that was one of the few times I ever woke up with a hangover and didn't regret some stupid thing I'd said or done the night before."

"So you're telling us that the Grand Duke of Austria came all the way to the United States just to hunt with my Uncle Tom?" Dixie said.

"That, young lady, as they say is the long and the short of it. And I'll even go you one better. Had it not been for that fancy sumbitch comin' to shoot every livin' critter he could put a rifle sight on, I would never have met Susanna's mama."

Elmer approached with several men carrying a table and chairs.

"Where do you want this, Boss?" he asked.

"Put 'er there in the shade, fellas. I'll take my comfort, thank you!"

Dixie and Susanna put bread and cold beef and chicken on the table.

"You never told me this story," Susanna said.

Tom smiled as he looked at the striking, dark haired young woman who looked so much like her mother.

"Well, you know, that was back in the olden days. And it don't seem that anyone was ever too interested to hear what I ever done till this here newspaper fella comes along and wants to write about it."

"Dad, you know that kids never want to hear about the olden days. Besides, to hear you tell it, I would have been just another squaw toting firewood and trying to avoid being killed while the army was running everyone onto the reservations," Susanna said.

Tom looked at Susanna. His thoughts drifted back to his own

childhood and the many things his father and mother had told him of their early lives. Their stories had been the olden days to him. It is unfortunate for human beings, he thought, that memories don't pass from generation to generation. He smiled to consider that for every generation, all things that occurred before your personal ability to recall were the olden days.

"Well, let me tell you about the 'olden days' when I met your mama. This here Grand Duke gave me an address and we corresponded for near a year. Then he wrote and told me that he was gonna be coming in the early summer of eighty-seven for his big adventure. By that time, your grand pappy and his people was gettin' the real shitty end of the stick in dealin' with the government.

Now seein' as how I'd been travelin' the world for a few years, I hadn't seen ol' Bloody Spear or his folks for quite some time. The government had rounded up all of the Blackfoot and sent 'em to the reservation at Browning. They had the army standin' by makin' sure they wasn't causing no problems and they had a Injun Agent who was a lyin' thief and a complete poltroon.

I hadn't never been up to the reservation and I had no idea as to what it was like...at least how bad it really was. So I get to figurin' what with this dandy Duke comin' for a buffalo hunt, he'd probably want some Injuns to guide him about and look real savage and all. So I figured to get Bloody Spear and some my old pals to be them real fierce Injun guides. It took me near about six weeks just to cut through the government knots before I could even find out where they was."

Tom looked into the distance as if he was seeing an image that only he could apprehend.

"I was heartbroken when I finally found 'em. There wasn't no village. It was just a collection of shanties that the generous Injun Agent for the Great White Father in Washington City had seen fit to build for 'em.

The people was dressed in ragged lookin' hand-me-down clothes that you wouldn't give to some alley crawlin' bum. They wasn't allowed to perform any ceremonies and the only weapons they had was for what little subsistence huntin' as the agent would allow.

The worse part of the whole affair was that the guards that was enforcin' the rules was all Blackfoot themselves. They called 'em the Reservation Police."

Tom looked at Grant.

"In fact, it was about this same time that Crazy Horse and Sittin' Bull was both kilt by their own people. Damnedest state of affairs as a man could have imagined. Just twenty years before, in the olden days, these men had been the Lords of the plains. Now they was dressed like stew bums in a hobo camp and bein' kilt by their own. It was one helluva state of affairs.

When I finally found Bloody Spear, it was like he was embarrassed to see me. And I can't say as how I blamed him. They'd took everything from him but his very life, and the way they was feedin' the 'tame Injuns,' as they called 'em, it didn't look to me like it was gonna be long before they'd have that too.

Now I'd brought some tobacco and gifts and such, but I guess what I should'a brung was food. Me'n Bloody Spear had us a sit down and smoke, and I explained to him what it was I had in mind. Now his eyes lit up like a Fourth of July rocket...but there was one big problem. He had to get permission from the Injun Agent."

Grant, who was taking notes in his usual hectic style, stopped and asked, "Weren't the agents assigned to see to the best interests of the Indians?"

"That was the way it was supposed to be when them Washington politicians made the law. But most of them agents was a bunch of politically appointed thieves who stole most of what was supposed to go to their inmates. I believe that most of them Eastern dandy agents considered them Injuns to be the lowest form of life on earth. They hated their charges worse than a honyocker hates a varmint. Watchin' Injuns die seemed to be a part of their sworn oath...at least it sure didn't seem to cause those bastards no distress.

Well, sir, I go and find this dog turd whose name was Ephraim Stiengey. I started right off callin' him Stingy, which he hated, and so from the get go we was off to a bad start. I told him what I had in mind and he dug in his heels and said them Injuns wasn't goin' nowhere and especially with me.

I guess I'd done my friends no favor bein' a smart mouth. I could see I wasn't gettin' no where with Stingy. As much as I hated doin' it, I sent a telegram to Mr. Roosevelt. I knew he had some contacts and I explained that this was for the betterment of international affairs, what with the Arch Duke comin' and all. In fact, Teedie sent back a telegram that he wished he could join us but that he had to go to London or some such thing. So anyway, he must'a leaned on the right functionary, because it wasn't long till I get word from Stingy that he's been ordered to allow twenty of the Blackfoot men to be put in my charge until further notice."

Tom looked at Susanna.

"And now I'm gonna get to the part about your mama. While I was waiting to get permission for Bloody Spear and the men to go with me on the huntin trip I had been easin' up around their camp, such as it was. Well now one'a the fellas that I'd known since we was kids...that'd be your grandpa who was called Bow Maker, now he had a daughter. I'd never seen her before because when I'd come back from the army, she wasn't yet born and when I'd last been to the village in the seventies, your grand pappy was livin' with another village over by the big lake that they call the Flathead.

Now I'll tell you this, when I saw that young woman, there was somethin' woke up in me that I hadn't felt for many a year. She was right near about the prettiest young thing as ever I had laid eyes upon."

Tom gestured with his hand in Susanna's direction.

"You can see for yourself what beautiful children she had. Susanna looks just like her mama."

Susanna blushed.

"You must have been a lot older than mom was."

"Now I wasn't no old man. However, I was sure enough older than Dancin' Fawn. But I reckon she thought I was still cuttin' a fine figure. Before too long she made it clear that she had an eye on me too."

Susanna walked around the table. Lifting Tom's hat she kissed her father on the forehead. "And you're still a fine looking gentleman...and if you weren't my father I'd have an eye for you myself," she said.

"I have heard that there were customs...traditions, which had to be followed as far as obtaining a bride and so forth?" Grant inquired.

"Like I told you, son, the government had taken everything away from these folks, includin' their traditions. Some of them Injun Agents wouldn't even let 'em speak their own language. Customs and traditions were just damned hard to honor under those conditions.

Had it been twenty years earlier, I would'a had to fight some young fella and come up with a whole herd of ponies and a pile'a hides to have a young bride like that. But my friend was so happy that his baby girl would be gettin' good food and a decent place to live and the protection of a white man, that he was more'n happy to give his blessings. Not only that, I took Bow Maker along on the last buffalo hunt he ever got, and I got him a new rifle besides. That didn't hurt my chances none either."

"So you took grandpa on the hunt with the Duke?" Susanna asked.

"Sure enough and he was one helluva tracker and guide. Just like your uncle. That's why I'm so glad that Derrick has got to spend some time with him. Derrick's learnin' a heap from Watches the Ground."

"Did I hear my name?" Derrick said.

They all turned to see Derrick walking toward them.

"Would you like something to eat?" Dixie asked.

"Sounds good," Derrick replied. "I was trying to help with the tires but they've got more hands than they need."

"Dad was just telling about taking the Arch Duke of Austria hunting with grandpa," Susanna said.

She leaned across the table and set a plate in front of Derrick.

"I heard a little about that from Watches the Ground and some of the old men," Derrick replied. "Did that guy really shoot everything he saw?"

"Yep! The man just couldn't get enough of killin'. He'd traveled the world to do his huntin' and this was a big adventure for him.

But I was just about to tell 'em about the camp these dandies set. Now I was expectin'...bein' the guide and all...to be responsible for the food and tents and such; which I figured would be comin' outta my one hundred thousand gold."

Derrick wrinkled his brow. Squinting he looked at his father.

"The Duke gave you a hundred thousand dollars for that hunt?" Derrick said.

"Sure enough did, and they brought all their own possibles besides. They had tents and beds and blankets and even china to eat off of. The Duke had him one whole wagon load of guns. He had muzzle stuffers and cartridge guns that had been custom built just for him...and revolvers; even a Gatling Gun just in case we got jumped by hostile redskins, I reckon.

He'd shoot anything from a prairie dog to a grizzly bear. Now I had just acquired a brand new Winchester Model 86. It shot a big .45-70 cartridge and the ol' Duke had never seen one'a them. After he shot 'er a few times he wanted to buy it from me. I decided that for the money he was payin', I'd just give it to him.

First chance I got, before we left to hunt, I ordered myself a new one and I also ordered new ones for all of Bloody Spear's men who'd come along. That's what I meant when I said I gave your grandpa a new rifle. Of course, I had to go kiss Stingy's ass so that they could keep them guns, and I had to make them promise they'd never use 'em in war...which they did!

In the evening, when we'd make camp, the Duke would set a table that was literally fit for a king...or at least for a Grand Duke. Except for the fresh meat, which we provided each day, he had brought all manner of groceries with him. He'd brought stuff that was pickled and preserved, peppered and dried. They ate a lot of sour stuff like sauerkraut and they liked sausages and such. His cook baked fresh bread everyday. Other than puttin' up with their foolishness, it was the easiest hundred thousand dollars a fella never earned."

Tom looked at Derrick and then Susanna.

"Your grandpa and the other men just shook their heads and made circles around their ears with their pointin' fingers. They figured these white men was really crazy. I can tell you this, it was a long three months for me, but for your Uncle Bloody Spear and grandpa Bow Maker, it was a real treat. They was livin' like the old times...exceptin' they couldn't scalp the white men.

When we finally got them dude wagons rollin' toward the railhead down by Billings for their departure to the East...man did we have us a party. I got all of Bloody Spear's men away from any kind'a settlements where there'd be some bitchin' about drunk Injuns and then we tied one on."

"How did you get mom out of the camp?" Susanna asked.

"Well, you see, after we got rid of them European dandies we headed back to the reservation, just like I promised. One thing I'd learned is that you don't cross the government. So when we rode in, there was ol' 'Stingy', waitin' like the snake in the grass that he was. He stood there with his hands on his hips like some schoolmarm and said 'I thought perhaps you were planning to harbor these men from the custody of the United States government.'

I can still remember that smile on his face. Of course, never knowin' when to shut up, I said, 'Actually I was plannin' to pull off your head and shit down your neck you unemployable piece'a government trash.' After I said it I was sorry 'cause I knew them poor people who had to live under the whip of that no good sumbitch would pay the price."

"What else could he do to them?" Grant asked.

"Cut their rations, withhold their blankets, refuse to let 'em hunt. That dirty little bastard had plenty'a ways to make their lives miserable."

Derrick finished his food and Tom could see that his hands were shaking. He stood up and turned to walk toward the trucks.

"I think I'll go kick some cowboys in the ass and see if we can't get this train movin'," he said.

Susanna watched her brother walk away.

"So what did you do about Stingy?" she asked.

"There wasn't much I could do...but on the way back to Browning, I had provisioned all the men with plenty'a grub for the people. I even bought 'em plenty of cartridges for them 86 Winchesters. I said a lot of prayers that they wouldn't go gettin' into no trouble with them rifles. I would'a surely felt responsible had that happened.

When we got back to Browning we had our feast, which was much to the dismay of ol' Stingy, and I married your mama in the traditional ceremony. We was blessed with the smoke and celebrated as best we could under the circumstances."

"But how did you get her out of that place?" Susanna asked again.

"Stingy didn't give a damn about how many women and children you took. His only concern was the young men of fightin' age. I told Bloody Spear and your grandpa that I would hide 'em out at my place if they chose to come. They both thought on it for some time and then they looked at the reality. First off, they didn't want to hide out the rest of their lives, and both of 'em had a responsibility to the people that looked to them for leadership. So the matter was closed. Bloody Spear and his folks would have to stay put, but I was real insistent about some of the women. Bloody Spear's woman didn't want to leave him and neither did Bow Maker's woman...that'd be your grandma...but there was still one girl that I figured to get outta that place. Dancin' Fawn's cousin."

Tom looked at Grant.

"I believe you know her as Koko."

"I am beginning to put things together," Grant said. Bloody Spear and Bow Maker must have been brothers?"

"That's right...and Koko and Dancin' Fawn was cousins. Koko had lost her husband to the pox the year before and she was still in mournin'...and her and Dancin' Fawn was near about inseparable. It occurred to me that Dancin' Fawn goin' to a strange place alone would probably not be the best thing to make my life happy neither. So I took 'em both along with me. It worked out well too. They was both homesick, of course, but they at least had each other and of course sister Sarah could palaver with 'em and started to teach 'em both enough American to get by."

"I can remember that mom spoke pretty good English," Susanna said.

"That's 'cause you was just a tyke and kids can understand damned near anything that their mama says."

Elmer and several of the men came to take away the table and chairs.

Derrick shouted from the back of the caravan, "Let's get on the road."

Slowly the vehicles lurched forward and soon the train of trucks and cars was making up lost time.

27

Susanna stopped the car beside the gas pump at the White Rose Filling Station on Front Street in Fort Benton. Roy Kearns began pumping gasoline into Tom's car and then looked at the line of vehicles.

"I hope I got enough for all of your outfits, Tom," Roy said.

"I do too, Roy. We still have to get out to The Buffalo Rock. At least get enough into each one to get us home."

Tom turned to Dixie and Susanna.

"Come on girls, let's go over to the hotel and you two can freshen up a bit. I got to see if'n I got an answer from Bernie."

Grant joined them as they walked to the Grand Union Hotel.

"Any telegraphs for me, Charlie?" Tom said, walking to the desk.

"Yes, sir, Tom, there is...and I was real sorry to hear about Howdy. I know he was a good hand and a fine young feller," Charlie said.

Charlie handed a telegram to Tom.

"UNCLE DRUNK – STOP – SAYS BURY THE BOY WHEREVER YOU LIKE – STOP – BERNIE – STOP."

"Tell the girls that we went back to the car, would you Charlie," Tom said.

Tom returned to the filling station and then walked the caravan from vehicle to vehicle.

"Do any of you fellas know what religion Howdy honored?"

Buck sat behind the wheel of one of the trucks and just shook his head when Tom walked by.

"I think I heard him say once that he'd gone to the 'Piscapalians' a time or two when he was a boy…but I don't know that he was devout about it," Elmer said.

"Buck," Tom said, "help Elmer take Howdy over to Beanblossum's Mortuary. I gotta go over to the church and talk to the preacher."

Tom drove to the Anglican Church where he knocked at the rectory door. Considering the exhaustion and emotional distress of the entire group, he arranged with the minister that the service be held two days hence. He then drove to the mortuary where arrangements were made with Barlow Beanblossum for the funeral service at The Buffalo Rock.

The following day the work of cleaning trucks and equipment began. Grant accompanied Tom as he walked through The Compound attempting to bolster moral. Crossing the main street to return to Tom's house, the sound of an automobile horn stopped them. Caleb was riding with Nick in his Ford.

"Would you like us to do something special tonight for a dinner? Sort'a have a memorial or somethin'?" Caleb asked.

"That's a damned good idea, Caleb," Tom replied. "Get some extra help if you need it and tell anyone who wants to join us that they're welcome to say a few words for the boy."

Grant spent the afternoon writing notes and recording his thoughts on what had occurred. It was evening when Dixie knocked at his door. Her eyes were still red and swollen.

"Are you going to the mess hall for dinner and the memorial?"

"Absolutely," Grant replied. "Let me get my jacket."

When they entered the mess hall, Grant saw Buck sitting with several other ranch hands at one of the long tables. Grant and Dixie took the last seats at the table with Tom, Nick, Susanna and Caleb.

After dinner, one after another, men rose to remember Howdy. Unaccustomed to speaking in public, the largely inarticulate memorials paid homage to his courage, loyalty, tenacity and work ethic. When all who wished to be heard had spoken, a long silence fell upon the assembly. The entire coterie then sat in anticipation of Buck offering words of honor for his departed friend.

Buck sat stolidly looking around him for a long moment at the expectant faces. Then he stood and left the room.

The slamming of the mess hall door resounded like thunder as cold silence followed Buck's exit. Tom arose, and immediately every eye fell upon him. He looked slowly around the room and allowed his gaze to come to pause on each person in turn.

Picking up a glass of water, Tom took a drink and cleared his throat.

"The Buffalo Rock has lost a good hand, a good man and a good friend. I have lost a good man and a good friend. Tomorrow, we're gonna lay that young man to rest here in the soil of The Buffalo Rock, right next to the only family he's known for quite some time. Seemed no one else wanted to claim him, so we will. He was a young man full of promise and he was always excited to take on challenges and I had great expectations of him. I guess you could say that he died fulfillin' some of those expectations."

Tom took another swallow of water and then gazed slowly at the crowd as if he was speaking to each individual.

"No one can ever know what's in another man's heart, and I affix no blame for this tragedy. Accidents happen when men play dangerous games and that's the truth of it. Now, I don't want to sound like a preacher.

I'll leave that to the man in the collar for tomorrow. But before we lay our little brother Howdy to rest, let's all go home and take a good look in the mirror.

I can still remember my mama readin' to us children from the Good Book when we'd get to complainin' about one another. If I recall correctly, I think it was from Mathew. He was tellin' the story of somethin' that Jesus said while he was preachin' on the mount. I don't recall exactly how it went but the gist of the thing was that we ought not to be lookin' at the splinter in the eye of our brother when we ought to be payin' heed to the telegraph pole stickin' outta our own eye."

Tom picked up his hat and walked out of the mess hall. The track of a tear was visible on his cheek. He hoped that his words might help defuse the animosity he could feel building in the crew of The Buffalo Rock.

Promptly at ten the next morning Barlow Beanblossum drove his shiny black and white Cadillac hearse through the gathered throng and parked beside the fenced graveyard. Six men, dressed in their cleanest shirts carried Howdy's casket to the open grave where the Episcopal minister presided over the short ceremony.

The casket was lowered into the grave and several men began filling the hole. Tom surreptitiously dropped three twenty dollar gold pieces into the pocket of the minister and then told Barlow to send him the bill to settle the account.

Grant had been standing with his arm around Dixie during the ceremony and each time he looked around he could feel Buck's glowering stare. When the minister finished the service, he watched Buck deftly vault the fence and walk toward the corrals.

Tom took Koko's hand and walked toward the house.

"You kids come on up to the house. We'll have us some iced tea and sit a while," he said.

Tom sat on the front porch swing. Grant and Dixie sat in chairs. Soon Koko reappeared with a tray of glasses and a pitcher of iced tea.

"Come here and sit with me, darlin'. Let's just take the day off today," he said.

Tom looked at Grant.

"You remember that first week you was here? I'm sure you had no idea as to who was who. You was talkin' about our eclectic group?"

Grant took a sip of tea and acknowledged with reddened cheeks that he remembered.

"Well, son...everyone here on the Buffalo Rock is kin of some sort. By blood or spirit. I know you probably won't understand, but I loved that boy like I love my own children."

Tom took Koko's hand gently in his own.

"Even though she acts like she don't like me sometimes, she really does. Hell, she's been more like a sister to me than my own blood kin."

Grant nodded, but his attention was diverted as he watched Buck mount a horse and ride onto the prairie. None of the others seemed to notice.

"Would everyone excuse me a moment," he said.

Grant walked into the house and then out the back door. He crossed the road behind the house and went to the stable where he saddled Nick's horse. Not sure as to just what he was planning to do he mounted and rode in the direction Buck had taken. When he crossed tracks that even his tyro's eye told him were the fresh prints of Buck's shod horse, he urged Nick's horse into a lope. He rode for nearly an hour. Riding into a grove of trees he recognized that he was getting close to the lake and tipi.

He slowed his mount to a walk. Tom's warnings rang in his ears. He asked himself just what he intended to do when he caught Buck. He realized that he had allowed his feelings of anger over Buck's intimidation and Howdy's death to spin out of control. Reason was quickly turning his anger to a knot in his stomach and a lump in his throat. Was it necessary that he test his own courage? His mind raced for answers.

He had wanted a confrontation, once and for all, when he began this pursuit. But what sort of confrontation did he want? Why hadn't he done this at the rodeo? Why hadn't he done this at the funeral? Why was he here in the middle of the wilderness, impulsively pursuing a brute of a man who could very likely kill him with his bare hands; and very likely would? He stopped his mount and sat staring into the timber for a long while.

Taking a deep breath of relief, he smiled to himself. This had certainly been one of the more childish, immature things he had ever done, he thought.

"Grow up," he said to himself, aloud.

He turned Nick's horse and rode toward The Compound.

The horse walked slowly, stepping carefully through the deadfalls and the timber as it picked its way down the hillside. Grant, still not totally comfortable on horseback, kept his eyes glued to the ground immediately in his path. When the horse stopped, Grant looked up. Buck was sitting on his horse immediately in Grant's path, calmly smoking a cigarette.

"Well, fuck me for an old heifer," Buck said a mirthless smile on tight lips. "Now just what in holy hell do you think you're doin' out here, Dude? I seen you was followin' me, so I circled around just in case you changed your mind...and I reckon you must'a."

Grant was too stunned with surprise to give an immediate answer.

Buck was sitting with his right leg crooked and resting on the saddle horn in a relaxed posture which completely unnerved Grant.

"I'll tell you what, Dude. I lost my pal and I thought I'd get myself a little time in the way out lonesome...just to think things over, but damned if you didn't just follow me out here to disturb my solitude. So as long as you're here, we may as well settle what's been goin' on. Don't you reckon?"

"And just what might that be?"

Grant's voice cracked as he asked the question.

"Well, that might be, that you're just some smart-assed, lacy pants dandy from New York City who come here and took my girl and made me look bad in front of my boss. That's what that's bein', and I been wantin' to beat the holy livin' shit right outta you since the day you got here. But you always got the boss to protect you."

Buck looked around casually and slipped his left foot from the stirrup. He slid from the saddle and onto the ground. Walking toward Grant he flipped his cigarette butt at Grant's face, causing him to flinch.

"Look around you now you fair-haired son-of-a-bitch! There ain't no one around here to protect you."

Buck walked his horse to a small tree where he tied the animal with a lead rope.

"Just want to make sure I got a ride home when we're done."

Grant thought for a moment of kicking his horse into a run and escaping as Buck walked toward him. Buck grabbed Grant's arm, pulling him from the saddle. Nick's riderless horse jumped a deadfall log and trotted down the hill.

"But you ain't gonna need a ride home. In fact, you ain't gonna need a ride no where when I'm done with you."

Buck had barely finished the sentence when Grant hit him squarely in the nose with a solid right hand punch, just as Tommy Gibbons had demonstrated for him. Buck fell backwards and tripped over the deadfall tree. To Grant's surprise he sprung to his feet in an animal-like move that set Grant aback.

Swinging wildly Buck missed Grant with two poorly aimed right hands, his vision blurred by the blow to his nose. As Buck regained his senses he jabbed a left, which connected and then a follow-up right hand, which knocked Grant onto his back. Instantly, Buck was on top of him pinning Grant's arms to the ground with his knees and pummeling Grant's face and chest with a flurry of blows from fists toughened by years of hard manual labor. Buck put his left hand on Grant's chin, holding his head still while delivering a hammer blow to Grant's face.

"Dixie ain't gonna think you look so pretty now, Dude."

Struggling to free himself, Grant was able to get his teeth around the meaty butt of Buck's left hand. Survival instinct was taking over. He bit down with all the strength his jaws could muster.

Buck's attention was immediately focused on the pain as a piece of his hand was severed by the bite. He focused momentarily on the blood that was squirting around Grant's teeth. Seeing the distraction, Grant rolled and was able to free his right arm. He aimed another punch at Buck's undefended nose.

Grant's teeth loosed their grip as the flesh of Buck's hand ripped. Buck began to beat a tattoo on Grant's face until he went limp. It appeared that Grant had lost consciousness.

Buck got to his feet and looked at his badly bitten hand. Cursing, he kicked Grant in the face and the ribs. Buck then pulled Grant to his feet. Holding Grant's wobbly legged form upright with his bloody left hand, Buck aimed several punches intended to crush the bones in Grant's face. He then released his grip and Grant collapsed on the ground.

Buck was looking at the bleeding bite in his left hand when Grant came to. He shook himself into consciousness and struggled to his feet. He caught a breath and repeating the Gibbon's taught technique he again landed a blow on Buck's nose. The larger man fell sideways onto the ground. Grant jumped onto Buck, maneuvering himself into position for another punch at Buck's nose.

Buck, the more experienced fighter, heaved Grant to the side and was again on top of him, beating his face with both fists until Grant again quit moving.

He then stood over Grant's prostrate body. His ribs were heaving with the exertion. Buck could see that his rival was now completely helpless. He removed a kerchief from his pocket and mopped the blood from his own face. He then wrapped the kerchief around his bleeding left hand.

Standing over his hated adversary on unsteady legs, he attempted to catch his breath. Reaching into his pocket, he took out a folding knife. Grant regained consciousness and tried to move. The beating had left him immobile. He could not get his arms and legs to obey his commands.

Buck opened the knife. He looked down at his fallen foe.

"Now I'm gonna find out if your liver is as yellow as I figure it to be."

Taking a step toward Grant, he smiled through bloody teeth.

"You know Dude, I seen where a grizzly been workin' on the calves hereabouts. I don't reckon it will take him long to make a picnic outta your refined ass, and them griz love liver, even if it's yellow."

Dropping to one knee, Buck ripped open Grant's shirt.

"By the time they find what's left'a your bony ass, there won't be enough to send home to your mama in a Luden's cough drop box."

Bracing the blade with his thumb, Buck raised the knife so that Grant could clearly see what he intended. Even in his half consciousness Grant's eyes were wide as he watched the blade moving inexorably toward his exposed abdomen.

Suddenly the knife flipped through the air and Grant watched in astonishment as Buck's hand seemed to explode. Mangled fingers spurted blood into Grant's face, blurring his vision. Buck's middle finger dangled momentarily on a thread and then fell onto Grant's chest.

Buck grabbed his still twitching digit and jumped to his feet. He looked down at Grant who was covered in blood and small chunks of flesh. His lips moved but no sound came forth. A look of pain and consternation painted his face. He began to jump around, attempting to reattach the severed finger. The surreal dance caused Grant, in his semi-consciousness, to believe it was all a dream.

The shock, which blurred Buck's comprehension, began to dissipate as the smell of a wispy cloud of gun powder smoke drifted down the hillside. As the reality of what had occurred overtook him, he sagged onto a log.

"Had this been thirty years ago, Buck, I would'a just kilt you. But I reckon we're getting' civilized...or else I'm just gettin' soft in my old age," Grant heard Tom say.

Grant could hear Tom's footsteps walking down the hill.

"You shot my hand off you old bastard. I ought'a kill you," Buck screamed.

Tom stood over Grant, looking at Buck. Grant then heard the unmistakable metallic click as Tom cocked his Colt revolver.

"Like I said, thirty years ago I would have kilt you outright. Looks to me like maybe you kilt this reporter fella here. He sure ain't lookin' none too good. So you're gonna likely enough be in jail till long after I'm dead and gone. Now it might just happen that bein' bent over a bunk rail by some big horny bastard who'll be usin' you for his one-armed Susie down in Deerlodge will mellow your intemperate ways. I don't know...I doubt it. But I'll tell you this, you can get on that horse and get back to The Compound as quick as you can. Then get your gear cleaned outta my bunkhouse. I never been one to take threats lightly Buck. You never know if a fella is serious or not, so I don't ever want to see you again. Since you was foolish enough to make that threat; if I ever see you again, I'll shoot you on sight like the mangy cur dog that you are."

Buck put his finger into his shirt pocket and then untied his horse. He mounted in a jump. Spinning the bald faced gelding in the direction of The Compound, he spurred the animal with all urgency.

Tom picked up Grant's hat and then knelt beside his young friend. Blood covered Grant from head to foot.

"How bad you hurt?"

"My ribs are pretty badly bent and my nose may be broken, but I don't think anything is fatal."

"Well, you just lay there a while till you feel better. I'll go catch your horse."

"Buck was right about one thing, I don't think my nose will never look the same."

Tom looked at the young man's face and grinned.

"Sort'a gives your boyish features a bit of character, if'n you ask me."

Tom walked up the hill and mounted Luke. In a short time he returned leading Nick's horse.

"You would'a sure enough had yourself some major surgery had I not happened along when I did. And somehow I don't think ol' Buck is none too particular about his medical procedure, neither. I told you that Buck was a mean one. What the hell was you thinkin' about goin' after him by yourself that way?"

Grant laughed through his aching jaw.

"Frankly, I don't know. It was a real lapse of judgment...but then, after all of the stories you have told me about the things you did when you were just a child, what would you expect a man to do?"

"I'd at least carry a gun! Let me assure you that it makes all the difference. You may not ever have heard this, but I'm gonna tell you one of life's little truisms. God created man, but it was ol' Sam Colt who brought about equality."

Tom pulled Grant to his feet and helped him mount. The ride to The Compound took several hours at the slow walk necessitated by Grant's injuries. They were met half way by Elmer and several of Tom's ranch hands.

"Nick drove Buck to town," Elmer shouted as he reined alongside. "Looks to me like that mean son-of-a-bitch had best learn to wipe his ass with his left hand."

"Let's hope we won't be seein' no more of Mr. Horton around The Buffalo Rock," Tom said. "I thought he'd kilt ol' Grant here. I figured we'd be sendin' Buck to the graybar hotel, but he slid through again. Maybe he'll leave this part of the country this time. When I get done talkin' to the ranchers, ain't no one gonna give him work."

Dixie and Koko were standing in front of the house when the men rode into The Compound.

Grant dismounted gingerly. Elmer took the reins of the horses and walked to the corral.

Dixie ran to Grant, a look of revulsion in her eyes when she saw Grant's nearly unrecognizable face.

"Buck took all of his things out of the bunkhouse and said he wouldn't be seeing us again. What happened?" Dixie asked.

"Buck and Grant had 'em a minor misunderstandin'. Nothin' serious," Tom said.

"Nothing serious!" Dixie shrieked. "Buck had a finger dangling by a thread and he was carrying another finger in his shirt pocket. Grant looks like he's been run down by a trolley car. Just when do you consider something serious?"

Dixie threw her arms around Grant, sobbing in near hysteria.

He moaned loudly as she squeezed his ribs, and she quickly stepped back realizing that he was in pain.

"What can I do?" she asked, allowing him to use her shoulder as a crutch.

Grant, taking full advantage of the sympathy, moaned with every step.

2 8

The next few weeks found Grant enjoying the attention of both Koko and Dixie. Taking full advantage of the serious look of his injuries, he allowed them to wait on him hand and foot. He also spent considerable time meticulously recording events, past and present.

After some weeks, Grant went to the dining room for breakfast.

"Been a few weeks now and you're still eatin' them eggs like you was chewin' buffalo hide," Tom said. "You reckon you're ever gonna get that jaw workin' right?"

"It's getting better by the day," Grant said.

"Well, you still look positively awful," Dixie said. "I don't think your beautiful nose will ever be the same. I hope you have learned a lesson."

"Yes ma'am, I have," Grant said, imitating Tom.

"Good! I wrote a poem...would you like to hear it tonight?"

"Yes, ma'am, I would," Grant said.

"Alright, Mr. Tornado Tom junior," she said. She stood to leave the table. "I'll see the two of you later. I have to go help Susanna. We have another party of rock hunters coming and then in a few weeks the elk hunters will be coming. We have a lot to get ready."

"Elk hunters?" Grant asked.

Dixie walked out of the dining room and Grant looked at Tom.

"Yes, sir...Elk hunters. It's comin' on fall and the Eastern dandies like to come out and hunt elk and deer. Too bad there ain't no buffalo no more. We take the dudes up into the mountains south of where that new Glacier Park is. I kind'a enjoy the huntin' myself. Derrick and his uncle, Watches the Ground, help out with the guidin' and I have a couple'a boys who tend the camps and do the cookin'."

"Do you go on the hunts?" Grant asked.

"Hell, yes! It kind'a takes me back to my younger days, gettin' out and puttin' the sneak on a big ol' bull elk. We even shoot us bear now and then," Tom replied."Come on in the office. We'll have some more coffee and talk a bit."

Koko brought a tray with cups and coffee.

"Thanks, darlin'. Would you go see if you can find Dannie's wedding dress and them pictures?" Tom asked.

Grant walked around the room looking at the numerous photos and artifacts.

"Was this taken while you were in Europe?" he asked, pointing to a picture of Tom with Buffalo Bill Cody.

"Yep, it was. Next to that is a picture of me and Mr. Roosevelt with one of the biggest griz ever killed up in this country. That ain't the one he had stuffed and kept in the White House. I shot the one there in that picture. I shot it with a rifle he gave to me, though."

Tom walked to his gun cabinet and took out a rifle. The bluing on the gun shone in the light from the window and the wood of the walnut stock reflected the hand-rubbed figuring and deep checkering.

"This here is a 1895 Winchester, caliber Four-oh-five."

Tom pushed the lever down to open the chamber. He then handed the gun to Grant.

Grant read the inscription on the side of the receiver.

"My Friend Tornado Tom Thomas. T. R."

"Teedie gave me that rifle on his last trip out to hunt just before the Cuban war. He took three of them guns to Africa on that big huntin' adventure just before he died. He thought it was the finest rifle ever made."

Just then Koko entered the room carrying a bundle wrapped in brown paper. Koko laid the bundle on the sofa and opened the package. Several faded photographs lay on top of a nearly pure white beaded buckskin leather dress. Tom handed the photos to Grant who looked at them one at a time.

"Were these photos taken at your wedding?"

"Yep. I brought a photographer from Fort Benton just to take them pictures. That was Dancin' Fawn wearin' this here dress. Pretty thing wasn't she? And that other pretty little maiden right there is this fine figure of a woman."

Tom put his arm around Koko.

"Those other pictures was taken later...obviously...that was Susanna and Derrick when they was little younkers; and of course, that bigger boy is Nick."

Grant held the dress, turning it to the window light to examine the beadwork and decoration.

"What a beautiful piece of art. I had never thought of Indian wedding dresses per se," he said.

"Dancin' Fawn's mama made it for her with the help of some others, includin' miss Koko here. Lot's of work went into that."

Tom pointed to a photo of two small dark haired children sitting on the laps of a man and woman in buckskin clothing.

"That there is Horse Sense and my sister Sarah with Romulus and

Remus."

"Did you all live in this house then?"

"No, we lived over there in the house where Remus and Rom live. We was just poor ranchers then. But that hundred thousand that I got from the Grand Duke made a world of difference in our lives."

"As you pointed out, back in the eighties and nineties that was a huge sum."

"I hope to shout it was huge! We wouldn't be sitting here today had it not been for that small fortune landin' in my lap."

Koko rewrapped the package and left the room.

"Thanks, hon," Tom said as she walked to the door. "And we'll have some more coffee if you have the time."

"Son...a hundred thousand is a lotta dollars in anybody's time. But that wasn't what put this ranch on the map, nor built this Victorian monstrosity I live in."

"Well, I'd just assumed with all of the cattle and sheep and crops and the guest ranch...so what did make your ranch a success?"

"Oil! Good old fashioned black gold. You see, back in the nineties they was just discoverin' that the oil outta the ground was cheaper and better than whale oil. They was also startin' to build engines that would burn the stuff. And guess what?"

Grant shrugged.

"Ol' Rockefeller and the boys was out figurin' ways to make the stuff pay and they was lookin' for where it was. Everyone talks about Texas and all the oil they have. But just like everything else I hear about them Texicans, they always seem to forget Montana. Hell boy, we got oil a plenty. The whole Hi-Line had oil by the tank car."

"And what was the Hi-Line?"

"This whole northern section of Montana, which stretches just south of the Canadian border was pretty much isolated until James Hill of the Great Northern Railroad got the big idea that he could find a shortcut to trade with the orient by building a railroad through this country. It was originally gonna go through Great Falls, but one of his engineers, the designin' kind, not the train drivin' kind, discovered that he could put the rails through Marias Pass. That opened the country to settlement and when they found that black gold...well, I guess you can see what happened."

"How did you find the oil?"

"I didn't find it. The oil fellas found it. I just happen to be lucky enough to have money in the bank, and I didn't have to sell no rights nor kiss no ass. So all of my oil is still my oil. And that's why I've made it possible for my family to live well, enjoy life and not have to worry about the price of beef. That's not to say that we don't work. We work hard and we live just like we always did. But I'll tell you this...if'n I decide I want a new car, I get a new car and if'n I wanted to take a trip to the Bahamas and see them bronze beauties showin' all that skin, I reckon I could afford the trip."

"Why does Derrick seem so angry at you...the world for that matter? It seems to me that he is a very wealthy young man."

"I reckon that every generation has to rebel against the standards of the one before. He see's himself as having been robbed of his Injun heritage, so he dresses Injun and acts like he ain't got good sense sometimes in protest. I ain't yet figured out what it is that he's protestin', but he lives on the reservation and tries to honor the old ones. But their times has gone. Things change. They're changing around us right now. I can only hope that some day he'll come to know that change is just the way of life. Hell, I hate to see the new life comin' just as much as he does. I am just like them old Injuns in a lotta ways. I look at all these cheechakos puttin' in new businesses and the honyockers buildin' houses and fences and roads and stickin' up telephone poles, and I always have to stop and think about the old chiefs. Sittin' Bull and Crazy Horse was raised in a land where they could ride from horizon to horizon and see nothin' but the glory that nature had laid before 'em...and that was in my lifetime.

But you got to remember that there was folks here before them even. Each time a stronger tribe moved in, they took the land from the weaker ones. Someday, there'll be another tribe that'll come and kick our asses off this land too. Just like the Barbarians became Rome...that's just the way of it. The whole history of the human existence is one bunch gettin' stronger than the next and takin' over.

Think about your history. The Romans conquered the world, right! Well, it is my belief that the United States is the Rome of today. Just look at the canal ol' Teedie built on foreign soil. Don't reckon George Washington or even Andy Jackson would have ever thought of takin' a chunk of Panama...and I reckon some day the United States will have a president who ain't strong like Teedie and we'll lose that canal. Unfortunately for Derrick and the Blackfoot, they'd best adapt or they'll live unhappy lives forever more."

"Derrick seems like a bright man. I hope he sees your reality. By the way, are you going to go hunting next month when the guests come?"

"You bet! Never miss it. How would you like to come along?"

"I would love that. I have never been on any sort of hunt and in fact I have never shot a gun. I had never really seen a gun fired until you shot Buck...and I really didn't see that."

"I reckon you was a bit punchy when the shot went off. I hated to shoot ol' Buck, but I reckon that had I not seen you ride out and followed, he would have been examinin' your innards. He was right, there is a big ol' griz workin' that country. Remember, we saw him from the Jenny the day she crashed?"

Grant shifted uneasily in his chair. He recalled the day he and Dixie had gone to the lake. The thought of the bear being somewhere close at hand sent a shiver down his spine.

"Before I forget, you never have told me about your sister and her husband. Sarah and Horse Sense. What happened to them?"

"It was a terrible thing and I don't like to talk about it much, but I reckon it's a part of the story. I would say it was late in the eighties, as I recall...after my trip to Europe. A steamboat had brought a bunch of minin' gear to Fort Benton for delivery to the gold strikes over in Idaho. We had plenty of men workin' for us by then but ol' Horse Sense just kind'a enjoyed drivin' a team now and then. So he took five outfits loaded to top heavy, and headed for Kellogg, over in Idaho, on the Mullan Road.

The boys, Romulus and Remus, was about half growed and they was both workin' by then, and there was plenty of help around with my new bride and Koko, so Sarah decided she would just go along for the ride, just to keep ol' Horse Sense company. They were gone about a week...and then ten days goes by...and then I get a message from Kellog that they'd been bushwhacked on the road. Horse Sense and sister Sarah was dead along with all of the other of our teamsters."

"How had they gotten word to you?"

"They'd sent a rider clear from Idaho over to let us know where the equipment was. The ridiculous part of the whole robbery was that the cargo they was haulin' wasn't nothin' you could make use of. You couldn't take this machinery to a pawn shop for Christ's sake. It was parts for hydraulic pumps and dredges. The whole robbery and the murders was just senseless.

Well, sir, I get a couple'a my best hands and impose on ol' Caldwell, my former deputy, and we ride out and see what is goin' on. We found the wagon's right where the fella told us they'd be. To add insult to injury the mean bastards had burned them wagons to the ground. The minin' gear was pretty much destroyed but we was able to salvage some parts...then we got some fellas from Kellogg to haul what was salvageable into the minin' camp.

I went and found what was passin' for a sheriff and he told me that there had been a bunch'a Texas waddies who'd come to try their hand at the minin' but that it hadn't worked out for 'em. They'd apparently got drunk and gone on a rampage and on their way outta the territory they'd decided to rob Horse Sense's freight wagon train.

They couldn't have got much, but the sheriff said it was a pretty ugly kind'a massacre. They'd tried to make it appear that Injuns had done it and they'd burned the bodies and of course they'd done what men do to women under them circumstances. The sheriff told us that the leader of the bunch was a wiry lookin' snake-eyed scoundrel with a harelip. They called him Thum. There was another they'd called Wink Eye Eddie and another with a scar from forelock to brisket that he'd supposedly got from a cavalry sword in the Civil War. The sheriff went on to tell us that the bunch had about a two-week start on us. He said, however, that what with the nature of their conduct, they would likely not be too difficult to follow, considerin' that they was spreadin' fear and discontent wherever they lit."

"With a two-week head start, weren't you a little disheartened?"

"Disheartened ain't the word, son. When I was with the Pony Express, we would cross the entire country in two weeks. I surely wasn't holdin' out much hope of gettin' these boys any too quick...but we started on the trail just the same.

I figured that if they was goin' back to Texas that they'd head straight east from where they'd killed my people to cross the divide. There had been about twenty-five or thirty people around where the wagons had been burnt, which made it difficult to near about impossible to pick up their tracks. So I just took it on a hunch and crossed the divide and headed south. Did you ever hear of the Hole-In-The-Wall-Gang?"

"You mean Butch Cassidy and the Wild Bunch?"

"The Hole-In-The-Wall wasn't really a hole in a wall at all, but rather a sort a series of canyons where scalawags could hide, and anyone pursuin' could be seen for miles. The miscreants could then set up an ambush for the unsuspectin' pursuers.

The-Hole-In-The-Wall is located right where Utah, Wyomin' and Colorado meet at the borders and it was a great place for lots of no good bastards to hang out. They could cross a border from one state to the other and if it was a Utah lawman he couldn't chase 'em into Wyomin' or Colorado and vice versa. I figured that this bunch was probably gonna head that way so we headed down to Helena to look around and resupply. We started inquirin' around Helena, and sure enough they'd come right through town about a week before. Six rode in but it seems that only five rode out. One'a the louts had got into a poker game with fella that apparently had just about as much compassion for his fella human bein's as these slime dippers. This one had got himself gutted on a poker table and the rest of the bunch had been nearly lynched. Under them circumstances they had decided to leave their dead pal and desert the inhospitable environs of Montana."

"That was still a lot of country to cover between Helena and Texas," Grant said.

"You bet it was. But now the trail was only about five days old and we started ridin' hard. The odds was a little better too, what with the one bein' killed and all. I sent the other men home and so it was just me and Caldwell against five of 'em. About a day outta Helena, I picked up the tracks of five riders. I figured it was our boys 'cause when we'd crossed the mountains to head south, I'd seen a set of hoof prints of an animal that hadn't had his hooves trimmed in a while, and the critter was in need of shoes.

Well, one of the hoof prints we was followin' was just like that. The fronts was a little long and the cayuse would kind'a drag on the left side when he was in a lope. Ol' Caldwell rides alongside and says, 'You notice anything funny about that one track we crossed back there?' I told him that I sure enough did and then we both know'd we was on the right track."

"It is just amazing to me that you can tell that much from tracks on the ground."

"Well, son, when that's how you make your livin', you learn the business or you don't last long. That's what a scout got paid for. But anyways, we really rode hard then, and seein' as how they didn't seem to be movin' too quick; we figured we'd catch 'em in a day or two. Then we got a real piece of good luck. Ol' drag foot, as we'd begun to call him, appeared to be lamin' up. It wasn't long and we could see that the drag foot rider was goin' double with one'a the others. But even leadin' the poor critter he was still lamin' up real fast, even without a load.

Then I noticed that they'd begun to zig and zag. I figured that they'd made us for doggin' their trail. But I knowed they was gonna have to do somethin' soon 'cause that lame animal and the ridin' double was really slowin' 'em down. Now just to show the kind'a honor you get among thieves, we all of a sudden come upon a track that really cheered us both. Damned if it wasn't ol' drag foot's rider walkin' along and leadin' the horse."

"So his companions had abandoned him?"

"Precisely, and the next mornin' we topped out on a butte and we could see the poor bastard out in the coulees walkin' along. So Caldwell went one way and I went the other and just about mid-day, we met up in the only natural low spot on that whole piece of prairie. Wasn't no place else for that vermin to go. So we tied our critters in a little willow patch and walked about a half mile and set our ambush in a spot that a skinny field shrew couldn't have squeezed through without bein' seen.

Sure enough I hear the clop drag, clop drag and I knowed our boy was a comin'. So me'n Caldwell set upon him and to say the least he was surprised. We disarmed him of both rifle and pistol, and you could tell right off that he was a tough sumbitch. Gettin' this boy to talk wasn't gonna be no easy matter so I decided that maybe a little Blackfoot medicine might freshen up his memory a bit.

We took him back up the trail to where we'd left our horses and I told Caldwell that maybe he ought not stick around 'cause I intended to get some information out of this hard case bastard, and I wasn't plannin' on bein' none too civilized about how I got it. Now ol' Caldwell surprised me. He was actually a kind'a gentle fella but seein' what they'd done to Horse Sense and my sister had apparently toughened his sensibilities. He says 'Go right ahead on with whatever you're gonna do, 'cause this sumbitch sure ain't worthy of no mercy in my book.' And no mercy was what I planned. I'd asked who his friends was and where they was goin, but he was one of those who'd spit in your eye quick as he'd answer a question.

First thing I done was strip that worthless scum to his bare hide. You know, there's somethin' about bein' naked that makes a man weak and kind'a vulnerable. At least for a white man who's accustomed to the wearin' of clothes. Now there was a half growed cottonwood tree in that coulee with a limb about fifteen feet in the air. It looked like it was strong enough to hold a man's weight so I got a rope, put him on his lame horse and gave this craven cowardly bag of guts every reason to believe that I was gonna hang him right there.

I got to give him credit. The sumbitch was tough. He still wouldn't talk. After a bit I jerked him off that horse and put a loop around his feet. Then I throwed that rope over the cottonwood limb and usin' my horse I dragged his naked ass up to where he was hangin' by his feet about head high off the ground. Now I don't care how strong a fella is, in a short time of hangin' like that he gets weak and can't do nothing but just hang. I knew it was painful and that it made your head all discombobulated because me'n them Injun boys used to do it to one another when we was kids...just for fun.

Then me and Caldwell begun to gather wood and brush. Had us a big pile stacked and ready. I reckon that cutthroat figured me for a civilized man 'cause he still didn't say nothin'. Pretty quick, we had us a good pile of wood and he'd had a chance to think things over a bit. Unfortunately, he was stickin' to his silence. Now the sun was hot and it wasn't long before the white hide on his bare ass cheeks began to show the effects of a real good sunburn. So I cut the latigo off of his saddle and gave his bare ass a few good whacks to give him a preview of things to come if'n he didn't start to talk.

The wind was real still and he just kind'a hung there wavin' his arms and pretty quick he didn't have the strength left to lift himself up in an attempt to relieve the weight on that rope, which was now cuttin' into his ankles somethin' awful.

So I leaned back against a big ol' rock, lit a cigarette and flipped the match right into that brush pile. Now I've seen some brave men, and I've seen some stupid men, but brave or stupid, no one wants to get burned. Even a grizzly bear will run from a fire."

"You mean you burned the man alive?"

"Not exactly, we didn't have to roast his worthless hide after all. He started singin' like Caruso before all his hair even got singed off. So I asked him real nice, 'If I put the fire out, will you tell us who your friends are?' Seems that he'd had a change of heart, 'cause he assured me that he would. I took my horse and pulled that smolderin' slime above the fire. Then we kicked the fire around a little so that he was just hangin' in the smoke. He was a might bit singed around the edges but he wasn't hurt too bad.

Seems that him and his partner, who was a quarter breed Apache goin' by the name of Galloway, had joined up with the gang in Denver. They was, in fact, as the sheriff had said, a bunch of Texicans who'd figured on some easy money in the Idaho gold fields. The one that had been gutted in Helena, as it turned out, had been partners with the one we'd captured. Now, he claimed his name was George somethin'. He also claimed that him and his partner, Galloway, had taken no part in the murders of Horse Sense and the teamsters, nor the rape and murder of my sister. I didn't believe a single word that came from betwixt his lyin' teeth. But he claimed that him and Galloway was kind'a outsiders with the group, which was why he'd got abandoned when his cayuse lamed up on him."

Tom lit a cigarette and looked at the match with a smile before he blew it out.

"I then explained that I had no time for sob stories. I wanted to know who the others were and where they was headed. So he says, 'The leader of the bunch is a beady-eyed skinny fella they call Thum.'

Now I'd been curious about that name since the sheriff had called it in Kellogg, so I asked, 'What in the hell does Thum mean?' To which he replies, 'Thum is a harelip. He can't say the word some.' Accordin' to George, when Thum asks for something he'll say 'give me 'thum.' I reckon the name had stuck from him gettin' teased as a kid. Except nobody was teasin' him in them days 'cause he'd killed near everyone that ever did…tease him that is. But George tells us that the skinny snake did let's his friends call him Thum. 'He's a scary sumbitch and meaner than Black Widow,' says George. So I ask him who this Wink Eye Eddie is. Well it turns out we got us a whole gaggle of misfits. This one's got some kind'a disorder that keeps him jerkin around and winkin' his left eye all the time. Ol' George said he didn't know how the guy could shoot 'cause he was jerkin' around all the time like he was havin' a fit.

He also told us that the other two with Thum's bunch was a young boy named Zeke, who wasn't but about fifteen and an older fella with a scar down his face. I then asked him where Thum was headed, and as I figured, they was headed for Hole-In-The-Wall. George told us that they knowed they was bein' dogged and that was why they'd put him afoot so as to move quicker. So much for honor among thieves…like I said. Our captured culprit reckoned that they'd be headed to Green River, a little town just to the south. They was goin' to pick up supplies and some whiskey. Then they was headin' on to Denver."

"What did you do with this 'George' after he talked?"

"Like I told you, this George fella was one hard-bitten, no good bastard and I wanted to kill him in the worst way. But Caldwell got soft on me so we threw some slack for him.

We rebuilt that fire and burned his saddle and his clothes so as to inconvenience him a bit, and then knowin' he'd be needin' some food, I shot that horse just in case he got hungry. And then, outta the goodness of my heart, I just turned that ol' boy loose."

Tom smiled and looked at Grant.

"I reckoned that the good Lord, in his infinite wisdom, would see to George. However, just in case he was busy, I built that fire big and smoky. I'd seen some sign, and I was pretty sure there was some Cheyenne workin' the area. If they missed that smoke and the buzzards that would soon be circling that horse carcass, them Injuns didn't deserve a good party.

So anyways, we said our goodbyes to George and took to trackin' the four others to Green River. We missed 'em by a day. The tracks led south headin' to Hole-In-The-Wall just like I'd figured. Now I'd wanted to head 'em off before they got to Hole-In-The-Wall, but they'd got the jump on us. We suspected that they'd likely stop in the only other little town down that way, which was a place called Burntfork. We knowed that they'd need to get some liquor before they headed back across the mountains.

Me'n Caldwell supplied ourselves sufficiently in Green River, so rather than catch 'em in Burtfork with them knowin' we was followin', we made straightaway for Gypsum down in Colorado. Now I was figurin' that they'd likely want to go through that little burg, which George had mentioned, to pay heed to the whore and the gamblin' on their way over to Denver. I also had it figured that without us trailin' they was more likely to relax and take 'er slow. Then we'd have a little edge on 'em.

Now me'n Caldwell skirted the trail so as to avoid them seein' our tracks and then we rode into Gypsum separately, actin' like we didn't know one another. Caldwell got a room at the boardin' house and I told the smith who ran the livery that I was short on money but I'd pay a bit to sleep in his loft. Well, of course, he was all for that and so we had the town pretty well covered no matter who came and went.

Sure enough, third day in Gypsum, here come the four we was seekin'. There was no doubt about it. The one with the scar was out front with the snake-faced Thum ridin' just behind. Then Wink Eye and the kid rode in the rear, side by side."

"Why had you chosen Gypsum?"

"It was far enough from Burntfork, which was the last place they could have provisioned, that it was near certain that they'd be stoppin' for eatin and drinkin' in Gypsum...at least to feed the stock before headin' to Denver. Gypsum, like ol' George had told us, was the only real town between Burntfork and Denver, and it was the only logical place they could go, if'n they was to be headin' to Denver, that is.

I was just bankin' that they was headin' that way. Had they not gone to Denver they'd have made 'er to Texas and we'd have been left holdin' an empty bag. But my gut was correct and sure enough they come ridin' right up to the livery, dismount and make an arrangement to livery and feed their stock. Caldwell had seen 'em come in and when they all headed to the boardin' house, he came to the livery so as to give me and him a chance to work out a strategy.

Now the first thing that occurs to ol' Caldwell, bein' a law abidin' fella and all, was the fact that there was no jurisdiction for takin' these men into custody for a crime which had been committed in Idaho. So I told Caldwell, as nice as I could, that I had no intentions for takin' 'em to Idaho or anywhere else for that matter. I made it clear that it was my aim too bury the lot of 'em all right there in Gypsum.

He was a bit squeamish about that idea so I told him that he should just stay clear of the doin's. After all, there was no reason for him to be goin' to jail in Colorado for a fight that was purely my own, or worse yet, gettin' himself kilt. I said to him, that it wasn't his sister raped and murdered and I figured it wasn't for him to risk life and limb over my fight. Especially not to get hanged over it. I thanked him for his help in the trackin' and his company on the trail and I told him I'd take care of the rest alone.

I guess it was somethin' in the way I said it that changed his mind. He said he'd do what he could. Had you been there you would'a understood just how good a friend ol' Caldwell really was. Keep in mind now that these were some dangerous and desperate men who had no scruples when it come to killin'. I wasn't sure about the kid who was with 'em, but

I had no doubt as to disreputable nature of those three grown men."

Grant shook his head.

"With the odds at two to one, I wouldn't have blamed Caldwell, or you for that matter, had you just gone home to Montana!" Grant said.

"I reckon that would have been the smart thing to do, alright. Hell's fire, I was one big raw nerve. But then men don't always do the smart thing, do they? As I recall you had yourself a real imprudent episode in the right recent past."

Grant smiled painfully as he looked up from his notebook.

"Point taken!" he said.

"Now we had to figure that any one of them no good bastards, includin' that kid, would'a kilt you for bottle'a whiskey. Facin' 'em to pay for what they'd done was gonna take a little thinkin'. One thing we had on our side was the element of surprise. We knew who they was and they didn't know us from twenty other drifters who were hangin' around that town. So Caldwell went over to the boardin' house to have dinner with 'em and see what he could learn as to their plans. I kept an eye out and waited to hear what he'd found. As soon as they'd finished dinner they all headed for the saloon, such as it was. The saloon wasn't no more than a shack with a couple'a tables and a burned out old whore who had a crib in the back.

Caldwell come right on over to the livery and told me, 'They're gonna spend the night and the scar face is gonna crib with the whore. Then they're gonna pull out real early and head to Denver.' So I figured if'n we was gonna do somethin', it was gonna have to be that night. They'd already been at the saloon for about an hour, so I'm figuring that we've got some edge, what with them swillin' rotgut and all.

Caldwell was gettin' ready to go to the saloon when Wink Eye comes outta the saloon and heads for the livery. The decision hit me so fast I don't even know where I came up with the idea. Right quick climbed up into the loft and hung a rope down about head high. I told Caldwell, 'Keep him busy, he knows you from the boardin' house. Just talk to him.'

Wink Eye comes into the livery and fortunately the fella that run the place had gone to eat. He sees Caldwell so he comes over and he's standin' there chitter chatterin' like they was old pals whilst I drop a loop right on his neck and jerk him off the floor. He was so surprised that he didn't even go for his gun. He just kept grabbin' at his neck and trying to get a breath. I was, all the while, wonderin' about what Sarah was thinkin' during her last few minutes. It happened so quick that the goofy lookin' brute never made a sound. Caldwell grabbed the gun out of his belt right quick and the odds was now three to two.

I climbed down from the loft and we put Wink Eye's worthless corpse in a stall and covered his carcass with hay. Laid him out right straight so's he'd stiffen nice for the coffin. Then we came up with another idea. I told Caldwell, 'I was judge, jury and executioner on this one, but I may still need a bit more help with the other three.'

He agreed, so we headed over to the saloon and I let Caldwell go in first. They knew him and I figured he wouldn't rouse no suspicion. Our plan was to have him say howdy to me when I came in. That way they'd figure him and me was acquainted. We figured it'd give us a chance to get 'em comfortable a little before we made our play.

Before we went to the saloon, we'd saddled and packed our critters figurin' that things might get a little unpleasant around that town when we started killin' these boys. We wanted to make a quick exit and ride hell bent for Montana.

So I walk in the door and look around. There's maybe ten or twelve men in the place. Caldwell says, 'Well, Sam...how the hell are you. I haven't seen you since we was in Denver,' to which the harelip asks me, 'You been down to Denver?' and I come back with 'Yep, and I think I might go back, too. It's a great town,' to which Thum says, 'They have thum good whoor houthes in Denver. I want thum good puthy. I don't want none of that ol' scab in this cwib.'

I tell him he's never gonna find any better than in Denver and then I offer to buy him a drink. Meanwhile, the big bastard with the scar is eyein' me up and down while he's contemplatin' the old toothless half-breed whore sittin' in the corner. I don't know what put the burr under his saddle but he looks me in the eye and says, 'Well, I'm gonna have a little of what's right here.' He started to walk away and then he looks at me again and says, 'What's your favorite place there in Denver anyway?'

I'd already told Caldwell to follow my play, and I figured that there was a test contained in that ugly bastard's question...and I don't mean no test for the purpose of gradin'...if'n you know what I mean. I figured that the time had come.

I jerked that Schofield and put one center of his chest. Of course, he was only four feet away so it wasn't really a great shot. My second shot missed snake face as he ducked behind the end of the bar, so I dropped and rolled as close to the bar as I could since it was the only cover available.

Men was runnin' out of that place and divin' under any available cover. Caldwell had tipped a table and jumped behind it, but before he could get off a shot, Thum put a forty-four right through that table top. That bullet hit Caldwell in the ribs right at his liver. Of course, I didn't know that at the time.

I looked amidst the chaos and saw the youngster was reachin' for his iron and I put a bullet right through his hips sideways, which sent him spinnin' to the floor and pretty much took the fight outta him. I always figured that even if he didn't die he was never much of a man after that hunk of forty-five lead went through his manly workin' parts.

In the meanwhile, ol' Thum was stickin' his Colt around the bar and firin' blind just as fast as he could. Unfortunately, he wouldn't stick his head out so as to give me a shot. Now Thum might'a been a pretty good criminal but he wasn't much of a mathematician."

Grant looked at Tom with a quizzical shrug.

"You see, I'd fired three. One had killed Scarface and the other had taken the hips out from under the boy. My second shot had missed Thum but I still had three more. All the while, I had been countin' the shots that little rat faced rapist behind the end of the bar had been shootin'. I figured he'd fired five and was layin' there with only one left in his gun. That is if my mathematics was servin' me correctly.

Now I didn't know but what he didn't have a second gun, but I was pretty sure he wasn't reloadin' 'cause I hadn't heard nothin' but that one gun bein' cocked and there wasn't no empty brass casin's hittin' the floor. I reckon he was confident in that one shot.

Now, when I rolled up against that bar, much to my dismay, I had rolled right into the spittoon…which spilled…naturally! But somehow, when you're choice is a bullet in brisket or rollin' in tobacco spit, you just don't seem to mind gettin' a bit befouled. I grabbed the spittoon in my free hand and wiggled myself around to where I could toss it over behind another table, which had got turned over in the fracas when the bystanders exited the premises. I tossed that spittoon just high enough in the air that when it hit the floor, it really made a hell of a noise. That rat faced murderin' son-of-a bitch let go his last bullet at the sound of that clatter.

I didn't wait to see if'n he had another gun or anything else for that matter. I jumped to my feet and run to the end of the bar. Lookin' that murderin' bag of shit right in his beady eyes I didn't give him time to beg. I put a hole in his forehead that must'a took that undertaker a couple'a ounces of putty to fill.

Fortunately for me, them boys didn't have no friends in that town. So no one seemed upset. Unfortunately for me, I lost one'a mine. Caldwell died where he'd been shot. I went and paid the local undertaker to care for Caldwell and see to his buryin'.

Then I went and explained the reason for killin' those men to the local marshal. As it turned out, that marshal wasn't no more than a part-time local drunk who'd had the blacksmith make him a badge from the end of a tin can. He reckoned, based on my story, that the killin's was for a good cause and decided not to interfere with my leavin' town.

The undertaker asked what should be done with the three miscreants and if'n I was gonna pay to see to 'em. I told him he could put 'em out for the buzzards. Then I got on my horse and rode north."

"I suppose that's when Romulus and Remus came to live with you?"

"They was about half growed by then and they both took it hard. They'd loved their mama and they'd loved ol' Horse Sense too. We all loved Horse Sense, but life went on. They come to live with us, and Dannie and Koko took good care of 'em. They both growed up to be real good men. They each take life for what it gives 'em. You'll never hear either of those men complainin' about nothin'. I'm real proud of both 'em and I love 'em like they was my sons.

I lost a real friend when Caldwell got himself kilt in Gypsum. I felt real bad about it. It wasn't his fight but he stuck 'er out and it cost him dearly. But like I said, life goes on.

Just remember when you write this here story that those were tough times and there was a lotta bad men runnin' around this country. Whenever I hear someone talk about justice I always think about little sister and Horse Sense. I suppose that story will offend the sensibilities of the Eastern folk, but Horse Sense and little sister would have had no justice had it not been for me'n Caldwell. And Caldwell gave everything he had to see that justice served. Maybe that's why you Easterners aren't always thought of in the highest regard when justice is discussed in places like Montana. I think you civilized folks like to call that kind of justice 'vigilantism.'"

Grant looked up from his notes as Dixie opened the door.

"Have you two been gabbing all day?" Dixie said.

"I'm filling volumes with stories that don't sound anything like Tom Mix. Your Uncle Tom is quite an incredible man."

"Well, you boys have fun...I'm going to go help Koko fix dinner."

Dixie closed the door behind her.

"Do you really think it's possible for me to go on a hunting trip with you next month?" Grant asked.

"This is almost next month," Tom replied. "When do you have to get back to Saint Louis?"

"Considering that I am on unpaid leave, I don't really have a time schedule."

"I'll tell you what, if you really want to hunt some deer and elk I'll even let you use that Four-oh-five Winchester. If it was good enough for the President of the United States I reckon it ought'a be good enough for you."

"Oh, I wouldn't want to use that rifle. That was a gift to you. Perhaps I could go buy a rifle to use."

"Don't be foolish. That rifle needs a little exercise. I would consider it a great honor if'n you was to use it...and one other thing..."

Tom walked to the gun cabinet. Removing a short barreled Smith and Wesson revolver, he opened the cylinder and handed the empty gun to Grant.

"I want you to wear this Lemon Squeezer wherever you go until you get on the train to go back to Saint Louis or until this Buck business is finished."

"I thought Buck had gone," Grant asked.

"He's gone, but not forgotten. I can tell you sure enough, he'll be around...and wherever he is there is gonna be trouble. I suspect that about now, in his mind, you are the cause of every bad thing ever happened to him. So do me a favor and wear this all the time. I hope you don't need it, but if'n you do, I'll feel a whole lot better if I know you got it.

"Why do you call it a Lemon Squeezer?"

"It's the safety.

Tom took the gun from Grant's hand and held it by the cylinder. He depressed the movable bar on at the back of the pistol grip with his thumb.

"This here is a real safe gun. That's why I gave it to you. It's pretty much idiot proof...no offense intended."

Tom pointed the gun out the window and squeezed the trigger on an empty chamber.

"See, it won't fire unless you push this bar with the palm of your hand while you pull the trigger. She don't even have a hammer to cock. You gotta squeeze the trigger and the grip or she won't go. So they called it a Lemon Squeezer."

Handing the revolver to Grant, he said, "You give it a try. You'll see what I mean."

Grant took the gun and squeezed the trigger of the unloaded revolver several times to get a sense of what Tom was explaining.

"If you think it is a good idea, I will carry it, but I must admit that it makes me very uncomfortable."

"Don't worry, boy, if you carry one long enough it becomes a part of you."

"Well, alright then…and I will altogether be looking forward to our hunting trip. It sounds very exciting."

"Good enough then. We'll show you some real wild country. But first we got to go over to Kalispell for the Cattleman's Ball. Give me a chance to give that ol' Widow Barnaby a whirl."

"How far is it to Kalispell?" Grant asked.

"On the other side of the Divide. Takes a bit to get there, but I have a lot of old friends over there, and the Cattleman's Ball is an excuse to get together once a year for a little socializin'."

"Are we driving over in your car?"

"No, sir, we'll be takin' the train. Then on the way back we'll get off the train in a little town just outside of that new Glacier Park. We're gonna be huntin' up in that country along the Two Medicine River, south of the park…just this side of the Divide. We'll take all our clothes and huntin' possibles with us and let Nick bring the women back to Fort Benton and The Buffalo Rock."

"Won't Nick be going on the hunt?"

"No. I don't reckon he will. You see, Nick is one helluva businessman, just like his grandpa. But he wasn't ever too keen about huntin' and fishin' and campin' and such. I'd take him along when he was a pup, but he never took a fancy to it. He took more after his mama's side. They was business people and city folks as far back as she knew. Much as I tried to pass on a love of the wild land and the open spaces, Little Nicky never could get past viewin' the entire operation with an eye on the business side. There's a lot of myself in Nicky, and I'm proud of ever bit of that. But he's a lot of his mama too…and so I don't reckon he'll be goin' hunting with us. It just ain't in him."

Grant appeared ready to speak, then hesitated.

"Yes, sir?" Tom said, looking at Grant. "You was gonna say

somethin'?"

"As I told you, I have never fired a gun."

"I'll tell you what let's do," Tom said. "How about the next day or so, you and me go out to the coulees and I'll teach you to shoot. How would you like that?"

"I would be most honored to learn the art of shooting from a marksman like yourself."

Dixie opened the door.

"Gentleman, would you care to join us...dinner is served."

29

The shrill blast of the locomotive's whistle sent an involuntary thrill down Grant's spine. It seemed a lifetime since he'd stepped down on this very spot. He watched a new group of homesteaders as they unloaded the last of the wagons and household goods from the freight car. Perhaps Tom was right. Perhaps the hills and prairie would soon be covered with homesteads. The land seemed so vast, but then Tom could speak of times within his memory when he could ride for days without encountering a fence. Things were changing quickly.

"All aboard!" the conductor shouted.

Nick put his hand on the conductor's shoulder.

"Can you hold 'er just a minute Hank? That's dad comin' up the hill. We'll be ready in a wink," Nick said.

Elmer parked Tom's Ford next to the platform.

Nick and Grant ran to assist with the mountainous pile of hatboxes and suitcases Elmer was hurriedly removing from Tom's car. Grant tipped his hat as he ran past a well-dressed woman whom Tom was helping from the back seat of the Ford.

The lady went to board the train while Tom helped with the luggage.

"We thought you were going to miss the train, Dad," Nick said.

"Kate's bringing accoutrement enough for a bevy," Tom grumbled under his breath.

The four men pitched boxes and cases to the trainman who was loading the baggage car.

"Easy, Grandpa," Nick said. "Those veins are gonna pop right outta your neck. Go ahead and get on board, we'll finish up and be right there."

Tom crossed the platform, stopping at the steps of the coach.

"Sorry...we got held up a little, Hank," he said to the conductor.

"Don't give it another thought, Mr. Thomas," the conductor said with a smile. "You folks have a nice trip."

Grant again found himself somewhat in awe of the deferential treatment Tom received. Trains, he thought, were never delayed...not for anyone...except his new friend Tornado Tom.

Elmer tossed the last of the cases into the baggage car as Grant ran with Nick to clamber up the steps onto the slowly moving train. When he entered the car, he was stunned to find that Tom's party was not traveling in a passenger car but rather in an elegantly outfitted Pullman.

"Come on over here and meet Mrs. Barnaby," he heard Tom say from the other end of the car.

Tom was seated on a comfortable sofa with the lady Grant had seen alighting from Tom's car.

"Grant Collins, I'd like you to meet one of the most beautiful women in the entire state of Montana, Mrs. Katherine Barnaby," Tom said.

"Mr. Collins. I've heard so much about you. It is a pleasure to, at last, make your acquaintance," Mrs. Barnaby said.

"Likewise, I'm sure, Mrs. Barnaby. And I have heard much about you...and please, call me Grant," he said, extending his hand.

Mrs. Barnaby took Grant's hand, holding it firmly as she studied his face.

"And you may call me Katherine," she replied. "I think I'm going to like you."

As Grant took a seat at the table with Nick, a porter appeared and asked, "Would you ladies and gentlemen care for some refreshment?"

"The Glenlivet with a water back for me and a sherry for the lady," Tom said.

Nick looked at Phoebe and Dixie who were seated on another sofa.

"Would you girls care for a refreshment?" he said.

"Tea," the two women said simultaneously.

"And tea for me also," Grant said.

"Hot or cold?" the porter asked, looking first at the ladies and then Grant.

"On ice...sweet, would be fine," Dixie replied.

Phoebe nodded her head.

"The same will be fine for me," Grant said.

Grant then turned to Katherine Barnaby.

"I understand you've been traveling in the East. How was your trip?"

"It was splendid," she replied, placing her hand on Tom's. "Except for the heat and humidity. I suppose I have become accustomed to this Western climate, and the air of Boston just seems to cling to one like a wet Turkish towel. I understand you are originally from Baltimore. I'm sure you understand what I mean."

"I've only been in Montana a short while, but I do agree. This summer climate with warm days and cool nights is quite agreeable. I have never slept so well."

"I won't bore you with stories of my beautiful daughter and my wonderful grandchildren," Katherine Barnaby said. "I would rather hear about your project. Are you really planning to write about this old scalawag?"

"Yes ma'am. That is my intention. I still have some holes to fill, but we are making significant progress on Tom's biography. My editor recently sent an inquiry as to my anticipated return to Saint Louis. I am ignoring it temporarily. Frankly, I have never enjoyed myself so much as I have these past few months."

The porter returned with the drinks. Dixie came to the table and sat beside Grant.

"He can't leave too quickly, he's been a considerable help to me. I'm taking advantage of his Columbia education to improve my writing," Dixie said.

"How simply marvelous. So the two of you share a commonality."

"Kindred spirits is the way I've described it in a poem," Dixie said.

"She is actually quite talented," Grant said, beaming as he turned to look at Dixie. "I am encouraging her to send an anthology to some of the publishing houses."

Mrs. Barnaby looked at the two of them and then at Tom.

"Mr. Thomas, I believe we have the flower of American literature right here in our midst. How absolutely wonderful! The best of my wishes will be with the both of you and your futures in a wonderful enterprise," Mrs. Barnaby said.

Grant took a sip of tea and looked at Tom.

"In fact, I was hoping that Tom could tell us about his relationship with President Roosevelt and his trip to Cuba while we have some hours to enjoy."

Katherine Barnaby turned to Tom and with a quizzical look.

"Do tell us about Cuba. In all these years you have never mentioned it to me. I had supposed that you just didn't want to talk about it."

"Goin' to Cuba was about the dumbest thing I ever done. First of all...as much as I hate to admit such a thing, I was gettin' too damned old for that sort'a foolishness. In addition to that, I never liked bein' in the army in the first place...and not only that, I had a young family that needed carin' for and I had plenty of responsibilities for my own business right here in Montana. Hell, Nick was still a young fella, and Susanna and Derrick was no more than tykes."

Tom looked around at the group.

"You seen that photograph of me and Roosevelt with the bear. That one in my office?"

Each of them acknowledged with a nod having seen the photo.

"It was on that very trip when I kilt that grizzly bear that Teedie talked me into that foolishness. He'd come up to Montana for a bit of huntin' in the fall of ninety-seven. He was some kind'a assistant to the Secretary of Navy, as I recall. Told me straight out that he was sure there was trouble'a brewin' with the Spaniards. He said there were some people in the government who thought we ought'a just go take Cuba and tell Spain where to go. Many of them politicians was considerin' it to be a strategic necessity. But then, I guess, there was those that just wanted to leave well enough alone. I personally didn't give it one helluva lotta thought. Cuba was a long way from Montana and I had a lot to do right here."

Tom took a sip from his glass.

"Teedie says to me, while we're sittin' around the campfire one evening, that if'n there was to be a war, he's gonna get together a bunch of volunteers. Said he was gonna call 'em the Rough Riders. Kind'a like what ol' Cody had done with his Wild West Show. Then he tells me that he's gonna need men like me to field such an outfit and asks would I come along if he was to do it."

Tom looked around, a sheepish expression painting his face.

"Now ol' Teedie didn't drink...but I did...and it was late of an evening. I'd poured down just about enough of the Ol' Blabbermouth to agree to anything. Besides which, whether ya liked ol' Roosevelt as a president or ya didn't, I'll tell you this, the little fella had one helluva persuasive personality. I swear that fast talkin' little sharpie could'a sold coconuts to them Hawaiians. Here I was an oil millionaire agreein' to go fight a war I didn't even care a damned thing about."

"Is it your belief that the government was preparing for the war with Spain before the Maine was sunk?" Grant asked.

"No doubt in my mind. Hell, Roosevelt was a high muckety-muck in the Navy. I guess if anyone would'a knowed, it would'a been him. He sure as hell convinced me."

Mrs. Barnaby raised an eyebrow and looked obliquely at Tom.

"You mean to tell us that you abandoned your wife and a young family on a drunken promise to your hunting pal?" No wonder you never told me this story."

Tom fidgeted for an uncomfortable moment. He took another sip from his glass and cleared his throat, ignoring Katherine's question.

"So comes the early spring of ninety-eight and damned if the Battleship Maine don't blow up right in Havana harbor. Now I won't say for sure that the Spaniards blew it up. If'n they did, it was near about as dumb a thing for them to do as it was for me to join the army. But the newspapers was beatin' the war drums by that time and bein' a man of my word I headed south to join up with ol' Teedie's Rough Riders. Compared to most, I was an old man, but I was still in pretty good shape and I could keep up with the younger boys. Even so, they all called me 'Pop.' That tweaked me just about as much as anything."

"How old were you, Uncle Tom?" Dixie asked.

"I reckon I was in my fifties at the time. Because of my age and former military experience they made me a Sergeant, thank God. At least I didn't have to put up with too much lip from those whipper snappers. From March until June we was engaged in the same ol' military training...hup, two, three, four...that I hated when I'd been in both the armies back in the War of the Rebellion. Drill and shoot, clean your gun, take care of your horse and drill and shoot some more. Exceptin' that I was the Sergeant doin' the drillin'."

Tom smiled, looking at Katherine.

"You're right darlin'. Sometimes it just don't pay to be a man of your word."

"Where were you doing all of this drilling and shooting?" Katherine asked.

"We were down in Arizona, which is where a goodly number of the Rough Riders was from. Arizona, New Mexico and Texas mostly.

I swear, that bunch of brush poppin' Texicans in our outfit was just as full of meadow muffins as them so-called cowpunchers I'd met back in the eighties when they was driving cows up from Texas to Montana for the free range. But at least they was better at soldering than they had been at cowboyin'."

"You mentioned April until June. Where did you go then?" Grant asked.

"They shipped us by train, horses and all down to Florida for the crossin' over to Cuba on ships. Have you ever been to Florida?"

Grant shook his head negatively.

"It is hotter than the hubs of runaway hell. And Cuba was even worse. Kate here was talkin' about hot and humid in Boston. Hell's bells, you ain't never seen hot and humid! Remember me tellin' you about roastin' that murderin' little cutthroat to get some information out of him?"

Grant nodded.

"Well, that bastard had a picnic in the shade compared to the soldiers in those uniforms...in the heat of the tropics no less. Shit oh dear, I don't think I'd ever been so miserable. Every man had rashes on their skin and there were critters that were rippin' off chunks of your hide faster than you could swat 'em. When we finally got to the fighting in Cuba you couldn't tell the buzz of the bullets from the buzz of the bugs. And I still ain't sure which was worse."

"What's this about roasting a man?" Dixie asked.

Tom looked at his niece and then at Mrs. Barnaby.

"That's a story for another time. You can read about it in Grant's book."

"Did you actually charge up San Juan Hill with Mr. Roosevelt?" Katherine Barnaby asked.

"You might say that, if'n ya take into account Teedie's version of the events. But as I recall, we was pinned down by the Spaniards at a place called Kettle Hill...or more accurately Kettle Heights. Now, as I've told you, ol' Roosevelt had a pretty high opinion of himself, kind'a in the tradition of Custer. He'd even brung along a historian and some reporters to ensure that his name got into the newspapers as often as possible back home.

Now, I ain't saying this to disparage ol' Teedie in any way. His personal courage was beyond question, and he was sure enough in the thick of it when the battle occurred, but just like Buffalo Bill Cody and in some ways like Custer and Hickock; he just had a sense of how to make himself famous.

When we got back from Cuba, I went out to celebrate with some of the officers and the newspaper fellas. One of those news hawks was jokin' around and said somethin' I recall to this day. He says, 'Roosevelt had never gone to a wedding where he hadn't wanted to be the bride, and he'd never been to a funeral where he hadn't wished he was the corpse.' Now remember, I loved the ol' boy like a brother, but damned if that wasn't the truth. He was, after all, a politician."

"Why weren't you an officer? You would certainly seem to have been qualified. And your pal was the organizer of this regiment as I understand," Katherine Barnaby said.

"I had no desire to be an officer. Teedie offered, but I turned that down. The majority of the officers in the Rough Riders was just like all the other army outfits. They was mostly well educated, some even from West Point and mostly upper crust rich boys. Not that I wasn't a rich boy, myself, but thank God I decided to stay a Sergeant. Before we left for Cuba, all of Teedie's officers swore an oath and gave a toast. 'May the war last until we are all dead, wounded or promoted.'

Like I've said, I'd take a drink to damned near anything, but there was no way you would'a caught me drinkin' to that foolishness.

But ol' Teedie was a real leader. He was one'a them rare military fellas who leads from the front. Tough as whang leather and I never saw him when he looked scared. I am sure he was puttin' on the dog for his troops but it still takes a special kind."

The porter entered the car carrying a tray of fresh drinks. Picking up the glasses, whether empty or not.

"Sorry to interrupt, but can I get you ladies and gentlemen anything else?"

There was no response. As the porter turned to leave he pointed to a tasseled cord hanging from the ceiling.

"If ya'll needs anything at all, just pull that," he said.

Tom pointed out the window and said, "Dixie, Grant. You haven't seen this country before. We're starting the climb up to the Divide. You can see how the country is starting to have more trees and it'll be real steep goin' here pretty quick."

"Is this where you go hunting?" Dixie asked.

"That's still a while yet. Up past Browning. There's a little whistle stop called East Glacier. Me'n Grant will get off there on the way back.

So, anyway, I guess I better get to this San Juan Hill business. We had a couple of problems in fighting that battle at Kettle Hill. Worst of all was that the Spaniards had the high ground with a fine array of artillery such as French seventy-fives lookin' down our throats. Our so-called leaders had sort'a disremembered to bring our artillery support, so before we even got to goin', we was pinned down. The Spaniards had also made good use of barbed wire strung low to the ground so as to trip us when we'd get up to move from place to place. Not only that, the bugs and the heat was unbearable and half the men was sick with typhoid or dysentery or cholera or malaria. Ain't nothin' worse than having a sour stomach and messin' your britches while some sumbitch is shootin' at you.

The army had started using a rifle called the Krag-Jorgensen. It was some fancy foreign made thing, Swedish or some such, with a side load flop-open box for a magazine. To say the least, I didn't like it. Shot a smokeless load but the rifle wasn't near as good as the Mausers, which the Spanish was usin'. When you loaded that Krag, that flop-down door would get full'a dirt and then she wouldn't shoot at all till you'd get 'er cleaned out.

Those Spaniards was sittin' up in the hills with rifles that could shoot the balls of'n a horse fly at four hunderd yards and we couldn't even see 'em. Pardon the vulgarity ladies but we're talking about a war here. Anyway, they were pickin' us off one at a time. Since the Spaniards was shootin' smokeless powder, we had no idea as to where they was shootin' from or where to shoot back."

Tom took a sip from the fresh drink and lit a cigarette.

"For some reason, the sumbitch in charge, I believe he was a General named Sumner, wasn't givin' no orders for anyone to move. So there we was, like gobblers at the turkey shoot just waitin' for someone to do somethin'.

Now, I told you that these young officers considered that they had to demonstrate real bravery, bein' as how we was all just volunteers you see. Most of them officers, being real military, I reckon they figured they'd get some glory at the first opportunity. So they was displayin' gallantry that, to my estimation, was way above and beyond the call of duty. In fact, it was nothin' but foolhardy. I remember this one Captain. This was too bad 'cause he was a good pal of ol' Teedie's and they hung out together quite a bit. There he was, strollin' along the line where me and the men was pinned down.

He was acting as if he was directin' men on the shootin' range or somethin'. He would walk along with the bullets whizzin' past and talk to the men, who were layin' face down in the dirt, tryin' to be as small as possible. He was actin' like there was nothin' to worry about. He come by me and I said 'Captain, I don't wish to sound cowardly but one'a them Spaniards is gonna get the range on you sooner than later and blow you right outta your boots.'

He walked about ten feet further down the line and then calmly lit himself a cigarette. He blowed out the smoke and then he looked back at me, and here he comes walking back to where I was making an imprint of my belly button in the dirt. He looked down at me and said, 'Sergeant, there isn't the Spanish bullet made that can kill me.' He had that same kind'a fancy Eastern accent that you got."

Tom looked at Katherine Barnaby and grinned.

"I have an accent?" she said, indignantly.

"Yeah, ya do...and he had one somethin' similar...but anyway, he took another big draw on that cigarette and turned to look up the hill. Just about then a gapin' red hole appeared in the back of his head. I swear that the smoke came outta that hole and then he fell over dead. He never knew what hit him."

"What a horrible story," Dixie said. "I'm not sure I want to hear any more."

"My word, O. F., that is quite macabre," Mrs. Barnaby agreed.

"O. F.?" Grant asked, looking at Mrs. Barnaby.

"Oscar Fineas. That's his name. Didn't he tell you that?" Mrs. Barnaby said.

"And I didn't tell you for a reason. She's the only one who calls me that! Keep that in mind," Tom said.

A huge smile covered Grant's face.

"Pseudonym duly noted, Tom. Now where was Roosevelt when his friend was shot?" Grant asked.

"He was walkin' the line himself. And sendin' messengers tryin' to get one'a them armchair generals to either lead, follow or get the hell outta the way. I figured that if the boys with the stars wasn't gonna help to push or pull, they ought to at least not drag their feet. Finally, some star wearin' sumbitch come by and said somethin' to Roosevelt, and ol' Teedie jumped on his horse and the race was on."

"Now this was or wasn't San Juan Hill?" Mrs. Barnaby asked.

"Like I said, it was actually a place called Kettle Heights. So the first thing that happened was that the fella carryin' the flag jumped up and got himself shot. I'll never know why I did this, but like a damned fool, I picked up that flag and start hollerin' for the dismounted cavalry to dress down the line. When they was on their feet and movin with the flag, I started movin' up the hill behind the bunch ahead of us. That was the bunch that was actually with Roosevelt.

I looked over and we had a group of Buffalo Soldiers on our right flank. They was takin' some really brutal fire from the edges of the jungle."

"You mean Negro soldiers?" Mrs. Barnaby asked.

"That's the ones."

Tom stood to stretch his legs.

"I had no idea that there were any Negroes in Cuba with Roosevelt," she said.

"They wasn't actually with Roosevelt, Kate. They were with another outfit. It just turned out that they was assigned to our right flank. Poor bastards took one helluva shellackin' too. I hadn't really thought much about it, but I guess they did sort'a get written right out of the history of that famous charge. Come to think about it, I ain't never seen any mention of them boys in anything I've read about the history of that battle. Fact is that them Buffalo Soldiers marched side by side with us and got to the top of the hill the same time we did."

"I declare," Mrs. Barnaby said. "I never saw a word about that in the papers."

"I reckon that being left outta the newspaper story ain't the worst that's happened to those folks since the end of the Great War of the Rebellion...and before."

"So you picked up the flag and charged up the hill?" Dixie said.

"Oh, yeah! Your Uncle Tom was a real unwillin' hero that day. But anyway, we had some units with Gatling Guns and they finally got themselves into position to spray the jungle edges, which cut the sniper fire in a hurry. Them Forty-Five-Seventy bullets were big and heavy and they'd cut right through the jungle. Pretty quick we'd pushed our way to the top of that hill and the Spaniards skedaddled.

When we finally got to the top, I looked at that flag I was totin' and wondered what in the name of sweet Jesus was I doin'. That thing had been shot to pieces. I lit up a cigarette and stood there ponderin' what had just happened, tryin' to make some sense of it in my own mind.

I looked back down the hill and there was a whole lotta soldiers, black and white layin' on that hill behind us. I wondered who got to choose which one lived and which one died. There wasn't no sense to be made of it.

I was lookin' at the men strewn on the hillside when a colored Sergeant who was checking his Buffalo Soldiers for casualties asked me somethin' and I turned to answer him. When he stopped, he stepped right in front of a bullet that I believe was intended for my dumb ass, seeing as how I was holdin' that flag and all. It was just one'a them real inequitable moments in life. That black Sergeant got a cross in Cuba and I got a hero badge from the future President."

"I can remember when you got home. You got back in the fall. Right?" Nick asked. "I remember when you left to go to Cuba, but I have never heard this story either. You've never talked about this. Was that battle close to the end of the war?"

"It wasn't the end. There was a few more battles, more like skirmishes. But I was lucky...never got a scratch. However, I did end up with one helluva case of malaria. I was scared to death I was gonna pass it to you, or Dancin' Fawn, or your brother and sister when I got home. Fortunately, they was using quinine by then and I finally got shed of it. Best of all, none of you got it when I came back."

"Why didn't you ever tell me this before?" Nick asked.

A smile lit Tom's face.

"Because it was in the 'olden days' and I didn't reckon you'd be interested."

Nick smiled at his father and then a serious look crossed his face.

"I do remember when you were gone. We were all worried about you, but I was real proud. I'd just started learnin' the ranchin' business. It was a big responsibility. Rom and Remus helped get me through that, though. Tellin' the other men that my dad was in the army with the Rough Riders; I got a lot of bang for that bullet. Got me some free drinks I reckon. You never found out about."

The porter quietly entered the car and waited for a break in the conversation.

"We'll be stopping in Browning, if you'd care to stretch your legs. About fifteen minutes is what they tell me."

The train slowed and then came to a jolting halt accompanied by the sound of grinding metal brakes.

Tom, Nick and Grant stepped out of the car to get some air. Grant looked around at the shacks and hovels of Browning. Several inebriated men were sitting on the platform and Tom could read the look of disgust on Grant's face.

"Yep, drunken Injuns. But they wasn't always like that. Was a time when their grand pappies owned this country. Now, all they got is worthless ground with no buffalo and too much cheap whiskey. But they're tame, and that makes the government happy. They only kill each other now, mostly after a drunken fight over nothin."

"I suppose they have nothing to motivate them," Grant said.

"Hopelessness. That's all they got. That's all we give 'em." Tom said.

"Let's get back on board. Looks like he's ready to go," Nick said.

"All aboard," the conductor shouted.

The train pulled out of Browning and began the ascent to the Continental Divide.

"Tom, is this your rail car?" Grant asked.

"Belongs to a friend of mine in Kalispell. He sent it over to get us,"

Tom answered. "Conrad Conlon. You can just call him C. C. Everyone does...partly because that's his initials and partly because that's what he drinks."

"C. C., is that a drink?" Dixie asked.

"Canadian Club. It's some mighty fine whiskey and it's only a few miles to Canada from Kalispell. Them Canucks ain't got no prohibition so it's perfectly legal over there. All you gotta do is to sneak some back across the border."

"Are we staying with Mr. Conlon?" Dixie asked.

"We are, and while we live in the luxury of C. C.'s fine domicile, Nick and your beau are gonna bunk in this here Pullman on the siding in Kalispell."

"Have you known Mr. Conlon long?" Dixie asked.

"Yes ma'am. Me and ol' C. C. go back a long way. He stayed in Fort Benton when he first come out to this country. He come by steamer. Hell, that's been forty maybe forty-five years I reckon. Then he came to Kalispell and built himself some ranchin' and lumber and bankin' sort'a things. Made a pile of money. Me and him have some holdings together and we've shared some tough times too...goin' way back to the freightin' days. He got to know Teedie. The three of us used to go huntin'."

"Was Conrad along on this ill-considered adventure to Cuba with your friend, Mr. Roosevelt?" Katherine Barnaby asked.

"No ma'am. C. C. was lucky enough that he wasn't on that huntin' trip with Teedie. He managed to talk himself out of that boat ride to Cuba. He wasn't never much of what you would'a called a Rough Rider anyway. His interests was more toward the makin' of money and runnin' of businesses and such. He only rode a horse to get from place to place when there wasn't no other transport available."

"I'll be looking forward to meeting your friend C. C. He must have been an interesting person to maintain your friendship all these years," Grant said.

"Ol' C. C. is a one-of-a-kind character," Tom said.

Grant and Dixie moved to a sofa at the far end of the car and spoke softly as they sat watching the scenery change from the coulee country of the prairie to snow capped peaks and sheer bluffs with cascading water falls. Ancient glaciers, lit by the midday sun, shown brightly through breaks in the trees and mountains. An occasional deer or elk could be seen scurrying into the forest, fleeing the noise of the laboring locomotive. The foliage was changing from grass and brush into conifer forests with stands of aspen and birch. The train whistle blew a warning as they approached a small settlement.

Tom walked to where Grant and Dixie were sitting.

"I reckon we ain't stoppin' in East Glacier. Like I told you, it's just a whistle stop. They don't stop here without someone wants on or off…or either they have some freight. But this is where we'll be takin' our leave on the trip home. Off on the left is the Two Medicine River country where we'll be goin' to hunt."

They watched a small cluster of buildings pass the window of the Pullman car as Tom returned to sit beside Katherine Barnaby.

"How unfortunate that Caleb had clients. It would have been nice had he and Susanna been able to come along. They are good company," Grant said.

Dixie rolled her eyes and looked over her shoulder to see if anyone was paying attention.

"They could have come had Susanna wanted."

"Why wouldn't she want to come?" Grant asked. "It is my understanding that this is the major social gathering of the year."

Dixie, again, rolled her eyes.

"Her mother was an Indian," she whispered into Grant's ear.

Grant sat in stunned silence as the malignant essence of Dixie's words enveloped him.

"But she's Tom's daughter," he said. "That hasn't seemed a problem since I've been here."

He stared at Dixie, still unwilling to grasp the nuance.

"Mr. Conlon was married to a Sioux woman. He has a half-breed son of his own."

"Then what earthly difference would it have made for Susanna and Caleb to have come along?" Grant asked.

"She and Caleb came here with Uncle Tom a couple of years ago. Apparently, she was not made to feel welcome and neither was Caleb. I understand that 'C. C.' does not even allow his own son to come into his house," Dixie whispered. "It broke my heart when she told me the story but that is the way it is and she has decided to accept the reality."

Grant felt his face turn warm in anger. He was beginning to dislike a man whom he had yet to meet. For the first time in his life, he was witnessing the subtle cruelty of social injustice through the eyes of people whom he knew and cared about.

Seeing his distress, Dixie took his hand.

"Susanna deals with it, you will have to do the same. It is just the way it is."

"Why would your uncle tolerate such treatment of his own child?"

"You may have noticed that Uncle Tom is a pragmatist to the end. There was no real affront to Caleb or Susanna. It was just a feeling of being slighted. So he wasn't about to have a shootout with his old friend. Besides, the attitude is pervasive. You may recall your own discomfort on the first night you were here?"

Grant's cheeks turned pink again.

"That was a very embarrassing moment. I was totally at a loss. I forgot to thank you for coming to my rescue."

"Well, keep that in mind during the next few days. As Uncle Tom would say, 'Life just ain't fair.' He is absolutely correct, but he does the best he can with life. I suppose that we need to do the same."

The porter entered the Pullman car.

"We'll be in Kalispell in about fifteen minutes. Can I get anything for ya'll before we get in?" he asked.

"No, thank you," Tom said looking at each of the others for any request. "I think we're fine. Hope we see you on the return."

Tom stood and dropped a ten dollar gold piece into the breast pocket of the porter's jacket.

A Packard limousine awaited Tom's party at the platform adjacent to a private siding.

"This is where C. C. maintains this rollin' mansion when it ain't on the road," Tom said.

Tom took Katherine Barnaby's hand and walked her to the limousine.

The uncomfortably liveried young driver opened the rear doors and stood at attention.

"Good afternoon, Mr. Thomas. I hope you and your folks had a nice trip over. Don't worry about that luggage. I'll see to it that it gets to your rooms."

"Thank you, Aaron. How's life treatin' you these days?" Tom said.

"Just fine, sir, never better," the chauffer replied.

"Aaron, I've told you before, you don't have to call me sir. I was old enough to enlist. If'n it makes you feel better, then you can do it when the boss is around. But just betwixt us boys, it don't matter to me."

"Yes sir...Tom," the young man said with a smile.

Aaron stopped the Packard next to the carriage house and opened the doors for his passengers. When they had all alighted, he began to escort the party to the guest entrance.

Tom stepped ahead of the group.

"I know how to get in, Aaron. You go take care of the bags so these ladies can pretty up, and leave the ones we marked for the Pullman. These two boys will be staying over there," Tom said.

Tom led the group as they walked into an elegant entryway of marble and travertine tile. A waterfall ornamented the alcove on one side while a fresco of angels attending the Blessed Virgin commanded the opposite wall.

"The old bastard thinks that's gonna get him into heaven, I reckon," Tom said.

They walked into a huge room filled with sturdy oak and leather furniture. The walls were adorned with mounted game heads, photos and, not surprisingly, paintings by Russell and sculptures by Remington. To Grant's surprise, however, he found works by Gauguin and Monet.

"Anyone care for a toddy?" Tom asked as he walked to the bar and began to prepare drinks.

"I know C. C. has some C. C.," Nick said.

"Sure enough."

Tom took a bottle of Canadian Club from the shelf.

"Would you care for some sherry, darlin'?" Tom asked Mrs. Barnaby.

"That would be delightful," she replied.

"How about you girls?" Tom asked.

"No, thank you," Dixie and Phoebe said in unison.

"How about you, son?" Tom said.

"No thank you. I'm doing fine," Grant replied.

As Tom poured the drinks, a broad shouldered man with a patch over his left eye entered the room. He was wearing a tweed shooting jacket with an ascot and Jodhpur style pants with riding boots.

"What are you doing in my liquor cabinet you old mooch?" the man roared in sham outrage.

"Well, I'll be damned, C. C. You know...you look a whole lot more like you do now than you did when I saw you just this time a year ago," Tom said.

Tom took the man's hand and they greeted one another warmly.

"And I'll be damned if you ain't just as full of nonsense," the man replied.

Grant looked at Dixie, uncertain if there was some meaning to what he had just heard.

The man then walked to Mrs. Barnaby and gave her a bear hug, lifting her from her feet.

"When are you gonna make an honest man outta that old reprobate, you pretty thing?"

"Con," she said, as she kissed his cheek, "you're just too anxious. You mind your own immortal soul and I will tend to his...and mine."

Turning quickly away from Katherine Barnaby, Conrad approached Nick.

"How are you doing, young man? You're looking well."

Without waiting for an answer, he turned and embraced Phoebe.

"And you're as beautiful as ever. Are you takin' good care of this boy?"

Phoebe's face reddened but she did not have to answer because Conrad had already crossed the room to take Dixie into his arms.

"And you must be this niece I have heard so much about?"

Holding her shoulders, he pushed her to arms length and looked at her face.

"You're not nearly as homely as your Uncle claims. In fact, if I was about twenty-five years younger, I might just be chasing you around the sofa."

Not knowing how to respond to the bombast, Dixie stared back in silence. She was about to speak when Conrad Conlon turned and walked to where Grant was standing.

"Don't worry; I won't give you a hug," he said. "Newspaper man, I hear! Have you found anything good to say about my old partner? He should have a lot to tell. He's a legend in his own mind you know."

"Well...uh, yes...I have learned quite a bit actually."

"That's good," Conrad Conlon said.

He then took Grant's hand in a firm grasp. He looked Grant in the eye.

"He's as good a man as you're likely to find. Me and him go way back. Do a good job on his story. He deserves it."

Grant considered the anger and disdain he had experienced following Dixie's revelations earlier on the train. Although he still felt the indignation, he found himself unable to genuinely dislike this grandiloquent character that Tom called friend.

When everyone had been seated, Tom and Conrad Conlon moved off into a corner to catch up on the gossip. Grant sat next to Dixie on a love seat sofa adjacent a huge stone fireplace.

"He seems like such a fine person," Dixie said. "I didn't think I would like him but I can't help myself. He is really charming."

"I know exactly how you feel," Grant said. "He should be called Tornado Conrad with that personality."

The train had arrived late in the afternoon. Following introductions and greetings, Tom and C. C. had continued an animated conversation.

Katherine Barnaby stood and set her empty glass on the end table.

"Con, would you have someone show us to our rooms? The ladies need to refresh before dinner."

"Kate, you'll be in your usual room and I'd appreciate it if you could show the other ladies where everything is," C. C. said without getting up. "They're gonna stay in the big room next to you."

"Come on, Grant," Nick said. "We'll head back over to the Pullman and get ready for dinner."

3 0

Grant laid his napkin on the table and took the last sip of warm tea from his cup. Whatever one might say of Conrad Conlon, Grant thought, he was not lacking as a host. The béarnaise sauce, generally overdone with vinegar in Grant's opinion, had gently prepared the pallet for Chateau Briand, which seemed to melt from fork to tongue. He was even tempted to gauchely request the recipe for the Baked Alaska, which had crowned the meal, and which Grant was sure would delight his mother.

Every chair at the dinner table, which seated twenty-four, was filled. The number of guests made it difficult to attempt conversation with any but a few fellow diners.

C. C. tapped on his glass with a spoon to get the attention of his guests and said, "Gentlemen, I suggest we retire for brandy and cigars... and ladies, if you will follow Mrs. Conlon, she will show you to the drawing room."

Conrad Conlon and his wife arose from their respective ends of the table and escorted the guests to the appropriate after dinner retreat.

As the men straggled into C. C.'s den, Tom introduced the various members of the aggregation to Grant, briefly explaining how he had come to know each of the men and what business interests they held.

Soon, cigar smoke filled the room. Grant walked through the French doors to a patio adjacent to the den to get some fresh air and collect his thoughts. The night air was cool and Grant was glad that he had packed warm clothing for his trip into the mountains.

"Grant," Tom's voice came from behind him.

Grant turned to see Tom walking through the door accompanied by a heavy set man with a badge pinned to his suit coat.

"This here is Cecil Burt," Tom said. "Cecil is the Sheriff of Flathead County. He was just telling me an interesting little story and I thought you'd best hear it too."

Grant shook the hand of the Sheriff and said, "I've only been here half a day Sheriff. I'm not in trouble, I hope."

"Not with me you're not," Cecil Burt replied. "But you might be in trouble, none the less. I understand that you ain't none too popular with a fella by the name of Buck Horton, who used to work over at Tom's outfit?"

Grant felt his stomach tighten as an involuntary rush of adrenaline brought his senses to keen awareness.

"Is he in Kalispell?" Grant asked, trying to control the quaver in his voice.

"I don't really know, son. He damned well may be. About a week ago, he robbed a man south of Missoula and took some money and the fella's horse. Then I got word yesterday that a miscreant fittin' his description had robbed the mercantile down at Ronan. Cut up old Ben Levy pretty bad for no good reason and left him for dead.

Now Ronan is just out of my jurisdiction, but puttin' two and two together, I would have to figure that he could be headed this way. I told the folks at the bank and the mercantile to be on the lookout."

Grant shifted his weight uncomfortably from foot to foot, his mind racing.

"You brought that gun I give you, right?" Tom asked.

"It's in the Pullman."

Cecil Burt put his hand on Grant's shoulder.

"Well, I reckon you had best start packin' it with you wherever you go," the Sheriff advised. "Seems ol' Buck has got himself a new gadget that sounds real scary."

Sheriff Burt held up the middle two fingers of his right hand.

"I understand that Horton lost his social finger and his ring finger when Tom shot him. Now I hear tell that before the wound had healed he'd got the saddle maker in Great Falls to fix up a leather cuff. It's supposed to be somewhat like the cuffs you see a lot of cowboys wearing on their wrists, except that this thing has a band that extends down the back of his hand. It wraps around the stubs of his missin' fingers and down the palm so as to be laced to that wrist cuff."

Holding out his right hand to demonstrate, Sheriff Burt folded his middle two fingers into his palm.

"This apparatus, I'm told, is rigged so that he can release a long knife blade which drops out of this contraption and locks into place."

Pointing at the middle knuckles of his right hand, he swept his left forefinger downward.

"The blade comes down like so and then locks tight against the leather on the back of his hand. It leaves his other two fingers free to use like a claw while he wields that weapon. The way I understand it, he apparently told the saddle maker he needed it for ranch work, cutting feed sacks and the like, but that poor sumbitch south of Missoula found out the hard way what else it was good for."

"How is that fella doing?" Tom asked.

"Deader'n dirt," Cecil replied. "Ol' Buck gutted the poor bastard and left him to bleed to death. He was just some threadbare honyocker on his way to town for supplies. They said it didn't look like he'd even put up a fight."

Grant's face blanched, remembering how close he had come to a similar fate. He recalled clearly seeing Buck's toothy grin, while that blade moved ever closer to completing its grisly chore.

"How does a person become so demented?" Grant asked, sensing his face flush and a lump in his throat.

"I don't have an idea," the Sheriff replied. "But you stay heads up now, young fella. From what Tom tells me, you should know better'n anybody what a mean son-of-a-bitch ol' Buck can be."

"You probably never knew Howdy Dunbar, did you Cecil?" Tom asked.

Sheriff Burt shook his head no.

"Well ol' Howdy was one of my best hands and a real nice young feller. He was Buck's only pal and I believe that Howdy kind'a kept a modest rein on Buck's natural inclinations."

"You're talking about him like he ain't with us no more, Tom. Was that the youngster who got killed up to Calgary a while back? Seems I recall the name Howdy in the newspaper," the Sheriff said.

"That was the one, and although it was an accident, it was sure as hell an avoidable accident. It was ol' Buck who run over him."

"It was in the paper but I never put together the people involved. It did say that he worked at The Buffalo Rock," the Sheriff said.

"A lot of my folks at the ranch thought that Buck had done it on purpose, but I tried to give him the benefit of the doubt. Never figured a man would be mean enough to kill his best pal to win a damned race. But then I caught the bastard about to eviscerate my very own biographer here. That's when my mind got made up."

"Keep a sharp eye, Mr. Collins, and good luck," Sheriff Burt said.

He stuck out his hand to offer another hand shake, and then turned to walk away.

When Cecil and Tom returned to the house, Grant sat for a long while staring into space.

Thinking aloud, he asked himself, "What did I do to warrant an unpleasant situation like this?"

Conrad Conlon's chauffeur drove Grant and Nick to the Pullman car. Grant retrieved the small pistol from his luggage and put it under his pillow as he lay down in the sleeper.

A slight wind created strange sounds as Grant tried to find a comfortable position to get some rest. After arising several times to look out the windows, he heard Nick from the other bunk.

"God damn, boy, if you aren't gonna sleep, would you at least lay still. Shit Marie, I haven't had a wink myself all night."

"Sorry. I'm just a little restless, I guess."

"And damned well you should be. But this Pullman coach has good locks and I have my Colt right under my pillow. So tuck yourself in, put that gun Dad gave you where you can get at it, and be still."

"Sorry. I won't make a sound the rest of the night."

Forsaking comfort, Grant lay silently, staring at the door of the Pullman. Every creak and groan of the rail car seemed to be the footsteps of doom. Every moving shadow wielded a long shining blade.

The hours passed. Grant became aware that he was unconsciously fondling the borrowed Smith and Wesson. In the reality of the half-lit early morning, it occurred to him how quickly he had become dependent on this small inanimate iron machine. He suddenly understood Tom's stories of clutching a gun and knowing it was the only thing between life and death.

"I give up," Nick said from the other sleeper. "We might just as well be gettin' some breakfast. We sure as hell ain't gettin' no sleep. Let's head over to C. C.'s place. I reckon at least that the cook should be stirrin'."

They dressed in silence and then walked to the Conlon mansion. As they entered the guest entrance they heard C. C.'s voice.

"You boys come on in and get some vittles."

As they walked into the dining area, they saw Tom and C. C. already seated at the table.

"What'll it be?" C. C. asked. "Pour yourself a cup and pull up a chair."

A young woman wearing a lace cap and apron entered the room.

"They'll have what we're havin'," Tom said.

The girl quickly scurried back to the kitchen.

Tom picked up a leather shoulder holster, which was setting on the table. He handed it to Grant.

"Gift from C. C. Try it out," Tom said.

Grant arose, removed the revolver from his pocket, and took off his coat. He slung the shoulder holster on his left shoulder and fastened it to his belt.

"It's perfect. Thank you very much, Mr. Conlon."

"It may come in handy," C. C., laughed. "Better'n carryin' the thing in your belt. You might drop it. Worse yet, you might shoot your pecker off trying to get it out of your pants."

Grant was sitting down when he heard Mrs. Barnaby.

"I suppose you gentlemen are keeping breakfast warm for us," she said.

She entered the room followed by Alice Conlon, Phoebe and Dixie.

Each of the men quickly rose to pull out a chair, seating the women.

When they had finished breakfast, Mrs. Conlon said, "The ladies and I will be making ourselves beautiful this afternoon. You gentlemen are free to do whatever suits your fancy."

"That's just fine, darlin'," Tom said. "We'll just head over to the Elks Lodge and make sure no one is makin' off with the good liquor."

"Small danger of that with you around," said Mrs. Conlon.

Katherine Barnaby brushed a kiss on Tom's cheek as she left the room.

"You fellers care to go for a swim?" C. C. asked, looking at each of the men.

"Sounds refreshing," Grant said. "But I don't have the attire."

"Not a problem," Tom said. "C. C. has everything we need."

Filing from the room, the men entered Conrad Conlon's Packard limousine for the short ride downtown.

Grant sat quietly, his head swiveling to take in as much of the thriving little city as he could. Many new and ornate Victorian style homes lined the streets and the business district bustled. Brick store fronts lined the main street, selling the latest clothing fashions, hardware, general mercantile and ice cream.

The massive three-story brick building, which housed the Kalispell Elks Lodge, was a surprise. Grant stepped from the car and stood admiring the unexpected structure.

"This must be quite a prosperous organization," Grant said as they walked to the entrance.

"We do pretty well," C. C. said.

Aaron, the liveried chauffer, removed a large canvas bag from the luggage compartment and carried it down an exterior stairwell into the basement.

The lobby of the building was decorated with granite floors and leather covered benches. The lounge was surrounded by leather covered booths. The room was filled with round marble topped tables on cast iron bases. A marble topped bar filled the length of one wall.

C. C. noticed Grant looking at the room in astonishment.

"It took a few barbecues and turkey shoots but we got 'er built," C. C. said.

"What we havin' boys? On me," Tom said.

"I'll just have a Coca-Cola. Perhaps it will pick me up a bit. I didn't sleep well last night," Grant replied.

"Boogie man keepin' you awake," Tom said. "He's kept me awake a night or two in my life."

"Kept me awake, too," Nick chided.

They walked to a table and sat down.

"Well, I don't blame him for being nervous," C. C. said. "I don't know this Buck fella, but from what I hear this boy has every reason to be a bit skittish."

They finished their drinks making idle chatter.

"Let's go for a plunge. It will clear our heads," C. C. said.

He stood and walked to the stairwell.

Grant followed the other men to the basement of the building. They entered a dressing room where towels and two piece bathing suits had been laid out neatly on benches.

"Grab that one there, Grant. I believe it should fit fine," C. C. said, pointing to a blue suit with white trim.

Grant stepped into one of the privacy stalls and put on the swim suit, which fit as if it had been made for him. When he came out, the others had left the room and were already in the water.

Nick climbed out of the pool and walked onto the diving board. He dived and began to porpoise the length of the pool.

"Well, jump on in," Tom said. "I don't think you're gonna melt."

"It feels great," Nick said. "Maybe you can sleep tonight."

Grant dived into the deep end, surprised that the water was quite warm. He swam the length of the pool. Indulging his tired muscles, he stopped to sit on the steps and leaned against the tile wall. Enveloped in the soothing water, he soon relaxed.

Listening to the unfamiliar conversation of his three companions was an education unto itself. Breeds of cattle and times to plow; government regulation of grazing lands and mineral rights; commodity futures and the price of oil; new fangled farm machines versus horse drawn equipment and stories of the days before the fences and plows. Each topic, which was punctuated by ubiquitous discussions of the weather, was lending context for Grant to build his story.

The swim, followed by an invigorating shower, had lifted Grant's spirits.

"Just put those wet things in the canvas bag when you're finished and set it by the door. Aaron will grab 'em before we leave," C. C. said.

Grant dressed quickly and they walked up the stairs toward the lounge.

When they were seated, Grant saw Sheriff Cecil Burt enter the room. He was accompanied by a younger man who was also wearing a badge on his suit jacket.

"Glad I caught you men," the Sheriff said. "I'm afraid I've got some bad news."

"Don't tell me you're gonna arrest us for drinking whiskey, Cecil," Tom laughed. "You even brought a big strong deputy for some help."

"It ain't quite that serious, Tom," Cecil replied.

Cecil smiled momentarily and then the look on his face turned serious.

"You know ol' Melvin Webster don't you, C. C.?" the Sheriff asked.

"He used to work for me. Went into business for himself selling some kind'a sock-knitting machines door to door during the big war. Said he was gonna make his fortune. I haven't seen him around in quite some while though. Why do you ask?" Conrad Conlon replied.

"The constable down at Bigfork called to tell me that they found him dead in a farm lane. Bill here went down to look things over. I'll let him tell you what he found," the Sheriff said.

Cecil Burt looked at the young man standing beside him.

"Oh, by the way Grant, this is my deputy, Bill Snow. Bill, this is Grant Collins, the newspaper man I was telling you about," Sheriff Burt interjected.

Grant nodded to acknowledge the introduction as the deputy spoke.

"Mr. Webster was found by a farmer who saw some crows flocking in a lane that runs back to his old orchard. Mr. Webster had been there a day or two, I would reckon from the look of it," Bill Snow said.

Bill Snow looked at C. C.

"Like you said, Mr. Conlon, he made his livin' goin' door to door sellin' cast iron sock-knittin' contraptions for some outfit in Pennsylvania. I went by to talk to his wife and according to her, he usually took a half a dozen machines with him. Five of them machines had been left with his body so I am guessing that he had sold one somewhere along the way. His wife said he'd been gone about six days and he was in that lane for a couple of those. Mrs. Webster told me that if he'd sold a machine, he must have had fifty to a hundred dollars with him."

"So how did Melvin end up in an orchard lane with five of his machines," C. C. asked.

"We're just puttin' pieces together right now, so I'll try to give you the short version. Mrs. Webster says that Melvin was sellin' more than just the knittin' machines. He was sellin' these ladies a little home business.

The ladies are supposed to make socks and mittens with the machine, and then this big outfit that Melvin worked for would buy the finished goods from the ladies, which they sell in catalogues and stores. Like you said Conrad, it started during the war and the idea was to make socks and mittens for the Doughboys. Well it appears that Melvin had delivered some yarn to a honyocker lady on a little spread down by the river. It also appears that sometime during his sales call, he was accosted by none other than Grant's ol' buddy Buck Horton."

"And how did we put those pieces together?" Tom asked.

"Well, sir, the horse that Buck was suspected of robbin' from the farmer south of Missoula was left at that farm. That woman's poor husband found her filleted like a trout...and she had of course been defiled. So the story fits like this, Buck was having his way with that farm lady when Melvin came callin' to deliver some yarn and buy her supply of socks. Buck must'a decided that Melvin's Model T was better transport than the nag he'd got from the honyocker and for some reason he took ol' Mel along for the ride. I suspect that he figured Mel for havin' a lot of money. Whatever the reason, he tortured the old boy somethin' horrible and then he finally finished him off."

"So Buck's now got a car and some money," Tom said.

"That's the way she looks," Deputy Snow said. "Worse yet, he got himself a gun. Mrs. Webster told me that Melvin carried one of them Army forty-five automatic pistols in a pouch under the seat of his Model T. Considering that all of his other things were throwed here and there in the farm lane, I would have to figure that Buck found the gun."

Sheriff Burt put his hand on Conrad's shoulder.

"I just got the word out to the newspaper and we'll be calling all of the other towns in the area, but it would help if you fellas would help pass along the information about Buck and the black Model T he's drivin'.

And tell everyone to keep an eye peeled tonight at the dance," the Sheriff said.

The four men followed the Sheriff out of the Elks Lodge and got into the limousine. Aaron stopped beside the Pullman car to drop off Nick and Grant.

"I'm sorry, Mr. Conlon, but I forgot the bag of swim suits at the Lodge," Aaron said.

"Don't worry about it now Aaron. We can get it tonight when we go to the dance," Conrad Conlon said.

Tom and Nick got out of the limousine.

"I'll send the car back to get you boys when you're dressed...say about an hour?" Conrad Conlon said.

Nick unlocked the door and looked around the inside of the car before he entered.

"I feel real bad about ol' Melvin Webster," Nick said. "Phoebe even bought one of his machines back during the war. Real nice fella. Wouldn't hurt a piss ant."

"I haven't seen these sock machines," Grant said. "Is Phoebe's of any value?

"She makes socks for me and she used to make them for the girls when they were still home and in school. She never tried to make any to sell so I don't know how it would be as a business. Looked to me to be mighty slow goin'," Nick replied. "But then we owned sheep and she knows how to spin so the wool didn't cost her nothin' either."

Looking into the mirror, Grant slicked down his hair and then brushed his new Stetson hat.

"I suppose this is proper attire for a Cattleman's Ball?"

"You bet! You'll see a whole bunch of them tonight," Nick said as he walked toward the door. "Let's go. I think I hear that big ol' Packard comin'. You got your pistol?"

"Unfortunately, it is right here under my arm," Grant said.

"Well, like it or not, it is really appropriate attire tonight."

Nick checked the locks on the Pullman doors a second time before getting into the limousine.

31

It was nearing seven o'clock when Grant and Nick walked into Conrad Conlon's parlor. Looking at Dixie, Grant's heart seemed to swell in his chest. Without thinking he walked directly to her and kissed her in front of the group.

"How impetuous, Mr. Collins," she smiled, in feigned indignation.

"You are, again, a vision," he said. "I have never seen a more beautiful woman."

"Now hold on here, son," C. C. laughed. "Just look around. Mrs. Conlon herself is a very portrait of pulchritude in her new gown. And just cast your eyes on these other visions of beauty who have kindly agreed to accompany us undeservin' rapscallions for an evening at the ball."

"Why, yes…of course…all of you ladies look absolutely stunning this evening," Grant stammered.

They all had a good laugh.

"You're off the hook young man," Mrs. Barnaby said. "Thirty years ago, I may have taken offense, but C. C. is just having you on. Your young lady is a vision in that gown."

"Kate is right," Alice Conlon said.

She walked to Grant and gave him a hug and a kiss on the cheek.

"Unfortunately, forty years won't treat you young people any more kindly than it has treated us," she said.

Finishing their sherry, the group crowded into the limousine for the ride to the Elk's Lodge.

The third floor of the Elk's Lodge was a gymnasium, which served as an open banquet hall and meeting room. Bunting and crepe paper adorned the walls and fixtures with clusters of toy balloons lending color to the otherwise bland open space. Tables with candles and flowers surrounded the spacious dance floor.

"Isn't this gorgeous?" Dixie said.

She and Grant followed the other couples to a table.

"A fitting frame for a lovely portrait," Grant said.

"Well, thank you kind sir," she said, squeezing his arm in delight. "And listen to the orchestra. Aren't they wonderful?"

"They sound very professional," Grant replied. "Are you on for a Charleston in that dress?"

"You lead, Mr. Collins, I will follow," she replied.

During dinner, Grant and Dixie listened as the murders and robberies were the main topic of conversation.

"I just can't believe that Buck would do such things," Dixie protested. "I know he hurt Grant but that was about jealousy. What reason has he for doing these horrible things?"

"Darlin'," Tom said. "Buck is just one mean sumbitch, if you'll pardon my French. You didn't hear the story from the Sheriff. It was enough to turn your stomach. We all thought we knew him, but we didn't. He's bad and that's all there is to it. He can only end up in jail or dead...and it was his call."

As they finished dinner, the lights dimmed and the band began to play a waltz.

"It's not the Charleston but we can still dance." Dixie said.

As they got up from the table, several other couples around the room rose and walked toward the dance floor. Momentarily forgetting everything around them, Grant and Dixie embraced, moving together to the strains of Beautiful Dreamer.

"Do you really think it was Buck who did all of those terrible things?" Dixie said.

"I have to believe it was. Sheriff Burt seemed pretty confident."

Grant held her closely as they moved slowly around the dance floor.

"Do you think he is coming here?" she asked.

"He is really angry at your Uncle and he obviously detests my innards... so yes, I have to think that he is seeking some sort of revenge after what happened during the fight. You heard at dinner about the device he had constructed for his injured hand?"

"I didn't quite understand what they were talking about."

"As I understand, it is a knife that is concealed in a leather wrist band, which he can deploy at will. He has allegedly used it to kill several of the people that C. C. and your uncle were talking about at dinner. The Sheriff told us today that there was also a gun in the car he stole."

"Grant. I'm frightened," she said.

She held him tightly, closing her eyes in an attempt to lose herself in the music. The cold steel of the gun butt pressed uncomfortably against her.

"I never thought I would be happy to have my escort carrying a firearm."

"Don't worry; everything is going to be fine. I'm not delighted about going around armed but there appears to be no alternative. Thank God we're all leaving tomorrow. I don't think Buck will be going back to The

Buffalo Rock, and your Uncle Tom and I are going to be in the mountains hunting. Buck doesn't know where we'll be going. I don't think there is anything to worry about."

The band began to play the Charleston.

"Grant, let's take a walk. It is close in here and I'm afraid that gun is going to go flying across the floor if you dance your usual unbridled version of the Charleston," Dixie said.

They walked to the table to retrieve Dixie's wrap.

"We're going to get some air. We'll be back in a bit," Grant said.

"Aaron is out there with the car if you kids want to go back to the house," C. C. winked.

Walking onto the sidewalk from the Elk's Lodge, Grant noticed that he could see his breath in the illumination of the newly installed electric street lamps. Being from the East, both he and Dixie were surprised by the cool air of late August in Montana. Dixie draped her shawl around her shoulders and pulled it tight, crossing her arms against the chill.

"This air may be a bit fresher than I had bargained for," Dixie said through chattering teeth.

Grant could see the Packard parked a short distance down the street.

"C. C. told me that we could use the car. Would you like to go back to his house?"

Pulling the shawl tighter she grabbed his arm.

"That is a good idea. I don't feel much like dancing any more tonight. I just want to be alone with you."

Her words warmed him and he walked tall as they hurried to the Packard.

Grant opened the door and followed Dixie onto the cool leather seat.

"Would you take us to Mr. Conlon's house, Aaron?" Grant said.

The engine roared and the headlights came on.

The Packard lurched forward in an unusually rough start.

"I think maybe Aaron has been nipping a few himself," Grant whispered in Dixie's ear.

The limousine turned into the Kalispell City Park.

Dixie whispered, "He has been drinking. I think he has forgotten the way home."

The Packard stopped beside a small lake in the middle of the park. Leaving the engine running and the lights on, the chauffer got out of the car and opened the passenger door.

"What is it, Aaron?" Grant asked.

"Get out of the car, flatlander," Buck's voice boomed through the darkness. "You and me got some unfinished business...and bring that bitch out here with ya. We're gonna have us a little fun."

Reflected in the glow from the headlights, Grant could now see a pistol held menacingly in Buck's left hand. He was wearing Aaron's hat and coat which appeared absurdly small on his large frame.

Tempted to reach for the Smith and Wesson under his coat, Grant sat frozen in place.

"Buck, why are you doing this? I've always thought we were friends," Dixie said.

"Shut up and get the hell out of that car," Buck growled.

Reaching into the car, Buck grabbed Grant's necktie and pulled him from the seat.

"Get out of that car you bitch or I'm gonna blow this college boy a couple of new assholes!" Buck shouted.

Dixie got out of the Packard, following as Buck dragged Grant by the necktie to the front of the car.

Buck released his grip and held his right hand in Grant's face. For the first time Grant could see the leather brace between Buck's forefinger and little finger.

"Take a good look you fancy pants son-of-a-bitch," Buck growled. "It's gonna be your first and last look at what ya done to me."

Stepping forward, Buck ripped away Dixie's shawl, staring at her bare shoulders.

"I do have to admit that you are looking one helluva lot better than the last piece of ass I got," Buck said. "That old honyocker bitch smelled like a damned goat. I think I am really gonna enjoy this."

Grant was slowly moving his hand to reach for the pistol hidden beneath his jacket. Doubting his competence with the revolver and fearing that Buck might fire and hit Dixie, he hesitated.

"What you got in mind there, dude?" Buck asked. "Let's see what you got under that there coat."

Buck took a step toward Grant. A voice from the darkness stopped him.

"Drop the gun, Horton."

Buck froze in place and slowly looked in the direction of the voice. He carefully measured the odds of getting off a shot.

"You're a cracker jack if you can get 'er done, Buck." The voice was calm. "I got you dead to rights with this here twelve gauge, and much as I hate to admit it, I think I might just enjoy blowin' your head off. I saw what you did to that farm lady and old Mr. Webster."

Grant recognized the voice of Deputy Bill Snow.

Buck slowly turned in the direction of the Deputy's voice. He raised he hands, pointing the forty-five into the air.

"I said to drop the gun, Horton. My trigger finger is gettin' real twitchy," Bill Snow said.

The Colt slid from Buck's left hand and hit the graveled road with a thud.

"Thank God you came!" Dixie shouted, as she bent down to pick up the shawl. "How did you know we were here?"

"We found Aaron's body floating in the Elk's Lodge swimmin' pool with his throat cut," Deputy Snow said. "I was just comin' up the stairs out of the basement when I saw Mr. Conlon's Packard drivin' off. Figured I'd best follow and see what was up, but I didn't have a car. Then I seen you turn into the park and I knew it wasn't good. I cut across...had to run all the way over here. I guess it's a good thing I did."

Bill Snow was still breathing heavily.

"Good thing indeed," Grant said. He breathed a sigh of relief causing his shoulders to sag.

Buck stood motionless, holding his hands at shoulder level. He studied Bill Snow's every move as the Deputy entered the area illuminated by the Packard's headlights.

The Deputy held a Model 97 Winchester pump shotgun in his right hand. Stepping behind Buck, he reached under his coat and withdrew a set of handcuffs.

"Okay Horton, put your hands behind your back."

Buck dropped his hands and put them behind him. Watching carefully to ensure compliance, Bill Snow lowered the barrel of the shotgun and stepped forward to place the handcuffs on Buck's wrists.

Grant heard a metallic click, which he thought was the sound of the handcuffs putting an end to the danger. To his horror he saw a flash of shiny steel as Buck's much discussed blade dropped from its crafted sheath, reflecting in the headlights. In an instant, Buck wheeled and plunged eight inches of razor sharp steel into the chest of Deputy Bill Snow.

The blast of the Deputy's shotgun hit the gravel road beside his feet.

A cloud of dust momentarily obscured the two men. Then Grant saw another flash of steel as Buck withdrew the blade and plunged it a second time into the Deputy's vital organs.

Grant's mind was reeling in a confused frenzy. Dixie's piercing screams intensified the confusion. He looked at Bill Snow who stood staring a sightless stare. The shotgun slipped slowly from his fingers onto the ground. He seemed to be mouthing words but an unnatural silence hung over the scene. The Deputy stood in place for a long moment. Buck pushed against his chest and Bill Snow fell dead on his back in the gravel road.

Grant looked at Buck's face. Fear burned through him like a lightning bolt as he realized that Buck was as calm as if at afternoon tea. Smiling at Grant, Buck bent down to pick up his pistol and the Deputy's shotgun.

Buck's move changed Grant's fearful immobility to reaction. He grabbed for the butt of the pistol under his coat and drew the gun. Pointing the Smith and Wesson at the pistol beneath Buck's fingers, he fired. The shot hit the ground beneath Buck's hand, moving the Colt. Startled, he stood erect and looked at Grant.

"Damned if you ain't got a little sand in your craw after all, Cheechako. That'll make it even more entertainin' to kill your miserable ass."

Buck again bent down to pick up the guns. Grant fired a second shot which hit Buck's revolver, spattering shards of lead into his left hand.

"I really don't want to kill you, Buck, but if you touch those guns I am going shoot you," Grant said.

The sound of his words rang hollow and distant in his ears, drowned by the beating of his heart.

The silence was broken by the roar of automobile engines. Headlights moving toward them gave Grant a renewed feeling of confidence.

"You're going to pay for what you did, Buck," Grant said. "I would imagine that this is the Sheriff coming with a couple of carloads of deputies."

"Well it's gonna take more than some skinny peckerwood like you to put me away, flatlander...but I will see you all again."

Buck turned and ran into the darkness. Grant took careful aim at the form of his fleeing nemesis, but could not bring himself to shoot the man in the back.

3 2

The Pullman car lurched, nearly knocking Nick off his feet, as the ten o'clock eastbound connected to Conrad Conlon's private car.

The porter approached Grant, who sat alone in one end of the car staring out the window. The others sat drinking their morning coffee as they discussed events of the previous evening.

"Could I bring the gentleman some coffee?" the porter asked.

"No, thank you...not right now," Grant said.

Dixie walked up behind Grant, massaging his neck and shoulders.

"Why don't you come and join us?"

"I just need a little time to think," he replied.

"Come on down here and join us son," Tom shouted. "Hell, there ain't no reason to feel bad."

Dixie took his hand and urged him to his feet. They walked toward the group.

"You know, Grant, I haven't ever killed a man and I don't particularly ever want to," Nick said. "I'm not just sure I would have shot Buck myself, if that makes you feel any better."

"I just feel very badly that he got away when I could have stopped him. If someone else gets hurt or killed; that is going to be my fault,"

Grant said.

"Don't punish yourself over it," Tom said. "Most of the men who ever went to war never killed anybody. It ain't an easy thing to do...killin' someone...especially someone you know. I had C. C. call over to The Buffalo Rock and warn everyone to be on the lookout. Buck's picture was on the front page of the paper this morning. So I don't reckon it'll be too long before someone gets him."

"Dixie and I had an opportunity to see first hand just what the man is willing to do to avoid apprehension," Grant said. "I feel so badly about Bill Snow and his family. I understand he had children."

"Even if'n you'd a shot the miserable bastard, it wouldn't have brought Bill back. So don't go pokin' yourself with a sharp stick. What's done is done! Now have some coffee and try to forget it," Tom said.

Grant poured a cup of coffee and then returned to his seat in the far end of the car. Dixie came to sit beside him and they watched in silence while the scenery of the open valley changed to rocky cliffs and forested hills as the train climbed its way toward the Continental Divide.

The porter entered the car and began to put empty cups and glasses on a tray.

"We'll be in East Glacier in just a few minutes. I understand that some of you gentlemens is gonna leave us. Best start gettin' ready," the porter said.

A blast of the train whistle accompanied the grinding sound of brakes as the Pullman car stopped beside the small railway station at East Glacier.

Tom and Grant picked up the canvas bags containing their clothing for the ride into the mountains.

"See you back at The Buffalo Rock," Nick said.

Tom and Grant stepped onto the platform followed by Katherine

Barnaby and Dixie.

"My word, it is cold here. I'm getting back on board before I catch my death," Katherine Barnaby said.

She kissed Tom a quick good-bye and scrambled up the steps.

Dixie held Grant in a long embrace. Tom stood by patiently as they shared a kiss.

"Good luck! Both of you, and don't get eaten by bears," she said.

Dixie climbed the steps as the train pitched forward with another blast of the whistle.

"And don't catch pneumonia," Dixie shouted from the door as the train pulled out of East Glacier.

A light rain mixed with snow was beginning to fall. The sound of thunder could be heard in the distant mountains. Grant could see that the far-off peaks were shrouded in white.

"Mrs. Barnaby was right. It is cold," Grant said.

"It'll be a whole lot colder up in the high lonesome where we're goin'," Tom said.

Elmer was waiting inside the station. When they entered he introduced a tall, thin man wearing spectacles.

"This here is Constable Olafsen. He's the law here in East Glacier. He got a telegram regardin' Buck. I reckon you ought to know about it before we go in the back country," Elmer said.

"What did ol' Buck do now?" Tom asked.

"According to the telegram," Constable Olafsen said, "he robbed the mercantile down at Hungry Horse and apparently outfitted himself right and proper. Took himself a rifle and some ammo, and food enough for a couple of weeks. Near about killed the clerk, but I'm told she'll survive. It was said that he'd also violated the poor girl. Damned ornery sort, that Horton."

"How was he travelin'," Tom asked.

"He was in a Ford that he'd stole from some salesman in Bigfork," Olafsen replied.

"Yeah, we know all about that! Were they able to give you any idea of which way he was headed?" Tom asked.

"This'a way! He don't have that Ford no more. He apparently accosted a young packer down by Apgar and took three head of horses. Took a tent and some cookin' gear and saddles for the stock. He even made that kid help him pack the outfit. But the boy had apparently heard about Buck's previous meanness and he lit out before Buck could do him any harm."

"Smart boy," Tom said. "I should hire him myself."

Tom walked out of the station followed by Grant and Elmer.

"Grant, maybe we had best head back to The Buffalo Rock. Buck knows where our camps are up in the hills. He helped set some of 'em, and he's gonna be a might hard for the laws to catch once he makes it into the high country. I don't think that bastard is gonna rest until he puts us both in the ground."

"Pshaw! I'll not let my first hunting trip be ruined by the likes of Buck. I'm betting they'll catch him before he gets too far. The Butch Cassidy days he's trying to relive are long since gone. Besides, we have firearms of our own," Grant said.

Tom's stories of outlaws and Indians flashed through his mind. He recalled a mental picture of Buck in his Butch Cassidy outfit at the summer dance.

"It will be like living the old days with you; when you had to keep an eye out for the hostiles or the bad men. This high drama should make for a real adventure," Grant said.

"Okey, dokey then. If'n you're game, I am. Let's get rollin'," Tom said.

Constable Olafsen had followed them onto the platform.

"If you hear anything Olafsen, we'll have a man at base camp. We've got a cabin at the trailhead into the Two Medicine River country. Give us a holler, huh!"

The rain pounded on the windshield of the truck. Elmer fought the wheel as the vehicle snaked a path on the muddy road.

"Like I told Olafsen, we've got a little cabin at the foot of the trailhead," Tom said. "It's warm and dry and if this don't let up, I think maybe we'll spend the night there before we head on in to our spike camp. You got that camp all set up...didn't you Elmer?"

"Yes, sir," Elmer said with a grin. "You'll be snug as bugs."

Elmer pulled the truck off the road into an open area and parked beside a small cabin. Grant noticed several horses standing fetlock deep in a muddy split rail corral. A smaller corral contained a canvas covered stack of hay bales. Saddles, covered with ponchos, hung on a rail next to the cabin where a neat pile of firewood reached to the eaves.

"Let's get us a fire goin', while Elmer feeds the stock," Tom said.

Tom jumped from the truck and ran toward the cabin. He stopped to grab an armload of firewood. Grant followed Tom's lead, getting firewood before they entered the log house.

Tom put several logs into the woodstove. Soon the kindling was ablaze. Grant sat on a bench beside the table which occupied the middle of the room. He looked around at the narrow rough hewn bunk beds standing against three walls. There would be little luxury on this trip, he thought to himself.

When Elmer entered, shaking rainwater from his hat, the cabin was warm.

Tom scooped a handful of coffee from the can and dropped it into the battered coffee pot boiling on the stove. He watched as the coffee grounds rolled vigorously in the boiling water and then set the pot onto the table.

"Looks like it might be clearin' a bit, Boss," Elmer said.

Tom walked outside to look at the clearing sky. He came back into the cabin and shut the door.

"I reckon you're right. I believe we'll get to camp before dark," Tom said.

Elmer dipped a ladle of cold drinking water from a bucket and dowsed the coffee grounds.

"That'll settle the grounds to the bottom," Elmer said, noting the quizzical look on Grant's face. "Would you care for a cup?"

"Yes, sir," Grant said. "I could use a little warm-up."

Tom poured a shot of brandy into his coffee, and then offered the flask to Grant.

"A little sweetenin'?"

"Oh, no," Grant laughed. "My head is already spinning from the altitude."

When they had finished their coffee, Tom again opened the door.

"Well Grant, looks like we might get a break in this weather. Let's get saddled and head on up the trail."

Elmer retrieved the canvas bags from the truck.

"Pack them possibles on ol' Banjo," Tom said.

Elmer entered the corral. Using a handful of oats as bait, he caught a long legged, appaloosa mule with a split ear.

"That mule takes to the mare you're gonna ride," Tom said. "We won't have to worry about him runnin' off, if'n she's in camp."

"What happened to his ear? It looks like it was cut," Grant said.

"He was born of an early spring. Had a cold spell and froze his ear. You see a lot of horses and mules up in this country with ears like that," Elmer said.

Tom busied himself with saddling Luke, while Grant saddled the mare Elmer had brought from the corral.

"You about ready to ride?" Tom asked.

"I think I have everything...everything but my rifle," Grant said.

Grant walked into the cabin, returning with his borrowed rifle.

Tom walked around Grant's horse, inconspicuously checking to ensure that the cinch was tight and that the mare was properly tacked. Tom held the scabbard open.

"Stick 'er in there and let's see how she'll ride."

Grant slid the Winchester into the scabbard and mounted the mare, noting that the rifle was slung stock up so as to be easily drawn with the right hand.

"It'll be a bit uncomfortable at first," Tom said. "The damned thing rides right under your knee and gets sore after a couple of hours. Six or eight months and a man can get used to it though."

Elmer finished tying a diamond hitch to hold the top packs on the mule. He then handed the lead rope to Tom who was mounted on Luke. Tom made a quick visual inspection and then started Luke into a walk up the worn trail.

"We'll see you tomorrow, Elmer," Tom shouted over his shoulder. "Don't forget to bring a couple of bags of grain. These animals are gonna earn it."

Grant's mare followed the mule at a steady walk. Soon the trail became steeper. As the horses climbed into the mountains, the trail narrowed. Grant was glad that Tom was leading. The path was, at times, barely visible as it crossed shale slides and rocky outcroppings. Then a sleety rain began, turning the trail to muddy slime, which defied the grasp of shod hooves.

When the trail widened, Tom stopped in a meadow. He dismounted and pulled two oil cloth ponchos from one of the panniers on the mule.

"Put this over ya," Tom said. "Don't want to get too wet. A man can freeze to death in this wind, real quick."

Grant slipped the poncho over his head.

"These are some steep hills. I haven't ever been in terrain like this," Grant said.

"You see how we'll be ridin' on some real steep cliffs and then the trail goes into these little meadows? Well, sir, these are the feeder creeks for the Two Medicine River drainage. These Rocky Mountains are some of the most beautiful country in the world, and they can be some of the most dangerous too."

"You know more of geography than my professor at school," Grant said. "This is really an education."

As they rode on, the storm increased, and lightening was soon streaking the sky with following claps of thunder that caused the horses to start nervously.

"We'll shelter in the sag up ahead," Tom said. "Don't want to be on this high ground when this lightening is sparkin'. A fella could get himself kilt."

Tom stopped the horses in a low spot below a high rock ledge.

"We'll just sit here a bit and let this pass. At least we're out of the wind. And them big pines up the ridge are kind'a like lightnin' rods."

Tom lit a cigarette as the clouds passed overhead.

"I don't like the lightnin'. Never have," he said. "Back when me and Horse Sense was freightin' on the Mullan Road, we had a fella workin' for us who was one helluva teamster. Never saw a man could use a whip like that fella could. He could part the hair on a mule's ass and not even touch the hide below. He was a real artist with that black snake. It was somethin' to behold."

Tom took a puff on his Lucky Strike.

Grant sat politely mute, wondering if Tom had forgotten to finish a story.

"Is there a point to that story?" he asked.

"Oh, yeah! I was thinkin' on somethin' else. Anyway, Horse Sense had several wagons in a train and they was toppin' out on ridge when a storm just like this one come upon 'em. Now I wasn't there, I'm just relatin' what Horse Sense told me. As they topped the ridge the lightening was poppin' all around and ol' Horse Sense said that he got down from his rig and hunkered among some rocks that was downhill and just off the trail. Well this here fella just sat there on his wagon yellin' that the mules was gonna run off, if'n they didn't keep a hand to 'em."

"Did the mules run away?" Grant asked.

"Some did, but not that fella's. Horse Sense told me that the man stood up in that wagon to get a rein on them critters when a bolt hit him like a blacksmith's hammer. Split him near about in two. It knocked them mules right to their knees so they wasn't runnin' nowhere. Took them other boys a day and a half to pick up all the pieces and round up the rest of the stock though. I haven't ever been too trustin' of lightnin' ever since I heard that yarn."

The lightening subsided as the clouds passed. Tom led the mule alongside Luke to check the pack and then nudged the horse into a walk.

"We should be in camp in about an hour, I'd reckon."

Soon, the path was little more than a game trail climbing the side of a steep canyon wall. Shaded areas beneath trees and the north sides of rocks held patches of snow the sun was unable to melt in the cold high mountain air.

Every muscle in Grant's body was tensed as he watched rocks, dislodged by Tom's horse, tumble and disappear into the canyon. He

568

fixed his eyes on the spotted rump of the pack mule, wondering how the animals were able to cling to this precarious footing. On his right he could touch the rocks and sparse vegetation with his stirrup. On his left was a sheer drop into a gorge with a roaring creek hundreds of feet below.

They rounded a bend in the trail where the shelf widened to allow the animals room to stand side by side. Tom stopped Luke and motioned Grant forward. The horses were wheezing heavily from the effort.

"Let's let 'em blow a little," he said. "That was a pretty good pull coming up that last grade."

"I noticed that one side of the trail seems to be filled with nothing but a lot of air."

"I reckon I forgot to tell you. Keep most of your weight in the uphill stirrup. If that ol' mare looks like she's gonna lose footin', just dive off on the high side and grab whatever you can get a hold on. A fella can always get another horse," Tom said.

They sat for several minutes with the whistling wind and the labored breathing of the animals the only sounds to be heard.

When the breathing of the horses returned to normal, Tom urged Luke forward.

Grant fell in behind the mule as the trail narrowed. He could faintly hear Tom singing an unfamiliar shanty:

MacTavish is dead and his brother don't know it

His brother is dead but MacTavish don't know it

They're both lyin' dead in the very same bed

And neither one knows that the other is dead.

Grant laughed to himself. He wondered how many times Tom had ridden a lonesome trail with only his own songs to entertain him.

The path turned sharply and then widened as they entered a canyon meadow. Grant urged his mare forward to walk beside Luke.

"I didn't know you were a singer amongst your many accomplishments."

"Well, son, I'll tell you somethin'."

Tom took off his hat and scratched his head.

"When a man spends a lot of time alone, especially in the company of nothin' but horses and cows, he sings to himself a whole bunch. I guess it's akin to whistlin' past the grave yard. Singin' sort'a gives a bit'a comfort to a fella when he's alone and it always seemed to calm the animals, so I reckon I just got in the habit."

As he put his hat back on his head he squinted as he looked up the trail.

"Damn! Did you see that?"

Grant looked up in time to see the whitish buff colored rumps of a dozen elk disappear into the trees.

"Sons-a-bitches was right in camp," Tom said. "Well, at least we ain't gonna have to go too far to find 'em...I hope."

They rode into the trees and Grant could see the white of the canvas tent in a clearing several hundred yards from the meadow.

"This is a good camp right here," Tom said. "Good stream right beside for water and some trees to keep us out of the wind."

Riding into camp Grant saw that firewood was piled beside the tent and a ring of rocks was ready for a campfire. A canvas tarpaulin covered a makeshift table built of saplings tied across two pine stumps.

Knee-high lengths of sawed pine rounds served as stools set around the fire ring. A hitch rail of lodge pole had been nailed between two large trees a few yards from the camp.

"Was the time I would'a had to do all this myself. That's the best thing about havin' some money. It makes for comfort. Now I can hire someone to come set this camp and come and take it out again. This is pure luxury. When I was your age I was happy to have a tarp, some flint and steel and a tin cup to cook in. Now I come to camp with pots and pans waiting for me on a sure enough table."

Grant and Tom unsaddled the horses and tied them to the rail. Grant then helped Tom remove the packs from the mule.

Tom took leather hobbles from the pack and tossed them to Grant.

"Put these on that old girl. We don't need her runnin' off and takin' this damned mule with her. We'll turn 'em out in the meadow to feed for the night. They won't go far from the creek, and Elmer will be bringing us supplies and grain tomorrow."

Taking a large cowbell from the pack, Tom attached it to a leather strap and walked to the mare. He buckled the bell around her neck and turned her loose to graze.

"That bell will make it harder for them to hide."

Tom winked at Grant as he released the hobbled animals.

"Grab a bunk, stow your gear and fix yourself a bed," Tom said. "Like I told ya, this is pure luxury. Sure one helluva lot better than sleepin' on the ground when you get to be my age."

Grant opened the tent flap and put his bag on one of the four cots which had been assembled of lodge pole pine and bailing wire. He then walked to the hitch rail to cover his saddle with the poncho and retrieve his rifle from the scabbard.

"I suppose it is best to put our guns in the tent?" Grant asked.

"You bet! There's still some bears in this country and we need to be thinkin' about other visitors...like Mr. Horton, if'n you know what I mean."

Grant walked toward the tent with his rifle.

"Don't forget to load that thing boy," Tom shouted.

"Oh...yes...I suppose that would be the best idea."

Grant put four cartridges into the rifle's magazine as Tom had shown him, then placed the rifle beside his bunk. When he came out of the tent, Tom was putting meat, potatoes and vegetables in a large Dutch oven.

"Soon as this here fire gets to goin' we'll have us some stew for supper."

Grant sat on one of the log round stools by the fire. He soon found his mouth watering. The smell of Tom's concoction was overpowering. He thought to himself how comfortable Tom was in this primitive environment. He envied the frontiersman's life of hardship and deprivation, feeling that he had somehow missed an important connection with the real world. All that Tom is, and everything that he has, Grant thought, are products of his own effort and two calloused hands. Few who live so well could make such a claim.

Tom lifted the lid from the bubbling stew.

"Get us some tin plates and eatin' irons from the table and let's get at it," he said.

Grant ate ravenously, mopping his plate with a piece of bread.

"Damn boy...don't eat the spoon too!" Tom laughed.

"I guess I was pretty hungry. It has been a long day."

Grant filled a basin and washed the dishes while Tom sat by the fire smoking a cigarette. As the darkness enclosed their camp, it became a tiny island of light in a sea of blackness. As the fire died, Grant could not recall ever having seen so many stars.

"I'd like to get an early start in the morning. I don't think those elk will go too far," Tom said.

Tom stood and stretched himself.

"That bunk is lookin' mighty comfortable right now," he said.

Grant followed as Tom walked into the tent with a lantern. When they were in their bunks, Tom blew out the light.

"See ya bright and early. About dark thirty," Tom chuckled.

Grant pulled his blankets tightly around his neck. He could feel the aches from the hours in the saddle and his sore right knee gave meaning to Tom's forewarning of earlier in the day. Although they were in the wilderness, he felt a certain security unlike any he had ever experienced. He listened to the sounds of the night punctuated by the reassuring clang of the bell on his mare. He tried to envision the comfort that would have been felt by the old plainsmen like Tom, knowing that their horses; their transportation; their very survival was still at hand.

He thrilled with the anticipation of experiencing for himself the hunt and stalking of game. How better to prepare to write of a man like Tom, he thought. What could be more appropriate than to be here in the rough country and taste the iron pot stew and smell campfire smoke, which lingered on sturdy clothing? His thoughts melted into the unfamiliar inky blackness of the mountain night.

"Come'on, boy! Those elk will be bedded by the time we get saddled. It's near about four already," Tom said.

Grant raised himself onto one elbow to watch Tom light the oil lantern. Seeing his steamy breath in its glow, Grant pulled the blankets tight under his chin and curled himself into a ball.

Tom pulled on his shirt and boots.

"You get a fire goin' and I'll catch the critters. There's some pitch beside the table," Tom said.

Grant sat up on the edge of the bunk. His cold long johns, damp with sweat, clung to his torso. Hurrying to put on his clothing he shivered so violently that he was unable to button his shirt. Pulling on his boots, he grabbed the lantern.

Still shaking, he stacked wood in the fire ring. He gathered a small mound of kindling chips and placed a sticky chunk of pine pitch on the pile, as he had seen Tom do the day before. The pitch blazed instantly when touched with the match. He piled more kindling onto the pitch and blew into the flame. Soon the fire was glowing brightly in the predawn darkness. He pulled his jacket tight and hunkered by the fire until his teeth quit chattering. He could hear the mare's bell moving closer to camp.

Tom walked into the light leading the mare. Luke and the mule rabbit hopped along behind in their hobbles. Tying the animals to the hitch rail he placed a bag with grain on the head of each.

"Might chilly this morning. These critters are gonna need a little hot food. Elmer should be bringin' us some more grain this afternoon," Tom said.

Tom set an iron skillet across two fresh logs he placed in the fire and then began slicing off chunks of bacon.

"Looks like that pot is a boilin'. Grab that bag on the table and throw some coffee in it, would ya."

Grant dropped a handful of coffee into the pot. Soon the smell of coffee and bacon tantalized his senses in the piney fragrance of the still morning air. He splashed a dipper of cold water into the coffee grounds and set the pot on a stone beside the fire.

They quickly finished the bacon with bread and coffee and then began to saddle the horses.

"We'll take the mule just in case we get an elk down. Then we can at least pack a couple of quarters in."

Grant could feel his excitement rising as he saddled his mare and then helped Tom with the pack saddle on the mule. Riding out of camp in the graying light of dawn his hand touched the walnut butt stock of the borrowed Winchester with an involuntarily affectionate caress.

The sun was rising as they entered a long open meadow, which held standing water. Grant heard a loud splash and saw a beaver dive beneath the surface of the pond. He marveled at the beaver's well maintained earthen dam.

"I had no idea that beavers built such large dams!" he said excitedly. "One would almost think this was man made."

"Hell, I've seen 'em a half mile across. That old story about 'busy as a beaver' didn't just pop up in someone's head. Notice how there ain't nothin' but stumps for five hundred yards in every direction?"

They dismounted and Grant followed as Tom walked to a flowering plant, which had begun to wilt and dry with the frosty fall mornings. Taking out his knife, Tom cut several twelve-inch lengths from the main stem and put them carefully into the breast pocket of his jacket.

"Cow parsnip," he said, without being asked.

He then walked the edge of the pond until he found a small willow bush, which he scrutinized. Carefully selecting several branches he cut lengths of willow twig and put those in the pocket with cow parsnip cuttings.

"Gonna make us an elk call," Tom said.

He walked the edge of the pond.

"Lot's of sign here. I'd say that ol' bull we saw with that bunch yesterday uses this meadow for his wallow. See all these tracks where he's been diggin' in the mud? Good feed and water for the cows. I reckon this will be the place."

Tom sat on a protruding rock and took the cuttings from his pocket. Using a willow twig he reamed the pith from the cow parsnip stem creating a hollow tube. He then cut another piece of willow at an angle, shaving a thin slice from one side and carefully fitting the willow into the end of the cow parsnip stem.

"That ought'a about do the trick."

He placed the tube to his lips and cupped his hands around the end. Taking a deep breath, he blew a musical whistling sound, which changed pitch and rose in intensity as he manipulated his hands.

Grant was about to speak when a similar noise could be heard echoing from the timber to their left a half mile away.

A smile lit Tom's face.

"I reckon she did the work," he said.

"My God. What was that?" Grant asked, never having heard the bugle of an elk.

"That was ol' Mister Bull Elk lettin' us know that he is the king of this here piece of real estate," Tom said.

He stood and walked toward the horses. As they mounted, another bull elk bugled from the opposite side of the meadow to their right.

"Now this might get real interesting," Tom said.

They crossed the creek below the dam and headed for a grove of heavy timber.

"Tie that ol' girl high enough so she can't get down and roll," Tom said.

Grant watched Tom tie Luke and the mule to lodge pole pine trees.

"Why don't you want her to roll?" he asked.

"Cause she'll bust the saddle and maybe her neck if she tangles in that rope. Either way, you'll be walkin' home."

Tom pointed and began to walk silently toward a rocky knoll overlooking the meadow. Grant followed, tripping over rocks and fallen limbs. Suddenly, Tom stopped and raised his hand.

"Try to sound like just a small heard of stampeding buffalos...would ya, son. We are tryin' to put the sneak on these critters ya know?"

Grant said nothing, amazed at Tom's quick silent movement across the rough terrain. Tom slowed his pace to give his greenhorn partner an opportunity to catch up.

He picked a spot among the rocks at the top of the outcropping and motioned for Grant to sit down.

"What a great spot. We can see the whole valley from here," he whispered.

Tom looked through his binoculars, searching the tree line surrounding the open grassy meadow.

The whistling bugle of a bull elk came from the timber to their right.

"That sounds like the second bull that answered us earlier. I reckon he must be the bachelor and he's tryin' to talk a few of the girls into coming over his way. The old boy with all the cows is stayin' quiet right now."

Tom scanned each detail of the trees. Movement caught his straining eyes. He fixed on the spot.

"There's our challenger," he said.

Tom handed Grant the glasses and pointed to a spot in the trees several hundred yards to the right. Grant's hands were shaking and he could feel his heart pounding. He looked through the binoculars and searched until a glint of morning sun on the antlers of the huge animal revealed its location.

"What a magnificent beast," he said.

"Let me see them glasses," Tom said, putting out his hand without looking at Grant.

Grant put the binoculars in Tom's hand. Without moving his eye Tom raised the glasses and fixed on a spot to their left.

"And there is the old man of the mountain," Tom said.

He handed the binoculars back to Grant.

The large herd bull was in a grassy cove in the tree line. Several cows were feeding close by.

"They're both huge," Grant said.

The bachelor bull bugled again. Grant turned the glasses and could clearly see the steam from bugling bull's breath in the morning sun.

"It looks like he's peeing on himself," Grant said.

"He is," Tom answered. "That's an elk's version of Bay Rum. He pisses all over himself and rolls in the mud and he thinks he's dressed for the ball. It must work. The worse they smell, the more the girls seem to like 'em."

Grant sat glued to the binoculars as the two animals, moving with nearly imperceptible purpose, closed the distance.

"The big fella with cows," Tom whispered, "he's tryin' to intimidate that other one. But I'd reckon this is gonna get hot, 'cause that boy off to the right is just near about as big as the herd bull."

As the animals drew closer to one another they were moving obliquely, coming ever nearer to the knoll where Tom and Grant sat watching. As they cleared the timber, the animals could at last see one another. Each time they exchanged bugles, Grant flinched as if startled.

Walking in a slow stiff-legged exhibition, the two large bull elk began an ancient ritual dance. They circled toward one another, each sizing up his opponent. First one and then the other would lay his antlers along his back in a display designed to intimidate his rival. Each ringing bugle now ended in deep guttural grunting sounds. Mucous, excreted from flared nostrils, hung in steaming streamers from the animal's mouths after each vocalization.

"Just like a couple of young fellers tryin' to impress the girls," Tom whispered.

Grant looked at the cows peacefully feeding in the meadow, oblivious to the impending battle.

"The girls don't look very interested."

"That's women for ya. You'll never know they're interested until it's a done deal."

To Grant's surprise, the two bulls stopped and turned to face one another. The bugling stopped and the entire meadow fell silent. The cows now raised their heads to look at the challenging monarchs. The two bulls stood momentarily, statue like, on the frosty meadow. As if a signal had been given they dropped their heads and charged, colliding in a reverberating clash.

"Ain't many folks will ever get to see a spectacle like that, my boy," Tom said.

Grant watched breathless as the violent ebb and flow of the well matched mêlée ripped the valley floor, shattering the idyllic silence of the mountain meadow. Colliding, then retreating; halting to paw the ground and then pursuing again. Out of the corner of his eye he saw that Tom had laid his rifle across his forearm on the rock in front of them.

"This is it, son! You don't get a chance like this very often. Get your gun up where we can do some business."

Shaking in uncontrolled excitement, Grant raised the Winchester to his shoulder being careful not to scratch the borrowed rifle against the rocks.

"I know you're excited...and it'll be hard to get a good breath. Take your time...aim real good," Tom instructed in a soothing voice. "I'm excited myself. This is somethin' a fella don't get to see every day."

Grant tried several times to get a good breath. Finally, he forced himself to relax. He closed one eye and looked through the sights of the rifle.

"You shoot first. I'll back you up," Tom said. "Now get a deep breath, hold 'er steady and squeeze that trigger."

Grant concentrated. This seemed, unexpectedly, the most important thing he had ever done. Taking careful aim at the bull on the right he slowly squeezed the trigger. He did not hear the shot. He knew that the rifle had fired but he felt momentarily detached. He did not feel the recoil. It was as if nothing had happened. The two animals stopped in place, standing like the bronze statue in front of the Elk's Lodge.

When Tom fired, Grant nearly dropped his rifle. The animal on the left, which he assumed Tom had shot, dropped in its tracks with the crack of Tom's rifle. Frozen momentarily, he frantically pushed the lever of the Winchester to chamber another round. How could he have missed? Quickly shouldering the rifle he aimed carefully and was about to squeeze the trigger, when the elk toppled onto its side, head to head with the animal Tom had shot.

"I thought you were going to back me up?" Grant said.

He sat back breathing heavily.

"Wasn't no need," Tom said. "I saw the dust fly when you let 'er rip and I knew you'd hit him right through the heart. He just didn't know he was dead there for a minute. Wasn't no use wastin' another bullet on that one, so I thought I'd just get mine too. This kind'a thing just don't happen too often. We were just right lucky this morning."

Tom walked around the rock and sat down to light a cigarette. The cow elk, which had milled around in confusion after the shooting, now saw him and galloped into the timber.

"We'll just sit here and watch 'em a minute. Make sure one of 'em don't get up and try to run off."

They both leaned back against the rock and Grant could feel himself beginning to relax and catch his breath.

"I could never have dreamed that the hunting of an animal would be such an emotional experience. I have always wondered why people wanted to hunt. Especially when one considers that the need to hunt no longer exists. We have modern farming and ranching and one can buy food. Frankly, I was one of those who opposed the idea of shooting animals as sport. Now I have to reconsider my thoughts. This is a genuine communion with the world and our ancestors. It will be very difficult for me to explain to my family and friends, the emotions involved in the experience. There has to be some primordial instinct left over from our days in the caves that brings about the rush of adrenaline at the scene of the kill," Grant said.

"I don't know about that, but the fun's all over now. From here on it ain't nothin' but hard work. However, you'll really enjoy a steak off'n these critters more than any you ever had, when you think that you did it all yourself."

They walked down the hill toward dead animals. Grant realized that the elk had to be drawn and skinned and taken back to camp.

"I guess you're right. It looks like a long day of hard work ahead," Grant said.

"I hope you got a sharp knife," Tom laughed.

Tom bent over his elk and prepared to open the carcass.

"I'll get started with the guttin' and you go get the horses. We'll need that saw and a sharpenin' stone before we're done here."

Grant walked to where they had left the animals tied. He put his rifle in the scabbard and walked back across the meadow leading all three.

Although, at first, he found the chore repulsive, Grant had learned enough anatomy from his father to make short work of dressing the game. He watched and emulated Tom's every move as they skinned the elk. It was early afternoon before the animals were quartered.

Tom used ropes tied to Luke's saddle to pull the quarters of meat into the high branches of a tree.

"That'll keep the bears off of the meat till we can get back tomorrow," Tom said.

He rode under the hanging meat to ensure it was too high for any bear to reach.

"Guess we'd best take your trophy," Tom said.

He wrapped the hind quarters of Grant's elk in tarpaulins and packed them with the antlers onto the mule.

"You'll be wantin' those horns to hang on your wall someday, I'd reckon. You might even want to make yourself a buckskin shirt from the hide."

Tom gave Grant a canvas tarpaulin.

"Go get those elk livers and wrap 'em in this mantee tarp. Ain't no use feedin' them to the magpies. We can have liver and onions with Elmer tonight."

Grant reluctantly retrieved the elk livers and packed them on the mule. Mounting his mare he followed Tom toward the trail back to camp.

Tom stopped at the creek below the beaver dam to water the horses. Grant rode to the creek and gave the mare her head to drink from the stream.

"Fuck ol' Roan and his farrier too," Tom said.

Grant rode to where Tom was sitting on Luke. He was looking at the mud below the dam.

"What's the matter?" Grant asked.

"See that," Tom said, pointing to the mud.

"I'm no woodsman but I would say that it looks like the track of a bear," Grant answered.

"Son, that ain't a bear. That's a beeeaar!" Tom roared. "That's about the biggest grizzly track I think I've ever seen. I hope to hell we got that meat high enough so that big bastard can't get at it. That is one critter you don't want to run into in a dark alley...I'll guarantee ya that. We'd best keep these horses close to camp tonight."

"Would he be a trophy as nice as President Roosevelt's White House bear?" Grant asked.

"Better'n that I reckon. This is one big sumbitch," Tom said. "Damned if he didn't cross since we were here this morning. That should be enough to scare hell outta ya. We might'a rode right up on him in the trail."

Tom looked at Grant, sensing his excitement.

"Would ya like to go after him?"

"I would, indeed," Grant said.

"In the morning, we'll bring Elmer out to pack in the rest of our elk, and then we'll take a look around and see if we can spot that monster. What the hell, we ain't in no hurry. We can stay up here a month if'n you're a mind. Besides, I'd like to get myself one of those Bighorn sheep for the wall in my den. All the years I've hunted these hills, I never have shot one of them. Tell ya the truth, I never cared much for eatin' mutton. But those old Rams are sure a pretty sight hangin' on the wall. Those big ol' horns have a majesty about 'em. Don't ya think?"

Grant nodded in agreement and then fell into line behind the mule as they headed back to camp.

It was nearing dark as they started down the last incline into the meadow where the camp was set.

"God dammit," Tom said.

"What's the problem? I don't see anything," Grant said.

"Well, you don't see it 'cause it ain't there. There's no smoke comin' outta camp, and I don't hear no horses whinnyin'. Which means that Elmer ain't there."

Riding into camp, Grant could see that things were just as they had been left. Tom dismounted and began to unpack the mule. Grant removed the saddles from all three animals.

"What do you suppose could have happened?" Grant asked.

"I don't know, but to tell ya the truth, I'm a might worried. Hope that damned Buck didn't come and cause Elmer no problems. Ol' Elmer is generally a pretty reliable kid. One thing's sure, he'd better have one hell of an excuse or I'm gonna chew him a new one," Tom said.

Grant hobbled the animals and put the bell on the mare. He then turned them into the grassy meadow.

"We got just about enough grain to catch 'em in the mornin'," Tom said.

Piling firewood in the rock ring, Grant lit a fire.

Tom threw a rope over a lodge pole tied high between two trees.

"Lend a hand in pullin' this quarter up onto the meat pole," Tom said.

Working together they hung both quarters of the elk and hung the antlers beside the meat.

"Put on the pot to boil and peel some of them spuds, huh," Tom said.

Tom unwrapped the elk livers, washing the meat to cut and cook.

"Elmer's gonna miss a treat."

Grant did not say anything but he was not looking forward to the dinner. He had not eaten liver since he was a child. Even then he had been forced to do so by his grandmother. However, the smell of the liver and onions soon had his juices flowing. The long day of hard work on a breakfast of bread and bacon had developed his appetite. When Tom began to dish up the disdainful plate he consumed his portion with relish.

After they had eaten, Grant washed the dishes while Tom lit a cigarette and leaned against his saddle on the ground close to the fire. He looked up at the starless sky.

"Looks like we might get a little rain or snow tonight, maybe," he said.

Grant placed his saddle by the fire and laid back in its cradle. As he relaxed he could feel the soreness in the seldom used muscles of his back and shoulders. His right knee ached from the bulge of the rifle under the stirrup fender, and the inside cheeks of his buttocks were rubbed raw.

"You don't think Buck would harm Elmer, do you?" Grant said.

"I just don't know. Buck has done some awful things. Bein' a friend seems to be no guarantee with that mean bastard."

Grant removed his worn notebook from the inside pocket of his jacket and began to write rapidly, attempting to capture the memories and emotions of the day. After some minutes of writing he looked up at Tom.

"I really want to thank you for bringing me on this adventure. This trip into the 'high lonesome,' as you call it, has given me an entirely new and enriched perspective on what life was like in your younger days when a good horse could mean life and death and your firearm and knife was not only security, but currency at your grocery store."

Tom looked at Grant's wind-burned face and smiled.

"Now by God, son, if you can write with the eloquence that you just spit out that fine description, I think you might just get your prize...what did you call that, a Pulitzer?

"Well, thank you kind sir! You know, Tom, in all the years that I have had this ambition to write, I have always lacked a single quality."

"And what's that?" Tom asked.

"Confidence! I have never really been confident, because I didn't have any real life experiences within which to frame my words. I think I have read every dime novel ever written and those descriptions were all I ever had as reference. Now I actually know what a horse smells like." Grant smiled and sniffed his clothing. "Maybe too well!"

"It grows on ya...in more ways than one," Tom said.

"I suppose you know that I have also grown quite fond of your niece."

"Hard for anyone not to have noticed that, son."

"Would you mind if I asked her to marry me?"

Tom looked at Grant with a wry grin.

"It would be to my everlasting pleasure, but I reckon you'd best ask her pa."

"I plan on that when I return to Saint Louis."

"I ain't never met the man, but I hear he is a highfalutin' legal eagle with some real connections...and he is real protective of his baby girl. I will say this...that's a marriage that ain't likely to hurt your career none."

"I wasn't really thinking of your niece as a career move."

"Didn't reckon you were, but you might one day down the road."

"May I ask you a personal question?"

"Shoot! That's what you're here for. You've heard all there is so far."

"May I ask what happened to Dancing Fawn?"

Tom dropped the butt of his cigarette into the fire and took a long breath.

"Well, son, it was one of those unexpected things that life visits upon...to remind us to be thankful for today."

Tom stared into the embers for a few moments and then looked at Grant.

"It was 1904. Susanna was about eight or nine, I reckon, and Derrick was comin' six. Things was goin' real good. Business was doin' well and me and Dancin' Fawn was about as happy as two folks can be. She was a darlin'. Looked after me like I was ol' King Tut himself. We never had a cross word as I can recall."

Tom lit another cigarette and flipped the match into the fire.

"They was havin' a World's Fair in Saint Louis. Dancin' Fawn had never been anywhere except the reservation and Fort Benton, and she was hintin' that she'd sure enough like to go see them doins'. She could speak pretty good American by then...and I was ready for a little fun myself. I figured we'd have us a real honeymoon and I could show her what the world looked like outside the prairies of Montana. So I booked us a Pullman sleeper and we headed down to Saint Louis in the early spring."

"My parents attended that World's Fair," Grant said. "They still speak of it today. They were there when President Roosevelt gave the opening address."

"Well, now, ain't that a coincidence. So was me and Dancin' Fawn. In fact, that was the first time I'd seen ol' Teedie since our little trip to Cuba. We didn't get to spend any time together but we had a chance to chew the fat for a few minutes before he gave that speech."

"I can't wait to tell my mother and father about that when I see them," Grant said.

"Well, after we heard ol' Teedie blab on about the brotherhood of man and all that falderal, we got on to seeing the fair. It was a sure enough spectacle. Dancin' Fawn was just thrilled. Various electrical devices and fancy mechanical doodads of all descriptions...things that she hadn't even been able to imagine."

"Did you take the children with you?" Grant asked.

"No...we left them at the ranch with Koko. She was real good at lookin' out for 'em. Koko had one baby of her own. He died on the reservation before he could walk. That was before I met Dancin' Fawn. Koko's husband died just shortly after the baby. She took care of our children as if they was her own. As it turned out, I reckon it was for the best...leavin' our kids at home and all."

A tear ran down Tom's cheek.

"We don't have to talk about this if you'd rather not."

"Well...I'll just make a long story real short. Dancin' Fawn, according to the pill peddler in Saint Louis, got the mumps. What I didn't know was that she was gonna have another child and the mumps was the worst thing that could'a happened to a woman with child. She got sicker by the day and died in the hospital in Saint Louis. Bled to death when she lost the little one."

A light rain was beginning to fall. Tom got to his feet and began putting tarpaulins over the groceries and cookware on the table. Picking up his saddle, he walked toward the tent.

"Better bring your saddle in," he said, choking back tears. "You think your ass hurts now...just wait till you ride a wet saddle."

"Was that the last time you saw Mr. Roosevelt?" Grant asked.

"No, sir. He come here huntin' two more times after that. Then in fourteen, I believe it was fourteen, he took a trip to the jungles of the Amazon. Him and his boy Kermit and some science fella from South America discovered a new river that they named after Teedie. But the old boy got so sick on that trip that they had to carry him outta there. Now I can tell you that if they carried Teedie out, he was really sick. Anyway, I never saw him again after that. I got a letter from him in sixteen, as I recall, but that Amazon trip seemed to take the fire out of him. He died a couple of years later."

"I understand now why you consider Koko a sister. She has been a valuable member of your family for many years," Grant said.

"She's a darlin'," Tom replied.

He pulled off his boots and blew out the lantern.

Grant lay in the inky darkness hoping that when the time came to put his pen to paper he would be able to capture the nuance and drama of the highs and lows, the joy and pain that Tom had recounted.

33

The morning dawned cloudy and windy. Although the rain had stopped, a damp wet chill pervaded the camp. Tom lit a fire and cut steaks from the elk quarters before Grant was out of bed. He emerged from the tent, his teeth chattering, shivering uncontrollably and stood by the fire, engulfed in smoke.

"Cut up some of those taters and onions, would you boy. We'll at least have a decent breakfast," Tom said.

"Are we going to ride down to the cabin to find Elmer?" Grant asked.

"Not yet. We'll eat somethin' and then I'll ride over to our other camp. Maybe Elmer went over there instead. The boy does get confused from time to time. I'll get one of the boys over there to bring in our elk. If'n Elmer ain't over there, we'll head back to the cabin."

Tom set a large skillet on the fire and dropped in a piece of bacon fat.

"Put the spuds in this skillet when you're done cuttin'," Tom said.

He then set a cast iron grill on the embers and put the elk steaks on to broil.

Grant could feel the clammy chill of worry hanging over breakfast. He washed the dishes in silence and waited for direction from Tom.

"Do you think you can find your way back to where we left them elk hangin'?" Tom asked.

A huge smile lit Grant's face.

"Like an Indian scout. I was trained by the best."

"Good enough. Like I told you, we have another camp just over this ridge in the next drainage. I'm gonna ride over there to check on Elmer. I'll get a couple of pack animals and someone to pack the elk back to the trail head. It's just past nine now. I should be back over to where the meat is hung at around two. You just tie that mare and mule by the beaver dam...right where they was yesterday. Then go hide yourself in amongst those same rocks. Set yourself up so you can watch those gut piles where we kilt them elk. You might just get a shot at that big ol' griz."

Grant mounted the mare and Tom handed him the pack mule's lead rope. The mule balked, then moved toward Luke, nearly pulling Grant from the saddle.

"Don't let that ornery bastard unseat you now. Dally on the horn so you can keep a grip on him. He'll settle down once you get on the trail," Tom said.

Tom mounted Luke.

"Sometimes, other hunters will come into this area to look for game. Keep an eye out and don't shoot until you know what your target is. Don't be killin' some hunter or his horse. Even more important yet, keep an eye out so that some flatlander don't shoot you."

"I'll be cautious," Grant said.

The mare moved into a walk pulling the mule.

"You're doin' fine. I'll see you about two this afternoon," Tom shouted.

He disappeared into the timber heading for the ridgeline high above.

Riding along in the mountain silence, Grant felt elated that Tom had trusted him to navigate the trail alone. It gave him a feeling of pride and again reminded him of what it must have been like for the young Tom to have ridden into Indian country alone, with nothing but a horse, a rifle and instinct to guide him.

Grant rode slowly, watching the trail for signs of game. Deer and elk tracks were clearly visible in the damp earth overlaying the hoof prints he and Tom had left the day before. Remembering Tom's mention of meeting the large bear in the trail, he began to alternate his gaze from the earth in the path of his horse to the trail and woods ahead. I surely don't want to meet that bear, while mounted on this horse with this mule jerking on me, he said to himself.

He was congratulating himself on his newly developed skill of reading game sign when it occurred to him that there were fresh horse shoe tracks overlaying all of the deer, elk and horse prints in the trail.

A burst of adrenaline pumped through him as he remembered following Buck into the woods. Buck did, after all, know where all of Tom's camps were set. He may have come in by a different trail to hide in ambush. Grant stopped his horse to study the tracks.

What a fool, he chided. Tom had told him that others did hunt this area. These tracks could belong to anyone. I surely don't want to get trigger happy and shoot some poor 'honyocker' who has come to the forest to feed his family, he chuckled to himself. That grizzly bear is my only nemesis on this trip, he thought.

He cleared the timber and rode into the large meadow where the elk had been the day before, straining his eyes for any movement. He watered the animals at the creek and then turned his horse toward the timber above the dam. He tied the mare and mule high on lodge pole pine trees as per Tom's instructions.

He removed the Winchester from the scabbard and took Tom's

binoculars from the saddle bags. Placing a small cloth bag containing some jerky in his jacket pocket, he slung his canteen over his shoulder. Marching toward the rocky promontory where they had sat the day before, he was conscious of the noise as his boots crunched loudly in the brush and gravel of the stream bed. He realized, being alone, just how loud the noises sounded in this silent wilderness. He began to walk lightly, one step at a time. He began to look around, swiveling his head as Tom had done. Take a step, look around, walk a step, look around. Now aware of the uneven terrain and foliage, he used the available cover, practicing techniques he had seen his expert teacher use.

Not perfect, he thought to himself, but not bad for the second day as a hunter. At least I am now aware of the commotion I'm making. He began to write scenes in his head as he crept along, selectively choosing the verbs and adjectives to describe the stalk when he wrote about it later.

Grant neared the rocks at the top of the promontory. Peering over the top he froze in place. A dark shape was moving at the upper end of the meadow. Hunkering behind the rise he raised the binoculars. His body quivered in an odd combination of fear and anticipation. It was a bear. It was a very large bear. Too far off for a shot he thought. The bear disappeared into the timber. Perhaps he didn't want to get close enough for a shot. He told himself to relax and get a grip on his emotions. What would Tom do?

Using the rise of the hill to conceal his movement, he crept into the rocks and sat where he and Tom had shot the elk the day before. Magpies and jays were swarming on the two mounds of intestines about seventy yards in front of him. From his vantage point he could see that the elk meat was still hanging in the tree several hundred yards to his left. Patience, my boy. Patience, he said to himself.

Time seemed to stop as his eyes strained to pick up any movement. At last he again saw motion in trees at the upper end of the meadow. He raised the glasses to see a small herd of Bighorn sheep break from the timber and cross the meadow in a four-footed hopping gait. They must be escaping the bear, he said to himself. I'll have to tell Tom about the huge ram that was with that herd. That would be a trophy for sure. Tom was correct, he thought, the ram was really a beautiful creature.

He felt the urge to leave his overlook and attempt to stalk the bear. Patience, he repeated to himself. Tom had told him that if the bear was close to where they had killed the elk, to wait him out. The old scout's counsel overruled Grant's youthful impetuosity. He sat and watched and waited.

Clouds were building over the mountains, blocking the sun. A chilled wind made the wait seem interminable. Time passed imperceptibly.

Grant took off his wrist-watch and placed it on the rock in front of him. The hands seemed not to be moving. He picked it up to listen and was reassured by the tick-tick-tick.

Another movement caught his eye. This time it was closer. Fixing the binoculars on the spot Grant strained to make out a shape. To his amazement, the enormous bear moved into the meadow just a few hundred yards away and began to graze on the vegetation like a cow. It then began digging and eating the roots of what appeared to Grant to be onions. Appearing startled, the bear rose up and stood on its hind legs. It sniffed the air, looking in the direction that the sheep had run. Dropping to all fours he began a slow meandering walk toward the hanging meat.

Grant looked at his watch. It was nearing twelve and Tom had promised to meet him at two. If Tom rode into the meadow it would surely send his trophy scampering for tall timber. He estimated the range. He knew enough about his skill with the borrowed rifle to realize that this was much too far for a sure and lethal shot. He waited.

Grant's gaze alternated between the giant grizzly, moving slowly and erratically across the meadow, and his watch, which was ticking down the time to Tom's arrival. The chill now elongated every minute as he waited for his quarry to come into range.

The elk quarters were hanging in a tree at the foot of a steep timber covered ridge. The ridge curved behind Grant's position and dropped into the canyon below the meadow. The great grizzly plodded toward the tree where the elk were hung. Standing on his hind legs, he could barely scratch the hanging meat with the tips of his claws.

Grant recalled that Tom had been at least a foot shy of touching the quarters of elk when he'd reached to his full extension while standing in the saddle stirrups on Luke. The size of this beast was now in full perspective.

The bear strained mightily to dislodge the meat. However, his best effort was futile as the swinging carcasses defied his grasp. At last, he gave up the effort and lumbered toward the flocking birds feeding on the elk entrails.

As the bear drew into the range of Grant's rifle, it again stood on its hind legs to test the wind. Grant could plainly see how large the animal really was. This was not like shooting an elk. The twinge of fear he had felt earlier was now outright alarm. He made a mental note to write of his ambivalence. He wanted to remember the trepidation mixed with the fervor to achieve the trophy.

His senses seemed to be sharper than at any time he could remember in his life. It's now or never, he said to himself as he laid the rifle across his forearm. The metallic click when he cocked the rifle rang in his ears like a blacksmith's hammer striking an anvil. The bear seemed to be looking him directly in the eye. He placed the front sight in the middle of the giant's chest.

Taking a deep breath, Grant put his finger on the trigger.

To his left and up the ridge he heard the crack of timber and the sound of rocks rolling down the steep hill. Before he could squeeze the trigger, his quarry bolted toward the timber on the ridge to his left and disappeared.

Grant cursed aloud in an unaccustomed display of anger. What in the hell could that have been, he wondered. Perhaps some elk? The Bighorn sheep he had seen earlier? They must have moved along the top of the ridge. But then, perhaps it was another bear or the hunter whose tracks he had seen that morning?

He looked at his watch. It was after one.

Slinging the binoculars around his neck, he picked up the rifle and began climbing the slope toward the source of the noise. I don't want to meet that bear in the timber, he thought. That animal ran faster than an automobile...but then I have a rifle.

Grant smiled to himself. I might get a chance at that Bighorn ram. Whatever it was that spooked my trophy bear, I have to satisfy my curiosity as to the culprit. I guess that's why they call it hunting. The bear had obviously been disturbed when it ran off. It would surely not come back to the meadow before Tom rode in.

In the thin air of the high altitude, Grant quickly became breathless. He stopped often to gasp for air as he clamored up the steep hill. Above the meadow floor the wind was sending a chill through his jacket as he began to sweat beneath his clothing.

His labored breathing and the increasing wind obscured the forest sounds. He thought that he heard the footfalls of a large animal walking in the thick vegetation above him. He stood stark still, holding his breath and attempting to hear.

The unfamiliar horse tracks he had seen earlier had left the trail and disappeared into the canyon below. Could it be Buck? Was Buck setting a trap? His stomach tightened and his mouth was suddenly dry. He took a swallow from his canteen.

How could Buck have come all the way to this ridge from the bottom of that canyon without being seen or heard? He scolded himself for acting like a small boy in the dark alone.

Grabbing the limbs of a deadfall treetop, he pulled himself up an exceptionally steep portion of the hill, and then sat on the log to rest and catch his breath.

He looked at his watch. It was nearly twenty after one. I had better hurry he thought. Tom will be expecting to find me in the rocks. The noise had to have come from the sheep, he thought.

"*Tempus fugit, ergo carpe diem*. I am going to go hunt that ram," he said aloud.

"What kind'a fancy talk is that, college boy?"

Grant grabbed his rifle as he jumped to his feet.

Buck rode from a thicket twenty yards up the hill. He smiled that cold toothy grin and crossed his right leg over the saddle in front of him. Resting his ankle on the saddle horn as he had done the day Tom shot him. His casual attitude sent a nauseating bolt of fear surging through Grant.

"It's Latin...how did you get up here?" Grant said.

"Been watchin' you," Buck said. "I reckon you think you're a real hunter now. Did you shoot them elk down there?"

"I shot one," Grant replied. "Tom's with me. He shot the other," Grant lied, hoping that Buck might be distracted.

"Tom went over to Derrick's camp. I watched you ride in here this morning. So he ain't gonna be here to save your ass this time. I would say we're pretty much alone out here. I do wish you had our sweetheart with you, though! I could give her what she really needs and then cut out her lyin' heart."

Grant could feel his fear turning to anger as he thumbed back the hammer of the Winchester and slowly moved the muzzle to point in Buck's direction.

"Ya know, college boy," Buck said, "seeing a slicker like you carrying a big bore hunk of hardware like that is just down right sceery. But I am comforted in knowin' that you ain't got the balls to actually shoot a man."

Never taking his eyes off of Grant, Buck took a small can of snuff from his pocket and placed a pinch under his lower lip.

"Now shootin' an elk don't take too much out of a fella. But killin' a man takes a special kind'a attitude. Somehow, I just don't think you've got any of that."

Still watching Grant, Buck leaned forward to spit. Without warning his horse spun and bolted down the hill. Caught unaware, in an ungainly position, Buck catapulted from the saddle. He hit the ground head first but scrambled quickly to his feet.

Buck shook his head and looked around, momentarily disoriented.

"Well, there went my rifle...and my pistol is in my saddle bag," he said, seeming to gather is faculties. "Now how did you manage to spook that cayuse, flatlander? That was a pretty good trick."

Buck dropped his right hand and the dreaded blade concealed in his leather wrist band deployed with a ringing click.

Grant stood stoically, his rifle held at his waist pointed at Buck's chest.

"You're right, Buck, it's hard to shoot a man. I learned that the last time we met. I have regretted my decision to let you get away. I won't make that mistake again."

"Talk is real cheap, Slicker. Now I been told that you should never bring a knife to a gunfight...but seein' as how that's all..."

Buck's voice tailed off as he turned quickly to his left.

In the corner of his eye, Grant caught a flash of brown fur as the giant grizzly bear burst from the brush and charged Buck at a run. He could hear a strange popping sound, the grizzly's jaws snapping rapidly together as the animal engulfed Buck. Flailing frantically, Buck kicked and screamed as the huge beast grabbed his head in its mouth. In an instant, blood covered the ground.

Grant looked for a moment at the rifle he had been pointing at his adversary. Without thinking he raised it to his shoulder. Brown fur filled his sights as he squeezed the trigger. A puff of dust erupted behind the bear's ribs. The giant immediately loosed its grip on Buck's head. It turned its attention to Grant.

Frantically, he levered a second cartridge into the chamber and raised the Winchester to fire again. Before the rifle was at his shoulder, the animal had crossed half the distance that separated them. Grant squeezed the trigger in the instant before the bear knocked him backward into the fallen tree.

Grant could feel the animal's teeth sink into the flesh of his shoulder. The full weight of the bear was on his chest. The rifle, which he held tightly in his right hand, was now pressed against the log. He could hear the wooden stock crack under the animal's bulk. His head slammed against the fallen tree and he was suddenly surrounded by a dreamy darkness.

When Grant came to, he did not know how long he had been unconscious. He could hear growling rumbles and knew that the bear was close. He attempted to sit up. His hand bumped the metal receiver of the rifle. Knowing it could be his only salvation, he grasped the broken weapon as he laboriously pulled himself upright so as to see where the animal was. To his amazement, the bear had renewed its attack on Buck. Grant could clearly hear the cracking of Buck's skull as the bear shook his lifeless body.

He levered a round into the chamber of the broken Winchester. Upon hearing the sharp metallic sound, the bear looked at Grant. Without hesitation it ran at him like a thing possessed. Holding the rifle in both hands, Grant fired into the dark specter descending upon him. He knew that the heavy bullet, fired point blank, had hit the bear. However, the animal struck him again, knocking him onto his back against the log. The giant then continued past Grant and down the hill.

He dare not move. He lay quietly to listen, waiting for the seemingly indestructible beast to return to complete its mission. His breath came with difficulty and he felt that he was going to drown in the blood coming from his lungs.

He attempted to rise, but immediately heard movement in the brush below. The monster wasn't dead. He looked around to find the Winchester. The crunch of pine needles was nearly upon of him. Completely drained, he made a futile effort to reach the broken rifle.

"Don't move around too much, son," he heard Tom say.

34

Tom was out of breath when he reached the horses where Derrick was waiting.

"What was all the shootin' about?" Derrick asked. "And what did ya do with your coat. It's freezin' out here. It's startin' to snow already."

"Grizzly," Tom grunted. "Killed Buck and pretty near kilt that kid too. We need to build a travois to get Grant outta here. We ain't gonna be able to pack him on a horse."

"If we're gonna drag him, we'll have to go the long way around," Derrick said. "Never be able to get a travois down the short cut trail."

"I reckon you're right," Tom said. "Too steep on that short trail."

Tom and Derrick rode up the hill. Tom stooped beside Grant, who was now unconscious.

"I'll skin that griz. We can wrap him in the hide. At least keep the wind off him. It's gettin' colder by the minute," Derrick said.

Tom and Derrick quickly assembled a travois.

"Let's put this travois on your paint," Tom said. "He's stout enough and I can follow and keep an eye on the boy as we go down the trail."

They wrapped Grant in the grizzly bear hide with the hair inside for warmth and tied it in place around his limp body.

Derrick cut the laces holding Buck's wrist band knife. He removed the device and pushed the blade back into the sheath.

"I don't want this thing falling out and cuttin' up this mule," he said.

Tom walked the mule to Buck's body. He and Derrick struggled to lift the large man across the mule's pack saddle. Derrick covered Buck's corpse with a tarpaulin and tied him securely to the saddle.

The trail down the river canyon was a gentle slope. However the terrain was rocky and Tom knew that the constant bumping of the travois was exaggerating any damage to Grant's broken bones. He watched the travois carefully hoping that the tightly bound bear hide would serve to splint Grant's injuries.

A bitter wind drove the now frigid air through their clothing. Half way down the canyon the spitting snow turned to a blizzard. The elusive trail became even more difficult to follow as the afternoon twilight turned to evening darkness.

The hours passed as they slowly picked their way over the rough, snow covered, trail. The only light was the dim reflection from the new snow.

"There's the road," Derrick said.

He turned his horse into a wide lane.

"Shouldn't be more than half an hour to the cabin. We'll get Grant loaded in the truck and have Elmer see to these animals," Tom shouted back.

It seemed to Tom an eternity until they could hear the horses in the corral, whinnying loudly. When they rode to the hitch rail, Tom could see the animals running wildly around in the enclosure. The cabin was dark and no smoke came from the chimney.

"These critters haven't been fed. They're about crazy with the hungries," Tom said.

Derrick took an armload of firewood and walked into the cabin. Through the window, Tom could see a dim glow as Derrick lit the oil lamp.

"Holy shit!" Tom heard Derrick say.

Tom ran to the cabin door, stared a moment and then turned away.

Elmer's lifeless eyes stared down from the far wall of the frigid cabin. Pole barn nails through his hands and feet held his naked body in an obscene replication of the crucifixion. A crusty brown residue of blood streaked his right side from a knife wound just below the ribs. A crown of barbed wire was wrapped around his head. Written in blood on a board above his head were the words, "He died for you."

"Ya know what, son...I ought'a do to ol' Buck what your grand pappy would'a done. I ought'a cut that no good sumbitch into little bitty pieces so that he can't come back in the next life as nothin' bigger than a piss ant," Tom said.

Derrick's hands were shaking as he struck a match and ignited the kindling in the wood stove.

"You get that fire goin' and we'll get Grant inside. After he warms up a bit we'll get him into town to the doc," Tom said.

Tom looked up at Elmer's staring eyes.

"Let's get poor Elmer out of here. The heat from this stove sure as hell ain't gonna do him any good."

Tom found a hacksaw in the tool box and handed it to Derrick.

"See if you can cut the heads off them nails while I go see to Grant."

Tom lit a second lantern and walked outside. As he approached Grant, something touched the back of his leg and he reflexively spun and grabbed for his pistol.

"Dawg," Tom said. "You near scared the shit outta me!"

The black and white collie wagged his tail.

"Where's your boy," Tom said, as he petted the dog's head.

"I'm comin'," he heard Little Tom shout from the trail above.

"We got worried when Derrick didn't come back to camp so they sent me down to see what had become of you."

"It's a good thing. We're gonna need some help here," Tom said.

Walking to the travois, Tom began to untie the lashings securing Grant's bearskin wrapped form.

"Who's that, Grandpa," Little Tom asked.

"It's Grant," Tom answered. "Grizzly hurt him real bad. Come on over here and give me a hand. We gotta get him inside."

Little Tom tied his horse and went to the travois. He put his hand on the bear hide.

"This hide is froze solid, Grandpa."

He touched Grant's face, and then withdrew his hand quickly.

"Don't reckon there's no use takin' him inside. He's froze too!" the boy croaked.

Tom put his hand on Grant's face, and then felt for a pulse on his neck. He choked back tears as he covered the young man's face with a red kerchief.

"I really liked this boy. Dixie is gonna be just broken hearted...and to tell you the truth, son, so am I."

Tom and his grandson walked back into the cabin as Derrick was finishing the gruesome task of sawing the heads from the pole barn nails.

"What happened to Elmer," the boy asked, tears pouring down his cheeks.

"Buck done killed him," Derrick said.

Derrick put his arm around the boy's shoulders.

"I know you really liked Elmer. He was your pal. Everybody liked him,"

Derrick said.

Tom watched his grandson dissolve in sobs of grief.

"Let it out, son. Ain't no shame in cryin' for your friend."

When Little Tom had gathered himself, the three pulled Elmer's unbending body from the headless nails, wrapped him in blankets and carried him outside.

Derrick made coffee and the men stood by the stove while Little Tom sat with his head resting on the table.

"I guess about all we can do now is load these boys into the truck and take them into East Glacier. The constable can call the sheriff," Tom said.

"I'll help you load them in the truck and then I'll see to the stock," Derrick said.

Derrick put his hand on Little Tom's shoulder.

"Why don't you go on in to town with Grandpa? I'll pack feed back up to the camp and see to the needs of the flatlanders," Derrick said.

The snow continued as they walked outside with the lanterns.

"We better load Elmer first," Tom said. "He's gonna take up a lot of room, spread eagled and stiff like he is."

Gently, they lifted Elmer's body and laid him in the back of the truck. Little Tom tucked blankets around the naked corpse of his friend.

Derrick walked over to the mule and pulled the tag end of the knot, which held Buck's body on the pack saddle. He then gave a tug, and Buck's body tumbled head first and landed with a thud.

"Kind'a stuck in the shape of a U, ain't he?" Little Tom said with a grimace.

"U for ugly," Tom said. "Lend a hand and we'll throw this dirty bastard in the truck."

Little Tom jumped up into the back of the truck as Tom and Derrick hoisted Buck's body up into the bed. He pushed Buck's U shaped form into one corner with his boot.

"He is sure one heavy son-of-a-bitch," Little Tom said.

Derrick walked to the travois and cut the bindings holding Grant's bear skin wrap. The heavy hide, frozen in place, could not be removed.

"I reckon that bear hide wasn't such a good idea," Derrick said.

Derrick and Tom sledded Grant's cocooned body to the truck.

"Seemed like a good idea at the time," Tom replied. "Who would'a figured it would freeze into a coffin? It sure ain't your fault. That bear hurt the boy real bad."

Tom and Derrick cradled the rawhide clad body between them and lifted him gently into the covered bed of the truck beside Elmer. Little Tom fastened the tail gate and tied the canvas door.

"If we get goin' now, we can get the midnight train out of East Glacier," Tom said.

Derrick again put his arm around his nephew's shoulders as they walked to the truck.

"I really am sorry about your pal, Elmer," he said.

Little Tom climbed into the cab of the truck beside his grandfather.

Derrick stepped onto the running board and touched his father's arm.

"I'm sorry about your friend too…Dad."

Tom smiled as he looked his son in the eye.

"Thank you, son. We'll leave the truck at the station. See ya in a couple of weeks."

3 5

The station agent was leaning back in his chair, mouth agape, snoring loudly.

"I need to send some telegrams and arrange passage to Fort Benton tonight, if that's possible," Tom said in a loud voice.

Leaping to his feet and straightening his hat, the agent stared in stunned surprise.

"Wha...wha...whatever we can do to accommodate you, Mr. Thomas."

"First thing...I need to book passage tonight for my grandson and me to Fort Benton."

The agent grabbed the pencil from behind his ear and began to write on a slip of paper.

"Will you have any baggage?"

"I got three dead men in the truck outside and I need them put in the baggage car for direct shipment to Fort Benton."

The agent squinted through sleepy eyes.

"Three dead men," the agent repeated. He then looked at Tom for some sign that it was a joke.

"And I need to send some telegrams when you're finished with the other arrangements. And I need to use your phone, if it's workin'."

"Would you like to step behind the counter, Mr. Thomas? The phone is over there on the wall."

Tom removed the receiver from its cradle and turned the crank on the side of the telephone.

"Give me Constable Olafsen," Tom said.

Constable Olafsen answered his telephone with a sleepy voice.

"Olafsen...this is Tom Thomas. I got three dead men over here at the train depot and I think you'd best come have a look."

Tom replaced the receiver and walked back to the front of the counter.

"That'll be six dollars for the tickets and nine dollars for your baggage, Mr. Thomas. That's a total of twelve dollars," the agent said.

Tom put the money on the counter and said, "Are you ready to send those telegrams?"

"Yes sir. Shoot," the agent replied, his pencil poised.

"I want these sent emergency status...with immediate delivery."

"Yes, sir...I'll see to it."

"First one is to Nick Thomas at The Buffalo Rock Ranch.

"BUCK ELMER GRANT ALL DEAD – STOP – BRINGING BODIES ON MORNING TRAIN – STOP – MEET ME AT TRAIN – STOP – DAD – STOP"

"Got it," the agent said.

"The next is to the Beanblossom Mortuary in Fort Benton.

"BRINGING THREE CLIENTS ON THE SEVEN O'CLOCK TRAIN – STOP – BODIES FROZEN – STOP – WILL REQUIRE SPECIAL ATTENTION – STOP – BRING TRANSPORT AND ASSISTANCE – STOP – TOM THOMAS – STOP"

"Read 'em back. The constable should be here in a minute."

Little Tom opened the back of the canvas covered truck bed as the midnight train ground to an unscheduled stop in East Glacier. Tom explained to the Constable how each of the three men had met his demise. Constable Olafsen checked for a pulse on each of the bodies.

"I'll notify the Sheriff, Mr. Thomas. I'm sure your word will be good enough with him. And I'm sure he'll be glad to be rid of that Buck fella," Olafsen said.

Tom and his grandson helped as several local men, who had been called by the station agent, began to load the bodies into the baggage car.

The substitute baggage handlers, finding it difficult to hold Elmer's unwieldy form, dropped the body breaking off three of Elmer's toes.

"Careful with that boy, unless you want to join him in the hereafter and give him back those toes," Tom shouted.

Throwing back his coat to expose the Colt, Tom walked toward the men.

"He's a human bein', ya know...even if he's dead."

The three looked at Tom, faces blanching. Without a word, one of the men ran into the depot. He returned with some brown paper and string. Picking up the digits, he wrapped them carefully. Keeping one eye on Tom, he tied the bundle around Elmer's neck.

Tom watched as the bodies were loaded into the baggage car. He and Little Tom then boarded for the ride to Fort Benton.

Nick, Susanna and Dixie were waiting on the platform when the train arrived. Little Tom jumped from the car and ran to put his arms around his mother, tears streaming down his face.

"Dad, you look absolutely wore out. We've got to get you home," Nick said.

Dixie put her arms around Tom, sobbing uncontrollably. Tom held her tenderly, not knowing what to say.

"I want to see him, Uncle Tom," Dixie said.

"Okay, darlin'," Tom assured. "Let Barlow get him laid out and then you can spend some time with him."

"No! I want to go see him now," she blurted.

Tom put his arm around Dixie and walked her toward Nick's car.

"What happened?" Susanna asked.

"Caleb's alright and Derrick helped me pack the boys out. Everyone else is fine," Tom said.

Tom opened the door for Dixie and then walked to the back of the car, motioning to Nick.

"I don't want the girls to see 'em takin' the bodies off the train," Tom whispered to Nick. "Ol' Elmer's all spread eagled and Buck looks like a horseshoe. It's a terrible thing to see. That's why Little Tom is so addlepated. We'll give Barlow some time to get 'em over to the mortuary."

Nick started the car and drove down the hill into town.

"Let's stop at the café and get a bite. Me and Little Tom ain't ate in a while."

Tom sat next to Dixie, who remained bereft. He lingered over his food, hoping to give Barlow Beanblossom sufficient time to prepare Grant's remains for viewing.

"You didn't answer Susanna, Uncle Tom. What happened?" Dixie asked.

"I wasn't there darlin', so I can't say for certain...but it looks like Buck had set an ambush for Grant...but then they both got bushwhacked by the biggest grizzly I ever seen. The bear killed ol' Buck outright, but it looks like Grant put up a pretty good fight. It appears that he shot that monster maybe three times before it finally got him. I don't know if there's any comfort in that for you, but the boy turned out to be a pretty good kind'a man. Looks like he stood his ground to the end. Now as to Buck, it appears that bear was his justice and that he got what was comin' to him. It looks like he'd kilt poor Elmer for no good reason whatsoever."

Dixie again broke down, racked with sobs of grief. Tom put his arm around her shoulders and they sat saying nothing.

Nick finished eating and finally broke the silence.

"You fellers get your fill?" he asked.

Although Tom and the boy had barely touched their food, they both nodded.

"Let's go on over to Beanblossum's and I'll finish gettin' the arrangements made," Tom said. "We've still got to notify Grant's people and The Morning Star in Saint Louis. If I remember right, I think his boss is a fella by the name of Kuntz."

"Jonathan Kuntz," Dixie said. "My parents are friends of the Kuntz family. I'm sure my childhood friend Melinda will be heart broken at the news. She knew Grant also. Her father owns the newspaper."

Nick paid the check and they drove in silence to the mortuary.

Walking into the reception room, Tom saw Barlow Beanblossum motioning to him from behind a half open door. Tom walked into the office and closed the door behind him.

"Tom, I have bad news. None of the decedents is ready for visitors. We'll not be prepared for viewing until tomorrow...and that will require working all night. Two of the departed are frozen into hideous caricature and one of the young men is encased in a frozen raw hide that will take a day to thaw without causing severe decomposition of the corpse."

"I know Barlow...I was the one that wrapped him in that hide," Tom said.

Fatigue and remorse lent a gravelly quality to Tom's voice.

"I thought that furry hide would help keep him warm, but that bear had hurt him too bad I reckon."

"I understand that he was from the East. Will you be shipping him?" Barlow asked.

"I suppose we will. I have to get in touch with his folks. I'd reckon his mama will want him shipped back to Baltimore."

"What about the other two? Will you be taking them to the ranch?"

"We'll be buryin' Elmer on The Buffalo Rock. He was one of mine. When you get him thawed out so he'll lay flat, we'll set the time for a funeral. As far as Buck Horton, just fix him up good enough to put in a pine box. Cheapest thing you got. If it was up to me, I'd put the mean bastard in the dump...but I reckon that wouldn't be the Christian thing to do. You can find a spot for him on potter's hill, and get a couple of pictures so I can send them to the Sheriffs in the counties where he done his meanness."

"Do you want the young man in the bear hide dressed and prepared? We'll need his best clothing, and it is going to take some time till the hide thaws."

"Yes, sir, I do...but in the meanwhile I want you to put him on a fancy decorated table and set him in your best viewin' parlor. My niece, Dixie, wants to sit with the boy. It'll bring her some comfort and it won't do no harm to you or him."

"That's quite an unusual request. You can't see anything but his face... and the smell is terrible."

"Be that as it may...do it!"

"I'll see to it immediately, Tom" Barlow said.

Barlow Beanblossum left Tom alone with his thoughts. He returned about ten minutes later.

"We've laid him out so that his face can be seen and cleaned it up a bit. My people put on a little powder and makeup. He'll be laid in The Ambassador room. You may take your party in to see him and they may stay as long as they like. I'll await instructions from his family."

Tom escorted Dixie to the viewing parlor and seated her next to the table. Nick, Susanna, and Little Tom had been joined by Koko, Romulus and Remus. Each walked past the table to pay their respects to this young man for whom they had all grown a genuine affection. Koko kissed Dixie's tear stained cheek while a trickle of tear ran down her own. One by one, they left Dixie to her solemn anguish.

Hours passed. Dixie sat immobile, staring at Grant's powdered face, wondering what might have been.

Tom silently entered the room. He pulled a chair next to Dixie.

"I sent a telegram to his folks. His father called a few minutes ago. They want the boy prepared and shipped back to Baltimore."

Dixie did not respond. She continued to sit, eyes transfixed on Grant's face in stolid silence.

Tom could see that the bear skin was thawing rapidly in the warmth of the Franklin stove in the corner of the room. Fatty liquid dripped from the warming hide, staining the velvet decorations. The foul odor of grizzly bear filled the room.

Tom lifted the now supple corners of the thawing raw hide. The folds fell away under their own weight and hung to the floor on the sides of the table. The strong odor of excrement immediately overwhelmed the senses. Tom had seen enough of violent death to understand.

"Come on, darlin'," Tom said, taking Dixie's arm. "Let Barlow fix the boy up right and proper, and then we'll come back and you can sit with him."

Dixie sat staring.

"Come on now," Tom cajoled. "Barlow is gonna need to clean this up... and you can come back after they get him all prettied and dressed. I'll go tell Barlow's folks that they can get started...okay!"

Tom walked from the room while Dixie continued her vigil. She ignored the stench, staring at the face of her young lover. She was inundated by another wave of grief as she understood this would be the last time she would see him as he had been in life. She buried her head in her hands and sobbed.

Footsteps outside the door told her they would soon take him away. She stood and bent to kiss his face.

A nearly imperceptible movement of Grant's shirt caused her to start. It is my imagination, she told herself. Then the pocket of Grant's shirt seemed to move as if he had taken a breath.

She closed her eyes and shook her head. She then stared intently. Nothing! It was wishful thinking after all, she said to herself. He is thawing out...that's all. I can't wish him back to me. She gazed another long moment and bent to kiss his face for the last time.

Grant's eyes opened. He looked around the room and back at Dixie in slow realization.

"How did you get here? I shot a bear you know," he said in a barely perceptible whisper.

She tried to scream but no sound came from her throat.

Grant tried to sit up but could only move his arm.

"Have I been asleep long?" he asked in a scratchy whisper. "This is very embarrassing...but I think I've soiled myself. Would you excuse me?"

Dixie ran from the room.

"He's alive...he's alive, call the doctor!" she screamed.

Epilogue

Two weeks passed with Grant again enjoying service, hand and foot, from Dixie and Koko. He was finishing his breakfast in bed when Tom knocked at the door.

"How you doin' this mornin'? It's beginnin' to look, by God, like you just might make it."

"I'm feeling just wonderful," Grant replied. "I doubt that better nursing care is available anywhere."

"Well, I'll tell you this much...you sure as hell put a scare in me. I didn't think my book was ever gonna get written."

Dixie entered the room.

"Uncle Tom, that is gauche."

"Maybe so, but it would'a been a lot gaucher if'n he'd died and my book didn't get wrote."

Dixie looked at her uncle and Grant. She laughed in spite of herself.

"I guess I will never understand the masculine sense of humor."

"I talked to Doc O'Brien. I was feelin' real bad about wrappin' you in that bear hide. I figured that's what near kilt you," Tom said.

"It didn't appear to have done him a lot of good," Dixie interrupted.

"Not so! The doc tells me that the hide turned out to be the lifesaver.

Seems that when the thing stiffened up it kept his whole body still...kind'a immobilized the injuries. It was like a splint on a broke leg. That stiff hide kept them ribs and shoulder from gettin' more damage than they got. O'Brien also thinks that the hide kept him warm for just a bit and then slowly cooled him down until he went into a state of what the doc called torpor. He likened it to a humming bird on a cold day...or a hibernatin' bear, slowly coolin' down for the winter. All his workin' parts, like his heart and such, just slowed down a little at a time until it appeared he was dead.

The warm air in that viewin' room sort'a restarted his motor. Any way you slice it, he was one lucky young fella. Had he stayed conscious, doc figures he would have died for certain, gettin' bounced out of the hills on that travois."

"Were you able to save my bear hide? I'll want that for a rug," Grant said.

Tom looked at Dixie and then at Grant.

"I sent it to the tanner for ya. It'll be done by the time the two of you are ready to set up housekeepin', I reckon."

Dixie looked at Tom.

"Well thank you, Uncle Tom...because that is the last one he'll ever have the opportunity to shoot."

She looked at Grant and squinched her face.

"Isn't that so, Mr. Collins?"

"Well...I...uh...I can't say for sure," Grant stammered, looking at Tom.

Tom winked at Grant.

"This here sounds like a family matter to me."

Tom walked from the room and closed the door behind him.

The End

About the *Author*

www.BobFaulkner.com

Following service in the United
States Marine Corps., author Bob
Faulkner joined the Los Angeles
Police Department. He later moved to
Montana where he enjoys fishing the
lakes and rivers, shooting skeet and
exploring the wild country.